" I, John, saw the holy city."

# *The Story of the Seer of Patmos*

By
Stephen N. Haskell

**TEACH Services, Inc.**
Brushton, New York

ISBN 0-945383-50-9
Library of Congress Catalog Card No. 95-61928

Published by

**TEACH Services, Inc.**
R.R. 1, Box 182
Brushton, New York 12916

# AUTHOR'S PREFACE.

PROPHECY is often considered dark and mysterious. The Lord describes how prophecy given in vision, will be looked upon by many people. "And the vision of all is become unto you as the words of a book that is sealed, which men deliver to one that is learned, saying, Read this, I pray thee; and he saith, I cannot; for it is sealed: and the book is delivered to him that is not learned, saying, Read this, I pray thee; and he saith, I am not learned." The book of Revelation was never sealed; for the angel said to John, "Seal not the sayings of the prophecy of this book, for the time is at hand."

God has given the book of Revelation a title different from any other book in the Bible, signifying that it is open to all. It is the "*revelation* of Jesus Christ." He has pronounced a blessing upon every one who reads it, or even hears it read. "Blessed is he that readeth, and they that hear the words of this prophecy, and keep those things which are written therein: for the time is at hand." It is adapted to every mind, and is full of choice illustrations and symbols, which will not only interest, but instruct the reader. It is a complete book in itself; for John was told "What thou seest, write in a book." He then said that he bear record of the Word of God, and "of all things that he saw."

The prophecies of Revelation cover the period of the time from the first advent of Christ to the earth made new. The history of the Christian church is repeated four times in different figures, illustrating almost every phase of experience the church will pass through. Portions of the history are repeated several times. The book of Revelation opens the portals of the city of God, and presents to the readers, Eden restored, with its tree of life bearing twelve manner of fruit.

The study of prophecy, by many, is considered uninteresting, and much that is written upon this subject is given in an argumentative style, which is unattractive to many minds. The "Story of the Seer of Patmos" is a treatise on the book of Revelation, given in a narrative style, interesting alike to old and young.

The "Story of the Seer of Patmos" is sent forth on its mission of love with earnest prayer to God that it may point all who read to the Lamb of God that taketh away the sin of the world. May the Bible student find treasure, the skeptics find ground for faith, and the thoughtless become acquainted with the thoughts of God by reading this book.

May the Lord bless it in its mission; and in love of the great Master, may it prove a blessing to thousands of souls who are struggling with the conflicts and ills of this life, and guide them to the pearly portals of the New Jerusalem.

# CONTENTS.

# FULL-PAGE ILLUSTRATIONS.

# INTRODUCTION.

One of the distinguishing features of the age of the world in which we live is the prevalence of light and knowledge. It is but a fulfillment of the divine words: "But thou, O Daniel, shut up the words, and seal the book, even to the time of the end: many shall run to and fro, and *knowledge shall be increased*." Dan. 12:4.

During the preceding century, more than in all the centuries of the past, a flood of light has been shed upon the prophetic page. The seal which metaphorically hid the true meaning of the book of Daniel has been removed by the fulfillment of nearly all its predictions, so that the records of history demonstrate its true meaning. Prophecy is history in advance. History is prophecy fulfilled. When both agree we have the genuine meaning. Therefore we know we are in the "time of the end," and very near its close.

The book of Revelation is introduced by the following words: "The Revelation of Jesus Christ, which God gave unto Him, to show unto His servants things which must shortly come to pass; and He sent and signified it by His angel unto His servant John." Rev. 1:1.

As the book of Daniel reaches to the "*time of the end*," and the book of Revelation contains "things which *must shortly come to pass*," before the end, the two books must be "*companion volumes*," closely related to each other. The book of Daniel, in point of time, precedes the book of Revelation upwards of six centuries. In short, the latter is largely an inspired commentary on the former, and as such, becomes a valuable aid to its correct understanding. Every earnest, intelligent student of prophecy will study these two books together. Each is mutually helpful to the understanding of the other.

There is an opinion extant, quite prevalent among those skeptically inclined, and a class of professed Christians who ignore the whole subject of prophecy, that the book of Revelation is mystical, foggy and cannot be understood. If so, the Spirit of God has misnamed it. God says it is a "Revelation of Jesus Christ." A revelation is not something *concealed.* It is something *made known.* In other words, this blessed book makes known to us the things God wishes us to know. He reveals to us the nature of the events to occur all through the Christian dispensation, and especially those connected with Christ's return to this earth at His second coming.

The "Revelation" is a book of symbols. The representation of mighty kingdoms by the symbols of beasts, as given in Daniel and Revelation, is common among the nations of the earth. We speak of the British lion, the Russian bear, the American eagle; and every intelligent person understands what is meant, because nations themselves have chosen these creatures to represent them on their flags and standards. Inspiration chooses symbols to represent various nations, and the Scriptures themselves plainly define their meaning.

There are no books in the Bible of greater interest to the earnest student than the visions of Daniel and John. This volume, "The Story of the Seer of Patmos," is a companion volume to "The Story of Daniel the Prophet," by the same author. We doubt not that this volume will equal or exceed the former in popularity.

The author is a devoted minister of the gospel of long experience; a deep and most earnest student of the holy Scriptures, and especially conversant with the subject of prophecy. He has given many years of careful study to the subjects contained in this volume. It is written for all classes of readers. The most intelligent professional man can find herein blessed food for thought, and precious instruction in the Bible truths for this remarkable age. The business man can be greatly profited by the perusal of this volume. Men need to have their attention called away from worldly themes, to the great things God is about to do in our world. The common people will read this volume with delight. It will open up great fields of thought which they have never before explored, while the Bible student will find in it a rich mine of treasure.

The apostle John was an old man when he wrote the book of Revelation. It was a special revelation from Jesus Christ Himself, and reveals the order of events commencing in John's time, and reaching to Christ's second coming, under various heads and series of events: The Seven Churches, The Seven Seals, The Seven Trumpets, The

Three Messages, etc. It ends with the glorious restitution of all things, spoken of by the "mouth of all the holy prophets since the world began." Here are themes worthy of the most careful study. The author has made these mysterious symbols so plain, that any one who will carefully follow him can understand the book of Revelation.

The study of this inspired book of Holy Writ is important. Christ Himself says, "Blessed is he that *readeth*, and they that *hear* the words of this prophecy, *and keep* those things which are written therein: *for the time is at hand*."

We are living at the close of the great prophetic periods revealed in Daniel and Revelation. We greatly need the light contained in this volume. We most gladly welcome every additional ray of light shining on our pathway. The perils of the last days are around us. Great changes are occurring. Satanic deceptions abound on every hand. The time has come, foretold by our Saviour, when if it be possible, even the elect are in danger of deception. Matt. 24:23, 26. The Revelator speaks of the same things. Let all become intelligent in reference to these things. "The Story of the Seer of Patmos" will enlighten all who will read and study it. Our Saviour informs us that when the signs of His coming begin to come to pass His people should look up and lift up their heads, for their redemption draweth nigh.

Ah! dear reader, do you not desire to be a citizen of that glorious city spoken of in the last chapters of Revelation, with its gates of pearl, streets of gold, wall of jasper, and foundations garnished with precious stones; where the tree of life shall grow, and the river of life flows out from beneath the throne of God; where Christ will ever dwell? Where God shall wipe away all tears from the eyes of His people; where death will never come, sorrow will never be felt, nor pain evermore exist? Study the blessed Revelation, and you will get new and blessed conceptions of these great divine realities.

GEO. I. BUTLER.

*Nashville, Tenn., April 24, 1905.*

# A WORD TO THE READER.

THE history of this world is fast closing. Events are taking place, in the physical, political, and spiritual world, which show that we are living in a crisis such as has never been since the creation of this world. The voice of innocent blood crieth from the ground. The nations are angry. Not one nation, but all the nations of earth, look forward with fearful apprehensions to what is coming.

The prophet, in view of this time, exclaims, "Watchman, what of the night? Watchman, what of the night?" The watchman said, "The morning cometh and also the night,"—the glorious morn of salvation that will bring deliverance to the people of God, and the night of eternal death to those who reject the repeated warnings given in the Word of God. Through John on the Isle of Patmos, the Lord lifts the veil, and lets us see the history of the church in its relation to the world. Seven times the prophet exhorts all who have an ear, to hear what the Spirit saith unto the churches.

We invite all to a careful perusal of the contents of this book, with the prayer that God will impress minds by His Holy Spirit. It is not the design of the writer of the "Story of the Seer of Patmos" to arouse discussion and awaken controversy upon theoretical points, but to tell the truth as it is in Jesus Christ.

The book is written in a narrative style, and the symbols are explained by the marginal references, so that the reader will readily find a mine of rich treasure in the book. The entire book of Revelation is printed in italics on the margin of the pages, together with several thousand other scriptures which throw light on the subject.

We earnestly pray that God's blessing may rest upon the readers, and that the book may help many to become better acquainted with the Book of all books, the Word of the living God.

Yours in the blessed hope,

S. N. H.

# CHAPTER I.

## THE SEER OF PATMOS.

THE men whom God has chosen as a means of communication between heaven and earth, form a galaxy of noted characters. The gift of prophecy is called the "best gift," and the church is exhorted to covet that "best gift." To be able to view scenes still future and to talk in the language of heaven, requires a closer walk with God than is attained by most men. But through all the ages, there have been those whose lives were so in unison with the laws of Jehovah that they became the channel of the Spirit of God.

It is not that such men have greater attainments than all others, but they are like the dense

Disallowed indeed of men, but chosen of God, and precious. 1 Peter 2:4.

By a prophet the Lord brought Israel out of Egypt, and by a prophet was he preserved. Hos. 12:13.

Gen. 20:7.

1 Cor. 14:1.

Enoch also, the seventh from Adam, prophesied of these, saying, Behold, the Lord cometh with ten thousand of his saints. Jude 14.

Gen. 5:24.

2 Cor. 12:1-5.

Elias was a man subject to like passions as we are. Jas. 5:17.

Amos 7:14, 15.

I delight to do thy will, O my God: yea, thy law is within my heart. Psa. 40:8.

---

NOTE:—In the margin are many passages of scripture that will direct the mind of the reader to those portions of the Bible which give light upon the story of the Seer of Patmos. In the texts quoted, marks of ellipsis are omitted; and frequently several verses are cited in the reference, though only one or more are printed in full.

When I bring a cloud over the earth, that the bow shall be seen in the cloud. Gen. 9:14.

Eze. 1:28.

1 Cor. 1:25-28.

I will look upon it, that I may remember the everlasting covenant. Gen. 9:16.

To see thy power and thy glory, so as I have seen thee in the sanctuary. Psa. 63:2.

Isa. 63:9.

Isa. 48:10, 11.

Beloved, think it not strange concerning the fiery trial which is to try you, as though some strange thing happened unto you. 1 Peter 4:12.

And when he had gone a little farther thence, he saw James the son of Zebedee, and John his brother, who also were in the ship mending their nets.

And straightway he called them: and they left their father Zebedee in the ship with the hired servants, and went after him. Mark 1:19, 20.

Rev. 1:9.

Dan. 1:1.

Dan. 2:31-45.

These great beasts, which are four, are four kings, which shall arise out of the earth.

But the saints of the Most High shall take the kingdom, and possess the kingdom forever, even forever and ever. Dan. 7:17, 18.

And after threescore and two weeks shall Messiah be cut off, but not for himself. Dan. 9:24-26.

Dan. 1:3, 6.

cloud with its falling rain drops, through which the sun shines to produce the rainbow in its glory. One forgets the cloud while watching the bow of promise. So with the prophet; one loses sight of the instrument through whom God speaks, by beholding the glory of the scene which He portrays. But lest the Spirit should be lost in its transmission, the chosen instrument must be purified in the furnace of affliction. Those tests which bring the human soul in touch with the divine are necessary experiences, before human eyes can see, or human tongues can speak of things yet future.

Genesis,—that condensed treatise on the plan of salvation,—the work which contains the Gospel in embryo,—was written in the Midian desert, probably near Mount Horeb, while Moses watched the flocks of Jethro. Every other book in the Bible is but the unfolding of the truths of Genesis. It is the Alpha, and the book of Revelation is the Omega, of the Word of God to man.

As God prepared Moses, by a life of forty years in the solitudes of Midian, so He called the Apostle John from the society of men, and led him along a strange path upward, and still upward, until at last on the rocky coast of Patmos, heaven was opened to his wondering gaze, and the future history of the church was made known.

About six hundred years before the advent of Christ, there lived another seer, Daniel. To him God revealed the history of the nations of the world. From his own day, when Babylon bore universal sway, until nations should be no more, Daniel was shown the world's history. In connection with the account of the rise and fall of nations, Daniel saw the history of his own people, the Hebrew race, from their captivity in Babylon, until they rejected the Anointed of God. Daniel was of the royal seed of Israel, and was prime minister in the Court of Babylon during the years when this history was revealed to him. He of all men was fitted by education and position to write the history of the world.

Luke 24:27.

The path of the just is as the shining light, that shineth more and more unto the perfect day. Prov. 4:18.

Then the king made Daniel a great man, and gave him many great gifts, and made him ruler over the whole province of Babylon, and chief of the governors over all the wise men of Babylon. Dan. 2:48.

Dan. 5:11, 12.

Dan. 1:17, 20.

Heb. 12:6.

Heb. 12:8.

Write the things which thou hast seen, and the things that are, and the things which shall be hereafter. Rev. 1:19.

Dan. 8:27.

Gen. 3:15.

Now Moses kept the flock of Jethro his father-in-law, the priest of Midian: and he led the flock to the back side of the desert, and came to the mountain of God, even to Horeb. Ex. 3:1.

Gen. 1:1.

**Genesis was written while Moses watched the flocks of Jethro.**

As foretold by ancient prophets, the Saviour came a servant of men. He was anointed at the very time predicted by the Prophet Daniel. "And Jesus when He was baptized, went up straightway out of the water: and lo, the heavens were opened unto Him, and He saw the Spirit of God descending like a dove, and lighting upon Him: and lo a voice from heaven, saying, This is My beloved Son, in whom I am well pleased."

MESSIAH.

Dan. 9:25. Sixty-nine weeks or 483 years from the commandment to restore Jerusalem unto Messiah.

Ezra 7:9–26. Command given 456 1-2 B. C.

John 1:41 [margin]. Messiah means Christ or anointed.

Acts 10:38. Jesus was anointed with the Holy Ghost.

Matt. 3:15–17. The Holy Ghost came on Christ at His baptism; 483 years added to 456 1-2 years B. C. reaches to 26 1-2 A. D., or 27 A. D., the date of Christ's baptism.

John 1:36-38.
Rev. 1:19.

And the king appointed them a daily provision of the king's meat, and of the wine which he drank: so nourishing them three years, that at the end thereof they might stand before the king.

Now among these were of the children of Judah, Daniel, Hananiah, Mishael, and Azariah.
Dan. 1:5, 6.

There is a God in heaven that revealeth secrets, and maketh known to the king Nebuchadnezzar what shall be in the latter days. Thy dream, and the visions of thy head upon thy bed, are these.
Dan. 2:28.

Luke 9:52-56.
Mark 9:38-40.

But go thou thy way till the end be: for thou shalt rest, and stand in thy lot at the end of the days.
Dan. 12:13.

If I will that he tarry till I come, what is that to thee? follow thou me. John 21:22.

The Revelation of Jesus Christ, which God gave unto him, to shew unto his servants things which must shortly come to pass. Rev. 1:1.

The disciples were called Christians first in Antioch.
Acts 11:26.

Rev. 2:1-29.
Rev. 3:1-22.
Rev. 6:1-17.
Rev. 8:1-13.
Rev. 9:1-21.
Dan. 2:48.
Dan. 6:1-3.
Mark 1:19, 20.

Standing on the banks of the Jordan, a witness to this anointing, was a young man chosen of Heaven, to continue the history begun by Daniel.

The Hebrew prophet Daniel, was in the schools of Chaldea three years, during which time God revealed to the wise men of Babylon the superiority of the wisdom of God over all the learning of the world. While in that school, Daniel received the inspiration of the Holy Spirit. John the fisherman, the first of Christ's disciples, spent three years at the side of the Master Teacher, receiving such instruction as fitted him, in spiritual things to become a leader of nations. Daniel will stand in his lot in the latter days, by his prophecies revealing the time of the end. John, according to the words of Christ, will by his prophecies tarry until the coming of the Saviour in the clouds of heaven. For, when in answer to Peter's question concerning the future of the beloved disciple, Jesus said, "If I will that he tarry till I come," He revealed the prophetic mission of that disciple. The Saviour saw him on Patmos receiving the Revelation.

The prophecy as given to John is a revelation of Jesus Christ, and is the history of God's dealings with the church which bears the name, Christian. Daniel is a history of nations; the Revelation is ecclesiastical history, and into it, nations are introduced only when they affect the growth of the church.

The life of Daniel shows how God can work through men in high positions: the preparation of John for his work as a prophet is the story of the transformation wrought in the heart of a fisherman by the Spirit of God. The extremes of society were represented by these two men The story of each life is the narration of the events of a life in which love worked, and is an object lesson of the development of Christian character.

In the town of Bethsaida, on the west shore

of the Sea of Galilee, lived the fisherman, Zebedee, with his wife, Salome, and two sons, James and John. The two young men were partners with their father in his business, and were accustomed to the toil and hardships of a fisherman's life. A spirit of piety characterized the home; for beneath the rough exterior, was a desire to understand the Word of God. The promise of the Messiah had been read, and when it was known that the Prophet of the Wilderness was preaching and baptizing at Enon, and proclaiming the advent of Christ, the younger son of Zebedee, in company with Andrew of Bethsaida, sought baptism. It was there that they witnessed the anointing, and heard the Baptist's words, "Behold the Lamb of God." John and Andrew were the two disciples who followed after Christ, and to whom He turned saying, "What seek ye?" They said unto Him, "Rabbi . . . where dwellest thou?" And when He led them to the place where He abode, they talked with Him, they believed, and the nucleus of the Christian church was formed.

Bethsaida of Galilee.
John 12:21.

Mark 6:45.

Matt. 4:21.

Matt. 27:56.

Going on from thence, he saw other two brethren, James the son of Zebedee, and John his brother, in a ship with Zebedee their father, mending their nets.
Matt. 4:21.

For Moses of old time hath in every city them that preach him, being read in the synagogues every sabbath day. Acts 15:21.

And John also was baptizing in Enon near to Salim, because there was much water there: and they came, and were baptized.
John 3:23.

Again the next day after, John stood, and two of his disciples;

And looking upon Jesus as he walked, he saith, Behold the Lamb of God!

And the two disciples heard him speak, and they followed Jesus.

Then Jesus turned, and saw them following, and saith unto them, What seek ye? They said unto him, Rabbi, (which is to say, being interpreted, Master,) where dwellest thou?

He saith unto them, Come and see. They came and saw where he dwelt, and abode with him that day: for it was about the tenth hour.

One of the two which heard John speak, and followed him, was Andrew, Simon Peter's brother.
John 1:35-40.

And I, if I be lifted up from the earth, will draw all men unto me.
John 12:32.

1 John 5:11, 12.
1 Tim, 3:16.
John 1:41.
John 1:42.

Come, see a man, which told me all things that ever I did: is not this the Christ?
John 4: 29.

Gen. 32:28.
Gen. 25:30.

Beloved, let us love one another: for love is of God; and every one that loveth is born of God, and knoweth God.
He that loveth not, knoweth not God; for God is love.
1 John 4:6–12.

1 John 3:1.

The soul of my lord shall be bound in the bundle of life with the Lord thy God. 1 Sam. 25:29.

And the whole multitude sought to touch him: for there went virtue out of him, and healed them all.
Luke 6:19.

Mark 5:30.
Luke 8:46.

Now there was leaning on Jesus' bosom one of his disciples, whom Jesus loved. John 13:23.

Whoso keepeth his word, in him verily is the love of God perfected hereby know we that we are in him.
1 John 2:5.

1 John 1:7.

Walk in the Spirit, and ye shall not fulfil the lust of the flesh.
For the flesh lusteth against the Spirit, and the Spirit against the flesh: and these are contrary the one to the other; so that ye cannot do the things that ye would.
Gal. 5:16, 17.

But Jesus called them to him, and saith unto them, Ye know that they which are accounted to rule over the Gentiles exercise lordship over them; and their great ones exercise authority upon them.
But so shall it not be among you: but whosoever will be great among you, shall be your minister:
And whosoever of you will be the chiefest, shall be servant of all.
Mark 10:35–45.

Christ, the center, the life, drew John, and the young man's heart responded to the quickening touch. This was the beginning of a new life,—a soul communion. Andrew, too, was convinced of the divinity of Christ, but Andrew represents those who accept because the mind is convinced of truth. He sought at once for his brother Peter, saying, "We have found the Messiah, . . . the Christ, the Anointed." And when Peter came to Christ he was convinced of the divine nature of Jesus, because the Saviour read his character and gave him a name in accord with Peter's nature.

But John represents those of the inner circle of discipleship. He was won by love, not argument. His heart was held by love, and the whole theme of all his writings is love. He saw only love in Christ, and he responded freely to that wondrous drawing power. It was like an electric current flowing from Christ, and John desired to be ever in the circuit. He kept close to Jesus, walked hand in hand with Him, sat next to Him at the table, lay on His bosom,—he was "that disciple whom Jesus loved."

As long as John kept in touch with the divine life of the Master, there was nothing in his life out of harmony with the Saviour. That there were times when the harmony was broken, is true, and this was due to the fact that the human in John had not yet been subdued. The human channel through which the spirit flowed, sometimes arrested the flow. This was the case when James and John asked to sit, one on the left, and the other on the right, of the throne in the new kingdom. Christ recognized the desire as a result of more than human affection, and so in place of a rebuke, He attempted only to deepen and purify that love.

The entire life of John tended to cleanse the soul temple, and to prepare him for his final work. The union between the soul of Christ and John, is shown by numerous incidents. During the temptation of Jesus in the wilderness, John sought Him out, longing to go with Him. But Christ bade John return, for He did not wish the young man to witness the fierce struggles with the prince of darkness. When not allowed to remain as companion in the wilderness, he sought out Mary of Nazareth, who was in doubt as to the whereabouts of her Son. Sitting by the side of the lonely mother, John related the story of Christ's baptism, and told her of His present condition. He won his way into the heart of the family, as well as into the heart of Jesus. This explains why the Saviour, when hanging on the cross, gave directions for John to make a home for this same mother.

Be ye clean, that bear the vessels of the Lord. Isa. 52:11.

Matt. 17:1.
Mark 5:37.
Mark 13:3.
Luke 8:51.
Luke 22:8.

Then saith Jesus unto him, Get thee hence, Satan: for it is written, Thou shalt worship the Lord thy God, and him only shalt thou serve. Then the devil leaveth him, and behold, angels came and ministered unto him. Matt. 4:10, 11.

Luke 3:21, 22.

John 19:26, 27.

**Sitting by the side of the lonely mother, John relates the story of Christ's baptism.**

Such gentleness was not altogether natural with the sons of Zebedee; for when they first became Christ's followers, He called James and John "Boanerges," "Sons of Thunder." They possessed an ambitious, hasty, outspoken spirit, which was subdued by association with the Saviour. The natural inclinations were replaced by contrition, faith, and love. John especially yielded to that power of the Christ.

Every experience of this disciple pointed unmistakably to the crowning work of his life. When the Saviour had returned to heaven, John

James the son of Zebedee, and John the brother of James; and he surnamed them Boanerges, which is, The sons of thunder. Mark 3:17.

1 John 3:23.

I am crucified with Christ: nevertheless I live; yet not I, but Christ liveth in me: and the life which I now live in the flesh I live by the faith of the Son of God, who loved me, and gave himself for me. Gal. 2:20.

NEW TESTAMENT PROPHETS.
Acts 7:37. Jesus.
Matt. 11:9–11. John the Baptist.
2 Cor. 12:1–7. Paul.
Rev. 1:10. John.
Acts 10:9–17. Peter.
Acts 11:27, 28. Agabus and one other.
Acts 21:8, 9. Philip's four daughters.
Acts 15:32. Judas and Silas.
Luke 1:67. Zacharias.
Luke 2:25–28. Simeon.
Luke 2:36. Anna.
James 5:1–5. James.

Take, my brethren, the prophets, who have spoken in the name of the Lord, for an example of suffering affliction, and of patience.
James 5:10.

Truly our fellowship is with the Father, and with his Son Jesus Christ. 1 John 1:3.

And this is life eternal, that they might know thee the only true God, and Jesus Christ, whom thou hast sent. John 17:2–4.

And he shall be as the light of the morning, when the sun riseth, even a morning without clouds.
2 Sam. 23:3, 4.

And John answered him, saying, Master, we saw one casting out devils in thy name, and he followeth not us; and we forbade him, because he followeth not us.

But Jesus said, Forbid him not: for there is no man which shall do a miracle in my name, that can lightly speak evil of me.
Mark 9:38, 39.

Rom. 2:1.

Matt. 7:1.

Rom. 14:3, 4.

And when his disciples James and John saw this, they said, Lord, wilt thou that we command fire to come down from heaven, and consume them, even as Elias did?

But he turned, and rebuked them, and said, Ye know not what manner of spirit ye are of.
Luke 9:54, 55.

would become the medium of communication between God and man. He was not the only prophet of the apostolic church, for sixteen others are named in the New Testament; but to him was given the most extended view of the future work of God in the earth. Bearing in mind that the eye of Heaven was upon John, and that he was in every act preparing for that noblest of callings, although he knew it not, the history of this disciple becomes a wonderful object lesson to those who live in the end of time.

He yielded himself fully to the teachings of the Man of God; his mind met the mind of Christ; his soul touched the soul of the Divine One. Life flowed from Christ, begetting life in the disciples. This is Christian experience; this will be the experience of all who live to see the Saviour coming in the clouds of Heaven; and this experience enabled John to say, "Of His fullness have we all received, and grace for grace."

The growth in grace was a gradual development, and, at times, an unholy zeal over-mastered the tenderness which Christ constantly sought to impart. There was one man who cast out devils, and John rebuked him because this man was not like the disciples a follower of the Saviour. This spirit of judging all others by a self-reared standard, was rebuked in the words of the Master, "Forbid them not." When the Samaritans offered insult to the Saviour, John was the one who wished to call down fire from heaven and destroy them. He was surprised when the Saviour revealed to him the fact that such a spirit was one of persecution, and that He, the Son of God. had not "come to destroy mens' lives, but to save them." Each correction was keenly felt, but it opened to the mind of John the principle of divine government, and revealed to him the depth of divine love.

Near the close of Christ's ministry, the mother of James and John came to ask for her sons the place of honor in His kingdom. Salome herself was a follower of Christ, and the great love of the family for the Saviour, led them all to desire to be near Him. Love always draws us near the object of our love. Jesus saw what the granting of the request would imply, and in tones of sadness, answered that the place nearest the throne would be occupied by those who endured most, who sacrificed most, and who loved most. In

**Salome asks for her sons the place of honor in His kingdom.**

later life John comprehended the meaning of the answer; for he was given a view of the redeemed as they will gather on the sea of glass about the throne.

These human desires came at times when the life current was partially broken. At other

Now no chastening for the present seemeth to be joyous, but grievous. Heb. 12:11.

Then came to him the mother of Zebedee's children with her sons, worshipping him, and desiring a certain thing of him.

And he said unto her, What wilt thou? She saith unto him, Grant that these my two sons may sit, the one on thy right hand, and the other on the left, in thy kingdom. Matt. 20:20, 21.

My beloved is white and ruddy, the chiefest among ten thousand. Sol. Songs 5:10.

I am my beloved's, and his desire is toward me. Sol. Songs 7:10.

To sit on my right hand, and on my left, is not mine to give, but it shall be given to them for whom it is prepared of my Father. Matt. 20:23.

And I saw as it were a sea of glass mingled with fire: and them that had gotten the victory over the beast, and over his image, and over his mark, and over the number of his name, stand on the sea of glass, having the harps of God. Rev. 15:1-3.

Thou hast made me to serve with thy sins. Isa. 43:24.

Thou art all fair, my love; there is no spot in thee. Sol. Songs 4:7.

Luke 9:28-36.
Matt. 17:1-13.
Mark 9:2-10.

Then cometh Jesus with them unto a place called Gethsemane, and saith unto the disciples, Sit ye here, while I go and pray yonder.

And he took with him Peter and the two sons of Zebedee, and began to be sorrowful and very heavy.

Matt. 26:36, 37.

times its flow was steady and strong. Thus it was when John stood with Christ on the Mount of Transfiguration, and heard the voices of Moses and Elijah, as they sought to strengthen the Saviour for His soon coming death. John sat at

**John pressed close to the Saviour's side.**

And he cometh unto the disciples, and findeth them asleep, and saith unto Peter, What, could ye not watch with me one hour?

Watch and pray, that ye enter not into temptation: the spirit indeed is willing, but the flesh is weak.

He went away again the second time, and prayed, saying, O my Father, if this cup may not pass away from me, except I drink it, thy will be done.

And he came and found them asleep again: for their eyes were heavy.

Matt. 26:40-43.

Knowing this, that the trying of your faith worketh patience.

Jas. 1:3.

And they all forsook him, and fled.

Mark 14:50.

And Simon Peter followed Jesus, and so did another disciple: that disciple was known unto the high priest, and went in with Jesus into the palace of the high priest.

But Peter stood at the door without. Then went out that other disciple, which was known unto the high priest, and spake unto her that kept the door, and brought in Peter.

John 18:15, 16.

the Saviour's left hand at the Passion Supper, and as the little company of twelve walked in the moonlight toward Olivet on that last night, John pressed close to the Saviour's side. As they entered the Garden of Gethsemane, eight of the disciples remained without the gate; while Peter, James, and John went on a little farther. The Son of Man longed to have John sit beside Him during that bitter struggle; and although John had lived so near to Jesus, yet he failed to grasp that last opportunity which would have placed him next the throne. While the Saviour pleaded in agony, and finally fell fainting to the ground, John was sleeping. The flesh was weak although the spirit was willing. His love so fervent, was still weakened by the clay channel through which it flowed. Still more bitter trials were needed to burn out all the dross.

Having slept, he too fled when the mob came for the Saviour, but his love drew him back. Ashamed of his cowardice, he returned, and entered the judgment hall, keeping close to the man condemned as a criminal. All night long he watched and prayed, and hoped soon to see a flash of divinity which would forever silence the accusers. He followed to Calvary. Every nail that was driven seemed to tear his own flesh. Faint, he turned away, but came back to support the mother of Jesus, who stood at the foot of the cross. That dying cry pierced to his very heart; the One whom he had loved was dead. Unable to comprehend the meaning of it all, yet he helped prepare the body for burial, and with the other sorrowing disciples passed a lonely Sabbath. Life seemed scarcely worth living; for He for whom they had given up everything, and whom they had believed to be the Son of God, was silent in death. The words which Christ had spoken concerning His own death, and which John should have understood, had fallen on deaf ears. Much as he loved his Lord he was dull of hearing.

On the morning of the resurrection John was the first of the twelve to reach the tomb; for he outran Peter, when Mary Magdalene reported that the body was gone. Seeing the folded napkin in the sepulchre, he recognized the familiar touch of a risen Saviour, and believed.

On the evening after the resurrection John received the benediction when Christ appeared; but since he could no longer see his Master with the physical eye, he returned to his fishing on the shores of the Sea of Galilee. But Jesus sought him again, and bade him go forth a fisher of men. In the last recorded interview between Christ and His disciples, the Saviour prophetically gave the work of Peter and John, those two earnest fol-

And all his a
women that foll
ilee, stood afar o ... these
things. Luke 23:49.

John 19:26, 27.

And about the ninth hour Jesus cried with a loud voice, saying, Eli, Eli, lama sabachthani? that is to say, My God, my God, why hast thou forsaken me?

Jesus, when he had cried again with a loud voice, yielded up the ghost. Matt. 27:46, 50.

Luke 23:50–53.

Mark 15:42–47.

And that day was the preparation, and the sabbath drew on.

And the women also, which came with him from Galilee, followed after, and beheld the sepulchre, and how his body was laid.

And they returned, and prepared spices and ointments; and rested the sabbath day according to the commandment. Luke 23:54–56.

Matt. 16:21–23.
Matt. 20:17–19.
Mark 8:31–33.
Mark 9:31, 32.
Mark 10:32–34.
Isa. 29:10.
Luke 9:21, 22.
Luke 18, 31–34.

And the napkin, that was about his head, not lying with the linen clothes, but wrapped together in a place by itself.

Then went in also that other disciple, which came first to the sepulchre, and he saw, and believed. John 20:4–9.

John 20:19–23.

Simon Peter saith unto them, I go a fishing. They say unto him, We also go with thee. They went forth, and entered into a ship immediately; and that night they caught nothing. John 21:1–3.

Verily, verily, I say unto thee, When thou wast young, thou girdedst thyself, and walkedst whither thou wouldest: but when thou shalt be old, thou shalt stretch forth thy hands, and another shall gird thee, and carry thee whither thou wouldest not.

Then spake he, signifying by what death he should glorify God. And when he had spoken this, he saith unto him, Follow me.

Then Peter, turning about, seeth the disciple whom Jesus loved following; which also leaned on his breast at supper, and said, Lord, which is he that betrayeth thee?

Peter seeing him saith to Jesus Lord, and what shall this man done

Jesus saith unto him, If I will that he tarry till I come, what is that to thee? follow thou me.

John 21:18–22.

lowers, who had passed through so many clouds, and yet had seen such bright rays of sunlight. Peter was told it would be his lot to follow his Lord to the cross. When he asked the fate of John, Christ replied, "If I will that he tarry till I come, what is that to thee?"

The life of John is but briefly referred to after the ascension. He remained in Jerusalem for a number of years, and was known as one of the pillars of that church as late as A. D. 58. John's

Her sins, which are many, are forgiven. for she loved much: but to whom little is forgiven. the same loveth little

Luke 7:47.

**Isle of Patmos. Distant View.**

And when James, Cephas, and John, who seemed to be pillars, perceived the grace that was given unto me, they gave to me and Barnabas the right hands of fellowship.

Gal. 2:9.

And the people of the prince that shall come shall destroy the city and the sanctuary.

Dan. 9:26.

fervent love for the Saviour grew stronger as he suffered oppression and imprisonment. His own brother, James. was among the first martyrs to the cause of Christianity. Living as John did at the center of the work, he witnessed the spread of the truth, and knew of its triumphs as well as its vicissitudes. Roman oppression became greater. The city of Jerusalem was destroyed by the army of Titus, and John was banished to the Isle of Patmos. He himself says that he was there for the "Word of God, and for the Testimony of Jesus Christ."

It is a beautiful thought that he whose heart was so bound up in Jerusalem and the Hebrew race, and who was always so true to both, should have been permitted to see the glories of the New Jerusalem, the city finally to take the place of his own earthly Zion. To him was given the entire history of the church of God, which must do the work rejected by his own race.

The road from the Jordan to the rocky height of Patmos was a steep and stony way; but when he sat alone upon the mountain side overlooking the sea, the intense love, the soul union with Christ, which those previous years had developed, enabled that "disciple whom Jesus loved" to become the connecting link between heaven and earth. Gabriel, Christ's own angel, stood by the side of the last survivor of the chosen twelve, and opened to his vision the glories of the future. A nature less spiritual would have failed to grasp the picture of eternity; a mind less consecrated could not have been the channel for such a flood of divine enlightenment.

In the Midian desert, where none but God was near, Moses wrote Genesis, the Alpha of all things. John wrote Revelation—the complete unfolding of that first book—the Omega—when alone on an island in the midst of the sea. The pen of him who wrote the history of creation, was guided by the same angel who bore to John the heavenly message concerning the consummation of the plan of redemption.

Rev. 1:9.

The testimony of Jesus is the spirit of prophecy. Rev. 19:10.

Pray for the peace of Jerusalem: they shall prosper that love thee. Psa. 122:6.

And I John saw the holy city, new Jerusalem, coming down from God out of heaven, prepared as a bride adorned for her husband. Rev. 21:2.

For if God spared not the natural branches, take heed lest he also spare not thee. Rom. 11:21.

Many waters cannot quench love, neither can the floods drown it: if a man would give all the substance of his house for love, it would utterly be contemned. Sol. Songs 8:7.

If there be a prophet among you, I the Lord will make myself known unto him in a vision, and will speak unto him in a dream. Num. 12:6.

Dan. 10:21.
Dan. 8:16.
Rev. 1:1.

But the natural man receiveth not the things of the Spirit of God: for they are foolishness unto him: neither can he know them, because they are spiritually discerned. 1 Cor. 2:14.

And beginning at Moses and all the prophets, he expounded unto them in all the Scriptures the things concerning himself. Luke 24:27.

And I John saw these things, and heard them. And when I had heard and seen, I fell down to worship before the feet of the angel which shewed me these things.

Then saith he unto me, See thou do it not: for I am thy fellow servant, and of thy brethren the prophets, and of them which keep the sayings of this book: worship God. Rev. 22:8, 9.

I will raise them up a Prophet from among their brethren, like unto thee, and will put my words in his mouth; and he shall speak unto them all that I shall command him. Deut. 18:18.

Acts 3:22, 23.
Deut. 34:1-4.
Rev. 21:1, 2.
Zech. 14:4, 5.
Gen. 1:1.
Rev. 22:10.

Moses recorded the story of Creation and the Fall, and by faith he grasped the promise of a Redeemer. John lived with that Redeemer, and as he stood on Patmos, he looked back into the past to the place where Moses stood on Pisgah, and then forward to the City of God, which he saw descending on the Mount of Olives. The two mountain peaks from which all history can be viewed are Genesis and Revelation, the beginning and the end, the first and the last.

# John the Beloved.

I'M growing very old. This weary head
That hath so often leaned on Jesus' breast
In days long past that seem almost a dream,
Is bent and hoary with its weight of years.
These limbs that followed Him—my Master—oft
From Galilee to Judah, yea, that stood
Beneath the cross, and trembled with His groans,
Refuse to bear me even through the streets
To preach unto my children. E'en my lips
Refuse to form the words my heart sends forth.
My ears are dull, they scarcely hear the sobs
Of my dear children gathered round my couch;
God lays His hand upon me,—yea, His *hand*
And not His *rod*,—the gentle hand that I
Felt, those three years, so often pressed in mine
In friendship such as passeth woman's love.

I'm old,—so old I can not recollect
The faces of my friends, and I forget
The words and deeds that make my daily life;
But that dear face and every word *He* spoke
Grow more distinct as others fade away,
So that I live with Him and holy dead
More than with the living.

Some seventy years ago
I was a fisher by the sacred sea.
It was at sunset. How the tranquil tide
Bathed dreamily the pebbles! How the light
Crept up the distant hills, and in its wake
Soft, purple shadows wrapped the dewy fields!
And then *He* came and called me. Then I gazed,
For the first time, on that sweet face. Those eyes,
From out of which, as from a window, shone
Divinity, looked on my inmost soul
And lighted it forever. Then His words
Broke on the silence of my heart, and made
The whole world musical. Incarnate Love
Took hold of me, and claimed me for its own.
I followed in the twilight, holding fast
His mantle.

O, what holy walks we had,
Through harvest fields and desolate, dreary wastes!
And oftentimes He leaned upon my arm,
Wearied and wayworn. I was young and strong,
And so upbore Him. Lord, now *I* am weak,
And old, and feeble! Let me rest on Thee!
So, put Thine arm around me. Closer still!
How strong Thou art! The twilight grows apace.
Come, let us leave these noisy streets, and take
The path to Bethany, for Mary's smile
Awaits us at the gate, and Martha's hands
Have long prepared the cheerful evening meal.
Come, James, the Master waits; and Peter, see,
Has gone some steps before.

What say you, friends?
That this is Ephesus, and Christ has gone
Back to His kingdom? Ay, 'tis so, 'tis so.
I know it all; and yet, just now I seemed
To stand once more upon my native hills,
And touch my Master. O, how oft I've seen
The touching of His garment bring back strength
To palsied limbs! I feel it has to mine.

"Oftentimes He leaned upon my arm, wearied and worn."

UP! bear me once more to my church! Once more
There let me tell them of a Saviour's love;
For, by the sweetness of my Master's voice
Just now, I think He must be very near,—
Coming, I trust, to break the veil, which time
Has worn so thin that I can see beyond,
And watch His footsteps.

So, raise my head.
How dark it is! I can not seem to see
The faces of my flock. Is that the sea
That murmurs so, or is it weeping? Hush,
My little children! God so loved the world
He gave His Son. So love ye one another.
Love God and man. Amen. Now bear me back.
My legacy unto an angry world is this.
I feel my work is finished. Are the streets so full?
What call the folk my name,—the Holy John?
Nay, write me rather, Jesus Christ's beloved,
And lover of my children.

Lay me down
Once more upon my couch, and open wide
The eastern window. See, there comes a light
Like that which broke upon my soul at eve,
When, in the dreary Isle of Patmos, Gabriel came
And touched me on the shoulder. See, it grows
As when we mounted toward the pearly gates.
I know the way! I trod it once before.
And hark! It is the song the ransomed sang
Of glory to the Lamb! How loud it sounds!
And that unwritten one! Methinks my soul
Can join it now. . . . . . . .
. . . . O my Lord, my Lord!
How bright Thou art! and yet the very same
I loved in Galilee. 'Tis worthy the hundred years
To feel this bliss! So lift me up, dear Lord,
Unto Thy bosom. There shall I abide.

—*Selected.*

# CHAPTER II.

## THE AUTHOR OF THE REVELATION.

THE first chapter of Revelation is an introduction to the entire book. The first three verses are a preface to the chapter, and the first verse is the key, not only to Revelation, but to every prophetic book in the Bible, showing how all prophecy is given. In this first verse is given the title of the book, the author of the prophecy, its object, the manner in which it came, and the agent of God in making known the history of future events.

It is "The Revelation of Jesus Christ." It is not the Revelation of John, as many seem to think; for then it would cease to be prophecy, and as a history, would rank no higher than the works of many other writers. John calls himself our "brother and companion in tribulation." It is the Revelation of Jesus Christ,—an unfolding of the life of the God-man. Jesus means *Saviour*. "Thou shalt call His name Jesus: for He shall save His people from their sins." Jesus was the name given by the angel when he talked with Mary, the mother of Jesus. *Christ* means

*The Revelation of Jesus Christ, which God gave unto him, to shew unto his servants things which must shortly come to pass; and he sent and signified it by his angel unto his servant John.*
*Rev. 1:1.*

For in him dwelleth all the fulness of the Godhead bodily.
Col. 2:9.

John 1:1.

And the Word was made flesh, and dwelt among us, (and we beheld his glory, the glory as of the only begotten of the Father,) full of grace and truth. John 1:14.

Heb. 2:14.

For there is one God, and one mediator between God and men, the man Christ Jesus. 1 Tim. 2:5.

Rev. 1:9.

Believe me that I am in the Father, and the Father in me: or else believe me for the very works' sake.
John 14:11.

Matt. 1:21.
John 1:41 [margin.]
Dan. 9:26.

Behold, a virgin shall be with child, and shall bring forth a son, and they shall call his name Emmanuel, which being interpreted is, God with us. Matt. 1:23.

anointed: Jesus Christ is the anointed Saviour; prophets of old had foretold of His mission on earth, and named Him *Emmanuel*, "God with us."

To John, then, was laid open, or made manifest, the mystery of Emmanuel, the union of the divine and human, the Christ. The entire book of Revelation is an explanation of the *divine life* which God placed in the human mold, and gave to man for all eternity. "Divinity needed humanity; for it required both the divine and the human to bring salvation to the world. Divinity needed humanity, that humanity might afford a channel of communication between God and man." Humanity was lost without divinity. Salvation came by the union of the two in Christ. The union formed in Him will never be severed, for the church to which His teachings gave birth is a child of God, and the history of the church is the history of Emmanuel,—the mystery of godliness. Adam was made in the image of God, and was a son of God; but sin severed the tie, and the children of Adam were born in sin. But Christ, the second Adam, was the Son of God; and the church, the only begotten of Christ, partakes of the nature of the Father, and stands before the world to perpetuate His name,—Emmanuel. This family name will never become extinct. "I [Paul] bow my knees unto the Father of our Lord Jesus Christ, of whom the whole family in heaven and earth is named."

The continued history of Emmanuel, as read in the life of the Christian Church, is what was revealed to John by the angel Gabriel, Christ's attendant,—that member of the heavenly host whose duty it has long been to make known the mystery of God to His servants. God desires

And without controversy great is the mystery of godliness: God was manifest in the flesh, justified in the Spirit, seen of angels, preached unto the Gentiles, believed on in the world, received up into glory.
1 Tim. 3:16.

To wit, that God was in Christ, reconciling the world unto himself, not imputing their trespasses unto them; and hath committed unto us the word of reconciliation.

Now then we are ambassadors for Christ, as though God did beseech you by us: we pray you in Christ's stead, be ye reconciled to God.
2 Cor. 5:19, 20.

Luke 19:10.

Having abolished in his flesh the enmity, even the law of commandments contained in ordinances; for to make in himself of twain one new man, so making peace.
Eph. 2:15, 16.

Eph. 3:10, 11.

So God created man in his own image, in the image of God created he him; male and female created he them. Gen. 1:27.

And so it is written, The first man Adam was made a living soul; the last Adam was made a quickening spirit. 1 Cor. 15:45.

Eph. 3:11-17.

Who is he that condemneth? It is Christ that died, yea rather, that is risen again, who is even at the right hand of God, who also maketh intercession for us.
Rom. 8:34.

Eph. 3:14, 15.

***Who bare record of the word of God, and of the testimony of Jesus Christ, and of all things that he saw. Rev. 1:2.***

Dan. 10:21.

Dan. 8:16.

**I have written to him the great things of my law, but they were counted as a strange thing.**
**Hos. 8:12.**

The secret things belong unto the Lord our God: but those things which are revealed belong unto us and to our children forever, that we may do all the words of this law.
Deut. 29:29.

I have also spoken by the prophets, and I have multiplied visions, and used similitudes, by the ministry of the prophets.
Hos. 12:10.

Num. 12:6-8.

And the Word was made flesh and dwelt among us, (and we beheld his glory, the glory as of the only begotten of the Father,) full of grace and truth. John 1:14.

that man should comprehend the nature of His law and the manner of His working.

Near the close of the first century, Gabriel was bidden to open to the Prophet on Patmos the signs, or symbols, by which John might understand the history of the work of God in the earth. God reveals Himself to man in various ways. "Nature is the mirror of divinity;" the Word of God is His character in human language; Christ was that Word lived in human form, and the body of Christ—the church—has, in addition to these methods, the providences, or leadings, of the

Heb. 4:12-15.

John 15:10.

John 16:7, 8.

Rev. 19:10.

But ye have an unction from the Holy One, and ye know all things. 1 John 2:20, 27.

**A Heavenly benediction is pronounced upon him that readeth.**

Spirit. Thus John "bare record of the Word of God," as written and as lived in Christ; and he bare record also "of the testimony of Jesus Christ," "which is the spirit of prophecy," and he likewise bare record of the signs which Gabriel presented to his vision,—the "all things that he saw."

Yea, if thou criest after knowledge, and liftest up thy voice for understanding;
If thou seekest her as silver, and searchest for her as for hid treasures;
Then shalt thou understand the fear of the Lord, and find the knowledge of God.
Prov. 2:3-5.

A heavenly benediction is pronounced upon him "that readeth, and they that hear the words of this prophecy," and upon those who "keep those things which are written therein." It must needs be that the things written by John can be understood, else why the blessing that is here pronounced? Since the book is a revelation of

***Blessed is he that readeth, and they that hear the words of this prophecy, and keep those things which are written therein: for the time is at hand.***
***Rev. 1:3.***

Jesus Christ to the servants of the Most High, all who are His servants will study and understand the prophecy. Every doctrine necessary for salvation was given in the revelation of Christ, and the book becomes a compendium of the whole Bible. The blessing pronounced upon the servants to whom it is sent, is an eternal blessing; "For thou blessest, O Lord, and it shall be blessed forever."

2 Tim. 3 : 15, 16.
John 5 : 39.

1 Chron. 17 : 27.

Thou shalt hide them in the secret of thy presence from the pride of man: thou shalt keep them secretly in a pavilion from the strife of tongues. Psa. 31 : 20.

John, while on the island, away from the work with which he had been so long and so intimately associated, away from friends and companions, often let his mind wander to the scene of his former labors. As he looked toward the shores of Asia Minor, there came up before him the picture of the companies of believers who were standing for the truth in the midst of pagan darkness. He loved those followers of his Lord, and through him, Christ sent a message to each of "the seven churches which are in Asia." The Spirit used each of those churches to represent a period in the history of the work of God on earth, the seven covering the time from the life of John to the closing events in the history of the world.

Jer. 15 : 15-18.
Deut. 33 : 3.

*John to the seven churches which are in Asia: Grace be unto you, and peace, from him which is, and which was, and which is to come; and from the seven Spirits which are before his throne;*
*And from Jesus Christ, who is the faithful witness, and the first begotten of the dead, and the prince of the kings of the earth. Unto him that loved us, and washed us from our sins in his own blood.*
*Rev. 1 : 4, 5.*

Rev. 12 : 17.

There was a peculiar significance in the location of these seven churches. Asia Minor, or more particularly the western portion of the peninsula to which the term *Asia* is applied in Rev. 1 : 4, held in the spread of Christianity, a position corresponding to that which was occupied by Palestine in the history of the Jewish nation. When God wished to make the Hebrew race the leading government of earth, He chose, for the seat of that government, a position unrivaled by any other portion of the globe. Palestine was

Beautiful for situation, the joy of the whole earth, is mount Zion, on the sides of the north, the city of the great King. Psa. 48 : 2.

Out of Zion, the perfection of beauty, God hath shined.
Psa. 50 : 2.

All that pass by clap their hands at thee; they hiss and wag their head at the daughter of Jerusalem, saying, Is this the city that men call The perfection of beauty, The joy of the whole earth?
Lam. 2:15.

Acts 19:8–10.
Acts 19:18–20.
Acts 2:5–11.

Go ye therefore, and teach all nations, baptizing them in the name of the Father, and of the Son, and of the Holy Ghost:
Teaching them to observe all things whatsoever I have commanded you: and, lo, I am with you alway, even unto the end of the world. Amen.
Matt. 28:19, 20.

Ex. 3:2-6.

And God said unto Moses, I AM THAT I AM: and he said, Thus shalt thou say unto the children of Israel, I AM hath sent me unto you. Ex. 3:14.

John 20:22.
1 Cor. 1:3.
2 Cor. 1:2.
2 Cor. 13:14.
Gal. 1:3.
Eph. 1:2.
Phil. 1:2.
Col. 1:2.
1 Thess. 1:1.
2 Thess. 1:2.
1 Tim. 1:2.
2 Tim. 1:2.
Titus 1:4.
Phil. 1:3.

He is despised and rejected of men; a man of sorrows, and acquainted with grief: and we hid as it were our faces from him; he was despised, and we esteemed him not.
Isa. 53:3.

the highway between the South and the East and between the East and the West. When the power of God passed from this nation to the Christian Church, Asia Minor became the center of activity and the base of operation. In those seacoast towns, and in Ephesus above all others, Jew and Gentile met on equal footing. Every nationality,—Parthians, Medes, Elamites, and dwellers in Mesopotamia, representing the far North and East, met in trade, with citizens of Rome, Egypt, and Cyrene, men from the South and the West. Into these busy marts the Christian faith penetrated, and from these centers, the knowledge of the Christ was spread to all the world.

Jehovah, the Great I AM, who appeared to Moses in the burning bush, the Father of us all, who meets us where we are,—He, the Ever Present, breathed His blessing on the church called by the name of His Son. And from "the seven spirits which are before His throne," and from Jesus Christ, the visible manifestation of that Spirit, came the greeting of grace and peace to the companies who should be known by the name of the Anointed.

Here is inscribed the name of the author of the Revelation. He, who to-day witnesses for us in the heavenly court, is the "faithful witness," "the first begotten of the dead," "the prince of the kings of the earth;" and above all He is the one who "loved us, and washed us from our sins in His own blood." He, who on earth was the despised and rejected of men, was in truth the Prince of the kings of the earth. Again and again this same Christ had, by His providences, caused men to acknowledge the fact that "the Most High ruleth in the kingdom of men." No ruler on earth reigns independent of the Lord of heaven; for all power belongs unto God, and "the powers that be, are ordained of God." For this reason men are exhorted to pray for governors and kings, that there may be peace in the land.

Dan. 4 : 17.

Psa. 44 : 5-8.
Psa. 33 : 6, 7.
Psa. 75 : 5-7.
1 Sam. 2 : 10.

Here is the position to which He calls us. He "hath made us kings," to sit on thrones and rule; "and priests" to minister "unto God and

1 Sam. 14 : 6.
Jer. 46 : 16-20.
Rom. 13 : 1.

Patmos. Near View.

*And hath made us kings and priests unto God and his Father; to him be glory and dominion for ever and ever. Amen. Rev. 1:6.*

I John, who also am your brother and companion in tribulation and in the kingdom and patience of Jesus Christ, was in the isle that is called Patmos, for the word of God, and for the testimony of Jesus Christ. Rev. 1 : 9.

His Father." And yet, when on earth, He had said, "He that is greatest among you, let him be . . . as he that doth serve." The joint-heirs with Christ rule while still on earth, but their authority here is by virtue of the "power of an endless life," and they are leaders, not in a physical sense, but in the spiritual realm. The scepter that they sway is not carnal and temporal, but eternal. The position is above earthly potentates, and the wonderful part of it all is, that, in the world, which is in the hands of the prince of evil, Christ has a nation of kings and priests.—a kingdom within a kingdom. "This

*Behold, he cometh with clouds; and every eye shall see him, and they also which pierced him: and all kindreds of the earth shall wail because of him. Even so, Amen.*

*I am Alpha and Omega, the beginning and the ending, saith the Lord, which is, and which was, and which is to come, the Almighty. Rev. 1:7, 8.*

2 Cor. 10:4.
Heb. 7:16.
Col. 1:12, 13.

is a great mystery: but I speak concerning Christ and the church."

The eye of the prophet swept over the company and as he saw the power of the gospel, in ecstasy he exclaimed, "To Him be glory and dominion forever and ever." He saw, in one glance, the closing of earth's history, the coming of the Son of man with power and great glory. He saw, again, that angry crowd who gathered in the Garden of Gethsemane, and rudely bore

Eph. 5:32.
Jude 25.

But the day of the Lord will come as a thief in the night; in the which the heavens shall pass away with a great noise, and the elements shall melt with fervent heat, the earth also and the works that are therein shall be burned up.
2 Pet. 3:10.

He came out, and went, as he was wont, to the mount of Olives; and his disciples also followed him. Mark 14:39.

They came to a place which was named Gethsemane: and he saith to his disciples, Sit ye here, while I shall pray.
Luke 22:32.

**Garden of Gethsemane.**

away his Master; he saw the jeering company about the cross, and the soldier who pierced His side; but as he watches this time, he hears the bitter wail of those who rejected the Saviour of mankind. And, as he looked, he heard the words: "I am Alpha, the beginning, and Omega, the ending, 'the Lord, which is, and which was, and which is to come, the Almighty.'" This expression, or its equivalent, occurs four times in this first chapter.

Luke 22:47, 48.
John 19:34.

Luke 23:27, 28.
Rev. 1:8, 11, 17, 18.

The Sabbath was a precious day to John, and it had been especially dear since that never to be forgotten Sabbath on which their Master rested

And hallow my sabbaths; and they shall be a sign between me and you, that ye may know that I am the Lord your God.
Eze. 20:20.

in the tomb. The preparation for that Sabbath was the bitter hours on Calvary; the day itself was one of utter loneliness; because the gospel of the resurrection was not comprehended. It should have been a day of joy; it was intended as such; and after the Saviour came from the grave, and the light of His countenance again rested upon His followers, they saw more clearly than ever before that the Sabbath was not only a reminder of Creation, but that it also commemorated Redemption. It became the central truth in giving the life of Christ. To John on Patmos it was a day of holy joy. The Saviour came divinely near, and as John contemplated scenes in his own association with Christ, the Man of God, his heart warmed with praise. In imagination he stood by Jordan, and saw the baptism of the Holy Spirit: again he was on the Mount of Transfiguration; he saw the pained face of the Master as they sat around the table on that last night; an agony of feeling passed over him as he recalled the trial, the condemnation, and the death; but it was replaced by the joy of the resurrection, and the remembrance of those last words as the clouds caught Him from the sight of men. John's love for Christ was so strong that it seemed his Master must surely speak to him again. And he heard behind him a great voice as of a trumpet, and Christ, his own Christ, stood by his side. "I am the first, but I am also the last. 'I am Alpha and Omega.' Write what thou seest in a book and send it unto the seven churches which are in Asia."

He spoke in trumpet tones, like the clearest music, and the voice was as the sound of many waters; but still, to John He was the same Jesus

Luke 23:54-56.
Isa. 58:13.

*I John, who also am your brother, and companion in tribulation, and in the kingdom and patience of Jesus Christ, was in the isle that is called Patmos, for the word of God, and for the testimony of Jesus Christ.*

*I was in the Spirit on the Lord's day, and heard behind me a great voice, as of a trumpet,*

*Saying, I am Alpha and Omega, the first and the last: and, What thou seest, write in a book, and send it unto the seven churches which are in Asia; unto Ephesus, and unto Smyrna, and unto Pergamos, and unto Thyatira, and unto Sardis, and unto Philadelphia, and unto Laodicea.* *Rev. 1:9-11.*

Col. 1:14-16.
John 13:21-25.
Luke 3:21, 22.
Matt. 17:1-3.

Ye shall receive power, after that the Holy Ghost is come upon you: and ye shall be witnesses unto me both in Jerusalem, and in all Judea, and in Samaria, and unto the uttermost part of the earth.

Acts 1:8-11.

O my dove, that art in the clefts of the rock, in the secret places of the stairs, let me see thy countenance, let me hear thy voice; for sweet is thy voice, and thy countenance is comely.

Sol. Song 2:14.

Rev. 1:10.
Eze. 42:2.
Eze. 1:24.
Rev. 19:5, 6.

*And I turned to see the voice that spake with me. And being turned, I saw seven golden candlesticks;*

*And in the midst of the seven candlesticks one like unto the Son of man, clothed with a garment down to the foot, and girt about the paps with a golden girdle.*

*His head and his hairs were white like wool, as white as snow; and his eyes were as a flame of fire.* *Rev. 1:12-14.*

**"The hoary head is a crown of glory, if it be found in the way of righteousness."**

Prov. 19:31.
Dan. 7:9.

*And his feet like unto fine brass, as if they burned in a furnace; and his voice as the sound of many waters.*

*And he had in his right hand seven stars: and out of his mouth went a sharp twoedged sword: and his countenance was as the sun shineth in his strength.* *Rev. 1:15, 16.*

Eze. 1:7.
Matt. 17:2.
Acts 26:13-15.
1 Pet. 1:7.

Lord, lift thou up the light of thy countenance upon us. Psa. 4:6.

Psa. 89:15.
Luke 9:29.

The light of the eyes rejoiceth the heart. Prov. 15:30.

The light of the body is the eye. Matt. 6:22.

whom he had known in Galilee and in Jerusalem. Not now despised, mocked, and rejected, but standing in the midst of the seven candlesticks, —the churches, their light being the reflection of His own. He was clothed, not in the cast-off purple robe, but in a garment of righteousness of dazzling whiteness, and girt about the loins with the golden girdle of truth. The purity of God Himself encircled His brow with a halo of light, for His head and His hairs were white like wool, as white as snow. The white hairs, which in old age are a crown of glory, even in the presence of sin and decay, are a token of salvation through a Saviour's love. The power of the life within shone through His eyes as a flame of fire, and the character is still further portrayed in the fact that His feet glowed like unto the most brilliant metal purified seven times. His footsteps were attended by light and heat, and His countenance shone above the brightness of the sun. The shining of our sun is a figure of the light of God shining in the face of Jesus Christ. In human beings, the light of the eye betrays the inner life, and a man's "countenance doth witness against him." Thus in every detail of John's description is revealed the depth of spirituality, the power of the God of life.

Although this is a description of the personal appearance of Christ, it portrays His character as well. Those who continue to reveal God in the earth must, through the merits of Christ, manifest the same character as living epistles known and read of all men. The robe of His righteousness must cover the human frailties and imperfections; the truth of God must be the rule of life; cleansed by the blood of Christ, the sinner becomes as white as snow. As He was made perfect through suffering, so the church will be purified by the fires of affliction; they will be brethren with John; "companions in tribulation, and in the kingdom and patience of Jesus Christ."

Isa. 3:9.

As ye have therefore received Christ Jesus the Lord, so walk ye in him. Col. 2:6.

2 Cor. 5:20.
1 Pet. 2:21.
2 Cor. 3:1, 2.
Isa. 6:10.
Rev. 19:8.
Jas. 2:12.
1 John 1:7.
Isa. 1:18, 19.
Heb. 10:35.
Rev. 1:9.

He who spoke to John was the One who commanded, and worlds stood forth in space. Christ

**Jesus laid His right hand upon him.**

now stood beside John, and the prophet, looking upon His glory, fell at His feet as one dead. He had walked with Him and talked with Him,—with this same *man*, Christ Jesus,—when He was on earth. He had asked to sit by His side in His kingdom. The glory of His presence now overcame John, but Jesus laid His right hand on him,—that hand which had so

Prov. 16:31.
Psa. 33:6-9.

*When I saw him I fell at his feet as dead. And he laid his right hand upon me, saying unto me, Fear not; I am the first and the last:*

*I am he that liveth, and was dead: and, behold, I am alive for ever more, Amen: and have the keys of hell and of death.*
*Rev. 1: 17, 18.*

*Write the things which thou hast seen, and the things which are, and the things which shall be hereafter:*
*The mystery of the seven stars which thou sawest in my right hand, and the seven golden candlesticks. The seven stars are the angels of the seven churches: and the seven candlesticks which thou sawest are the seven churches.*
*Rev. 1:19, 20.*

Mal. 2:7.

The Lord thy God in the midst of thee is mighty; he will save, he will rejoice over thee with joy; he will rest in his love, he will joy over thee with singing.
Zeph. 3:17.

Heb. 2:12.

Zech. 2:5.

And it shall come to pass in the last days, saith God, I will pour out of my Spirit upon all flesh: and your sons and your daughters shall prophesy, and your young men shall see visions, and your old men shall dream dreams.
Acts 2:17.

Luke 15:10.
Luke 2:7–14.
Matt. 4:11.
Luke 22:43.

Now therefore ye are no more strangers and foreigners, but fellow-citizens with the saints, and of the household of God;
And are built upon the foundation of the apostles and prophets, Jesus Christ himself being the chief corner stone.
Eph. 2:19–21.

Col. 1:28, 29.
1 Cor. 3:3, 15, 16.
Rev. 1:3.

often rested there before, and in a voice which John recognized as the same with which the Master spoke to the stormy waves of Galilee, He said, "Be not afraid, 'I am He that liveth and was dead; and, behold, I am alive forevermore.' You saw me in the grave, but I now have the keys of hell and of death." And so the message which John was commanded to give unto the churches is a message of triumph over sin, over death and the grave. It is the victory of truth over error.

Christ appeared, walking in the midst of the candlesticks, which symbolize the churches; and He held in His hand the seven stars or angels, which direct the work of the churches, and which are light-bearers from His throne to those who represent the work of heaven on earth. God looks upon the Christian Church as He looked upon Christ in the days of His sojourn on earth. As He was attended by an angel, so the church is guided by the Spirit of God, and by the testimony of that Spirit. In days of triumph, the angel attendants sing the song which filled the plains of Bethlehem on the night of the birth of Jesus: in days of persecution, trials, and despondency, angels lift the weary heads, as Gabriel ministered to Christ in the wilderness and in Gethsemane. The church completes the work begun by Christ in the flesh. His life studied will give the history of the church. His life as recorded in the Revelation of Jesus Christ is but a further unfolding of that same mystery of the incarnation,—the Emmanuel. "Blessed is he that readeth, and they that hear the words of this prophecy, and keep those things which are written therein."

# CHAPTER III.

## THE MESSAGE TO THE CHURCHES.

### EPHESUS.

THE message to the seven churches covers a period in ecclesiastical history, extending from the time of Christ's first advent to His second coming. To John, Christ appeared walking in the midst of the churches,—the candlesticks; and it is a most beautiful truth that the Divine Presence has never been withdrawn from the earth. One of the last promises made by Christ to His disciples was, "Lo, I am with you alway, even unto the end of the world," and it matters not how torn or scattered His people may have been, that promise, reverberating from age to age, has been the comfort and solace of each individual Christian, and of the church as a body. Heaven looks upon the earth as one vast mission field, and the church is a beacon light in the midst of darkness. The incarnation of Christ drew the sympathies of all the universe earthward, and "the whole creation groaneth," waiting for our adoption. Christ, attended by the host of heaven—His ministering spirits—is always

He which testifieth these things saith, Surely I come quickly. Amen. Rev. 22:20.

Rev. 1:19.

Rev. 1:13; Ruth 4:4.

For he hath said, I will never leave thee, nor forsake thee. Heb. 13:5.

But when the Comforter is come, whom I will send unto you from the Father, even the Spirit of truth, which proceedeth from the Father, he shall testify of me. John 15:26.

Matt. 28:20.

I will heal their backsliding, I will love them freely: for mine anger is turned away from him. Hosea 14:4.

Fear thou not; for I am with thee: be not dismayed; for I am thy God: I will strengthen thee; yea, I will help thee; yea, I will uphold thee with the right hand of my righteousness. Isa. 41:10.

Matt. 5:13–17.

Suddenly there was with the angel a multitude of the heavenly host praising God. Luke 2:13.

Rom. 8 : 22.

I was daily his delight, rejoicing always before him ;

Rejoicing in the habitable part of his earth ; and my delights were with the sons of men.

Prov. 8 :29-31.

Zech. 2 : 8.

Psa. 17 : 8.

Deut. 32 : 10.

Rev. 2 : 1.

**The church is a beacon light in the midst of darkness.**

**Page 39.**

Be not deceived : evil communications corrupt good manners.

1 Cor. 15 :33.

Behold, I send you forth as sheep in the midst of wolves : be ye therefore wise as serpents, and harmless as doves.

Matt. 10 : 16.

1 Tim. 1 : 1-7.

Avoiding profane and vain babblings, and oppositions of science falsely so called :

Which some professing have erred concerning the faith.

1 Tim. 6 :20, 21.

found in the midst of the church, and he that toucheth the church, toucheth the apple of the eye of Christ.

The first message which John was bidden to deliver was to the church of Ephesus. There were other churches in Asia Minor, but there were reasons why Ephesus was first addressed, and why it should be taken to represent the church in general during the first years of its existence. The word "*Ephesus*" means "*first*," or "*desirable*." In the first century, Ephesus was the capital of Asia Minor, and the center of trade from both the east and the west. It was strongly under Greek influence, and in position, corresponded to Corinth in Greece, and Alexandria in Egypt. It has been called the "rallying place of paganism," and was a stronghold of the recognized religion and the popular education of the world, when, soon after the death of the Saviour, it was first visited by the apostles. It may well be taken to symbolize that period of ecclesiastical history when the Gospel in its purity met, in open conflict, the darkest forms of pagan worship. Side by side with the Greeks, dwelt Jews, men who ought to have held aloft the worship of Jehovah, but who had lost the Spirit by mingling with the idol worshipers. It was into this city, restless and turbulent and easily wrought upon, that Paul, as a missionary, went to preach of a risen Saviour. He met with difficulties. Opposed on one side by science, falsely so called, and on the other side by a religion which had the form of godliness, but which had lost the power thereof, Paul offered the crucified Son of God. Miracles attended his preaching. In the synagogue of the Jews, he reasoned three months concerning "the kingdom of God;" and when men hardened their hearts against the Word, he entered the school of Tyrannus, where he taught for two years with such power that the Word of the Lord Jesus went abroad throughout all Asia, among both Jews and Greeks. The Greeks were scholars, and exalted the power of intellectual culture.

God wrought special miracles by the hands of Paul. Acts 19:11.

He went into the synagogue, and spake boldly for the space of three months, disputing and persuading the things concerning the kingdom of God.

But when divers were hardened, and believed not, but spake evil of that way before the multitude, he departed from them, and separated the disciples, disputing daily in the school of one Tyrannus.

And this continued by the space of two years; so that all they which

**Ephesus. Present State.**

Paul, as a Christian missionary, first taught in the synagogue, then in the schools, where the Gospel of Jesus Christ was offered in place of the philosophy of Plato, whom the Greeks deified. Said he, "The Jews require a sign, and the Greeks seek after wisdom: but we preach Christ crucified, unto the Jews a stumbling-block, and unto the Greeks foolishness; but unto them which are called, both Jews and Greeks, Christ the power of God and the wisdom of God." So powerful was this teaching of the apostle that many who owned books of sorcery, or magic, which passed for wisdom in the eyes of the

dwelt in Asia heard the word of the Lord Jesus, both Jews and Greeks. Acts 19:8–10.

For all the Athenians, and strangers which were there, spent their time in nothing else, but either to tell or to hear some new thing. Acts 17:16–21.

2 Cor. 10:5.

Many that believed came, and confessed, and shewed their deeds.

Many of them also which used curious arts brought their books together, and burned them before all men: and they counted the price of them, and found it fifty thousand pieces of silver.

So mightily grew the word of God and prevailed. Acts 19:18–20.

Acts 18 : 4–6.

For a certain man named Demetrius, a silversmith, which made silver shrines for Diana, brought no small gain unto the craftsmen;

Whom he called together with the workmen of like occupation, and said, Sirs, ye know that by this craft we have our wealth.

Moreover ye see and hear, that not alone at Ephesus, but almost throughout all Asia, this Paul hath persuaded and turned away much people, saying that they be no gods, which are made with hands:

So that not only this our craft is in danger to be set at nought; but also that the temple of the great goddess Diana should be despised, and her magnificence should be destroyed, whom all Asia and the world worshippeth.

And when they heard these sayings, they were full of wrath, and cried out, saying, Great is Diana of the Ephesians. Acts 19 : 24–28.

Dan. 2 : 10–19.

*Unto the angel of the church of Ephesus write; These things saith he that holdeth the seven stars in his right hand, who walketh in the midst of the seven golden candlesticks;*

*I know thy works, and thy labour, and thy patience, and how thou canst not bear them which are evil: and thou hast tried them which say they are apostles, and are not, and hast found them liars.*
*Rev. 2 : 1, 2.*

*And hast borne, and hast patience, and for my name's sake hast laboured, and hast not fainted.*
*Rev. 2 : 3.*

Acts 5 : 41, 42.
Acts 8 : 4.
Acts 11 : 24, 25.
Acts 13 : 2–5.

Elymas the sorcerer (for so is his name by interpretation) withstood them, seeking to turn away the deputy from the faith.

Then Saul, (who also is called Paul,) filled with the Holy Ghost, set his eyes on him,

And said, O full of all subtilty

world, brought their books and burned them before all men. Students from this school of Tyrannus became earnest workers in Asia Minor, and through them the Gospel was made known. Not only was the learning of the Greeks, who were the intellectual lights of the world, opposed by Paul and his disciples, but the trades were affected; so much so that there was an uprising of the people, who with one voice cried, "Great is Diana of the Ephesians." Diana, the patron goddess of Ephesus, was a personification of fecundity. In this city, Christianity—the power of God unto salvation—came in open and bitter conflict with the false religion and the false education of the world.

He who walked among the churches, watched the lighting of the torch of truth in Ephesus, and so the first words addressed to the church are, "I know thy works, and thy labor, and thy patience." Those, who, on the day of Pentecost, received the baptism of the Spirit, and those who heard the Gospel from their lips, were filled with a burning desire to spread the news of a Saviour. They were married unto Christ, and in the ardor of their first love, the converts sought for their friends and relatives, pleading with them to forsake evil and to accept salvation. There was no work too arduous, no journey too difficult, to be undertaken for Him whom they loved.

It can be seen that the power of God and the power of evil were in each other's grasp. By the side of pagan temples, were erected Christian churches; Christian schools sprang up in the very shadow of the Greek institutions of learning. In spite of the power of the enemy, the spread of truth was rapid, so rapid, indeed, that paganism trembled for its life. Among the converts to the new doctrine, were some who were convinced of the truth, but who failed to experience the change of heart which comes with the new birth. There were others, who, for policy's sake, sought fellowship with the Christians; but as long as the church maintained a close connection with God, a clear and distinct line separated believers from impostors. "Thou hast tried them which say they are apostles, and are not, and hast found them liars."

The power which attended even the common converts, and their ready spirit of discernment, is seen in the case of Priscilla and Aquila, when Apollos, who received the Gospel, or at least a part of it, in Alexandria, came to Ephesus. Apollos was fervent in the Spirit, and taught with power; for he was an eloquent man, and mighty in the Scriptures; but he knew only of the baptism of John. When he preached in the

**By the side of pagan temples were erected Christian churches.**

and all mischief, thou child of the devil, thou enemy of all righteousness, wilt thou not cease to pervert the right ways of the Lord?

And now, behold, the hand of the Lord is upon thee, and thou shalt be blind, not seeing the sun for a season. And immediately there fell on him a mist and a darkness; and he went about seeking some to lead him by the hand.
Acts 13:8–11.

Acts 16:16–18.
Acts 8:18–24.
2 Tim. 1:15.

This witness is true. Wherefore rebuke them sharply, that they may be sound in the faith;

Not giving heed to Jewish fables, and commandments of men, that turn from the truth.
Titus 1:13–16.

1 Tim. 1:20.
2 Tim. 2:17, 18.
Rev. 2:2.

A certain Jew named Apollos, born at Alexandria, an eloquent man, and mighty in the Scriptures, came to Ephesus.

This man was instructed in the way of the Lord; and being fervent in the spirit, he spake and taught diligently the things of the Lord, knowing only the baptism of John.

And he began to speak boldly in the synagogue: whom when Aquila and Priscilla had heard, they took him unto them, and expounded unto him the way of God more perfectly. Acts 18:24–26.

Blessed is the man that heareth me, watching daily at my gates, waiting at the posts of my doors.
Prov. 8:34, 35.

He said to them all, If any man will come after me, let him deny himself, and take up his cross daily, and follow me. Luke 9:23.

If any man walk in the day, he stumbleth not, because he seeth the light of this world.

But if a man walk in the night, he stumbleth, because there is no light in him. John 11:9, 10.

The remnant of Jacob shall be among the Gentiles in the midst of many people, as a lion among the beasts of the forest, as a young lion among the flocks of sheep: who, if he go through, both treadeth down, and teareth in pieces, and none can deliver. Micah 5 8.

Matt. 28:19, 20.
Mark 16:15-18.
Rev. 6:2.
Acts 19:1-7, 9, 10.

Those that be planted in the house of the Lord shall flourish in the courts of our God. Psa. 92:13.

Gal. 2:9.

Acts 19:10.

For a day in thy courts is better than a thousand. I had rather be a doorkeeper in the house of my God, than to dwell in the tents of wickedness. Psa. 84:10.

Rev. 2:2.

Acts 5:1-11.

Rom. 5:3-5.

I am the Lord: that is my name: and my glory will I not give to another, neither my praise to graven images. Isa. 42:8.

Christianity walked as a spotless virgin clothed in white.

hearing of those with whom Paul abode in Corinth, and who had studied with the great Apostle, Aquila and Priscilla detected his ignorance of the outpouring of the Spirit, and the eloquent man received instruction from those who had recently come into the truth. One can, in imagination, picture the sacrifice which seems necessary on the part of those who accepted Christ in this central stronghold of paganism. Light and darkness met face to face, and paganism made a desperate struggle for existence. It is for these reasons, that the first message, addressed to Ephesus, is applicable to the first era of the Christian religion. Into the darkness of the worst forms of heathenism, the religion and culture of the Greeks, backed by the government of Rome,—Christianity walked as a spotless virgin clothed in white. By preaching and by teaching, two methods which are divinely ordained for the spread of the truth, Paul and his fellow laborers raised up a church at Ephesus.

John had known of the work at this place; for he, as a pillar in the Jerusalem church, was acquainted with the progress of the light as it spread from that center, and from Patmos his heart turned to the believers on the mainland. The angel said, "Unto the church of Ephesus write: 'I know thy works, and thy labor, and thy patience, and how thou canst not bear them which are evil: and thou hast tried them which say they are apostles, and are not, and hast found them liars.'" The message is sent by the One who in heaven "holdeth the seven stars in His right hand, who walketh in the midst of the seven golden candlesticks." God Himself had watched each soul as it had separated from the world and linked itself with Christ. The power of Christ Himself attended the spread of the Gospel in those early days; for it was carried

**There were no idols, no outward forms, only a spiritual worship.**

by men who had received of the Pentecostal showers.

Christianity was a strange power as viewed by the heathen, for there were no idols, no outward forms, only a spiritual worship which they could not comprehend. The kingdom of Christ was invading the realm of the enemy, and there were no weapons which could attack it. In the space of thirty years, the Gospel went to every creature under heaven. Rich and poor alike heard the glad tidings of the Desire of all Nations,

Wherefore come out from among them, and be ye separate, saith the Lord, and touch not the unclean thing; and I will receive you. 2 Cor. 6:17.

Acts 2:1-4.

Acts 5:1-11.

Acts 10:44-48.

Acts 19:6.

Ex. 20:4-6.

The Lord spake unto you out of the midst of the fire: ye heard the voice of the words, but ye saw no similitude; only ye heard a voice. Deut. 4:12.

God is a Spirit: and they that worship him must worship him in spirit and in truth. John 4:24.

For we can do nothing against the truth, but for the truth. 2 Cor. 13:8.

Rom. 1:5, 8.

Rom. 16:19.

Col. 1:6, 23.

The rich and poor meet together: the Lord is the maker of them all Prov. 22:2.

Luke 3:1.

So that my bonds in Christ are manifest in all Cæsar's court, and in all other places.
Phil. 1:13 [margin.]
Phil. 4:22.

Blessed is the man that endureth temptation: for when he is tried, he shall receive the crown of life, which the Lord hath promised to them that love him.
Jas. 1:12.

Love is strong as death.
Sol. Songs 8:6.

The Lord thy God in the midst of thee is mighty; he will save, he will rejoice over thee with joy; he will rest in his love, he will joy over thee with singing.
Zeph. 3:17.

Howbeit certain men clave unto him, and believed: among the which was Dionysius the Areopagite, and a woman named Damaris, and others with them.
Acts 17:34.

Canst thou by searching find out God? canst thou find out the Almighty unto perfection?
It is as high as heaven; what canst thou do? deeper than hell; what canst thou know?
Job. 11:7–9.

*Nevertheless I have somewhat against thee, because thou hast left thy first love.*

*Remember therefore from whence thou art fallen, and repent, and do the first works; or else I will come unto thee quickly, and will remove thy candlestick out of his place, except thou repent.*

*But this thou hast, that thou hatest the deeds of the Nicolaitanes, which I also hate.*
*Rev. 2:4–6.*

who had been born in Judea. Cæsar ruled with unlimited power at Rome. No hand was raised against the throne; and yet Christianity crept within those palace walls, and Paul preached to some of Nero's household. This growth is recognized in the message. Thou "hast borne, and hast patience, and for My name's sake hast labored, and hast not fainted." This was the experience of the first century of the Christian religion. The power by which it grew was that of love,—the first love, which in its ardor knew no bounds. It was the love of which Paul writes when he says that "Love is the fulfilling of the law." Christ watched over the believers with the joy of a bridegroom, and they in return gave Him their heart's devotion.

There were many among the pagans who listening to Paul, were convinced of the truth in their minds, but retained their Greek manner of reasoning. Indeed, they applied to the Scriptures the same interpretation which they had formerly placed upon their own Greek writings. These converted Greek philosophers stood side by side with the simple Gospel teachers, and in trying to refute paganism by argument, Christianity was in danger of weakening. The shadow of the enemy was falling upon the church. God called after these first believers, "Remember therefore from whence thou art fallen, and repent, and do the first works; or else I will come unto thee quickly, and will remove thy candlestick out of his place."

The Nicolaitanes, referred to in verse six, are said by Mosheim to have been a branch of the Gnostics, a sect living in Asia, who denied the divinity of Christ, and "boasted of their being able to restore to mankind the knowledge of the true and Supreme Being." Their belief concerning the creation of the world, conflicted with the writings of Moses, and led to a denial of the divine authority of the Old Testament. Still other beliefs, contrary to the teachings of Christ, the result of a mixture of Greek and Oriental philosophy, led to practices which the church of Christ could not tolerate. He does not say they hated the presence of the Nicolaitanes, and could not endure them; but that they hated their deeds, "which I also hate." This church was in a position where they could hate the sin, and not the sinner, where they could have patience, and labor long for the erring, and love them; while they hated the deeds that separated them from the Lord. The Lord closes with a message to every one: "He that hath an ear let him hear." The message comes to all ages in all time, to every one who receives the gift of hearing. It is the Spirit of God speaking to the church. "To him that overcometh will I give to eat of the tree of life, which is in the midst of the paradise of God." Adam was overcome by Satan, and thus lost his right to the tree of life; but to every son of Adam the message comes, "I give to eat of the tree of life." It is the privilege of every child of God to claim the victory, and to overcome every attack of the enemy through the strength given by Christ. To the tree of life, the faithful are promised access, in contradistinction to the fruit of the tree of knowledge of good and evil. The tree of life was transplanted from the garden of Eden to heaven, but its boughs hang over the wall for all who will

Through faith we understand that the worlds were framed by the word of God, so that things which are seen were not made of things which do appear. Heb. 11:3.

For had ye believed Moses, ye would have believed me: for he wrote of me.

But if ye believe not his writings, how shall ye believe my words? John 5:46, 47.

Who concerning the truth have erred, saying that the resurrection is past already; and overthrow the faith of some. 2 Tim. 2:18.

**The message comes to every one who receives the gift of hearing.**

God commendeth his love toward us, in that, while we were yet sinners, Christ died for us. Rom. 5:8.

2 Cor. 2:5-11.

Acts 28:18-23.

*He that hath an ear, let him hear what the Spirit saith unto the churches; To him that overcometh will I give to eat of the tree of life, which is in the midst of the paradise of God. Rev. 2:7.*

Behold, I have refined thee, but not with silver; I have chosen thee in the furnace of affliction.

For mine own sake, even for mine own sake, will I do it: for how should my name be polluted? and I will not give my glory unto another. Isa. 48 : 10, 11.

Rev. 2: 10.

reach upward for its fruit. As the experience of the church is applicable to each denomination, to each organization, and to each individual, so to the end of time, Christians will be placed in positions where they must choose between the wisdom of God, and the philosophy of the world,—the wisdom which is pure, peaceable, gentle, full of mercy and good fruits; and the philosophy which, if adhered to, brings loss of light, and eventually death.

**Smyrna. Present State.**

SMYRNA.

Having food and raiment let us be therewith content.

But they that will be rich fall into temptation and a snare, and into many foolish and hurtful lusts, which drown men in destruction and perdition.

Smyrna, the second church addressed, was only about fifty miles from Ephesus, and doubtless knew of the conditions at the central church of Asia Minor; but as it was not a great trade center, many of the perplexities with which Ephesus had to contend were not present in Smyrna. Its members were poor, but still they worked earnestly for others. The wealth of Ephesus was one of the greatest drawbacks to the spirituality of that church; but Smyrna, though poor in worldly goods, was rich in the eyes of the Lord. Through false teachers, claiming to be the children of God, persecution came to those who wished to follow the teachings of Christ. The true Jew is an heir by faith of the inheritance promised to Abraham, but many pride themselves on the inheritance of the flesh. Such belong to the synagogue of Satan; for righteousness by works is the devil's counterfeit of the Lord's plan of salvation through faith alone in the merits of the Son of God. The words written by Paul in his letter to the Galatians, who had this same false teaching to meet, makes clear the difference between those who are children of promise and those who are Jews in name only. Paul illustrates the truth by repeating the life experience of Abraham. Ishmael, the son of Hagar, the Egyptian bondwoman, represents in allegory, those who hope to obtain righteousness by their own efforts. Such are the Jews against whom the church at Smyrna was warned. Isaac, the son of Sarah and Abraham, was the child of promise, and represents those who accept Christ by faith. "But as then he that was born after the flesh persecuted him that was born after the Spirit, even so it is now." So to the Smyrna church God said, "Fear none of those things which thou shalt suffer: behold, the devil shall cast some of you into prison, that ye may be tried; and ye shall have tribulation ten days: be thou faithful

For the love of money is the root of all evil: which while some coveted after, they have erred from the faith, and pierced themselves through with many sorrows.
But thou, O man of God, flee these things; and follow after righteousness, godliness, faith, love, patience, meekness.
1 Tim. 6:8–11.

Ye shall be betrayed both by parents, and brethren, and kinsfolks, and friends; and some of you shall they cause to be put to death.
And ye shall be hated of all men for my name's sake.
Luke 21:12–17.

Titus 1:9–11.

For he is not a Jew, which is one outwardly; neither is that circumcision, which is outward in the flesh:
But he is a Jew, which is one inwardly; and circumcision is that of the heart, in the spirit, and not in the letter; whose praise is not of men, but of God.
Rom. 2:28, 29.

Rom. 9:31.
Rom. 4:3–7.

Wilt thou know, O vain man, that faith without works is dead?
Was not Abraham our father justified by works, when he had offered Isaac his son upon the altar?
Seest thou how faith wrought with his works, and by works was faith made perfect?
Jas. 2:14–26.

Gal. 3:8–10, 26–29.
Gal. 4:22–31.

We are all as an unclean thing, and all our righteousnesses are as filthy rags. Isa. 64:6.

Rom. 3:23.
Gal. 4:29.

*And unto the angel of the church in Smyrna write; These things saith the first and the last, which was dead, and is alive.* *Rev. 2:8.*

Num. 14:34.
Eze. 4:6.
Rev. 1:18.

Beloved, think it not strange concerning the fiery trial which is to try you, as though some strange thing happened unto you:

But rejoice, inasmuch as ye are partakers of Christ's sufferings; that, when his glory shall be revealed, ye may be glad also with exceeding joy. 1 Pet. 4:12, 13.

1 Pet. 1:5–9.

Take heed therefore unto yourselves, and to all the flock, over the which the Holy Ghost hath made you overseers, to feed the church of God, which he hath purchased with his own blood.

For I know this, that after my departing shall grievous wolves enter in among you, not sparing the flock. Acts 20:28, 29.

2 Thess. 2:2–7.

*I know thy works, and tribulation, and poverty, (but thou art rich) and I know the blasphemy of them which say they are Jews, and are not, but are the synagogue of Satan.* *Rev. 2:9.*

Dan. 11:34.
Zech. 3:6, 7.

The law is no more; her prophets also find no vision from the Lord. Lam. 2:9.

unto death, and I will give thee a crown of life." The message was signed by Him "which was dead, and is alive." Christ's sacrifice of life and His victory over death, was pointed to by Gabriel as a special lesson and source of encouragement to those followers who would be called to pass through the fire of persecution. By faith the martyrs could see the crown of eternal life held out to them by the Son of God.

**The devil shall cast some of you into prison.**

The message came to Smyrna, a church in Asia Minor, and likewise to the Christian church as a whole, during the second and third centuries. It was a time when paganism was making its final stand for supremacy in the world. Christianity had spread with wonderful rapidity, until it was known throughout the world. Some embraced the faith of Christ because of heart conversion, others, because of the might of argument brought to bear, and still others, because they could see that the cause of paganism was waning, and policy led them to the side that promised to be victorious. These conditions weakened the spirituality of the church. The Spirit of Prophecy, which characterized the apostolic church, was gradually lost. This is a gift which brings the church to which it is entrusted, into the unity of the faith. When there were no longer true prophets, false teachings spread rapidly; the philosophy of the Greeks led to a false interpretation of the Scriptures, and the self-righteousness of the ancient Pharisees, so often condemned by Christ, again appeared in the midst of the church. The foundation was laid during the two centuries preceding the reign of Constantine for those evils which were fully developed during the two centuries following. During this period, martyrdom became popular in many parts of the Roman Empire. Strange as this may seem, it is none the less true. It was the result of the relationship existing between Christians and pagans.

In the Roman world the religion of all nations was respected, but the Christians were not a nation, they were but a sect of a despised race. When they therefore persisted in denouncing the religion of all classes of men, when they held secret meetings, and separated themselves entirely from the customs and practices of their nearest relatives and most intimate friends, they became objects of suspicion, and often of persecution, by the pagan authorities. Often they brought persecution upon themselves, when there was no spirit of opposition in the minds of the rulers. In illustration of this spirit, history gives the details of the execution of Cyprian, bishop of Carthage. When his sentence was read, a general cry arose from the listening multitude of Christians, who said, "We will die with him."

The spirit with which many professed Christians accepted death, and even needlessly provoked the enmity of the government, probably had much to do with the passage, in 303, A. D., of

He gave some, apostles; and some, prophets; and some, evangelists; and some, pastors and teachers;

For the perfecting of the saints, for the work of the ministry, for the edifying of the body of Christ.
Eph. 4:11-16.

When Peter was come to Antioch, I withstood him to the face, because he was to be blamed.

For before that certain came from James, he did eat with the Gentiles: but when they were come, he withdrew and separated himself, fearing them which were of the circumcision. Gal. 2:11, 12.

They that are unlearned and unstable wrest, as they do also the other scriptures, unto their own destruction.

Ye therefore, beloved, seeing ye know these things before, beware lest ye also, being led away with the error of the wicked, fall from your own steadfastness.
2 Pet. 3:16, 17.

Titus 1:9-13.
2 Tim. 2:19, 20.
Phil. 1:12-19.

We desire to hear of thee what thou thinkest: for as concerning this sect, we know that every where it is spoken against. Acts 28:22.

Ye men of Athens, I perceive that in all things ye are too superstitious. Acts 17:22.

Be not conformed to this world: but be ye transformed by the renewing of your mind. Rom. 12:2.

Love not the world, neither the things that are in the world.
1 John 2:15.

As obedient children, not fashioning yourselves according to the former lusts in your ignorance.
1 Pet. 1:14.

Now the brother shall betray the brother to death, and the father the son; and children shall rise up against their parents, and shall cause them to be put to death.

And ye shall be hated of all men for my name's sake.
Mark 13:12, 13.

Psa. 31:11-13.

Heb. 11:35-38.
Rev. 13:7.

*Fear none of those things which thou shalt suffer: behold, the devil shall cast some of you into prison, that ye may be tried; and ye shall have tribulation ten days: be thou faithful unto death, and I will give thee a crown of life.*
*Rev. 2:10.*

Sweet smelling myrrh.
Sol. Song 5:13.

**Like the smoke from the altar of incense.**

Precious shall their blood be in his sight. Psa. 72:14.

Having received the things which were sent from you, an odour of a sweet smell, a sacrifice acceptable, well-pleasing to God.
Phil. 4:18.

A bundle of myrrh is my well-beloved unto me. Sol. Song 1:13.

For I bear them record that they have a zeal of God, but not according to knowledge. Rom. 10:2.

Happy is that people, that is in such a case: yea, happy is that people, whose God is the Lord.
Psa. 144:15.

the edict of persecution, by the emperor Diocletian, and his assistant, Galerius. The edict was universal in its spirit, and was enforced with more or less strenuousness for ten years.

Many Christians suffered death. The sacrifice of a child of God opens afresh the wound made in the Father's heart when Christ was slain. The death of Christ was a sign of separation from sin, on the part of him who accepted the sacrifice. Like the smoke from the altar of incense in the sanctuary service, a life given for the Saviour becomes a sweet savor in the sight of Jehovah. *Smyrna* means "*myrrh*" or "*sweet scent*." This name is applied to those who willingly offered their lives for their faith. The mercy of God is shown in this message in a most wonderful way; for although some doubtless suffered needlessly, and brought persecution upon themselves, yet God does not condemn them for mistaken zeal. This is a message that contains no reproof, and it would seem that the tenderness of our Father causes Him to lose sight of the fact that death was sought; because He sees the earnestness in the heart of the one who offers his life. It is the same in individual experience. The over-zealous ofttimes suffer when there is no need of suffering, and yet God reads the motive of the heart, and measures out the reward in accordance with what He finds there. Fellowmen may criticize and condemn, but God accepts any sacrifice made in His name; and He says to such a follower as He did to King David, "Thou didst well that it was in thine heart."

"He that hath an ear, let him hear what the Spirit saith unto the churches;" "He that overcometh shall not be hurt of the second death." The second death is the only death that the people of God need to fear. Satan may bring physical death to the faithful followers of Christ, but they will be shielded from the second death. God's people will rejoice in life everlasting; while the decree of the second death will be passed upon Satan and his emissaries. The Smyrna church immediately followed the time of Christ and His disciples, and was often referred to prophetically in their teachings.

But he shall receive an hundredfold now in this time, with persecutions; and in the world to come eternal life. Mark 10:28-30.

2 Chron. 6:8

*He that hath an ear, let him hear what the Spirit saith unto the churches; He that overcometh shall not be hurt of the second death. Rev. 2:11.*

Rev. 20:12-15.

Forasmuch then as the children are partakers of flesh and blood, he also himself likewise took part of the same; that through death he might destroy him that had the power of death, that is, the devil. Heb. 2:14.

**Pergamos. Present state.**

PERGAMOS.

The condition of Christianity for two or more centuries following the accession of Constantine the Great, to the Roman throne may be learned from the message delivered to the church of Pergamos. The ten years' persecution, which took place during the reign of Diocletian, failed to accomplish the design of its instigator, and a wonderful reaction followed. Constantine, wishing to gain favor above the very men who were foremost in the opposition to Christianity, espoused the cause of that despised sect, and

There are many devices in a man's heart; nevertheless the counsel of the Lord, that shall stand. Prov. 19:21.

Because they rebelled against the words of God, and contemned the counsel of the most High:

Therefore he brought down their heart with labour; they fell down, and there was none to help. Psa. 107:11, 12.

Herein thou hast done foolishly: therefore from henceforth thou shalt have wars. 2 Chron. 16:9.

Heb. 11:15, 16.

*And to the angel of the church in Pergamos write; These things saith he which hath the sharp sword with two edges.*
*Rev. 2:12.*

Samuel said, Hath the Lord as great delight in burnt offerings and sacrifices, as in obeying the voice of the Lord? Behold, to obey is better than sacrifice, and to hearken than the fat of rams.
1 Sam. 15:22.

*I know thy works, and where thou dwellest, even where Satan's seat is: and thou holdest fast my name, and hast not denied my faith, even in those days wherein Antipas was my faithful martyr, who was slain among you, where Satan dwelleth.* *Rev. 2:13.*

The dragon gave him his power, and his seat, and great authority.
Rev. 13:2.

Whoso shall offend one of these little ones which believe in me, it were better for him that a millstone were hanged about his neck, and that he were drowned in the depth of the sea. Matt. 18:6.

1 Cor. 5:1–6.

Num. 31:16.

Num. 25:1–5.

Num. 22:15–22.

*But I have a few things against thee, because thou hast there them that hold the doctrine of Balaam, who taught Balac to cast a stumblingblock before the children of Israel, to eat things sacrificed unto idols, and to commit fornication.* *Rev. 2:14.*

through him, Christianity was raised to the throne of Rome. *Pergamos* means "*exaltation*," or "*elevation*," and it was when nominal Christianity became popular, and swayed the civil government, that the two-edged sword of the Word was necessary to separate between the true and the false. Naturally the number of converts increased rapidly, and church buildings multiplied. Officers in the church, under favor of the government, spread themselves like the green bay tree. The doctrine of Him who said, "He that is greatest among you shall be your servant," was reversed, and the papal hierarchy grew apace. This was peculiarly true of the Roman See. Other dioceses attempted the same exaltation. Constantinople, Jerusalem, Ephesus and Alexandria,—all contended for supremacy, but Rome, the seat of the dragon, was finally the acknowledged head of the Christian church. God watched the church as it trod this dangerous path to worldly exaltation, and to Pergamos He sent this message: "I have a few things against thee, because thou hast there them that hold the doctrine of Balaam, who taught Balac to cast a stumbling-block before the children of Israel, to eat things sacrificed unto idols, and to commit fornication."

During the period of ecclesiastical history, when the message to Pergamos is applicable, the church was guilty of idolatry and fornication. Lest Christians should misunderstand the application, and be led to deny the charge, the Spirit of God cites them to the experience of Balaam with Balac, the king of the Moabites, at a time when Israel was about to enter the promised land. The following quoted paragraphs throw

" Balaam answered and said, Told not I thee, saying, All that the Lord speaketh, that I must do ? "

light on the work of Balaam in teaching Balac to cast a stumbling-block before Israel :—

"Balaam was once a good man and a prophet of God; but he had apostatized, and had given himself up to covetousness; yet he still professed to be a servant of the Most High. He was not ignorant of God's work in behalf of Israel; and when the messengers (from Balac) announced their errand, he well knew that it was his duty to refuse the reward of Balac, and to dismiss the ambassadors. But he ventured to dally with temptation, and urged the messengers to tarry with him that night, declaring that he could give no decided answer till he had asked counsel of the Lord. Balaam knew that his curse could not harm Israel. . . . The bribe of costly gifts and prospective exaltation excited his covetousness. He greedily accepted the offered treasures, and did not change his course when met by the angel. While professing strict obedience to the will of God, he tried to comply with the desire of Balac."

If in reading this paragraph the word "Balaam" is replaced by the "Church," in the fourth and fifth centuries, and for "Balac" is read "Constantine," or "the Roman Emperor," the exact history of the church is portrayed. The church had known God, but it became covetous; while it still professed allegiance to the Most High. The church, tempted by the rich offers of the government, parlied with its ambas-

Josh. 13:22.

Woe unto them! for they have gone in the way of Cain, and ran greedily after the error of Balaam for reward, and perished in the gainsaying of Core. Jude 11.

Balaam answered and said unto the servants of Balak, If Balak would give me his house full of silver and gold, I cannot go beyond the word of the Lord my God, to do less or more. Num. 22:15-21.

For every one of the house of Israel, or of the stranger that sojourneth in Israel, which separateth himself from me, and setteth up his idols in his heart, and putteth the stumblingblock of his iniquity before his face, and cometh to a prophet to enquire of him concerning me; I the Lord will answer him by myself. Eze. 14:7.

**Balaam did not change his course when met by the angel.**

The thing that hath been, it is that which shall be; and that which is done is that which shall be done: and there is no new thing under the sun.

Is there any thing whereof it may be said, See, this is new? it hath been already of old time, which was before us. Eccl. 1:9, 10.

This people draweth nigh unto me with their mouth, and honoureth me with their lips; but their heart is far from me. Matt. 15:8.

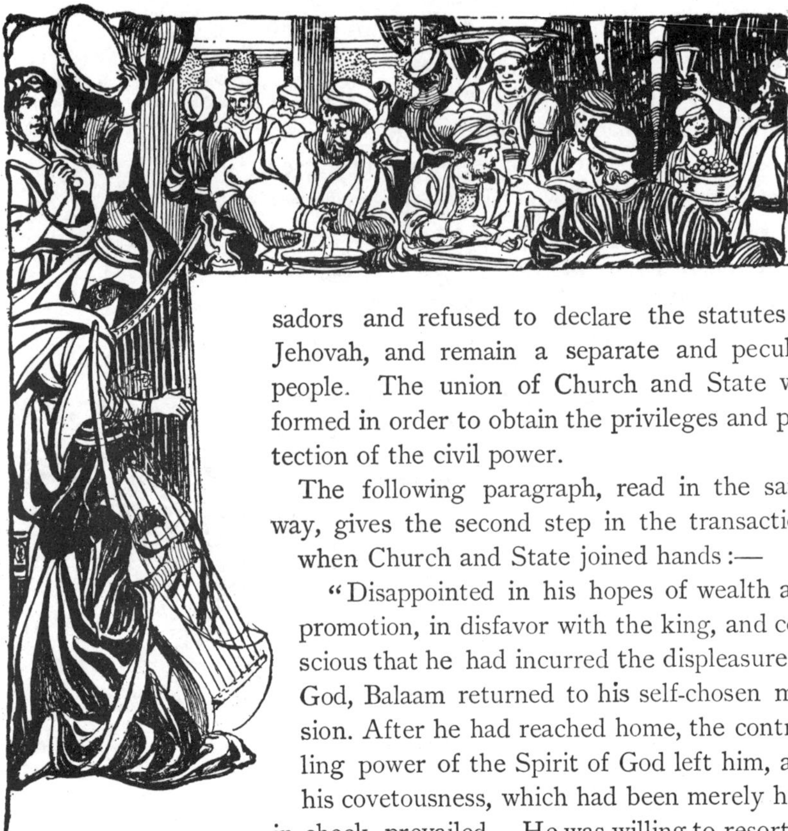

**Israel invited to a feast of the Moabites.**

This is a rebellious people, lying children, children that will not hear the law of the Lord. Isa. 30:9.

Ye adulterers and adulteresses, know ye not that the friendship of the world is enmity with God? Jas. 4:4.

Num. 23:11.
Num. 24:10, 11.

sadors and refused to declare the statutes of Jehovah, and remain a separate and peculiar people. The union of Church and State was formed in order to obtain the privileges and protection of the civil power.

The following paragraph, read in the same way, gives the second step in the transaction, when Church and State joined hands:—

"Disappointed in his hopes of wealth and promotion, in disfavor with the king, and conscious that he had incurred the displeasure of God, Balaam returned to his self-chosen mission. After he had reached home, the controlling power of the Spirit of God left him, and his covetousness, which had been merely held in check, prevailed. He was willing to resort to any means to gain the reward promised by Balac. . . . He immediately returned to the land of Moab, and laid his plans before the king. . . The plan proposed by Balaam was to separate them (Israel, the church) from God by enticing them into idolatry. . . . This plan was readily accepted by the king, and Balaam himself remained to assist in carrying it into effect. Balaam witnessed the success of his diabolical scheme."

The scheme was that Israel should be invited

to a feast of the Moabites, where meats sacrificed to the heathen gods, were eaten, and that Israel should be caused to commit adultery with the inhabitants of Moab.

The church between 312 and 538 A.D. joined hands with the civil power. It took of the wealth of the State, and asked for civil protection. Then it was that the spiritual sins of idolatry and fornication were introduced. Idolatry was the love of money, the world, and all false worship which took the place of the worship of Jehovah. It is fornication in the eyes of God when His people are wedded to any power save the arm of Omnipotence.

If ancient Israel had remained true to the teachings of their leader, the temptations of the Moabites would have fallen on deaf ears. The same is true of the church to which all this history is sent as an allegory. The doctrine of the Nicolaitanes, as described under the church of Ephesus, was a mingling of the pure teachings of Christ with the philosophy of the Greeks. If this doctrine had not been accepted in the church which claimed to be following the Saviour; if the children and the young people had been fed on *truth* instead of the mixture of good and evil, as represented by the doctrine of the Nicolaitanes, the church would never have fallen. The message to Pergamos applies in the fourth and fifth centuries; it has also been the experience of each separate Protestant denomination, and it is a warning to all churches to the end of time. Any interpretation of this period that does not correspond with the history of Balaam is not according to the mind of the Lord, for God has given Balaam's history as a

For if after they have escaped the pollutions of the world through the knowledge of the Lord and Saviour Jesus Christ, they are again entangled therein, and overcome, the latter end is worse with them than the beginning.

For it had been better for them not to have known the way of righteousness, than, after they have known it, to turn from the holy commandment delivered unto them.
2 Pet. 2:20, 21.

Matt. 12:43-46.

Behold, these caused the children of Israel, through the counsel of Balaam, to commit trespass against the Lord in the matter of Peor, and there was a plague among the congregation of the Lord.
Num. 31:16.

They called the people unto the sacrifices of their gods: and the people did eat, and bowed down to their gods.

And Israel joined himself unto Baal-peor: and the anger of the Lord was kindled against Israel.
Num. 25:1-3.

Having eyes full of adultery, and that cannot cease from sin; beguiling unstable souls: an heart they have exercised with covetous practices; cursed children:

Which have forsaken the right way, and are gone astray, following the way of Balaam the son of Bosor, who loved the wages of unrighteousness. 2 Pet. 2:14, 15.

O my people, remember now what Balak king of Moab consulted, and what Balaam the son of Beor answered him from Shittim unto Gilgal; that ye may know the righteousness of the Lord. Mic. 6:5.

Rev. 17:2-5.

Rev. 18:2, 3.

For the love of money is the root of all evil: which while some coveted after, they have erred from the faith, and pierced themselves through with many sorrows. 1 Tim. 6:10.

test by which we may know the true interpretation.

"Repent; or else I will come unto thee quickly, and will fight against them with the sword of my mouth," which is the two-edged sword. From the midst of the church, which fell because of its union with the State, God separated, by His Spirit, a little company whose history may be read in a part of the message sent to the church of Thyatira.

O that thou hadst hearkened to my commandments! then had thy peace been as a river, and thy righteousness as the waves of the sea. Isa. 48:18.

Psa. 119:11.

God calls to each church, no matter how low the ebb of spirituality, and those who have an ear turned heavenward, hear. "To him that overcometh will I give to eat of the hidden manna, and will give him a white stone, and in the stone a new name written, which no man knoweth saving he that receiveth it." As the sins of the church of Pergamos are given in the form of a parable, so the blessings to the repentant ones of this period are offered in figure. Those who had in sin partaken of food offered to idols, are offered in exchange the "hidden manna." Manna is the bread of heaven, and as it was the only food necessary to nourish the multitudes of Israel during their forty years' journey, it became a fit emblem of Christ, the bread sent down to the world. Eating flesh sacrificed to idols brings death, but hidden manna brings life. "Jesus said unto them, Verily, verily, I say unto you, Moses gave you not that bread from heaven; but My Father giveth you the true bread from heaven. For the bread of God is He which cometh down from heaven, and giveth life unto the world." A union of Church and State crushes the spiritual life of any church. Why will men eat the food of idolatry when the

*So hast thou also them that hold the doctrine of the Nicolaitanes, which thing I hate. Rev. 2:15.*

Num. 23:1-6, 14-17, 29, 30.

No man can serve two masters: for either he will hate the one, and love the other; or else he will hold to the one, and despise the other. Ye cannot serve God and mammon. Matt. 6:24.

Jer. 7:17-19.

Deut. 4:23-28.

That which hath been is now; and that which is to be hath already been; and God requireth that which is past. Eccl. 3:15.

Heb. 4:12.

bread of heaven is free to all? Why do Christians in the education of their children, cultivate in them an appetite for "food sacrificed to idols," instead of spreading the table with manna which will give life to the soul?

*Repent; or else I will come unto thee quickly, and will fight against them with the sword of my mouth. Rev. 2:16.*

Deut. 13:6–11.
Isa. 17:6.

Ruins near ancient Pergamos.

The Lord did not set his love upon you, nor choose you, because ye were more in number than any people; for ye were the fewest of all people. Deut. 7:7.

Luke 12:32.
Isa. 1:18.
Isa. 43:26.

Moses said unto Aaron, Take a pot, and put an omer full of manna therein, and lay it up before the Lord, to be kept for your generations. Ex. 16:32, 33.

Rev. 19:12.

*He that hath an ear, let him hear what the Spirit saith unto the churches; To him that overcometh will I give to eat of the hidden manna, and will give him a white stone, and in the stone a new name written, which no man knoweth saving he that receiveth it. Rev. 2:17.*

Our fathers did eat manna in the desert; as it is written, He gave them bread from heaven to eat. John 6:31.

I am the living bread which came down from heaven: if any man eat of this bread, he shall live for ever: and the bread that I will give is my flesh, which I will give for the life of the world. John 6 51.

The lesson for the church as a whole is total separation from the civil power. The lesson to the home and to the individual is complete separation from the world. Cling to God; for He has the hidden manna. Feed the children on

Isa. 52:11, 12.
Jer. 50:8.

Jer. 51:6, 45.
2 Cor. 6:14–18.

2 Tim. 3:15, 16.

Corn shall make the young men grow, and new wine the maids.
Zech. 9:17 [margin.]

In the divisions of Reuben there were great searchings of heart.
Judges 5:15, 16 [margin.]

Eph. 6:17.
Rev. 2:17.
Hag. 2:23.

Set me as a seal upon thine heart, as a seal upon thine arm: for love is strong as death.
Sol. Songs 8:6.

Mal. 3:17.

We all, with open face beholding as in a glass the glory of the Lord, are changed into the same image from glory to glory, even as by the Spirit of the Lord. 2 Cor. 3:18.

O my dove, that art in the clefts of the rock, in the secret places of the stairs, let me see thy countenance, let me hear thy voice; for sweet is thy voice, and thy countenance is comely. Sol. Song 2:14.

Matt. 11:27.
1 Pet. 3:4.
1 Cor. 6:18–20.
Gen. 32:24–29.

Yea, he had power over the angel, and prevailed: he wept, and made supplication unto him: he found him in Beth-el, and there he spake with us. Hos. 12:4.

hidden manna; for it is well adapted to supply every need. God is teaching in these words a wonderful lesson on the laws of physical growth by simplicity of food; of mental growth by purity of food,—food unadulterated with heathen teachings,—and a spiritual lesson of marriage with the Lamb, instead of with the dragon.

The keen heart searching of the Spirit, represented by the sword with the double edge, is shown in the second reward which is offered the repentant soul. To him is given a white stone, and in the stone a new name, which is known only to the one who receives it. As Zerubbabel was called a signet, or stone of sealing, represented as worn upon the hand of the Lord, so is each one who chooses to follow Christ in preference to the world. The stone is white, of dazzling purity. There are seen in it none of the tints which are admired by human eyes, but it is a stone free from all signs of impurity, and on it is impressed, by the power of God, the name which is known only to the individual and his Redeemer. Others may pronounce that name, it is true, but its significance is a secret between Christ and the individual. The one who receives it has been guilty of idolatry and fornication, and none other save his Lord can know the soul experience which brought the new name. Once it was Jacob, supplanter. None but the bearer knew how applicable was the name. Every time it was pronounced by friend or foe, it was an open rebuke from God. And when at the close of the night of wrestling, the angel said, "Thy name shall be called no more Jacob, but Israel"—a prince of God,—

none but Israel knew the depth of meaning in that new name.

Gen. 23 : 28.
Gen. 16 : 11.

When the Jewish nation lived near to God, and the voice of Jehovah could be heard, every child was named under the direction of the Spirit. To-day heaven has a new name carved on a pure white stone for each sinner who repents, and the deeper the crimson dye of sin, the purer the stone will appear by contrast. "Blessed is he whose transgression is forgiven, whose sin is covered. Blessed is the man to whom the Lord imputeth not iniquity, and in whose spirit there is no guile."

Matt. 1 : 21.
Ex. 2 : 10.

Rom. 5 : 20.

Come now, and let us reason together, saith the Lord : though your sins be as scarlet, they shall be as white as snow ; though they be red like crimson, they shall be as wool. Isa. 1 : 18.

Rom. 4 : 7, 8.

**Thyratira. Present state.**

THYATIRA.

The message to Pergamos carries ecclesiastical history to the year 538 A. D., at which time the union between civil and ecclesiastical power, begun in the days of Constantine, was consummated. During the period covered by Pergamos, the

Israel is swallowed up : now shall they be among the Gentiles as a vessel wherein is no pleasure. Hos. 8 : 8.

The iniquity of Ephraim is bound up ; his sin is hid. Hos. 13 : 12.

Deut. 32:32-34.

O Israel, thou hast destroyed thyself; but in me is thine help. Hos. 13:9.

We will eat our own bread, and wear our own apparel: only let us be called by thy name, to take away our reproach. Isa. 4:1.

Eph. 2:3, 4.

For if we sin wilfully after that we have received the knowledge of the truth, there remaineth no more sacrifice for sins. Heb. 10:26, 27.

Whosoever therefore will be a friend of the world is the enemy of God. Jas. 4:4.

*And unto the angel of the church in Thyatira write; These things saith the Son of God, who hath his eyes like unto a flame of fire, and his feet are like fine brass. Rev. 2:18.*

Rev. 2:19.
Rom. 3:15.
Matt. 23:15.
Rev. 13:3.
Rev. 18:9-11.

All that dwell upon the earth shall worship him, whose names are not written in the book of life of the Lamb slain from the foundation of the world. Rev. 13:8.

Be sober, be vigilant; because your adversary the devil, as a roaring lion, walketh about, seeking whom he may devour. 1 Pet. 5:8.

Rom. 3:20, 28.

Spirit of the Lord was with the church as a church; but near the end of that period, a separation began to take place. In the years following, there was formed an organization still carrying the name of Christian; and another company, separating from that first organization, because of the practices of Balaam,—the idolatry and fornication practiced by those who were once Christians indeed. Thus improper education was the cause of the apostasy of the church, and the one sign of its fall was that, in its spiritual weakness, it sought the civil power for support.

It is under these conditions that the message comes to the church of Thyatira. It is sent by "the Son of God, who hath His eyes like unto a flame of fire, and His feet are like fine brass." Christ still walks among the candlesticks, but to Thyatira He comes with "eyes like unto a flame of fire" to search the very hearts of those who profess to be His followers. To these He says, "I know thy works, and charity, and service, and faith, and thy patience, and thy works." This was not an idle period; their works are thrice mentioned in the one list. Those who established a state religion, replacing paganism by the papacy, were most diligent workers. The church absorbed every government, every industry, all the educational institutions,—everything. There was not a corner of Europe which was not under the direct inspection of that all-absorbing organization known as the papacy. Not only kings on their thrones, but every private individual in his own home, was amenable to the power of Rome. The church stood between the king and his subjects; it stood between parents and children; it came even between husband and wife. The secrets of men's hearts were open to the confessor. Works, works of all kinds were advocated; for the church taught that men were saved by works. Long pilgrimages across continents paid many a debt of sin. Penance and indulgences took bread from many a hungry mouth. The strongest government that ever bore sway was seated on the throne. Nevertheless the masses thought that in their works for the church, their service, their charities and their faith, they served the Christ. "Notwithstanding I have a few things against thee, because thou sufferest that woman Jezebel, which calleth herself a prophetess, to teach and to seduce my servants to commit fornication, and to eat things sacrificed unto idols." The sins imputed to the church of Pergamos are repeated in the message to Thyatira, but they are introduced by a different character. The woman Jezebel is taken as an object lesson.

*I know thy works, and charity, and service, and faith, and thy patience, and thy works; and the last to be more than the first.* *Rev. 2:19.*

Dan. 2:40.

I said, Lord, they know that I imprisoned and beat in every synagogue them that believed on thee. Acts 22:19, 20.

Gal. 1:13.

**The secrets of men's hearts were open to the confessor.**

Jezebel was a Zidonian princess, a prophetess of the god Baal. Unlike Balaam, who before his fall worshiped the true God, Jezebel never made any pretensions of worshiping the Lord. Ahab, the king of Israel, married her for the sake of her influence, but found himself completely under the control of a headstrong, wicked woman. At her table, in the kingdom of Israel, sat the prophets of Baal. In the capital were erected temples, groves, and altars, to the heathen god; sun-worship took the place of the worship of Jehovah. The prophets

*Notwithstanding I have a few things against thee, because thou sufferest that woman Jezebel, which calleth herself a prophetess, to teach and to seduce my servants to commit fornication, and to eat things sacrificed unto idols.* *Rev. 2:20.*

It came to pass, as if it had been a light thing for him to walk in the sins of Jeroboam the son of Nebat, that he took to wife Jezebel the daughter of Ethbaal king of the Zidonians. 1 Kings 16:31-33.

Prov. 5:3-6.
Prov. 7:21-27.
1 Kings 18:19.
1 Kings 18:4.
2 Chron. 14:5 [margin].

She wrote in the letters, saying, Proclaim a fast, and set Naboth on high among the people:
And set two men, sons of Belial, before him, to bear witness against him, saying, Thou didst blaspheme God and the king. And then carry him out, and stone him, that he may die. 1 Kings 21:8-13.

Elias was a man subject to like passions as we are, and he prayed earnestly that it might not rain: and it rained not on the earth by the space of three years and six months. Jas. 5:17.

1 Kings 17:1.
Luke 4:25.
1 Kings 21:23, 24.
2 Kings 9:30-37.
Jas. 2:14-26.
1 John 5:4.
Rom. 5:13-17.

But there was none like unto Ahab, which did sell himself to work wickedness in the sight of the Lord, whom Jezebel his wife stirred up.
And he did very abominably in following idols, according to all things as did the Amorites, whom the Lord cast out before the children of Israel. 1 Kings 21:25, 26.

Lam. 5:12.
Dan. 7:21, 25.
Rev. 13:7.
Lam. 4:18, 19.
Rev. 17:1-6.
Rev. 16:13, 14.

Who opposeth and exalteth himself above all that is called God, or that is worshipped; so that he as God sitteth in the temple of God, shewing himself that he is God. 2 Thess. 2:4.

of God were put to death by order of the queen; even Elijah fled before her face. She was a propagator of whoredom and witchcraft, and in the name of the king, she wrote a letter causing innocent men to be put to death. Israel had war, bloodshed, and finally captivity, as the result of the evil of this woman. It was during her lifetime that the heavens were stayed so that it rained not for three years and a half. The history of Jezebel is an unerring guide to the interpretation of the prophetic history of the church during the Dark Ages.

In every detail, even to this last period of years, the history of Jezebel is a parable of the church history during the time, times, and half a time—the three and one half years of the papal supremacy, the period covered by the message to Thyatira. As a result of the doctrine of justification by works, which was the stronghold of the church during this period, Europe had over a thousand years of darkness, known in all history as the Dark Ages. It was a tyranny of the most absolute kind,—a tyranny of theology over thought. Whosoever raised a hand against the church, fell as did Naboth whom Jezebel slew. Sorcery, witchcraft, idolatry, and fornication took the place of the religion of Jesus Christ. Antichrist, or the "mystery of iniquity," had full control of the world. As Jezebel wrote in the king's name, and in his name slew an innocent man, so the apostate church opposed and exalted itself above the King of heaven, and while speaking in His name, it changed the law of Jehovah, and put to death thousands who were, indeed, followers of Christ.

Jezebel had an opportunity to repent, so also had Ahab her husband; for there were many prophets in Israel, and the truth of God was taught; but the royal family were so under the control of the mother that there was no salvation for them. So God said of Thyatira, or the church of the Dark Ages, "I gave her space to repent of her fornication; and she repented not." But as there was a day of recompense with Jezebel, so there will be with the oppressive

Dan. 7 :25

*And I gave her space to repent of her fornication; and she repented not.* *Rev. 2 :21.*

1 Kings 18 : 17-39.
1 Kings 21 : 23-29.
2 Kings 9 : 7-10.
Dan. 7 : 7-11.
Rev. 2 : 21.
Rev. 19 : 20.

**The End of Jezebel.**

Wherefore they came again, and told him. And he said, This is the word of the Lord, which he spake by his servant Elijah the Tishbite, saying, In the portion of Jezreel shall dogs eat the flesh of Jezebel. 2 Kings 9 : 36.

2 Kings 9 : 30-37.
1 Kings 22 : 37-39.
2 Kings 10 : 1-7.

power of the papacy. Jezebel was thrown from a window and dashed to pieces, and dogs ate her body. Ahab was slain, and dogs licked up his blood, and his sons were also killed. Of the "mystery of iniquity" it is recorded, "Behold, I will cast her into a bed, and them that commit adultery with her into great tribulation, except they repent of their deeds. And I will kill her children with death; and all the churches shall know that I am He which searcheth the reins and hearts: and I will give unto every one

*Behold, I will cast her into a bed, and them that commit adultery with her into great tribulation, except they repent of their deeds. And I will kill her children with death; and all the churches shall know that I am he which searcheth the reins and hearts: and I will give unto every one of you according to your works.* *Rev. 2 : 22, 23.*

of you according to your works." Herein is given the final destruction of the apostate church. The civil power of the papacy was broken in 1798, when Pope Pius VI. was taken prisoner by the French; but the influence continues. Thyatira is Babylon itself, and the churches spoken of elsewhere as "daughters of Babylon," will meet with the fate of the mother, Thyatira; for when the history of all churches is over, Babylon and her daughters will be destroyed in the lake of fire. The time of trouble spoken of by Daniel, the prophet (Dan. 12 : 1), will be the time of tribulation for Thyatira. Of this the dreadful death of Jezebel is a symbol; as her life and deeds are taken to typify the church itself.

Mention has already been made of a separation from the church as a church in the days of Pergamos and the early days of Thyatira. Individuals, who recognized the leadings of the Spirit, gathered in little companies, hidden away in the caves, mountain fortresses, and dens, like the prophets of God in the days of Jezebel. In these secluded spots were thousands who did not bow the knee to Baal. Among these were the Waldenses of Italy, and others scattered all through Europe, who retained the Word of God, and trusted in His promises. Of these scattered, yet faithful ones, the message speaks in the following words: "But unto you I say, and unto the rest in Thyatira, as many as have not this doctrine (of Jezebel), and which have not known the depths of Satan, as they speak; I will put upon you none other burden."

The name *Thyatira* means "*sacrifice of contrition*," and appears to have direct application

He that leadeth into captivity shall go into captivity: he that killeth with the sword must be killed with the sword. Here is the patience and the faith of the saints.
Rev. 13 : 10.

Dan. 7 : 26.
Rev. 17 : 5.

And the beast was taken, and with him the false prophet that wrought miracles before him, with which he deceived them that had received the mark of the beast, and them that worshipped his image. These both were cast alive into a lake of fire burning with brimstone.
Rev. 19 : 20.

There shall be a time of trouble, such as never was since there was a nation even to that same time: and at that time thy people shall be delivered, every one that shall be found written in the book.
Dan. 12 : 1.

To the woman were given two wings of a great eagle, that she might fly into the wilderness, into her place, where she is nourished for a time, and times, and half a time, from the face of the serpent
Rev. 12 : 6, 14.

1 Kings 18 : 4, 13.

Yet I have left me seven thousand in Israel, all the knees which have not bowed unto Baal, and every mouth which hath not kissed him.
1 Kings 19 : 18.

Rejoice not against me, O mine enemy: when I fall, I shall arise; when I sit in darkness, the Lord shall be a light unto me.

I will bear the indignation of the Lord, because I have sinned against him, until he plead my cause, and execute judgment for me: he will bring me forth to the light, and I shall behold his righteousness.
Micah 7 : 8, 9.

to those, who, in the eyes of their persecutors and the world, were looked upon as heretics and outlaws—fit subjects for the stake. Their sacrifice was in truth a "sacrifice of contrition." The contrite heart is the heart which God honors. As the ages passed, much of the light and truth which shone upon the Apostolic Church had been lost; but the Saviour does not rebuke the ones who were sacrificing for the truth which they knew and lived out, because they did not have the light of the first centuries.

*But unto you I say, and unto the rest in Thyatira, as many as have not this doctrine, and which have not known the depths of Satan, as they speak; I will put upon you none other burden.*
*Rev. 2:24.*

Though I have afflicted thee, I will afflict thee no more.
Nah. 1:12.

Thou hast made us as the offscouring and refuse in the midst of the people.
All our enemies have opened their mouths against us.
Lam. 3:45, 46.

Justification by faith was the doctrine which broke the power of the papacy. Christ and Him crucified, a truth so long forgotten, or replaced by faith in the head of the church, was given to the people of the world in the sixteenth century. Many other truths, long hidden by the darkness, or buried under the traditions of the church, were brought forward in the early days of the Reformation. The Sabbath of the decalogue was acknowledged; some preached upon the true meaning of baptism, and others made known the proper relation of the church to the state; but these subjects were too strong for minds so long held in subjection. The age was not ripe for the fullness of truth. But as watchmen of the night hail the dawn when the morning star arises, so the early Reformers, from Wycliffe to Luther and his contemporaries, opened the Scriptures, and the first rays of light brought joy and gladness to those who sat in darkness. The

**When the morning star arises.**

Acts 24:14.
Heb. 11:38.

For he said, Surely they are my people, children that will not lie: so he was their Saviour.
Isa. 63:8.

This is the victory that overcometh the world, even our faith.
1 John 5:4.

For I am determined not to know any thing among you, save Jesus Christ, and him crucified.
1 Cor. 2:2.

Psa. 119:18.

Making the word of God of none effect through your tradition, which ye have delivered: and many such like things do ye. Mark 7:8–13.

Ex. 20:8-11.
Rom. 6:3-5.
Acts 8:38, 39.
Matt. 3:15, 16.
Matt. 22:21.

For when for the time ye ought to be teachers, ye have need that one teach you again which be the first principles of the oracles of God; and are become such as have need of milk, and not of strong meat.

For every one that useth milk is unskilful in the word of righteousness: for he is a babe.
Heb. 5:12, 13.

Psa. 130:6.
Dan. 11:33.

Thy words were found, and I did eat them; and thy word was unto me the joy and rejoicing of mine heart: for I am called by thy name, O Lord God of hosts.
Jer. 15:16.

The entrance of thy words giveth light; it giveth understanding unto the simple. Psa. 119:130.

Matt. 24:29.

When these things begin to come to pass, then look up, and lift up your heads; for your redemption draweth nigh. Luke 21:28.

*But that which ye have already hold fast till I come.*
*Rev. 2:25.*

For he knoweth our frame; he remembereth that we are dust.
Psa. 103:14.

1 Cor. 10:13.
Matt. 24:42.
Prov. 4:18.

Light is sown for the righteous, and gladness for the upright in heart. Psa. 97:11.

Matt. 5:14-16.
Psa. 147:15.
Luke 13:21.
Psa. 2:8, 9.

very ones who saw the darkness break before the light of God's Word, saw also the sign of the coming of the Son of man, which was hung in the heavens. In 1780 the sun was darkened. This was the first of a series of celestial signs (see chapter VII., Sixth Seal), and it was given to encourage those who had been oppressed.

Christ says, "I will put upon you none other burden. But that which ye have already hold fast till I come." How merciful is our God. He measures out to humanity its burdens of life, and no burden is made heavier than can be borne. "Only hold fast till I come," are His words of encouragement. To others, more accustomed to the light, greater truths would be made known.

**Holding up the torch of truth.**

To the little companies thus addressed, was given the privilege of holding up the torch of truth. As a beacon on a hill, seen from afar, the light shone from the valleys of the Piedmont. Many came in contact with this light, and soon fires were kindled throughout Europe. "He that overcometh, and keepeth My works unto the end, to him will I give power over the nations." Truth was bound to triumph, though trampled to the ground for over a thousand years. At last the faithful ones will reign as kings. The hand of the oppressor will be broken to pieces, as a potter's vessel. There was a time when the clay was soft and yielding, when it could have been remolded; but as the fires of persecution kindled, those who remained hardened in sin became so set that any attempt to change them resulted in breaking them to pieces. "I will give him the morning star." Christ is the light, and the faithful ones at the close of the years of persecution were told to lift up their heads, for their "redemption draweth nigh." This is the first church which is pointed forward to the second coming of Christ. The message to Thyatira is in harmony with the Psalmist's words, "My soul waiteth for the Lord more than they that watch for the morning; I say, more than they that watch for the morning."

It should be remembered that, as the experiences of Ephesus, Smyrna, and Pergamos, will be repeated in the last church before the second coming of Christ, so the history of Thyatira will have its counterpart in the last generation. The power of Jezebel will again be felt. What was once done by a church in days of intellectual darkness will be repeated in days of great light. The union of the church and state will be followed by laws compelling obedience to man-made laws, instead of the laws of God. The law of God will be trampled under foot; for a church with civil power always works the works of Jezebel. Just as Elijah fled before ancient Jezebel, so those proclaiming the last warning message, of which Elijah was a type, will be persecuted by this power. This message is impressed upon the minds of those living in the latter days by the oft-repeated words, "He that hath an ear, let him hear what the Spirit saith unto the churches."

*And he that overcometh, and keepeth my works unto the end, to him will I give power over the nations:*

*And he shall rule them with a rod of iron: as the vessels of a potter shall they be broken to shivers: even as I received of my Father.* *Rev. 2:26, 27.*

Jer. 18:1-4.

For ye know how that afterward, when he would have inherited the blessing, he was rejected: for he found no place of repentance, though he sought it carefully with tears. Heb. 12:15-17.

1 Pet. 4:12, 13.

*And I will give him the morning star.* *Rev. 2:28.*

I am the light of the world: he that followeth me shall not walk in darkness, but shall have the light of life. John 8:12.

Titus 2:13.
Psa. 130:6.

Is there any thing whereof it may be said, See, this is new? it hath been already of old time, which was before us. Eccl. 1:10.

Dan. 7:21, 22.

He had power to give life unto the image of the beast, that the image of the beast should both speak, and cause that as many as would not worship the image of the beast should be killed. Rev. 13:15.

That no man might buy or sell, save he that had the mark, or the name of the beast, or the number of his name. Rev. 13:17.

Rev. 17:3-6.
Rev. 12:17.

*He that hath an ear, let him hear what the Spirit saith unto the churches.* *Rev. 2:29.*

# CHAPTER IV.

## THE MESSAGE TO THE CHURCHES.—Continued.

### SARDIS.

The Lord bless thee, O habitation of justice, and mountain of holiness. Jer. 31 : 23.

Because they have committed villany in Israel, and have committed adultery with their neighbours' wives, and have spoken lying words in my name, which I have not commanded them ; even I know, and am a witness, saith the Lord. Jer. 29 : 19, 23.

I have given the dearly beloved of my soul into the hand of her enemies. Jer. 12 : 7–11.

Jer. 11 : 15–17.
Acts 5 : 29.
Eze. 20 : 35, 37.

If ye be willing and obedient, ye shall eat the good of the land. Isa. 1 : 19.

THE message to Sardis is addressed to Protestantism. The period covered by Thyatira was the era of papal persecution. This church was once the church of God, one of the candlesticks among which the Son of man was seen to walk, but when that organization prostituted itself by joining hands with the state, when, in other words, it followed the example of Balaam and worked the works of Jezebel, the oil was withheld from the candlestick, and given to those who were willing to obey God in preference to the head of the church. God regards character, not name ; and the faithful few to whom the light was entrusted, were mentioned in a part of the message to Thyatira. They were the ones who knew not the works of Jezebel.

These became the forerunners of Protestantism. The darkness was first broken when Wycliffe, "the morning star of the Reformation," translated the Bible into the English language. The first streaks of dawn lighted up the sky, and in the course of two hundred years, the sun had arisen in its splendor. The church came out of the wilderness, leaning on the arm of her Beloved. The twelve hundred and sixty years of darkness ended. It was like the return of spring after a severe winter. Life of every kind sprang into existence. Energy, long dormant, seemed suddenly imbued with a hitherto unknown activity. Discovery followed discovery; inventions were multiplied; men, accustomed to spending a lifetime in one village, now found the world opening before them through publications and increased facilities for travel. Every branch of science was explored, governments bestirred themselves, and the dust of the Middle Ages was shaken off. America was discovered and settled. Men knew not why it happened at such a time and under such circumstances; but God was preparing a cradle for the new-born cause of Protestantism. Germany might have nourished it; England had an opportunity to cherish it; but it was in America that the new church found congenial environments for growth: and while all nations receive the Sardis message, it is particularly applicable in the United States, or at least, the United States becomes the center for the movement therein mentioned.

*Sardis* means "*prince of joy*"; and the name is most appropriate for those who received the light of the eighteenth century, and the first half of the nineteenth century. Protestantism

If thou doest well, shalt thou not be accepted? Gen. 4:7.

He shall be as the light of the morning, when the sun riseth, even a morning without clouds; as the tender grass springing out of the earth by clear shining after rain. 2 Sam. 23:4.

**Wycliffe.**

Many shall run to and fro, and knowledge shall be increased. Dan. 12:4.

Hos. 2:14–22.

The chariots shall rage in the streets, they shall justle one against another in the broad ways: they shall seem like torches, they shall run like the lightnings.

He shall recount his worthies: they shall stumble in their walk; they shall make haste to the wall thereof, and the defence shall be prepared.

The gates of the rivers shall be opened, and the palace shall be dissolved. Nahum 2:4–6.

Psa. 40:13, 14.

Go, ye swift messengers, to a nation scattered and peeled, to a people terrible from their beginning hitherto; a nation meted out and trodden down, whose land the rivers have spoiled!

All ye inhabitants of the world, and dwellers on the earth, see ye, when he lifteth up an ensign on the mountains; and when he bloweth a trumpet, hear ye. Isa. 18:1–4, 7.

is an active, living principle, based upon eternal truths. It came as the result of the opening of the Scriptures to the common people. The doctrine of justification by faith makes every man responsible to God alone, and necessitates freedom of conscience. When it is once made known that every man is equal in the sight of God, a deathblow is struck to all tyranny in government; and with freedom of conscience, comes also a government by the people and for the people. In the days of Luther, Germany and the other countries of Europe, had an opportunity to develop this twofold nature of Protestantism. For a time it seemed that all Europe would be transformed; but gradually, there was a return to papal principles in Germany, and nearly all of the other countries, which had espoused the cause of Protestantism, followed her example. The return was largely due to the educational work of the Jesuits, who arose to counteract the teachings of the Reformers.

Since the days of Wycliffe, there had been in England followers of God, walking in all the light which they had received. Upon these God placed "none other burden"; but as the light increased, Protestantism in its broadest sense, was offered to England. The history of England was, for a time, a struggle between the papacy, and Protestantism under the name of Puritanism. The Commonwealth was Puritanism in power; and it was then demonstrated that there was not yet strength enough to resist the crown of tyranny when it lay within the grasp of man. England returned allegiance to her own royal family; but so strong were the principles of Protestantism that her government

Neither be ye sorry; for the joy of the Lord is your strength. Neh. 8:10.

In him was life; and the life was the light of men. John 1:4.

Whosoever will, let him take the water of life freely. Rev. 22:17.

For there is no respect of persons with God. Rom. 2:11.

I will overturn, overturn, overturn, it: and it shall be no more, until he come whose right it is; and I will give it him. Eze. 21:26, 27.

The small and great are there; and the servant is free from his master. Job 3:19.

Prov. 29:2.
Isa. 9:2.

It is happened unto them according to the true proverb, The dog is turned to his own vomit again; and, the sow that was washed to her wallowing in the mire. 2 Pet. 2:22.

2 Cor. 6:14.
Isa. 8:20.
Deut. 6:6–9.

If we walk in the light, as he is in the light, we have fellowship one with another, and the blood of Jesus Christ his Son cleanseth us from all sin. 1 John 1:7.

Acts 15:28.
Prov. 11:5,
Luke 19:20–23.

How long halt ye between two opinions? if the Lord be God, follow him: but if Baal, then follow him. 1 Kings 18:21.

My son, fear thou the Lord and the king: and meddle not with them that are given to change:
For their calamity shall rise suddenly; and who knoweth the ruin of them both? Prov. 24:21, 22.

| A.D 27. | 100. | 323. | 538. | 1798. | 1833. | 1844. |
|---|---|---|---|---|---|---|
| Pure. 73 Years. | Bloody. 223 Years. | Corrupt. 215 Years. | Death. 1260 Years. | Lack of Zeal. 35 Years. | Love. 11 Years. | Lukewarm. To the End. |
| EPHESUS. | SMYRNA. | PERGAMOS. | THYATIRA. | SARDIS. | PHILA-DEL-PHIA. | LAODICEA. |
| First, or Desirable. | Myrrh, or Sweet-smelling Savor. | Height, or Elevation. | Savor of labor, or Sacrifice of contrition. | Song of Joy, or that which remains. | Brotherly Love. | A just people, or judging the people. |
| History in the New Testament. | The Saviour prophesied of this period. | Parallel with the history of Balaam. | Parallel with the history of Jezebel. | History given from Father to Son. | | Present Generation. |

THE messages to the seven churches cover the period from the beginning of Christ's ministry to His second coming. This line of prophecy follows the church from the purity of the first century, until it unites with the state and persecutes the true people of God, and finally emerges from the Dark Ages and separating from the world prepares to meet its Lord and Master in the clouds of heaven.

The history of the first period is found in the New Testament, the second was plainly foretold by Christ. During the Pergamos and Thyatira periods the darkness was so dense that the historians of this period are unreliable, therefore the Lord gives the parallel history of the times of Balaam and Jezebel as guides for these periods. The history of the fifth and sixth periods can be received from the preceding generation, while the last period is present time.

DIAGRAM OF THE SEVEN CHURCHES.

has been, since the days of the Commonwealth, a government by the people. It was in England that the first Anglo-Saxon branches of Protestantism had birth, and it was because of lack of freedom in the mother country, that separatists from the English church sought homes in America.

It is true that freedom was not always granted in those early days; for the very ones who crossed the ocean because of oppression at home, oppressed, in America, those who did not worship God in the prescribed way. Nevertheless, America was destined to be the home of Protestantism; and gradually, the shackles of the Dark Ages were dropped off, and the equal rights of mankind were acknowledged. The Constitution of the United States was the first document ever granting complete freedom of worship, and placing in the hands of the people the sole power of the government. It was a world-wide wonder, not the work of any man, but the culmination of those principles born in Germany in the sixteenth century. The Constitution was adopted in 1789; the sun was darkened in 1780. These events, taking place as they did, were as if God saw the end hastening on, and as a source of encouragement to His followers, placed the sign of His approval in the heavens. A few years later the papal power was completely broken, and then the countries of southern Europe, France, Spain, Italy, and others, were free to choose between the principles of the papacy and those of Protestantism. America responded with its free government. During the fifty years following the adoption of the principles of Protestantism in America, the various branches

Whoso causeth the righteous to go astray in an evil way, he shall fall himself into his own pit: but the upright shall have good things in possession. Prov. 28:10.

When the wicked rise, men hide themselves: but when they perish, the righteous increase. Prov. 28:28.

The anointed of the Lord, was taken in their pits, of whom we said, Under his shadow we shall live among the heathen. Lam. 4:19, 20.

Every way of a man is right in his own eyes: but the Lord pondereth the hearts. Prov. 21:2.

I beheld another beast coming up out of the earth; and he had two horns like a lamb, and he spake as a dragon. Rev. 13:11.

Through wisdom is an house builded; and by understanding it is established. Prov. 24:3.

The nations shall see and be confounded at all their might: they shall lay their hand upon their mouth, their ears shall be deaf. Mic. 7:16.

In those days, after that tribulation, the sun shall be darkened, and the moon shall not give her light. Mark 13:24.

Luke 21:25.
Gen. 1:14.

He that leadeth into captivity shall go into captivity: he that killeth with the sword must be killed with the sword. Here is the patience and the faith of the saints. Rev. 13:10.

The earth helped the woman, and the earth opened her mouth, and swallowed up the flood which the dragon cast out of his mouth Rev. 12:16.

of the Protestant church had their period of probation. One by one the denominations arose, separating farther and farther from the physical, intellectual, and spiritual tyranny of the papacy. To each denomination was offered the law of God and the faith of Jesus. The time came when each had an opportunity to accept or reject, as seemed good to them; but the decision then made, decided their eternal destiny.

Luther searching for light.

In the early days of the nineteenth century God took a man, hitherto unacquainted with the Bible, and opened to him the beauties of the prophecies. As Luther found in Christ a Sav-

Let my counsel be acceptable unto thee, and break off thy sins by righteousness, and thine iniquities by shewing mercy to the poor; if it may be a lengthening of thy tranquillity. Dan. 4:27.

I heard another voice from heaven, saying, Come out of her, my people, that ye be not partakers of her sins, and that ye receive not of her plagues. Rev. 18:4.

If it seem evil unto you to serve the Lord, choose you this day whom ye will serve; whether the gods which your fathers served that were on the other side of the flood, or the gods of the Amorites, in whose land ye dwell: but as for me and my house, we will serve the Lord. Josh. 24:15.

I will make a man more precious than fine gold; even a man than the golden wedge of Ophir. Isa. 13:12.

God, who commanded the light to shine out of darkness, hath shined in our hearts, to give the light of the knowledge of the glory of God in the face of Jesus Christ. 2 Cor. 4:6.

iour, and with the light that entered his mind, attacked the papacy, so William Miller, in 1818, saw light in the books of Daniel and Revelation. He studied with care the twenty-three hundred days, spoken of by Daniel, and became convinced that the second coming of Christ was near at hand. He applied every test, but all pointed forward to the year 1843 as the time when the world must welcome its Saviour. The condition of the people at the first advent of Christ, was now repeated; when the time approached for the message of His second coming, the world lay in ignorance: and not the world only, but the church which bore the name of Christian. Nay, more! the very churches which in their zeal for truth had faced hardship and persecution, in protesting against the errors of the papacy,—these churches were quiet when great changes were right upon them. But unto the church of Sardis, John was bidden write: "These things saith He that hath the seven Spirits of God, and the seven stars; I know thy works, that thou hast a name that thou livest, and art dead."

He, who walked among His churches, and who sought diligently for signs of life, searching among the seven stars,—the leaders of the churches,—found that, although Sardis claimed to have life, it was dead. Strange condition! So quietly had this life been lost, that, looking back upon the activity of the past, and priding itself upon what great things had been done by Protestantism, this church had allowed the very principles of the papacy to twine about it until its life was choked.

There was a time in the history of Pergamos,

Study to shew thyself approved unto God, a workman that needeth not to be ashamed, rightly dividing the word of truth. 2 Tim. 2:15.

Dan. 8:14.
Matt. 24:33.

Prove all things; hold fast that which is good. 1 Thess. 5:21.

He came unto his own, and his own received him not.
John 1:11.

I saw the wicked buried, who had come and gone from the place of the holy, and they were forgotten in the city where they had so done: this is also vanity.
Eccl. 8:10.

*And unto the angel of the church in Sardis write; These things saith he that hath the seven Spirits of God, and the seven stars; I know thy works, that thou hast a name that thou livest, and art dead.*
*Rev. 3:1.*

Isa. 1:11–15.
Matt. 6:5.

This people draweth nigh unto me with their mouth, and honoureth me with their lips; but their heart is far from me.
Matt. 15:8, 9.

Know ye not, that to whom ye yield yourselves servants to obey, his servants ye are to whom ye obey; whether of sin unto death, or of obedience unto righteousness?
Rom. 6:16.

Her priests have violated my law, and have profaned mine holy things: they have put no difference between the holy and profane, neither have they shewed difference between the unclean and the clean, and have hid their eyes from my sabbaths, and I am profaned among them. Eze. 22:26-28.

The heads thereof judge for reward, and the priests thereof teach for hire, and the prophets thereof divine for money: yet will they lean upon the Lord, and say, Is not the Lord among us? none evil can come upon us. Mic. 3:11.

Because, even because they have seduced my people, saying, Peace; and there was no peace; and one built up a wall, and, lo, others daubed it with untempered morter. Eze. 13:10-12.

*Be watchful, and strengthen the things which remain, that are ready to die: for I have not found thy works perfect before God. Rev. 3:2.*

He hath shewed thee, O man, what is good; and what doth the Lord require of thee, but to do justly, and to love mercy, and to walk humbly with thy God? Mic. 6:8.

*Remember therefore how thou hast received and heard, and hold fast, and repent. If therefore thou shalt not watch, I will come on thee as a thief, and thou shalt not know what hour I will come upon thee. Rev. 3:3.*

when Christianity thought Paganism was dead; but in reality, the religion which was apparently vanquished, had conquered. Paganism baptized, stepped into the church. In the days of Sardis this history was repeated. Protestantism thought itself free from the principles of the Dark Ages; but the plant was sturdy and long lived, and although Protestantism reared itself aloft like a mighty oak, the rootlets of the papacy were planted with the oak, and soon the vine encircled the tree, and sapped its very life. Protestantism reared the structure, and the papacy is supported by it. "Be watchful," says the divine message to Sardis, "and strengthen the things which remain, that are ready to die: for I have not found thy works perfect before God." There was, at the time this message came, some life still in the oak, but unless haste was made to "strengthen the things which remain," death would follow.

**Like a mighty oak.**

"Remember, therefore, how thou hast received and heard, and hold fast, and repent." The truths already received were indeed life; but a church, as well as an individual, must make constant progress, or they will suffer spiritual death.

For nine years William Miller was convinced that he ought to give his message to the churches; but he waited, hoping that some recognized authority would proclaim the glad news of a soon-coming Saviour. In thus waiting, he but proved the truth of the message; there was a name that they lived, but they were fast dying. In 1831 Miller gave his first discourse on the prophecies. He was a member of the Baptist church, and in 1833, he received from this church, license to preach. This was the very year in which appeared another sign in the heavens,—the third spoken of by the Saviour in Matthew 24:29. In November, 1833, "the stars of heaven fell unto the earth, even as a fig tree casteth her untimely figs, when she is shaken of a mighty wind." God was calling to the dying church of Sardis by the voice of man and by signs in the heavens. "If therefore thou shalt not watch, I will come on thee as a thief, and thou shalt not know what hour I will come upon thee."

As the time, which was supposed to be the time of the second advent approached, men of learning and position helped spread the message. The light of this message flashed throughout the world. "Thou hast a few names even in Sardis which have not defiled their garments." Three years after Miller was convinced of the near coming of Christ, that is, in 1821, Joseph Wolff, known as the "missionary to Asia," began to give the same message. He visited Egypt, Abyssinia, Palestine, Syria, Persia, Bokhara, and India,—everywhere proclaiming the soon coming of the Messiah. In 1837 he was in America; and after preaching in several large

Heb. 2:1 [margin.]

Quench not the Spirit. 1 Thess. 5:19.

Grieve not the holy Spirit of God, whereby ye are sealed unto the day of redemption. Eph. 4:30.

The remnant of Jacob shall be in the midst of many people as a dew from the Lord, as the showers upon the grass, that tarrieth not for man, nor waiteth for the sons of men. Mic. 5:7.

The stars of heaven fell unto the earth, even as a fig tree casteth her untimely figs, when she is shaken of a mighty wind. Rev. 6:13.

**Joseph Wolff.**

That was the true Light, which lighteth every man that cometh into the world. John 1:9.

*Thou hast a few names even in Sardis which have not defiled their garments; and they shall walk with me in white: for they are worthy. Rev. 3:4.*

Go ye therefore, and teach all nations, baptizing them in the name of the Father, and of the Son, and of the Holy Ghost. Matt. 28:19.

The Lord said unto him, Go thy way: for he is a chosen vessel unto me, to bear my name before the Gentiles, and kings, and the children of Israel. Acts 9:15.

How hear we every man in our own tongue, wherein we were born? Cretes and Arabians, we do hear them speak in our tongues the wonderful works of God. Acts 2:8, 11.

William Miller.

Said unto him, Hearest thou what these say? And Jesus saith unto them, Yea; have ye never read, Out of the mouth of babes and sucklings thou hast perfected praise? Matt. 21:16.

Saying to the sixth angel which had the trumpet, Loose the four angels which are bound in the great river Euphrates.
And the four angels were loosed, which were prepared for an hour, and a day, and a month, and a year, for to slay the third part of men. Rev. 9:14, 15.

Blow ye the trumpet in Zion, and sound an alarm in my holy mountain: let all the inhabitants of the land tremble: for the day of the Lord cometh, for it is nigh at hand. Joel 2:1.

cities, he visited Washington, where, in the presence of all the members of the Congress of the United States, he preached on the personal reign of Christ.

In England the same message was given by Edward Irving, a minister of the Church of England. South America heard of Christ's soon coming from the pen of Lacunza, formerly a Spanish Jesuit. Gaussen, finding that many mature minds claimed that prophecy could not be interpreted, gave the message of the soon coming of Christ to the children of Geneva. In Scandinavia, the truth was proclaimed by children; for God used child-preachers, when older persons were restricted by law.

In 1838 Josiah Litch and William Miller published an exposition of the ninth chapter of Revelation, in which it was predicted that the Ottoman Empire would fall in 1840. The exact fulfillment of this prophecy on August 11, 1840, when the Turkish government surrendered its independence, and has since been known as "the sick man of the East," was a startling proof to many that prophecy could be understood, and that men were living in the end of time.

This message of the personal appearance of Christ was one of the most world-wide proclamations ever given. Every kindred, nation, and people were suddenly aroused from their lethargy by the cry,—"Behold the Bridegroom cometh, go ye out to meet Him." This truth is inseparably connected with the wording of the message to Sardis. "Thou hast a few names even in Sardis which have not defiled their garments; and they shall walk with Me in white: for they are worthy." The very sins of idolatry and fornication, which characterized the mother church in the days of Thyatira, were staining the garments of her daughters during the Sardis period. But "he that overcometh, the same shall be clothed in white raiment." The white raiment is the righteousness of Christ,—"the fine linen clean and white." "And I will not blot out his name out of the book of life, but I will confess his name before My Father, and before His angels." A most precious promise, and a most solemn

Woe unto you, scribes and Pharisees, hypocrites! because ye build the tombs of the prophets, and garnish the sepulchres of the righteous,

And say, If we had been in the days of our fathers, we would not have been partakers with them in the blood of the prophets.

Matt. 23:29-32.

Acts 7:52, 53.
Rev. 19:8.
Isa. 61:10.

**Sardis. Present state.**

*He that overcometh, the same shall be clothed in white raiment; and I will not blot out his name out of the book of life, but I will confess his name before my Father, and before his angels.*

*Rev. 3:5.*

Isa. 4:3 [margin.]
Rev. 3:5.
Luke 9:26.

warning, are combined in these closing words of the message to Sardis. The second coming of the Son of man had been proclaimed to all the world. To him that accepted truth, it was promised that his name should remain in the book of life, and should be confessed in the presence of God. The books of heaven are opened. Christ promises to witness for all who are true to His cause on earth. The church of Sardis lived in the period when Daniel saw

I saw another angel fly in the midst of heaven, having the everlasting gospel to preach unto them that dwell on the earth, and to every nation, and kindred, and tongue, and people. Rev. 14:6.

Matt. 10:33.
Mark 8:34.

A fiery stream issued and came forth from before him: thousand thousands ministered unto him, and ten thousand times ten thousand stood before him: the judgment was set, and the books were opened.

Dan. 7:9, 10.

I saw in the night visions, and, behold, one like the Son of man came with the clouds of heaven, and came to the Ancient of days, and they brought him near before him. Dan. 7:13, 14.

For Christ is not entered into the holy places made with hands, which are the figures of the true; but into heaven itself, now to appear in the presence of God for us. Heb. 9:24.

The books were opened: and another book was opened, which is the book of life: and the dead were judged out of those things which were written in the books, according to their works. Rev. 20:12.

Matt. 22:9-14.
Rev. 6:11.

Into the second went the high priest alone once every year, not without blood, which he offered for himself, and for the errors of the people. Heb. 9:7.

Heb. 8:5.

Every man that hath this hope in him purifieth himself, even as he is pure. 1 John 3:3.

2 Pet. 1:4.
Isa. 25:9.

Which hope we have as an anchor of the soul, both sure and steadfast, and which entereth into that within the veil;
Whither the forerunner is for us entered, even Jesus, made an high priest for ever after the order of Melchisedec. Heb. 6:19, 20.

Heb. 7:24, 25.

*He that hath an ear, let him hear what the Spirit saith unto the churches. Rev. 3:6.*

"One like the Son of man [who] came . . . to the Ancient of Days." It was at the end of the twenty-three hundred days of Daniel 8:14, that Christ was brought in before the Father. He entered the Holy of Holies in the sanctuary above. "The judgment was set, and the books were opened." Then there came before Him all who had ever named the name of Christ, and to those whose garments were unspotted, was given the fine linen of Christ's righteousness.

This great change in the heavenly sanctuary, corresponding to the entering in of the high priest in the earthly, or typical service, on the day of atonement, was made known to the church of Sardis. Those who opened the prophecies where this truth is made known, misinterpreted the cleansing of the sanctuary to be the second coming of Christ. Nevertheless, while mistaken in the event which transpired, they were not mistaken in the time; and the heart cleansing necessary to prepare a people for the beginning of the investigative judgment, which has been going on in heaven since 1844, is the same preparation necessary to welcome the Son of God in the clouds of heaven. Although Christ did not then come to the earth,—the outer court of the heavenly sanctuary,—but entered within the most holy place before the Ancient of Days, to act as mediator in the investigative judgment, the message to prepare for His coming, will continue to the end of time. Some of those who witnessed the signs given to Sardis and listened to the advent message, will see Him when He comes in the clouds of heaven. So near is Sardis to the end.

**Philadelphia. Present state.**

PHILADELPHIA.

The Saviour, walking in the church of Sardis, found a few whose garments were undefiled. They were those in whom life remained after the body was dead; and to these the call came to separate from the lifeless form, that their own life might be saved. The message of the soon coming of Christ was a universal message. It offered an opportunity to all to repent, and as many as believed, took up the cry with the enthusiasm which characterized the Apostolic Church. They were experiencing their "first love," and those who welcomed Christ were bound together with a love surpassing that of Jonathan for David. The oneness of spirit which Christ prayed might be found among His followers was more perfectly developed among those

Though ye have lien among the pots, yet shall ye be as the wings of a dove covered with silver, and her feathers with yellow gold. Psa. 68 : 13.

Depart ye, depart ye, go ye out from thence, touch no unclean thing; go ye out of the midst of her; be ye clean, that bear the vessels of the Lord. Isa. 52 : 11.

Jer. 51 : 6, 45.
Rev. 14 : 6.

Repent ye therefore, and be converted, that your sins may be blotted out, when the times of refreshing shall come from the presence of the Lord. Acts 3 : 19.

Thou art beautiful, O my love, as Tirzah, comely as Jerusalem, terrible as an army with banners. Song Sol. 6 : 4.

6

Jesus answered them and said, Verily, verily, I say unto you, Ye seek me, not because ye saw the miracles, but because ye did eat of the loaves, and were filled. John 6:26.

Behold, thou art fair, my beloved, yea, pleasant. Song Sol. 1:16.

Now ye are the body of Christ, and members in particular. 1 Cor. 12:27.

Dan. 7:13.

*And to the angel of the church in Philadelphia write; These things saith he that is holy, he that is true, he that hath the key of David, he that openeth, and no man shutteth; and shutteth, and no man openeth. Rev. 3:7.*

**The glory of God appeared in the shekinah above the mercy seat.**

Speak unto Aaron thy brother, that he come not at all times into the holy place within the vail before the mercy seat, which is upon the ark; that he die not: for I will appear in the cloud upon the mercy seat. Lev. 16:2.

The temple of God was opened in heaven, and there was seen in his temple the ark of his testament: and there were lightnings, and voices, and thunderings, and an earthquake, and great hail. Rev. 11:19.

who heeded the closing message to Sardis, than among any others since the day of Pentecost; and to this company of believers scattered every where, yet united in heart and purpose, the name *Philadelphia* signifying *"brotherly love"* is applicable.

Some who heard the advent message, accepted it through fear; others were attracted by the forcible arguments; but whatever may have been the motive, all were tested, and those who accepted because of real love for the Saviour, composed the Philadelphia church. Of this church no complaint is made; and as love is the ruling power of the throne of God, the Saviour appears to recognize the Philadelphian church as a part of His own being,—heirs with Christ of the everlasting promises made to David. "These things saith He that is holy, He that is true, He that hath the key of David."

When the call was made, saying, "the Bridegroom cometh," Christ, the Heavenly Bridegroom, passed into the presence of His Father, there to receive dominion and power; and a door in heaven was opened to the faithful and true ones on earth. This door was the entrance into the most holy place in the temple, where Jehovah sat enthroned over the mercy seat. He is surrounded by His angels, and the law of God is the foundation of His throne. This was shown in type and shadow in the tabernacle, built by Moses. To Israel in the wilderness, the glory of God appeared in the shekinah above the mercy seat. The attention of the Philadelphian church is directed to the heavenly sanctuary. It was opened by the Saviour Himself, as He entered the most holy place at the close of the twenty-three hundred days. He sends the message to all, "I have set before thee an open door, and no man can shut it." The door stands open to all, who by faith, will enter, and no combination of circumstances, instigated by men or demons, can shut out the soul that keeps the eye of faith centered upon the Saviour within that shining portal. The time of test for those who were looking for their Lord, came in the autumn of 1844. At first the expiration of the twenty-three hundred days was thought to be in the spring of 1844. On further investigation, it was found that the decree of Artaxerxes, from which the prophetic period is reckoned, went into effect in the autumn of the year 457 B. C.; hence, this reckoning would cause those days to expire in the autumn of 1844 A. D. Here was a waiting time, in which those who loved the Lord, prepared, by deep heart searching, to receive Him. Many inquired, "What must I do to be saved?" Those who were looking upward received the light of the investigative judgment, when, in the autumn of 1844, the door in heaven opened, and Christ approached the Father. But many who had only professed to believe in the advent, changed when the time passed and He did not come, and now scoffed at those who still clung to the message, "Fear God, and give glory to Him; for the hour of His judgment is come." The heavenly door opened, but those who turned back to the world were left in darkness; while those who sought earnestly for their mistake in interpreting prophecy, received a flood of light, straight from the throne. Through this open door in the heavenly temple, there was seen "the ark of His testament," containing the ten commandments: and

Now of the things which we have spoken this is the sum: We have such an high priest, who is set on the right hand of the throne of the Majesty in the heavens.
Heb. 8:1.

*I know thy works: behold, I have set before thee an open door, and no man can shut it: for thou hast a little strength, and hast kept my word, and hast not denied my name.* *Rev. 3:8.*

All thine enemies have opened their mouth against thee: they hiss and gnash the teeth: they say, We have swallowed her up: certainly this is the day that we looked for; we have found, we have seen it.
Lam. 2:16.

John 10:28, 29.
Jude 24.
Heb. 11:27.
Dan. 8:14.
Dan. 8:16–27.
Dan. 9:20–27.
Ezra 7:11–26.
John 1:41 [margin.]
Luke 3:21, 22.
Acts 10:38.
Acts 8:4.
Ezra 7:9.
Dan. 9:25.
Matt. 25.7.
Heb. 10:32–34.

From that time many of his disciples went back, and walked no more with him. John 6:66.

2 Pet. 3:3, 4.
Rev. 14:6, 7.
Matt. 25:10.
Matt. 6:23.
1 Pet. 3:15.
Psa. 119:105.
Rev. 11:19.

Ex. 31 : 18.
Ex. 32 : 15.
Deut. 10 : 1–5.
Ex. 40 : 3.
Heb. 9 : 2–5.
1 John 5 : 3.

**Every open door should be a reminder of the heavenly door opened by Christ, which no man can close.**

Making the word of God of none effect through your tradition, which ye have delivered: and many such like things do ye. Mark 7 : 13.

If thou turn away thy foot from the sabbath, from doing thy pleasure on my holy day; and call the sabbath a delight, the holy of the Lord, honourable; and shalt honour him, not doing thine own ways, nor finding thine own pleasure, nor speaking thine own words:
Then shalt thou delight thyself in the Lord. Isa. 58 : 13, 14.

***Behold, I will make them of the synagogue of Satan, which say they are Jews, and are not, but do lie; behold, I will make them to come and worship before thy feet, and to know that I have loved thee. Rev. 3 : 9.***

from that time, the Sabbath of the Fourth Commandment became a test to the people of God. The God who had led His people thus far, was still leading them by His Word. Many precious rays of light that had been hidden by tradition during the Dark Ages, now opened up to their understanding. The Sabbath reform now became the message to the world. The traditions which connected the Philadelphian church with the Dark Ages, were portrayed in vivid colors; and man was called to exalt the law of God, and remove his foot from desecrating the Sabbath of Jehovah. Hitherto, all the Protestant churches opened their doors to receive the message; but when the Sabbath truth was proclaimed, the churches closed their doors against those who accepted the new doctrine. When the door in heaven opened, the doors of the Protestant churches closed. Every open door should be a reminder of the heavenly door opened by Christ, which no man can close, from whose portals shines forth a stream of light upon the pathway of all whose minds are staid upon Him. Those who forsook the new light, that came with the "open door," are referred to as those "of the synagogue of Satan, which say they are Jews, and are not."

As the Jewish nation, at the first advent, turned from the Saviour, and rejected the Son of God, so many in 1844 crucified the Son of man afresh. But He will one day be lifted up in the eyes of all men; and those who have followed close beside Him, entering by faith, within the second veil, will be seated on thrones and will reign with Him. To the disciples in Gethsemane, was given an opportunity to drink of the cup of which He drank. To the faithful ones in 1844, it was, likewise, given to drink of the cup of the world's scorn. To such is the promise, "Because thou hast kept the word of my patience, I also will keep thee from the hour of temptation, which shall come upon all the world, to try them that dwell upon the earth." Before His second coming, there will be such a time as the world has never seen. God's people will be saved from this; for He will hide them in His "pavilion." "Here is the patience of the saints: here are they that keep the commandments of God, and the faith of Jesus." Patience will be developed by keeping the commandments and by clinging to the faith of Jesus. If He tarry, wait for Him; for He says to Philadelphia, "Behold, I come quickly."

To the faithful in Thyatira, the angel said, "That which ye have already, hold fast till I come." To Philadelphia came the words, "Hold that fast which thou hast, that no man take thy crown." The people in Thyatira may have had but a few rays of light, compared with those living in the later period; for the light was but dawning in Thyatira, while its midday rays shone in Philadelphia; but the crown is the reward of character, and he who receives one, will have been faithful to all the light which shone upon his pathway. Heaven can be enjoyed by those only, who have developed a character in harmony with the truth. Every man is a candidate, but only he who striveth lawfully, will inherit the crown. It belongs to him who receives a white stone with a new name. For six thousand years the angelic hosts have been watching for the circle of perfection to be completed,

*Because thou hast kept the word of my patience, I also will keep thee from the hour of temptation, which shall come upon all the world, to try them that dwell upon the earth. Rev. 3:10.*

Dan. 12:1.
Jer. 30:7.

**Patience will be developed by keeping the commandments.**

For in the time of trouble he shall hide me in his pavilion: in the secret of his tabernacle shall he hide me; he shall set me up upon a rock. Psa. 27:5.

Rev. 14:12.

*Behold, I come quickly: hold that fast which thou hast, that no man take thy crown. Rev. 3:11.*

**The crown is the reward of character.**

For as many as have sinned without law shall also perish without law: and as many as have sinned in the law shall be judged by the law. Rom. 2:12.

Henceforth there is laid up for me a crown of righteousness, which the Lord, the righteous judge, shall give me at that day. 2 Tim. 4:8.

Rev. 21:7 [margin.]
Rev. 22:17.
Isa. 55:1.
Zech. 9:16.

Thou shalt also be a crown of glory in the hand of the Lord, and a royal diadem in the hand of thy God. Isa. 62:3.

1 Pet. 2:5
Gal. 2:9.

Whereby are given unto us exceeding great and precious promises: that by these ye might be partakers of the divine nature, having escaped the corruption that is in the world through lust. 2 Pet. 1:4.

*Him that overcometh will I make a pillar in the temple of my God, and he shall go no more out: and I will write upon him the name of my God, and the name of the city of my God, which is new Jerusalem, which cometh down out of heaven from my God: and I will write upon him my new name. Rev. 3:12.*

Jerusalem which is above is free, which is the mother of us all. Gal. 4:26.

For we are his workmanship, created in Christ Jesus unto good works. Eph. 2:10.

Isa. 45:23.
Matt. 25:34.

If a man also strive for masteries, yet is he not crowned, except he strive lawfully. 2 Tim. 2:5.

Rev. 14:12.

*He that hath an ear, let him hear what the Spirit saith unto the churches. Rev. 3:13.*

Rev. 3:14.
Rev. 3:3, 11.

and when the last character mold is filled, time will cease to be.

Some from the Philadelphian church will become pillars in the temple of God,—living pillars, holding up a structure of life. The most wonderful promises are made to those living in this period; for heaven itself was spread out before the overcomer; and yet this is true for all who overcome. The message to the Philadelphian period reaches to the end of time, and all who receive the crown will have passed through its experiences. The patience, faith, and love of Jesus, will characterize those who sit at last on the left, and on the right, of the throne in heaven. "He that hath an ear, let him hear what the Spirit saith unto the churches."

**Laodicea. Present state.**

LAODICEA.

The last church to which John was bidden to send a message was Laodicea. The messages to Sardis and to Philadelphia, separately cover a period extending to the second coming of Christ; but in addition to the experiences portrayed in the fifth and sixth messages, that which is directed to Laodicea is also applicable. It is given by the Amen, the One with whom yea is yea, and nay is nay,—the One who changeth not. He is also "the faithful and true Witness"; for the Laodicean message is given to the people at the time when the investigative judgment is in progress; and while the message is going forth, the names of the very ones who receive it, will be called in the court of heaven, and Christ will stand as the faithful and true Witness; but Satan as the accuser of the brethren. "The Beginning of the Creation of God," who gave His life at the foundation of the world, is watching His people in the closing hours of probationary time. The cry, "Babylon is fallen," was proclaimed when the churches rejected the advent message; and as in the Thyatira period, the true separated from those who turned from the light; so in the days when the principles of Protestantism are again disregarded, this time by the daughters of Babylon, a separation is necessary. The light of the sixteenth century came from an opened Bible. Justification by faith was made known as opposed to justification by works. Later the temple in heaven was opened, and the true Sabbath was made known. This had long been trampled in the dust; but its observance was a cross too heavy for many to lift, and they turned back toward the Dark Ages. The principles of Protestantism were repudiated by the churches, and the principles of Republicanism by the state; while the nominally Protestant denominations returned to the days of Pergamos. But some went forward to proclaim the third angel's message,

Jesus Christ the same yesterday, and to day, and for ever.
Heb. 13:8.

From Jesus Christ, who is the faithful witness, and the first begotten of the dead, and the prince of the kings of the earth. Unto him that loved us, and washed us from our sins in his own blood.
Rev. 1:5.

Rev. 3.5.

*And unto the angel of the church of the Laodiceans write; These things saith the Amen, the faithful and true witness, the beginning of the creation of God.*
*Rev. 3:14.*

**The light of the sixteenth century came from an opened Bible.**

What agreement hath the temple of God with idols? 2 Cor. 6:16.

The entrance of thy words giveth light; it giveth understanding unto the simple. Psa. 119:130.

Six days thou shalt work, but on the seventh day thou shalt rest.
Ex. 34:21.

Blessed is the man that doeth this, and the son of man that layeth hold on it; that keepeth the sabbath from polluting it.
Isa. 56:1, 2.

The kings of the earth, and all the inhabitants of the world, would not have believed that the adversary and the enemy should have entered into the gates of Jerusalem.
Lam. 4:12,

Lam. 5:6.
Isa. 1:9.
Rev. 12:17.
Isa. 1:3.

They regard not the work of the Lord, neither consider the operation of his hands. Isa. 5:12.

*I know thy works, that thou art neither cold nor hot: I would thou wert cold or hot. Rev. 3:15.*

When pride cometh, then cometh shame: but with the lowly is wisdom. Prov. 11:2.

Rom. 8:22.

The devil is come down unto you, having great wrath, because he knoweth that he hath but a short time. Rev. 12:12.

2 Thess. 2:9, 10.
Gen. 19:16.
Rev. 7:1-3.
Heb. 1:14.
Gen. 33:14.
Rev. 1:13.
Rev. 2:1.
Deut. 3:28.

Walk while ye have the light, lest darkness come upon you: for he that walketh in darkness knoweth not whither he goeth. John 12:35.

What man is there that is fearful and fainthearted? let him go and return unto his house, lest his brethren's heart faint as well as his heart. Deut. 20:8.

His word was in mine heart as a burning fire shut up in my bones, and I was weary with forbearing, and I could not stay. Jer. 20:9.

Matt. 26:51-55.
2 Sam. 7:1-13.

*So then because thou art lukewarm, and neither cold nor hot, I will spew thee out of my mouth. Rev. 3:16.*

Jer. 3:32-36.

as given in the fourteenth chapter of Revelation.

Upon this last church—the remnant,—shine the accumulated rays of all past ages. It is a church highly favored, and one of which heaven and earth have a right to expect great things. But like the churches of the past, it has disappointed heaven, and Christ sorrowfully says of them, 'I know thy works, that thou art neither cold nor hot." Spiritual pride is the worst of evils, and the hardest to reach. Heaven and earth are waiting for the closing up of history. The climax has been reached in the controversy. Satan is preparing for the final struggle. The armory of heaven awaits the signal of its Leader. The church of God on earth, is the only object which can retard the progress of events. It becomes the center of interest for the universe. The Saviour still bids the hosts hold till the servants of God are sealed. Angels are hurrying to and fro between heaven and earth, but God will go no faster than His church. For centuries He has walked with it, holding its star in His right hand. Every encouragement has been offered to speed the work; but when the church hesitates, He goes no faster than it can go, lest the light be so far in advance that His followers will lose their way.

A spirit of lukewarmness rests upon God's people. Says the Witness, "I would thou wert cold or hot." If very cold, something could warm them, or if too hot, their ardor could be controlled; but "because thou art lukewarm, and neither cold nor hot, I will spew thee out of My mouth." There is danger that those who have seen the signs of His coming; those who have heard the advent message, and have followed in the light which shone from the open door; and those who have sacrificed for the cause in many ways, will, near the close, when just about ready to receive the crown, rest satisfied in their past experiences. They say they are "rich, and increased with goods, and have need of nothing;" and forget that he who receives most, is accountable for the most. "And knowest not that thou art wretched, and miserable, and poor, and blind, and naked." Think of it. He who prides himself on his wealth is, in the eyes of heaven, poverty-stricken, blind and naked. Heaven pities such a church, and the true Witness, who longs to plead for, and not against them, in the presence of the angels, counsels them, "Buy of Me gold tried in the fire, that thou mayest be rich." Faith and love is the wealth offered by Christ, and with these the possessor can purchase the treasures of heaven. "Buy of Me white raiment, that thou mayest be clothed, and that the shame of thy nakedness do not appear." The raiment offered is the righteousness of Christ. It is a garment of light, which will attract the world to Christ. This will clothe all the redeemed who are living on the earth when Christ appears. It is a reflection of the holiness of God, and comes to him only, who lives in constant communication with the Lord of Life. The life of him who is in touch with heaven, is like the glow of the incandescent light. When this counsel is heeded, the "loud cry" of Revelation 18:1 will sound throughout the world.

"I counsel thee to anoint thine eyes with eyesalve, that thou mayest see." The oil for anointing, is the oil of His grace, which will give

Therefore thus saith the Lord, If thou return, then will I bring thee again, and thou shalt stand before me: and if thou take forth the precious from the vile, thou shalt be as my mouth: let them return unto thee; but return not thou unto them. Jer. 15:19.

Mark 10:31.
Luke 12:47, 48.
Hosea 12:8.

*Because thou sayest, I am rich, and increased with goods, and have need of nothing; and knowest not that thou art wretched, and miserable, and poor, and blind, and naked.* *Rev. 3:17.*

Now ye are full, now ye are rich, ye have reigned as kings without us: and I would to God ye did reign, that we also might reign with you. 1 Cor. 4:8.

Hosea 12:14.

The Lord said unto Satan, The Lord rebuke thee, O Satan; even the Lord that hath chosen Jerusalem rebuke thee: is not this a brand plucked out of the fire? Zech. 3:1–6.

Prov. 8:18–21.
Rev. 19:8.

If so be that being clothed we shall not be found naked. 2 Cor. 5:3.

2 Cor. 5:21.
2 Cor. 4:4–6.
2 Cor. 3:18.

*I counsel thee to buy of me gold tried in the fire, that thou mayest be rich; and white raiment, that thou mayest be clothed, and that the shame of thy nakedness do not appear; and anoint thine eyes with eyesalve, that thou mayest see.* *Rev. 3:18.*

Psa. 104:2.

All that sat in the council, looking steadfastly on him, saw his face as it had been the face of an angel. Acts 6:15.

As truly as I live, all the earth shall be filled with the glory of the Lord. Num. 14:20, 21.

spiritual eyesight to the soul in blindness and darkness, that he may distinguish between the workings of the Spirit of God and those of the spirit of the enemy. The way which these souls must travel, is a narrow way. Satan, as his time grows short, uses every device to deceive, if possible, the very elect; and as his deceptions become more delusive, only those eyes which are anointed with the oil of grace, can discern the spirits. The heavenly Merchantman opens His wares, and counsels us to buy of Him. He addresses those who have lost their first love, those who have lost their zeal and interest in spiritual things, and urges them to buy of the heavenly store. Many will be reproved for the sins mentioned in the Laodicean message, and such reproofs, unheeded, will cause those to be shaken out who are unwilling to receive the reproof of the Spirit.

Eternal interests are at stake; the time of probation is almost over; and Christ, as if loath to lose one single soul, reproves and rebukes, that sin may be discarded. There is no other time for preparation, for the Laodicean message covers ecclesiastical history to the very end of time. "As many as I love, I rebuke and chasten: be zealous therefore, and repent."

To those hearts that have not yet admitted Christ as the one Ruler in the soul-temple, He says, "Behold, I stand at the door, and knock." He does not force Himself in, although His own heart is breaking over our hardness. He pleads in gentleness, and if allowed to enter, in the capacity of an intimate friend, He will sup with us. The very closest relationship is seen to exist between God and His remnant church. It

Then shall ye return, and discern between the righteous and the wicked, between him that serveth God and him that serveth him not. Mal. 3:18.

For there shall arise false Christs, and false prophets, and shall shew great signs and wonders; insomuch that, if it were possible, they shall deceive the very elect. Matt. 24:24.

For which things' sake the wrath of God cometh on the children of disobedience. Col. 3:6.

Luke 1:17.

Cast away from you all your transgressions, whereby ye have transgressed; and make you a new heart and a new spirit: for why will ye die, O house of Israel? Eze. 18:31.

The harvest is past, the summer is ended, and we are not saved. Jer. 8:20.

Rev. 22:11, 12.
Rev. 22:10.

*As many as I love, I rebuke and chasten: be zealous therefore, and repent. Rev. 3:19.*

John 16:8, 9.

Ye have set at nought all my counsel, and would none of my reproof. Prov. 1:25.

John 17:23.
Song Sol. 5:2.

*Behold I stand at the door, and knock: if any man hear my voice, and open the door, I will come in to him, and will sup with him, and he with me. Rev. 3:20.*

Which doeth great things past finding out; yea, and wonders without number. Job. 9:10.

*To him that overcometh will I grant to sit with me in my throne, even as I also overcame, and am set down with my Father in his throne. Rev. 3:21.*

*He that hath an ear, let him hear what the Spirit saith unto the churches. Rev. 3:22.*

is as a brand plucked from the burning. Weak, trembling, and sin-laden, this remnant of the race, is taken by the Saviour to sit with Him on His throne, even as He overcame, and sat down on the throne of the Father. Angels see the place, made vacant by the fall of Lucifer, filled by those whom sin had marred and defaced more than any other race. The Majesty of heaven reaches to the lowest depths of earth, and exalts man to the highest place in heaven,—a seat beside the King on His throne. The redeemed occupy a position nearer the Creator than they could have occupied, had there been no sin. Such is the wondrous love of Christ! To-day angels and inhabitants of unfallen worlds are watching the consummation of the plan. We who live to-day are the objects of their interest. "He that hath an ear, let him hear what the Spirit saith unto the churches."

**"Behold I stand at the door and knock."**

# CHAPTER V.

## A GLIMPSE OF HEAVEN.

For he endured, as seeing him who is invisible. Heb. 11:27.

John 14:21.
John 17:20-23.
Song Sol. 2:16.

Many waters cannot quench love, neither can the floods drown it: if a man would give all the substance of his house for love, it would utterly be contemned. Song Sol. 8:6, 7.

*After this I looked, and, behold, a door was opened in heaven: and the first voice which I heard was as it were of a trumpet talking with me, which said, Come up hither, and I will shew thee things which must be hereafter. Rev. 4:1.*

Acts 7:55, 56.

In all their affliction he was afflicted. Isa. 63:9.

He that toucheth you toucheth the apple of his eye. Zech. 2:8.

Rev. 1:10.

Soul communion with the Redeemer was sweet to the prophet John, as he lived alone on Patmos; and the actual meeting with Christ in that first vision, which opened before his mind the future history of the church, had drawn him very near to the object of his love. "After this I looked, and, behold, a door was opened in heaven." Stephen, while men were killing the body, looked, and the heavens opened; and he said, "Behold, I see . . . the Son of man standing on the right hand of God." As Christ rose in sympathy with that suffering disciple, so the yearning felt by John, touched the heart of Christ, and the prophet heard again the trumpet tone saying, "Come up hither, and I will show thee things which must be hereafter."

Only the spiritual eye can gaze on things of God; and few mortals have allowed the spiritual side of their natures to be developed until it is possible to leave earthly scenes, and view the realms above. John was one, who, when God said "Come," could go. Ezekiel was another who had the privilege of visiting heaven; and he describes, as best the human language can portray, the glories of the throne of God. When Christ called, Gabriel conducted John into the sanctuary above, into the very presence of Jehovah. He says, "Immediately I was in the Spirit: and, behold, a throne was set in heaven, and One sat on the throne" "A glorious high throne from the beginning is the place of our sanctuary." As Moses, before the burning bush, was commanded to take off his shoes; "for," said the Lord, "the place whereon thou standest is holy ground;" so one feels to step lightly when in the presence of the scenes which John portrays.

Heaven, from whatever standpoint it may be viewed, presents the plan of Redemption. This plan is the one all-absorbing theme of the universe of God; and heaven reflects it in all its works. Only the sinful heart of man, is unmindful of the work of God in overcoming the effects of the fall. The things presented to John show that the activity of the heavenly beings is spent in the service of man. "He that sat was to look upon like a jasper and a sardine stone: and there was a rainbow round about the throne, in sight like unto an emerald." The light of the glory of God, as it shines in the face of Jesus Christ, is a light of dazzling whiteness, its rays are unbroken.

The rainbow in the clouds is but a symbol of the rainbow which has encircled the throne from eternity. Back in the ages, which finite mind cannot fathom, the Father and Son were alone in the universe. Christ was the first begotten of the Father, and to Him Jehovah made known

Rom. 11:33, 34.

How that he was caught up into paradise, and heard unspeakable words, which it is not lawful for a man to utter. 2 Cor. 12:3, 4.

*And immediately I was in the spirit: and, behold, a throne was set in heaven, and one sat on the throne. Rev. 4:2.*

Jer. 17:12.
Ex. 3:2-5.

Who is able to stand before this holy Lord God? and to whom shall he go up from us? 1 Sam. 6:20.

Num. 4:5, 19, 20.
2 Sam. 6:7-11.
1 Kings 21:27.
Heb. 12:29.

God commendeth his love toward us, in that, while we were yet sinners, Christ died for us. Rom. 5:8.

We are made a spectacle unto the world, and to angels, and to men. 1 Cor. 4:9.

Heb. 1:14.

The ox knoweth his owner, and the ass his master's crib: but Israel doth not know, my people doth not consider. Isa. 1:3.

The living creatures ran and returned as the appearance of a flash of lightning. Eze. 1:14.

Dan. 9:20-23.

*And he that sat was to look upon like a jasper and a sardine stone: and there was a rainbow round about the throne, in sight like unto an emerald. Rev. 4:3.*

2 Cor. 4:4.
Eze. 1:28.
Matt. 17:1-3.
Luke 9:28, 29.
Rev. 10:1.

And above the firmament that was over their heads was the likeness of a throne, as the appearance of a sapphire stone: and upon the likeness of the throne was the likeness as the appearance of a man above upon it. Eze. 1:26, 27.

the divine plan of Creation. The plan of the creation of worlds was unfolded, together with the order of beings which should people them. Angels, as representatives of one order, would be ministers of the God of the universe. The creation of our own little world, was included in the deep-laid plans. The fall of Lucifer was foreseen; likewise the possibility of the introduction of sin, which would mar the perfection of the divine handiwork. It was then, in those early councils, that Christ's heart of love was touched; and the only begotten Son pledged His life to redeem man, should he yield and fall. Father and Son, surrounded by impenetrable glory, clasped hands. It was in appreciation of this offer, that upon Christ was bestowed creative power, and the everlasting covenant was made; and henceforth Father and Son, with one mind, worked together to complete the work of creation. Sacrifice of self for the good of others was the foundation of it all. As angels came into being at the command of Jehovah, heaven was so arranged that the plan of salvation could be read by them in everything. The arrangement of the angels in their work about the throne, is a picture of the redeeming love of God. Angelic beings know nothing different. Thus all heaven waits for the redemption of man. Even the stones which compose the foundation walls, have voices which speak of the atonement. The colors reflected from every object in the heavenly court speak louder of the power and infinite mercy of God than mortal tongue can speak. Human language cannot tell the story. It is beyond description. Throughout eternity, as one thing after another reveals the love of the

I do set my bow in the cloud, and it shall be for a token of a covenant between me and the earth. Gen. 9 : 13.

Even he shall build the temple of the Lord; and he shall bear the glory, and shall sit and rule upon his throne; and he shall be a priest upon his throne: and the counsel of peace shall be between them both. Zech. 6 : 12, 13.

And God said, Let us make man in our image, after our likeness. Gen. 1 : 26.

Who verily was foreordained before the foundation of the world, but was manifest in these last times for you. 1 Pet. 1 : 19, 20.

2 Tim. 1 : 9, 10.
Eph. 1 : 4, 5.
Heb. 1 : 13, 14.
Rev. 5 : 7.
Isa. 14 : 12–14.

Col. 1 : 20.
Col. 1 : 14–17.
Heb. 13 : 20.

I am in the Father, and the Father in me: the words that I speak unto you I speak not of myself: but the Father that dwelleth in me, he doeth the works. John 14 : 10.

But made himself of no reputation, and took upon him the form of a servant, and was made in the likeness of men. Phil. 2 : 6–11.

Rom. 8 : 22, 23.

For the stone shall cry out of the wall, and the beam out of the timber shall answer it. Hab. 2 : 11.

Josh. 24 : 27.
Rev. 21 : 19–21.

Father, the redeemed, like the living creatures now about the throne, will sing, "Holy, holy, holy." Upon the face of our own world, is reflected this story; for nature is "the mirror of divinity;" but man is blind, and he misinterprets those things which point unmistakably to a God of love. The purpose of this revelation of Jesus Christ to the apostle John is to show men how near God is to the creatures of His hand; that Jehovah's voice may be heard explaining the plan of Redemption.

For the invisible things of him from the creation of the world are clearly seen, being understood by the things that are made, even his eternal power and Godhead; so that they are without excuse.
Rom. 1:20.

Deut. 30:11-13.

The bow shall be in the cloud; and I will look upon it, that I may remember the everlasting covenant between God and every living creature of all flesh that is upon the earth. Gen. 9:16.

As a token of the covenant between Father and Son, the bow was placed about the throne. "Justice and judgment are the habitation of thy throne: mercy and truth shall go before thy face," for "mercy and truth are met together; righteousness and peace have kissed each other." After the flood, the rainbow in the cloud was but a faint reflection of the constant reminder in heaven of the everlasting covenant made for the salvation of man before the foundation of the world.

**Upon the face of our own world is reflected this story.**

Psa. 89:14.
Psa. 85:10.

Sin hides God's love from us, shutting out from the soul the rays of light from the throne of mercy. As the cloud gives forth the rain, and the sun, shining through the drops, produces the rainbow, so "the tears of the penitent are only the rain drops that precede the sunshine of holiness." The Sun of Righteousness, shining upon the tears of the penitent, makes manifest the glory of God, of which "the bow that is in

Through the blood of the everlasting covenant,
Make you perfect in every good work to do his will.
Heb. 13:20, 21.

Your iniquities have separated between you and your God, and your sins have hid his face from you, that he will not hear.
Isa. 59:2.

Behold, for peace I had great bitterness: but thou hast in love to my soul delivered it from the pit of corruption: for thou hast cast all my sins behind thy back.
Isa. 38:17.

It shall come to pass, when I bring a cloud over the earth, that the bow shall be seen in the cloud:
And I will remember my covenant, which is between me and you and every living creature of all flesh. Gen. 9:14, 15.

*And round about the throne were four and twenty seats: and upon the seats I saw four and twenty elders sitting, clothed in white raiment; and they had on their heads crowns of gold.*
*Rev. 4:4.*

1 Chron 24:1-5, 19.
Luke 1:8.
Rev. 5:9.
2 Tim. 4:7, 8.
1 Cor. 9:24, 25.

Blessed is the man that endureth temptation: for when he is tried, he shall receive the crown of life, which the Lord hath promised to them that love him. Jas. 1:12.

Matt. 27:51-53

Wherefore he saith, When he ascended up on high, he led a multitude of captives, and gave gifts unto men.
Eph. 4:8 [margin.]

Psa. 68:18.

*And out of the throne proceeded lightnings and thunderings and voices: and there were seven lamps of fire burning before the throne, which are the seven Spirits of God.* *Rev. 4:5.*

And above the firmament that was over their heads was the likeness of a throne, as the appearance of a sapphire stone. Eze. 1:4-26.

Hath in these last days spoken unto us by his Son, whom he hath appointed heir of all things, by whom also he made the worlds.
Heb. 1:2.

the cloud in the day of rain" is a likeness. When God looks upon the bow, He remembers the everlasting covenant. In our own storm clouds, God and man look upon the same bow; to man it is a promise of forgiveness; to God a reminder of mercy.

Turning from the Father, who sat upon the throne, John saw four and twenty seats round about the throne. These seats were occupied by four and twenty elders, "clothed in white raiment; and they had on their heads crowns of gold." These also represent the atoning work of Christ. They represent men from every kindred, tongue, and people, redeemed by the blood of Christ, clothed with the white raiment of His righteousness, and wearing on their heads the crowns of victory, which are promised to every overcomer. They were of that company who arose from the grave when Christ came from the tomb, and who are spoken of by Paul as a "multitude of captives," offered to the Father as the first fruits from the dead. The work of these four and twenty elders is described in the fifth chapter, and for that reason, they are but mentioned in this connection as sitting near the throne.

The throne of God is a throne of life; not an inanimate throne of stones, but a living and moving throne. As John looked, he saw lightnings and heard thunderings and voices. He is viewing the center of creation,—the throne of God. It is the great body of life, the source of all law. By the power which centers there, worlds are held in space, and suns complete their circuits. The power which holds the universe in space, and binds atoms together, emanates from this throne of life. Angels are the ministers sent forth to do the will of Him who sits as King. Some are light-bearers to worlds, others are guardian angels for little children upon earth; but whatever the mission, whether great or small, as measured in humanity's scales, there is the same obedience to the mandates of Jehovah. Issuing from the presence of the Father, clothed in the reflection of His own light, those messengers disappear like flashes of lightning. The commands given, when spoken in an unknown tongue, sounded like the roar of the sea, or like deep and distant thunder. Other men have heard God speak when His voice sounded like thunder. This was so at Sinai, and also, when, near the close of His ministry, men gathered about Christ in the temple court. To the Son it was the voice of God; to men it was thunder. John heard other voices which he understood. He saw also the seven spirits of God, which, in the earthly tabernacle, were typified by the seven lamps upon the golden candlestick. These stood before the throne. This was the ever present, all-pervading Spirit of Jehovah, in which all life has its origin.

Upholding all things by the word of his power. Heb. 1:3.

He is before all things, and by him all things consist. Col. 1:17.

Bless ye the Lord, all ye his hosts; ye ministers of his, that do his pleasure. Psa. 103:21.

Father, glorify thy name. Then came there a voice from heaven, saying, I have both glorified it, and will glorify it again.

The people therefore, that stood by, and heard it, said that it thundered: others said, An angel spake to him. John 12:28, 29.

**Some are light-bearers to worlds, others are guardian angels for little children.**

The throne was high and lifted up, as Jeremiah saw it. Ezekiel describes the throne as above a firmament, having the appearance of "terrible crystal." And this crystal firmament, or expanse, rested above the heads of four living creatures, which were full of eyes. John was accustomed to the placid waters of the Mediter-

For with thee is the fountain of life: in thy light shall we see light. Psa. 36:9.

He giveth to all life, and breath, and all things. Acts 17:25.

A glorious high throne from the beginning is the place of our sanctuary. Jer. 17:12.

*And before the throne there was a sea of glass like unto crystal: and in the midst of the throne, and round about the throne, were four beasts full of eyes before and behind. Rev. 4:6.*

Eze. 1:26, 27.
Ex. 24:10.
Eze. 10:1.
Rev. 15:2.
Eze. 10:8–22.
Eze. 1:5–14.

*And the first beast was like a lion, and the second beast like a calf, and the third beast had a face as a man, and the fourth beast was like a flying eagle.*

*And the four beasts had each of them six wings about him; and they were full of eyes within: and they rest not day and night, saying, Holy, holy, holy, Lord God Almighty, which was, and is, and is to come.* *Rev. 4:7, 8.*

Luke 3:23–33.
Gen. 49:9, 10.
Isa. 9:6, 7.
Rev. 19:16.

On the east side toward the rising of the sun shall they of the standard of the camp of Judah pitch. Num. 2:3.

In the first place went the standard of the camp of the children of Judah according to their armies. Num. 10:14.

The book of the generation of Jesus Christ, the son of David, the son of Abraham. Matt. 1:1.

Behold, a virgin shall be with child, and shall bring forth a son, and they shall call his name Emmanuel, which being interpreted is, God with us. Matt. 1:23.

John 1:18.
Heb. 1:6.
Gen. 49:3.
1 Tim. 3:16.

When the fulness of the time was come, God sent forth his Son, made of a woman, made under the law. Gal. 4:4.

ranean, and the space about the throne is described by him as "a sea of glass like unto crystal." "And in the midst of the throne, and round about the throne, were four beasts [or living creatures] full of eyes before and behind."

These four living creatures represent four phases of the character of God. The first was like a lion, the second like a calf, or an ox, as Ezekiel says, the third had the face of a man, and the fourth was like a flying eagle. This again establishes the fact that when the plan of redemption was laid, all heaven was in unison with the plan. Ezekiel and John, one before Christ's advent, the other after, describe the same thing, showing that the New Testament is but the unfolding of the Old.

Christ in His life upon earth combined these four natures. He is the Lion of the tribe of Judah, of whom it was prophesied, "The sceptre shall not depart from Judah, nor a lawgiver from between his feet, until Shiloh come." As lawgiver and governor, Christ represented the kingly nature of the Father. When the tribes were given their places about the sanctuary, Judah was located on the east; and as they journeyed, the standard of Judah went before them. In the Gospels, Matthew begins with the genealogy, showing the right of Christ to the throne of David. There was, in the life of Emmanuel, a union of divinity with humanity. Christ was the firstborn in heaven; He was likewise the firstborn of God upon earth, and heir to the Father's throne. Christ, the firstborn, though the Son of God, was clothed in humanity, and was made perfect through suffering. He took the form of man, and through eternity, He will remain a a man. Every firstborn into human families is a type of the offering made by Christ. Mark, in his life of Christ, gives the servant side. The second face was that of the calf, or the ox, the servant of men. This represents the priesthood,—the Levites who were chosen for service. Christ is both the slain lamb, and the priest who ministers in the sanctuary on high. He bore the sins of the world in His own body on the cross, and the burden crushed Him to death. The most exalted position, and the most lowly position are here represented,—God in the heavens, and God on the cross. As Levites always accompanied the tabernacle, so Christ ministers constantly to man. Heaven will know no other story till man is redeemed from the earth. Every beast of burden beneath its load, every overworked child of God, is a reminder of the Christ who became the servant of men. Although He stepped into the lowliest place, yet He was still the giver of the law, and He is judge of all. The Gospel of Luke describes the man side of the Son, giving that part of His life work, which appeals most forcibly to the mind of man. As God took the form of man, there is, in the gift, a promise that man may have the nature of his God. The keen eye of the flying eagle is taken to represent the searching gaze of Him whose eyes, as a flame of fire, "run to and fro throughout the whole earth, strongly to hold with them whose heart is perfect toward Him." Among the different writers, it was John, the beloved disciple, who saw the character of Christ portrayed as the glorious Word, One equal with the Father in might, power, and glory, and his gospel completes the inspired record of the

The beginning of the gospel of Jesus Christ, the Son of God;
As it is written in the prophets, Behold, I send my messenger before thy face, which shall prepare thy way before thee. Mark 1 : 1, 2.

Who his own self bare our sins in his own body on the tree, that we, being dead to sins, should live unto righteousness : by whose stripes ye were healed. 1 Pet. 2 : 24.

But made himself of no reputation, and took upon him the form of a servant, and was made in the likeness of men. Phil. 2 : 7.

Heb. 2 : 10.
Ex. 13 : 2.
Num. 3 : 14-51.

Wherefore in all things it behoved him to be made like unto his brethren, that he might be a merciful and faithful high priest in things pertaining to God, to make reconciliation for the sins of the people.
For in that he himself hath suffered being tempted, he is able to succour them that are tempted. Heb. 2 : 17, 18.

There is one lawgiver, who is able to save and to destroy. Jas. 4 : 12.

Forasmuch as many have taken in hand to set forth in order a declaration of those things which are most surely believed among us,
Even as they delivered them unto us, which from the beginning were eyewitnesses, and ministers of the word;
It seemed good to me also, having had perfect understanding of all things from the very first, to write unto thee in order, most excellent Theophilus. Luke 1 : 1-3.

In the beginning was the Word, and the Word was with God, and the Word was God.
The same was in the beginning with God. John 1 : 1, 2.

*And when those beasts give glory and honour and thanks to him that sat on the throne, who liveth for ever and ever. Rev. 4 : 9.*

***The four and twenty elders fall down before him that sat on the throne, and worship him that liveth for ever and ever, and cast their crowns before the throne, saying,***

***Thou art worthy, O Lord, to receive glory and honour and power: for thou hast created all things, and for thy pleasure they are and were created. Rev. 4:10, 11.***

I heard the voice of harpers harping with their harps:

And they sung as it were a new song before the throne, and before the four beasts, and the elders: and no man could learn that song but the hundred and forty and four thousand, which were redeemed from the earth. Rev. 14:2, 3.

Saviour's life. He portrayed the divine character more fully than any other writer. This is represented by the eagle flying heavenward.

In the heavenly court, there is such an overpowering sense of the infinite work of God that the four living creatures cry constantly, "Holy, holy, holy, Lord God Almighty, which was, and is, and is to come." And in the song of heaven, those redeemed from among men, take up the response; and casting their crowns before the throne, they sing, "Thou art worthy, O Lord, to receive glory and honor and power: for Thou hast created all things, and for Thy pleasure they are and were created."

# CHAPTER VI.

## WHO IS WORTHY TO OPEN THE BOOK?

JOHN had been taken in the Spirit into the presence of God. In the fourth chapter he describes the appearance of the throne; this is followed by a view of the work of Christ and others connected with the plan of salvation. The fifth chapter is only a continuation of the subject introduced in the fourth;—it is an introduction to the history given in the sixth chapter.

Rev. 4:1-3.

All things are of God, who hath reconciled us to himself by Jesus Christ, and hath given to us the ministry of reconciliation.
2 Cor. 5:18.

Finite man may think himself separated from his Creator; but "there is not a word in my tongue, but, lo, O Lord, Thou knowest it altogether." "Whither shall I go from Thy Spirit? or whither shall I flee from Thy presence?" John was made to understand this truth in a most solemnly impressive way. He says, "I saw in the right hand of Him that sat on the throne a book written within and on the back side, sealed with seven seals." The right hand of the Father holds the record of our lives, and unless one can approach within the inner circle of the majesty

Psa. 139:1-12.

Seeing his days are determined, the number of his months are with thee, thou hast appointed his bounds that he cannot pass. Job 14:5.

*And I saw in the right hand of him that sat on the throne a book written within and on the backside, sealed with seven seals.*
*Rev. 5:1.*

The secret of the Lord is with them that fear him; and he will shew them his covenant.
Psa. 25:14.

Then hear thou in heaven thy dwelling place, and forgive, and do, and give to every man according to his ways, whose heart thou knowest; (for thou, even thou only, knowest the hearts of all the children of men.) 1 Kings 8:39

Eph. 3:16.

This is a great mystery: but I speak concerning Christ and the church. Eph. 5:32.

*And I saw a strong angel proclaiming with a loud voice, Who is worthy to open the book, and to loose the seals thereof? Rev. 5:2.*

*And no man in heaven, nor in earth, neither under the earth, was able to open the book, neither to look thereon.*

*And I wept much, because no man was found worthy to open and to read the book, neither to look thereon. Rev. 5:3, 4.*

Rev. 19:14.
Gen. 32:1, 2.
Psa. 103:19–22.

*And one of the elders saith unto me, Weep not: behold, the Lion of the tribe of Juda, the Root of David, hath prevailed to open the book, and to loose the seven seals thereof. Rev. 5:5.*

of the Eternal One, he cannot look within this book. It is written both within and without. Within, is the life which is known only to God, —the secret, known only to the soul and its Creator. Without, is the reflection of that inner life, the outward part which is open to the gaze of others. As the condition of the individual, so is the condition of the church of God. The one created in the image of Jehovah, has received of His Spirit, and the soul history can be understood only by Him of whom it is a part. This connection between God and man, is the mystery of the Gospel.

As the host of heaven gazed upon the One on the throne, a strong angel proclaimed with a loud voice, "Who is worthy to open the book, and to loose the seals thereof?" Heaven's arches rang as the challenge was given. It was not a reproof, but a call to all the universe of God, to witness anew the glory of the Son of man. This was a fresh unfolding of the plan of salvation. John, a representative of the fallen race, was near, and he wept when "no man in heaven, nor in earth, neither under the earth, was able to open the book, neither to look thereon." Must the work of earth cease? Was the sacrifice a failure? Would history cease even after Christ had died? Hosts of angels, marshaled under their leaders, bowed before the throne. They had known of the mighty power of Jehovah, they had watched the work of creation, and had ministered in the utmost bounds of space; but they were silent when the herald's voice was heard.

Though angels held their peace, one of the elders broke the silence. He who had once lived on earth, who was born in sin, who had fought and conquered in the name of Christ, and who had risen with Him a victor over that last and greatest enemy—death—spoke to his fellow man. He knew the full meaning of life on earth; he knew the terrors of the grave, and he could also speak from experience of the righteousness of Christ, for he was clothed in the white garment, and on his head was the golden crown of victory. He approached John, saying, "Weep not: behold, the Lion of the tribe of Juda, the Root of David, hath prevailed to open the book." The elder, who had seen the mighty power of Christ so often manifested, took the strongest objects in the vegetable and animal kingdoms to represent His power,—the root and the lion. Massive rocks are torn asunder by the noiseless power of the root. Hidden beneath the soil its power is mighty. So the power of the Root of David, hidden in the heart, can break the strongest bands of sin. The Saviour speaks of those who had no root in themselves as not being able to endure tribulation. The Root of David bears the tree of righteousness. None can be trees of righteousness who have not this pure and holy Root hidden in the soil of the heart. The elder used language familiar to the prophet, for John was a Jew, and from infancy, had listened to the prophecy of Christ read from the book of the law. He was promised as the "Lion of the tribe of Juda," the King for whom the nation looked as temporal ruler. The sure mercies of David were repeated in the synagogue services as the prophecies of Jeremiah were read. "Behold . . . I will raise unto David a righteous Branch, . . . and this is

Matt. 27:52–53.
1 Cor. 15:26.

When the chief Shepherd shall appear, ye shall receive a crown of glory that fadeth not away.
1 Pet, 5:4.

I Jesus have sent mine angel to testify unto you these things in the churches. I am the root and the offspring of David, and the bright and morning star. Rev. 22:16.

What is stronger than a lion?
Judges 14:18.

That he would grant you, according to the riches of his glory, to be strengthened with might by his Spirit in the inner man;
That Christ may dwell in your hearts by faith; that ye, being rooted and grounded in love.
Eph. 3:16, 17.

Matt. 13:6, 21.

The root of the righteous shall not be moved. Prov. 12:3.

The root of the righteous yieldeth fruit. Prov. 12:12.

Gal. 5:22, 23.

That they might be called trees of righteousness, the planting of the Lord, that he might be glorified
Isa. 61:3.

For Moses of old time hath in every city them that preach him, being read in the synagogues every sabbath day. Acts 15:21.

Jer. 23:5, 6.
Zech. 3:8.
Isa. 11:10.

His name whereby He shall be called, The Lord Our Righteousness." "I will bring forth My servant the Branch," the Lord had said through the prophet Zechariah. "In that day there shall be a Root of Jesse, which shall stand for an ensign of the people." Christ, in the presence of John, had used these same symbols to designate His own work in the earth. As a lion of the forest, He was born to rule, and the power of the Spirit within drew all men unto Him. Like the tree, which, springing from a seed hidden in the cemented vault-burst asunder the tomb of the dead, so the Root of David prevailed to loosen the seals and to open the book. It was not the simple reading of the book that was called for. The angel's call was for one whose life could accomplish what was written therein. There, was written the work of God in the earth. This is seen when the seals are broken, as given in the following chapter.

And the remnant of Jacob shall be among the Gentiles in the midst of many people as a lion among the beasts of the forest, as a young lion among the flocks of sheep: who, if he go through, both treadeth down, and teareth in pieces, and none can deliver. Mic. 5:8.

I am he that liveth, and was dead; and, behold, I am alive for evermore, Amen; and have the keys of hell and of death. Rev. 1:18.

**The tree burst asunder the tomb.**

As the Father knoweth me, even so know I the Father: and I lay down my life for the sheep. John 10:15.

As John watched, "lo, in the midst of the throne and of the four beasts, and in the midst of the elders, stood a Lamb as it had been slain." In the center of all the glory, in the very presence of Life, before adoring angels and witnesses from earth, stood a Lamb, slain, its life-blood dripping from its veins.

*And I beheld, and, lo, in the midst of the throne and of the four beasts, and in the midst of the elders, stood a Lamb as it had been slain, having seven horns and seven eyes, which are the seven Spirits of God sent forth into all the earth. Rev. 5:6.*

There was a time when sin did not exist;

when the harmony of perfection reigned supreme. Man broke the chord. Life began to ebb. All nature mourned. Slowly, one by one, the stately trees shed their leaves; the flowers faded. Each blossom as it fell, sounded a death knell throughout the universe of God. But Christ had already covenanted with the Father. His life was offered for this very time. And man,—penitent, sorrowful man,—brought a lamb from the flock, slew it; and its life-blood became a token of the life of Christ. Every creature, from the highest form of creation, down to the insect mote in the sunbeam, lives in the life of God; and when death occurs, a vibration is felt in the heart of the Eternal. In every lamb, slain in all the sacrificial offerings, God saw the blood of His own Son. The heart of the Father was broken when the first lamb was slain; and every time the knife was stained with the blood of an offering, it brought afresh to the mind of God the death of His Son. Christ died of a broken heart. Heaven knows the meaning of a broken heart,—of a life spent,—of hopes blasted. "A broken and a contrite heart, O God, thou wilt not despise."

So when John watched for one to open the the book, there appeared, as it were a Lamb slain. That all power was given to the Lamb, that all heaven was poured out in this sacrifice, is shown by its seven horns and its seven eyes. "He came and took the book out of the right hand of Him that sat upon the throne"; for not even Christ could do the work alone. The power came from the Father. Father and Son unite in the work of Redemption. "And when He had taken the book, the four beasts (living

Gen. 1:31.
Gen. 3:1–7.
1 Tim. 2:14.

Cursed is the ground for thy sake; in sorrow shalt thou eat of it all the days of thy life;
Thorns also and thistles shall it bring forth to thee. Gen. 3:17, 18.

Rev. 13:8.
Gen. 4:4.

In whose hand is the soul of every living thing, and the breath of all mankind. Job 12:10.

For God sent not his Son into the world to condemn the world; but that the world through him might be saved. John 3:17.

Hope deferred maketh the heart sick: but when the desire cometh, it is a tree of life. Prov. 13:12.

Psa. 51:17.

Being fully persuaded that, what he had promised, he was able also to perform. Rom. 4:21.

*And he came and took the book out of the right hand of him that sat upon the throne. Rev. 5:7.*

Matt. 28:18.

*And when he had taken the book, the four beasts and four and twenty elders fell down before the Lamb, having every one of them harps, and golden vials full of odours, which are the prayers of saints. Rev. 5:8.*

Rev. 8:3–8.

Wherefore he is able also to save them to the uttermost that come unto God by him, seeing he ever liveth to make intercession for them. Heb. 7:25.

The whole multitude of the people were praying without at the time of incense. Luke 1:10.

He shall burn incense upon it, a perpetual incense before the Lord throughout your generations. Ex. 30:8.

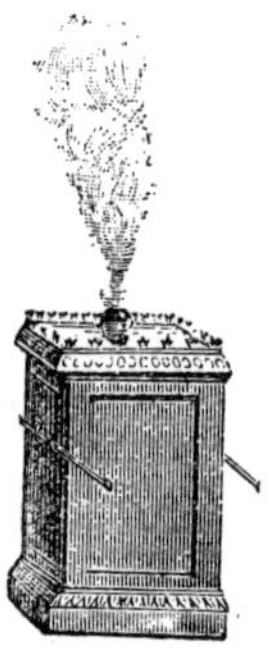

**In the tabernacle service on earth, the altar of incense burned continually.**

Lev. 16:2.

And he shall take a censer full of burning coals of fire from off the altar before the Lord, and his hands full of sweet incense beaten small, and bring it within the vail:

And he shall put the incense upon the fire before the Lord, that the cloud of the incense may cover the mercy seat that is upon the testimony, that he die not. Lev. 16:12, 13.

Rev. 8:3, 4.
Rev. 5:8.

Let my prayer be set forth before thee as incense; and the lifting up of my hands as the evening sacrifice. Psa. 141:2.

Evening, and morning, and at noon, will I pray, and cry aloud: and he shall hear my voice. Psa. 55:17.

creatures) and four and twenty elders fell down before the Lamb, having every one of them harps, and golden vials full of odors (incense), which are the prayers of saints." Here is given the work of the elders and the living creatures. As the Lamb ministers constantly before the throne of God, these who have been redeemed to God "out of every kindred, and tongue, and people, and nation," bow before the throne, offering to Him who sits thereon the prayers which ascend from the earth. With the prayers, is a cloud of incense. "This holy incense is the merits and intercession of Christ, His perfect righteousness, which, through faith, is imputed to His people, and which alone can make the worship of sinful beings acceptable to God."

In the tabernacle service on earth, the altar of incense burned continually before the ark of the covenant, where shone the visible presence of God. When the high priest entered on the day of atonement into the Holy of Holies, he made his offering for the people with much incense, a cloud ascended from the censer as long as he remained in Divine Presence. To-day in heaven those who once lived on earth, representatives from every kindred, nation, and people, having passed through every phase of earthly experience, take the prayers offered by penitent sinners, and present them before the Lamb. Repentance is a sweet odor before our God; for it tells of sorrow for sin, and the acceptance of the life of Christ. Since the death of Christ, the lamb is no longer slain; but the morning and evening prayers, when the blood of Christ is presented by faith, touch the heart of God, and from His throne angels speed their way on rapid wings to fulfill the petition. If to prayer there does not seem to come an immediate answer, there is still the assurance that no earnest petition escapes the notice of our Father. They are represented as preserved in vials, in "bottles," as David says; and when the family of the redeemed is at last gathered on that crystal sea with the Lamb and the four and twenty elders, it will be found that every prayer of faith is answered. The lowliest believer, the most burdened sinner, who turns his face heaven ward, can see the rainbow of promise above the throne. For him the Lamb was slain, and in his behalf, some one in that company of elders, who surround the throne, can plead, "I have passed over this same road and I have been rescued by the Saviour." Look up, and take heart; for all heaven is working for the redemption of man!

In anticipation of the final cleansing of the universe from sin, and the restoration of man to his place beside the Father, there is sung in heaven the song of the redeemed. The four beasts and the four and twenty elders sing a new song,—a song of Redemption; for they have been raised from the depths of sin to the position of kings and priests unto God. Those now in heaven, look forward to their reign with Christ on the earth made new. When the plan is completed, the few who now minister in heaven, together with the multitudes who come forth at the first resurrection, will reign as kings and priests on the earth. "Thine is the kingdom, Thine is the power, and Thine the glory," will be the grand chorus when Christ as King of kings receives His everlasting dominion, and the redeemed reign with Him. To the earth

Gabriel, whom I had seen in the vision at the beginning, being caused to fly swiftly, touched me about the time of the evening oblation. Dan. 9:21.

Jer. 10:25.

Rev. 5:8.

But thou, when thou prayest, enter into thy closet, and when thou hast shut thy door, pray to thy Father which is in secret; and thy Father which seeth in secret shall reward thee openly. Matt. 6:6.

The Lord is nigh unto them that are of a broken heart; and saveth such as be of a contrite spirit.

Many are the afflictions of the righteous: but the Lord delivereth him out of them all. Psa. 34:18, 19.

Dan. 8:14.

*And they sung a new song, saying, Thou art worthy to take the book, and to open the seals thereof: for thou wast slain, and hast redeemed us to God by thy blood out of every kindred, and tongue, and people, and nation;*

*And hast made us unto our God kings and priests: and we shall reign on the earth*

*And I beheld, and I heard the voice of many angels round about the throne and the beasts and the elders: and the number of them was ten thousand times ten thousand, and thousands of thousands. Rev. 5:9-11.*

Rev. 11:15.
Isa. 35:1–10.

renewed, and reflecting again the glory of God as when it first came forth from the hand of its Creator; with the discord all gone, and the music of the spheres rolling in ceaseless pæans through endless space; is the scene which heaven looks forward to in anticipation.

He will make her wilderness like Eden, and her desert like the garden of the Lord; joy and gladness shall be found therein, thanksgiving, and the voice of melody.
Isa. 51:3.

The redeemed sang, "Thou art worthy," and from ten thousand times ten thousand of angel voices there rang the response: "Worthy is the Lamb that was slain to receive power, and riches, and wisdom, and strength, and honor, and glory, and blessing."

*Saying with a loud voice, Worthy is the Lamb that was slain to receive power, and riches, and wisdom, and strength, and honour, and glory, and blessing.*
*Rev. 5:12.*

And then in the chorus of voices, angels, elders, and every creature from earth and sea and sky, joined in singing, "Blessing, and honor, and glory, and power, be unto Him that sitteth upon the throne, and unto the Lamb for ever and ever." And the four beasts answered, "Amen. And the four and twenty elders fell down, and worshiped Him that liveth for ever and ever." If man but caught a glimpse of the joy of salvation, his lips would repeat the songs of heaven. Angelic beings are looking forward to the completion of the plan. So may we.

*And every creature which is in heaven, and on the earth, and under the earth, and such as are in the sea, and all that are in them, heard I saying, Blessing, and honour, and glory, and power, be unto him that sitteth upon the throne, and unto the Lamb for ever and ever.*
*And the four beasts said, Amen. And the four and twenty elders fell down and worshipped him that liveth for ever and ever.*
*Rev. 5:13, 14.*

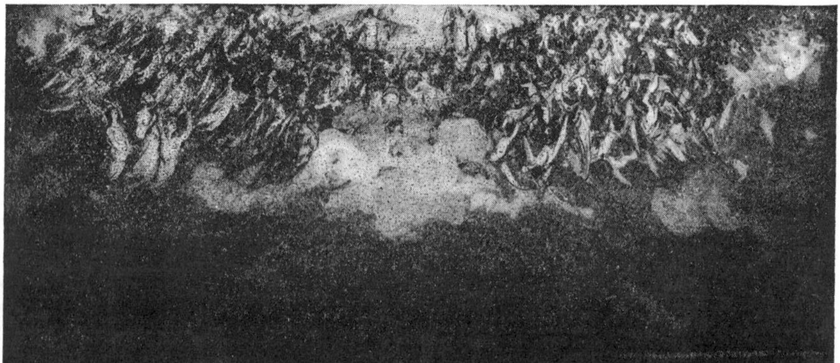

# CHAPTER VII.

## HISTORY IN THE SEALS.

THE book of Revelation is introduced as a "revelation of Jesus Christ"; the first five chapters verify the truthfulness of the name. The sixth chapter opened to John a new phase of the divine character as revealed in the life of the Son, and in His attitude toward the people upon whom His love is bestowed.

The secret history of those on earth, between whom and the Father no being can intervene, is held in the right hand of that Father, and the Lamb alone is able to fulfill what is written within the scroll. The seals, opened, reveal the life of the church, the child of God; and beginning at the birth of Christianity, the seals extend to the end of time. Others may know somewhat of the life; but only the Father knows the environments, the place of birth, the inherited tendencies of His child, He alone is able to appreciate the character, and to form righteous judgment concerning it.

When the first seal was broken by the Lamb, one of the four living creatures, whose voice was

The Revelation of Jesus Christ, which God gave unto him, to shew unto his servants things which must shortly come to pass; and he sent and signified it by his angel unto his servant John. Rev. 1:1.

John 15:13.
Eph. 5:23-25.
Rev. 2:17.

For there is one God, and one mediator between God and men, the man Christ Jesus.
1 Tim. 2:5.

Of Zion it shall be said, This and that man was born in her: and the highest himself shall establish her.
The Lord shall count, when he writeth up the people, that this man was born there. Psa. 87:5, 6.

John 16:27.

*And I saw when the Lamb opened one of the seals, and I heard, as it were the noise of thunder, one of the four beasts saying, Come and see.*
*And I saw, and behold a white horse: and he that sat on him had a bow; and a crown was given unto him: and he went forth conquering, and to conquer.*
*Rev. 6:1, 2.*

Rev. 12:11.
Zech. 6:5.

The eyes of the Lord run to and fro throughout the whole earth, to shew himself strong in the behalf of them whose heart is perfect toward him. 2 Chron. 16:9.

like thunder, bade John behold. Those living creatures, as they surround the throne, reflect the character of God, they are interested in those upon earth, whose lives also reflect the Divine Image. "And I saw, and behold a white horse: and he that sat on him had a bow; and a crown was given unto him: and he went forth conquering, and to conquer." Zechariah was told that horses symbolized the "spirits of the heavens, which go forth from standing before the Lord of all the earth." God's Spirit is seeking for those who will give it full control in their lives, and the Apostolic Church was blessed with a double portion of the Spirit. The horse upon which it rode was white, representing the simple faith and trust of those who accepted the baptism of the Spirit in its purity. All the gifts of the Spirit were manifested in the church of the first century. The followers of Christ separated themselves from the midst of the world, from friends and relatives and all that earth counts dear, and God pronounces His richest blessing "On the crown of the head

**He went forth conquering, and to conquer.**

Moreover I have given to thee one portion above thy brethren. Gen. 48:22.

1 Cor. 1:1-7.

Acts 2:1-17.

Luke 9:23.

Gen. 49:26.

of him that was separate from his brethren."

A crown denotes victory. A crown was given to him that sat on the horse, and he went forth "conquering, and to conquer." During the first century, it mattered not whether there was an appearance of defeat, or whether triumph was seen in the healing of the sick, and the delivering of the tried and tempted. The name of Jesus Christ of Nazareth was health to the afflicted and life to the dead. Victory was written upon every move of the disciples. In prison, with their backs lacerated, their songs of praise and thanksgiving brought victory and resulted in the conversion of souls. Peter was sentenced to death, shut up in the inner prison; but that last night in prison was a victory; for the angel of the Lord brought deliverance. Truly wonderful was the story of the Gospel during the first century, as it went forth "conquering, and to conquer."

Like the tree planted by the fountain, whose branches grow beyond all bounds, so the church of the first century spread throughout the world. Its very loneliness and spirit of sacrifice was its most attractive feature to those hitherto unacquainted with the power of the Gospel. It was indeed planted by the Fountain of Life, and so long as it remained in connection with that living water, no amount of opposition could retard its growth.

The unparalleled rapidity attending the propagation of the gospel of the Cross, is witnessed to by writers of that age. To the Roman church Paul wrote: "I thank my God . . . that your faith is spoken of throughout the whole world;" and again, "Your obedience is come abroad unto all men."

2 Tim. 4:7, 8.
Rev. 2:10.

Acts 5:40, 42.

In the name of Jesus Christ of Nazareth rise up and walk.

And he took him by the right hand, and lifted him up: and immediately his feet and ankle bones received strength. Acts 3:6, 7.

Acts 9:36–41.
Acts 16:19–39.

Behold, the angel of the Lord came upon him, and a light shined in the prison: and he smote Peter on the side, and raised him up, saying, Arise up quickly. And his chains fell off from his hands. Acts 12:7.

Rom. 1:8.

Joseph is a fruitful bough, even a fruitful bough by a well; whose branches run over the wall. Gen. 49:22.

Jer. 17:7, 8.

He shall be like a tree planted by the rivers of water, that bringeth forth his fruit in his season; his leaf also shall not wither; and whatsoever he doeth shall prosper. Psa. 1:3.

Rom. 1:8.
Rom. 16:19.

When the apostle had been preaching but little more than thirty years, he said to the Colossians that the Gospel had been "preached to every creature which is under heaven." What stronger expression could be used than "it went forth conquering, and to conquer." But it was "not by army, nor by power, but by My Spirit, saith the Lord of Hosts." This was the soul experience of those children of the living God when they felt the warmth of "their first love."

Rom. 1:5.
Col. 1:23.
Rev. 6:2.

Not by army, nor by power, but by my spirit, saith the Lord of hosts. Zech. 4:6 [margin.]

The Gospel of Christ brings peace on earth, but when men fail to receive the truth, it brings sword and bloodshed. The second beast said, "Come and see." "And there went out another horse that was red, and power was given to him that sat thereon to take peace from the earth, and that they should kill one another." Peace was taken from the earth; blood was shed upon the right hand and upon the left, and the saints were led as a lamb to the slaughter. Nothing could more vividly describe this period than the "horse that was red: and power was given to him that sat thereon to take peace from the earth." This carries us through the period known as the triumph of paganism, corresponding to the Smyrna church. In the eyes of the world, the experience of God's people through this age, was one of great defeat, but in the eyes of Him, who has power to give victory in the smallest things of earth, and to bring to naught things that are, by things that are not, this experience was a triumph. The very witness borne by the sacrifice of the lives of the saints became seed that sprang up and bore fruit. God's infinite power is made manifest in every sacrifice made by men upon earth. In their

These things I have spoken unto you, that in me ye might have peace. In the world ye shall have tribulation. John 16:33.

*And when he had opened the second seal, I heard the second beast say, Come and see.*

*And there went out another horse that was red: and power was given to him that sat thereon to take peace from the earth, and that they should kili one another: and there was given unto him a great sword. Rev. 6:3, 4.*

Rev. 2:8-11.
Rom. 4:17.

Heb. 11:4.

**Power was given to him that sat thereon to take peace from the earth.**

Fear none of those things which thou shalt suffer: behold, the devil shall cast some of you into prison, that ye may be tried; and ye shall have tribulation ten days; be thou faithful unto death, and I will give thee a crown of life.

He that hath an ear, let him hear what the Spirit saith unto the churches; he that overcometh shall not be hurt of the second death.

Rev. 2:10, 11.

These things I have spoken unto you, that in me ye might have peace. In the world ye shall have tribulation: but be of good cheer; I have overcome the world.

John 16:33.

utter helplessness lay their strength. It was then that the power of Christ rested upon them. Even the smallest act, performed in behalf of Christ, multiplies not only a hundredfold in this life, but its influence, like a stone thrown into a smooth surface of water, extends until it reaches the ocean of eternity.

Therefore I take pleasure in infirmities, in reproaches, in necessities, in persecutions, in distresses for Christ's sake: for when I am weak, then am I strong.

2 Cor. 12:10.

Matt. 10:42.
Mark 10:29, 30.
Matt. 26:6-13.

Seeing they crucify to themselves the Son of God afresh, and put him to an open shame. Heb. 6:6.

He said to me, These are they which came out of great tribulation, and have washed their robes, and made them white in the blood of the Lamb. Rev. 7:14.

The man that wandereth out of the way of understanding shall remain in the congregation of the dead. Prov. 21:16.

*And when he had opened the third seal, I heard the third beast say, Come and see. And I beheld, and lo a black horse; and he that sat on him had a pair of balances in his hand Rev. 6:5.*

Therefore thou art inexcusable, O man, whosoever thou art that judgest: for wherein thou judgest another, thou condemnest thyself; for thou that judgest doest the same things. Rom. 2:1.

Ex. 32:30–35.
Rom. 9:1–3.
Ex. 32:31, 32.
Jas. 4:12.

Speak not evil one of another, brethren. He that speaketh evil of his brother, and judgeth his brother, speaketh evil of the law, and judgeth the law: but if thou judge the law, thou art not a doer of the law, but a judge. Jas. 4:11.

2 Thess. 2:4.
Isa. 14:13, 14.

To live a spiritual life requires a ceaseless climbing, higher and still higher; but humanity is prone to take an easier part. Sad as it may seem, we find the church, which for years sacrificed its life for the sake of the Gospel, beginning to compromise the truth of God. The church turned its eyes from Christ, and was allured by the world into strange paths. What Satan could not do by persecution, he accomplished by flattery. When the third seal was opened, the third beast was heard to say, "Come and see." "And I beheld, and lo a black horse; and he that sat on him had a pair of balances." It is strange that, when men lose the Spirit of God, they at once become self-appointed judges of other men. The Spirit of Christ is, "in honor preferring one another." The life of the Saviour exemplifies this; the lives of those who have followed closely in His footsteps show that the same spirit has dwelt in men. The prayer of Moses was that God would blot out his name from the book of life, but save Israel. "Oh, this people have sinned a great sin. . . . Yet now, if Thou wilt forgive their sin;—and if not, blot me, I pray Thee, out of Thy book which Thou hast written." "There is one Lawgiver, who is able to save and to destroy: who art thou that judgest another?" When, however, men cease to obey the law of God, they at once exalt self above the Lawgiver, and seated on the throne of justice, they attempt to weigh men's deeds. This is the "mystery of iniquity," which "opposeth and exalteth himself above all that is called God, or that is worshiped; so that he as God sitteth in the temple of God, showing himself that he is God." It is the spirit of him who

**He that sat on him had a pair of balances in his hand.**

said, "I will ascend into heaven, I will exalt my throne above the stars of God . . . I will ascend above the heights of the clouds; I will be like the Most High."

But the balances held by man are false balances; and while man is passing judgment, God, from the throne, is watching those who are being weighed, and in His infinite kindness, limits the power of the self-made judge. This judge may say "a measure of wheat for a penny, and three measures of barley for a penny;" he may, it is true, judge somewhat from outward appearances, he may weigh out the physical actions, but the Divine command is, "See thou hurt not the oil and the wine." The oil of His grace, and the wine, the emblem of the inner spiritual life, must not, and cannot be touched.

The church during the fourth and fifth centuries, began dictating to men what they should believe, and how they should worship. This was the period when Christianity was replaced by the papacy, and man was exalted as vicegerent of God on earth.

TEKEL; Thou art weighed in the balances, and art found wanting. Dan. 5:27.

*And I heard a voice in the midst of the four beasts say, A measure of wheat for a penny, and three measures of barley for a penny; and see thou hurt not the oil and the wine. Rev. 6:6.*

*And when he had opened the fourth seal, I heard the voice of the fourth beast say, Come and see. Rev. 6.7.*

**His name that sat on him was Death, and Hell followed with him.**

The fourth beast bade John come, and see the opening of the fourth seal, which was the culmination of the scenes begun under the third seal. "I looked, and behold a pale horse: and his name that sat on him was Death, and Hell followed with him." The pale horse was an indication of still greater departure from the spirit of truth than the black one. Thousands have been put to death by the sword, by starvation, and by wild beasts; and what is worse than killing the body, many more have suffered spiritual death because of the hiding of the Word of Life. Whenever the church is clothed with civil power, it weighs out to mankind Christian experience. If that experience is not according to the prescribed religion, the thumbscrew and other instruments of torture are brought forth to extort confessions from the penitent. But God, even in the midst of the severest persecution, watches over every afflicted soul.

*And I looked, and behold a pale horse: and his name that sat on him was Death, and Hell followed with him. And power was given unto them over the fourth part of the earth, to kill with sword, and with hunger and with death, and with the beasts of the earth.*
*Rev. 6:8.*

Jer. 2:22.
Hos. 13:12.
Gen. 4:4-8.

It might seem that God would have prevented

such seeming cruelty durıng the Dark Ages; but the view given to John, shows that Christ suffered in the person of His saints. At the time of the crucifixion angels were restrained from rescuing the Saviour from His agony. It was suffered to be so for the time, that the greater glory might be seen thereafter. So in the martyrdom of the Middle Ages, and in any form of persecution, Christ identifies Himself with the sufferer, and all heaven stands ready to succor him.

John 18:36, 37.
Luke 12:4-7.

The King shall answer and say unto them, Verily I say unto you, Inasmuch as ye have done it unto one of the least of these my brethren, ye have done it unto me.
Matt. 25:40.

"When He had opened the fifth seal," John "saw under the altar the souls of them that were slain for the Word of God and for the testimony which they held." God does not forget those who have suffered for His name, but their names are written in the Book of Life. The lamb in the tabernacle service was slain on the earth; Christ left the courts of heaven, and the earth became the altar where His blood was shed; the rock-hewn sepulchre became the grave in which His dead body was laid; so the earth has drunk the blood of martyrs, and their bodies lie buried in its bosom. Representatives of all classes of men, from the lowly tradesman to the men of brilliant intellect, fell before the power of him who sat on the pale horse. Such men as Huss and Jerome, Ridley, Cranmer, and Latimer, suffered for the Word of God. But there were others, such as Galileo, who were persecuted because they advocated principles, which, when weighed in the balances of him who sat enthroned, were deemed to be dangerous to the government.

Isa. 41:10-12.

*And when he had opened the fifth seal, I saw under the altar the souls of them that were slain for the word of God, and for the testimony which they held:*

*And they cried with a loud voice, saying, How long, O Lord, holy and true, dost thou not judge and avenge our blood on them that dwell on the earth?*
*Rev. 6:9, 10.*

Luke 22:44.
Num. 35:33, 34.
Josh. 24:26, 27.

Others had trial of cruel mockings and scourgings, yea, moreover of bonds and imprisonment:

They were stoned, they were sawn asunder, were tempted, were slain with the sword: they wandered about in sheepskins and goatskins; being destitute, afflicted, tormented;

(Of whom the world was not worthy.) Heb. 11:36-38.

The blood of Abel cried unto God, so the earth bears witness before Jehovah of every life

Gen. 4:10.
Psa. 50:4.
Rom. 8:23, 24.

**" How long, O Lord, holy and true, dost thou not judge and avenge our blood ? "**

which has been taken in His name. This witness is true, one that can never be suborned; and it matters not what may be the verdict of him who holds the balance. God knows, and gives righteous judgment. When the history of nations was revealed to Daniel, the angels of heaven cried, "How long, O Lord, how long till the end of these things?" The whole creation suffers because of the curse which sin has brought; and in addition to these voices, which plead for the end of all things, the blood of the martyrs is heard by the sensitive ear of Jehovah.

The eyes of the Lord are upon the righteous, and his ears are open unto their cry. Psa. 34:15.

*And white robes were given unto every one of them; and it was said unto them, that they should rest yet for a little season, until their fellowservants also and their brethren, that should be killed as they were, should be fulfilled. Rev. 6:11.*

Heb. 11:35-38.

When asked why there is such long-suffering on the part of God, John saw the white robes of Christ's righteousness, prepared for every one who has given up life for the sake of the truth. They have been despised, rejected, and killed by men; but on the record books of heaven, every sin is covered by the character of their Lord. They were the company who were "destitute, afflicted, tormented: of whom the world was not worthy;" but heaven has a home for them, and in the restoration of all things, they will be given a place near the throne. Their numbers will be increased by those who are called to suffer a similar death in the period of time preceding the second coming of Christ. What was done under the cover of darkness in the Middle Ages, will be repeated when the sun is at its zenith. All who are slain for conscience' sake, sleep together in their graves until called forth by the trumpet tones of Him, who is the resurrection and the life. Then will white robes be given them, together with palms of victory. To-day they are seen clothed in white robes; for the world, forgetting the crimes of which they were basely accused, assigns them a martyr's crown.

If we suffer, we shall also reign with him: if we deny him, he also will deny us. 2 Tim. 2:12.

This is the condemnation, that light is come into the world, and men loved darkness rather than light, because their deeds were evil. John 3:16-19.

Job 14:12-15.

This inner life history, as revealed by the opening of the seals, was not for the benefit of those who lived during the period in ecclesiastical history, when it was especially applicable; for at those times the prophecies were not understood; but it is for those who live in the time of the end, especially under the sixth seal, that the wondrous love of Him who ruleth in the heavens, may be read in the events which occur.

Understand, O son of man: for at the time of the end shall be the vision. Dan. 8:17.

The words are closed up and sealed till the time of the end.

Many shall be purified, and made white, and tried; but the wicked shall do wickedly: and none of the wicked shall understand; but the wise shall understand. Dan. 12:9, 10.

The sixth seal covers history until the end of time; therefore the generation now living will witness at least some events shown to the prophet when this seal was opened. It differs from the first four seals, by showing events which mark prophetic time, rather than by showing the condition of the church. Those who recognize the signs therein given, as omens of the second coming of the Son of man, will welcome Him under the seventh seal. Those who

Song Sol. 4:7.
Mark 13:28-31.

Luke 21:29-31.
Eccl. 3:1.
Eph. 5:26, 27.
Col. 1:28, 29.

The great day of the Lord is near, it is near, and hasteth greatly, even the voice of the day of the Lord: the mighty man shall cry there bitterly. Zeph. 1:14.

Amos 1:1.
Zech. 14:5.
Ex. 10:21–23.

do not thus read the language of God, as given in signs and wonders, will have the experience recorded in Rev. 6:15–17.

There shall be signs in the sun, and in the moon, and in the stars; and upon the earth distress of nations, with perplexity; the sea and the waves roaring. Luke 21:25.

At the beginning of the sixth seal, a mighty earthquake shook the earth. This doubtless refers to the earthquake of 1755, felt with greatest severity at Lisbon, Portugal, and known in history as the Lisbon earthquake. Its influence was felt as far north as Greenland, also in the north of Africa. This was to be followed by the darkening of the sun, and the moon, and the falling of the stars of heaven. There have been many earthquakes in the history of the world, and the sun has often been darkened; but a definite earthquake was to be considered as a sign of the times in which men were living. A definite darkening of the sun and moon would be used by the Lord as a token of His near approach. That men might know which events to accept and which to reject, the Word of God has described with divine minuteness the ones referred to under the sixth seal. Eight writers of the Bible give the signs in the sun, moon, and stars, as heralds of the last day. Four of these, Joel, Amos, Isaiah, and Ezekiel, wrote before the time of Christ; the other four are Matthew, Mark, Luke, and John, three of whom repeat the words given by the Saviour Himself. The description of the signs in the heavenly bodies, given by these eight writers, points out at least thirteen peculiarities, which unmistakably indicate the time and nature of their occurrence. The time when men might look for signs in the heavens is given by Matthew. He says, "Immediately after the tribulation of those days shall the sun be darkened, and the moon shall not

Joel 2:31.
Amos 8:9.
Isa. 13:9, 10.
Eze. 32:7, 8.
Matt. 24:29.
Mark 13:24.
Luke 21:25.
Rev. 6:12, 13.

And except that the Lord had shortened those days, no flesh should be saved: but for the elect's sake, whom he hath chosen, he hath shortened the days. Mark 13:20.

*And I beheld when had he opened the sixth seal, and, lo, there was*

give her light," etc. The "tribulation of those days" is the period of darkness and persecution, known as the "abomination of desolation spoken of by Daniel the prophet." It began with the establishment of the papacy in 538 A.D., and continued twelve hundred and sixty years, or until 1798. But God in mercy shortened the time of persecution; for "except those days be shortened there should no flesh be saved." The persecuting power of the papacy was broken about 1776 A.D. "Immediately after the tribulation of those days shall the sun be darkened and the moon shall not give her light." The prophesied dark day must then be looked for soon after 1776. Mark adds another item which helps in the location of the time. He says, "In those days, after that tribulation," etc. That is, within the period of the twelve hundred and sixty years, or before 1798 and after 1776, "the sun shall be darkened and the moon shall not give her light." History records the extraordinarily dark day of May 19, 1780; and the student of prophecy finds that in point of time, this meets the requirements of Matthew and Mark.

**" He is even at the door."**

*a great earthquake; and the sun became black as sackcloth of hair, and the moon became as blood.*
*Rev. 6:12.*

**The following are thirteen peculiarities which indicate the time and nature of the signs in the heavens:**

Immediately after the tribulation of those days shall the sun be darkened and the moon shall not give her light, and the stars shall fall from heaven. Matt. 24:29.

In those days, after that tribulation, the sun shall be darkened, and the moon shall not give her light. Mark 13:24.

When these things begin to come to pass, then look up, and lift up your heads; for your redemption draweth nigh.

So likewise ye, when ye see these things come to pass, know ye that the kingdom of God is nigh at hand. Luke 21:28, 31.

The sun shall be turned into darkness, and the moon into blood, before the great and the terrible day of the Lord come. Joel 2:31.

Maketh the day dark with night. Amos 5:8.

The sun shall be darkened in his going forth. Isa. 13:10.

I will cause the sun to go down at noon. Amos 8:9.

I will darken the earth in the clear day. Amos 8:9.

I will cover the sun with a cloud. Eze. 32:7.

The sun became black as sackcloth of hair. Rev. 6:12.

The moon became as blood. Rev. 6:12.

The stars of heaven fell unto the earth, even as a fig tree casteth her untimely figs, when she is shaken of a mighty wind. Rev. 6:13.

I beheld when he had opened the sixth seal, and, lo, there was a great earthquake. Rev. 6:12.

Luke, the Gospel writer, who appeals especially to the lover of logic, so states facts that the reader is at once convinced that the signs in the sun, moon, and stars, are consecutive events. In Luke 21:25–33, the signs are mentioned. The 28th verse says, "When these things begin to come to pass, then look up, and lift up your heads; for your redemption draweth nigh." It is not yet nigh, but it draweth nigh. The 31st verse continues, "When ye see these things [Matthew says, 'all these things,'] come to pass, know ye that the kingdom of God is nigh at hand." There is a lapse of time between the first and the last signs. When they begin to appear, redemption draweth nigh; when all have appeared, redemption is nigh, "even at the door." Those who endured the afflictions of the Dark Ages, who had seen friends tortured on the rack, or burned at the stake; or had themselves endured imprisonment or persecution, when the light of the Reformation scattered the darkness, were bidden to look forward; for the morning star was to be seen. A little later came the darkening of the sun. Then they were encouraged to lift up the head, for "redemption draweth nigh." Those living since the fulfillment of all the signs, should rejoice; for "He is even at the door." One characteristic of the darkening of the sun, which is given as a sign of His coming, is found in Joel 3:15. That prophet states that the sun, the moon, and the stars, should all be darkened. "The sun and the moon shall be darkened, and the stars shall withdraw their shining." The accounts of the dark day in 1780 agree with this. It appeared to those who witnessed the phenom-

THE DARKENING OF THE SUN AND MOON.

enon, that the darkness at its height could not have been more dense, had every luminary been blotted out of existence. One writer says, "The darkness of the following evening was probably as deep and dense as ever had been observed since the Almighty first gave birth to light. . . . A sheet of white paper, held within a few inches of the eyes, was equally invisible with the blackest velvet. . . . The denseness of this evening darkness was a fact universally observed and recorded." (Devens, in "Our First Century.")

Amos witnesses to the fact that the night following the darkening of the sun, would be dark also. That is to say, that the darkening of the sun and moon, to which the sixth seal has reference, would be within the same twenty-four hours; one day would be dark, and the night following, the moon would be dark also. The paragraph quoted above shows that the darkening of the sun and moon on May 19, 1780, met these specifications.

The prophet Isaiah gives one point to which none of the other writers refer. He says, "The sun shall be darkened in his going forth," that is, in the morning. Amos 8:9 states that the darkest portion of the day would be at noon, and that this would take place on a clear day. Ezekiel states that a cloud would cover the face of the sun. Here are four peculiarities worthy of notice. The sign which the Lord placed in the heavens, could be easily read. Of all the dark days which history records, none, but the one in 1780, meets all these specifications. The morning would be clear, but during the morning a cloud would obscure the face of the sun. The darkness would

Now learn a parable of the fig tree; When his branch is yet tender, and putteth forth leaves, ye know that summer is nigh:

So likewise ye, when ye shall see all these things, know that it is near, even at the doors.

Matt. 24:32, 33.

Then shall be great tribulation, such as was not since the beginning of the world to this time, no, nor ever shall be. Matt. 24:21.

Luke 21:28–33.

Gen. 1:14.

The Lord said unto Moses, Stretch out thine hand toward heaven, that there may be darkness over the land of Egypt, even darkness which may be felt.

And Moses stretched forth his hand toward heaven; and there was a thick darkness in all the land of Egypt three days.

Ex. 10:21, 22.

The fifth angel poured out his vial upon the seat of the beast; and his kingdom was full of darkness; and they gnawed their tongues for pain. Rev. 16:10.

Shall a trumpet be blown in the city, and the people not be afraid? shall there be evil in a city, and the Lord hath not done it?

Surely the Lord God will do nothing, but he revealeth his secret unto his servants the prophets.

Amos 3:6, 7.

Hold thy peace at the presence of the Lord God: for the day of the Lord is at hand: for the Lord hath prepared a sacrifice, he hath bid his guests.

And it shall come to pass in the day of the Lord's sacrifice, that I will punish the princes, and the king's children, and all such as are clothed with strange apparel.

In the same day also will I punish all those that leap on the threshold, which fill their masters' houses with violence and deceit.

Zeph. 1:7–9.

increase until it reached its greatest density about noon. On these points "Our First Century," the work before referred to, states: "The time of the commencement of this extraordinary darkness, was between the hours of ten and eleven in the forenoon on Friday, of the date already named [May 19, 1780]. As to the manner of its approach, the darkness seemed to appear first of all in the southwest. The wind came from that quarter, and the darkness appeared to come on with the clouds. . . . The sun, rising towards the zenith, gave no increase of light, as usual; but, on the contrary, the darkness continued to increase until between eleven and twelve o'clock, at which time there was the greatest obscurity in that place." Speaking of another locality the same writer says, "At twelve the darkness was greatest. Lights were seen burning in all the houses; . . . the birds in the midst of their blithesome forenoon engagements, stopped suddenly, and singing their evening songs, disappeared and became silent; the fowls retired to their roosts, the cocks were crowing in their accustomed manner at the break of day." The day was not intensely black as if there were no sun, but as stated in Rev. 6:12, "the sun became black as sackcloth of hair." Sackcloth of hair is made of goat hair, and is black mingled with gray. John is the only one who mentions this feature.

Joel and John prophesied that the moon would be turned into blood. Those who witnessed the dark night, say that when the moon appeared, near the morning, it was a blood-red ball in the heavens.

The peculiar features of the special falling of

Gather yourselves together, yea, gather together, O nation not desired;

Before the decree bring forth, before the day pass as the chaff, before the fierce anger of the Lord come upon you, before the day of the Lord's anger come upon you.

Seek ye the Lord, all ye meek of the earth, which have wrought his judgment; seek righteousness, seek meekness: it may be ye shall be hid in the day of the Lord's anger.
Zeph. 2:1-3.

The earth shall quake before them; the heavens shall tremble the sun and the moon shall be dark, and the stars shall withdraw their shining:

And the Lord shall utter his voice before his army: for his camp is very great: for he is strong that executeth his word: for the day of the Lord is great and very terrible; and who can abide it?
Joel 2:10, 11.

"The dark day of Northern America was one of those wonderful phenomena of nature which will always be read of with interest, but which philosophy is at a loss to explain."—*Herschel.*

Therefore thus will I do unto thee, O Israel: and because I will do this unto thee, prepare to meet thy God, O Israel. Amos 4:12.

***And the stars of heaven fell unto the earth, even as a fig tree casteth her untimely figs, when she is shaken of a mighty wind.***
***Rev. 6:13.***

the stars, which God gave as a sign, are given by John. They should fall from heaven "as a fig tree casteth her untimely figs, when she is shaken of a mighty wind." Extensive and magnificent showers of shooting stars have been known to occur at various places in modern times; but the most universal and wonderful which has ever been recorded is that of the 13th of November, 1833, the whole firmament, over all the United States, being then for hours in fiery commotion. As a fig tree covered with green fruit being violently shaken sends the fruit in all directions, so from one center in the sky, the stars fell in showers in every direction.

The great day of the Lord is near, it is near, and hasteth greatly, even the voice of the day of the Lord: the mighty man shall cry there bitterly. Zeph. 1:14.

**"As a fig tree casteth her untimely figs."**

Since 1755 the inhabitants of the earth have been living under the sixth seal. In the heavens and on the earth, signs have appeared, which show that time is short. This period has been a time of great intellectual light. Men, by their discoveries and inventions, have made rapid transit and speedy communication between different lands possible. Since "the tribulation of those days," the light of truth has been shining in steady rays upon God's people. At no time, save when Christ was born, has greater light shone upon the world. Some will accept a spiritual life, while others will find very soon that should the Lord come, it would be to them a time of darkness and despair. The sixth seal

Every man that hath this hope in him purifieth himself, even as he is pure. 1 John 3:3.

Dan. 12:4.

The chariots shall rage in the streets, they shall justle one against another in the broad ways: they shall seem like torches, they shall run like the lightnings.
Nahum 2:4.

I will bring distress upon men, that they shall walk like blind men, because they have sinned against the Lord: and their blood shall be poured out as dust, and their flesh as the dung.

Neither their silver nor their gold shall be able to deliver them in the day of the Lord's wrath.
Zeph. 1:17, 18.

*And the heaven departed as a scroll when it is rolled together: and every mountain and island were moved out of their places.*
*Rev. 6:14.*

Psa. 82 : 5.
Gen. 2 : 6.
Gen. 7 : 11.

*And the kings of the earth, and the great men, and the rich men, and the chief captains, and the mighty men, and every bondman, and every free man, hid themselves in the dens and in the rocks of the mountains;*

*And said to the mountains and rocks, Fall on us, and hide us from the face of him that sitteth on the throne, and from the wrath of the Lamb:*

*For the great day of his wrath is come; and who shall be able to stand? Rev. 6:15-17.*

looks forward to the very end, when the heavens depart as a scroll rolled together; and when the mountains and islands are moved out of their places. When sin entered the world, the course of nature was changed. The atmosphere, once agreeable to the senses of man, now chilled him; the moisture, at first distilled as the dew, finally came in torrents from the sky, and the fountains of the great deep were broken up. The earth itself was turned from its original position, at the time of the flood; vast portions were made uninhabitable on account of the cold and the vast amount of water left on the surface. At the sound of the voice of the Son of man, the elements of the atmosphere will be rearranged, the high places will be brought low, and islands will be moved from their positions.

2 Pet. 3 : 10.

They shall go into the holes of the rocks, and into the caves of the earth, for fear of the Lord, and for the glory of his majesty, when he ariseth to shake terribly the earth.

In that day a man shall cast his idols of silver, and his idols of gold, which they made each one for himself to worship, to the moles and to the bats. Isa. 2 : 19, 20.

At that time those who have put their trust in idols of gold rather than in their Maker, and those who have exalted humanity above Divinity, will in terror seek to be hidden by rocks and mountains from the piercing gaze of Him who sits upon the throne. There is now a time of probation. All may know the time of God's visitation, for we are walled about by the signs given by Jehovah. We cannot lose ourselves; for the dates 1755, 1780, and 1833, are as clearly marked as the close of the twelve hundred and sixty years, and the twenty-three hundred years of the book of Daniel.

Isa. 33 : 15.
Psa. 24 : 4-6.

"Who shall be able to stand?" "He that hath clean hands, and a pure heart; who hath not lifted up his soul unto vanity, nor sworn deceitfully. He shall receive the blessing from the Lord, and righteousness from the God of his salvation."

" The great day of His wrath is come; and who shall be able to stand? "

# CHAPTER VIII.

## THE SEALING WORK.

THE seventh chapter of the book of Revelation continues the description of events taking place under the sixth seal. Already the signs, which prophecy foretold would appear in the heavens, have been seen. Not only did men witness the phenomena, but as early as 1844, and since that time, these things have been recognized as signs of the second appearing of the Son of man, and as such, have been preached before all the world. When the Saviour was giving the signs by which men should know of the approach of the second advent, He mentions, in addition to the strange appearance in the heavens, "upon the earth distress of nations, with perplexity." This distress of nations follows the falling of the stars, and as it is the subject with which the seventh chapter of Revelation is introduced, it places that chapter, when considered chronologically, between the thirteenth and fourteenth verses of the sixth chapter of Revelation.

Let them bring them forth, and shew us what shall happen: let them shew the former things, what they be, that we may consider them and know the latter end of them; or declare us things for to come. Isa. 41:22, 26.

Go ye therefore, and teach all nations. Matt. 28:19.

There shall be signs in the sun, and in the moon, and in the stars; and upon the earth distress of nations, with perplexity; the sea and the waves roaring;

Men's hearts failing them for fear, and for looking after those things which are coming on the earth: for the powers of heaven shall be shaken. Luke 21:25, 26.

*And after these things I saw four angels standing on the four corners of the earth, holding the four winds of the earth, that the wind should not blow on the earth, nor on the sea, nor on any tree.*
*Rev. 7:1.*

Zech. 14:9.

God is the King of all the earth.
Psa. 47:7.

Heb. 1:14.
Psa. 103:20.

I will shew thee that which is noted in the scripture of truth: and there is none that holdeth with me in these things, but Michael your prince. Dan. 10:21.

Psa. 34:7.
Matt. 18:10.

The king of the north shall come against him like a whirlwind, with chariots, and with horsemen, and with many ships; and he shall enter into the countries, and shall overflow and pass over.
Dan. 11:40.

Woe to the multitude of many people, which make a noise like the noise of the seas; and to the rushing of nations, that make a rushing like the rushing of mighty waters!
The nations shall rush like the rushing of many waters: but God shall rebuke them, and they shall flee far off, and shall be chased as the chaff of the mountains before the wind, and like a rolling thing before the whirlwind.
Isa. 17:12, 13.

Rev. 13:8.
Gen. 4:3, 4.
Rev. 12:14-16.
Isa. 60:16.
Isa. 61:6.

"After these things," that is, after the occurrence of the signs mentioned in Rev. 6:12, 13, "I saw four angels standing on the four corners of the earth, holding the four winds of the earth." John's view of heaven had opened to his mind the workings of the government of God, and the work of the angels was revealed as he watched the loosening of the seals. "Are they not all ministering spirits, sent forth to minister for them who shall be heirs of salvation?" Angels who excel in strength, do the bidding of Jehovah, hearkening unto the voice of His word. Gabriel, the angel of prophecy, is by no means the only one who has a specifically assigned task. To John are shown four of these heavenly beings, standing on the four corners of the globe, holding the winds that they might not blow. Winds symbolize war or contention. There has been more than one war in the past, as well as more than one dark day; but at a certain period of time, there should be a distress of nations differing from all previous international troubles.

In the opening of the fifth seal, when the church as a church came from the Dark Ages, two great principles born of the Reformation, and cutting short the persecuting power, finally made martyrdom impossible. These two principles then came into existence under the names of Protestantism and democracy. Protestantism, representing the religious phase of society; democracy, or the principle which recognizes the equal rights of all mankind, representing the civil government. In other words, the results of the sixteenth century Reformation were not seen alone in the organization of Protestant churches;

but there was at the same time a protest against the absolute monarchy which had borne sway for a thousand years. Under these conditions the salvation of the cause demanded a new soil for the cultivation of freedom. For this purpose God had already opened America and Southern Africa. The South African colonies failed to profit by their opportunities, but in America both Protestantism and democracy—freedom to worship, and the equal rights of men in civil affairs,—blossomed and bore fruit in the Constitution of the United States. During the first half century of this nation's existence, it was watched with a most critical eye by monarchs and statesmen of Europe. But as the government grew stronger, and one state after another was added; as its ministers received recognition in foreign courts; and as its products were sought in foreign markets, the people of European governments saw, that democracy was no longer an experiment, but a possibility.

There was restlessness in Europe. From the days of Napoleon, France was divided in its opinions, and the desire for a representative government, was more than once made known. Any manifestation on the part of subjects in all European countries was jealously watched by the sovereigns, and all uprisings were put down with unusual severity. The elements were gathering for a storm, the low mutterings of distant thunder were heard; yet each ruler tried to convince himself that his throne was secure. France, fortunate or unfortunate, as one may choose to view the matter, appears, however, to have been the center from which the waves of commotion started. In 1830 the French minis-

He increaseth the nations, and destroyeth them: he enlargeth the nations, and straiteneth them again.

He taketh away the heart of the chief of the people of the earth, and causeth them to wander in a wilderness where there is no way.

Job. 12:23, 24.

Rulers are not a terror to good works, but to the evil. Wilt thou then not be afraid of the power? do that which is good, and thou shalt have praise of the same:

For he is the minister of God to thee for good. But if thou do that which is evil, be afraid; for he beareth not the sword in vain: for he is the minister of God, a revenger to execute wrath upon him that doeth evil. Rom. 13:3, 4.

As a roaring lion, and a ranging bear; so is a wicked ruler over the poor people. Prov. 28:15.

Thou hast increased the nation, O Lord, thou hast increased the nation: thou art glorified: thou hadst removed it far unto all the ends of the earth. Isa. 26:15.

There is one come out of thee, that imagineth evil against the Lord, a wicked counsellor.

Nahum 1:11.

Thou hast multiplied the nation, and not increased the joy: they joy before thee according to the joy in harvest, and as men rejoice when they divide the spoil. Isa. 9:3.

He stretched out his hand over the sea, he shook the kingdoms.

Isa. 23:11.

This matter is by the decree of the watchers, and the demand by the word of the holy ones: to the intent that the living may know that the most High ruleth in the kingdom of men, and giveth it to whomsoever he will, and setteth up over it the basest of men.

Dan. 4:17.

All people, nations, and languages, trembled and feared before him: whom he would he slew; and whom he would he kept alive; and whom he would he set up; and whom he would he put down.

Dan. 5:19.

Shall the throne of iniquity have fellowship with thee, which frameth mischief by a law?

They gather themselves together against the soul of the righteous, and condemn the innocent blood.

But the Lord is my defence; and my God is the rock of my refuge.

And he shall bring upon them their own iniquity, and shall cut them off in their own wickedness; yea, the Lord our God shall cut them off. Psa. 94 : 20.

The wrath of a king is as messengers of death. Psa. 94: 20–23.

try, fearing that too much authority was being exercised by the Chamber of Deputies, issued an ordinance declaring all recent elections illegal, restricting suffrage, and limiting the freedom of the press. This act was met by mob violence, and resulted in the unseating of the reigning monarch and the enthroning of a new French king, who, because he was crowned by the middle classes, was called the "citizens' king." The name was significant. The common people were coming into power, and had nations followed the leadings of Providence, there might have been, in the next few years, a peaceful reorganization of Europe. Instead, however, the people, especially of dependent countries and provinces, were oppressed. But the French uprising had its effect.

**Arch of Triumph, Paris.**

He who smote the people in wrath with a continual stroke, he that ruled the nations in anger, is persecuted, and none hindereth. Isa. 14:6.

Therefore shall evil come upon thee; thou shalt not know from whence it riseth: and mischief shall fall upon thee; thou shalt not be able to put it off: and desolation shall come upon thee suddenly, which thou shalt not know. Isa. 47:11.

"In Saxony and in the minor states of Germany, disturbances were consequent on the tidings of the revolution at Paris." In Poland there was an uprising, a result of the movement in Paris. One result traceable to the French trouble, occurred in the year 1832, when "eight thousand Poles were sent to Siberia." In Germany, unity was foretold by the formation of the customs-union between 1828 and 1834. Uprisings occurred in Italy, demanding independence and unity. In 1833 the system of slavery in the British colonies was abolished. In 1837 Victoria became ruler of England; and the repeal in 1846 of the Corn Laws, which imposed duties on imported grains, was an omen of the increasing liberality of the British government. Events might be multiplied, to show the sharp division between those who favored popular rights and those who still fought for the divine right of kings.

The internal pressure became greater. It was recognized by all that some settlement must soon be reached. The climax came, when in 1848, mob violence again broke out in France. For two years there had been a scarcity of food, and the rabble rebelled against all authority. The king, Louis Phillippe, abdicated, and escaped to England. Except for the courage and firmness of a few French statesmen, who guided affairs through this critical period, the scenes of the Revolution of 1789, would have been repeated. The soldiers fraternized with the mob. Only through the wisest management, a socialistic Directory was avoided. Instead, the motion for a provisional government, prevailed. A constitution was adopted which provided for a president who should serve for a term of four years. Louis Napoleon was elected first president of the new French Republic. This was the eventful year of 1848. Judson, in his work entitled "Europe in the Nineteenth Century," says this revolution "was like a lighted match touched to the dry prairie grass after a drought. The flam ..shed at once throughout the continent." In Germany "new ministries were installed which were pledged to a liberal policy." "Prus-

Righteousness exalteth a nation: but sin is a reproach to any people. Prov. 14:34.

Thou, O king, art a king of kings: for the God of heaven hath given thee a kingdom, power, and strength, and glory. Dan. 2:37.

The balances of deceit are in his hand: he loveth to oppress. Hos. 12:7.

So I returned, and considered all the oppressions that are done under the sun: and behold the tears of such as were oppressed, and they had no comforter; and on the side of their oppressors there was power; but they had no comforter. Eccl. 4:1.

Eze. 14:13.

Her princes are become like harts that find no pasture, and they are gone without strength before the pursuer Lam. 1:6.

There was a little city, and few men within it; and there came great king against it, and besieged it, and built great bulwarks against it:

Now there was found in it a poor wise man, and he by his wisdom delivered the city; yet no man remembered that same poor man.

Then said I, Wisdom is better than strength. Eccl. 9:14-16.

He that handleth a matter wisely shall find good. Prov. 16:20.

But mine enemies are lively, and they are strong: and they that hate me wrongfully are multiplied.

They also that render evil for good are mine adversaries. Psa. 38:19, 20.

Wisdom and knowledge shall be the stability of thy times.
Isa. 33 : 6.

Lift not up your horn on high : speak not with a stiff neck.
For promotion cometh neither from the east, nor from the west, nor from the south.
But God is the judge : he putteth down one, and setteth up another.
Psa. 75 : 5-7.

There is no king saved by the multitude of an host : a mighty man is not delivered by much strength.
Psa. 33 : 16.

sia and Austria were thoroughly disturbed by the movement for freedom and national unity." In Germany nearly five hundred men gathered, determined to organize a provisional government. The disturbances in Prussia, forced the king to swear to maintain a new constitution. Both Hungary and Vienna revolted, and this furnished the long coveted occasion for the Italians to throw off Austrian rule. Thus, in a brief period of time, many crowned heads of Europe submitted themselves to the people.

**Louis Napoleon.**

*And I saw another angel ascending from the east, having the seal of the living God : and he cried with a loud voice to the four angels, to whom it was given to hurt the earth and the sea,*
*Saying, Hurt not the earth, neither the sea, nor the trees, till we have sealed the servants of our God in their foreheads.*
*Rev. 7 : 2, 3.*

Rev. 14:9-12.

In the midst of the turmoil and strife, came a sudden calm. No man could assign any reason for it. Like the troubled waters of Gennesaret when Christ spoke peace out of the storm, tumult and confusion ceased. The four angels had been stationed on the earth to hold the winds of strife till the servants of God could be sealed. Europe had been wrought upon until the power of an absolute monarchy was practically a thing of the past. There was now an opportunity for the ripening of the principles of the Reformation. The closing work in the earth, will be a continuation of the movement set on foot when the darkness of the Middle Ages was broken. God has prepared the earth for the rapid spread of the Gospel, and the sealing work is now going on.

" And I saw another angel ascending from the east, having the seal of the living God : and he cried with a loud voice to the four angels, . . saying, 'Hurt not the earth, neither the sea, nor the trees, till we have sealed the servants of our

God in their foreheads.'" Nations are represented as being held in check by the angels of heaven until the servants of God are sealed. Men are led to ask, "What is this seal placed upon the foreheads by which God recognizes His servants?" God's chosen people are always a peculiar people; they are called to be a nation of kings, a royal priesthood, who show forth the virtues of their Commander. Jehovah looks not on the outward appearance, but weighs character, and places His seal on those whose hearts are right toward Him. When Abraham was called to become the founder of a nation, God gave to him "the sign of circumcision, a seal of the righteousness of the faith which he had." To the seed of Abraham, who live in the time of the end, the same God gives a sign, or seal, of the righteousness of the faith which they have. This seal comes not because of boasted pride, or self-supremacy, but by simple faith in the promises of God, as a child learns from its mother. Christ, looking up to heaven, said, "I thank thee, O Father, Lord of heaven and earth, because thou hast hid these things from the wise and prudent, and hast revealed them unto babes." This sign or seal, is a direct revelation from God, to those who will accept with the faith of a little child. "Flesh and blood hath not revealed it unto thee, but My Father which is in heaven." That which the Father and Son alone can reveal is a knowledge of God, and this knowledge of God, is the seal placed in the foreheads of the chosen generation. To this, Paul testifies in the words, "The foundation of God standeth sure, having this seal, the Lord knoweth them that are His." The seal then is the knowledge

Who gave himself for us, that he might redeem us from all iniquity, and purify unto himself a peculiar people, zealous of good works. Titus 2:14.

1 Pet. 2:9.

Look not upon his countenance, or on the height of his stature; because I have refused him: for the Lord seeth not as man seeth; for man looketh on the outward appearance, but the Lord looketh on the heart. 1 Sam. 16:7.

Rom. 4:11.

Verily I say unto you, Except ye be converted, and become as little children, ye shall not enter into the kingdom of heaven. Matt. 18:3.

Matt. 11:25.

Matt. 16:17.

This is life eternal, that they might know thee the only true God, and Jesus Christ, whom thou hast sent. John 17:3.

2 Tim. 2:19.

Eze. 20:20.

If ye love me, keep my commandments. John 14:15.

Eze. 20:12.

He that hath my commandments, and keepeth them, he it is that loveth me: and he that loveth me shall be loved of my Father, and I will love him, and will manifest myself to him. John 14:21.

Ex. 31:13.

Ex. 31:17.

The gods that have not made the heavens and the earth, even they shall perish from the earth, and from under these heavens.

He hath made the earth by his power, he hath established the world by his wisdom, and hath stretched out the heavens by his discretion. Jer. 10:11, 12.

John 4:24.

The Lord said unto him, Go through the midst of the city, through the midst of Jerusalem, and set a mark upon the foreheads of the men that sigh and that cry for all the abominations that be done in the midst thereof.
Eze. 9:4.

Remember the sabbath day, to keep it holy.
Six days shalt thou labour, and do all thy work:
But the seventh day is the sabbath of the Lord thy God: in it thou shalt not do any work, thou, nor thy son, nor thy daughter, thy manservant, nor thy maidservant, nor thy cattle, nor thy stranger that is within thy gates:
For in six days the Lord made heaven and earth, the sea, and all that in them is, and rested the seventh day: wherefore the Lord blessed the sabbath day, and hallowed it. Ex. 20:8–11.

Gen. 2:2, 3.
Ex. 34:21.

If thou turn away thy foot from the sabbath, from doing thy pleasure on my holy day; and call the sabbath a delight, the holy of the Lord, honourable; and shalt honour him, not doing thine own ways, nor finding thine own pleasure, nor speaking thine own words:
Then shalt thou delight thyself in the Lord. Isa. 58:13, 14.

of the true God, and this, Jehovah has placed in His Sabbath. "Hallow My Sabbaths; and they shall be a sign between Me and you, that ye may know that I am the Lord your God." "Moreover also I gave them My Sabbaths, to be a sign between Me and them, that they might know that I am the Lord that sanctify them." This seal is a sign of sanctification, and it is a sign forever. "Verily My Sabbaths ye shall keep: for it is a sign between Me and you throughout your generations." Again He says, "It is a sign between Me and the children of Israel forever: for in six days the Lord made heaven and earth, and on the seventh day He rested, and was refreshed." This was spiritual rest, for "God is a Spirit," and knows no rest but spiritual rest. The rest, the blessing, and the sanctification of the Sabbath of Jehovah are all spiritual, and only such as are living in a condition symbolized by the first seal, can rest as God rested. Such, and such alone, have a knowledge of God. The seal placed in the forehead by the angel, cannot be read by man; only God and heavenly beings can read it. For this reason, no civil law can enforce Sabbath keeping. Man may keep the form one day in seven, but only a knowledge of God can give the seal in the forehead. Christ was a living commentary on true Sabbath observance, and the things which He did on that day, reveal the mind of God toward the children of men. "The seventh day is the Sabbath of the Lord thy God." "On the seventh day God ended His work which He had made; and He rested on the seventh day from all His work which He had made. And God blessed the seventh day, and sanctified it."

In these texts, the day upon which God rested, and which He subsequently blessed and sanctified, is plainly stated to be the seventh day. And from that seventh day on which Jehovah rested, all future seventh days have in them the blessing and the sanctification. The use of the word *seal* directs the mind to a legal document. When a ruler's seal is attached to a legal paper, that seal contains the name of the one in authority, his right to rule, and the territory over which he rules. These features are all made prominent in the seal contained in the law of God. To-day the seal is usually placed, either at the beginning, or at the close of the decree or law; but in the divine law it is placed in the center, that nothing may be taken from, or added thereto. The fourth commandment reads: "Remember the Sabbath day, to keep it holy. Six days shalt thou labor, and do all thy work: but the seventh day is the Sabbath of the Lord thy God: in it thou shalt not do any work. . . . For in six days the Lord made heaven and earth, the sea, and all that in them is, and rested the seventh day: wherefore the Lord blessed the Sabbath day, and hallowed it." Herein lie the three specifications of a seal: first, the name,—the Lord thy God, Jehovah; second, the authority,—Creator; third, the extent of territory,—the heavens and earth. Take away this command from the decalogue, and it would contain no seal. God's right to rule rests in the fourth commandment, and the seal will be placed in the foreheads of those who thus know God. The knowledge of the creative and the redeeming power of God, is revealed by Christ in the fourth commandment of the decalogue.

Matt. 24:20.

Wherefore the law is holy, and the commandment holy, and just, and good. Rom. 7:12.

Write ye also for the Jews, as it liketh you, in the king's name, and seal it with the king's ring: for the writing which is written in the king's name, and sealed with the king's ring, may no man reverse. Esther 8:8.

Bind up the testimony, seal the law among my disciples. Isa. 8:16.

Think not that I am come to destroy the law, or the prophets: I am not come to destroy, but to fulfil.

For verily I say unto you, Till heaven and earth pass, one jot or one tittle shall in no wise pass from the law, till all be fulfilled. Matt. 5:17, 18.

Thus saith the Lord God; The gate of the inner court that looketh toward the east shall be shut the six working days; but on the sabbath it shall be opened, and in the day of the new moon it shall be opened. Eze. 46:1.

Ye shall keep my sabbaths, and reverence my sanctuary: I am the Lord. Lev. 19:30.

That day was the preparation, and the sabbath drew on.

And the women also, which came with him from Galilee, followed after, and beheld the sepulchre, and how his body was laid.

And they returned, and prepared spices and ointments; and rested the sabbath day according to the commandment. Luke 23:54–56.

*And I heard the number of them which were sealed: and there were sealed an hundred and forty and four thousand of all the tribes of the children of Israel.*

*Rev. 7:4.*

Here is the patience of the saints: here are they that keep the commandments of God, and the faith of Jesus. Rev. 14:9–12.

Madest known unto them thy holy sabbath, and commandedst them precepts, statutes, and laws, by the hand of Moses thy servant.

Neh. 9:14.

Blessed is the man that doeth this, and the son of man that layeth hold on it; that keepeth the sabbath from polluting it.

Isa. 56:2.

If some of the branches be broken off, and thou, being a wild olive tree, wert graffed in among them, and with them partakest of the root and fatness of the olive tree;

Boast not against the branches. But if thou boast, thou bearest not the root, but the root thee.

Rom. 11:17, 18.

Rom. 11:20.

Blessed are they that do his commandments, that they may have right to the tree of life, and may enter in through the gates into the city. Rev. 22:14.

In 1848 thc Angel from the East called to the four angels to hold the winds of war until the servants of God were sealed in their foreheads. Since 1848, in the quiet which has prevailed among nations, light upon the Sabbath of Jehovah's law, has been going to every nation of the earth. It began gently as the rising sun; it shines to-day with the clearness of the noonday rays. Thousands, in all quarters of the globe testify to the saving health in the Sabbath observance.

The number of the servants of our God is now being made up. "I heard the number of them which were sealed: and there were sealed an hundred and forty and four thousand of all the tribes of the children of Israel." Character alone is the basis of the sealing work. The promise of the new earth was made to Abraham, Isaac, and Jacob; but the literal descendants of these patriarchs, failed to develop a character which would place upon them a seal of the living God, and they were rejected as a nation. Then the Gentiles, like branches from a wild olive tree, were, contrary to nature, grafted into the Jewish root; and those who bear fruit unto righteousness will partake of the inheritance once promised to Jews of the flesh. The places in the twelve tribes, which might have been filled by the direct descendants of Abraham, will be occupied by children by adoption. The attention of all heaven is directed toward this sealing work; for when it is over, the plan of redemption is completed. The one hundred and forty-four thousand are divided into classes called by the names of the twelve tribes of Israel. These are character names, and those who develop the character, will be classed under the tribe bearing a name indicating that character. To illustrate; "Issachar is a strong ass couching down between two burdens: and he saw that rest was good, and the land that it was pleasant; and bowed his shoulder to bear, and became a servant unto tribute." Burden bearers are here described. Those, who, looking forward to the promised future home are willing to couch often beneath heavy burdens; and like the patient ass, even bear double burdens, that the cause of God may prosper. They are free and happy in this service; and the cause of God would never move forward in the earth if it were not for these loyal burden bearers,—these faithful Issachars, spending their lives "couching down between two burdens," while close by perhaps, are the representatives of Naphtali, who bear no burdens. "Naphtali is a hind let loose: he giveth goodly words." Free and lighthearted, he sees a thousand places where he can speak goodly words, and spring hastily to give a helping hand, that the representatives of Issachar, bowed down under their heavy burdens, would never see, neither does God expect it of them. All are needed to make the number com-

**"Naphtali is a hind let loose."**

How often would I have gathered thy children together, as a hen doth gather her brood under her wings, and ye would not! Luke 13:34.

Behold, the man clothed with linen, which had the inkhorn by his side, reported the matter, saying, I have done as thou hast commanded me. Eze. 9:11.

*Of the tribe of Juda were sealed twelve thousand. Of the tribe of Reuben were sealed twelve thousand. Of the tribe of Gad were sealed twelve thousand.*

*Of the tribe of Aser were sealed twelve thousand. Of the tribe of Nepthalim were sealed twelve thousand. Of the tribe of Manasses were sealed twelve thousand.*

*Of the tribe of Simeon were sealed twelve thousand. Of the tribe of Levi were sealed twelve thousand. Of the tribe of Issachar were sealed twelve thousand.*

*Of the tribe of Zabulon were sealed twelve thousand. Of the tribe of Joseph were sealed twelve thousand. Of the tribe of Benjamin were sealed twelve thousand.* *Rev. 7:5-8.*

Gen. 49:14, 15.
Gal. 2:9.
Isa. 9:6.
Isa. 22:22.

Of the children of Issachar, which were men that had understanding of the times, to know what Israel ought to do; the heads of them were two hundred; and all their brethren were at their commandment. 1 Chron. 12:32.

Judges 5:15.
Gen. 49:21.

The words of the pure are pleasant words. Prov. 15:26.

Prov. 16:24.
Psa. 119:103.

A soft answer turneth away wrath. Prov. 15:1.

Naphtali were a people that jeoparded their lives unto the death in the high places of the field. Judges 5:18.

plete. Let not the burden bearer think, that because he bears the heavy burdens he is the most important. He is only one twelfth part of the whole. One company will represent Levi, whose life seemed a failure through sin; and yet through victory in God, the Levites became teachers in Israel. And of unstable Reuben it is said, "Let Reuben live, and not die." He became the "excellency of dignity, and the excellency of power." Judah represents the leaders, those before whom the others bow down. Every phase of the work is represented, and the name of each tribe will be placed on one of the gates of the city of God. The tribe of Dan is omitted in the final count, and two portions are given to the family of Joseph to make up the twelve. Of Dan it was said: "Dan shall judge his people, as one of the tribes of Israel. Dan shall be a serpent by the way, an adder in the path, that biteth the horse heels, so that his rider shall fall backward." God purposed that Dan should judge Israel righteously. Keen observation, and quick discernment are necessary for a judge. These gifts were given to Dan, but instead of using them aright, he was "a serpent by the way, an adder in the path, that biteth the horse heels, so that his rider shall fall backward." In

**Dan shall be a serpent by the way, that biteth the horse heels.**

But now are they many members, yet but one body.

And the eye cannot say unto the hand, I have no need of thee: nor again the head to the feet, I have no need of you. 1 Cor. 12:20, 21.

Gen. 49:5-7.

They shall teach Jacob thy judgments, and Israel thy law: they shall put incense before thee, and whole burnt sacrifice upon thine altar. Deut. 33:8-11.

Gen. 49:3, 4.
Deut. 33:6.
Gen. 49:8-12.
Deut. 33:7.

At the gates twelve angels, and names written thereon, which are the names of the twelve tribes of the children of Israel. Rev. 21:12.

Rev. 7:5-8.
Rev. 7:6-8.
Gen. 49:16, 17.

Thou sittest and speakest against thy brother; thou slanderest thine own mother's son. Psa. 50:20-22.

Whoso privily slandereth his neighbour, him will I cut off. Psa. 101:5.

1 Kings 3:7-28.

Then he which had received the one talent came and said, Lord, I knew thee that thou art an hard man, reaping where thou hast not sown, and gathering where thou hast not strawed:

And I was afraid, and went and hid thy talent in the earth: lo, there thou hast that is thine.

His lord answered and said unto him, Thou wicked and slothful servant, thou knewest that I reap where I sowed not, and gather where I have not strawed:

Thou oughtest therefore to have put my money to the exchangers, and then at my coming I should have received mine own with usury.

Take therefore the talent from him, and give it unto him which hath ten talents. Matt. 25:24-28.

other words, he became a backbiter, a cruel critic. The gift intended for a blessing, when perverted, became an injury, causing others to fall. The cruel critic, the one who always detects the evil in others and speaks of it first, has the gift of judgment misdirected. None who persist in this work, can ever enter the kingdom of heaven; for the "accuser of our brethren" was cast out of heaven once, and neither he, nor his representatives, will ever enter its shining portals again.

Rev. 12:10.

*After this I beheld, and, lo, a great multitude, which no man could number, of all nations, and kindreds, and people, and tongues, stood before the throne, and before the Lamb, clothed with white robes, and palms in their hands;*

*And cried with a loud voice, saying, Salvation to our God which sitteth upon the throne, and unto the Lamb.*

*And all the angels stood round about the throne, and about the elders and the four beasts, and fell before the throne on their faces, and worshipped God.*

*Rev. 7:9-11.*

Once more the prophet John was shown the end of the sixth seal. The creatures of God's love were gathered from all ages. An innumerable company of the redeemed were seen standing before the throne and before the Lamb. They were clothed with the robes of Christ's righteousness; but throughout eternity, they will remember that both robes and palms are the result of the sacrifice of the Son of God. With one voice the song rings through heaven, "Salvation to our God which sitteth upon the throne, and unto the Lamb." The redeemed host sing the song of their experience; and the angels who are acquainted with each individual, the four and twenty elders, and the four beasts who have had a similar experience, respond to the mighty chorus.

*Saying, Amen: Blessing, and glory, and wisdom, and thanksgiving, and honour, and power, and might, be unto our God for ever and ever. Amen.*

*And one of the elders answered, saying unto me, What are these which are arrayed in white robes? and whence came they?*

*And I said unto him, Sir, thou knowest. And he said to me, These are they which came out of great tribulation, and have washed their robes, and made them white in the blood of the Lamb.*

*Therefore are they before the throne of God, and serve him day and night in his temple: and he that sitteth on the throne shall dwell among them.*

*Rev. 7:12-15.*

Then, as if again to call attention to the little company who have suffered most, one elder, pointing to the one hundred and forty-four thousand, said, "What are these which are arrayed in white robes? and whence came they?" He answers his own question, saying, "These are they which came out of great tribulation, and have washed their robes and made them white

Heb. 5:8, 9.

To him that overcometh will I grant to sit with me in my throne, even as I also overcame, and am set down with my Father in his throne. Rev. 3:21.

in the blood of the Lamb." The Saviour Himself was made perfect through suffering, and, as a man, gained the place on the throne beside the Father; because He overcame. The life of the one hundred and forty-four thousand is pictured in the experiences of the apostles who lived nearest to the Saviour when He was upon earth. Because they have lived as He lived, and passed through the trials which He endured, and Satan has been forced to acknowledge that he found none of his own nature in them, "therefore are they before the throne of God, and serve Him day and night in His temple: and He that sitteth on the throne shall dwell among them."

Before the rebellion in heaven, Lucifer was a covering cherub, standing always in the presence of God. In his fall he took with him a multitude of angels. The place once occupied by Satan and his angels, will be filled by the hundred and forty-four thousand, when they gather at last about the throne, where they serve God day and night in His temple, with God Himself dwelling in their midst. This is their reward for the hunger and thirst endured on earth. They form the bodyguard of their Saviour, and He leads them to the fountain of living waters. They, who, on earth clung to the knowledge of God when the world was given over to idolatry, have an infinity of truth to learn, and endless ages for growth and development. "The fear of the Lord is the beginning of wisdom." That beginning was made here on earth, when, to be true to the knowledge of God, men ofttimes suffered hunger and thirst, tribulation and persecution.

The Lord said unto Satan, Hast thou considered my servant Job, that there is none like him in the earth, a perfect and an upright man, one that feareth God, and escheweth evil? Job 1:8.

1 John 3:2, 3.

The prince of this world cometh, and hath nothing in me. John 14:30.

Thou art the anointed cherub that covereth; and I have set thee so: thou wast upon the holy mountain of God; thou hast walked up and down in the midst of the stones of fire. Eze. 28:14.

The great dragon was cast out, that old serpent, called the Devil, and Satan, which deceiveth the whole world: he was cast out into the earth, and his angels were cast out with him. Rev. 12:9.

I heard a great voice out of heaven saying, Behold, the tabernacle of God is with men, and he will dwell with them, and they shall be his people, and God himself shall be with them, and be their God. Rev. 21:3.

Because thou hast kept the word of my patience, I also will keep thee from the hour of temptation, which shall come upon all the world, to try them that dwell upon the earth. Rev. 3:10.

They shall feed in the ways, and their pastures shall be in all high places.

They shall not hunger nor thirst; neither shall the heat nor sun smite them: for he that hath mercy on them shall lead them, even by the springs of water shall he guide them. Isa. 49:9, 10.

Heb. 11:27.

*They shall hunger no more, neither thirst any more; neither shall the sun light on them, nor any heat.*

*For the Lamb which is in the midst of the throne shall feed them, and shall lead them unto living fountains of waters: and God shall wipe away all tears from their eyes. Rev. 7:16, 17.*

But he who endures as seeing Him who is invisible,—the Lamb, who is in the presence of God, will one day be filled with the knowledge of the Lord. In that day the tears of earth will be wiped away by the joys of eternity. "Neither shall the sun light on them, nor any heat." On earth they have felt the heat of the sun's rays, and although, after the restoration, the sunshine is sevenfold brighter than at present, yet the little company stand so near the throne, and are so enshrouded by the intense light of the Father and Sòn, that the sunlight is no longer noticeable. The appearance of one angel on earth dazzled the eyes of the centurion's guard at the Saviour's tomb, and they fell like dead men. Light is the result of an abundance of life. What must be the purity of those who partake of divinity to such a degree that they walk in the very presence of the Creator?

These are redeemed from among men. They come from the last generation,—that race which is almost extinct because of the prevalence of disease and sin. But the blood of the Lamb is all powerful, and places these next the throne. "Where sin abounded grace did much more abound." The matchless love of Christ, who can understand!

Moreover the light of the moon shall be as the light of the sun, and the light of the sun shall be sevenfold, as the light of seven days. Isa. 30:26.

Then shall the righteous shine forth as the sun in the kingdom of their Father. Matt. 13:43.

The angel of the Lord descended from heaven, and came and rolled back the stone from the door, and sat upon it.

His countenance was like lightning, and his raiment white as snow:

And for fear of him the keepers did shake, and became as dead men. Matt. 28:2, 3.

Who is a God like unto thee, that pardoneth iniquity, and passeth by the transgression of the remnant of his heritage? he retaineth not his anger for ever, because he delighteth in mercy. Mic. 7:18.

Rom. 5:20.

# CHAPTER IX.

## THE TRUMPETS.

Hurt not the earth, neither the sea, nor the trees, till we have sealed the servants of our God in their foreheads. Rev. 7 : 3.

Thou shalt love the Lord thy God with all thy heart, and with all thy soul, and with all thy mind. Matt. 22 : 37.

That Christ may dwell in your hearts by faith ; that ye, being rooted and grounded in love. Eph. 3 : 17.

Then shall the King say unto them on his right hand, Come, ye blessed of my Father, inherit the kingdom prepared for you from the foundation of the world. Matt. 25 : 34.

And I looked, and, lo, a Lamb stood on the mount Sion, and with him an hundred forty and four thousand, having his Father's name written in their foreheads. Rev. 14 : 1.

The closing work of the earth is the sealing of the servants of God. The universe is now waiting for that work to be completed. The only thing in heaven or earth that can hinder the work of God, is a lack of spirituality on the part of His chosen people. The kingdom over which Christ will reign will be a spiritual kingdom, and while many serve God in the mind, the subjects for whom Christ is now waiting, are those who serve with the whole heart. When it is fully demonstrated that the Spirit of the Eternal Father can dwell in man, then those who have overcome as Christ overcame, will inherit the kingdom prepared from the foundation of the world. The one hundred and forty-four thousand, together with the multitude of the saved, gathered about the throne and the Lamb on Mount Zion, were shown to the prophetic eye of John. The sixth seal closes when the one hundred and forty-four thousand have received the seal of God, and are waiting for the appearance of Christ in the clouds of heaven. The opening of the seventh seal is the ushering in of eternity. "And when He had opened the seventh seal, there was silence in heaven about the space of half an hour." God's dwelling place is the center of life and the scene of constant activity. Music ever echoes from the vaults of heaven, and choruses composed of ten thousand times ten thousand of angel voices, sing the praises of the Lamb and of Him who sitteth on the throne. When the little company on earth are prepared, the sealing angel speeds back to heaven with the message that the work is done. Christ in the sanctuary above, lays aside His priestly robes, and the Lamb appears as the King of kings. Angel leaders marshal the hosts of heaven. The throne of Omnipotence is moved. God accompanies His Son to earth. Attended by myriads of angels, the Rulers of heaven and earth leave heaven empty, drawn earthward by the faithful ones whose hearts have become the abiding place of His eternal Spirit. The time for the fulfillment of the promise of the Saviour, has come. He said, "It is expedient for you that I go away." "I go to prepare a place for you. And if I go and prepare a place for you, I will come again, and receive you unto Myself; that where I am, there ye may be also." Never before has there been such a scene.

This is the cause of the silence in heaven. Those who have been torn asunder by the ruthless hand of death, meet in the air around their Deliverer. Some had been burned at the stake; others had perished in dungeons; others had been buried in the sea. Happy families, rent asunder by the cruel hand of death, are now

Lo, this is our God; we have waited for him, and he will save us: this is the Lord; we have waited for him, we will be glad and rejoice in his salvation. Isa. 25:9.

*And when he had opened the seventh seal, there was silence in heaven about the space of half an hour. Rev. 8:1.*

Isa. 42:5.
Job 33:4.

His throne was like the fiery flame, and his wheels as burning fire.

A fiery stream issued and came forth from before him: thousand thousands ministered unto him, and ten thousand times ten thousand stood before him. Dan. 7:9, 10.

And, behold, the man clothed with linen, which had the inkhorn by his side, reported the matter, saying, I have done as thou hast commanded me. Eze. 9:11.

Lev. 16:23.
Isa. 63:3.

And he hath on his vesture and on his thigh a name written, KING OF KINGS, AND LORD OF LORDS. Rev. 19:16.

Rev. 19:14.

Looking for that blessed hope, and the glorious appearing of the great God and our Saviour Jesus Christ. Titus 2:13.

When the Son of man shall come in his glory, and all the holy angels with him. Matt. 25:31.

John 16:7.
John 14:1-3.

This same Jesus, which is taken up from you into heaven, shall so come in like manner as ye have seen him go into heaven. Acts 1:9-11.

Deut. 4:32, 33.
Heb. 12:22-24.

That he might be the firstborn among many brethren. Rom. 8:29.

Rejoice, because your names are written in heaven. Luke 10:20.

Heb. 9:15.

For the Lord himself shall descend from heaven with a shout, with the voice of the archangel, and with the trump of God: and the dead in Christ shall rise first:

Then we which are alive and remain shall be caught up together with them in the clouds, to meet the Lord in the air: and so shall we ever be with the Lord.

1 Thess. 4:16, 17.

Heb. 11:33–39.

He will swallow up death in victory; and the Lord God will wipe away tears from off all faces; and the rebuke of his people shall he take away from off all the earth: for the Lord hath spoken it.

Isa. 25:8.

Rev. 8:1.

I have appointed thee a day for a year, a day for a year.

Eze. 4:6 [margin.]

1 day = 1 year.

1 hour, or 1-24 of a day = 15 days.

1-2 hour = 7 1-2 days.

Blessed are they that do his commandments, that they may have right to the tree of life, and may enter in through the gates into the city. Rev. 22:14.

Rev. 14:1.

united around Christ. Husbands and wives, parted in this life, who slept in Jesus, meet at the voice of Him who died for them. Oh, what a meeting that will be! Friends will recognize friends. All will unite in thanksgiving and praise to Him who died and rose again, and has now come to give them everlasting rest and peace. The cruel monster death has no power over them. "And God shall wipe away all tears from their eyes; and there shall be no more death, neither sorrow, nor crying, neither shall there be any more pain: for the former things are passed away." This is heavenly reunion. Together, for seven successive days, they are traveling to their glorious home. They are a company of Sabbath-keepers, and the first Sabbath in their redeemed state will be spent on the way to the city of God. This is the company that sing the response given in the twenty-fourth Psalm; and it is the same company, who, as they gather about the throne with white robes and palms of victory, join in the chorus which John heard.

And mount Sinai was altogether on a smoke, because the Lord descended upon it in fire: and the smoke thereof ascended as the smoke of a furnace, and the whole mount quaked greatly. Ex. 19:18.

The law of thy mouth is better unto me than thousands of gold and silver. Psa. 119:72.

And the Lord spake unto you out of the midst of the fire: ye heard the voice of the words, but saw no similitude; only ye heard a voice.

And he declared unto you his covenant, which he commanded you to perform, even ten commandments; and he wrote them upon two tables of stone.

Deut. 4:12, 13.

The giving of the law on Mount Sinai may be considered as a symbol of Christ's coming for the redeemed. Moses, an eyewitness of the giving of the law, says, "The Lord came from Sinai, and rose up from Seir unto them; He shined forth from Mount Paran, and He came with ten thousands of saints: from His right hand went a fiery law for them. Yea, He loved the people; all His saints are in Thy hand: and they sat down at Thy feet; every one shall receive of Thy words." Then it was that His law, the guide of life, was spoken in the hearing of all the people. Only those who have known this same fiery law, the righteousness of Jehovah, and have had its seal implanted in their foreheads, will hear the law spoken, again, by Jehovah.

Rev. 7:9.

Declaring the end from the beginning, and from ancient times the things that are not yet done, saying, My counsel shall stand, and I will do all my pleasure.
Isa. 46:10.

The prophet on Patmos was given a threefold view of events which would take place between the time in which he lived, and the time when the redeemed gather about the throne. The messages to the seven churches are ecclesiastical history, showing the spread of the religion of Jesus Christ, and the errors which crept in. The seven seals reveal the inner workings of the church,—the individual experience—and foretell the signs of Christ's coming. In the messages to the churches, Christ was seen as the Light walking in their midst: in the seals, He is the Lamb who was slain that man might live. Another phase of history, not wholly national, but having to do with nations, is revealed in the sounding of the trumpets. The sounding of the seven trumpets extends to the close of the eleventh chapter, the seventh trumpet carrying history into eternity, like the seventh church and the seventh seal. The work of the trumpets is first introduced to John in the second verse of chapter eight. Seven angels stood before God, "and to them were given seven trumpets." The trumpet, or bugle sound, is the call to war; and the history of the trumpets is one long story of war and bloodshed, but in order that men might learn that the hand of God is overruling in every army, and that He guides in every war, the story of the trumpets is left on record.

**The giving of the law.**

Hear, ye that are far off, what I have done; and, ye that are near, acknowledge my might.
Isa. 33:13.

In the midst of the seven candlesticks one like unto the Son of man. The seven candlesticks which thou sawest are the seven churches.
Rev. 1:13, 20.

Rev. 5:6.
Rev. 11:15-19.

*And I saw the seven angels which stood before God; and to them were given seven trumpets.*
*Rev. 8:2.*

And if ye go to war in your land against the enemy that oppresseth you, then ye shall blow an alarm with the trumpets. Num. 10:9.

He shall take a censer full of burning coals of fire from off the altar before the Lord, and his hands full of sweet incense beaten small, and bring it within the vail:

And he shall put the incense upon the fire before the Lord, that the cloud of the incense may cover the mercy seat that is upon the testimony, that he die not.

Lev. 16:12, 13.

Lest men, in following the details of national history, should, in the chronicle of all the distress of nations, lose sight of the work in heaven, a most precious phase of the Redeemer's work, is revealed, before the work of the trumpeters is described. Instead of introducing Christ as a sacrifice, bleeding in the presence of the heavenly beings, He is here shown as our great High Priest, ministering in the presence of the Father. John saw Him standing at the altar, having a golden censer. In the shadowy service of the earthly tabernacle, the altar of incense burned continually before the inner veil. The smoke ascended before the glory of the shekinah, which shone above the mercy seat. On the Day of Atonement, when the high priest entered into the Most Holy place, he carried with him a censer filled with precious odors, the fragrance of which was wafted by the breezes far beyond the tabernacle court. The priest entered the presence of Jehovah, bearing the sins of the people, and carrying with him their prayers. These prayers were acceptable with God because offered by faith in the righteousness of Christ. So in the heavenly court, God is enthroned and Christ stands before Him in behalf of His people. He pleads His own righteousness which is acceptable with God. There is an inexhaustible fund of perfect obedience,

**The glory of the shekinah shone above the mercy seat.**

*And another angel came and stood at the altar, having a golden censer; and there was given unto him much incense, that he should offer it with the prayers of all saints upon the golden altar which was before the throne.*

*And the smoke of the incense, which came with the prayers of the saints, ascended up before God out of the angel's hand.*

*Rev. 8:3, 4.*

which is the "much incense" which He offers. This "perfect obedience," or righteousness, meets every need, covers every case. As He was tempted in all points, yet yielded in none, so where sin abounds grace more than meets the need.

The offering which the High Priest makes, is the prayers of all saints. From the time of the fall, heart yearnings have been felt in heaven. Every prayer has been recorded in the record books; never has one soul-longing been passed by unheeded. Parents have prayed for the conversion of their children, and children have pleaded for their parents. The burden for souls in distant lands, has often rested heavily on some faithful follower of God; and although the ones prayed for may never have been conscious of the fact, a connection was made between heaven and earth, and the needy ones were within the circuit. Heaven always responds to the call of a soul; it is pledged to do so, and will fulfill the promise. So the prayers which are ascending daily are as sure to be answered as the truth is sure that God's throne is eternal. Angels are rearranging environments, changing circumstances, weaving about disinterested souls a network of influences which will some day lead to a surrender. God never forces Himself upon a single life, but there is one way to connect a man with heaven in spite of himself, and that way is through prayer.

Will none who are prayed for reject light?—Certainly they will; but when those upon whom the light has shone, do reject, they will be broken off like the dead branch of a tree, and some one else will be grafted in. Those who offered the prayers may be quiet in death, but the prayers

Rom. 5:20.
1 Sam. 1:17.

Thou tellest my wanderings: put thou my tears into thy bottle: are they not in thy book? Psa. 56:8.

The prayer of the upright is his delight. Prov. 15:8.

Thy prayers and thine alms are come up for a memorial before God. Acts 10:4.

The prayer of faith shall save the sick, and the Lord shall raise him up; and if he have committed sins, they shall be forgiven him. Jas. 5:15.

Jas. 5:17, 18.

Then the priests the Levites arose and blessed the people: and their voice was heard, and their prayer came up to his holy dwelling place, even unto heaven. 2 Chron. 30:27.

The prince of the kingdom of Persia withstood me one and twenty days: but, lo, Michael, one of the chief princes, came to help me; and I remained there with the kings of Persia. Dan. 10:13.

Behold, I stand at the door, and knock: if any man hear my voice, and open the door, I will come in to him, and will sup with him, and he with me. Rev. 3:20.

Matt. 8:34.

Well; because of unbelief they were broken off, and thou standest by faith. Be not highminded, but fear. Rom. 11:20.

It was necessary that the word of God should first have been spoken to you: but seeing ye put it from you, and judge yourselves unworthy of everlasting life, lo, we turn to the Gentiles. Acts 13:46.

Therefore also now, saith the Lord, turn ye even to me with all your heart, and with fasting, and with weeping, and with mourning:

And rend your heart, and not your garments, and turn unto the Lord your God: for he is gracious and merciful, slow to anger, and of great kindness, and repenteth him of the evil. Joel 2:12–14.

*And the angel took the censer, and filled it with fire of the altar, and cast it into the earth: and there were voices, and thunderings, and lightnings, and an earthquake.* *Rev. 8:5.*

*And the seven angels which had the seven trumpets prepared themselves to sound.* *Rev. 8:6.*

Neither is there salvation in any other: for there is none other name under heaven given among men, whereby we must be saved.
Acts 4:12.

We are all as an unclean thing, and all our righteousnesses are as filthy rags; and we all do fade as a leaf; and our iniquities, like the wind, have taken us away.
Isa. 64:6.

Whatsoever is not of faith is sin.
Rom. 14:23.

Now will I return to fight with the prince of Persia: and when I am gone forth, lo, the prince of Grecia shall come. Dan. 10:20.

The king spake, and said, Is not this great Babylon, that I have built for the house of the kingdom by the might of my power, and for the honour of my majesty?

While the word was in the king's mouth, there fell a voice from heaven, saying, O king Nebuchadnezzar, to thee it is spoken; The kingdom is departed from thee.
Dan. 4:30, 31.

To all that be in Rome, beloved of God, called to be saints: Grace to you and peace from God our Father, and the Lord Jesus Christ.

First, I thank my God through Jesus Christ for you all, that your faith is spoken of throughout the whole world. Rom. 1:7, 8.

Jer. 17:24–27.
Jer. 38:17–20.

are lodged on heaven's altar, and will be answered before the censer is thrown down.

Thus John sees Christ pleading for sinners, while the sealing work is going on in the earth. When the angel returns to heaven with the message that all are sealed, Christ casts the censer to the earth, and the thunderings, the lightnings, and the earthquake, proclaim that the end is at hand. Having seen Christ as man's intercessor, John follows the work of the seven angels which had the seven trumpets.

Belief in the imputed righteousness of Christ, is the only means of salvation for man. Self-righteousness was the cause of Satan's fall, and it has ever been the studied plan of his satanic majesty to lead men from faith in the righteousness of Christ to a faith in their own works. When this is accomplished, destruction is inevitable. To an individual this means the loss of eternal life; to a church, it means the withdrawing of the Spirit of God; to a nation, it means subjugation by some stronger nation. This lesson was taught by Nebuchadnezzar, the Babylonian monarch. When he walked in his palace, saying with lordly pride, "Is not this great Babylon, that I have built?" destruction waited at the door. The same truth has been taught in the downfall of every nation which has risen to prominence in past ages. God, in the voice of the first four trumpets, taught this lesson to the Roman Empire.

Rome, the universal kingdom at the time of Christ's first advent, was wonderfully blessed with a knowledge of the truth, but in proportion to the greatness of her privileges, so her fall was terrible.

In the days of Constantine the empire was divided, Rome being the western capital, and Constantinople the eastern. At the death of Constantine, three divisions were made in order to seat each one of his three sons on a throne; this triple division is recognized throughout the trumpet history. Of these divisions, Italy, or the Western Roman Empire, was known as one third. While the three divisions are referred to, the first division into an eastern and western empire, is also preserved, until the capture of Constantinople by the Turks.

For the kingdom is the Lord's: and he is the governor among the nations. Psa. 22:28.

When the Most High divided to the nations their inheritance, when he separated the sons of Adam, he set the bounds of the people. Deut. 32:8.

**Ancient effigies of Constantine and his wife Fausta.**

"The first angel sounded, and there followed hail and fire mingled with blood, and they were cast upon the earth." This is a most concise statement of a long series of terrible events; but brief as it is, the most forcible language is chosen; hail and fire are mingled with blood and cast upon the earth. As early as the days of Constantine, hordes of barbarians pressed upon the frontiers of the Roman territory. Europe had, from prehistoric times, been subject to an influx of barbarians, and a spirit of emigration periodically swept like an undulating wave, over all the continent. When pressure came on the eastern frontier from the Scythians of northern Asia, the more western tribes were forced to seek broader fields in the populous southern countries. Largely because of this pressure, Constantine divided the empire, in order that there might be greater strength to resist invasions. The time came when all the resources which Rome could muster, were insufficient to repel the invaders.

*The first angel sounded, and there followed hail and fire mingled with blood, and they were cast upon the earth: and the third part of trees was burnt up, and all green grass was burnt up.* *Rev. 8:7.*

An ungodly man diggeth up evil: and in his lips there is as a burning fire. Prov. 16:27.

The heathen raged, the kingdoms were moved. Psa. 46:6.

The lords of the heathen have broken down the principal plants thereof, they are come even unto Jazer, they wandered through the wilderness: her branches are stretched out, they are gone over the sea. Isa. 16:8.

The adversary hath spread out his hand upon all her pleasant things: for she hath seen that the heathen entered into her sanctuary, whom thou didst command that they should not enter into thy congregation. Lam. 1:10.

Except the Lord build the house, they labour in vain that build it: except the Lord keep the city, the watchman waketh but in vain. Psa. 127:1.

For their feet run to evil, and make haste to shed blood. Prov. 1:16.

Many seek the ruler's favour; but every man's judgment cometh from the Lord. Prov. 29:26.

There is a generation, whose teeth are as swords, and their jaw teeth as knives, to devour the poor from off the earth, and the needy from among men. Prov. 30:14.

If thou seest the oppression of the poor, and violent perverting of judgment and justice in a province, marvel not at the matter: for he that is higher than the highest regardeth; and there be higher than they. Eccl. 5:8.

But if a man live many years, and rejoice in them all; yet let him remember the days of darkness; for they shall be many. All that cometh is vanity. Eccl. 11:8.

The wrath of a king is as messengers of death. Prov. 16:14.

All thy strong holds shall be like fig trees with the firstripe figs: if they be shaken, they shall even fall into the mouth of the eater. Nahum 3:12.

In the year 395, the Goths, with their renowned leader, Alaric, invaded the Eastern Roman Empire. As they crossed the Danube, the dividing line between the territory of the Romans and the wilds of Germany, in the middle of a winter of uncommon severity, they came like the hail from the north, and one of the Roman poets has said, "They rolled their ponderous wagons over the broad and icy back of the indignant river." Alaric was no mean leader; but bold, artful, and more than a match for any general in the degenerate Roman army. For a number of years, the Goths remained in the eastern division of the empire; part of the time at peace, at other times, at variance with the emperor. In the year 408 Alaric descended upon Italy. He hastily passed the Alps and the Po, pillaged the cities of northern Italy, and advanced a constantly increasing army to the city of Ravenna, where the pusillanimous emperor had his capital. Without meeting any resistance, he proceeded along the Adriatic until he came near Rome. Alaric took Ostia, the port of Rome at the mouth of the Tiber, and demanded unconditional surrender of the city itself. The senate yielded without reluctance, and Alaric placed the purple robe of the emperor on Attalus, the prefect of the city. Rome, the proud monarchy, was in the hands of a barbarian army, which could crown its emperor at will and insult its senate at pleasure. Later, Attalus, the tool of Alaric, was degraded in the presence of the people; his diadem was taken from him, and as if to offer insult to injury, the haughty barbarian sent the ensigns of royalty to Honorius, the real emperor, who was trembling behind the fortifications of Ravenna. Folly and imprudence provoked the Goths, and the city of Rome was awakened one night in the year 410 by the tremendous trumpet of the barbarian soldiers. Rome was ravaged. The gold and the silver, the silver plate and costly furniture from Roman palaces, were loaded on the Gothic wagons. Fire and bloodshed filled the city with terror. For six days the city was in the hands of the invaders. At the end of that time, "at the head of an army, encumbered with rich and weighty spoils, their intrepid leader advanced along the Appian Way into the southern provinces of Italy, destroying whatever dared to oppose his passage, and contenting himself with the plunder of the unresisting country." On the death of Alaric, in 410, he was succeeded by his brother-in-law, Adolphus, who allied himself with the Romans; he assumed the character of a Roman general, and later, married the sister of Honorius, the emperor. Thus, the conquest of the Goths over the weakened Roman Empire, was complete.

"The second angel sounded, and as it were a great mountain burning with fire was cast into the sea: and the third part of the sea became blood." The power here brought to view is distinguished from the Goths by the fact that its force was felt upon the sea instead of on the land. While Honorius, who had experienced the invasion of the Goths, was still nominally the emperor of Rome, the Vandals were making their presence felt in Spain. They were a horde of barbarians who had come from the northeast and for a time halted in the western provinces of Rome. In 428 the terrible Genseric be-

The nations shall see and be confounded at all their might: they shall lay their hand upon their mouth, their ears shall be deaf. Mic. 7:16.

Woe to him that coveteth an evil covetousness to his house, that he may set his nest on high, that he may be delivered from the power of evil!

Thou hast consulted shame to thy house by cutting off many people, and hast sinned against thy soul. Hab. 2:9, 10.

Woe to him that buildeth a town with blood, and stablisheth a city by iniquity! Hab. 2:12.

*And the second angel sounded, and as it were a great mountain burning with fire was cast into the sea: and the third part of the sea became blood. Rev. 8:8.*

There is a vanity which is done upon the earth; that there be just men, unto whom it happeneth according to the work of the wicked; again, there be wicked men, to whom it happeneth according to the work of the righteous: I said that this also is vanity. Eccl. 8:14.

This is an evil among all things that are done under the sun, that there is one event unto all: yea, also the heart of the sons of men is full of evil, and madness is in their heart while they live, and after that they go to the dead. Eccl. 9:3.

Woe to the bloody city! it is all full of lies and robbery; the prey departeth not;

The noise of a whip, and the noise of the rattling of the wheels, and of the pransing horses, and of the jumping chariots.

The horseman lifteth up both the bright sword and the glittering spear: and there is a multitude of slain, and a great number of carcases; and there is none end of their corpses; they stumble upon their corpses. Nahum 3:1–3.

Yea, they shall not be planted, yea, they shall not be sown: yea; their stock shall not take root in the earth: and he shall also blow upon them, and they shall wither, and the whirlwind shall take them away as stubble. Isa. 40:24.

Behold, the nations are as a drop of a bucket, and are counted as the small dust of the balance: behold, he taketh up the isles as a very little thing.

And Lebanon is not sufficient to burn, nor the beasts thereof sufficient for a burnt offering.

All nations before him are as nothing; and they are counted to him less than nothing, and vanity. Isa. 40:15–17.

Thou art become guilty in thy blood that thou hast shed; and hast defiled thyself in thine idols which thou hast made; and thou hast caused thy days to draw near, and art come even unto thy years: therefore have I made thee a reproach unto the heathen, and a mocking to all countries.

Those that be near, and those that be far from thee, shall mock thee, which art infamous and much vexed. Eze. 22:4, 5.

Yet was she carried away, she went into captivity: her young children also were dashed in pieces at the top of all the streets: and they cast lots for her honourable men, and all her great men were bound in chains. Nahum 3:10.

became their leader, and at once the Vandals assumed the aggressive. Of Genseric it is said, "His slow and cautious speech seldom declared the deep purposes of his soul; he disdained to imitate the luxury of the vanquished; but he indulged the sterner passions of anger and revenge. The ambition of Genseric was without bounds and without scruples." "The experience of navigation, and perhaps, the prospect of Africa" placed the Vandals on the sea. They were at first invited into Africa by Count Boniface, one of the Roman generals. The fatal step had been taken. The enemy once in Africa, Rome was confronted by a most formidable foe. It was in 431 that the Vandals crossed the Straits of Gibraltar. A few years later, they were sole possessors of Carthage and northern Africa. Rome could ill afford to lose her African possessions; for they furnished both wealth and food to the cities of Italy. Nevertheless Genseric and the Vandals grew strong on the southern shore of the Mediterranean. Soon their borders were too narrow, and the success of their fleet added Sicily and other places to the barbarians. In June of the year 455, A. D., Genseric and his Vandals disembarked at the mouth of the Tiber, and Rome was again at the mercy of the barbarians. The pillage lasted fourteen days and nights; and all that yet remained of public or private wealth, of sacred or profane treasure, was diligently transported to the vessels of Genseric The Empress Eudoxia, with her two daughters, was compelled as captive to follow the haughty Vandal. Thousands of Romans were likewise transported as slaves to the capital of the Vandal empire. "Their distress," says Gibbon, "was aggravated by the unfeeling barbarians, who, in the division of the booty, separated the wives from their husbands, and the children from their parents." The sack of Rome by the Goths had been a terrible calamity; but that by the Vandals, forty-five years later, was still worse. However, the devastation of the city itself was but a small part of the destructive work of these barbarians. The prophet was shown a great mountain burning with fire, cast into the sea. It was like a mighty stone cast into the waters, causing wave after wave to beat against the defenseless shores; or like an active volcano in the midst of the sea which periodically caused the waters to boil. This agrees with the description of the inroads of the Vandals. "In the spring of each year [between 461 and 467] they equipped a formidable navy in the port of Carthage; and Genseric himself, though in a very advanced age, still commanded in person the most important expeditions. . . . The Vandals repeatedly visited the coasts of Spain, Liguria, Tuscany, Campania, Lucania, Bruttium, Apulia, Calabria, Venetia, Dalmatia, Epirus, Greece, and Sicily. . . . Their arms spread desolation and terror, from the columns of Hercules to the mouth of the Nile." They took with them horses, so that their terror spread inland from the port at which the fleet landed the

They shall take up a lamentation for thee, and say to thee How art thou destroyed, that wast inhabited of seafaring men the renowned city, which wast strong in the sea, she and her inhabitants, which cause their terror to be on all that haunt it! Eze. 26:17, 18.

Thou shalt ascend and come like a storm, thou shalt be like a cloud to cover the land, thou, and all thy bands, and many people with thee.

**The ruins of Carthage.**

Thus saith the Lord God; It shall also come to pass, that at the same time shall things come into thy mind, and thou shalt think an evil thought:

And thou shalt say, I will go up to the land of unwalled villages; I will go to them that are at rest, that dwell safely, all of them dwelling without walls, and having neither bars nor gates,

To take a spoil, and to take a prey; to turn thine hand upon the desolate places that are now inhabited, and upon the people that are gathered out of the nations, which have gotten cattle and goods, that dwell in the midst of the land. Eze. 38:9-12.

Shall not all these take up a parable against him, and a taunting proverb against him, and say, Woe to him that increaseth that which is not his! how long? and to him that ladeth himself with thick clay!

Shall they not rise up suddenly that shall bite thee, and awake that shall vex thee, and thou shalt be for booties unto them? Hab. 2:6, 7.

That they may do evil with both hands earnestly, the prince asketh, and the judge asketh for a reward; and the great man, he uttereth his mischievous desire: so they wrap it up.

The best of them is as a brier: the most upright is sharper than a thorn hedge: the day of thy watchmen and thy visitation cometh; now shall be their perplexity. Micah 7:3, 4.

savage warriors. So hidden were the designs of Genseric that the Roman world never knew where to look for the next attack. As wealth and an abundance of plunder were the objects of their greed, the Vandals usually avoided fortified cities.

Rome was at last aroused to take active measures against her constant and most persistent enemy. She spent months in preparation of a fleet. The forces of the East and the West united in invading Africa. The Roman army stood under the walls of Carthage. Genseric asked and obtained a five days' truce. The wind became favorable to the warrior of the Mediterranean. His vessels were manned with the bravest of the Vandals and Moors, who in the darkness of the night, towed a large number of ships loaded with combustibles, into the very midst of the Roman fleet. The fire spread from vessel to vessel. "The noise of the wind, the crackling of the flames, the dissonant cries of the soldiers and mariners, who could neither command nor obey, increased the

*And the third part of the creatures which were in the sea, and had life, died; and the third part of the ships were destroyed. Rev. 8:9.*

**The fire spread from vessel to vessel.**

Notwithstanding the land shall be desolate because of them that dwell therein, for the fruit of their doings. Micah 7:13.

They shall come all for violence: their faces shall sup up as the east wind, and they shall gather the captivity as the sand.

And they shall scoff at the kings, and the princes shall be a scorn unto them: they shall deride every strong hold; for they shall heap dust, and take it. Hab. 1:9, 10.

horror of the nocturnal tumult." Many who might have escaped the flames, met death at the hands of the Vandal warriors. Historians state that eleven hundred Roman vessels were destroyed. The burning mountain had fallen upon the sea.

Genseric was again recognized as the tyrant of the sea. He lived to see the final extinction of the Roman Empire of the West in 476. His was the work which was permitted to be done at the sounding of the second trumpet, in that nation where apostasy replaced the true worship of God, and where the mystery of iniquity was fast coming into power.

But the end was not yet. "The third angel sounded, and there fell a great star from heaven, burning as it were a lamp." For nearly one hundred years previous to the final downfall of Rome, the Huns, one of the wildest of the Scythian tribes, had pressed upon the empire, spreading themselves from the Volga to the Danube. For a time they commanded the alternative of peace or war, with both the eastern and western divisions of the empire. In the days of Ætius, a general of the West, sixty thousand Huns marched to the confines of Italy; but retreated when paid the sum which they cared to demand. Theodosius, the emperor of the East, bought peace by paying an annual tribute of three hundred and fifty pounds of gold, and bestowing the title of general upon the king of the Huns. There was still a senate at Rome, and it purchased peace of the Huns. This was a part of the "wormwood" which Rome was caused to drink. In 433 Attila and his brother became joint rulers of the barbarians, and in a treaty

They make the king glad with their wickedness, and the princes with their lies. Hosea 7:3.

I have written to him the great things of my law, but they were counted as a strange thing. Hosea 8:12.

*And the third angel sounded, and there fell a great star from heaven, burning as it were a lamp, and it fell upon the third part of the rivers, and upon the fountains of waters. Rev. 8:10.*

For thus saith the Lord God; Because thou hast clapped thine hands, and stamped with the feet, and rejoiced in heart with all thy despite against the land of Israel;
Behold, therefore I will stretch out mine hand upon thee, and will deliver thee for a spoil to the heathen; and I will cut thee off from the people, and I will cause thee to perish out of the countries: I will destroy thee; and thou shalt know that I am the Lord. Eze. 25:6, 7.

Yea also, because he transgresseth by wine, he is a proud man, neither keepeth at home, who enlargeth his desire as hell, and is as death, and cannot be satisfied, but gathereth unto him all nations, and heapeth unto him all people. Hab. 2:5.

Strangers have devoured his strength, and he knoweth it not: yea, gray hairs are here and there upon him, yet he knoweth not. Hosea 7:9.

*And the name of the star is called Wormwood: and the third part of the waters became wormwood; and many men died of the waters, because they were made bitter Rev. 8:11.*

> The house of the wicked shall be overthrown. Prov. 14:11.

> He shall lean upon his house, but it shall not stand: he shall hold it fast, but it shall not endure. Job. 8:15.

> The lot is cast into the lap; but the whole disposing thereof is of the Lord. Prov. 16:33.

> They were haughty, and committed abomination before me: therefore I took them away as I saw good. Eze. 16:50.

> I will pour out mine indignation upon thee, I will blow against thee in the fire of my wrath, and deliver thee into the hand of brutish men, and skilful to destroy.
> Thou shalt be for fuel to the fire; thy blood shall be in the midst of the land; thou shalt be no more remembered: for I the Lord have spoken it. Eze. 21:31, 32.

> Ye have ploughed wickedness, ye have reaped iniquity; ye have eaten the fruit of lies: because thou didst trust in thy way, in the multitude of thy mighty men.
> Therefore shall a tumult arise among thy people, and all thy fortresses shall be spoiled, as Shalman spoiled Beth-arbel in the day of battle: the mother was dashed in pieces upon her children. Hosea 10:13, 14.

with the emperor, the Huns "dictated the conditions of peace; each condition was an insult on the majesty of the empire. Besides the freedom of a safe and plentiful market on the banks of the Danube, they required that the annual contribution should be augmented from three hundred and fifty pounds of gold to seven hundred pounds of gold; that a fine, or ransom, of eight pieces of gold should be paid for every Roman captive who had escaped from his barba-

**Ruins of the Forum.**

rian master; that the emperor should renounce all treaties and engagements with the enemies of the Huns; and that all the fugitives who had taken refuge in the court, or provinces of Theodosius, should be delivered to the justice of their offended sovereign." Thus was the Roman Empire made to realize that its power was gone, and that the proud Romans were subject to the most cruel of all barbarians. This was "wormwood" indeed.

After concluding such a treaty with the emperor of the East, Attila gathered his hordes and marched into Gaul. Here he was defeated by the Visigoths and the Huns retreated to northern Italy. One barbarian horde might repel another, but there was little danger of defeat when once within the confines of Italy. Attila crossed the Alps, "the fountain of waters." Aquileia, the richest and most populous city of the Adriatic, fell, and the succeeding generation could scarcely discover the ruins, so complete was the overthrow. Many cities were reduced to heaps of stones and ashes. Milan, the city of the royal palace, submitted. Rome was the next point of attack, but the city escaped the hand of Attila, its salvation being purchased by the gift of the princess Honoria, with an immense dowry. The bitterness of the portion which Rome drank is well described as wormwood. The "star" which fell upon the fountains of waters, retreated to his home in Hungary, where his light was extinguished.

Attila, king of the Huns, died in 453. His light went out like the snuffing of a candle. He was a lamp burning on the earth. But Rome was not delivered from her enemies. The Vandal king, Genseric, was in the height of his power, and continued to ravage the southern coasts until the final overthrow, about twelve years later.

Roman power was lost, although in name the Western Empire still existed. A Roman, Attalus, was seated on the throne by Alaric, the Goth, and recognized as sovereign by the rightful heir to the throne. The Vandals tormented the government until life was a burden. In order to complete the overthrow, nothing remained to be done, except to seat a barbarian on the throne in the place of the royal family.

There shall the fire devour thee; the sword shall cut thee off, it shall eat thee up like the cankerworm: make thyself many as the cankerworm, make thyself many as the locusts.
Nahum 3:15.

Because thou hast spoiled many nations, all the remnant of the people shall spoil thee; because of men's blood, and for the violence of the land, of the city, and of all that dwell therein. Hab. 2:8.

In the time when thou shalt be broken by the seas in the depths of the waters thy merchandise and all thy company in the midst of thee shall fall. Eze. 27:34.

Yea, I will make many people amazed at thee, and their kings shall be horribly afraid for thee, when I shall brandish my sword before them; and they shall tremble at every moment, every man for his own life, in the day of thy fall.
Eze. 32:10.

***And the fourth angel sounded, and the third part of the sun was smitten, and the third part of the moon, and the third part of the stars; so as the third part of them was darkened, and the day shone not for a third part of it, and the night likewise.***
***Rev. 8:12.***

**Attila.**

I have set the point of the sword against all their gates, that their heart may faint, and their ruins be multiplied: ah! it is made bright, it is wrapped up for the slaughter. Eze. 21:15.

In thee have we taken gifts to shed blood; thou hast taken usury and increase, and thou hast greedily gained of thy neighbors by extortion, and hast forgotten me, saith the Lord God. Eze. 22:12.

Ye which rejoice in a thing of nought, which say, Have we not taken to us horns by our own strength? Amos 6:13.

For the rich men thereof are full of violence, and the inhabitants thereof have spoken lies, and their tongue is deceitful in their mouth. Micah 6:12.

Behold, therefore I will stretch out mine hand upon thee, and will deliver thee for a spoil to the heathen; and I will cut thee off from the people, and I will cause thee to perish out of the centuries: I will destroy thee: and thou shalt know that I am the Lord. Eze. 25:7.

"The fourth angel sounded, and the third part of the sun was smitten, and the third part of the moon, and the third part of the stars." The prophetic history given under the fourth trumpet, represents the dense darkness that would exist if the sun, moon, and stars all refused to emit light. Its fulfillment was the extinction of the light of Western Rome.

During the last twenty years of the existence of the Western Empire, nine emperors had successively disappeared. The third from the last was murdered, and his successor, Nepos, was expelled. Orestes was a Pannonian by birth, and for years a faithful follower of Attila, the Hun. On the death of Attila he entered the service of the Roman princes. Step by step he advanced in the army until he was granted the title of patrician by Nepos, and made master-general of the troops. On the expulsion of Nepos, Orestes was offered the purple, but refused it; consenting, however, that his son, Augustulus, should become emperor of the West. Augustulus was a mere tool in the hands of the numerous barbarians who were now in Italy and upon her borders. The confederate tribes demanded one-third of the land of Italy, and when the request was refused, they united their forces under the leadership of Odoacer, the son of a barbarian, who had himself followed the great leader of the Huns, and then accepted a position in the Roman army. He was noted among the barbarians for his courage and ability. By the confederate tribes, he was saluted as the king of Italy. Augustulus offered his resignation, which was accepted by the Senate. This was its last act of obedience to its prince. Zeno, ruler of the

East, was recognized as sole emperor, and he awarded to Odoacer the title of "Patrician of the Diocese of Italy."

"Odoacer was the first barbarian who reigned in Italy over a people who had once asserted their just superiority above the rest of mankind." He reigned fourteen years, from 476 to 490, A. D., but the Roman Empire of the West was a thing of the past. The territory once held by the ruling kingdom of the world, was divided among the barbarians who had assisted in its overthrow.

Rome was now broken into fragments, and the ten divisions presented to the prophet Daniel were each given power. As iron and miry clay refuse to unite, so the fragments of the Western Roman Empire will remain separate until the end of time. With the year 476, which marks the fall of Rome, begins the history of the Middle Ages. Within the next few years every obstacle was cleared away, and the papacy had a clear road to the throne. Odoacer was by faith an Arian, and his kingdom, that of the Heruli, was the first of the horns, according to Daniel 7:8, to be plucked up by the little horn, which exalted itself, and spoke great words against the Most High.

In the distress caused by the numerous invasions of the barbarians, the bishop of the Roman diocese had acted well his part. When nations fell, and emperors ceased to grant protection, men sought safety in the shadow of the church. Daily the power of the bishop increased, and from the decaying ruins of ancient Rome, the papacy arose. The church had the name of life, but it was dead. To the one who followed the Saviour, He appeared as the High Priest in

As they gather silver, and brass, and iron, and lead, and tin, into the midst of the furnace, to blow the fire upon it, to melt it; so will I gather you in mine anger and in my fury, and I will leave you there, and melt you.

Yea, I will gather you, and blow upon you in the fire of my wrath, and ye shall be melted in the midst thereof.

As silver is melted in the midst of the furnace, so shall ye be melted in the midst thereof; and ye shall know that I the Lord have poured out my fury upon you.

Eze. 22:20–22.

Whereas thou sawest the feet and toes, part of potters' clay, and part of iron, the kingdom shall be divided; but there shall be in it of the strength of the iron, forasmuch as thou sawest the iron mixed with miry clay.

And as the toes of the feet were part of iron, and part of clay, so the kingdom shall be partly strong, and partly broken.

And whereas thou sawest iron mixed with miry clay, they shall mingle themselves with the seed of men: but they shall not cleave one to another, even as iron is not mixed with clay. Dan. 2:41–43.

Remember ye not, that, when I was yet with you, I told you these things?

And now ye know what withholdeth that he might be revealed in his time.

For the mystery of iniquity doth already work: only he who now letteth will let, until he be taken out of the way. 2 Thess. 2:5–7.

I considered the horns, and, behold, there came up among them another little horn, before whom there were three of the first horns plucked up by the roots: and, behold, in this horn were eyes like the eyes of man, and a mouth speaking great things. Dan. 7:8.

Rev. 13:2.

Whosoever will, let him take the water of life freely. Rev. 22:17.

I will shake all nations.
Hag. 2:7.

There shall be a time of trouble, such as never was since there was a nation even to that same time: and at that time thy people shall be delivered, every one that shall be found written in the book.
Dan. 12:1.

And he shall speak great words against the most High, and shall wear out the saints of the most High, and think to change times and laws: and they shall be given into his hand until a time and times and the dividing of time. Dan. 7:25.

*And I beheld, and heard an angel flying through the midst of heaven, saying with a loud voice, Woe, woe, woe, to the inhabiters of the earth by reason of the other voices of the trumpet of the three angels, which are yet to sound!*
*Rev. 8:13.*

His lips are full of indignation, and his tongue as a devouring fire:
And his breath, as an overflowing stream, shall reach to the midst of the neck, to sift the nations with the sieve of vanity.
Isa. 30:27, 28.

1 Tim. 4:1-3.
2 Tim. 3:1-8.

the heavenly court, offering His own righteousness to all of every nationality who would accept.

The fall of Rome was a mighty shaking up of nations, divinely symbolized by the trumpets blown by angels who stand in the presence of God. Its fall is a type of the time of trouble, preceding the final destruction of the world. God loved His people then, and through the darkness, His hand was leading. So it will be at the sounding of the seventh trumpet. The history of the fourth trumpet evidently covers the events of a number of years; for the next time the Roman Empire is brought to view, it is presented as the persecuting power which bore sway a thousand two hundred and three score years.

When the fourth angel had sounded, John beheld another "angel flying through the midst of heaven, saying with a loud voice, Woe, woe, woe, to the inhabiters of the earth by reason of the other voices of the trumpet of the three angels, which are yet to sound!"

Barbarian warfare is terrible; the crushing of a nation calls out the armory of heaven, and angels veil their faces from the scenes of cruelty and bloodshed. But the false doctrines which crush the sons of God, and the errors which hide the righteousness of Christ, are especially designated as woes. To these woes the student of prophecy is next introduced.

# CHAPTER X.

## THE BEGINNING OF WOES.

The struggle between truth and error has always been a bitter one. No great light has ever shone upon the earth for which the arch-enemy has not had a counterfeit, containing enough of the truth to make it palatable to those whose taste for spiritual food is not the keenest; and yet, with all this, God has used these very deceptions, to reveal the greatness of His love. The student of prophecy should bear in mind that before John was allowed to hear the trumpets, Christ was presented as full of righteousness.

And there was war in heaven: Michael and his angels fought against the dragon; and the dragon fought and his angels. Rev. 12:7.

Heb. 12:4.
Luke 2:32.
Matt. 24:24.
2 Cor. 11:14, 15.
2 Thess. 2:10–12.
Prov. 4:18, 19.
Rev. 8:3.
Matt. 22:11, 12.
Rom. 4:5–7.
Matt. 6:22, 23.
Mark 4:4, 14.
Psa. 19:4.
Rom. 10:18.
Rom. 1:19, 20.
Acts 13:47.

God plans from eternity; and while Satan worked hard for the utter destruction of all things, yet the guiding hand of Jehovah still controlled affairs; and preceding the setting up of the papacy, the eye of the Infinite One saw those who would give the last message to the world and see the triumph of truth. Thus

He said, It is a light thing that thou shouldest be my servant to raise up the tribes of Jacob, and to restore the preserved of Israel: I will also give thee for a light to the Gentiles, that thou mayest be my salvation unto the end of the earth. Isa. 49:6.

Because thy rage against me and thy tumult is come up into mine ears, therefore will I put my hook in thy nose, and my bridle in thy lips, and I will turn thee back by the way by which thou camest.
2 Kings 19:28.

Isa. 37:29.

I say unto you, That many shall come from the east and west, and shall sit down with Abraham, and Isaac, and Jacob, in the kingdom of heaven. Matt. 8:11.

Jesus knew from the beginning who they were that believed not, and who should betray him.
John 6:64.

Isa. 37:26–29.

While they promise them liberty, they themselves are the servants of corruption: for of whom a man is overcome, of the same is he brought in bondage. 2 Pet. 2:19.

I will deliver them to be removed into all the kingdoms of the earth for their hurt, to be a reproach and a proverb, a taunt and a curse, in all places whither I shall drive them. Jer. 24:9, 10.

***And the fifth angel sounded, and I saw a star fall from heaven unto the earth: and to him was given the key of the bottomless pit.***
***Rev. 9:1.***

Eze. 26:20.

Eze. 39:2–4.

The Gentiles shall see thy righteousness, and all kings thy glory: and thou shalt be called by a new name, which the mouth of the Lord shall name. Isa. 62:1, 2.

The princes are rebellious, and companions of thieves: every one loveth gifts, and followeth after rewards: they judge not the fatherless, neither doth the cause of the widow come unto them.
Isa. 1:23.

when the "mystery of iniquity" thought to reign supreme, it found that the seed of truth, which would inevitably cause its overthrow, had already been planted by God, in the Western Empire. Events which took place in the eastern third of the world, and which finally centered about Constantinople, the capital of the Eastern Empire, show, with equal clearness, the wonderful foresight and wisdom of the Saviour. Satan may be rich in resources, but the God of heaven knows a thousand ways to thwart his every scheme. The history of the fifth trumpet is another exemplification of this fact.

The barbarian hordes had spent their strength in the overthrow of the Western Empire, and had, in the course of a few years, laid aside their savage ways, and assumed the manners of the conquered people with whom they lived. But the Eastern Empire was as full of weakness and pollution as the Western, and its downfall was just as certain, although it came in an entirely different way. "The fifth angel sounded, and I saw a star fall from heaven unto the earth: and to him was given the key of the bottomless pit." The north of Asia had sent forth its hordes of barbarians, who passed like waves of the sea over the entire continent of Europe, even to the British Isles. From the central portion of western Asia, the Gospel was spread as the life and light of all mankind.

Near the close of the sixth century there was born in Mecca, of the princes of Arabia, a man who claimed direct descent from Ishmael, the son of Abraham. This man was Mohammed, the son of Abdallah, and the founder of a faith, which, to-day has many thousand adherents. "Arabia," says Gibbon, "was free; the adjacent kingdoms were shaken by the storms of conquest and tyranny, and persecuted sects fled to the happy land where they might profess what they believed, and practice what they professed." In Arabia were gathered, at this time, Christians, Jews, Persian fire-worshipers, and representatives of all sects and beliefs.

But were mingled among the heathen, and learned their works. Psa. 106 : 35-42.

Therefore speak unto them and say unto them, Thus saith the Lord God; Every man of the house of Israel that setteth up his idols in his heart, and putteth the stumbling-block of his iniquity before his face, and cometh to the prophet; I the Lord will answer him that cometh according to the multitude of his idols;

Mohammed was acquainted with them all as he mingled in the thoroughfares of Mecca, and in his journeys to Damascus, and seaports of Syria.

**Flight from Mecca.**

Mohammed was of a serious mind, and it was his custom to retire one month each year to a cave, a few miles from Mecca, where he gave himself to fasting and prayer. On his return from one of these seasons of seclusion he announced his belief in one God, and that Mohammed was the prophet of God. This was the beginning of Islamism. The prophet first taught in his own family, and gradually gained a number of converts. His flight, from Mecca, called the *Hegira*, [A. D. 622] is the era of his glory, and the date from which the Mohammedans compute their time. In opposition to the forms and ceremonies of the numerous worshipers who congregated at Mecca, and to the professed Christians who revered the images of saints and martyrs, the simple principles of the new religious leader called for prayer, fasting, and alms. Five times a day, his followers all over the world turn their eyes toward Mecca, and lift their hearts in prayer.

That I may take the house of Israel in their own heart, because they are all estranged from me through their idols.

And if the prophet be deceived when he hath spoken a thing, I the Lord have deceived that prophet, and I will stretch out my hand upon him, and will destroy him from the midst of my people Israel.

And they shall bear the punishment of their iniquity: the punishment of the prophet shall be even as the punishment of him that seeketh unto him. Eze. 14 : 4-10.

The way of peace they know not; and there is no judgment in their goings: they have made them crooked paths: whosoever goeth therein shall not know peace.
Isa. 59:3-8.

Wherefore have we fasted, say they, and thou seest not? wherefore have we afflicted our soul, and thou takest no knowledge? Behold, in the day of your fast ye find pleasure, and exact all your labours.

**Mohammed.**

Behold, ye fast for strife and debate, and to smite with the fist of wickedness: ye shall not fast as ye do this day, to make your voice to be heard on high. Isa. 58:3-7.

There came forth a spirit, and stood before the Lord, and said, I will persuade him.

And the Lord said unto him, Wherewith? And he said, I will go forth, and I will be a lying spirit in the mouth of all his prophets. And he said, Thou shalt persuade him, and prevail also: go forth, and do so. 1 Kings 22:21, 22.

Paradise, where the pleasures of this life are enjoyed in an exaggerated form throughout eternity, is the reward held out to the faithful. Wherever the followers of Mohammed met the foreigner, there was a single rule of action. "Confess," said the Mussulman, "that there is but one God, and that Mohammed is His prophet; pay tribute, or choose death." The atoning blood of Christ was spurned. Jesus was a prophet, they thought; but He, like Moses, was inferior to Mohammed. The Bible of the Christians was replaced by the Koran. True, the simple faith and austere practices of the Mohammedans were, to all outward appearances, a reform over the apostasy of the Greek Catholics; but in the rejection of Christ, the Mohammedan had nothing in which to place his faith, save in his own ability to obtain righteousness by works. So while the papacy was exalting man in the West, and perfecting its system of self-righteousness, the new religion of the East was propagating, under another name, the same device of the devil to destroy the souls of men.

The Arabs, or the Saracens, had never exercised any influence in the earth. In the history of nations, these free men of the desert had passed with scarcely a notice. Mohammedanism united the scattered tribes, and sent them forth as the conquerors of nations. The rapid progress which attended the Saracen arms was due, in great measure, to the strife between the Romans and Chosroes, the head of the modern Persian Empire. This strife resulted in the fall of the latter. Modern Persia had stood as a barrier wall, keeping in check the power of Mohammed; but when that power fell, the barrier was gone, the "bottomless pit" opened, and the Saracens deluged the world. When the "bottomless pit" was opened, there arose a smoke which hid the face of the sun. The figure is a strong one, representing the darkening effect of Mohammedanism, as it spread over the face of the earth.

*And he opened the bottomless pit; and there arose a smoke out of the pit, as the smoke of a great furnace; and the sun and the air were darkened by reason of the smoke of the pit. Rev. 9:2.*

*And there came out of the smoke locusts upon the earth: and unto them was given power, as the scorpions of the earth have power. Rev. 9:3.*

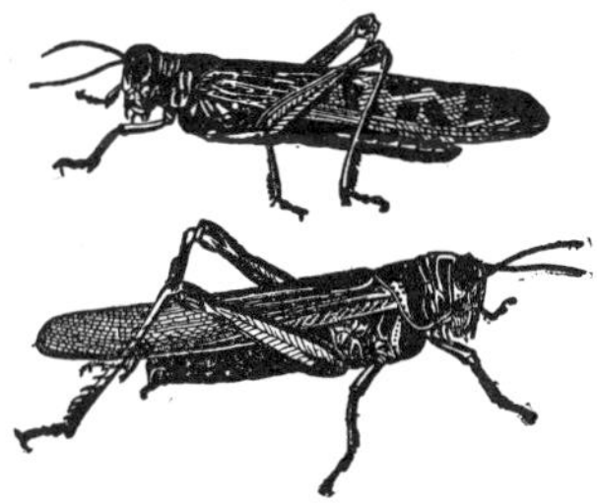

**"The locusts have no king, yet go they forth all of them by bands."**

This same characteristic is emphasized in the symbols used throughout the history. "There came out of the smoke locusts upon the earth." The Saracens themselves are called locusts by the prophet John, and the doctrine which impelled their actions was as a dense smoke, issuing out of a furnace. The work of these locust-like warriors is described in the eighth plague, sent upon the land of Egypt in the days when Pharaoh refused to let Israel go. "I will bring the locusts into thy coast: and they shall cover the face of the earth, that one cannot be able to see the earth: and they shall eat the residue of that which is escaped, . . . and shall eat every tree which groweth for you out of the field: and they shall fill thy houses, and the houses of all thy servants, and the houses of all the Egyptians."

The wisdom of Solomon led him to say, "The locusts have no king, yet go they forth all of them by bands." In using this one figure the divine historian tells the whole story of the Saracen conquest. There was no king, there was no organized government; but there was one common faith which bound the hordes of Arabia to their caliph. When Mohammed first advo-

And the locusts went up over all the land of Egypt, and rested in all the coasts of Egypt: very grievous were they; before them there were no such locusts as they, neither after them shall be such.

For they covered the face of the whole earth, so that the land was darkened; and they did eat every herb of the land, and all the fruit of the trees which the hail had left: and there remained not any green thing in the trees, or in the herbs of the field, through all the land of Egypt. Ex. 10:12-15.

He gave also their increase unto the caterpillar, and their labour unto the locust. Psa. 78:46.

He spake, and the locusts came, and caterpillars, and that without number. Psa. 105:34.

Prov. 30:27.

In those days there was no king in Israel, but every man did that which was right in his own eyes. Judges 17:6.

Thus saith the Lord concerning the prophets that make my people err, that bite with their teeth, and cry, Peace ; and he that putteth not into their mouths, they even prepare war against him.

Therefore night shall be unto you, that ye shall not have a vision ; and it shall be dark unto you, that ye shall not divine ; and the sun shall go down over the prophets, and the day shall be dark over them.

Then shall the seers be ashamed, and the diviners confounded : yea, they shall all cover their lips ; for there is no answer of God.

Micah 3 : 4-7.

That I have set before you life and death. Deut. 30 : 19.

*And it was commanded them that they should not hurt the grass of the earth, neither any green thing, neither any tree ; but only those men which have not the seal of God in their foreheads.*

*Rev. 9 : 4.*

No weapon that is formed against thee shall prosper ; and every tongue that shall rise against thee in judgment thou shalt condemn. This is the heritage of the servants of the Lord, and their righteousness is of me, saith the Lord.

Isa. 54 : 17.

cated his doctrine, he gained adherents by the power of argument; but this process soon became too slow for his ambition, and arms were taken to defend and extend the territory of the new religion. In the course of a few years, Persia, Syria, Egypt, Africa and Spain had been conquered by Saracen arms. It was in 632 that Caled, the lieutenant of the first caliph, began the conquest of Persia. His efforts were crowned with victory. To every man was offered death, or the acceptance of the Mohammedan doctrine. With the sword above their heads, multitudes thanked God for Mohammed, His prophet.

When the tribes of Arabia were gathered for the conquest of Syria, the caliph Abubeker instructed the chiefs of the army as follows: "When you fight the battles of the Lord, acquit yourselves like men, without turning your backs; but let not your victory be stained with the blood of women or children. Destroy no palm trees, nor burn any fields of corn. Cut down no fruit trees, nor do any mischief to cattle, only such as you kill to eat. . . . As you go on, you will find some religious persons who live retired in monasteries, and propose to themselves to serve God that way; let them alone, and neither kill them nor destroy their monasteries: and you will find another sort of people that belong to the synagogue of Satan, who have shaven crowns; be sure you cleave their skulls, and give them no quarter till they either turn Mohammedan or pay tribute."

It would seem that God put a spirit of gentleness into the hearts of these warriors toward those Christians, who, in the solitudes of Syria, were keeping the law of God; but the tonsured priests and monks were to be slain without mercy, unless they accepted the faith of Mohammed and paid tribute. Syria was soon wholly in the hands of the Saracens.

In 638 the conquest of Egypt was begun. The conquest of Africa, from the Nile to the Atlantic, was attempted by the caliph Othman in 647; but the Moors were not conquered until the beginning of the next century, and then the Moslem faith was accepted from Syria to the Straits of Gibraltar. In 711 the Arabs crossed these straits into Spain, and the horn of the Crescent, the Moslem standard, reached the Pyrenees. Thus the power of their arms was extended. They had hoped to encircle the Mediterranean, and, having driven out the papacy, to seat Mohammedanism in place of Christianity in the City of Seven Hills. But in 732 A. D., the onward progress of the Saracens was checked by Charles Martel, in the battle of Tours, in France, and relinquishing the hope of gaining Europe on the west, the Mohammedans retreated into Spain. Here they established schools, and by the cultivation of the arts and sciences, won, by the intellect, what they had failed to gain by the sword. It was from Toledo, Salerno, and other Spanish centers of learning, that the light of scientific knowledge shone into the darkness of Europe during the Middle Ages, and acted its part in breaking the strength of the papacy at the dawn of the Reformation.

This is the history of the Saracens as they marched south and west. They gradually lost

When a man's ways please the Lord, he maketh even his enemies to be at peace with him.
Prov. 16:7.

For before these days rose up Theudas, boasting himself to be somebody; to whom a number of men, about four hundred, joined themselves: who was slain; and all, as many as obeyed him, were scattered, and brought to nought.

After this man rose up Judas of Galilee in the days of the taxing, and drew away much people after him: he also perished; and all, even as many as obeyed him, were dispersed.

And now I say unto you, Refrain from these men, and let them alone: for if this counsel or this work be of men, it will come to nought.
Acts 5:36–38.

They have spoken words, swearing falsely in making a covenant: thus judgment springeth up as hemlock in the furrows of the field.
Hos. 10:4.

Though he be fruitful among his brethren, an east wind shall come, the wind of the Lord shall come up from the wilderness, and his spring shall become dry, and his fountain shall be dried up: he shall spoil the treasure of all pleasant vessels.
Hos. 13:15.

Destroy, O Lord, and divide their tongues: for I have seen violence and strife in the city.

Day and night they go about it upon the walls thereof: mischief also and sorrow are in the midst of it.

Wickedness is in the midst thereof: deceit and guile depart not from her streets. Psa. 55:9–11.

Their poison is like the poison of a serpent: they are like the deaf adder that stoppeth her ear. Psa. 58:4.

They have sharpened their tongues like a serpent; adders' poison is under their lips. Psa. 140:3.

Which long for death, but it cometh not; and dig for it more than for hid treasures;

Which rejoice exceedingly, and are glad, when they can find the grave. Job 3:21, 22.

For the love of money is the root of all evil: which while some coveted after, they have erred from the faith, and pierced themselves through with many sorrows. 1 Tim. 6:10.

He casteth forth his ice like morsels: who can stand before his cold? Psa. 147:17.

An inheritance may be gotten hastily at the beginning; but the end thereof shall not be blessed. Prov. 20:21.

their warlike characteristics, and conquered by the power of the intellect. The attacks on the Eastern Empire were of a different character. The constant pressure and oft-repeated assaults of the Saracens led men to wish for death. To the Saracens who fell in battle was given the sure promise of a life in paradise. This made

**They lost their warlike characteristics, and conquered by the power of the intellect.**

them unmindful of death, and especially in the East the Saracens stung men with their false doctrines, and tormented them by repeated attacks.

Only forty-six years after the flight of Mohammed from Mecca, (A.D. 668), the Saracen army appeared under the walls of Constantinople. They were especially anxious to gain possession of this center of wealth and commerce, and there was a saying among the followers of the prophet, that the first army which besieged the city should have its sins forgiven. With this inducement ever before them, the troops landed and formed the siege. But they had underestimated the strength of the fortress, and were dismayed by the use of fire, recently introduced into Grecian warfare. On the approach of winter, they retreated; but for six summers, in succession, the siege was carried on without success.

Finally in 677 a thirty years' truce was signed by the Greeks and Saracens at Damascus.

During the years 716 and 718 a Saracen army again overran Asia Minor, crossed the Hellespont, and for the first time, landed on European soil. History states, that the general stood at the head of one hundred and twenty thousand Arabs and Persians, and that one thousand eight hundred ships approached the Bosporus, both armies intending to attack the capital at the same moment. Again Greek fire saved the threatened empire. The citizens of Constantinople loaded ships with combustibles, sent these into the midst of the fleet of the enemy, and the Arabs with their arms and vessels were consumed by the flames or the waves. The following winter was unusually severe, and this, together with the aid rendered the Greeks by an army of Bulgarians, and the report of still stronger forces who were arming in the West, made it advisable to give up, this second attempt, to capture Constantinople. These were the "locusts" that spread over the face of the earth. Like the insect from which they are named, they devoured everything that came in their way, and stung men as a scorpion stings with its tail.

The failure of the Arabs to capture Constantinople during these years was due to the absence of a centralized government; for the Saracens were still controlled by caliphs; and jealousy had led to the elevation of several leaders, each faction having its following. They went, as Solomon said of the locusts, in bands without a king. The dash of the Arab cavalry is proverbial in history. Arabia is considered to

**The Alhambra.**

Behold, therefore I will deliver thee to the men of the east for a possession, and they shall set their palaces in thee, and make their dwellings in thee: they shall eat thy fruit, and they shall drink thy milk. Eze. 25:4.

Thy crowned are as the locusts, and thy captains as the great grasshoppers, which camp in the hedges in the cold day, but when the sun ariseth they flee away, and their place is not known where they are. Nahum 3:17.

Thou shalt carry much seed out into the field, and shalt gather but little in; for the locust shall consume it. Deut. 28:38.

Without counsel purposes are disappointed: but in the multitude of counsellors they are established. Prov. 15:22.

They said, Nay; but we will have a king over us;
That we also may be like all the nations; and that our king may judge us, and go out before us, and fight our battles.
1 Sam. 8:19, 20.

Their horses also are swifter than the leopards, and are more fierce than the evening wolves: and their horsemen shall spread themselves, and their horsemen shall come from far; they shall fly as the eagle that hasteth to eat. Hab. 1:8.

Zech. 10:3.

I hearkened and heard, but they spake not aright: no man repented him of his wickedness, saying, What have I done? every one turned to his course, as the horse rusheth into the battle. Jer. 8:6.

The horse is prepared against the day of battle: but safety is of the Lord. Prov. 21:31.

*And to them it was given that they should not kill them, but that they should be tormented five months; and their torment was as the torment of a scorpion, when he striketh a man.*

*And in those days shall men seek death, and shall not find it; and shall desire to die, and death shall flee from them.*

*And the shapes of the locusts were like unto horses prepared unto battle; and on their heads were as it were crowns like gold, and their faces were as the faces of men.*

*And they had hair as the hair of women, and their teeth were as the teeth of lions.*

*And they had breastplates, as it were breastplates of iron; and the sound of their wings was as the sound of chariots of many horses running to battle.*

*And they had tails like unto scorpions, and there were stings in their tails: and their power was to hurt men five months.*

*Rev. 9:5-10.*

Death and life are in the power of the tongue. Prov. 18:21.

If a man have long hair, it is a shame unto him. 1 Cor. 11:14.

He will be a wild man; his hand will be against every man, and every man's hand against him; and he shall dwell in the presence of all his brethren. Gen. 16:12.

be the home of the horse; and Gibbon says (chapter 50): "These horses are educated in the tents, among the children of the Arabs, with a tender familiarity, which trains them in the habits of gentleness and attachment. They are accustomed only to walk or to gallop; their sensations are not blunted by the incessant abuse of the spur and the whip; their powers are preserved for the moments of flight and pursuit; but no sooner do they feel the touch of the hand, or the stirrup, than they dart away with the swiftness of the wind; and if their friend be dismounted in the rapid career, they instantly stop till he has recovered his seat." Since so much of the success of these human locusts depended upon the steeds which they rode, it is not surprising that the prophet John saw them "like unto horses prepared unto battle;" and it is also not surprising to find that the tail of a horse was often used as an ensign by the Bedouin chiefs. The crown worn by the Arab, was the turban which was unfurled when Mohammed became prince of Medina, and "to assume which is proverbially to turn Mussulman." Personally the Arab is grave and dignified; "his speech is slow, weighty, and concise; he is seldom provoked to laughter, his only gesture is that of stroking his beard, the venerable symbol of manhood." Though they wore long hair, which to the European has the appearance of effeminacy, yet from the days of Ishmael, a tenderness mingled with the savage nature of the lion, seems to have characterized the men of the desert Gibbon, in his graphic description of the Arab, nicely illustrates this fact in these words: "If a Bedouin discovers from afar a solitary traveler, he rides furiously against him, crying with a loud voice, 'Undress thyself, thy aunt [my wife] is without a garment.' A ready submission entitles him to mercy; resistance will provoke the aggressor, and his own blood must expiate the blood which he presumes to shed in legitimate defence. A single robber, or a few associates, are branded with their genuine name; but the exploits of a numerous band assume the character of a lawful and honorable war. The temper of a people thus armed against mankind, was doubly inflamed by the domestic license of rapine. murder, and revenge." The breastplates of iron, spoken of by John, refer to the cuirasses with which the soldiers were provided from the days of Mohammed.

Enough has been said to show the vividness of the prophetic description of the charge of the Arab cavalry, who were armed with scimiters, protected by cuirasses, and seated on horses swift as the wind.

"They had a king over them, which is the angel of the bottomless pit, whose name is . . . Destroyer." This character might in truth be imputed to the Arab caliphs, who directed the armies for so many years after the death of Mohammed; but it is especially applicable to Othman, the founder of the Ottoman Empire. This, the first attempted centralization of government was the outgrowth of the doctrines of Mohammed. "Othman," says the historian, "possessed, and perhaps surpassed, the ordinary virtues of a soldier; and the circumstances of time and place were propitious to his independence and success." The close of the thirteenth century was near. The Crusades had

And unto him that smiteth thee on the one cheek offer also the other; and him that taketh away thy cloke forbid not to take thy coat also.

Give to every man that asketh of thee; and of him that taketh away thy goods ask them not again.
Luke 6:29, 30.

An evil man seeketh only rebellion: therefore a cruel messenger shall be sent against him.
Prov. 17:11.

A man that hath friends must shew himself friendly: and there is a friend that sticketh closer than a brother. Prov. 18:24.

Order ye the buckler and shield, and draw near to battle.

Harness the horses; and get up, ye horsemen, and stand forth with your helmets; furbish the spears, and put on the brigandines.
Jer. 46:3, 4.

*And they had a king over them which is the angel of the bottomless pit, whose name in the Hebrew tongue is Abaddon, but in the Greek tongue hath his name Apollyon. Rev. 9:11.*

He beholdeth all high things: he is a king over all the children of pride. Job 41:34.

I chose out their way, and sat chief, and dwelt as a king in the army. Job 29:25.

The residue of the number of archers, the mighty men of the children of Kedar, shall be diminished: for the Lord God of Israel hath spoken it. Isa. 21:17.

Tell ye, and bring them near; yea, let them take counsel together: who hath declared this from ancient time? who hath told it from that time? have not I the Lord? and there is no God else beside me; a just God and a Saviour; there is none beside me. Isa. 45:21.

FIVE MONTHS.

Gen. 7:11. The flood began the 17th day of the 2nd month.

Gen. 8:3, 4. Waters abated the 17th day of the 7th month.

Gen. 7:24. The flood continued 150 days, hence 150 days=5 months.

Each day for a year. Num. 14:34.

July 27, 1299 plus 150 years=July 27, 1449.

Ezra 9:8.

Calling a ravenous bird from the east, the man that executeth my counsel from a far country: yea, I have spoken it, I will also bring it to pass; I have purposed it, I will also do it. Isa. 46:11.

Ye have plowed wickedness, ye have reaped iniquity; ye have eaten the fruit of lies: because thou didst trust in thy way, in the multitude of thy mighty men. Hosea 10:13.

thrust Europe against the Turks in a most reckless manner. Constantinople had numerous emperors, but the Greek government grew weaker, and the time of its destruction was stealthily approaching. "It was on July 27, A.D., 1299," says Gibbon, "that Othman first invaded the territory of Nicomedia; and the singular accuracy of the date seems to disclose some foresight of the rapid and destructive growth of the monster." More than human foresight recorded this date with such definiteness. To the prophet on Patmos, it had been revealed that "their power was to hurt men five months."

Five prophetic months is the equivalent of one hundred and fifty literal years, one day meaning a year, and counting thirty days to the month. Since the exact day for the beginning of this power is given, the expiration of the five months may be reckoned to the day. It closed July 27, 1449. It is these dates which enable the student of the trumpets, to locate the events which take place under each trumpet. These dates are "nails in a sure place" for both the first and the second woe.

To show that in 1299 power was given "to hurt men five months" we have the testimony of historians. After speaking of the invasion by Othman of Nicomedia, which was the eastern frontier of the Greek Empire, Gibbon continues: "The annals of the twenty-seven years of his reign would exhibit a repetition of the same inroads; and his hereditary troops were multiplied in each campaign by the accession of captives and volunteers." The successors of Othman, the founder of the Ottoman Empire, each pushed his conquests nearer to the coveted seat of power. A regular standing army of twenty-five thousand Moslems was organized by the son of Othman. Asia Minor was completely in his hands, and the seven churches referred to in the first chapter of Revelation were desecrated by the religion of Mohammed. So near was the Turkish rule to the throne that in 1346 Orchan, the successor of Othman, demanded and obtained, as a wife, the daughter of the Greek emperor, and the princess left her home in Constantinople to live in the harem of the Turk. Between 1360 and 1389, the third sovereign of the Turks, conquered Thrace, and fixed the capital of his empire and his religion at Adrianople, almost within the shadow of Constantinople. Never before had the Greek Empire been surrounded on all sides by the foe.

He shall enter also into the glorious land, and many countries shall be overthrown: but these shall escape out of his hand, even Edom, and Moab, and the chief of the children of Ammon.

He shall stretch forth his hand also upon the countries: and the land of Egypt shall not escape.

But he shall have power over the treasures of gold and of silver, and over all the precious things of Egypt: and the Libyans and the Ethiopians shall be at his steps.
Dan. 11:41-43.

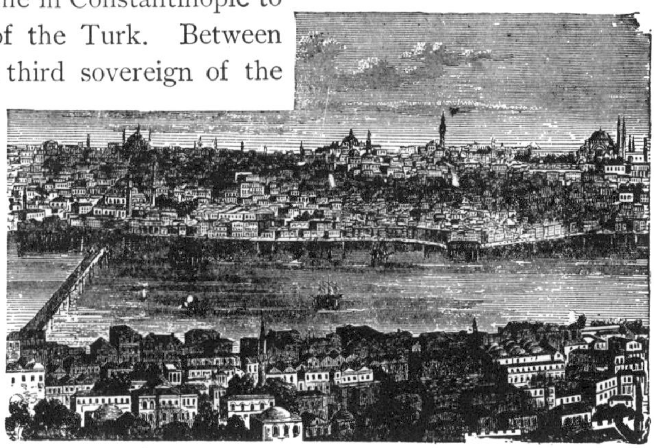

**Constantinople.**

The fourth king, Bajazet by name, was surnamed Ilderim, or "the lightning," because of the fiery energy of his soul, and the rapidity of his destructive marches. Constantinople was sorely pressed, and were not the hand of God recognized, the fact that the downfall was delayed for another fifty years might seem a mere accident. Called to contend with a Scythian force from the East, the Turks were obliged to postpone activities in Greece for a number of years. The Byzantine court, instead

And he said unto them, I beheld Satan as lightning fall from heaven.
Luke 10:18.

Heaven and earth shall pass away, but my words shall not pass away.
Matt. 24:35.

His lord was wroth, and delivered him to the tormentors, till he should pay all that was due unto him. Matt. 18:34.

*One woe is past; and, behold, there come two woes more hereafter.* *Rev. 9:12.*

In the fourth generation they shall come hither again: for the iniquity of the Amorites is not yet full. Gen. 15:16.

Another angel came and stood at the altar, having a golden censer; and there was given unto him much incense, that he should offer it with the prayers of all saints upon the golden altar which was before the throne. Rev. 8:3.

Who can bring a clean thing out of an unclean? not one.

Seeing his days are determined, the number of his months are with thee, thou hast appointed his bounds that he cannot pass;

Turn from him, that he may rest, till he shall accomplish, as an hireling, his day. Job 14:4-6.

The steps of his strength shall be straitened, and his own counsel shall cast him down.

For he is cast into a net by his own feet, and he walketh upon a snare.

The gin shall take him by the heel, and the robber shall prevail against him.

The snare is laid for him in the ground, and trap for him in the way. Job 18:7-10.

*And the sixth angel sounded, and I heard a voice from the four horns of the golden altar which is before God,*

*Saying to the sixth angel which had the trumpet, Loose the four angels which are bound in the great river Euphrates.*

*Rev. 9:13, 14.*

of profiting by the imminent danger, grew weaker. The one hundred and fifty years of torment, not destruction, was about to close. "One woe is past; and, behold, there come two woes more hereafter." The restraining hand of God had held contending forces in check, waiting, waiting, until the extreme limit of time, for men to acknowledge the righteousness of Jehovah. But at the sounding of the sixth trumpet a voice was heard from the four horns of the altar,—the altar before which Christ offers the prayers of saints,—saying, "Loose the four angels which are bound in the great river Euphrates." During the one hundred and fifty years, the Turks had power to torment, but when their armies seemed on the very verge of victory over the Greek Empire, their force was abated by troubles from the regions of the Euphrates. (See Gibbon, Chap. 65). The time was coming when they would not only torment, but kill. In 1448 the death of John Palæologus left the throne of Constantinople in a weak and precarious condition. Constantine, his successor, could claim no territory beyond the limits of the city, and the throne was already held by virtue of the grace of Amurath, the Turkish ruler. The gracious approbation of the Turkish sultan announced the supremacy of Constantine, and the approaching downfall of the Eastern Empire. The Turkish power had been bound, in a measure, by Rome; for as long as Rome held Constantinople, the Saracen power was limited in the East. When the sultan dictated to Rome, then, were fulfilled the words, "Loose the four angels which are bound in the great river Euphrates." These words seem especially to refer to Bagdad, Damascus, Aleppo and Iconium,—four sultanies bordering on the region of the Euphrates. No power could now resist, and the Moslem ruler soon gained the long coveted fortress on the Bosporus. The death of Amurath in 1451, and the succession of Mohammed II., a wily man full of ambition and restless of restraint, did not retard the conquest. Mohammed's one design was to capture Constantinople. "Peace was on his lips but war was in his heart," and every energy was bent toward the accomplishment of this design. At midnight he once started from his bed, and demanded the immediate attendance of his prime vizier. The man came trembling, fearing the detection of some previous crime. He made his offering to the sultan, but was met with the words, "I ask a present far more valuable and important,—Constantinople." Mohammed II. tested the loyalty of his soldiers, warned his ministers against the bribery of the Romans, studied the art of war and the use of firearms. He engaged the services of a founder of cannon, who promised weapons that could batter down the walls of the city. In April, 1453, the memorable siege was formed. At the sound of the war trumpet, the forces of Mohammed II. were increased by swarms of fearless fanatics until, as Phranza has said, the besieging army numbered two hundred and fifty-eight thousand. Constantinople fell; the last vestige of Roman greatness was gone, and the Moslem conquerors trampled the religion of Rome in the dust. This memorable event affected all future history. The fall shocked Europe; and the convulsions had not passed, before the light of the Reformation broke the

So I returned, and considered all the oppressions that are done under the sun: and behold the tears of such as were oppressed, and they had no comforter; and on the side of their oppressors there was power; but they had no comforter.
Eccl. 4:1.

My horn shalt thou exalt like the horn of an unicorn. Psa. 92:10.

Moreover I saw under the sun the place of judgment, that wickedness was there; and the place of righteousness, that iniquity was there. Eccl. 3:16.

For a dream cometh through the multitude of business. Eccl. 5:3.

Lo, this only have I found, that God hath made man upright; but they have sought out many inventions. Eccl. 7:29.

Dan. 2:40, 41.

Thus saith the Lord God; Remove the diadem, and take off the crown: this shall not be the same: exalt him that is low, and abase him that is high.

I will overturn, overturn, overturn, it: and it shall be no more, until he come whose right it is; and I will give it him.
Eze. 21:26, 27.

*And the four angels were loosed, which were prepared for an hour, and a day, and a month, and a year, for to slay the third part of men.*

*And the number of the army of the horsemen were two hundred thousand thousand: and I heard the number of them.*

*And thus I saw the horses in the vision, and them that sat on them, having breastplates of fire, and of iacinth, and brimstone: and the heads of the horses were as the heads of lions; and out of their mouths issued fire and smoke and brimstone.* *Rev. 9:15-17*

*By these three was the third part of men killed, by the fire, and by the smoke, and by the brimstone, which issued out of their mouths. For their power is in their mouth, and in their tails: for their tails were like unto serpents, and had heads, and with them they do hurt. Rev. 9:18, 19.*

Hast thou given the horse strength? hast thou clothed his neck with thunder? Job 39:19-25.

darkness which shrouded the Western Empire. While the smoke from the "bottomless pit" was settling over the East, streaks of light heralded a coming dawn in the nations of Europe

The characteristics, given by the prophet in describing the Turkish forces under the second woe, are similar to the description of the cavalry who fought for Mohammed under the first woe. The breastplate of iron and the scimiter of the Saracens, had been replaced by the firearms of the Turks, but the fury of the charge in the fifteenth century had lost none of the terrors of those earlier horsemen. Fire, smoke, and brimstone issued from the mouths of these warriors. The discharge of the firearms, as seen by the prophet in vision, appeared like fire issuing from the mouths of the horses. The power was also in their tail. Isaiah says, "The ancient and honorable, he is the head; and the prophet that teacheth lies, he is the tail." Their military valor was one thing in favor of the Turks; the unity of the faith in Mohammed and the zeal inspired by that prophet to kill the "infidels" (Christians), was a factor equally as potent.

**The discharge of the firearms appeared like fire issuing from the mouths of the horses.**

EXPLANATION OF REV. 9:15.

I have appointed thee each day for a year. Eze. 4:6.

1 prophetic day=1 year, or 360 literal days.

1 prophetic hour=1-24 of 360 days, or 15 days.

1 prophetic day=1 literal year.

1 prophetic month=30 literal years.

1 prophetic year=360 literal years.

360 years plus 30 years plus 1 year=391 years.

Total, 391 years and 15 days.

July 27, 1449, plus 391 years, 15 days=Aug. 11, 1840.

The power which came on the stage of action July 27, 1449, was to bear sway for an hour and a day and a month and a year,—three hundred ninety-one years and fifteen days, literally speaking. This is a wonderful prophecy, the only one in the Bible where the time of the fulfillment is given to the very day. At the end of this period, Turkey would cease to be an independent power. Three hundred and ninety-one years and fifteen days from July 27, 1449, brings us to August 11, 1840. There are four great waymarks in the world's history connected with Constantinople. First, when it was founded in 330 A.D. second, its capture by the Turks July 27, 1449; third, when the sultan of Turkey signed away his independence August 11, 1840. There is no date given for the fourth great waymark; namely, when the capital of Turkey will be removed from Constantinople to Jerusalem "between the seas in the glorious holy mountain."

In 1838 Josiah Litch and William Miller, after a careful study of the prophecies, came to the conclusion that on this last date nations might expect to see the Turkish sultan surrender his power. This prophecy was published to the world, but there were events transpiring which also called the attention of nations to Constantinople. The sultan of Turkey and Mehemet Ali, pasha of Egypt, were at war, the pasha refusing an indemnity demanded by the ruler of Turkey. In 1839 the pasha was victorious in battle over the Turkish army, and he sent another force under command of his son into Syria and Asia Minor, and threatened to carry his victorious arms against Constantinople. At this juncture, England, Austria, Prussia and Russia, combined in the demand that the pasha should confine himself to Syria and Egypt. A council of these four powers was held July 15, 1840. The ruler of Turkey agreed to abide by their

FOUR WAYMARKS IN THE HISTORY OF CONSTANTINOPLE.

1st. The dragon gave him his power, and his seat, and great authority. Rev. 13:2.

2nd. Loose the four angels which are bound in the great river Euphrates. Rev. 9:14.

3rd. And the four angels were loosed, which were prepared for an hour, and a day, and a month, and a year. Rev. 9:15.

4th. And he shall plant the tabernacles of his palace between the seas in the glorious holy mountain yet he shall come to his end, and none shall help him. Dan. 11:45.

I have declared the former things from the beginning; and they went forth out of my mouth, and I shewed them; I did them suddenly, and they came to pass. Isa. 48:3-6.

Whoso is wise, and will observe these things, even they shall understand the lovingkindness of the Lord. Psa. 107:43.

For they know not to do right. saith the Lord, who store up violence and robbery in their palaces.
Therefore thus saith the Lord God; An adversary there shall be even round about the land; and he shall bring down thy strength from thee, and thy palaces shall be spoiled. Amos 3:10, 11.

All the men of thy confederacy have brought thee even to the border: the men that were at peace with thee have deceived thee, and prevailed against thee; they that eat thy bread have laid a wound under thee: there is none understanding in him. Obad. 7.

His mischief shall return upon his own head, and his violent dealing shall come down upon his own pate. Psa. 7:16.

—

He shall spread forth his hands in the midst of them, as he that swimmeth spreadeth forth his hands to swim: and he shall bring down their pride together with the spoils of their hands.

And the fortress of the high fort of thy walls shall he bring down, lay low, and bring to the ground, even to the dust. Isa. 25:11, 12.

Dan. 11:45.

He shall come to his end, and none shall help him.

And at that time shall Michael stand up, the great prince which standeth for the children of thy people: and there shall be a time of trouble, such as never was since there was a nation even to that same time: and at that time thy people shall be delivered, every one that shall be found written in the book. Dan. 11:45; 12:1.

Rev. 7:1.

There shall be signs in the sun, and in the moon, and in the stars; and upon the earth distress of nations, with perplexity; the sea and the waves roaring;

Men's hearts failing them for fear, and for looking after those things which are coming on the earth: for the powers of heaven shall be shaken.

And then shall they see the Son of man coming in a cloud with power and great glory. Luke 21:25–27.

decision, and was only too glad to have his life saved by their intervention. He thereby voluntarily surrendered all rights into the hands of the combined forces of Western Europe. In the official document drawn up by the representatives of the nations concerned, are these words: "It having been felt that all the zealous labors of the conferences of London in the settlement of the pasha's pretensions were useless, and that the only public way was to have recourse to coercive measures to reduce him to obedience in case he persisted in not listening to pacific overtures, the powers have, together with the Ottoman plenipotentiary, drawn up and signed a treaty whereby the sultan offers the pasha the hereditary government of Egypt, . . . the pasha, on his part, evacuating all other parts of the sultan's dominions now occupied by him and returning the Ottoman fleet. . . . If the pasha refuses to accede to them, it is evident that the evil consequences to fall upon him will be attributable solely to his own fault."

This treaty was signed, and the ultimatum was officially put in the power of Mehemet Ali on August 11, 1840. Since that time Turkey has been known everywhere as the "Sick Man of the East." Daniel prophesied concerning him, saying, "He shall plant the tabernacles of his palace between the seas in the glorious holy mountain; yet he shall come to his end, and none shall help him." At any moment, when the jealous powers of Europe can decide, either peaceably, or in battle, which one of them shall occupy Constantinople, the "Sick Man" will speedily take his departure from Europe. That movement, for which nations are now on the alert, will be the sign of still more important changes in the heavenly court.

The importance of the prophecy, and the exactness with which it was fulfilled, to the very day, should lead to a careful investigation of that divine history, which circles about the years 1840 to 1844. Its study will lead men to look for changes in the heavens as well as upon earth; for when the capital of Turkey is removed to Palestine, then Christ, finishing His work in the sanctuary, throws His censer on the earth as a signal for the final dissolution of all things.

The closing words of the ninth chapter are a sad commentary on the condition of the world, and although the revelation of Jesus Christ is given in the Word, in nature, and may be read in the relation of nations to each other, yet "the rest of the men which were not killed by these plagues yet repented not of the works of their hands, that they should not worship devils, and idols of gold, and silver, and brass, and stone, and of wood. . . . Neither repented they of their murders, nor of their sorceries, nor of their fornication, nor of their thefts."

As the end draws near iniquity waxes greater. The fall of nations has ever been used as a symbol of the final destruction of the earth. Men see these things and yet continue in their idolatry, their theft, and their fornication. How precious in the sight of the Lord is that little company who by faith see Jesus, and following Him in His work above, reflect His character to the world! The faithful ones are to-day being sealed; for we are nearing the close of time, and eternity will soon open to the redeemed.

But sanctify the Lord God in your hearts: and be ready always to give an answer to every man that asketh you a reason of the hope that is in you with meekness and fear.
1 Pet. 3:15.

The angel took the censer, and filled it with fire of the altar, and cast it into the earth: and there were voices, and thunderings, and lightnings, and an earthquake.
Rev. 8:5.

John 15:5.
Isa. 5:12.

*And the rest of the men which were not killed by these plagues yet repented not of the works of their hands, that they should not worship devils, and idols of gold, and silver, and brass, and stone, and of wood: which neither can see, nor hear, nor walk:*
*Neither repented they of their murders, nor of their sorceries nor of their fornication, nor of their thefts.* *Rev. 9:20, 21.*

Evil men and seducers shall wax worse and worse, deceiving, and being deceived. 2 Tim. 3:13.

They shall be mine, saith the Lord of hosts, in that day when I make up my jewels; and I will spare them, as a man spareth his own son that serveth him.
Mal. 3:17.

The Lord said unto him, Go through the midst of the city, through the midst of Jerusalem, and set a mark upon the foreheads of the men that sigh and that cry for all the abominations that be done in the midst thereof.
Eze. 9:4.

# CHAPTER XI.

## THE VOICE OF A MIGHTY ANGEL.

THE prophet John watched the sounding of the sixth trumpet, and saw the woes and terrors of national strife, and the darkening of the earth by the smoke from the "bottomless pit." He saw men buried beneath the weight of their own sins, and although the Son of God was waiting, like the father of the prodigal son, for the return of the sinful, yet they repented not of their murders and sorceries, their fornications and thefts. Justice and mercy are inseparably mingled in the dealings of God with man, and great woes call forth from Jehovah a great overflowing of His love. So when the world lay in darkness, unmindful of the voice of God which they might have heard in the very din of battle or the councils of nations, there came to the world a most thrilling message. John heard this message before seeing the further events of the third woe.

There came from heaven a mighty angel clothed with a cloud. He was an ambassador from the courts of Jehovah, and his might cor-

Blow ye the trumpet in Zion, and sound an alarm in my holy mountain: let all the inhabitants of the land tremble: for the day of the Lord cometh, for it is nigh at hand.
Joel 2:1.

They shall pass through it, hardly bestead and hungry: and it shall come to pass, that when they shall be hungry, they shall fret themselves, and curse their king and their God, and look upward.

And they shall look unto the earth; and behold trouble and darkness, dimness of anguish; and they shall be driven to darkness.
Isa. 8:21, 22.

Luke 15:11-22.
Rev. 16:9.

Justice and judgment are the habitation of thy throne: mercy and truth shall go before thy face.
Psa. 89:14.

Hab. 3:2.
Rev. 14:6, 7.
Rom. 10:15.

How beautiful upon the mountains are the feet of him that bringeth good tidings, that publisheth peace; that bringeth good tidings of good, that publisheth salvation; that saith unto Zion, Thy God reigneth! Isa. 52:7.

responded with the court which he represented and the power and extent of the message which he bore. He was resplendent with the glory of the King, from whose presence he came. His face shone with the brightness of the sun, and his feet as pillars of fire. Here is a description of creative power; and the King's message which he came to deliver had in it the power, the brilliancy, and the light of Him who spake, and worlds stood forth. But the glory, lest it should dazzle men's eyes, was veiled with a cloud. As God covered Himself with a cloud, lest Israel beholding His brightness should be slain, so the glory of the message of the mighty angel was softened for mortal eyes by the cloud which clothed his form. Men living in harmony with their Maker are permitted at times to see the cloud withdrawn, and to behold more and more of His grandeur. In eternity only, the fulness of the message will be comprehended. Breadth of experience in the things of God, measures the ability ot each individual to penetrate the cloud.

"And a rainbow was upon his head." A rainbow encircles the throne of God, but the carnal eye will see little significance in the fact. To the one from whose eyes the veil has dropped, there is an infinite depth of meaning in the rainbow about the angel's head, and the appearance of the bow in our own heavens is, to the spiritual soul, a reminder of the everlasting covenant made in heaven. The divine historian gives the story of the rainbow as it appears in our heavens. Back in eternity, God and Christ covenanted for the redemption of the race, if man should sin after his creation, and so separate from his Maker, and the bow about the throne

***And I saw another mighty angel come down from heaven, clothed with a cloud: and a rainbow was upon his head, and his face was as it were the sun, and his feet as pillars of fire. Rev. 10:1.***

He that receiveth you receiveth me, and he that receiveth me receiveth him that sent me. Matt. 10:40.

His body also was like the beryl, and his face as the appearance of lightning, and his eyes as lamps of fire, and his arms and his feet like in colour to polished brass, and the voice of his words like the voice of a multitude. Dan. 10:6.

Psa. 33:6, 9.
Gen. 1:1–3.

Moses went into the midst of the cloud, and gat him up into the mount: and Moses was in the mount forty days and forty nights. Ex. 24:18.

1 John 2:20, 27.
Matt. 17:1–5.

Of his fulness have all we received, and grace for grace. John 1:16.

Eph. 1:7, 8.
Col. 2:9, 10.
1 Cor. 2:14–16.

As the appearance of the bow that is in the cloud in the day of rain, so was the appearance of the brightness round about. This was the appearance of the likeness of the glory of the Lord. Eze. 1:28.

Acts 9:18.

The bow shall be in the cloud; and I will look upon it, that I may remember the everlasting covenant between God and every living creature of all flesh that is upon the earth. Gen. 9:12–17.

Gen. 6:18–20.

Thus saith the high and lofty One that inhabiteth eternity, whose name is Holy; I dwell in the high and holy place. Isa. 57:15.

The Lamb slain from the foundation of the world. Rev. 13:8.

Psa. 103:19, 20.

For this is as the waters of Noah unto me: for as I have sworn that the waters of Noah should no more go over the earth; so have I sworn that I would not be wroth with thee, nor rebuke thee.

My kindness shall not depart from thee, neither shall the covenant of my peace be removed, saith the Lord that hath mercy on thee. Isa. 54:9, 10.

was made the token of the covenant. Ever since, it has had its place about the throne, and it became an eternal token of the redemption of man. Angels and beings of unfallen worlds behold the bow, and bow in reverence to the One on the throne. But the human eye cannot look into heaven, so when the Lord saved Noah and his family from the flood, He placed this same sign in the clouds of earth as a token of redemption. Like a little piece of heaven transported to the earth the bow is a reminder to man that God has toward him constant thoughts of peace and thoughts of righteousness. But the story is yet more wonderful; for God not only looks upon the bow about the throne, and is reminded of man; but He looks upon the bow in the clouds, and is drawn in heart toward earth. Every cloud that floats in the sky contains a bow. The cloud may appear dark and threatening to us; but the sun shining upon the other side forms the bow, and God looks upon it, and "remembers the everlasting covenant between God and every living creature," the covenant that makes "you perfect in every good work to do His will, working in you that which is well pleasing in His sight, through Jesus Christ." Every cloud should be a reminder to us that God is willing to help and strengthen us. If sunshine floods the path of mortals, its glory is God's smile. If through tears we look heavenward, the light, shining through the drops on our eyelashes,

An eternal token of the redemption of man.

It shall come to pass, when I bring a cloud over the earth, that the bow shall be seen in the cloud:

And I will remember my covenant, which is between me and you. Gen. 9:14, 15.

For I know the thoughts that I think toward you, saith the Lord, thoughts of peace, and not of evil, to give you an expected end. Jer. 29:11-13.

Now the God of peace, that brought again from the dead our Lord Jesus, that great shepherd of the sheep, through the blood of the everlasting covenant,

Make you perfect in every good work to do his will, working in you that which is wellpleasing in his sight, through Jesus Christ; to whom be glory for ever and ever. Amen. Heb. 13:20, 21.

forms the colors of the rainbow of promise. So near is God to man. The rainbow about the mighty angel's head, shows the loving kindness of the Father, and pledges redemption in the message that he brings. The insignia of earthly potentates sink into insignificance before those worn by the messenger of the King of kings. Jehovah was in the burning bush by the wayside; the same God, with ten thousand of His saints, proclaimed His fiery law from Sinai. God revealed Himself to the prophets and writers of the Old Testament, and the same Father of us all spoke through Christ to the apostles, and opened the eyes of the prophet on Patmos. And in order that men may see the oneness of the divine word, the mighty angel binds together the Old and the New Testaments. The one prophet, who, before Christ, gave the date of His first advent, and who also gave the time of His second coming and of the end, was Daniel. Daniel's prophecy was preeminently a time message, and when he sought to understand the times, which had been revealed to him, he was told to "shut up the words, and seal the book, even to the time of the end." The message was not for Daniel to comprehend, but in the time of the end, many would "run to and fro," knowledge would increase, and the wise, instructed of the Lord, would understand what had for ages been sealed. The period of time which Daniel sought to understand, was the two thousand three hundred days, at the end of which time, the sanctuary would be cleansed. This is the only sealed message of the Word, and yet the last promise made to Daniel, was that he should stand in his lot "at the end of the

Jer. 31:3.
Isa. 63:7.
Psa. 92:2.

The angel of the Lord appeared unto him in a flame of fire out of the midst of a bush: and he looked, and, behold, the bush burned with fire, and the bush was not consumed. Ex. 3:2.

Searching what, or what manner of time the Spirit of Christ which was in them did signify, when it testified beforehand the sufferings of Christ, and the glory that should follow.

Unto whom it was revealed, that not unto themselves, but unto us they did minister the things, which are now reported unto you by them that have preached the gospel unto you with the Holy Ghost sent down from heaven; which things the angels desire to look into.
1 Pet. 1:11, 12.

Dan. 9:25-27.
Dan. 8:13, 14.

Many shall run to and fro, and knowledge shall be increased.
Dan. 12:4.

Dan. 12:10.

But go thou thy way till the end be: for thou shalt rest, and stand in thy lot at the end of the days.
Dan. 12:13.

*And he had in his hand a little book open: and he set his right foot upon the sea, and his left foot on the earth.* *Rev. 10:2.*

Go to now, ye rich men, weep and howl for your miseries that shall come upon you.

Your riches are corrupted, and your garments are motheaten.

Your gold and silver is cankered; and the rust of them shall be a witness against you, and shall eat your flesh as it were fire. Ye have heaped treasure together for the last days. Jas. 5:1-5.

As thy servant was busy here and there, he was gone. And the king of Israel said unto him, So shall thy judgment be; thyself hast decided it. 1 Kings 20:40.

*And cried with a loud voice, as when a lion roareth: and when he had cried, seven thunders uttered their voices.* *Rev. 10:3.*

Wherefore he saith, Awake thou that sleepest, and arise from the dead, and Christ shall give thee light. Eph. 5:14.

Isa. 5:29, 30.

Rev. 14:6, 7.

He said unto them, Go ye into all the world, and preach the gospel to every creature. Mark 16:15.

Jer. 25:15, 16.

Jer. 15:16.

*And when the seven thunders had uttered their voices, I was about to write: and I heard a voice from heaven saying unto me, Seal up those things which the seven thunders uttered, and write them not.* *Rev. 10:4.*

*And the angel which I saw stand upon the sea and upon the earth lifted up his hand to heaven,*

*And sware by him that liveth for ever and ever, who created heaven, and the things that therein are, and the earth, and the things that therein are, and the sea, and the things which are therein, that there should be time no longer.* *Rev. 10:5, 6.*

days." John saw the mighty angel descend to earth, having in his hand a little book open. Not closed, not sealed, but open. It was at the close of the second woe, in 1840, that this angel with the open book of Daniel, set one foot on the land and one on the sea. Men were busy with their idolatry, they were heaping gold together, rushing to and fro, neither seeing nor hearing anything, save that which ministered to their earthly desires. Nations were busy with their own schemes, unmindful of the overruling hand of Providence. But the angel's message embraced the whole earth: standing with one foot on the earth and the other on the sea, "he cried with a loud voice" like the roar of a lion in the forest, and this cry awoke men from their slumber, and startled nations. No man was too humble, no place too secluded; that voice penetrated everywhere. It echoed, and re-echoed through the world. Men might think themselves secure, but the sound shook the very earth, causing many a heart to quake with fear. Though the voice was so penetrating, those who turned their faces toward the divine messenger, saw on his brow, the rainbow of promise.

Nature herself seemed to respond to the cry; for as the sound rolled through the earth, seven thunders uttered their voices as if in response. It is useless to speculate on the meaning of the thunderings; for while John understood, he was bidden not to write the things which he had heard.

The mighty angel, having the little book open in one hand, lifted up the other hand to heaven and "sware by Him that liveth for ever and ever,

" He had in his hand a little book open."

. . . that there should be time no longer." Jewish history was divided into distinct periods by the prophetic writers. The bondage in Egypt was revealed to Abraham; it was also plainly prophesied that the Babylonish captivity would continue seventy years. The birth of Christ was foretold by the prophets, the very year of His baptism was foretold by the prophet Daniel; His crucifixion and rejection by the Jewish nation was also given in an unmistakable way. Christians have taunted the Jews with blindness because they did not see and understand, but the dates which cluster about the life of Christ are a part of the time prophecy to which the mighty angel pointed the world; they are a part of the same two thousand three hundred days which Daniel sought to understand, but which were sealed until the time of the end.

A few years previous to 1840, men began the study of the prophecies of Daniel, and came to the conclusion that the two thousand three hundred days of the eighth chapter must end in 1844. Thinking that the cleansing of the sanctuary, spoken of in Daniel 8:14, referred to the cleansing of the earth at the advent of Christ, the second coming of the Saviour was, in 1840, and onward, preached with wonderful power throughout the world. In America the movement was led by William Miller, in England, by Edward Irving; in Asia, by Joseph Wolff, a Christian Jew; in Sweden, where the laws prohibited adults from giving the message, children preached. The Spirit of God took possession of the little ones, and their words sank deep into the hearts of men as they proclaimed "the hour of His judgment is come." "Prepare to meet your Lord."

Time of bondage in Egypt. Gen. 15:13–16; Ex. 12:40, 41.

Length of Babylonish captivity. 2 Chron. 36:21; Jer. 29:10.

Baptism of Christ foretold. Dan. 9:25; John 1:41 [margin.] Acts 10:38; Matt. 3:13–16.

The year of Christ's crucifixion. Dan. 9:26, 27.

Ye men of Israel, hear these words; Jesus of Nazareth, a man approved of God among you by miracles and wonders and signs, which God did by him in the midst of you, as ye yourselves also know: Him, being delivered by the determinate counsel and foreknowledge of God, ye have taken, and by wicked hands have crucified and slain. Acts 2:22, 23.

John 5:39.

Seek ye out of the book of the Lord, and read: no one of these shall fail. Isa. 34:16.

2 Pet. 3:7–10.

For I am the Lord: I will speak, and the word that I shall speak shall come to pass; it shall be no more prolonged: for in your days, O rebellious house, will I say the word, and will perform it, saith the Lord God.

Again the word of the Lord came to me, saying,

Son of man, behold, they of the house of Israel say, The vision that he seeth is for many days to come, and he prophesieth of the times that are far off.

Therefore say unto them, Thus saith the Lord God; There shall none of my words be prolonged any more, but the word which I have spoken shall be done, saith the Lord God. Eze. 12:25–28.

When the chief priests and scribes saw the wonderful things that he did, and the children crying in the temple, and saying, Hosanna to the son of David; they were sore displeased. Matt. 21:15.

Let these sayings sink down into your ears. Luke 9:44.

Rev. 14:6, 7.
Amos 4:12.

In 1838 the termination of the second woe of Rev. 9:13–21 was interpreted to end in 1840. Said those who were proclaiming the second advent: "If the Turkish power ceases in 1840, that may be considered a sign that the correct interpretation has been placed upon the prophetic periods of Daniel, and we may look for the Lord in 1844." Therefore, in 1840, when the world realized that the Turks had fulfilled the prophecy to the very day, (see chapter X), men of wealth, education, and position, were startled to find that they were nearing events which seemed to foretell the immediate closing up of earth's history. It was at this time, 1840, that the voice of the mighty angel awoke the earth with the message, "Fear God and give glory to Him, for the hour of His judgment is come." This was a message from the Creator of the heavens and the earth, the sea and all living creatures. And he swore "that there should be time no longer." The close of the long prophetic period was near at hand. The feet of the messenger were like pillars of fire, and his message burned its way into the hearts of even the most worldly. The sunlight of his countenance lighted up the page of the open book which he held out to the world; men read a new and living meaning in these prophecies. To scoff was to defy God Himself. To remain indifferent was impossible; for men seemed on the brink of eternity. Earthly possessions lost their value; homes were sold and men went forth to proclaim everywhere the coming of the Son of man. Books and papers were scattered broadcast like the leaves of autumn. As Elisha was called from his oxen, so farmers at the

The Lord answered me, and said, Write the vision, and make it plain upon tables, that he may run that readeth it.

For the vision is yet for an appointed time, but at the end it shall speak, and not lie: though it tarry, wait for it; because it will surely come, it will not tarry.
Hab. 2:2, 3.

In the day when the keepers of the house shall tremble, and the strong men shall bow themselves.
Eccl. 12:3.

The great day of the Lord is near, it is near, and hasteth greatly, even the voice of the day of the Lord: the mighty man shall cry there bitterly.

Neither their silver nor their gold shall be able to deliver them in the day of the Lord's wrath; but the whole land shall be devoured by the fire of his jealousy: for he shall make even a speedy riddance of all them that dwell in the land.
Zeph. 1:14–18.

Rev. 14:6, 7.
Rev. 10:6.
1 Pet. 4:4, 12, 15.

That the trial of your faith, being much more precious than of gold that perisheth, though it be tried with fire, might be found unto praise and honour and glory at the appearing of Jesus Christ. 1 Pet. 1:7.

Mal. 3:1, 2.

Behold, they say unto me, Where is the word of the Lord? let it come now. Jer. 17:15.

2 Pet. 3:3, 4.
Joel 2:6–11.

In that day a man shall cast his idols of silver, and his idols of gold, which they made each one for himself to worship, to the moles and to the bats. Isa. 2:20.

The Lord gave the word: great was the company of those that published it. Psa. 68:11.

1 Kings 19:19–21.

plow were greeted by strangers with the words, "Prepare to meet your Lord." So widespread was this truth that school children could be heard repeating the familiar quotation from the prophecy, "Unto two thousand three hundred days then shall the sanctuary be cleansed."

The exactness with which the time is given is noted in the seventh verse. After proclaiming that there should be time no longer, the angel said, "But in the days of the voice of the seventh angel when he shall begin to sound, the mystery of God should be finished, as He hath declared to His servants the prophets." The seventh trumpet, as is the case with the seventh church and the seventh seal, begins in time, and extends into eternity. It bridges, as it were, the gulf between this world and the next: but when the seventh trumpet shall begin to sound, "the mystery of God should be finished," as declared by the prophets. The sixth trumpet ended in 1840. Between the sixth and seventh trumpets is a short interval, designated by the word "quickly" in Rev. 11:14, and it is in this interval that the loud cry of the mighty angel was given. The close of the prophetic period was 1844, so that the "quickly" would be the time between 1840 and 1844, and the seventh trumpet began to sound when prophetic time was at an end, that is, in 1844. The mystery of God is the Gospel of Jesus Christ; the sacrifice of the Lamb of God.

When the prophecy was more fully comprehended than it was between 1840 and 1844, in other words, when the cloud was pierced by eyes which searched for Christ, the truth in regard to the heavenly sanctuary was discovered.

Out of the mouth of babes and sucklings hast thou ordained strength because of thine enemies, that thou mightest still the enemy and the avenger. Psa. 8:2.

Dan. 8:14.

The kingdom and dominion, and the greatness of the kingdom under the whole heaven, shall be given to the people of the saints of the most High, whose kingdom is an everlasting kingdom, and all dominions shall serve and obey him.

Hitherto is the end of the matter. Dan. 7:27, 28.

Dan. 7:17.

Dan. 2:44, 45.

*But in the days of the voice of the seventh angel, when he shall begin to sound, the mystery of God should be finished, as he hath declared to his servants the prophets. Rev. 10:7.*

Now to him that is of power to stablish you according to my gospel, and the preaching of Jesus Christ, according to the revelation of the mystery, which was kept secret since the world began. Rom. 16:25.

To make all men see what is the fellowship of the mystery, which from the beginning of the world hath been hid in God, who created all things by Jesus Christ. Eph. 3:3-9.

Heb. 9:2, 3, 7, 23.

For Christ is not entered into the holy places made with hands, which are the figures of the true; but into heaven itself, now to appear in the presence of God for us. Heb. 9:24.

Matt. 22 : 11–13.
Luke 19 : 12.

The judgment was set, and the books were opened. Dan. 7 : 9, 10.

The dead were judged out of those things which were written in the books, according to their works. Rev. 20 : 12.

Counting one by one, to find out the account. Eccl. 7 : 27.

Luke 21 : 36.

For he will finish the account and cut it short in righteousness: because a short work will the Lord make upon the earth. Rom. 9 : 28 [margin.]

Luke 22 : 31, 32.

For, lo, I will command, and I will sift the house of Israel among all nations, like as corn is sifted in a sieve, yet shall not the least grain fall upon the earth. Amos 9 : 9.

For a great door and effectual is opened unto me. 1 Cor. 16 : 9.

2 Cor. 2 : 12.

*And the voice which I heard from heaven spake unto me again, and said, Go and take the little book which is open in the hand of the angel which standeth upon the sea and upon the earth.*

*And I went unto the angel, and said unto him, Give me the little book. And he said unto me, Take it, and eat it up; and it shall make thy belly bitter, but it shall be in thy mouth sweet as honey.* *Rev. 10 : 8, 9.*

Thy words were found, and I did eat them; and thy word was unto me the joy and rejoicing of mine heart: for I am called by thy name, O Lord God of hosts. Jer. 15 : 16.

Eze. 3 : 1, 2.

Then opened he their understanding that they might understand the scriptures. Luke 24 : 45.
John 6 : 48–51.

In 1844 the antitypical work of the day of atonement was begun in the heavenly sanctuary. That is, Christ at that time passed within the veil, to make up the subjects of His kingdom from those who had accepted of the Divine Offering. The investigative judgment was opened, and in the first case decided before the throne, the work of finishing the Gospel was begun, which will be completed when the last name has passed the heavenly court. These events were veiled by the cloud between 1840 and 1844, that men's hearts might be tested. This period was a testing time, and when it passed, many were shaken out. The sixth and seventh verses of the tenth chapter of Revelation are parallel with the sixth and seventh verses of the fourteenth chapter.

With joy the advent message that time should be no more went to the world. It was preached to high and low, and the churches throughout the world opened their doors to receive it. But there came a voice from heaven saying, "Go and take the little book which is open in the hand of the angel which standeth upon the sea and upon the earth." The mighty angel did not close the open book when he had once cried, but still stood upon the earth and the sea with the pages open in his hand, and John, symbolizing God's people, was bidden to take it out of the angel's hand. John approached the angel with the words, "Give me the book," and he said, "Take it, and eat it up." Eating the Word of God implies a careful study until the meaning is fully comprehended. Jesus often used the figure in a spiritual sense, referring to His body and the "bread of life." Now was the time to penetrate deeper into the cloud that overshadowed the message. As the time for what was supposed to be the second advent, but which in reality meant the beginning of the investigative judgment, drew near, there was a searching of the prophecies such as had never been before. Then, when the spring of 1844 came and passed, and no Saviour had appeared, there was not only heart searching, but deeper, more intense study of the Word. The delay could not at first be understood; but soon it was seen that the decree of Artaxerxes, in 457 B. C., from which the two thousand three hundred days were reckoned, did not take effect until the year was half gone. This extended the prophetic period from the spring to the autumn of 1844. The joy of those who longed to see their Lord increased.

The message was, "It shall make thy belly bitter, but it shall be in thy mouth sweet as honey." They had tasted the sweetness of the message. The world never before witnessed such manifestations of brotherly love, such sacrifice and such devotion. The autumn of 1844 came and went, and the intensity of the disappointment was beyond description. No earthly inducement ever seemed so sweet as the message of His coming; no disappointment was ever so bitter as that experienced by the believers in the second coming of Christ. The disciples, weeping at the tomb over a crucified Saviour, seemed to drain the cup of bitterness, but a potion no less galling was drunk by the disciples in 1844. "We thought that it was He that would save Israel," was echoed eighteen hundred years later in the words, "We looked for Him to save us, but He has not come." In this period of

For the time is come that judgment must begin at the house of God: and if it first begin at us, what shall the end be of them that obey not the gospel of God?

And if the righteous scarcely be saved, where shall the ungodly and the sinner appear?

1 Pet. 4:17, 18.

Prov. 2:2-7.

I sat not in the assembly of the mockers, nor rejoiced; I sat alone because of thy hand: for thou hast filled me with indignation.

Why is my pain perpetual, and my wound incurable, which refuseth to be healed? wilt thou be altogether unto me as a liar, and as waters that fail? Jer. 15:17,18.

The decree of Artaxerxes.

Ezra 7:11-26.

This decree went into effect six months after it was issued.

Ezra 7:9.

Acts 2:44-47.

***And I took the little book out of the angel's hand, and ate it up; and it was in my mouth sweet as honey: and as soon as I had eaten it, my belly was bitter.***

***Rev. 10:10.***

For ye had compassion of me in my bonds, and took joyfully the spoiling of your goods, knowing in yourselves that ye have in heaven a better and an enduring substance.

Heb. 10:34-37.

The Almighty hath dealt very bitterly with me. Ruth 1:20.

2 Kings 14:26.
Luke 24:19-21.

Like as a woman with child, that draweth near the time of her delivery, is in pain, and crieth out in her pangs; so have we been in thy sight, O Lord.

We have been with child, we have been in pain, we have as it were brought forth wind; we have not wrought any deliverance in the earth; neither have the inhabitants of the world fallen.

Isa. 26:17, 18.

While they went to buy, the bridegroom came; and they that were ready went in with him to the marriage: and the door was shut. Matt. 25:10.

anguish and disappointment, the churches that had opened their doors for the message, now turned away from those who still clung to the belief in the prophecies and the second coming of the Lord. This closing of the doors, and the rejection of further light, caused the second message of Rev. 14:8 to be proclaimed.

There followed another angel, saying, Babylon is fallen, is fallen, that great city, because she made all nations drink of the wine of the wrath of her fornication. Rev. 14:8.

Many expected that those who passed through the disappointment, would forever sink out of sight, but the angel said, "Thou must prophesy again, before many peoples, and nations, and tongues, and kings." This foretells the third message of Rev. 14:9–12, which will go to all the world, increasing as it goes, until it swells into a loud cry.

***And he said unto me, Thou must prophesy again before many peoples, and nations, and tongues, and kings. Rev. 10:11.***

Rev. 18:1.

Many peoples, the nations of earth, representatives from every tongue, rich and poor, even kings on their thrones, will hear this last message of mercy which goes to the earth in the beginning of the sounding of the seventh trumpet. The angel's face was like the sun, and a rainbow was upon his head. The message is one of peace and joy, of mercy and triumph, which begins with the glory veiled, but increases in grandeur until what is begun on earth, mingles with the song of the redeemed on the other shore. As the people of God, by faith followed their Lord into the heavenly sanctuary, the bitter disappointment passed, and they realized that "Though ye have lien among the pots, yet shall ye be as the wings of a dove covered with silver, and her feathers with yellow gold."

Therefore thus saith the Lord, If thou return, then will I bring thee again, and thou shalt stand before me: and if thou take forth the precious from the vile, thou shalt be as my mouth: let them return unto thee; but return not thou unto them.

And I will make thee unto this people a fenced brazen wall: and they shall fight against thee, but they shall not prevail against thee: for I am with thee to save thee and to deliver thee, saith the Lord. Jer. 15:19, 20.

Isa. 57:18, 19.

Hear the word of the Lord, ye that tremble at his word; Your brethren that hated you, that cast you out for my name's sake, said, Let the Lord be glorified: but he shall appear to your joy, and they shall be ashamed. Isa. 66:5.

Psa. 68:13.

# CHAPTER XII.

## THE THIRD WOE.

THE record contained in the three preceding chapters is the world's history from the stand point which could be best presented to the human mind by the symbol of the trumpet. The eighth chapter portrays the fall of the Western Roman Empire. The prophet, in the ninth chapter, follows events which occurred in connection with the downfall of the Greek Empire and the setting up of the Ottoman power, clearly portraying the four periods in Turkish history: first, its rise; second, the one hundred and fifty years, during which time its power was restricted; third, the three hundred and ninety-one years and fifteen days of supreme rule; fourth, its existence by sufferance, until driven from Europe. The tenth chapter of Revelation gives the loud cry of the first angel's message, which was proclaimed by believers in God just at the time of the ending of the second woe. It foretells also the greater work to follow in the form of another message, which is given in detail in the fourteenth chapter of the book of Reve-

I saw the seven angels which stood before God; and to them were given seven trumpets.
Rev. 8:2.

FOUR PERIODS IN TURKISH HISTORY.
1st. Rev. 9:1-4.
2nd. Rev. 9:5-10.
3rd. Rev. 9:14, 15.
4th. Dan. 11:45.

Saying with a loud voice, Fear God, and give glory to him; for the hour of his judgment is come: and worship him that made heaven, and earth, and the sea, and the fountains of waters. Rev. 14:7.

The third angel followed them, saying with a loud voice, If any man worship the beast and his image, and receive his mark in his forehead, or in his hand,
The same shall drink of the wine of the wrath of God.
Rev. 14:9-13.

lation. The eleventh chapter, the one now before us, goes back to the Western Empire, and shows what was going on in that part of the world during the time that the Turkish Empire was making history in the eastern division.

The barbarians in 476 left Rome in a divided state. The ten tribes, namely, the Ostrogoths, the Lombards, the Heruli, the Vandals, the Visigoths, the Suevi, the Saxons, the Huns, the Burgundians, and the Franks, were by that time, or a few years later, settled within the borders of the Western Empire True, the Vandals, Heruli, and Ostrogoths were of short duration, having been, before the year 538, "plucked up" to make way for the enthroning of the ecclesiastical power, according to the prophetic history of Dan. 7 : 8. But from the other seven developed the nations of Europe which are in existence to-day. The smoke from the "bottomless pit" beclouded the eastern sky, and the consideration of the Eastern Empire necessitates a study of Mohammedanism instead of Christianity. The condition was different in the western division, that portion of Europe still claimed to be ruled by the precepts of Christ. Mohammedanism in its attempt to conquer the western nations met with a telling defeat in the eighth century, and never renewed the attempt. So the West stood before the world as the representative of the Christian religion. Here the principles of civil and religious liberty, to-day held dear, were born: and here, likewise, was committed to these nations, in a special manner, the everlasting Gospel, with the commission to make it known to the world. God was preparing, from afar, for the spread of the last message to the world.

The fourth kingdom shall be strong as iron: forasmuch as iron breaketh in pieces and subdueth all things: and as iron that breaketh all these, shall it break in pieces and bruise.

And whereas thou sawest the feet and toes, part of potters' clay, and part of iron, the kingdom shall be divided; but there shall be in it of the strength of the iron, forasmuch as thou sawest the iron mixed with miry clay. Dan. 2:40, 41.

The ten horns out of this kingdom are ten kings that shall arise: and another shall rise after them; and he shall be diverse from the first, and he shall subdue three kings. Dan. 7:24.

I considered the horns, and, behold, there came up among them another little horn, before whom there were three of the first horns plucked up by the roots: and, behold, in this horn were eyes like the eyes of man, and a mouth speaking great things. Dan. 7:8.

He opened the bottomless pit; and there arose a smoke out of the pit, as the smoke of a great furnace; and the sun and the air were darkened by reason of the smoke of the pit. Rev. 9:2.

Having a form of godliness, but denying the power thereof: from such turn away. 2 Tim. 3:5.

The earth helped the woman, and the earth opened her mouth, and swallowed up the flood which the dragon cast out of his mouth. Rev. 12:16.

To John was given a measuring reed, "and the angel stood, saying, Rise, and measure the temple of God, and the altar, and them that worship therein." Men have as many standards for measuring their fellow-beings as there are different individuals, but the one absolute rule by which men's actions are measured for eternity, is an infinitely perfect and unvarying standard. It cannot be comprehended by the finite mind; for it is infinite. "Let us hear the conclusion of the whole matter: Fear God, and keep His commandments: for this is the whole duty of man. For God shall bring every work into judgment, with every secret thing, whether it be good, or whether it be evil." The "reed like unto a rod," with which John was bidden to measure, was the commandments of God. With his angel guide, the prophet was shown the church of God and the world, and the wisdom of God was given to him that he might record the results of the measurements. God's law is but an expression of His own character, and John's mind was opened to an appreciation of the principles upon which the government of God is established. There was the temple where the Father sits enthroned, Himself the center of all law, all life, all love; His presence pervading all things, upholding all things, controlling all things. The temple was to be measured, and when measured, it told the story of absolute love, the power of the Creator, who made all beings to reflect His own perfection. Then John was to measure the altar. Here he saw the High Priest, with His censer, offering the prayers of His saints. Only the Infinite mind can grasp the breadth and length and depth and

*And there was given me a reed like unto a rod: and the angel stood, saying, Rise, and measure the temple of God, and the altar, and them that worship therein.*
*Rev. 11:1.*

So speak ye, and so do, as they that shall be judged by the law of liberty. Jas. 2:12.

Rom. 2:12, 13.

Because the carnal mind is enmity against God: for it is not subject to the law of God, neither indeed can be. Rom 8:7.

I say unto you, That every idle word that men shall speak, they shall give account thereof in the day of judgment.

For by thy words thou shalt be justified, and by thy words thou shalt be condemned.
Matt. 12:36, 37.

Judgment also will I lay to the line, and righteousness to the plummet: and the hail shall sweep away the refuge of lies, and the waters shall overflow the hiding place.
Isa. 28:17.

Wherefore the law is holy, and the commandment holy, and just, and good. Rom. 7:12.

For we know that the law is spiritual: but I am carnal, sold under sin. Rom. 7.14.

Ye shall keep my sabbaths, and reverence my sanctuary: I am the Lord. Lev. 19:30.

Upholding all things by the word of his power. Heb. 1:3.

Another angel came and stood at the altar, having a golden censer; and there was given unto him much incense, that he should offer it with the prayers of all saints upon the golden altar which was before the throne. Rev. 8:3.

Rom. 8:26, 27.

That Christ may dwell in your hearts by faith; that ye, being rooted and grounded in love,

May be able to comprehend with all saints what is the breadth, and length, and depth and height;

And to know the love of Christ, which passeth knowledge, that ye might be filled with all the fulness of God.

Now unto him that is able to do exceeding abundantly above all that we ask or think, according to the power that worketh in us.

Eph. 3:17-20.

For thou wast slain, and hast redeemed us to God by thy blood out of every kindred, and tongue, and people, and nation;

And hast made us unto our God kings and priests: and we shall reign on the earth. Rev. 5:9, 10.

Ye also, as lively stones, are built up a spiritual house, an holy priesthood, to offer up spiritual sacrifices, acceptable to God by Jesus Christ.

1 Pet. 2:5.

Thus he shewed me: and, behold, the Lord stood upon a wall made by a plumbline, with a plumbline in his hand.

And the Lord said unto me, Amos, what seest thou? And I said, A plumbline. Then said the Lord, Behold, I will set a plumbline in the midst of my people Israel: I will not again pass by them any more.

Amos 7:7, 8.

Isa. 61:10.

When he had opened the third seal, I heard the third beast say, Come and see. And I beheld, and lo a black horse; and he that sat on him had a pair of balances in his hand. Rev. 6:5.

height, and know the love of Christ which "passeth knowledge"; but this theme will be man's study throughout eternity, for when it is known, it reveals the fullness of God. Again it is infinite love. And as it is measured, it must be measured in every direction; there is length and breadth and height and depth; and in it all, the measures read, Love! infinite, far-reaching love!

The prophet was told to measure them that worship in the temple; for the creatures of His hand reflect His image, and are measured by the same standard. Angels worship in that temple, and they reflect the character of Him who is love. There were also men in that temple as worshipers; saints, who, while still on earth, were by faith within the inner veil; and they too were measured by the same reed of His law. Not an outward measure of stature, nor an external weighing of motives, as viewed by the human eye, but character was the test, with the rule of heaven for a standard. The character which is rewarded with a place near the throne is not shallow, but deep; it is not narrow, but broad; and in length it must measure with the life of God. A long experience, a deep experience, a broad experience in divine things, even while living here on earth; this is the life which develops a character that will stand the test of the "measuring reed."

Under the third seal was revealed a power on the earth which carried a pair of balances, to weigh the deeds of men. While a self-righteous standard was being erected on the earth, God was measuring according to the rule of heaven; and when character was measured by the divine rod, eternal life was often given to those, who according to the balances in the hands of man, were accounted worthy of death.

It would seem that the attention of the prophet was called to the measuring in the outer court, which the loosened seals had revealed to him; and he is told to leave out "the court which is without the temple, and measure it not; for it is given unto the Gentiles," those who know not God; and the holy city shall they tread under foot forty and two months. This locates the scene definitely in what was the Western Empire, for the same period of time is given by Daniel. In the seventh chapter of that prophecy, the power which plucked up the three barbarian tribes before referred to, "shall speak great words against the Most High, and shall wear out the saints of the Most High, and think to change times and laws: and they (times, laws, and saints) shall be given into his hand until a time and times and the dividing of time."

In prophecy one day stands for a year, and time is reckoned thirty days to the month. Forty-two months is equivalent to twelve hundred and sixty days of prophetic time, or twelve hundred and sixty years of literal time. The "time and times, and the dividing of time," is the same period as the "forty and two months," or twelve hundred and sixty years. The power which trod the people of God under foot for twelve hundred and sixty years was the papacy. This power was established in Rome in 538 A. D. on the ruins of the Western Empire, and continued until 1798 A. D. This was the period known as the Dark Ages for Europe. During this period the smoke of Mohammedanism hid the light of

I saw the souls of them that were beheaded for the witness of Jesus, and for the word of God, and which had not worshipped the beast, neither his image, neither had received his mark upon their foreheads, or in their hands; and they lived and reigned with Christ a thousand years. Rev. 20:4.

*But the court which is without the temple leave out, and measure it not; for it is given unto the Gentiles: and the holy city shall they tread under foot forty and two months. Rev. 11:2.*

Dan. 7:25.

Num. 14:34.

There was given unto him a mouth speaking great things and blasphemies; and power was given unto him to continue forty and two months. Rev. 13:5.

Dan. 12:7.
Rev. 12:14.

The woman fled into the wilderness, where she hath a place prepared of God, that they should feed her there a thousand two hundred and threescore days. Rev. 12:6.

The dragon gave him his power, and his seat, and great authority. Rev. 13:2.

Rev. 9:2, 3.

Let no man deceive you by any means: for that day shall not come, except there come a falling away first, and that man of sin be revealed, the son of perdition.
2 Thess. 2:3.

Seemeth it a small thing unto you to have eaten up the good pasture, but ye must tread down with your feet the residue of your pastures? and to have drunk of the deep waters, but ye must foul the residue with your feet?

the sun in the East. Mohammedanism in the East, and the "man of sin" in the West, both brought darkness and despair. Mohammedanism tormented men like the sting of a scorpion; the "man of sin" held men's minds in such subjection that they saw nothing above the exalted man on the throne. In the East, the Koran and a false prophet bore sway; in the West, precisely the same thraldom existed; for while there was no Koran, the Word of God was suppressed just as effectually. As Mohammedanism substituted the sixth day of the week for the Sabbath, and accepted a false prophet instead of Christ, so the "man of sin" thought to change the law of God, and attempted to change the times which were created by the Word of Jehovah, as surely as man himself was so created. In the East, the Koran wholly replaced the Bible; in the West, God said, "I will give power unto my two witnesses, that they shall prophesy a thousand two hundred and three-score days, clothed in sackcloth." For twelve hundred and sixty years [days] the light of God was hidden as beneath a covering of sackcloth. Men think that with the advanced knowledge of the twentieth century, human reason has outgrown the Word of God; but history proves, without the shadow of a doubt, that when the Word is replaced by

**At that very time God was measuring character by the law.**

And as for my flock, they eat that which ye have trodden with your feet; and they drink that which ye have fouled with your feet.
Eze. 34:18, 19.

Think to change times and laws: and they shall be given into his hand until a time and times and the dividing of time. Dan. 7:25.

*And I will give power unto my two witnesses, and they shall prophesy a thousand two hundred and threescore days, clothed in sackcloth. Rev. 11:3.*

the products of man's mind, both moral and intellectual darkness are brought upon the world. In this darkness the balances were held by those who believed that man was above God, that reason was the ultimate standard for judgment; but at that very time God was measuring character by the measuring reed of heaven,—the law which man in his blindness had set aside.

The "two witnesses" are the Old and the New Testaments. In the mouth of two witnesses every word is established. The Old Testament told of the God, who strove to live in man; the New Testament told of the God, who had lived in the human form, and the two agree. The same mystery is revealed to each individual heart in the providences of God. Christ, the God-man, sat on the curbing of Jacob's well at the hour of noon, when the Samaritan woman came to draw water. Likewise the Divine Spirit drew the woman of Samaria to the well at the very hour when the Son of man was there. These two witnesses agree. They agree in lives to-day. When the spiritual eye is opened, the testimony of the two witnesses will be accepted.

For they are the "two olive branches which through the two golden pipes empty the golden oil out of themselves." By the prophet Zechariah, the church is represented as a golden candlestick having seven branches, each bearing aloft a light for the world. These seven branches receive their oil from a single bowl, and the oil for this bowl is supplied by two olive trees, one on either side. The purity of the oil they burn is represented by the close connection with living, growing trees. This oil

Making the word of God of none effect through your tradition, which ye have delivered: and many such like things do ye. Mark 7:13.

Her priests have violated my law, and have profaned mine holy things: they have put no difference between the holy and profane, neither have they shewed difference between the unclean and the clean, and have hid their eyes from my sabbaths, and I am profaned among them. Eze. 22:26.

*These are the two olive trees, and the two candlesticks standing before the God of the earth.*
*Rev. 11:4.*

Zech. 4:2-6.

When the fulness of the time was come, God sent forth his Son, made of a woman, made under the law. Gal. 4:4.

Now Jacob's well was there. Jesus therefore, being wearied with his journey, sat thus on the well: and it was about the sixth hour.

There cometh a woman of Samaria to draw water: Jesus saith unto her, Give me to drink.
John 4:6, 7.

Zech. 4:12.
Rev. 1:20.

And said unto me, What seest thou? And I said, I have looked, and behold a candlestick all of gold, with a bowl upon the top of it, and his seven lamps thereon, and seven pipes to the seven lamps, which are upon the top thereof:

And two olive trees by it, one upon the right side of the bowl, and the other upon the left side thereof.
Zech. 4:2, 3.

It is the spirit that quickeneth; the flesh profiteth nothing: the words that I speak unto you, they are spirit, and they are life.
John 6:63.

I am the vine, ye are the branches: He that abideth in me, and I in him, the same bringeth forth much fruit: for severed from me ye can do nothing.
John 15:5 [margin.]

The foolish said unto the wise, Give us of your oil; for our lamps are gone out. Matt. 25:8.

*And if any man will hurt them, fire proceedeth out of their mouth, and devoureth their enemies: and if any man will hurt them, he must in this manner be killed.*
*These have power to shut heaven, that it rain not in the days of their prophecy: and have power over waters to turn them to blood, and to smite the earth with all plagues, as often as they will.*
*Rev. 11:5, 6.*

So shall my word be that goeth forth out of my mouth: it shall not return unto me void, but it shall accomplish that which I please, and it shall prosper in the thing whereto I sent it. Isa. 55:11.

Jas. 5:17.
The emptiers have emptied them out, and marred their vine branches.
Nahum 2:2.

I saw the woman drunken with the blood of the saints, and with the blood of the martyrs of Jesus: and when I saw her, I wondered with great admiration.
Rev. 17:6.

is the oil of grace, the truth of God. The unity of the seven candlesticks is typified by the common bowl from which each gains its supply of oil. How beautiful a picture of the work of God's Word in ministering to the needs of the church on earth. Life flows from the Old as well as the New Testament to those whose hearts are open channels for the Spirit. When connection with the living trees is severed, spiritual death is the result. The lights may burn for a time, but they soon exhaust the supply in the bowl, and gradually the flame dies out. Extinguishing a light does not affect the olive trees. Indeed they are trees of life, guarded by flaming swords, like the tree of life in the garden of Eden after the fall; and the flashes of light destroy the life of those who lift a hand against the witnesses. Men may claim to receive light, independently of these witnesses; but there are no channels for the communication of the spirit of wisdom and knowledge, except these two trees, or some of their branches, through which the life, the golden oil, is constantly flowing. It is thus that they have power to stay the heavens that it rain not. It is for this reason that the three and a half years of drought in the days of Elijah are used by the divine historian to illustrate the three and one-half prophetic years, the twelve hundred and sixty years of darkness, brought about by severing the connection between the church and the two witnesses. When the connection was broken the restraining power of God was withdrawn; and as in the natural world, so in the spiritual, there was nothing to prevent bloodshed, famine, and persecution. The time of great persecution was the period during which the witnesses prophesied covered with sackcloth. The Reformation removed the sackcloth from the two witnesses. From the close of the fourteenth century, when Wycliffe's translation placed the Word of God in the hands of the common people of England, until the full dawn of the Reformation, the restraint which had long been placed upon the Scriptures was gradually removed. The light was spread largely through the schools. In Germany, the University of Wittenberg made the study of the Word its most prominent feature, and at the educational centers in England, Germany, and France the heralds of truth received their inspiration and their training. In the preparation of laborers, the Scriptures formed the basis of all instruction; and as the classics and false sciences of the Dark Ages gave way to the Bible as a textbook, so the formal, lifeless methods of theological instruction were exchanged for teaching which fed the souls of the students. The remarkable swiftness with which society was remolded when the Word of God was restored is witnessed to by all historians. The historian, Ranke, states that in the short period of forty years the darkness had been broken from the Baltic to the Mediterranean, and Germany sat at the feet of Protestant teachers. Error trembled before a few teachers armed with the invincible Word of God. At this juncture the speedy overthrow of the false system was prevented by a counter educational movement. The organization of the order of Jesuits, in reality a papacy of the papacy, sent into the world a body of active workers, shrewd, well educated, and armed with

For now will I break his yoke from off thee, and will burst thy bonds in sunder. Nahum 1:13.

Thou through thy commandments hast made me wiser than mine enemies: for they are ever with me.

I have more understanding than all my teachers: for thy testimonies are my meditation.

I understand more than the ancients, because I keep thy precepts. Psa. 119:98–100.

Many of them also which used curious arts brought their books together, and burned them before all men: and they counted the price of them, and found it fifty thousand pieces of silver.

So mightily grew the word of God and prevailed. Acts. 19:19, 20.

Keep therefore and do them; for this is your wisdom and your understanding in the sight of the nations, which shall hear all these statutes, and say, Surely this great nation is a wise and understanding people.

For what nation is there so great, who hath God so nigh unto them, as the Lord our God is in all things that we call upon him for? Deut. 4:6–8.

For such are false apostles, deceitful workers, transforming themselves into the apostles of Christ.

And no marvel; for Satan himself is transformed into an angel of light.

Therefore it is no great thing if his ministers also be transformed as the ministers of righteousness; whose end shall be according to their works. 2 Cor. 11:13–15.

Unto the pure all things are pure: but unto them that are defiled and unbelieving is nothing pure; but even their mind and conscience is defiled. Titus 1:15.

Ye compass sea and land to make one proselyte, and when he is made, ye make him twofold more the child of hell than yourselves. Matt. 23:13-15.

Whose mouths must be stopped, who subvert whole houses, teaching things which they ought not, for filthy lucre's sake. Titus 1:11.

Avoiding profane and vain babblings, and oppositions of science falsely so called:
Which some professing have erred concerning the faith. 1 Tim. 6:20, 21.

If any man teach otherwise, and consent not to wholesome words, even the words of our Lord Jesus Christ, and to the doctrine which is according to godliness;
He is proud, knowing nothing, but doting about questions and strifes of words, whereof cometh envy, strife, railings, evil surmisings,
Perverse disputings of men of corrupt minds, and destitute of the truth, supposing that gain is godliness: from such withdraw thyself. 1 Tim. 6:3-5.

*And when they shall have finished their testimony, the beast that ascendeth out of the bottomless pit shall make war against them, and shall overcome them, and kill them. Rev. 11:7.*

a double-faced conscience, which enabled them to penetrate anywhere and assume any role. One of their most efficient methods of procedure was in the schools. They founded new schools in the very shadow of the Protestant institutions, and drew from their patronage; or when this was impossible, they entered Protestant schools under the guise of Protestant teachers. Everywhere they gained the children and the youth. They were more zealous, more ambitious than the Protestants, consequently the succeeding generation surprised the Reformers by turning a large part of Europe back under papal control. Their work was most fully developed in France. That country had received the light of the Reformation, but on this ground the Jesuits found excellent material. The universities of France clung to their old methods, and they likewise clung to the subjects taught during the Dark Ages. Under the forms and ceremonies of Mediævalism, pa al principles of government lurked, ready to spring into active service at the first opportunity. The renewal of these teachings wrought the same effect in the sixteenth century that the false teachings of the Alexandrian philosophers did in the church of the early Christians.

One cannot condemn the Jesuit teaching as wholly evil. It was as subtile a mixture of the good and evil as the devil ever compounded. It was when the two witnesses were escaping from the bondage of the Dark Ages, where they had finished their testimony in sackcloth, that the beast, which ascended out of the bottomless pit, made war against them and overcame them, and killed them.

The Counter-Reformation, known as such by all historians, was felt throughout Europe; but France was unfortunate enough to have sown an abundance of seed, and consequently reaped a bountiful harvest. France is the only nation that ever openly denied the existence of the Deity, and set up a worship recognizing no other ruler than the "Goddess of Reason." A woman, a profligate opera singer, was set up in Paris as a personification of reason, the god which France acknowledged. No other government ever made so base a movement. Men and women danced and sang in honor of the base idolatry. Other parts of France imitated the example set by Paris. The woman, veiled and worshiped in form, was but a type of what men will do when reason is enthroned above God. The decree prohibiting the Bible, changing the week, and establishing the worship of the "Goddess of Reason," was issued in 1793. For three years and a half, the two witnesses,—the two olive trees, which alone bring life to man or nation,—lay dead in the streets of Paris. The licentiousness of Sodom in the days of Lot, was repeated in France, especially in her capital The gross idolatry of Egypt, with its proverbial darkness, was to be found again in modern France. As the Jews, by rejecting the Word of God sent by the prophets, severed their connection with heaven and crucified their Lord, so France repeated the sin, and crucified again the Son of God.

The Reign of Terror had established itself in France. Whoever was suspected of hostility toward the tyranny, was immediately hurried to the scaffold; to be lukewarm was no protection.

For they have sown the wind, and they shall reap the whirlwind. Hosea 8:7.

Neither shall he regard the God of his fathers, nor the desire of women, nor regard any god: for he shall magnify himself above all.

But in his estate shall he honour the God of forces: and a god whom his fathers knew not shall he honour with gold, and silver, and with precious stones, and pleasant things. Dan. 11:37, 38.

Hear, O earth: behold, I will bring evil upon this people, even the fruit of their thoughts, because they have not hearkened unto my words, nor to my law, but rejected it. Jer. 6:19.

*And their dead bodies shall lie in the street of the great city, which spiritually is called Sodom and Egypt, where also our Lord was crucified. Rev. 11:8.*

Gen. 19:4-11.

They crucify to themselves the Son of God afresh, and put him to an open shame. Heb. 6:6.

The wise men are ashamed, they are dismayed and taken: lo, they have rejected the word of the Lord; and what wisdom is in them?

Therefore will I give their wives unto others, and their fields to them that shall inherit them: for every one from the least even unto the greatest is given to covetousness, from the prophet even unto the priest every one dealeth falsely. Jer. 8:9, 10.

Samaria shall become desolate; for she hath rebelled against her God: they shall fall by the sword: their infants shall be dashed in pieces, and their women with child shall be ripped up. Hos. 13:16.

Lam. 4:12.

*And they of the people and kindreds and tongues and nations shall see their dead bodies three days and an half, and shall not suffer their dead bodies to be put in graves.*

*And they that dwell upon the earth shall rejoice over them, and make merry, and shall send gifts one to another; because these two prophets tormented them that dwelt on the earth.*

*And after three days and an half the spirit of life from God entered into them, and they stood upon their feet; and great fear fell upon them which saw them.*

*And they heard a great voice from heaven saying unto them,*

Old age and youth alike suffered. Wild license was given to divorce and to profligacy. "There were seen, even in the hall of the convention, throngs of coarse and fierce men, and coarser and fiercer women with their songs and wild outcries and gestures." "Crowds escorted the batch of victims carried on carts each day to the place of execution, and insulted them with their brutal shouts." Men of other nations looked on in utter astonishment. The worship of reason was abolished, and the convention passed a resolution acknowledging the existence of God, but denouncing Christianity as a base superstition. Thus the Reign of Terror went on. "The deaths from want," says one historian, "much exceeded a million. France was on the brink of a great famine on the Asiatic scale." But men grew weary of bloodshed, and "great fear fell upon them which saw" these things. The God of heaven called a halt. Nations of the earth had seen the consequences of rejecting the Word of Jehovah; they had had before them, in the Reign of Terror, a most terrible example of the rejection of the principles of the Reformation. The Spirit of God was again recognized as residing in the "two witnesses," and before all nations the Scriptures have since been exalted. Those nations, which adhered most closely to the truths developed in the withdrawal from Roman tyranny, have taken the lead in the work of education, in invention, in judiciary matters, and in all lines of progress. Copies of the Word of God have been multiplied until the

**Before all nations the Scriptures have since been exalted.**

poorest are without excuse, if they remain unsupplied. Before the terrors in France, little attention was given to foreign missions; but in 1804 the British Bible Society was organized. Thirteen years later, the American Bible Society came into existence, and millions of copies of the Word have been printed. Its translation into hundreds of different languages has placed ignorance of the Scriptures entirely out of the question.

The restoration of the Christian religion in France, marked the beginning of its modern history. The Revolution of 1798 is spoken of as "a great earthquake," in which the "tenth part of the city fell." The "beast" received its deadly wound. Not only was the reign of papal tyranny at an end, but the power of the monarchy was shaken; and the vast army of nobles, which some historians give as seven thousand, lost their titles. The government was in the hands of the middle classes, or the common people. The exaltation of the Scriptures is always followed by a government which recognizes the equal rights of all men, and by a religion which grants the privilege to every man to worship according to the dictates of his own conscience. Men who advocate a system of government that rejects the atoning blood of Christ, or an educational system which exalts reason above faith, place themselves on the very verge of a precipice, and the next step will produce a repetition of the Terrors of France. The blindness with which men repeat the experiences of the past is amazing. The Jesuits may not be responsible to-day for the trend which many public institutions are taking, but,

*Come up hither. And they ascended up to heaven in a cloud; and their enemies beheld them.*
*Rev. 11:9-12.*

When wisdom entereth into thine heart, and knowledge is pleasant unto thy soul;
Discretion shall preserve thee, understanding shall keep thee:
To deliver thee from the way of the evil man, from the man that speaketh froward things.
Prov. 2:10–12.

The entrance of thy words giveth light; it giveth understanding unto the simple. Psa. 119:130.

*And the same hour was there a great earthquake, and the tenth part of the city fell, and in the earthquake were slain of men seven thousand: and the remnant were affrighted, and gave glory to the God of heaven. Rev. 11:13.*

But there is a spirit in man: and the inspiration of the Almighty giveth them understanding.
Great men are not always wise: neither do the aged understand judgment. Job 32:8, 9.

That which hath been is now; and that which is to be hath already been; and God requireth that which is past. Eccl. 3:15.

She is empty, and void, and waste: and the heart melteth, and the knees smite together, and much pain is in all loins, and the faces of them all gather blackness. Nahum 2:10.

As they were increased, so they sinned against me: therefore will I change their glory into shame.
Hosea 4:7.

The Pharisees and lawyers rejected the counsel of God against themselves, being not baptized of him. Luke 7:30.

Know ye not that a little leaven leaveneth the whole lump?
Purge out therefore the old leaven, that ye may be a new lump.
1 Cor. 5:6, 7.

without doubt, the methods the Jesuits used, are repeated in the twentieth century. Education which leaves out God, is putting the government into the hands of statesmen who will eventually exalt the Goddess of Reason.

Give ear, O ye heavens, and I will speak; and hear, O earth, the words of my mouth. Deut. 32:1.

The second woe, as already seen, ended in 1840. The close was marked by the transfer of Turkish power into the hands of the western nations. In heaven is witnessed the sending forth of the mighty angel of Rev. 10:1–11. The earth responded to his loud cry, and men, thinking that time was about to close, prepared to meet their God. But the seventh angel had not yet sounded. He was held in heaven for a little space, that men might be prepared for the events about to come in connection with the completion of the earth's history. "The second woe is past; and behold, the third woe cometh quickly." The little period between 1840 and 1844, during which the message of Rev. 10:1–11 was delivered, was the time between the close of the sixth trumpet and the sounding of the seventh. In the tenth chapter of Revelation John was told that "in the days of the voice of the seventh angel, when he shall begin to sound, the mystery of God should be finished." When the seventh angel "begins to sound," in the first part of the period of time set apart for his work, the mystery of God would be finished. "And the seventh angel sounded; and there were great voices in heaven, saying, The kingdoms of this world are become the kingdoms of our Lord and of His Christ; and He shall reign forever and ever." A kingdom can never be truly said to pass into the hands of another power, while either the territory, the capital, or the subjects,

*The second woe is past; and, behold, the third woe cometh quickly. Rev. 11:14.*

There was given him dominion, and glory, and a kingdom, that all people, nations, and languages, should serve him: his dominion is an everlasting dominion, which shall not pass away, and his kingdom that which shall not be destroyed.
Dan 7 14.

*And the seventh angel sounded; and there were great voices in heaven, saying, The kingdoms of this world are become the kingdoms of our Lord, and of his Christ; and he shall reign for ever and ever. Rev. 11:15.*

are beyond its control. It takes the three: subjects, capital, and territory, to make the full kingdom. The work of the investigative judgment, is Christ making up the number of the subjects, or in other words, taking one-third part of His kingdom; when the judgment is ended, then is given to Him the Holy City, the capital of the kingdom,—the second third part. When He comes to the earth, He takes possession of the territory, and possesses the kingdom in all its fullness forever. The enrollment for the new kingdom is made by Christ in the presence of the Father, while angels are watching. The books are open, the judgment begins; the measuring reed is applied to character. Christ offers the prayers of all His saints,—those whose names are written in the book of life,—together with the fragrant incense of His own righteous life; in this way the heirs of the kingdom are enrolled.

Again the prophet sees the work completed; and the four and twenty elders, who have long waited for the redemption of their fellow beings, fall before the throne, and worship Him who is crowned King of Kings. These are the beings who, with the host of the redeemed, will finally have the renewed earth for their home. A part of their song before the Father is, "Thou hast made us unto our God kings and priests, and we shall reign on the earth," showing that in the midst of heavenly glory, they yet look forward to the restoration of the earth at the end of the thousand years, during which time, the cases of the wicked are tried.

In 1844 the third woe began. It extends into eternity, covering all the corruption of the

Come hither, I will shew thee the bride, the Lamb's wife.

And he carried me away in the spirit to a great and high mountain, and shewed me that great city, the holy Jerusalem, descending out of heaven from God.

Rev. 21:9, 10.

As therefore the tares are gathered and burned in the fire; so shall it be in the end of this world.

The Son of man shall send forth his angels, and they shall gather out of his kingdom all things that offend, and them which do iniquity.

Matt. 13:40, 41.

Rev. 3:5.
Luke 9:26.

Help those women which laboured with me in the gospel, with Clement also, and with other my fellowlabourers, whose names are in the book of life. Phil. 4:3.

Isa. 4:3.

*And the four and twenty elders, which sat before God on their seats, fell upon their faces, and worshipped God,*

*Saying, We give thee thanks, O Lord God Almighty, which art, and wast, and art to come; because thou hast taken to thee thy great power, and hast reigned.*

*And the nations were angry, and thy wrath is come, and the time of the dead, that they should be judged, and that thou shouldest give reward unto thy servants the prophets, and to the saints, and them that fear thy name, small and great; and shouldest destroy them which destroy the earth.*

*Rev. 11:16-18.*

Now go, write it before them in a table, and note it in a book, that it may be for the time to come for ever and ever:

That this is a rebellious people, lying children, children that will not hear the law of the Lord:

Which say to the seers, See not; and to the prophets, Prophesy not unto us right things, speak unto us smooth things, prophesy deceits.

Isa. 30:8-10.

For I am with thee, saith the Lord, to save thee: though I make a full end of all nations whither I have scattered thee, yet will I not make a full end of thee: but I will correct thee in measure, and will not leave thee altogether unpunished. Jer. 30:7, 11.

Rev. 20:9, 10.

Ye shall tread down the wicked; for they shall be ashes under the soles of your feet in the day that I shall do this, saith the Lord of hosts. Mal. 4:1-3.

*And the temple of God was opened in heaven, and there was seen in his temple the ark of his testament: and there were lightnings, and voices, and thunderings, and an earthquake, and great hail. Rev. 11:19.*

He said unto me, Unto two thousand and three hundred days; then shall the sanctuary be cleansed. Dan. 8:14.

Prove all things; hold fast that which is good. 2 Thess. 5:21.

If thou turn away thy foot from the sabbath, from doing thy pleasure on my holy day; and call the sabbath a delight, the holy of the Lord, honourable; and shalt honour him, not doing thine own ways, nor finding thine own pleasure, nor speaking thine own words:

Then shalt thou delight thyself in the Lord. Isa. 58:13:14.

last days,—the anger or distress among nations, which was one sign of the second advent, as given by the Saviour. During the sounding of the seventh trumpet, the seven last plagues are poured out; men, having rejected God, drink of the wine of His wrath. During this sounding, the righteous and wicked pass through the last great time of trouble, in comparison with which the Reign of Terror in France was a light affliction. During this woe, the saints of God welcome the Lord in the clouds of heaven, for He comes to give reward unto the faithful. This period continues over the one thousand years following the second coming of Christ, and ends when Satan and all the wicked are reduced to ashes upon the surface of the new earth, and all sorrow and sin are forever vanquished.

As foretold in the Scriptures, the ministration of Christ in the most holy place began at the termination of the prophetic days in 1844. The words of the revelator apply to this time. "The temple of God was opened in heaven, and there was seen in His temple the ark of His testament." At the beginning of the work of the investigative judgment, when Christ entered the most holy place, the door in heaven was opened, and the law of God was seen as the foundation of His throne. It was immediately after the bitter disappointment of 1844, when earnest souls were still searching the Scriptures, that the sacredness of the law was revealed. As the decalogue was presented, a special glory shone about the Fourth Commandment. The seal of the law stood out as if written in letters of fire, and a new significance was given to the measuring reed which the angel offered. The

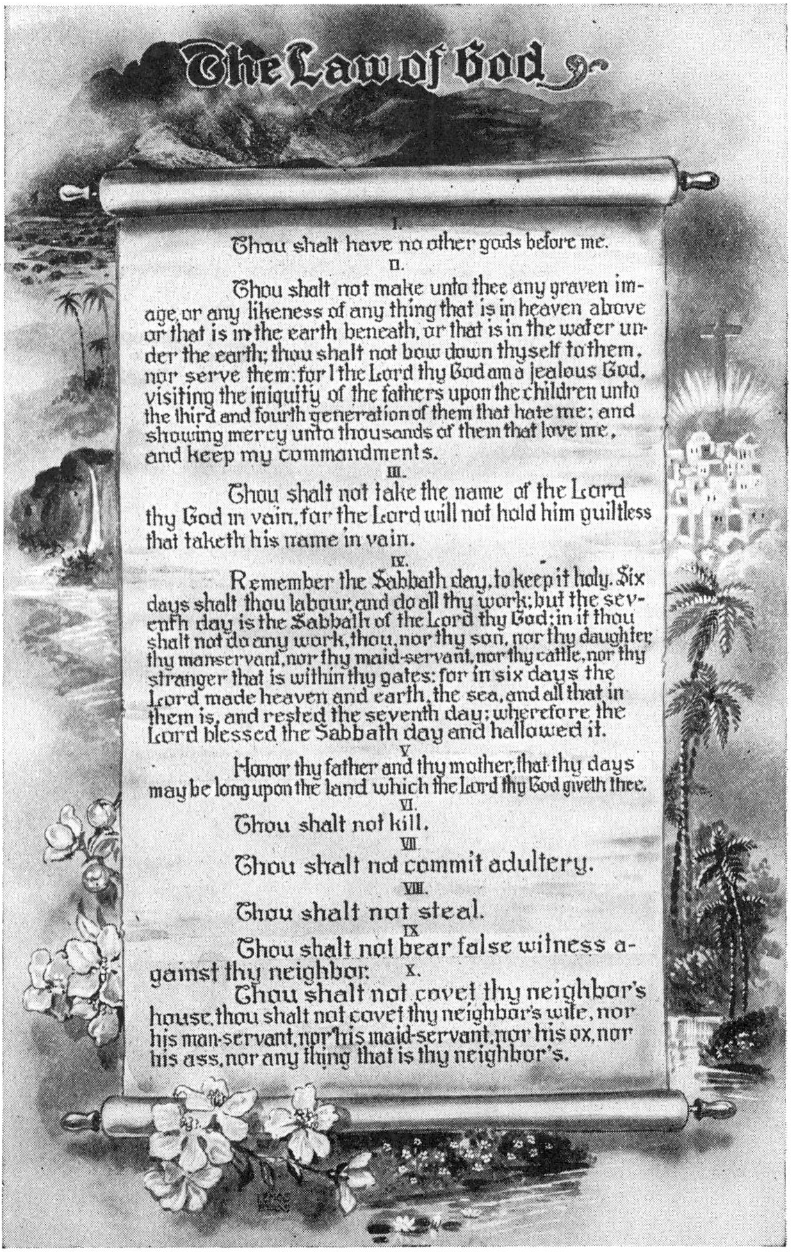
The Law of God
I.
Thou shalt have no other gods before me.
II.
Thou shalt not make unto thee any graven image, or any likeness of any thing that is in heaven above or that is in the earth beneath, or that is in the water under the earth; thou shalt not bow down thyself to them, nor serve them: for I the Lord thy God am a jealous God, visiting the iniquity of the fathers upon the children unto the third and fourth generation of them that hate me; and showing mercy unto thousands of them that love me, and keep my commandments.
III.
Thou shalt not take the name of the Lord thy God in vain, for the Lord will not hold him guiltless that taketh his name in vain.
IV.
Remember the Sabbath day, to keep it holy. Six days shalt thou labour, and do all thy work; but the seventh day is the Sabbath of the Lord thy God; in it thou shalt not do any work, thou, nor thy son, nor thy daughter, thy manservant, nor thy maid-servant, nor thy cattle, nor thy stranger that is within thy gates: for in six days the Lord made heaven and earth, the sea, and all that in them is, and rested the seventh day: wherefore the Lord blessed the Sabbath day and hallowed it.
V
Honor thy father and thy mother, that thy days may be long upon the land which the Lord thy God giveth thee.
VI.
Thou shalt not kill.
VII.
Thou shalt not commit adultery.
VIII.
Thou shalt not steal.
IX
Thou shalt not bear false witness against thy neighbor.
X.
Thou shalt not covet thy neighbor's house, thou shalt not covet thy neighbor's wife, nor his man-servant, nor his maid-servant, nor his ox, nor his ass, nor any thing that is thy neighbor's.

Lev. 26:2.

fuller significance of the trampling under foot of the law, and of the thinking to change the times and laws of Jehovah by an earthly power, filled the people of God with reverential awe; and again the two witnesses were exalted to heaven. The sealing work began at this very time, and those who were looking heavenward, saw the light streaming from that open door. Upon those to whom these rays are shining, the sealing angel places the mark of God. This sealed company make up the one hundred and forty-four thousand, who are a part of the host for whom the "four and twenty elders" are now waiting.

I saw another angel ascending from the east, having the seal of the living God. Rev. 7:2.

I heard the number of them which were sealed: and there were sealed an hundred and forty and four thousand of all the tribes of the children of Israel. Rev. 7:4.

As the proclamation is made in heaven that the work is over, the commandments are again seen; this time written on the clouds of the sky in the eyes of all men,—a sign of the near approach of Christ.

The heavens shall declare his righteousness: for God is judge himself. Psa. 50:6.

My tongue shall speak of thy word: for all thy commandments are righteousness. Psa. 119:172.

Under the sounding of the seventh trumpet are the thunderings, lightnings, voices, earthquake, and hail, which will shake the very foundations of the earth. With the close of the third woe, the earth is freed forever from the least taint of sorrow and sin. The Lord has pledged His word that affliction shall not rise up the second time, but joy and peace will reign forever in the redeemed earth.

For the Lord himself shall descend from heaven with a shout, with the voice of the archangel, and with the trump of God: and the dead in Christ shall rise first:

Then we which are alive and remain shall be caught up together with them in the clouds, to meet the Lord in the air: and so shall we ever be with the Lord. 1 Thess. 4:16, 17.

What do ye imagine against the Lord? he will make an utter end: affliction shall not rise up the second time. Nahum 1:9.

# CHAPTER XIII.

## THE GREAT CONTROVERSY.

THE salvation of souls is the end of an infinite plan. The object of all creation was the pleasure of God, and enjoyment comes to Jehovah when He sees the harmonious working of all the laws of the universe. Through the prophets, God has, from time to time, made known as much of the plan as the human mind could grasp. Each generation has received new revealing of that infinite plan of salvation. At each new manifestation, angels have exclaimed in wonder, and bowed in adoration before the throne; for it was the opening to their view of a new phase of the divine character. Beginning

Eze. 18:23, 31, 32.

Thou hast created all things, and for thy pleasure they are and were created. Rev. 4:11.

Col. 1:15, 16.

2 Pet. 1:20, 21.

ANGELS BOWED IN ADORATION.

1st. At the birth of Christ. Luke 2:9–14; Heb. 1:6.

2nd. At the death of Christ. John 12:31–33; Rev. 12:10.

3rd. At the resurrection of Christ. Matt. 27:51–53; Rom. 8:29; Eph. 4:8 [margin]; 1 Cor. 15:20.

4th. When the seventh angel sounded. Rev. 11:15; Dan. 7:13.

**Humble shepherds heard the angels singing at the birth of Christ.**

in Eden, God manifested His love in the relationship He sustained to the holy pair. The whole plan for peopling the earth with a race that could develop a spiritual nature like unto His own, was a revelation of His love.

The interest of heaven was centered upon humanity, and angels were commissioned to watch over them. This ministration of angels has linked heaven and earth by a tie which no power can sever. The enemy has offset each blessing of the Father by a hellish scheme; hence while some accept the workings of the Spirit of God, there are others who yield to the influence of the contrary spirit; and the earth has become a great battlefield. Every offering, from the first one at the gate of the Garden of Eden to the time of Christ, shadowed forth the one great sacrifice of the Saviour.

Many times, sin so blinded men's eyes that the form of the ceremony hid from them the real object of the service. Through Egyptian bondage, wilderness wanderings, prosperity, and captivity, the one hope buoyed up the spirits of the children of God. Their spiritual eyesight searched the future, ever expecting the appearance of the long-promised seed of the woman,

For thus saith the high and lofty One that inhabiteth eternity, whose name is Holy; I dwell in the high and holy place, with him also that is of a contrite and humble spirit, to revive the spirit of the humble, and to revive the heart of the contrite ones. Isa. 57:15.

1 Cor. 6:19, 20.
Psa. 34:7.
Psa. 91:11:12.

He dreamed, and behold a ladder set up on the earth, and the top of it reached to heaven: and behold the angels of God ascending and descending on it. Gen. 28:12.

All that dwell upon the earth shall worship him, whose names are not written in the book of life of the Lamb slain from the foundation of the world. Rev. 13:8.

Gen. 3:1-6.
Matt. 12:7.

that would bruise the serpent's head. True, they were often mistaken in their ideas of the Coming One; but in their individual need, they always pictured Him as their Deliverer. The self-righteous Jews, who had lost all the spiritual power in the sacrifices, while they multiplied forms, looked only for a mighty Prince who would deliver them from the Roman yoke. The prophecies concerning the meek and lowly One had no charm for them. These prophecies not only portrayed the character of the Messiah to come, but also revealed the time of His appearing. Satan is familiar with the Word of God, and trembles before its fulfillment. As the time drew near for the Son of man to appear, Satan used every art to absorb the children of men in the forms and ceremonies and sophistries of the world, in order that they might give no place for the lowly Jesus. But Satan was not permitted to bring confusion; for strange as it may seem, the whole world was at peace, when the Prince of Peace was born in a manger at Bethlehem.

True, the race which claimed to follow God, had lost the power of the Spirit, and the sway of evil was nearly universal. The connecting link, however, was not wholly severed; else the earth would have been destroyed, and neither Rome, with its boasted grandeur, nor Satan, with all his power, could have saved the wreck. Ministering at the altar in the temple in Jerusalem, was Zacharias, the priest. He and his wife Elizabeth prayed daily for the advent of the Son of God. Jehovah stopped to listen, and answered those prayers by giving to the aged priest and his wife a son, the forerunner of the Messiah.

I will put enmity between thee and the woman, and between thy seed and her seed; it shall bruise thy head, and thou shalt bruise his heel. Gen. 3:15.

When they therefore were come together, they asked of him, saying, Lord, wilt thou at this time restore again the kingdom to Israel? Acts 1:6.

Isa. 9:6, 7.
Dan. 9:25.

There were in the same country shepherds abiding in the field, keeping watch over their flock by night.
And, lo, the angel of the Lord came upon them, and the glory of the Lord shone round about them: and they were sore afraid.
And the angel said unto them, Fear not: for, behold, I bring you good tidings of great joy, which shall be to all people.
For unto you is born this day in the city of David a Saviour, which is Christ the Lord. Luke 2:8–12.

1 Cor. 1:26–29.
1 Pet. 3:3–5.
Rom. 3:10–18.

As Esaias said before, Except the Lord of Sabaoth had left us a seed, we had been as Sodoma, and been made like unto Gomorrha. Rom. 9:29.

There was in the days of Herod, the king of Judæa, a certain priest named Zacharias, of the course of Abia: and his wife was of the daughters of Aaron, and her name was Elisabeth.
And they were both righteous before God, walking in all the commandments and ordinances of the Lord blameless.
But the angel said unto him, Fear not, Zacharias: for thy prayer is heard; and thy wife Elisabeth shall bear thee a son, and thou shalt call his name John. Luke 1:5, 6, 13, 17.

In the sixth month the angel Gabriel was sent from God unto a city of Galilee, named Nazareth,

To a virgin espoused to a man whose name was Joseph, of the house of David; and the virgin's name was Mary.

And the angel came in unto her, and said, Hail, thou that art highly favoured, the Lord is with thee: blessed art thou among women.

And when she saw him, she was troubled at his saying, and cast in her mind what manner of salutation this should be.

And the angel said unto her, Fear not, Mary: for thou hast found favour with God.

And, behold, thou shalt conceive in thy womb, and bring forth a son, and shalt call his name JESUS.

Luke 1:26–38.

**Wise men of the East recognized the star.**

He came by the Spirit into the temple: and when the parents brought in the child Jesus, to do for him after the custom of the law,

Then took he him up in his arms, and blessed God. Luke 2:26–32.

There was one Anna, a prophetess, the daughter of Phanuel, of the tribe of Aser: she was of a great age.

And she coming in that instant gave thanks likewise unto the Lord, and spake of him to all them that looked for redemption in Jerusalem. Luke 2:36–38.

In the town of Nazareth, noted for its wickedness, lived a young woman. Daily her heart was lifted to God, asking for the advent of the promised Saviour. Again Jehovah's ear was reached, and that prayer was answered. Gabriel came from the presence of God, and made known to Mary that she, a virgin in Israel, should become the mother of the Son of God. The spirituality of her life is shown in her response to the angel. Taking her God-given responsibility, with all the sorrow and shame it entailed, she said: "Behold the handmaid of the Lord."[1] Three had been found who were true to the God of Heaven. There were still others. Humble shepherds, tending their flocks, heard the angels singing at the birth of Christ; wise men of the East, searching the prophecies, recognized the star as a herald of the Saviour.

On the day that the Babe was presented in the temple, Simeon, an aged man upon whom the Holy Ghost rested, and who saw with spiritual insight, recognized in the little One the Redeemer of men. And Anna, a prophetess, an aged widow, who lived in the temple, and who sought God day and night for the fulfillment of His promise, recognized divinity in the Babe, and giving thanks, "spake of Him to all them that looked for redemption in Jerusalem." This increased the number who in deed and in truth were waiting for the Messiah. They, while the world was in darkness and unconcern, travailed in birth for the world's Redeemer.

The faithful ones, the church of the living God,—few as their numbers may be, are represented as the "woman clothed with the sun, and the moon under her feet, and upon

" A woman clothed with the sun, and the moon under her feet."

her head a crown of twelve stars." It is the closing of one era, the age of types and shadows, which, like the moon, reflect the light of the true. The moon is under the feet of the church, and the glorious sunrising of a new day is ushered in. The paler light of the moon seems dim in that more glorious day. The types and ceremonies of the sanctuary service, which had been a shadow of the real, were passing away; for type met antitype in the Child that was born. Every sacrifice from the Garden of Eden to the cross, shadowed forth the great Sacrifice, and taught the everlasting Gospel. By faith, the sinner confessing his sins over the head of the innocent lamb, saw the real Sacrifice, and the light from Calvary reflected from the sacrifice shone into his heart. This service typified the Gospel in its fullness. This is the foundation upon which the church stands. It is not a stone slipping away, a sliding foundation, but a solid foundation upon which the living church rests. To-day the record of that typical service, emits light to the one who will search it. True, it does not have the full blaze of sunlight like the record of the antitypical Offering, but there is a mild and gentle light emitted from it that well repays the searcher after truth.

Around the head of the church clustered twelve stars, representing the twelve apostles, who became the fathers of the Christian church, their names are also on the twelve foundation stones of the New Jerusalem.

The followers of Christ are the special objects of care in the courts of heaven, and there never was a time when the interest was more intense

*And there appeared a great wonder in heaven; a woman clothed with the sun, and the moon under her feet, and upon her head a crown of twelve stars:*

*And she being with child cried, travailing in birth, and pained to be delivered. Rev. 12:1, 2.*

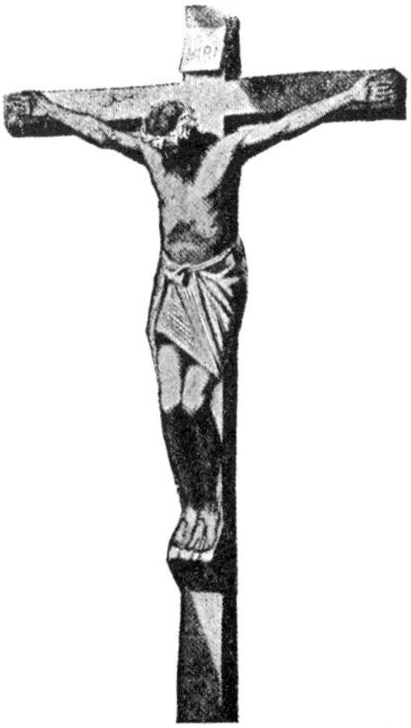

**By faith the sinner saw the real Sacrifice.**

The Holy Ghost this signifying, that the way into the holiest of all was not yet made manifest, while as the first tabernacle was yet standing:

Which was a figure for the time then present, in which were offered both gifts and sacrifices, that could not make him that did the service perfect, as pertaining to the conscience;

But Christ being come an high priest of good things to come, by a greater and more perfect tabernacle, not made with hands, that is to say, not of this building.

Heb. 9:8-11.

And are built upon the foundation of the apostles and prophets, Jesus Christ himself being the chief corner stone. Eph. 2:20, 21.

The devil said unto him, All this power will I give thee, and the glory of them: for that is delivered unto me; and to whomsoever I will I give it. Luke 4:6.

*And there appeared another wonder in heaven; and behold a great red dragon, having seven heads and ten horns, and seven crowns upon his heads. Rev. 12:3.*

than when the fullness of time was at hand, and the Son laid aside His God form, and clothed Himself in human flesh,—flesh subject to all the weaknesses of the frailest child on earth. Into the territory of Satan, into the nation which was the very essence of all untruth and deceit, the deepest, strongest compound of error, Christ came as a helpless child to show the power of truth and love.

**Cæsar Augustus.**

"There appeared another wonder in heaven;" it was the opposing power of Satan embodied in the ruling monarchy of earth—the empire of Rome, with Cæsar Augustus at its head. It is plainly stated in Rev. 12:9 that the great red dragon is the devil; and the seven heads with the ten horns represent the Roman Empire, in which the devil dwelt. This power during the reign of paganism, crucified the Saviour; and in its modified form, known as the papacy, held the church of God in bondage for twelve hundred and sixty years.

Luke 2:1.
Eph. 2:2.

I stood upon the sand of the sea, and saw a beast rise up out of the sea, having seven heads and ten horns, and upon his horns ten crowns, and upon his heads the name of blasphemy. Rev. 13:1.

Dan. 7:25.

Rome, at the time of the first advent, had, in her conquest about the Mediterranean, gained control of Palestine, the home of the Jews. Herod sat as king, but only by consent of the emperor, to whom he paid tribute. Herod was the last king who ruled over the Jews. "In his first will, he [Herod] appointed Antipas his successor; in his last, Archelaus." The people were ready to receive Archelaus, but afterwards revolted. Both he and Antipas went to Rome, each to present his claim to Cæsar for decision. Cæsar confirmed neither, but sent Archelaus back to Judea with the title of ethnarch; also with the promise of the crown, if he deserved it.

Search the Scriptures; for in them ye think ye have eternal life: and they are they which testify of me. John 5:39.

But his conduct was such that he never obtained it." This was the fulfillment of the prophecy concerning the Christ-child. Over seven hundred and fifty years before the Saviour's birth, Isaiah wrote: "Before the Child shall know to refuse the evil, and choose the good, the land that thou abhorrest shall be forsaken of both her kings." The death of Herod occurred when the Jewish nation was ruled by its king, aided by the Sanhedrin and the priests; and in the removing of the kings, the "dragon," through Rome, cast the third part of the stars of heaven to the earth. The divine hand which wrote this history cannot be hidden; for the very language which was literally fulfilled in Jerusalem, describes, with equal accuracy, the great fall in heaven, when Satan was cast out together with one-third of the angels,—those who adhered to his principles.

When he heard that Archelaus did reign in Judæa in the room of his father Herod, he was afraid to go thither: notwithstanding, being warned of God in a dream, he turned aside into the parts of Galilee. Matt. 2 : 22.

Isa. 7 : 16.

*And his tail drew the third part of the stars of heaven, and did cast them to the earth: and the dragon stood before the woman which was ready to be delivered, for to devour her child as soon as it was born. Rev. 12 : 4.*

**Bethlehem.**

Satan knew the time for the advent of the Son of man, and he determined to slay Him at birth. The history of the decree of Herod, who caused the slaying of "all the children that were in Bethlehem, and in all the coasts thereof," may be read in the Gospel of Matthew and in the prophecy of Jeremiah. The Child was guarded by an angel band, and He escaped the sword of the angry king. Throughout the lifetime of Christ, repeated attempts were made to take His life; and failing to do this, Satan haunted His every step, seeking to entrap Him

Matt. 2 : 16–18.

Thus saith the Lord; A voice was heard in Ramah, lamentation, and bitter weeping; Rachel weeping for her children refused to be comforted for her children, because they were not.

Thus saith the Lord; Refrain thy voice from weeping, and thine eyes from tears: for thy work shall be rewarded, saith the Lord; and they shall come again from the land of the enemy. Jer. 31 : 15, 16.

And rose up, and thrust him out of the city, and led him unto the brow of the hill whereon their city was built, that they might cast him down headlong. Luke 4 : 29.

Isa. 9 : 6.

For he is our peace, who hath made both one, and hath broken down the middle wall of partition between us. Eph. 2:14.

Gen. 49:10.
Heb. 1:8.
Psa. 2:6-9.

We see Jesus, who was made a little lower than the angels for the suffering of death, crowned with glory and honour; that he by the grace of God should taste death for every man. Heb. 2:9.

Let the saints be joyful in glory: let them sing aloud upon their beds.
Let the high praises of God be in their mouth, and a twoedged sword in their hand;
To execute vengeance upon the heathen, and punishments upon the people;
To bind their kings with chains, and their nobles with fetters of iron;
To execute upon them the judgment written: this honour have all his saints. Praise ye the Lord.
Psa. 149:5-9.

For even hereunto were ye called: because Christ also suffered for us, leaving us an example, that ye should follow his steps.
1 Pet. 2:21.

Whom God hath raised up, having loosed the pains of death: because it was not possible that he should be holden of it.
Acts 2:24.

*And she brought forth a man child, who was to rule all nations with a rod of iron: and her child was caught up unto God, and to his throne. Rev. 12:5.*

Looking unto Jesus the author and finisher of our faith; who for the joy that was set before him endured the cross, despising the shame, and is set down at the right hand of the throne of God. Heb. 12:2.

through the weakness of human flesh, or cause Him to exercise His divine power for His own protection.

"Unto us a Child is born, unto us a Son is given: and the government shall be upon His shoulder; and His name shall be called Wonderful, Counsellor, The Mighty God, The Everlasting Father, The Prince of Peace." Of Judah it had been said in the days of Jacob, "The scepter shall not depart from Judah, nor a lawgiver from between his feet, until Shiloh come; and unto Him shall the gathering of the people be." This was fulfilled in the birth of Christ. Of Him alone, Jehovah, the Father, said, "Thy throne, O God, is forever and ever: a scepter of righteousness is the scepter of Thy kingdom." To this Child King, and to Him alone, has been given the right to rule with a rod of iron. "I have set My King upon My holy hill of Zion. I will declare the decree: the Lord hath said unto Me, Thou art My Son; this day have I begotten Thee. Ask of Me, and I shall give Thee the heathen for Thine inheritance and the uttermost parts of the earth for Thy possession. Thou shalt break them with a rod of iron."

The Saviour lived among men for thirty-three years, an example in childhood, youth, and manhood, of the possibilities of a life with God. He was crucified, yet He triumphed over death. Satan thought that he held Christ securely, but the moment of exultation was a signal for his eternal defeat. Even then, a shout rang through heaven as the victory over death was seen. He broke the fetters of the tomb, and "her Child was caught up unto God and to His throne." Again heaven resounded with praise;

for the triumph was seen, and the terrors of evil were recognized as never before.

*And the woman fled into the wilderness, where she hath a place prepared of God, that they should feed her there a thousand two hundred and threescore days.*
*Rev. 12:6.*

Only the mountain peaks, in the history of the Christian church, are revealed in this view. There is the glorious rising of the sun; then, a lapse of over five hundred years. The days of papal tyranny and persecution are shown when the "woman" was in the wilderness for twelve hundred and sixty years; and the last peak is when the sun again shines upon the Remnant church in all its splendor. There are three steps from the moonlight of the typical sanctuary service until the day of triumph and salvation is completed; but oh, what those steps imply! The emptying of heaven in the gift of its Prince; the crushing of the light under the feet of him who thought to exalt his throne above that of the Most High, and lastly, the gathering of a little company with whom the dragon is still wroth, but who keep the commandments of God and cherish the light of His Spirit.

For thou hast said in thine heart, I will ascend into heaven, I will exalt my throne above the stars of God: I will sit also upon the mount of the congregation, in the sides of the north:

I will ascend above the heights of the clouds; I will be like the most High. Isa. 14:13, 14.

He said unto them, I beheld Satan as lightning fall from heaven. Luke 10:18.

It may, at first, seem strange that this far-reaching view of the church, should at once bring before the prophet's mind the whole history of Satan,—the power behind the throne of Rome in its evil doings toward the Christ. And yet, when the spirit of heaven is caught, this is the most natural view. Before the creation of our world, "there was war in heaven." Christ and the Father covenanted together; and Lucifer, the covering cherub, grew jealous because he was not admitted into the eternal councils of the Two who sat upon the throne. He, the light-bearer, standing so close to God that he reflected the glory of the throne, allowed jealousy to rankle in his heart.

*And there was war in heaven: Michael and his angels fought against the dragon; and the dragon fought and his angels,*

*And prevailed not; neither was their place found any more in heaven. Rev. 12:7, 8.*

Thou art the anointed cherub that covereth; and I have set thee so. Eze. 28:14.

*And the great dragon was cast out, that old serpent, called the Devil, and Satan, which deceiveth the whole world: he was cast out into the earth, and his angels were cast out with him.*
*Rev. 12:9.*

For the first time, the harmony of heaven was broken. The discord spread; and when love failed to win, Lucifer and his followers were cast beyond the gates of heaven, and Satan was permitted to make the earth his abiding place. Justice called for death; but Mercy pleaded for a testing of the principles upon which the divine government was founded. The rainbow about the throne promised long-suffering. The charge was made that God ruled with an arbitrary hand. The controversy was begun. Satan claimed that if permitted to do so, he could establish a government where tyranny would be forever absent. Heaven granted him the earth in which to test his principles. So true is God to the law of love, so sure are the foundations of His throne, that, although it cost the life of His Son, He yet gave permission for the trial.

Then Satan answered the Lord, and said, Doth Job fear God for nought?
Hast not thou made an hedge about him, and about his house, and about all that he hath on every side? thou hast blessed the work of his hands, and his substance is increased in the land.
But put forth thine hand now, and touch all that he hath, and he will curse thee to thy face.
Job. 1:9–11.

The governments of earth became the instruments through which Satan worked. Our little planet became the center of interest among the angels, and the beings of unfallen worlds. According to the government of heaven, representatives from each world meet in council at the gate of heaven as the men of earth, for centuries after Adam was driven from the Garden, brought their offerings to the gate of Paradise. Among the sons of God who gathered there, Satan came also. Satan was a son of God by creation, and likewise, because of the earth over which he had usurped power, and bore sway. As a representative of the earth, he claimed the right to meet at the gate. There, in the midst of the heavenly assembly, he stood an accuser of the brethren. The case of Job and that of

Now there was a day when the sons of God came to present themselves before the Lord, and Satan came also among them.
Job 1:6.

Luke 3:38.
Rom. 6:16.
1 Tim. 22:19–23.
2 Chron. 18:18–21.

The Lord said unto Satan, Whence comest thou? Then Satan answered the Lord, and said, From going to and fro in the earth, and from walking up and down in it.
Job 1:7.

Rev. 12:10.
Job 1:9, 10.
Job 2:1–5.

Joshua are examples of the complaints which he brought against the government of God. Over and over again, angels had listened to the accusations made against the men of earth. When Christ was living here as a man, the heavenly host watched the deep-laid plots for His overthrow; they saw the jealousy among Jewish rulers, the cruelty of the Romans; and as the cross was approached, the pain which pierced them was akin to that of their suffering Master

He shewed me Joshua the high priest standing before the angel of the Lord, and Satan standing at his right hand to resist him.

And the Lord said unto Satan, The Lord rebuke thee, O Satan; even the Lord that hath chosen Jerusalem rebuke thee: is not this a brand plucked out of the fire?

Now Joshua was clothed with filthy garments, and stood before the angel. Zech. 3:1-3.

John 12:31, 32.

Jesus, sitting in the temple court but a few days before the end, looked forward to the cross, and with feelings too deep for human heart to sense, said, "Now is the judgment of this world: now shall the prince of this world be cast out." At the cross, the fate of Satan was forever sealed. "I, if I be lifted up, will draw all unto Me." Darkness covered Calvary on that awful day, but the eye of faith could pierce the cloud; for the hour that seemed the darkest, was, for the universe, the hour of greatest victory. "At the cross of Calvary love and selfishness stood face to face. Here was their crowning manifestation. Christ had lived only to comfort and bless, and in putting Him to death, Satan manifested the malignity of his hatred against God. He made it evident that the real purpose of his rebellion was to dethrone God and to destroy Him through whom the love of God was shown."

**Darkness covered Calvary on that awful day.**

Now from the sixth hour there was darkness over all the land unto the ninth hour. Matt. 27:45.

When from the depths of anguish, the dying Son of man exclaimed, "It is finished," in spite of the sympathy which could scarcely bear restraint, a shout of victory rang through heaven. Christ's "ear caught the distant music and the

At the ninth hour Jesus cried with a loud voice, saying, Eloi, Eloi, lama sabachthani? which is, being interpreted, My God, my God, why hast thou forsaken me? Mark 15:34.

John 19:30.

Mercy and truth are met together; righteousness and peace have kissed each other.

Truth shall spring out of the earth; and righteousness shall look down from heaven.

Psa. 85:10, 11.

*And I heard a loud voice saying in heaven, Now is come salvation, and strength, and the kingdom of our God, and the power of his Christ: for the accuser of our brethren is cast down, which accused them before our God day and night.* *Rev. 12:10.*

And as Moses lifted up the serpent in the wilderness, even so must the Son of man be lifted up:

That whosoever believeth in him should not perish, but have eternal life. John 3:14, 15.

*And they overcame him by the blood of the Lamb, and by the word of their testimony; and they loved not their lives unto the death.* *Rev. 12:11.*

For by thy words thou shalt be justified, and by thy words thou shalt be condemned. Matt. 12:37.

So speak ye, and so do, as they that shall be judged by the law of liberty. Jas. 2:12.

*Therefore rejoice, ye heavens, and ye that dwell in them. Woe to the inhabiters of the earth and of the sea! for the devil is come down unto you, having great wrath, because he knoweth that he hath but a short time.* *Rev. 12:12.*

shouts of victory in the heavenly courts. He knew that the death knell of Satan's empire had sounded, and the name of Christ would be heralded from world to world throughout the universe." "And I heard a loud voice saying in heaven, Now is come salvation, and strength, and the kingdom of our God, and the power of His Christ; for the accuser of our brethren is cast down, which accused them before our God day and night." Wonderful triumph! One loses much of the force of Christ's life, unless he sees the actual triumph at the cross. He who had given up His power and His strength, taking human weakness instead, and "trodden the winepress alone" regained all at the cross.

The life of Christ as a man, formed the strongest bonds between angels and human beings, so that in heaven, men are spoken of as "our brethren." "They overcame him by the blood of the Lamb, and by the word of their testimony, "and in their love for Christ, they willingly sacrificed life itself." "Rejoice, ye heavens, and ye that dwell in them." This was a dark hour for the disciples, who stood blinded by grief beside a sealed sepulcher; but angels, who knew the power of eternal life, witnessing the exaltation of the Son of God and the final casting out of Satan, sang halleluiahs. No longer would Satan, "the prince of this world," be admitted to their councils. No longer could he accuse the brethren in their presence. "Rejoice, ye heavens, and ye that dwell in them."

This was at the time of the crucifixion; and while joy rang through heaven, and the strains echoed and re-echoed again at His ascension, the world was not yet free from the wiles of the devil. Having been cast to the earth, he put forth redoubled efforts to overthrow the truth, as it was heralded by followers of the Man of Nazareth. Through the various governments he had worked, only to meet with defeat in the end. Subtlety took the place of opposition. Paganism melted away before the increasing light of the Gospel; but pagan principles were accepted by Christians, and clothed in the garb of Christianity. Here again is the story of the churches of Pergamos and Thyatira and the fourth seal. "Woe to the inhabiters of the earth and of the sea! for the devil is come down unto you, having great wrath, because he knoweth that he hath but a short time." With the intensity of despair he pushed his destructive plans. "And when the dragon saw that he was cast unto the earth, he persecuted the woman which brought forth the man child." The papacy was established at Rome in 538 A. D. for twelve hundred and sixty years,—the "thousand two hundred and three score days" of Rev. 12:6, the "time, and times, and half a time" of Rev. 12:14. It was the period during which the "two witnesses" of the eleventh chapter of Revelation prophesied in sackcloth. It is the period called the Dark Ages. Hidden from sight in mountain fastnesses, and obscure corners of the earth, some secretly, through the long night, held fast to the Word of God. From the mouth of the "dragon" was cast out a flood of iniquity, of false doctrines, of false teachings, of persecutions, in the hope of forever drowning the truth. In the East, this flood was "smoke" from the "bottomless pit" in the form of Mohammedanism; in the West, it was the papacy.

Now is the judgment of this world: now shall the prince of this world be cast out.

And I, if I be lifted up from the earth, will draw all men unto me.

This he said, signifying what death he should die.

John 12:31-33.

For I know this, that after my departing shall grievous wolves enter in among you, not sparing the flock.

Also of your own selves shall men arise, speaking perverse things, to draw away disciples after them.

Acts 20:29, 30.

*And when the dragon saw that he was cast unto the earth, he persecuted the woman which brought forth the man child.*

*Rev. 12:13.*

It shall be for a time, times, and an half; and when he shall have accomplished to scatter the power of the holy people, all these things shall be finished. Dan. 12:7.

*And to the woman were given two wings of a great eagle, that she might fly into the wilderness, into her place, where she is nourished for a time, and times, and half a time, from the face of the serpent.*

*And the serpent cast out of his mouth water as a flood after the woman, that he might cause her to be carried away of the flood.*

*Rev. 12:14, 15.*

Thou hast made us as the offscouring and refuse in the midst of the people.

All our enemies have opened their mouths against us.

Lam. 3:45, 46.

Howbeit in vain do they worship me, teaching for doctrines the commandments of men.

For laying aside the commandment of God, ye hold the tradition of men, as the washing of pots and cups: and many such like things ye do.

And he said unto them, Full well ye reject the commandment of God, that ye may keep your own tradition. Mark 7:7-9.

*And the earth helped the woman, and the earth opened her mouth, and swallowed up the flood which the dragon cast out of his mouth.* *Rev. 12:16.*

God setteth the solitary in families: he bringeth out those which are bound with chains: but the rebellious dwell in a dry land. Psa. 68:6.

The Lord gave the word: great was the company of those that published it.

Kings of armies did flee apace: and she that tarried at home divided the spoil. Psa. 68:11, 12.

He had in his hand a little book open: and he set his right foot upon the sea, and his left foot on the earth,

And cried with a loud voice, as when a lion roareth. Rev. 10:2, 3.

*And the dragon was wroth with the woman, and went to make war with the remnant of her seed, which keep the commandments of God, and have the testimony of Jesus Christ.* *Rev. 12:17.*

Rev. 14:12.

The voice of the Lord is powerful; the voice of the Lord is full of majesty. Psa. 29:4, 5.

Hallow my sabbaths; and they shall be a sign between me and you, that ye may know that I am the Lord your God. Eze. 20:20.

The testimony of Jesus is the spirit of prophecy. Rev. 19:10.

Rev. 22:7.
2 Cor. 11:14, 15.

At last the earth itself grew weary of the evil. God broke the power of the tyranny. He raised up rulers who opposed the power of the papacy, and who espoused the cause of the reformers, and sheltered them from the anathemas hurled after them. This was especially true among the German princes at the Diet of Spires, and the same spirit characterized William of Orange in the Netherlands, and some of the English rulers; and the help which the earth gave, was seen especially in the refuge offered to the persecuted souls on the shores of America.

The power of the Reformation is still felt in the earth; and the nations of Western Europe, together with the people of the United States, have the privilege of giving the last messages of the Gospel of Christ to the world. The mighty angel of the tenth chapter of Revelation had a message for the Remnant church, and the fourteenth chapter brings to light more fully the last work of the "woman" with whom the "dragon" is wroth. The purity and power of the sunlight characterized the Apostolic Church. There are two characteristics of the Remnant; they keep the commandments of God,—the law which forms the foundation of the eternal throne, and which Lucifer considered an arbitrary code. In the midst of this law, is the seal which the "dragon" sought to destroy, but which is restored to the last true church. The second distinguishing mark of theRemnant is that they have the testimony of Jesus Christ, which is the Spirit of Prophecy. As time grows short, the anger of the devil increases, and his deceptions assume their most subtle forms. He finally personates the Son of man, and appears on earth as an angel of light. At that time his exceeding great wrath will be manifested toward those who keep the commandments of God, and who have the testimony of Jesus Christ. These two tests, and these alone, distinguish between those who are accepted of God and those who are not.

John, to whom was made known the Revelation of Jesus Christ, was bidden by the Son of God to take the opened prophecies of Daniel. The testimony of Jesus Christ is added to the testimony of these two great prophets through a chosen prophet in the Remnant church. Though the gift of prophecy was long silent, it is in the Remnant church; though the law of God was long degraded and suppressed, it is again obeyed by the Remnant.

The wrath of Satan may be great, but He who preserved Christ will preserve His people till the end. The book of Revelation reveals the fact that the Remnant church is now in existence and that the time is short.

Even him, whose coming is after the working of Satan with all power and signs and lying wonders,

And with all deceivableness of unrighteousness in them that perish; because they received not the love of the truth, that they might be saved. 2 Thess. 2:9, 10.

The voice which I heard from heaven spake unto me again, and said, Go and take the little book which is open in the hand of the angel which standeth upon the sea and upon the earth.

And I went unto the angel, and said unto him, Give me the little book. And he said unto me, Take it, and eat it up. Rev. 10:8, 9.

Her king and her princes are among the Gentiles: the law is no more; her prophets also find no vision from the Lord.

Lam. 2:9.

For the Lord will not cast off for ever:

But though he cause grief, yet will he have compassion according to the multitude of his mercies.

For he doth not afflict willingly nor grieve the children of men.

Lam. 3:31-33.

# CHAPTER XIV.

## THE BEAST FROM THE SEA AND THE BEAST FROM THE EARTH.

He that is spiritual judgeth all things. 1 Cor. 2:15.

John 12:28, 29.
Heb. 1:1.

How is the gold become dim! how is the most fine gold changed! the stones of the sanctuary are poured out in the top of every street.

The precious sons of Zion, comparable to fine gold, how are they esteemed as earthen pitchers, the work of the hands of the potter! Lam. 4:1, 2.

Rom. 8:35.
Eccl. 3:11.
Rom. 11:31.

I have declared the former things from the beginning; and they went forth out of my mouth, and I shewed them; I did them suddenly, and they came to pass. Isa. 48:3.

For the kingdom is the Lord's: and he is the governor among the nations. Psa. 22:28.

WHEN a human mind can put itself in the channel of divine thought, then and only then, can the events of the world's history be rightly interpreted. To John was given a many-sided history of the church on earth. He saw it in its purity, and watched it until it was wholly corrupt. In every case the love of God was unmistakably written on every page. The story of nations reveals the infinite love of the Creator no less than the history of the church reveals His love. The twelfth chapter of Revelation is a bird's-eye view of the church from the days of Christ until the plan of redemption is complete. The thirteenth chapter bears more directly on the nations which are the chief actors in the Great Controversy, related in the previous chapter.

Patmos is described as a desolate, rocky

island; but it had a sandy beach, and at times the prophet-exile stood upon the sands of the sea, and watched the dashing of the waves of the Mediterranean. The ceaseless lapping, the ebb and flow of the tide, spoke forcibly to the spiritual mind of the holy seer. Everything in nature reminded him of his God, and taught some deep, hidden lesson. His Master, when walking among men, had pointed to the clusters on the vine, to the setting sun, to the fig tree, or to the sower, and the apostle never saw these objects without hearing afresh the sacred story of heaven. But now when the scene is changed, the same God used the objects which daily met the eye of John to tell him of the glories of the world to come, or to illustrate the divine hand in all human history. The ear that can hear, will find a voice in leaf and stone, in rosy sunset and in falling twilight. "Lo, these are parts of His ways . . . but the thunder of His power who can understand?"

Fear ye not me? saith the Lord: will ye not tremble at my presence, which have placed the sand for the bound of the sea by a perpetual decree, that it cannot pass it: and though the waves thereof toss themselves, yet can they not prevail; though they roar, yet can they not pass over it? Jer. 5:22.

Psa. 104:6-8.
Psa. 19:1-4.

For the invisible things of him from the creation of the world are clearly seen, being understood by the things that are made, even his eternal power and Godhead; so that they are without excuse. Rom. 1:20.

John 15:5.
Josh. 24:27.
Job 26:14.

As John stood upon the sand of the sea, his mind was opened to the influence from above, and he received a new revelation. He saw "a beast rise up out of the sea;" from the midst of the waves a form appeared. It had the lithe and spotted body of a leopard, the feet of a bear, and the mouth of a lion. The Lord had before represented the history of nations by beasts; and the symbols here used, are the same which were given to Daniel, and were interpreted for that prophet by Gabriel, the angel of revelation. In the history of the world four beasts, or kingdoms, cover the time from the days when Israel lost its standing as a nation until Christ sets up His everlasting kingdom. These four, speaking

*And I stood upon the sand of the sea, and saw a beast rise up out of the sea, having seven heads and ten horns, and upon his horns ten crowns, and upon his heads the name of blasphemy. Rev. 13:1.*

Rev. 17:4-6.

The wicked have drawn out the sword, and have bent their bow, to cast down the poor and needy, and to slay such as be of upright conversation. Psa. 37. 14.

Babylon hath been a golden cup in the Lord's hand, that made all the earth drunken: the nations have drunken of her wine; therefore the nations are mad.
Jer. 51:7.

Thou art this head of gold.
Dan. 2:38.

Then shall his mind change, and he shall pass over, and offend, imputing this his power unto his god.
Hab. 1:11.

Dan. 4:23.
Dan. 7:5.
Isa. 13:16-18.

of them in the order of their existence, were Babylon, Medo-Persia, Greece, and Rome. Babylon was the lion, the king of beasts, which ruled by the power of worldly grandeur. Compared with other kingdoms, this kingdom was as gold among the baser metals. Babylon was overthrown; but her religious principles lived on, and, like the roots of a fallen tree, sent forth a cluster of new fruit-bearing branches. Babylon's crowning sin was that of imputing all her wisdom and power unto false gods.

Medo-Persia succeeded Babylon, and the bear was taken to represent that nation. Not so noble in appearance as the lion, but stronger, and more savage. With its feet it stamped and crushed its foe. The strength of Medo-Persia lay in its tyrannical government. It was a monarchy of the most absolute form, and the fact that the laws of the Medes and Persians changeth not, was known not only by the nation itself, but by all who fell under its power. A terrible tyranny was the result,—an example of which is recorded in the book of Esther, where the law passed by Xerxes, the greatest of Persian monarchs, would have blotted the people of God from the earth if the Lord had not brought deliverance. This history will be repeated in the closing scenes of earth.

Corinth.

Now, O king, establish the decree, and sign the writing, that it be not changed, according to the law of the Medes and Persians, which altereth not. Dan. 6:8.

Touching the Almighty, we cannot find him out: he is excellent in power, and in judgment, and in plenty of justice: he will not afflict. Men do therefore fear him: he respecteth not any that are wise of heart. Job 37:23, 24.

Shall the throne of iniquity have fellowship with thee, which frameth mischief by a law? Psa. 94:20.

" I stood upon the sand of the sea, and saw a beast rise up out of the sea."

The Medo-Persian government likewise fell when the life-giving Spirit of God was withdrawn; and the Greek Empire followed. Through Greece, "the prince of the power of the air," the "old dragon," who was cast into the earth, attempted a new scheme for enslaving the truth. Greek culture and intellectual development carried men farther away from the simple truth of God's Word than any form of religion, or any oppression from the government. The teachers of Greek philosophy followed in the wake of the Alexandrian conquests. The beauty and æsthetic nature of their learning deceived men as nothing else has ever done. The mixture of good and evil was divinely represented by the spotted leopard, and its universal acceptance, by the lithe form and agile movements.

The letters were sent by posts into all the king's provinces, to destroy, to kill, and to cause to perish, all Jews, both young and old, little children and women, in one day, even upon the thirteenth day of the twelfth month, which is the month Adar, and to take the spoil of them for a prey. Esther 3:13.

(For all the Athenians and strangers which were there spent their time in nothing else, but either to tell, or to hear some new thing. Acts 17:21.

Jer. 13:23.

John saw a beast coming up out of the sea, rising in the midst of the nations of the earth, and it combined the characteristics of the leopard, the bear, and the lion. The successor of Greece was Rome, and profiting by past failures, the devil combined the strength of all preceding kingdoms in this fourth. A false religion, a tyrannical government, upheld and propagated by a flattering, insinuating, false system of education,—this was the body of the beast.

*And the beast which I saw was like unto a leopard, and his feet were as the feet of a bear, and his mouth as the mouth of a lion: and the dragon gave him his power, and his seat, and great authority Rev. 13:2.*

It had seven heads and ten horns, and ten crowns upon these horns. Besides building a nation with the quintessence of the evil of all the past, the power which was controlling in the growth of Rome, experimented on that nation, seeking for that form of administration which would best accomplish his designs. The gov-

2 Sam. 12 30

Thus saith the Lord God; Remove the diadem, and take off the crown: this shall not be the same: exalt him that is low, and abase him that is high. Eze. 21:26.

Ruth 4:2.
Prov. 20:18.

ernment began with a king, but the people were able to dethrone the monarch; the wealthy ruled for a time as consuls; but there was discord and weakness. Ten men were chosen to make laws adapted to all classes; then, all the people tried holding the reins of government, and Rome became a sort of republic or tribunate. The greedy heart of man repeated the story of Lucifer in heaven, and a political ring of three prominent citizens ruled. This was the triumvirate. To find three men in Rome who would be of one mind, was as impossible as it would be to find such to-day; and shortly the triumvirs disappeared, and Rome became an empire. Constant change was the only means of perpetuity, and the throne which Satan hoped to see an eternal one, was weakened by constant modifications.

For riches are not for ever: and doth the crown endure to every generation? Prov. 27:24.

Oh that my people had hearkened unto me, and Israel had walked in my ways!
I should soon have subdued their enemies, and turned my hand against their adversaries.
Psa. 81:13, 14.

Thus it was at the advent of Christ; but the end of changes was not yet. The very foundations of the pagan empire tottered as the Gospel spread. Paul himself preached Christ to the household of the Cæsars; and emperors found that though they might spurn the teachings of the Christ, yet their wives believed, their servants accepted Christianity, and even their soldiers, accepted the teachings of Jesus. A new and unheard of power had arisen which could not be met and vanquished, as Cæsar had subdued the foes of Rome. Then the wisdom of past ages was brought into play, and paganism stealthily crept under the garments of Christianity. The prince of darkness clothed himself in the garments of light, and the "mystery of iniquity" was established! The pagan Roman Empire was broken into ten divisions as described in the

All the saints salute you, chiefly they that are of Cæsar's household. Phil. 4:22.

Luke 8:1–3.
Acts 25:10.
Acts 10:1–7.
2 Cor. 11:13–15.
Matt. 7:15.
2 Thess. 2:4–7.

Of the ten horns that were in his head, and of the other which came up, and before whom three fell; even of that horn that had eyes, and a mouth that spake very great things, whose look was more stout than his fellows. Dan. 7:20.

seventh chapter of Daniel, but each division was a branch nourished by the same old root. Seven of the ten divisions developed into the nations of modern Europe, and bear the fruits formerly borne by the kingdoms which prophecy describes under the symbols of the four beasts. Each horn wore a crown, showing that each is an independent kingdom or nation. These horns cluster about the last head which arose in their midst, taking the place once occupied by three which it plucked up. This plucking up of three horns to give place to the papacy, the seventh head, is made clear in the seventh chapter of Daniel. That each of the various forms of government under which Romans have lived, was controlled by the enemy of God, is signified by the expression that upon each head was written the name of blasphemy. Each was an attempt to seat a man above the God of heaven. The seventh head most fully accomplished the design of the enemy of truth; for to the beast, the dragon himself gave power, and his seat, and great authority.

In 330 A. D. Constantine removed his capital from Rome to Constantinople. The ancient city was left to the papal power and the pope occupied in Rome a throne higher than any occupied by the Cæsars. Constantine laid the foundation of the papacy; but it remained for Justinian to complete the edifice in 533 A. D., by declaring that memorable decree which constituted the pope the head of all the churches. The Heruli, the Vandals, and the Ostrogoths were of the Arian faith and opposed to the bishop of Rome. The decree could not go into effect until 538 A. D., when the last of the

There are seven kings: five are fallen, and one is, and the other is not yet come; and when he cometh, he must continue a short space. Rev. 17:10.

Rev. 17:3.

I will sit also upon the mount of the congregation, in the sides of the north:

I will ascend above the heights of the clouds; I will be like the most High. Isa. 14:13, 14.

*And I saw one of his heads as it were wounded to death; and his deadly wound was healed: and all the world wondered after the beast.*

*And they worshipped the dragon which gave power unto the beast: and they worshipped the beast, saying, Who is like unto the beast? who is able to make war with him?*

*And there was given unto him a mouth speaking great things and blasphemies; and power was given unto him to continue forty and two months. Rev. 13:3-5.*

The pride of thine heart hath deceived thee, thou that dwellest in the clefts of the rock, whose habitation is high; that saith in his heart, Who shall bring me down to the ground? Obadiah 3.

Num. 22:8, 9, 22.
Num. 23:1, 2.
Num. 31:16.

O my people, remember now what Balak king of Moab consulted, and what Balaam the son of Beor answered him from Shittim unto Gilgal; that ye may know the righteousness of the Lord. Mic. 6:5.

*And he opened his mouth in blasphemy against God, to blaspheme his name and his tabernacle, and them that dwell in heaven.* *Rev. 13:6.*

He shall think himself able to change times and laws: and they shall be delivered into his hands until a time and times and an half a time. Dan. 7:25 [Catholic Trans.]

Hos. 4:17–19.
Rom. 1:5, 8.
Col. 1:5, 6, 23.

I beheld, and the same horn made war with the saints, and prevailed against them;

Until the Ancient of days came, and judgment was given to the saints of the most High; and the time came that the saints possessed the kingdom. Dan. 7:21, 22.

*And it was given unto him to make war with the saints, and to overcome them: and power was given him over all kindreds, and tongues, and nations.*

*And all that dwell upon the earth shall worship him, whose names are not written in the book of life of the Lamb slain from the foundation of the world.*

*If any man have an ear, let him hear.*

*He that leadeth into captivity shall go into captivity: he that killeth with the sword must be killed with the sword. Here is the patience and the faith of the saints.* *Rev. 13:7-10.*

Gen. 3:15.

opposing powers was overthrown by the armies of Justinian.

From 538 A. D. may be reckoned that absolute power which lasted for forty and two prophetic months, during which time the mouth speaking great blasphemies was practically unchecked. "He opened his mouth in blasphemy against God." He "opposeth and exalteth himself above all that is called God, or that is worshipped; so that he as God sitteth in the temple of God, showing himself that he is God." He soon claimed power to forgive sin, and the church became sole interpreter of God's Word; the consciences of all men were made amenable to the church or to those to whom the church delegated the right to sit in judgment.

With unbounded audacity, the attempt was made to change the immutable law of God. The Sabbath was trodden underfoot, the second commandment was dropped from the decalogue, and the tenth was divided into two. The memorial of creation and redemption was thus denied to man, the atoning work of Christ was set aside, and the worship of idols was instituted. Any who dared lift a voice in opposition, or who denied, by word or act, the right of the church to control the conscience of man, found death a welcome relief,—a thing to be sought in preference to the incessant torture inflicted by the ecclesiastical tyranny which held the world with an iron grip.

The Gospel of Jesus Christ reached the ears of every nation under heaven; and, likewise, before the death of the seventh head, every kindred, nation, and tongue, will feel its oppression.

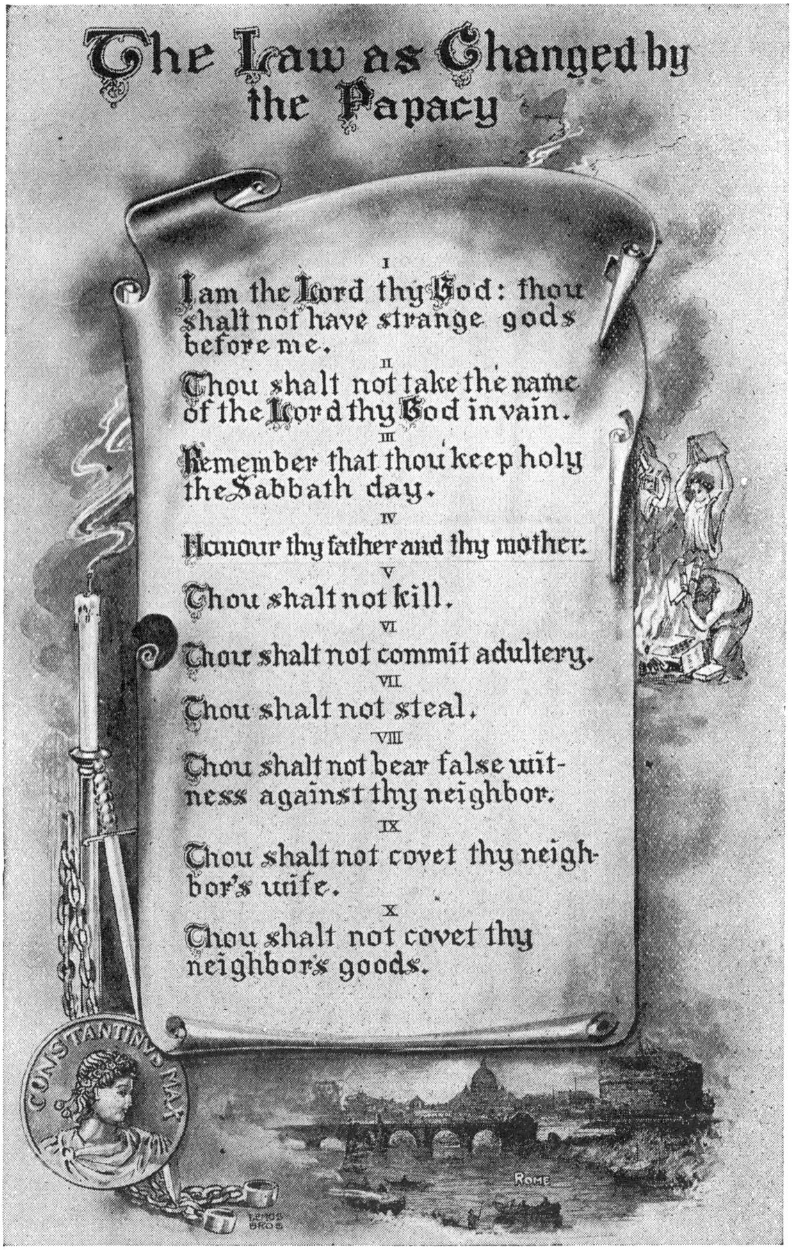
The Law as Changed by the Papacy
I
I am the Lord thy God: thou shalt not have strange gods before me.
II
Thou shalt not take the name of the Lord thy God in vain.
III
Remember that thou keep holy the Sabbath day.
IV
Honour thy father and thy mother.
V
Thou shalt not kill.
VI
Thou shalt not commit adultery.
VII
Thou shalt not steal.
VIII
Thou shalt not bear false witness against thy neighbor.
IX
Thou shalt not covet thy neighbor's wife.
X
Thou shalt not covet thy neighbor's goods.
CONSTANTINVS MAX
ROME
LEMOS BROS

Hos. 6:3.

So let all thine enemies perish, O Lord: but let them that love him be as the sun when he goeth forth in his might. Judg. 5:31.

Isa. 14:15-19.
Dan. 7:12.

When I shall say to the righteous, that he shall surely live; if he trust to his own righteousness, and commit iniquity, all his righteousnesses shall not be remembered; but for his iniquity that he hath committed, he shall die for it. Eze. 33:13.

If it seem evil unto you to serve the Lord, choose you this day whom ye will serve; whether the gods which your fathers served that were on the other side of the flood, or the gods of the Amorites, in whose land ye dwell: but as for me and my house, we will serve the Lord. Josh. 24:15.

Rev. 17:8.

One of his heads was wounded to death; for Truth rose up in its majesty and broke the tyrant's head. The seed of the woman put His heel upon the serpent's head, and would have crushed out all the life, had the plan of salvation been fully complete. The world emerged from the darkness gradually. The light of the Reformation shone forth in the sixteenth century; the last public execution for conscience' sake was in Seville, Spain, in 1776; and in 1798, the closing year of the forty and two months, Pope Pius VI, the representative of that power which had crowned and uncrowned kings, which had spoken, and Europe, almost *en masse*, had arisen to defend the holy sepulcher, which had extracted money from all nations, was captured by the French army, and died, shortly after, a prisoner, in fulfillment of the words "He that leadeth into captivity shall go into captivity." But the deadly wound was healed. The seventh head had not yet done its full work in the earth. According to the prophecy of Daniel, it lives until the close of time.

Although it seemed that a deathblow had been dealt in the early days of the Reformation; although for a time it was believed that the nations of Europe would accept Protestantism instead of the papacy; notwithstanding bloody battles were fought for the cause of Protestantism, yet life came back into the beast and into the wounded head; and before the end, all nations, kindreds, and people that dwell upon the earth, will be called to decide whether they will enroll under the banner of Prince Emmanuel, or whether they will acknowledge the leadership of a power that speaketh blasphemous words against the Most High. Those who choose the standard of Christ will have their names entered in the Lamb's Book of Life; they are the ones who accept the message of the tenth chapter of Revelation, and who are sealed as described in the seventh chapter. They will eventually join in the song of redemption which is sung before the throne of heaven. Those who voluntarily choose to follow the other power will receive the mark of the beast, and in the time of the final judgment, will go with their leader into everlasting death.

Psa. 40:7.

The Lord said unto him, Go through the midst of the city, through the midst of Jerusalem, and set a mark upon the foreheads of the men that sigh and that cry for all the abominations that be done in the midst thereof. Eze. 9:4.

Rev. 7:1-3.
Rev. 14:9-12.

He who has long led men into captivity, who has claimed the right to rule the hearts of men, and who has attempted to overthrow the eternal God of heaven, will finally be destroyed. The Lion of the tribe of Judah will reign as king; not by force, but by the power of love.

I beheld then because of the voice of the great words which the horn spake: I beheld even till the beast was slain, and his body destroyed, and given to the burning flame. Dan. 7:11.

Death follows the footprints of the beast. Some may wonder why a God of power does not, at once, blot out a rival who brings only distress and destruction; but mercy lingers that man may be saved. Here is needed, and here will be seen, in these closing days of the great controversy, the "patience of the saints." These things must be met by men now living, therefore, "if any man have an ear, let him hear."

I looked, and behold a pale horse: and his name that sat on him was Death, and Hell followed with him. And power was given unto them over the fourth part of the earth, to kill with sword, and with hunger, and with death, and with the beasts of the earth. Rev. 6:8.

The student of the book of Revelation has by the time he reaches the thirteenth chapter, met, a number of times, the power which would bear sway for twelve hundred and sixty years. In giving earth's history, that terrible period plays an important part; in the great controversy between good and evil, it was a marked era. It has been viewed from the standpoint of the church of God, from that of the false

Because thou hast kept the word of my patience, I also will keep thee from the hour of temptation, which shall come upon all the world, to try them that dwell upon the earth. Rev. 3:10.

The woman fled into the wilderness, where she hath a place prepared of God, that they should feed her there a thousand two hundred and threescore days. Rev. 12:6.

Dan. 12:6.
Dan. 11, 2, 3.
Dan. 7:25.
Dan. 11:33-35.
Dan. 12:5-7.

Except those days should be shortened, there should no flesh be saved: but for the elect's sake those days shall be shortened. Matt: 24:22.

Micah 3:6.

Behold, the days come, saith the Lord God, that I will send a famine in the land, not a famine of bread, nor a thirst for water, but of hearing the words of the Lord:

And they shall wander from sea to sea, and from the north even to the east, they shall run to and fro to seek the word of the Lord, and shall not find it. Amos 8:11, 12.

Their line is gone out through all the earth, and their words to the end of the world. In them hath he set a tabernacle for the sun. Psa. 19:4.

Behold ye among the heathen, and regard, and wonder marvellously: for I will work a work in your days, which ye will not believe, though it be told you. Hab. 1:5.

Isa. 29:13-15.

Let mine outcasts dwell with thee, Moab; be thou a covert to them from the face of the spoiler: for the extortioner is at an end, the spoiler ceaseth, the oppressors are consumed out of the land.

And in mercy shall the throne be established: and he shall sit upon it in truth in the tabernacle of David, judging, and seeking judgment, and hasting righteousness. Isa. 16:4, 5.

He will lift up an ensign to the nations from far, and will hiss unto them from the end of the earth: and, behold, they shall come with speed swiftly. Isa. 5:26.

or apostate church, and from the civil side as well. In all its aspects, it was a terrible time;—a time when angels trembled for the few faithful souls, and the heart of God longed for the time of their deliverance. "The noontide of the papacy was the world's moral midnight." The sad thing to contemplate is that the oppression, which, during the twelve hundred and sixty years was so galling, will be repeated just before the second coming of Christ. The last half of the thirteenth chapter deals with the history from the sixteenth century to the end of time.

The Reformation, in which Luther played such an important part, was more far reaching in its results than its most sanguine advocates could imagine, in the days when the light began to shine. It was the proclamation of a great truth, twofold in its mission. As the papacy must be considered, and had to be met, both as a civil and as an ecclesiastical power, so the Reformation gave birth to, or revived, the principles which were both civil and ecclesiastical in nature. The fact is stated in the words of the twelfth chapter, "The earth helped the woman." The church was in the hands of a persecuting power; and when the dragon sent forth a great flood, hoping to drown the truth, the earth came to the rescue of the church. The protest of the princes of Germany at the Diet of Spires, was like a pebble thrown into a lake; a wave was started, and the circles widened until man could not compass them.

John had another and more definite view of the help given by the earth. Turning from the sea, from which he had seen the great and terrible beast arise, with its seven heads and ten horns and the names of blasphemy, he saw "another beast coming up out of the earth." It was at the time the papal power was being led into captivity, that the prophet saw this new power "coming up." Rome sprang into existence in the midst of many peoples; the beast arose from the sea, but away from all the strife, outside the bounds of European darkness, arose another nation. It was brought into existence by the Lord Himself; at the very time it was most needed for the development of the principles of the Gospel, and of the final struggle for truth.

**He saw another beast coming up out of the earth.**

*And I beheld another beast coming up out of the earth; and he had two horns like a lamb, and he spake as a dragon. Rev. 13:11.*

From 1492 and onward, Europe heard reports of a new land beyond the seas. Navigators, usually in search of gold or glory, explored the shores and established colonies. But neither wealth nor honor was to have a hand in the final settlement; God reserved the territory, afterwards known as the United States of America, for the planting of downtrodden truth. When Germany refused full liberty, and clung to some forms of papal tyranny, Protestantism passed on to England. England and Holland for a time gave freer scope for the development of these principles; but space was limited in the Low Countries; and the British returned at last to their kings, and those seeking liberty of conscience, passed to the eastern shores of North America. In America the oppressed had freedom of worship, the right to educate their chil-

The people that walked in darkness have seen a great light: they that dwell in the land of the shadow of death, upon them hath the light shined.

Thou hast multiplied the nation, and not increased the joy: they joy before thee according to the joy in harvest, and as men rejoice when they divide the spoil. Isa. 9:2, 3.

They have turned unto me the back, and not the face: though I taught them, rising up early and teaching them, yet they have not hearkened to receive instruction. Jer. 32:33.

Afterwards they turned, and caused the servants and the handmaids, whom they had let go free, to return, and brought them into subjection for servants and for handmaids. Jer. 34:11.

I will bring you out from the people, and will gather you out of the countries wherein ye are scattered, with a mighty hand, and with a stretched out arm, and with fury poured out.

And I will bring you into the wilderness of the people, and there will I plead with you face to face. Eze. 20:34, 35.

Ex. 3:7.
Ex. 6:9.

Where the word of a king is, there is power: and who may say unto him, What doest thou? Eccl. 8:4.

So shall they fear the name of the Lord from the west, and his glory from the rising of the sun. When the enemy shall come in like a flood, the Spirit of the Lord shall lift up a standard against him. Isa. 59:19.

Go through, go through the gates: prepare ye the way of the people; cast up, cast up the highway; gather out the stones; lift up a standard for the people. Isa. 62:10.

dren according to their ideas of God, and the privileges of a free government. These were the things sought by the Pilgrim Fathers.

On the bleak New England shores, principles of Protestantism and republicanism struggled for existence. These two went hand in hand. Historians recount the hardships of braving the sea and making new homes; but these were light trials, compared with the soul-strivings against bondage and oppression. So strongly ingrained were the principles of monarchy and the spirit to dictate in religious matters—the two foundation stones of the papacy—that only by dint of perseverance and strong determination on the part of a few souls who were open to heaven-born convictions, there gradually grew up in New England a representative form of government. The towns about Boston refused to be taxed unless they had a voice in the legislative body. Thomas Hooker, with his whole congregation, emigrated to the wilds of Connecticut for greater liberty; and as a result, the first written constitution ever known to exist in America, was framed in 1633. Rhode Island had an existence solely, because of the attempt of man to oppress the conscience of his fellow man; and it stands in the Union to-day as a monument of the struggle for religious liberty.

In the more Southern Colonies the same battles were fought. Finally, in 1776, the Declaration of Independence published to the world the purpose of the new and growing states to cut loose from the tie which bound them to the mediæval forms of government. The step appeared rash; but this was the thing necessary, to bring unity and united effort among the people of America. With one common enemy, all internal strife was forgotten; but when the new nation was acknowledged free and independent, the problem of ages was just before it. Having thrown off the fetters of monarchy, and with no definite ideas as to the actual workings of an administration by the people, the ship of state was in the greatest danger of foundering on the rocks of anarchy; or, tired of the open sea, of again seeking shelter in the harbor from which it had sailed. There were men who advocated return; but God had His angels in the meetings of statesmen, and His Spirit guided the minds of those who sought to follow the light of the Reformation.

Stand fast, and prepare thee; for the sword shall devour round about thee. Jer. 46:14.

We have heard with our ears, O God, our fathers have told us, what work thou didst in their days, in the times of old.

How thou didst drive out the heathen with thy hand, and plantedst them; how thou didst afflict the people, and cast them out.

For they got not the land in possession by their own sword, neither did their own arm save them: but thy right hand, and thine arm, and the light of thy countenance, because thou hadst a favour unto them. Psa. 44:1-3.

**Hall of Independence Philadelphia, 1776.**

The Federal Convention, which convened in Philadelphia in the year 1787, was no common meeting; for from the work done by the men who sat there, a wave was set in motion which has influenced every nation of the earth. It was by the fifty-five representatives from the states which formed the nucleus of the nation to-day recognized as one of the leading powers of the world, that the American Constitution was framed. Of this document Gladstone says: "The American Constitution is the most wonderful work ever struck off at a given time by the brain of man." The words of the Declaration of Independence state the principles upon

He hath shewed thee, O man, what is good; and what doth the Lord require of thee, but to do justly, and to love mercy, and to walk humbly with thy God? Micah 6:8.

The Lord shall help them, and deliver them: he shall deliver them from the wicked, and save them, because they trust in him. Psa. 37:40.

God is in the midst of her; she shall not be moved: God shall help her, and that right early. Psa. 46:5.

Psa. 97 : 11.

The nations shall see and be confounded at all their might: they shall lay their hand upon their mouth, their ears shall be deaf.
Micah 7 : 16.

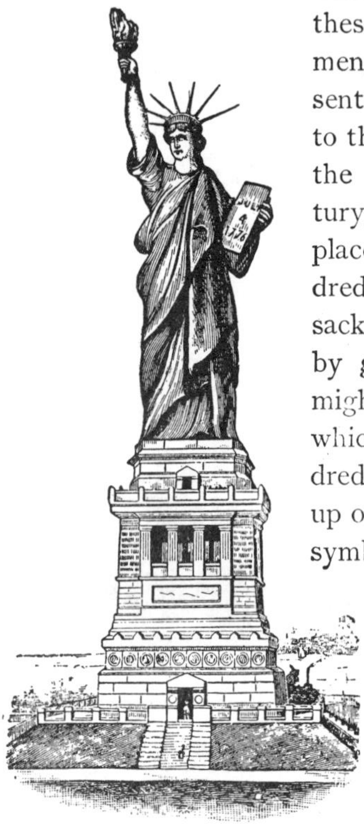

**The Statue of Liberty.**

The Gentiles shall come to thy light, and kings to the brightness of thy rising.

Lift up thine eyes round about, and see: all they gather themselves together, they come to thee: thy sons shall come from far, and thy daughters shall be nursed at thy side. Isa. 60 : 3, 4.

which the new government was founded. "We hold these truths to be self-evident, that all men are created equal, that they are endowed by their Creator with certain unalienable rights. . . . That, to secure these rights, governments are instituted among men, deriving their just powers from the consent of the governed." This was a deathblow to the papal hierarchy; it was the outgrowth of the principles advocated in the sixteenth century,—the result of restoring to their proper place the Two Witnesses, that for twelve hundred and sixty years prophesied, clothed in sackcloth. Thus the earth helped the woman, by giving to her a home where the sunlight might shine unobstructed by the darkness which covered Europe during the twelve hundred and sixty years. The beast which came up out of the earth in the sight of the prophet, symbolizes the United States; and the two horns represent the two foundation principles of the government, Protestantism and republicanism. The seed of the Reformation, having been planted in congenial soil, soon grew into a mighty tree, sheltering the oppressed of all nations. Glorious as the sun rising was the establishment of the new government. It was a wonder to all the world; but when its freedom and stability once became known, America became the center of progress. All nations have been molded, more or less by the example of this country. Her constitution has been the model for the reorganization of nations, especially since 1840. The monarchs of Europe were forced to relax their hold upon their subjects, and America is the place toward which all eyes have been directed in these crises. Even the Orient has relaxed to the warming influence of the United States.

But the world is not yet free from the influence of him who was "cast unto the earth," and the dragon, who had worked through each preceding nation, works in this. When unable to check the onward march of freedom, as it was started in America, the more wary plans, which had been combined in Rome, were introduced into America. A government by the people, for successful management requires a constituency educated in the principles of both Protestantism and republicanism. The schools played a most important part in the growth of the constitution, and the educational system of the United States has been the real support of the nation.

Gradually, however, the philosophy of Greece has, in the education of children and youth, almost wholly supplanted the truths of God. Graduates to-day are better able to interpret the mythology of Greece than they are to read the handwriting of the Creator in nature about them. They are prepared to believe the false theories of scientists in preference to direct statements of inspiration. The whole trend of their education is evolutionary in character, and develops doubt, not faith,—higher criticism instead of simple faith in the Word of God. The organization of society into guilds, trusts, rings, corporations, and unions, is a reflection of the spirit of the educational system. Monarchy is rapidly replacing democratic principles, and the dragon's voice sounds through the earth in the

Keep therefore and do them; for this is your wisdom and your understanding in the sight of the nations, which shall hear all these statutes, and say, Surely this great nation is a wise and understanding people.

And what nation is there so great, that hath statutes and judgments so righteous as all this law, which I set before you this day?

Deut. 4:6, 8.

Howbeit we speak wisdom among them that are perfect: yet not the wisdom of this world, nor of the princes of this world, that come to nought:

But we speak the wisdom of God in a mystery, even the hidden wisdom, which God ordained before the world unto our glory:

Which none of the princes of this world knew. 1 Cor. 2:6-8.

(For the weapons of our warfare are not carnal, but mighty through God to the pulling down of strong holds;)

Casting down imaginations, and every high thing that exalteth itself against the knowledge of God, and bringing into captivity every thought to the obedience of Christ.

2 Cor. 10:4, 5.

For the Jews require a sign, and the Greeks seek after wisdom.

1 Cor. 1:22.

Associate yourselves, O ye people, and ye shall be broken in pieces; and give ear, all ye of far countries: gird yourselves, and ye shall be broken in pieces; gird yourselves, and ye shall be broken in pieces.

Take counsel together, and it shall come to nought; speak the word, and it shall not stand: for God is with us.

For the Lord spake thus to me with a strong hand, and instructed me that I should not walk in the way of this people, saying,

Say ye not, A confederacy, to all them to whom this people shall say, A confederacy; neither fear ye their fear, nor be afraid. Isa. 8:9-12.

Amos 8:4-6.

dictation of the labor unions to their members; in the controllers of the oil and the grain; in the strikes and the exchanges. Wall Street dictates to thousands; and the masses pay their Peter's pence to the moneyed classes as surely as it was ever exacted in Rome. As the cry of the oppressed during the Dark Ages reached heaven, so in this day of apparent light and progress, and of boasted freedom, the voice of oppression is heard. "Behold, the hire of the laborers who have reaped down your fields, which of you is kept back by fraud, crieth: and the cries of them which have reaped are entered into the ears of the Lord of Sabaoth."

America, according to prophecy, would repudiate the fundamental principles of the nation, and from the lamblike beast, the voice of the dragon is heard. "And he exerciseth all the power of the first beast before him, and causeth the earth and them which dwell therein to worship the first beast, whose deadly wound was healed." America has already repudiated her first principles of liberty. In form, the government remains the same as when established, but the spirit and life of the beast speak through the form. The life of Protestantism is gone; the life of democracy is lost. The professed Protestant nation is imitating the papal power of Rome, thus forming the image to the beast. As time progresses, it will be seen that the image will receive, more and more, the life of the beast. The return to papal principles in Europe, is the partial healing of the wounded head; but the fuller development of all the powers of that beast, which combined the char-

Go to now, ye rich men, weep and howl for your miseries that shall come upon you.

Your riches are corrupted, and your garments are motheaten.

Your gold and silver is cankered; and the rust of them shall be a witness against you, and shall eat your flesh as it were fire. Ye have heaped treasure together for the last days. Jas. 5:1-3.

Ye have lived in pleasure on the earth, and been wanton; ye have nourished your hearts, as in a day of slaughter.

Ye have condemned and killed the just; and he doth not resist you. Jas. 5:5, 6.

Jas. 5:4.

*And he exerciseth all the power of the first beast before him, and causeth the earth and them which dwell therein to worship the first beast, whose deadly wound was healed.* *Rev. 13:12.*

Isa. 19:11-15.

They did cry there, Pharaoh king of Egypt is but a noise; he hath passed the time appointed. Jer. 46:17.

*And he doeth great wonders, so that he maketh fire come down from heaven on the earth in the sight of men,*

*And deceiveth them that dwell on the earth by the means of those miracles which he had power to do in the sight of the beast; saying to them that dwell on the earth, that they should make an image to the beast, which had the wound by a sword, and did live.* *Rev. 13:13, 14.*

For he saith, By the strength of my hand I have done it, and by my wisdom; for I am prudent: and I have removed the bounds of the people, and have robbed their treasures, and I have put down the inhabitants like a valiant man. Isa. 10:13.

acteristics of Babylon, Persia and Greece, in the once free and liberty loving America, will be the complete healing of the deadly wound.

America is the home of Protestantism, but her churches to-day are Protestant only in name. The exaltation of man above God, the enthroning of human intellect, the hope of righteousness by works, the trampling underfoot of the law of God,—these are some of the things which mark the Protestant churches as daughters of the Babylon, which swayed the world from her seat at Rome.

Two things characterize the Remnant people during the formation of the image to the beast. According to Rev. 12:17, they keep the commandments of God and have the spirit of prophecy. These two characteristics belong to all true Protestants, and are presented to Protestant denominations for their acceptance or rejection.

As the beast trampled upon the law of God, and sought to change times and laws, the image to the beast repeats these acts, and passes laws enforcing the observance of its mark,—the false Sabbath.

The spirit of prophecy is given to guide the church through the darkness; but this is counterfeited by the working of miracles, and by manifestations of a false spirit. Through human agents, the devil seeks to imitate the workings of the Spirit of God; and finally, at the very end of time, he appears in person claiming to be the Christ. "Satan himself is transformed into an angel of light. Therefore, it is no strange thing if his ministers also, be transformed as the ministers of righteousness."

For ye see your calling, brethren, how that not many wise men after the flesh, not many mighty, not many noble, are called:

But God hath chosen the foolish things of the world to confound the wise; and God hath chosen the weak things of the world to confound the things which are mighty;

And base things of the world, and things which are despised, hath God chosen, yea, and things which are not, to bring to nought things that are. 1 Cor. 1:26–28.

This is a rebellious people, lying children, children that will not hear the law of the Lord:

Which say to the seers, See not; and to the prophets, Prophesy not unto us right things, speak unto us smooth things, prophesy deceits:

Get you out of the way, turn aside out of the path, cause the Holy One of Israel to cease from before us. Isa. 30:9–11.

2 Tim. 3:5.
Rev. 12:17.
Rev. 19:10.
Lam. 2:9.
1 Thess. 5:20.

We have also a more sure word of prophecy; whereunto ye do well that ye take heed, as unto a light that shineth in a dark place, until the day dawn, and the day star arise in your hearts. 2 Pet. 1:19.

2 Cor. 11:14.

For of this sort are they which creep into houses, and lead captive silly women laden with sins, led away with divers lusts,

Ever learning, and never able to come to the knowledge of the truth.

Now as Jannes and Jambres withstood Moses, so do these also resist the truth: men of corrupt minds, reprobate concerning the faith. 2 Tim. 3:6–8.

Matt. 24:24.

Then Herod, when he saw that he was mocked of the wise men, was exceeding wroth, and sent forth, and slew all the children that were in Bethlehem, and in all the coasts thereof, from two years old and under, according to the time which he had diligently enquired of the wise men.

Then was fulfilled that which was spoken by Jeremy the prophet, saying,

In Rama was there a voice heard, lamentation, and weeping, and great mourning, Rachel weeping for her children, and would not be comforted, because they are not.
Matt. 2:16–18.

Heb. 12:2.
Heb. 8:1.

I saw three unclean spirits like frogs come out of the mouth of the dragon, and out of the mouth of the beast, and out of the mouth of the false prophet.

For they are the spirits of devils, working miracles, which go forth unto the kings of the earth and of the whole world, to gather them to the battle of that great day of God Almighty. Rev. 16:13, 14.

Rev. 13:13, 14.
Rev. 19:20.

*And he had power to give life unto the image of the beast, that the image of the beast should both speak, and cause that as many as would not worship the image of the beast should be killed.*
*Rev. 13:15.*

Dan. 6:8.

The letters were sent by posts into all the king's provinces, to destroy, to kill, and to cause to perish, all Jews, both young and old, little children and women, in one day, even upon the thirteenth day of the twelfth month, which is the month Adar, and to take the spoil of them for a prey. Esther 3:13.

If any man worship the beast and his image, and receive his mark in his forehead, or in his hand.
Rev. 14:9.

Through his human instruments, he will have power to make fire come down from heaven in the sight of men. "There shall arise false Christs, and false prophets, and shall show great signs and wonders; insomuch that, if it were possible, they shall deceive the very elect." These are the Saviour's own words, spoken as He looked forward to the time of His second appearing.

At the birth of the Son of God, the dragon stood ready to devour the Child. When the Child was caught up into heaven, the dragon drove the woman (the church) into the wilderness. His last and most daring act, will be, coming to the earth in person, clothed in garments of light, and claiming to be the Saviour. For this final scene, the work of Spiritualism, which, in its modern forms, arose in the United States, is now preparing the world. When Satan thus appears, he demands the life of all who have not the mark of the beast, and who refuse to worship his image. The tyranny of government will be complete. It will be as the laws of the Medes and Persians, from which there was no appeal. The decree of Xerxes, which demanded the slaying of all the Jews, on one day, throughout all the realm, in the days of Queen Esther, will be repeated by the powers that be, and the lives of the followers of God, those who have received His mark,—the seal of His law,—will be demanded.

Not only in the forehead, as a sign of acceptance, but also in the hand, as typical of actual service for the "beast," the mark will be required. There will be no spot too secluded for that power to reach. The present perfection of organization, the census taking, the enrollment for voting, etc., bring every individual under the eye of the government as truly as the enrollment of Augustus Cæsar, the taxgatherer of Rome, brought the parents of Jesus to the attention of the nation.

Luke 2 : 1.

*And he causeth all, both small and great, rich and poor, free and bond, to receive a mark in their right hand, or in their foreheads: And that no man might buy or sell, save he that had the mark,*

Once it would have seemed impossible to so boycott a class of individuals that they could neither buy

**Joseph and Mary on the way to Bethlehem.**

nor sell, but the history of recent years shows that this has been done by the labor unions of our large cities. This perplexing situation grows steadily worse, and the end is given only by the divine recorder.

*or the name of the beast, or the number of his name.*
*Rev. 13 : 16, 17.*

Eccl. 1 : 9, 10.
Isa. 24 : 2.

The history of the beast is given again and again, that God's people may know what to expect of the image to the beast. As the beast bore sway over the known world in its day, so the image will set the example to the world in the end of time. America once took the lead in propagating the principles of religious and civil freedom; to-day that nation leads the world in its strife for power and recognition, and the very principles of its own Declaration of Independence are overridden in dealing with subject provinces. Rome has been portrayed from all sides, and so definitely described that it cannot be mistaken. When the image is compared with the real, in the thirteenth

The time is come, the day draweth near: let not the buyer rejoice, nor the seller mourn: for wrath is upon all the multitude thereof.
Eze. 7 : 12.

For that the dream was doubled unto Pharaoh twice; it is because the thing is established by God, and God will shortly bring it to pass.
Gen. 41 : 32.

He exerciseth all the power of the first beast before him, and causeth the earth and them which dwell therein to worship the first beast, whose deadly wound was healed.
Rev 13 : 12.

***Here is wisdom. Let him that hath understanding count the number of the beast: for it is the number of a man; and his number is Six hundred threescore and six.*** ***Rev. 13:18.***

| VICARIUS FILII DEI. | | |
|---|---|---|
| V | - | 5 |
| I | - | 1 |
| C | - | 100 |
| A | - | 0 |
| R | - | 0 |
| I | - | 1 |
| U | - | 5 |
| S | - | 0 |
| F | - | 0 |
| I | - | 1 |
| L | - | 50 |
| I | - | 1 |
| I | - | 1 |
| D | - | 500 |
| E | - | 0 |
| I | - | 1 |
| | | 666 |

Know ye not, that to whom ye yield yourselves servants to obey, his servant ye are to whom ye obey. Rom. 6:16.

Dan. 12:1.
Rev. 12:12, 13.

Yea, all kings shall fall down before him. Psa. 72:11.

At the noise of the tumult the people fled; at the lifting up of thyself the nations were scattered. Isa. 33:3.

I saw as it were a sea of glass mingled with fire: and them that had gotten the victory over the beast, and over his image, and over his mark, and over the number of his name, stand on the sea of glass, having the harps of God. Rev. 15:2.

The judgment shall sit, and they shall take away his dominion, to consume and to destroy it unto the end. Dan. 7:26, 27.

chapter of Revelation, the very number, six hundred and sixty-six, which is worn on the insignia of the head of the papal hierarchy, is given, that men may be left without excuse. He who is acknowledged as the vicegerent of the Son of God (*Vicarius Filii Dei*), in his name carries the number six hundred and sixty-six, for the sum of the numerical value of the Roman letters in his title, equals that number. That power which again exalts man above the God of heaven, forms the image to the beast, and bears the number of his name.

The time of trouble, spoken of by Daniel, is right upon the world. "The devil is come down unto you, having great wrath, because he knoweth that he hath but a short time."

Nations have risen, and fallen, in the controversy between Christ and Satan; but the last leading nation to arise is now in existence; it will be the battlefield for the final struggle. From its borders, will be heralded the last great message, and from its people will be gathered a remnant church. The members of this church will join with those of other countries, who, in the very presence of the beast, stand true to the God of heaven and earth when the Saviour comes to receive His subjects.

The time of the fall of all nations approaches. They will be succeeded by the kingdom of God. Christ and the Father will reign forever, and the subjects will be those who have developed a character in harmony with Jehovah; and they will have done this when surrounded on all sides by the concentrated iniquity of Babylon, Persia, Greece, and Rome. Lucifer claimed that it was impossible to serve God in heaven. The controversy closes when it has been demonstrated, before the universe, that it is possible to serve God, and obey His law on the enemy's ground, and in the midst of all the evil which it is possible for him to invent. Such is the power of our God. May "Thy kingdom come. Thy will be done in earth as it is in heaven."

Who is a God like unto thee, that pardoneth iniquity, and passeth by the transgression of the remnant of his heritage? he retaineth not his anger for ever, because he delighteth in mercy. Micah 7:18.

Who is God save the Lord? or who is a rock save our God? Psa. 18:31.

# CHAPTER XV.

## THE THREE ANGELS' MESSAGES.

*And I looked, and, lo, a Lamb stood on the mount Sion, and with him an hundred forty and four thousand, having his Father's name written in their foreheads.*
*Rev. 14:1.*

Isa. 51:1.

And after these things I saw four angels standing on the four corners of the earth, holding the four winds of the earth, that the wind should not blow on the earth, nor on the sea, nor on any tree. Rev. 7:1.

Zech. 7:14.
Rev. 7:4.

I saw one of his heads as it were wounded to death; and his deadly wound was healed: and all the world wondered after the beast.
Rev. 13:3.

He had power to give life unto the image of the beast, that the image of the beast should both speak, and cause that as many as would not worship the image of the beast should be killed.
Rev. 13:15.

Except those days should be shortened, there should no flesh be saved: but for the elect's sake those days shall be shortened.
Matt. 24:22.

AFTER the strife and the turmoil of the great controversy, in which the oppression of the seven headed beast was followed by the lamb-like government,—the government which formed an image to the beast, and caused all men to worship the beast, or the image, John had his attention called to scenes where the conflict was all ended. The One whom Lucifer had held before the eyes of the world as a cruel despot, stands a Lamb on Mount Zion. He is no longer the slain Lamb once seen before the throne, but the King in His beauty, the true Conqueror, who has triumphed by the power of truth. He, who might have uttered a single word, and the enemy of truth would have been blotted out of existence, chose rather to be exalted through suffering. Love is the ruler of the universe; "love never faileth," and through six thousand years of conflict, it has come forth victorious with garments unsullied. The Lamb stood on Mount Zion, where the city of the living God stands. There in the heavenly temple, the work of the sanctuary is carried on. Christ entered the first apartment when He ascended from earth and presented His own blood for a lost race. In 1844 the door into the inner apartment was opened, and Christ and the Father then took up the cases of those whose names appeared in the Book of Life. While Christ is still in that apartment, the closing events of chapter thirteen take place. The sealing, as described in the seventh chapter of Revelation, is going forward, while the beast and his image, the ruling powers of earth, are striving to gain the recognition of all. The interest of heaven centers in those few who receive the mark of the great Jehovah. In fact, this little company, numbering one hundred and forty-four thousand, is the most interesting class of people brought to view in the Word of God. John, in the opening verse of chapter fourteen, sees them as they gather about the Saviour on Mount Zion. God's Word traces their history very minutely.

In the year 1848, the four angels of the seventh chapter of Revelation took their stand upon the four corners of the earth, to hold the winds of strife until the servants of God were sealed. "And there were sealed an hundred and forty and four thousand." Between 1798 and the close of time, the wound of the beast is fully healed, and he renews his work of oppression through the powers of the earth. In America the image to the beast is formed, and given life within that same period; and it exerciseth all the power of the first beast before it. Its special work of oppression is against those who have received the seal of God in the fore-

The field is the world; the good seed are the children of the kingdom; but the tares are the children of the wicked one. Matt. 13:38.

Likewise, I say unto you, there is joy in the presence of the angels of God over one sinner that repenteth. Luke 15:10.

Deut. 3:11.

Where sin abounded, grace did much more abound:

That as sin hath reigned unto death, even so might grace reign through righteousness unto eternal life by Jesus Christ our Lord. Rom. 5:20, 21.

I in them, and thou in me, that they may be made perfect in one; and that the world may know that thou hast sent me, and hast loved them, as thou hast loved me. John 17:23.

When he was strong, his heart was lifted up to his destruction: for he transgressed against the Lord his God. 2 Chron. 26:16.

The Lord will give strength unto his people; the Lord will bless his people with peace. Psa. 29:11.

1 Kings 19:12, 13.

Mark the perfect man, and behold the upright: for the end of that man is peace. Psa. 37:37.

Thinkest thou that I cannot now pray to my Father, and he shall presently give me more than twelve legions of angels? Matt. 26:53.

Psa. 11:4.
Heb. 9:24.
Gal. 3:6-8.

I will clothe him with thy robe, and strengthen him with thy girdle, and I will commit thy government into his hand: and he shall be a father to the inhabitants of Jerusalem, and to the house of Judah.

And the key of the house of David will I lay upon his shoulder; so he shall open, and none shall shut; and he shall shut, and none shall open. Isa. 22:21, 22.

Rev. 20:12.
Rev. 3:5.
Eze. 9:4.

I heard the number of them which were sealed: and there were sealed an hundred and forty and four thousand of all the tribes of the children of Israel.

And I said unto him, Sir, thou knowest. And he said to me, These are they which came out of great tribulation, and have washed their robes, and made them white in the blood of the Lamb.

Therefore are they before the throne of God, and serve him day and night in his temple: and he that sitteth on the throne shall dwell among them. Rev. 7:4, 14, 15.

For both he that sanctifieth and they who are sanctified are all of one: for which cause he is not ashamed to call them brethren,

Saying, I will declare thy name unto my brethren, in the midst of the church will I sing praise unto thee. Heb. 2:11, 12.

Psa. 48:2.

For thou hast said in thine heart, I will ascend into heaven, I will exalt my throne above the stars of God: I will sit also upon the mount of the congregation, in the sides of the north. Isa. 14:13.

head. America and the European nations control the world, and were it not that the winds of strife are restrained by the four mighty angels, time would end before the sealing work is accomplished. But among all nations, and unto every tribe and language, the sealing angel makes his way. As far as the gospel of truth is proclaimed, so wide is the field from which he gathers. The interest of all heaven is centered in his work. When one compares the last race on earth with man as he came forth in strength and grandeur from the hand of his Creator, the work of redemption seems more wonderful than ever. From degraded, degenerate humanity, reeking with disease and crime; God chooses the last little company who, because of the soul communion which they have had with Him, will have characters which admit them into the closest relationship with their Maker. Many acknowledge Jehovah in their minds, and many worship Him outwardly; only the few pass through Gethsemane with the Christ; but those who do know the realities of spiritual life, receive the name of the Father in their foreheads. These are the one hundred and forty-four thousand,—the chosen company, who reveal to the fullest extent the depths of redeeming love. John saw these surrounding the Saviour on the Mount of God,—"the mount of the congregation, in the sides of the North," where Satan once stood, and where he attempted to raise a throne for himself. The one hundred and forty-four thousand occupy the place once filled by Lucifer and his angels. Oh what a commentary to the universe on the glorious triumph of truth, over error! of love over selfishness!

These men were redeemed from the earth, from among men,—the first fruits unto God and the Lamb. They have been snatched as brands from the burning. "They were not defiled with women; for they are virgins." The prophet Isaiah, in describing the condition of the churches in the days when the sealing work is in progress, says: "In that day seven women shall take hold of one man, saying, We will eat our own bread, and wear our own apparel: only let us be called by thy name, to take away our reproach." The church is represented by a woman; and the relation of Christ to the true church, as the relation of the husband to his wife. The husband gives his name to the wife, and supplies her food and raiment; but apostate churches, while claiming the name of Christ, (Christian), eat their own bread and wear their own apparel, spurning the instruction Christ has given concerning the food and raiment of His bride. But the redeemed will be as virgins, undefiled, and Christ will present them to the Father as chaste virgins. During the last days the earth will be drunk with the wine of fornication offered by Babylon and her daughters, and the sealing angel places the name of the Father on the foreheads of those who turn from the world and all it offers. It will be known that bands of angels overshadow those who are pure in soul. "The Lord will create upon every [such] dwelling place of Mount Zion, and upon her assemblies, a cloud and smoke by day, and the shining of a flaming fire by night: for above all, the glory shall be a covering." In the secret of His tabernacle He will hide them till the indignation be overpast.

Zech. 3:2.
Rev. 14:4.
Isa. 4:1.

Jer. 6:2.
2 Cor. 11:2.
Eph. 5:23.
Isa. 54:4, 5.

APPAREL OF THE APOSTATE WIFE OF CHRIST.

Isa. 3:16–24. Fashions of the world.
Isa. 64:6. Self-righteousness.

APPAREL OF THE TRUE WIFE.

1 Pet. 3:1–5. Free from unnecessary ornaments.
1 Tim. 2:9, 10. Modest apparel.
Isa. 61:10. Robe of righteousness.

DIET OF THE APOSTATE WIFE OF CHRIST.

Isa. 65:3, 4. Swine's flesh.
Isa. 66:17. Swine's flesh.
Isa. 22:12–14. Flesh of sheep and oxen.
Prov. 23:20. Wine and flesh.
Prov. 23:29–32. Mixed wine.
Eze. 22:26–28. Traditions.

DIET OF THE TRUE WIFE.

Gen. 1:29. Fruits, nuts, and grains.
Lev. 11:1–28. Clean food.
John 6:51, 63. Feed on the Word of God.
1 Tim. 4:15. Meditate on the Word.
Psa. 119:103. God's Word sweet to the taste.

Psa. 27:5.

Come, my people, enter thou into thy chambers, and shut thy doors about thee: hide thyself as it were for a little moment, until the indignation be overpast. Isa. 26:20.

The remnant of Israel shall not do iniquity, nor speak lies; neither shall a deceitful tongue be found in their mouth: for they shall feed and lie down, and none shall make them afraid. Zeph. 3:13.

Ex. 4:15, 16.

I am crucified with Christ: nevertheless I live; yet not I, but Christ liveth in me: and the life which I now live in the flesh I live by the faith of the Son of God, who loved me, and gave himself for me. Gal. 2:20.

By faith Enoch was translated that he should not see death; and was not found, because God had translated him: for before his translation he had this testimony, that he pleased God. Heb. 11:5.

In his days Judah shall be saved, and Israel shall dwell safely: and this is his name whereby he shall be called, THE LORD OUR RIGHTEOUSNESS. Jer. 23:6.

He answered and spake unto those that stood before him, saying, Take away the filthy garments from him. And unto him he said, Behold, I have caused thine iniquity to pass from thee, and I will clothe thee with change of raiment.

And I said, Let them set a fair mitre upon his head. So they set a fair mitre upon his head, and clothed him with garments. And the angel of the Lord stood by.

And the angel of the Lord protested unto Joshua, saying,

Thus saith the Lord of hosts; If thou wilt walk in my ways, and if thou wilt keep my charge, then thou shalt also judge my house, and shalt also keep my courts, and I will give thee places to walk among these that stand by.

Hear now, O Joshua the high priest, thou, and thy fellows that sit before thee: for they are men wondered at: for, behold, I will bring forth my servant the BRANCH. Zech. 3:4-8.

The soul of my lord shall be bound in the bundle of life with the Lord thy God. 1 Sam. 25:29.

In their mouth was found no guile; for the soul temple had been so thoroughly cleansed before leaving earth that the human mouth became a channel for the words of God. When the mind of Christ takes full possession of a man, he thinks and speaks and acts as Christ Himself would act. Mortals may have such close and constant communion with Jehovah that they have the assurance that they walk with Him. This was the Christ-life while on earth, and He lived to show that the same is also possible to-day. This will be the mind of those who are sealed. They are without fault; because Christ's righteousness covers them as a garment. Walking untainted in the midst of self-righteousness, these have been clothed with the heavenly garments. Associated with those whose mouths are full of guile, these have been free from guile. They overcame by the blood of the Lamb. What wonder that they can sing a song in which no other beings can unite! They are given a place next to Christ; they alone of the redeemed can enter the temple. The new name which each one receives is there graven on a living tablet of stone, and they become pillars in that temple of life; living stones of a spiritual house. In that heavenly service they are called pillars, as James and Cephas by their faithfulness were termed pillars in the earthly church; and when the Lamb goes from place to place, this company follow Him as a trophy of grace. They are one with Him, as He is one with the Father; and being one, their souls are inseparably knit together. No power can separate them; for experience has made them what they are; and throughout eternity, they minister to Jehovah, showing forth forever the depths of redeeming love.

Listening, John heard music from the Holy Mount; for this company are clothed in white and wear crowns of gold, and have harps in their hands. Music, such as mortal ear never heard, comes from those harps swept by the hands of the redeemed. Music is the voice of inspiration,—the melody of a soul when it communes with the great Spirit of life. Those who have known Him best will bring forth the clearest notes from the instruments, and each chord will tell the history of their lives. Their voices blend with these strains. In talking, the voices of Christ and His company sound as the voice of many waters. The melody is beyond description.

If we be dead with him, we shall also live with him :

If we suffer, we shall also reign with him : if we deny him, he also will deny us. 2 Tim. 2 : 11, 12.

1 Cor. 2 : 9, 10.

Rev. 15 : 3, 4.

The Lord thy God in the midst of thee is mighty ; he will save, he will rejoice over thee with joy ; he will rest in his love, he will joy over thee with singing.

Zeph. 3 : 17.

*And I heard a voice from heaven, as the voice of many waters, and as the voice of a great thunder : and I heard the voice of harpers harping with their harps :*

**Music, such as mortal ear never heard comes from those harps swept by the hands of the redeemed.**

Entering the temple, the one hundred and forty-four thousand sing a new song before the throne and before the four beasts and before the four and twenty elders. Song, with the redeemed, is not only the repetition of words, but the pouring forth of the inmost soul. Only he who knows of soul-development can tune his voice to the melody of heaven. And of all the choirs which make heaven's arches ring, none compare with the music which issues from this little company. No other voice can join their song. Heaven is silent as they lift their voices, and tell the story of their redemption.

*And they sung as it were a new song before the throne, and before the four beasts, and the elders : and no man could learn that song but the hundred and forty and four thousand, which were redeemed from the earth.*

*These are they which were not defiled with women ; for they are virgins. These are they which follow the Lamb whithersoever he goeth. These were redeemed from among men, being the firstfruits unto God and to the Lamb.*

*And in their mouth was found no guile : for they are without fault before the throne of God.*

*Rev. 14 : 2-5.*

Deut. 34:1-7.
Rev. 14:13.

Yet Michael the archangel, when contending with the devil he disputed about the body of Moses, durst not bring against him a railing accusation, but said, The Lord rebuke thee. Jude 9.

Many of them that sleep in the dust of the earth shall awake, some to everlasting life, and some to shame and everlasting contempt. Dan. 12:2.

I the Lord will be their God, and my servant David a prince among them; I the Lord have spoken it.

And I will make with them a covenant of peace, and will cause the evil beasts to cease out of the land: and they shall dwell safely in the wilderness, and sleep in the woods. Eze. 34:24, 25.

For the Lord himself shall descend from heaven with a shout, with the voice of the archangel, and with the trump of God: and the dead in Christ shall rise first:

Then we which are alive and remain shall be caught up together with them in the clouds, to meet the Lord in the air: and so shall we ever be with the Lord. 1 Thess. 4:16, 17.

This gospel of the kingdom shall be preached in all the world for a witness unto all nations; and then shall the end come. Matt. 24:14.

Their song is called the song of Moses and the Lamb. Moses, the servant of God, who gazed into the land of promise from the height of Pisgah, and then lay down to sleep on the very borders of the inheritance, is the type of those who in the closing message look into eternity, but lie down in the grave until the appearing of their Lord. Christ Himself came to earth, and claimed the body of Moses. He did not wait until all came from their graves. So those who have fallen asleep, having the seal of God, will have a special resurrection, and will be called forth to hear the covenant of peace, and to behold their Lord as He comes in the clouds of heaven. These join their voices with those who tell their life story of Christ the Lamb,—a story of sacrifice and love. "Great and marvelous are Thy works, Lord God Almighty," and the response comes, "Just and true are Thy ways, Thou King of saints." This is a song of "victory over the beast, and over his image, and over his mark, and over the number of his name." Standing on the crystal sea, resplendent with the glory of God, they sing the songs of soul union with Jehovah. This is the consummation of the history as related in the thirteenth chapter of Revelation.

*And I saw another angel fly in the midst of heaven, having the everlasting gospel to preach unto them that dwell on the earth, and to every nation, and kindred, and tongue, and people.*

*Saying with a loud voice, Fear God, and give glory to him; for the hour of his judgment is come: and worship him that made heaven, and earth, and the sea, and the fountains of waters.* *Rev. 14:6, 7.*

Rev. 10:6.

With the sixth verse of chapter fourteen begins a view of the last work of the Gospel in the earth. A glimpse of the spread of truth during the last days is given in the tenth chapter. Rev. 14:6–12 is a further development of the message given by the mighty angel which came down from heaven, and stood upon the earth with an open book of prophecy in his hand. This angel proclaimed that time should be no more, and the prophetic time to which he referred was the twenty-three hundred days of Daniel 8:14. The message was given between 1833 and 1844. When the twenty-three hundred days closed in 1844, Christ entered the second apartment of the heavenly sanctuary. When this change was about to take place in heaven, God commissioned an angel to fly earthward with a message to mankind that would prepare the human heart for the closing work on the earth. The angel flew in the midst of heaven, that the divine word which he brought might be heard by all the world; for the message was universal. He carried the everlasting Gospel to every nation, kindred, tongue, and people. Every habitable portion of the globe was overshadowed by his wings; the most secluded peoples were awakened by his loud voice as he cried, "Fear God, and give glory to Him; for the hour of His judgment is come."

The everlasting Gospel, the power of God unto salvation, has been the point of controversy since the days of Eden. This is the same everlasting Gospel, which was covered up by the corruption of the antediluvians. The earth was destroyed, and the gospel promises were renewed to Noah and his sons, the bow in the clouds being the token of the everlasting covenant. In the time of Babylonian supremacy it was the avowed object of Satan to hide the everlasting Gospel beneath a flood of false worship; and thus through all time and all powers, the Gospel of Jesus Christ has been trampled down, and

Into the second went the high priest alone once every year, not without blood, which he offered for himself, and for the errors of the people:

It was therefore necessary that the patterns of things in the heavens should be purified with these; but the heavenly things themselves with better sacrifices than these. Heb. 9:7, 23, 24.

**"Fear God, and give glory to Him: for the hour of His judgment is come."**

He said unto them, Go ye into all the world, and preach the gospel to every creature. Mark 16:15.

It came to pass, that after three days they found him in the temple, sitting in the midst of the doctors, both hearing them, and asking them questions.

And all that heard him were astonished at his understanding and answers. Luke 2:46, 47.

He answered and said unto them, Why do ye also transgress the commandment of God by your tradition? Matt. 15:3-6.

Therefore we ought to give the more earnest heed to the things which we have heard, lest at any time we should let them run out as leaking vessels.
Heb. 2:1 [margin.]

Blow ye the trumpet in Zion, and sound an alarm in my holy mountain: let all the inhabitants of the land tremble: for the day of the Lord cometh, for it is nigh at hand. Joel 2:1.

For with thee is the fountain of life: in thy light shall we see light. Psa. 36:9.

man alone exalted. Christ put in a new setting, the truths which had been made known by prophets and typified by the Jewish services. Even as a child of twelve, in the presence of the learned doctors in the temple, the questions He asked, flashed new light upon Scriptures often used by those teachers of the Jewish nation. False doctrines had been introduced, and the traditions of men had been accepted by the world until the everlasting Gospel was unknown.

**Christ in the Temple.**

The sixteenth century Reformation was a revival of truth. Ministers and teachers saw light and beauty in the Scriptures. Again the living seed was sown, and Protestantism, was seen to be trees of the Lord's own planting. But scarcely had the living trees begun to yield fruit, when they were encircled by a parasitic vine. It crept round and round until its branches took the form of the growing tree. It spread its green leaves to the air until passers-by admired the foliage, but the tree had been choked to death, and stood a mere support for a stolen life. When this vine of error was steadily growing about Protestantism, especially in America, the angel flew in the midst of heaven, proclaiming the everlasting Gospel. Men, startled by the proclamation that time was about to close, turned to the Word of God for truth. The book of Daniel was studied as never before in the history of the world. The culminating point was the fourteenth verse of the eighth chapter. "Unto two thousand and three hundred days; then shall the sanctuary be cleansed." Careful study revealed that this prophetic period ended in the year 1844. In the one hundred and forty-five times the word "sanctuary" is used in the Bible, it does not once refer to the earth, yet they understood the sanctuary of Dan. 8:14 to be this earth. With this interpretation in mind they made the verse read, "'Unto two thousand and three hundred days; then shall the' Lord come." Wm. Miller, in America, Edward Irving, in England, Joseph Wolff, in Asia, with hundreds of colaborers, heralded to the world the glad news of the Saviour's return.

When the autumn of 1844 passed and the Saviour did not come, bitter sorrow filled the hearts of the people. Some lost their faith and turned to the world; but others said, "There is a mistake somewhere, God is true and faithful, the mistake must be on our part." While searching the Scriptures prayerfully, light from the heavenly sanctuary flashed into their minds. As they turned their eyes heavenward, by faith they saw the heavenly temple, and realized that they had truthfully given the message, "The hour of His judgment is come"; for Christ entered the most holy place of the heavenly sanctuary, at the end of the two thousand three hundred days and commenced the work of the investigative judgment.

The message went to the world; there was not a missionary station in the earth, where they

Thou, O Daniel, shut up the words, and seal the book, even to the time of the end: many shall run to and fro, and knowledge shall be increased. Dan. 12:4.

Study to shew thyself approved unto God, a workman that needeth not to be ashamed, rightly dividing the word of truth. 2 Tim. 2:15.

Behold, the Lord cometh with ten thousands of his saints,

To execute judgment upon all, and to convince all that are ungodly among them of all their ungodly deeds which they have ungodly committed, and of all their hard speeches which ungodly sinners have spoken against him.

Jude 14, 15.

The temple of God was opened in heaven, and there was seen in his temple the ark of his testament.

Rev. 11:19.

For Christ is not entered into the holy places made with hands, which are the figures of the true; but into heaven itself, now to appear in the presence of God for us.

Heb. 9:24.

When he was come nigh, even now at the descent of the mount of Olives, the whole multitude of the disciples began to rejoice and praise God with a loud voice for all the mighty works that they had seen;

Saying, Blessed be the King that cometh in the name of the Lord: peace in heaven, and glory in the highest. Luke 19:37, 38.

did not hear the message, "The hour of His judgment is come." Some may inquire, "Why was the message of Christ's coming given at that time?" We may also ask, "Why did Christ permit His followers to escort Him into Jerusalem, intending to crown Him as King, when He knew He was going there to be crucified?" His followers fulfilled the prophecy of Zech. 9:9. If they had known the truth they could not have given the shouts of rejoicing that fulfilled the prophecy. Likewise, the announcement of the opening of the judgment was to be given with a loud voice to the whole world. If the people of God had understood all at first they would never have given the message with power.

*And there followed another angel, saying, Babylon is fallen, is fallen, that great city, because she made all nations drink of the wine of the wrath of her fornication. Rev. 14:8.*

The Spirit and the bride say, Come. And let him that heareth say, Come. And let him that is athirst come. And whosoever will, let him take the water of life freely. Rev. 22:17.

This is the first angel's message of the fourteenth chapter of Revelation, and it will continue to sound till time shall close. In 1843 and 1844 it swelled into the loud cry by the added voice of the angel with the time message. In the very end of time, when oppression is again almost unbearable, just before the close of probation, it will again swell into a loud cry. In the meantime, the message of the first angel goes steadily forward, and those whose ears are listening for a voice from heaven, will join in giving the everlasting Gospel.

At midnight there was a cry made, Behold, the bridegroom cometh; go ye out to meet him.

Then all those virgins arose, and trimmed their lamps. Matt. 25:6, 7.

While the first angel continues to sound, a second angel follows saying, "Babylon is fallen, is fallen, that great city, because she made all nations drink of the wine of the wrath of her fornication." The preaching of the everlasting Gospel was a test of life. Those who truly loved the Saviour rejoiced to hear that His second advent was near and hastened to prepare for His coming, but many turned a deaf ear to the call of the first angel. The love of the world had so benumbed their sense of spiritual things that they could even scoff at the idea of the Saviour's return.

The preaching of the first angel's message drew a line among the professed followers of the Lord. Over those who showed they had lost their love for Christ by disregarding the message of His return, the angel pronounced the words, "Babylon is fallen, is fallen." Those who longed for a higher spiritual development, drank of the pure water of life, as given by the first angel; but in the hands of the church, a golden cup was filled with the wine of fornication; and, in place of offering the life-giving drink from the fountain, the churches, when the time passed in 1844, closed their doors against the everlasting Gospel; and ministers gave their flocks to drink of the wine of fornication,—a mixture of truth and error, which like any intoxicant, benumbs the sensibilities, and causes him who drinks to turn from that which would revive.

Babylon, the universal kingdom which offered the worship of idols for the worship of Jehovah, is used by the Spirit to symbolize the churches, which, like the Jewish nation in the days of Christ, mix the philosophy of the world with the truth of God, and offer this wine to men in place of the everlasting Gospel. The church which does this, realizes its inability to reach the souls of men, and unites with the state and attempts to compel the conscience. There is a form of godliness, but no power therein. This is the papacy renewed, the making of an image to the beast. "Babylon is

Therefore thus saith the Lord God unto them; Behold, I, even I, will judge between the fat cattle and between the lean cattle.

Because ye have thrust with side and with shoulder, and pushed all the diseased with your horns, till ye have scattered them abroad;

Therefore will I save my flock, and they shall no more be a prey; and I will judge between cattle and cattle.

And I will set up one shepherd over them, and he shall feed them, even my servant David; he shall feed them, and he shall be their shepherd. Eze. 34:20–23.

A drought is upon her waters; and they shall be dried up: for it is the land of graven images, and they are mad upon their idols. Jer. 50:38.

Looking diligently lest any man fail of the grace of God; lest any root of bitterness springing up trouble you, and thereby many be defiled;

Lest there be any fornicator, or profane person, as Esau, who for one morsel of meat sold his birthright.

For ye know how that afterward, when he would have inherited the blessing, he was rejected: for he found no place of repentance, though he sought it carefully with tears. Heb. 12:15–17.

John answered and said, Master, we saw one casting out devils in thy name; and we forbad him, because he followeth not with us.

And Jesus said unto him, Forbid him not: for he that is not against us is for us. Luke 9:49, 50.

Rev. 14:8.

Behold, here cometh a chariot of men, with a couple of horsemen. And he answered and said, Babylon is fallen, is fallen; and all the graven images of her gods he hath broken unto the ground.
Isa. 21:9.

Jer. 51:8.
Rev. 18:2.
Gen. 41:32.

fallen, is fallen," said the angel. His message began in 1844, and will continue until there is no longer time in which to withdraw from the fated city. The message "is fallen, is fallen," is twice repeated—"because the thing is established by God, and God will shortly bring it to pass." Like the warning sent to Babylon of old when the Jews were in captivity,—that those who were within the city might escape before the final overthrow, so is the warning concerning the churches. God has given warning, and those who desire life, will heed the call, and separate themselves. This message will also swell into a loud cry just before the close of probation. Those who hear to-day will obey to-day; others may be snatched from the burning as Lot and his family were hurried out of Sodom. But the effect of drinking the wine of fornication will be to deaden the spiritual senses until, like the physical drunkard, there will be no possibility of returning. Then, in one case, as in the other, a drunkard's grave will be the end. "To-day if ye will hear His voice, harden not your heart." The pure water of Lebanon is offered in the everlasting Gospel, the power of God unto salvation. "Whosoever will, let him take the water of life freely." "The water that I shall give him shall be in him a well of water springing up into everlasting life."

**Lot and his family were hurried out of Sodom.**

Flee out of the midst of Babylon, and deliver every man his soul: be not cut off in her iniquity; for this is the time of the Lord's vengeance.
Jer. 51:6.

Luke 19:41-44.

I call heaven and earth to record this day against you, that I have set before you life and death, blessing and cursing: therefore choose life, that both thou and thy seed may live. Deut. 30:19.

Repent ye therefore, and be converted, that your sins may be blotted out, when the times of refreshing shall come from the presence of the Lord;

And he shall send Jesus Christ, which before was preached unto you. Acts 3:19, 20.

The first angel turned hearts to the everlasting Gospel as the only means of salvation; for there is none other name under heaven given among men, whereby we must be saved.'

Man has tried to save himself, and the devil has invented innumerable ways for him to evade the Gospel; but only the one ladder connects heaven and earth. "I am the door:" said Christ, "by Me if any man enter in, he shall be saved." The second angel gives the warning, that destruction hangs over those who claim to be representatives of God on earth, but do not love His appearing.

Shortly after the giving of the first angel's message, the sealing work brought to view in chapter seven was begun. The glory shining from the law of God, enables angels to place the seal of God on the foreheads of those who obey the everlasting Gospel. But a counter sealing goes on at the same time. As Jehovah recognizes in the lives of His people the reflection of the law of His own eternal throne and the seal, His name or mark which is His Sabbath, so he who has, from the beginning, striven to thwart the Gospel of Jesus, has a seal of his own which gives his name, his title, and his dominion over which he rules. He who opposeth and exalteth himself above God, puts his seal in the place of the seal of the King of heaven. The image to the beast enforces the observance of Sunday, the first day of the week, instead of the Sabbath of the fourth commandment. The fourth commandment is the only one of the decalogue that the papacy has really thought to change, and those who in the face of light and truth, choose to keep the first day of the week as a Sabbath, are obeying the power that has "thought himself able to change times and the law," just as truly as those receive the seal of God, who take up their cross and keep

Neither is there salvation in any other: for there is none other name under heaven given among men, whereby we must be saved.
Acts 4:12.

Hereafter ye shall see heaven open, and the angels of God ascending and descending upon the Son of man. John 1:51.

John 10:9.

Now then we are ambassadors for Christ, as though God did beseech you by us: we pray you in Christ's stead, be ye reconciled to God.
2 Cor. 5:20.

Therefore thus saith the Lord, If thou return, then will I bring thee again, and thou shalt stand before me: and if thou take forth the precious from the vile, thou shalt be as my mouth: let them return unto thee; but return not thou unto them. Jer. 15:19.

Rev. 14:9-12.

*And the third angel followed them, saying with a loud voice, If any man worship the beast and his image, and receive his mark in his forehead, or in his hand,*

*The same shall drink of the wine of the wrath of God, which is poured out without mixture into the cup of his indignation; and he shall be tormented with fire and brimstone in the presence of the holy angels, and in the presence of the Lamb:*

*And the smoke of their torment ascendeth up for ever and ever: and they have no rest day nor night, who worship the beast and his image, and whosoever receiveth the mark of his name.*

*Here is the patience of the saints: here are they that keep the commandments of God, and the faith of Jesus. Rev. 14:9-12.*

Think not that I am come to destroy the law, or the prophets: I am not come to destroy, but to fulfil.

For verily I say unto you, Till heaven and earth pass, one jot or one tittle shall in no wise pass from the law, till all be fulfilled.
Matt. 5:17, 18.

Blessed is the man that doeth this, and the son of man that layeth hold on it; that keepeth the sabbath from polluting it, and keepeth his hand from doing any evil.
Isa. 56:2.

Isa. 58:12-14.

holy the Sabbath of Jehovah, the seventh day of the week. The law which is passed compelling men to receive the mark of the beast, will give life to the image of the beast, and the prophecy of Rev. 13:15-17 will be a reality. For six thousand years, God has pleaded with man to accept salvation. In the close of earth's history, the everlasting Gospel is preached with renewed power, and all are given an opportunity to stand with God or with the enemy. Those who accept Jehovah as King are sealed, and fill the ranks of the one hundred and forty-four thousand.

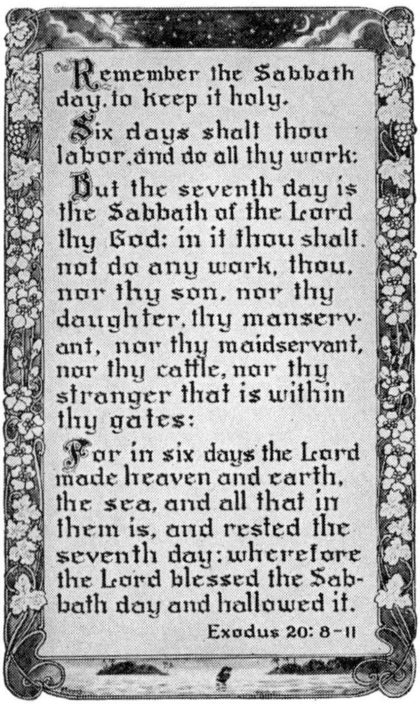


Another angel was seen flying in the midst of heaven, proclaiming with a loud voice, "If any man worship the beast and his image, and receive his mark in his forehead, or in his hand, the same shall drink of the wine of the wrath of God, which is poured out without mixture into the cup of His indignation; and he shall be tormented with fire and brimstone in the presence of the holy angels, and in the presence of the Lamb: and the smoke of their torment ascendeth up forever and ever: and they have no rest day nor night, who worship the beast and his image, and whosoever receiveth the mark of his name."

The wicked, through the pride of his countenance, will not seek after God: God is not in all his thoughts.
Psa. 10:4.

Put me in remembrance: let us plead together: declare thou, that thou mayest be justified.
Isa. 43:26.

After these things I saw another angel come down from heaven, having great power; and the earth was lightened with his glory.
Rev. 18:1.

The seventh and eighth verses of the fourteenth chapter state that the first angel went to every nation, kindred, tongue and people. The

The Three Messages.

second angel followed the first, and the third angel *followed them.* Every nation under heaven will hear the warning against worshiping the beast. Each individual will be given an opportunity to honor the Creator by obeying His law and keeping holy the Sabbath of the Lord. All will receive sufficient light to decide intelligently. Those who reject the warning receive the unmixed wrath of God, which is filled up in the seven last plagues. There will be a company who will heed the warning. Of this company the Lord has said, "Here is the patience of the saints: here are they that keep the commandments of God, and the faith of Jesus."

Those who have received the mark of the beast and his image, who have lived under the influence of the wine of the fornication held to the lips of Babylon, will now drain to the dregs the cup of God's wrath. Satan has claimed that in himself was light and life, and men, echoing his teachings, have thought themselves independent of heaven. When the Sun of Righteousness withdraws His shining, men left without Christ are as the world without the sunlight. This is the time of Jacob's trouble, spoken of by the prophets; it is the time of the outpouring of the plagues; for when Christ turns from the world, all the elements are broken up, and man is left to contend, single-handed, with disease and death. The plagues described in the sixteenth chapter of Revelation are the unmingled wrath of God. Men, living under the warming influence of the sun, cannot imagine what existence would be, were the sun blotted out. So the human race,

As truly as I live, all the earth shall be filled with the glory of the Lord. Num. 14:21.

For in the hand of the Lord there is a cup, and the wine is red; it is full of mixture; and he poureth out of the same: but the dregs thereof, all the wicked of the earth shall wring them out, and drink them. Psa. 75:8.

Rev. 14:12.

How art thou fallen from heaven, O day star, son of the morning! how art thou cut down to the ground, which didst weaken the nations! Isa. 14:12 [margin.]

Then Jesus said unto them, Yet a little while is the light with you. Walk while ye have the light, lest darkness come upon you: for he that walketh in darkness knoweth not whither he goeth. John 12:35.

Jer. 30:7.

The angel took the censer, and filled it with fire of the altar, and cast it into the earth: and there were voices, and thunderings, and lightnings, and an earthquake. Rev. 8:5.

If a man walk in the night, he stumbleth, because there is no light in him. John 11:10.

1 John 2 : 11.
Rev. 16 : 17–21.

The rest of the dead lived not again until the thousand years were finished. This is the first resurrection. Rev. 20 : 5.

The heavens shall pass away with a great noise, and the elements shall melt with fervent heat, the earth also and the works that are therein shall be burned up. 2 Pet. 3 : 10.

They went up on the breadth of the earth, and compassed the camp of the saints about, and the beloved city : and fire came down from God out of heaven, and devoured them. Rev. 20 : 9.

Rev. 15 : 8.
1 Tim. 2 : 5.

Because he hath set his love upon me, therefore will I deliver him : I will set him on high, because he hath known my name. Psa. 91 : 14.

Psa. 27 : 5.

A man shall be as an hiding place from the wind, and a covert from the tempest ; as rivers of water in a dry place, as the shadow of a great rock in a weary land. Isa. 32 : 2.

Rev. 14 : 12.
Psa. 102 : 19.
Heb. 11 : 27.

Then shall appear the sign of the Son of man in heaven : and then shall all the tribes of the earth mourn, and they shall see the Son of man coming in the clouds of heaven with power and great glory. Matt. 24 : 30.

1 Kings 18 : 44.

For I am with thee, saith the Lord, to save thee : though I make a full end of all nations whither I have scattered thee, yet will I not make a full end of thee :

Therefore all they that devour thee shall be devoured ; and all thine adversaries, every one of them, shall go into captivity ; and they that spoil thee shall be a spoil, and all that prey upon thee will I give for a prey. Jer. 30 : 11, 16, 17.

which has known life only with the light of love shining on it, cannot foretell the awfulness when conditions change. The seventh plague destroys all life upon the earth, those who are destroyed, will sleep in unconsciousness until the end of the thousand years, when the voice of Christ will call them forth to receive their final punishment. Fire comes down from God out of heaven, and devours them, and they become ashes upon the earth.

During the outpouring of the plagues, when Christ has left the temple, those in whose foreheads the seal of God is found, will stand without an intercessor. To the wicked, that time will bring the unmingled wrath of God, but the righteous are hidden under the shadow of the Almighty. In His tabernacle, he will hide them "until the indignation be over past." "Here is the patience of the saints: here are they that keep the commandments of God, and the faith of Jesus." With eyes fixed upon the sanctuary above, they "live as seeing Him who is invisible." Soul union with Jehovah before the time of trouble, hides these saints in Christ, and thus they await the sign of His appearing in the sky.

While watching the little companies who hover together through that time of trouble,—the only living representatives of God on earth when the wine of His wrath is being drunk by the world,—John heard a voice from heaven. The universe is watching, waiting; for the end has almost come. God Himself said to John, "Write." And he said, "What shall I write?" And God said, "Write, Blessed are the dead which die in the Lord." God pronounced the blessing, upon those who die in the Lord during the sealing work, and the Spirit answers, "Yea, blessed are they." "Thou blessest, O Lord, and it shall be blessed forever." So through this time of trouble, when those who live, will find their patience tested to the utmost, when death is upon every side, and anguish, too deep for utterance, fills every heart, some will sleep, free from the strife; and these are pronounced blessed by God and by the Spirit; because, they "rest from their labors; and their works do follow them." Having begun a good work, having accepted the everlasting Gospel with all the consequences that would follow, and having fought a good fight, Christ Himself completes what they have begun, and they rest until the announcement is made that He is coming. Then those who have fallen asleep under the sealing message come forth to meet their Redeemer.

*And I heard a voice from heaven saying unto me, Write, Blessed are the dead which die in the Lord from henceforth: Yea, saith the Spirit, that they may rest from their labours; and their works do follow them.*

*And I looked, and behold a white cloud, and upon the cloud one sat like unto the Son of man, having on his head a golden crown, and in his hand a sharp sickle.*
*Rev. 14:13, 14.*

**Some will sleep, free from strife.**

On leaving the temple, before the outpouring of the plagues, the Son of man exchanges His priestly garments for those of a king. The royal diadem is placed upon His brow,—the brow once pierced by a crown of thorns. Heaven's hosts are marshaled; the inhabitants of other worlds draw near. From the temple, flies an angel crying to Him who is crowned King, "Thrust in Thy sickle, and reap: for the time is come for Thee to reap; for the harvest of the earth is ripe."

I have fought a good fight, I have finished my course, I have kept the faith.
2 Tim. 4:7, 8.

Isa. 63:1–3.
John 19:2.

*And another angel came out of the temple, crying with a loud voice to him that sat on the cloud, Thrust in thy sickle, and reap: for the time is come for thee to reap; for the harvest of the earth is ripe. Rev. 14:15.*

The angel that had power over fire cried, "Thrust in Thy sharp sickle, and gather the

*And he that sat on the cloud thrust in his sickle on the earth; and the earth was reaped.*

*And another angel came out of the temple which is in heaven, he also having a sharp sickle.*

*And another angel came out from the altar, which had power over fire; and cried with a loud cry to him that had the sharp sickle, saying, Thrust in thy sharp sickle, and gather the clusters of the vine of the earth; for her grapes are fully ripe.*

*And the angel thrust in his sickle into the earth, and gathered the vine of the earth, and cast it into the great winepress of the wrath of God.*

*And the winepress was trodden without the city, and blood came out of the winepress, even unto the horse bridles, by the space of a thousand and six hundred furlongs.* *Rev. 14:16-20.*

For the Lord himself shall descend from heaven with a shout, with the voice of the archangel, and with the trump of God.

1 Thess. 4:16.

clusters of the vine of the earth; for her grapes are fully ripe." Two vines have been growing in the earth, one of heavenly origin; the other of the earth, earthy. Christ is the true vine, and His people are the branches. The vine of the earth, Satan, has many branches; its growth is far more luxuriant than the heavenly one, but it is the vine of Sodom,—its "grapes are grapes of gall; their clusters are bitter; their wine is the poison of dragons." Terrible is the vintage when the angels gather the clusters, and throw them into the great wine press of the wrath of God.

Ancient wine press.

Nation rises against nation; because the angels no longer hold the winds of strife. The whole earth gathers to fight in the great battle of Armageddon; and so great is the slaughter that for miles about the city, blood flows to the horse bridles. At last the Father's throne is moved, and heaven's gates are thrown open, as Christ and the Father, seated together on thrones of life, surrounded by ten thousand times ten thousands of angels, approach the earth. There is silence in heaven.

The waiting saints hear the voice of Jehovah as it rolls through the earth. They look upward toward a small cloud which appears in the eastern horizon. It comes nearer and nearer; and as its glory unfolds, earth beholds her King, seated upon it. In the hand of the

King, is the law of God, which is as a sharp two-edged sword, and the wicked fall before the brightness of His countenance. Those who are one with Christ, will be drawn upward to the Lord of life, and will mingle with the hosts about the throne.

Redemption's story is complete. The redeemed from every kindred, tongue, and people, ascend with Christ to the holy city. Broken families are reunited, the sorrows of earth are forgotten in the joys of eternity. Adam, the first son of God, meets the second Adam, Christ, who sees the travail of His soul, presents the offering to the Father, and is satisfied. The story has been a long, sad one,—a terrible conflict with error, but creation takes up the song of love, and the triumph of truth and the eternal principles of Jehovah are forever acknowledged.

Behold, he cometh with clouds. Rev. 1:7.

All thy commandments are righteousness. Psa. 119:172.

The heavens shall declare his righteousness: for God is judge himself. Psa. 50:6.

His righteousness hath he openly shewed in the sight of the heathen. Psa. 98:2.

The heavens declare his righteousness, and all the people see his glory. Psa. 97:6.

Then we which are alive and remain shall be caught up together with them in the clouds, to meet the Lord in the air: and so shall we ever be with the Lord. 1 Thess. 4:17.

For, behold, I create new heavens and a new earth: and the former shall not be remembered, nor come into mind. Isa. 65:17.

There is hope in thine end, saith the Lord, that thy children shall come again to their own border. Jer. 31:17.

# CHAPTER XVI.

## PREPARATION FOR THE PLAGUES.

After this I looked, and, behold, a door was opened in heaven: and the first voice which I heard was as it were of a trumpet talking with me; which said, Come up hither, and I will shew thee things which must be hereafter.

And immediately I was in the Spirit: and, behold, a throne was set in heaven, and one sat on the throne.

And he that sat was to look upon like a jasper and a sardine stone: and there was a rainbow round about the throne, in sight like unto an emerald. Rev. 4:1-3.

How that he was caught up into paradise, and heard unspeakable words, which it is not possible for a man to utter.
2 Cor. 12:4 [margin.]

John 14:1-3.
Rev. 21:9, 10.
Heb. 9:6.

HEAVEN may seem like a far away world, but inspiration has given vivid descriptions of the abode of Jehovah. Human language but faintly conveys the splendor of spiritual purity, and the mortal mind, because of its narrowness, fails to grasp even the glimpses that are given; nevertheless, some idea may be gained of the capital of the universe, where dwells the King of kings. Outside the city of the New Jerusalem, the place which Christ promised to prepare for His people, and which is called the bride, the Lamb's wife, is Mount Zion, on which stands the living temple, the great council chamber of the most High.

Between the ascension of Christ and 1844, the Saviour ministered His own shed blood in the first apartment of the heavenly sanctuary.

He, the Lamb slain in the court of the congregation as a sin offering, presented His own blood before the Father in the holy place of the sanctuary. In 1844, when the prophetic period of twenty-three hundred days of Daniel 8 : 14, closed, the mighty angel of the tenth chapter of Revelation, made known the fact to the waiting congregation in the earth, which is the outer court of the heavenly sanctuary. At that time, Christ entered into the most holy apartment, where the investigative judgment began before the throne of God. The judgment work continues until the sealing angel returns from the earth with the words that his work has been accomplished. Then Christ rises from the judgment throne, and with a loud voice proclaims, "It is finished." Every man has heard the everlasting Gospel, and has accepted, or rejected it. If he has answered the call of God, his spirit has responded to the wooings of Jehovah, and the seal of the living God rests in his forehead. He is numbered with the one hundred and forty-four thousand. If, on the other hand, he has spurned the Spirit's pleadings, he has received the mark of the beast, and his destiny is likewise sealed.

Christ casts to the earth the censer which He holds in His hand. He lays aside the garments of His priesthood, and passes from the temple. Probation is closed. Christ's work is finished; and as He, with those who have ministered with Him for fallen man, passes from the temple, the glory of God bursts forth in all its grandeur, until His train fills the temple. "The temple was filled with smoke from the glory of God, and from His power; and no man was able to

By his own blood he entered in once into the holy place, having obtained eternal redemption for us.
Heb. 9 : 12.

Luke 1 : 9, 10.

Saying with a loud voice, Fear God, and give glory to him; for the hour of his judgment is come: and worship him that made heaven, and earth, and the sea, and the fountains of waters. Rev. 14 : 7.

For the time is come that judgment must begin at the house of God: and if it first begin at us, what shall the end be of them that obey not the gospel of God?
1 Pet. 4 : 17.

Behold, the man clothed with linen, which had the inkhorn by his side, reported the matter, saying, I have done as thou hast commanded me. Eze. 9 : 11.

Matt. 24 : 14.

He that is unjust, let him be unjust still: and he which is filthy, let him be filthy still: and he that is righteous, let him be righteous still: and he that is holy, let him be holy still. Rev. 22 : 11.

Rev. 7 : 1-4.

The angel took the censer, and filled it with fire of the altar, and cast it into the earth: and there were voices, and thunderings, and lightnings, and an earthquake.
Rev. 8 : 5.

Lev. 16 : 23.
Isa. 6 : 1-4.
Rev. 15 : 8.
Ex. 40 : 34, 35.

It came to pass, when the priests were come out of the holy place, that the cloud filled the house of the Lord,

So that the priests could not stand to minister because of the cloud: for the glory of the Lord had filled the house of the Lord.
1 Kings 8 : 10, 11.

So that the priests could not stand to minister by reason of the cloud: for the glory of the Lord had filled the house of God.
2 Chron. 5:14.

2 Tim. 2:5.
Rev. 22:11, 12.

Father, I will that they also, whom thou hast given me, be with me where I am; that they may behold my glory, which thou hast given me: for thou lovedst me before the foundation of the world.
John 17:24.

Thine eyes shall see the king in his beauty: they shall behold the land that is very far off.
Isa. 33:17.

For our God is a consuming fire.
Heb. 12:29.

Behold, the veil of the temple was rent in twain from the top to the bottom; and the earth did quake, and the rocks rent;
And the graves were opened; and many bodies of the saints which slept arose. Matt. 27:51, 52.

Beloved, now are we the sons of God, and it doth not yet appear what we shall be: but we know that, when he shall appear, we shall be like him; for we shall see him as he is. 1 John 3:2.

The same shall drink of the wine of the wrath of God, which is poured out without mixture into the cup of his indignation; and he shall be tormented with fire and brimstone in the presence of the holy angels, and in the presence of the Lamb. Rev. 14:10.

enter into the temple, till the seven plagues of the seven angels were fulfilled." When the Son of God was offered for the sins of the world, when He became a man, and afterwards ministered in heaven as a man, God, the Father, had veiled His exceeding great glory until the work of redemption was complete. But when the Saviour utters the triumphant shout, "It is finished," the restrained glory bursts forth in the splendor which was seen before the fall. Human language is so weak that words fail to express the thought; but for six thousand years, even the God of the universe. has mourned for the lost world; and when at last the redeemed are gathered out, although they are still on earth, the pent up glory of Jehovah flashes forth,—a living, consuming fire. This was typified in the temple at Jerusalem, when at the words, "It is finished," uttered by the Saviour on the cross, the veil was rent from top to bottom. With the announcement of these words this second time, the man Jesus Christ, with the four living creatures and four and twenty elders, who for centuries have represented the re deemed, leave the temple altogether, and enter no more, until Christ returns from earth, bringing with Him the host of the redeemed. Then with the hundred and forty-four thousand, glorified, and reflecting the character of Christ, He enters the temple, and this company minister there.

In these closing events two distinct views are given to John. Before the Saviour leaves the temple, seven angels are seen standing before the altar. To them are given seven vials containing the unmingled wrath of God.

The elements of the earth are under the control of mighty angels, and although Satan, "the prince of the power of the air," has had partial control of these mighty forces, yet the power of God has held them in check; else destruction would have come, and man would have been destroyed. As Christ rises to leave the temple, these seven commanding angels stand awaiting the command of Jehovah.

While they are waiting, for heaven has seemed to pause, John sees the same company, precious in the eyes of the Lord, standing, as they will stand on the sea of glass, when the seven last plagues have been poured out. Lest it should seem that these were lost in the terror of the plagues, with one sweeping glance, the prophet sees beyond the time of trouble, when this same company stand on Mount Zion with the Lamb. It is wonderful how often this company is mentioned, and with what care it is described, before the terrors are portrayed! Its numbers come up out of great tribulation; they stand through the time of trouble without an intercessor; for Christ is without the temple, and only God remains within.

For them the time of the plagues, through which they pass unharmed, is as when Israel stood between the mountain and the Red Sea, with an Egyptian army pressing hard after them. There was no visible way of escape, and casting themselves on the arm of Jehovah, they awaited His deliverance. Their deliverance was a marvel in the eyes of the nations round about, and all men feared the God of Israel. The song in which Moses led the hosts of the delivered, will be repeated when the one hundred and

The Lord said unto Satan, Behold, all that he hath is in thy power; only upon himself put not forth thine hand. So Satan went forth from the presence of the Lord.

And there was a day when his sons and his daughters were eating and drinking wine in their eldest brother's house:

And there came a messenger unto Job, and said, The oxen were plowing, and the asses feeding beside them:

And the Sabeans fell upon them, and took them away; yea, they have slain the servants with the edge of the sword; and I only am escaped alone to tell thee.

Job 1 : 12–19.

*And I saw another sign in heaven, great and marvellous, seven angels having the seven last plagues; for in them is filled up the wrath of God.*

*And I saw as it were a sea of glass mingled with fire: and them that had gotten the victory over the beast, and over his image, and over his mark, and over the number of his name, stand on the sea of glass, having the harps of God.*

*Rev. 15 : 1, 2.*

I looked, and, lo, a Lamb stood on the mount Sion, and with him an hundred forty and four thousand, having his Father's name written in their foreheads. Rev. 14 : 1.

Rev. 7 : 14.
Isa. 61 : 2.
Isa. 63 : 4.

It came to pass, when all the kings of the Amorites, which were on the side of Jordan westward, and all the kings of the Canaanites, which were by the sea, heard that the Lord had dried up the waters of Jordan from before the children of Israel, until we were passed over, that their heart melted, neither was there spirit in them any more, because of the children of Israel.

Josh. 5 : 1.

Ex. 15 : 1, 21.

*And they sing the song of Moses the servant of God, and the song of the Lamb, saying, Great and marvellous are thy works, Lord God Almighty; just and true are thy ways, thou King of saints.*

*Who shall not fear thee, O Lord, and glorify thy name? for thou only art holy: for all nations shall come and worship before thee; for thy judgments are made manifest.*

*And after that I looked, and, behold, the temple of the tabernacle of the testimony in heaven was opened:*

*And the seven angels came out of the temple, having the seven plagues, clothed in pure and white linen, and having their breasts girded with golden girdles.*

*And one of the four beasts gave unto the seven angels seven golden vials full of the wrath of God, who liveth for ever and ever.*
*Rev. 15:3-7.*

2Tim. 4:8.

Suddenly there was with the angel a multitude of the heavenly host praising God, and saying,

Glory to God in the highest, and on earth peace, good will toward men. Luke 2:13, 14.

Rev. 15:3.

Thy dead men shall live, together with my dead body shall they arise. Awake and sing, ye that dwell in dust: for thy dew is as the dew of herbs, and the earth shall cast out the dead. Isa. 26:19.

forty-four thousand stand on Mount Zion. "I will sing unto the Lord, for He hath triumphed gloriously. . . . The Lord is my strength and song, and He is become my salvation: He is my God, and I will prepare Him an habitation; my father's God, and I will exalt Him. . . . Thy right hand, O Lord, hath dashed in pieces the enemy. And in the greatness of Thine excellency Thou hast overthrown them that rose up against Thee: Thou sentest forth Thy wrath, which consumed them as stubble." The song of Moses is the song of deliverance from impending destruction; the song of the Lamb is one of triumph over sin and the grave.

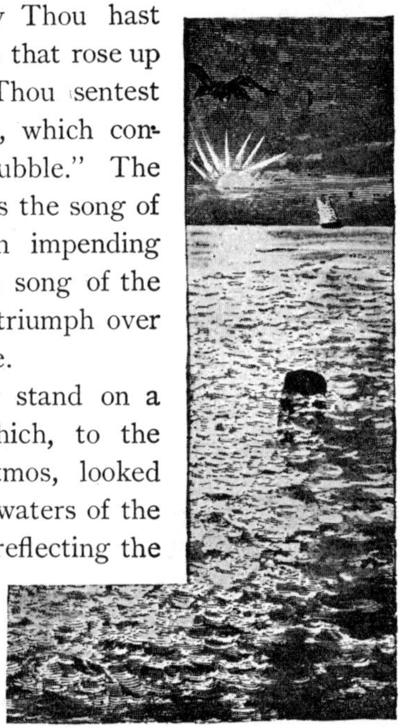

**The smooth waters of the Mediterranean, reflecting the glories of a sunset.**

This company stand on a sea of glass, which, to the prophet on Patmos, looked like the smooth waters of the Mediterranean, reflecting the glories of a sunset. It was a sea of glass mingled with fire. The Saviour Himself places crowns on their heads and harps in their hands.

Earth has heard music; but never has this world heard any music which can compare with celestial strains. Heaven has resounded with songs; but since the fall, the key has been lowered. When the redeemed gather about the throne, the leader of the angel choir strikes a note higher than before; and the harps are swept by fingers guided by souls filled with love and thanksgiving. "Great and marvelous are Thy works, Lord God Almighty," rings forth as the works of God are viewed by eyes once dimmed by sin. "Just and true are Thy ways, Thou King of saints," echoes and reechoes as the plan of salvation unfolds to minds, newly touched with immortality. "Who shall not fear Thee, O Lord, and glorify Thy name?" And the answer comes, "All nations shall come and worship before Thee; for Thy judgments are made manifest."

So when this corruptible shall have put on incorruption, and this mortal shall have put on immortality, then shall be brought to pass the saying that is written, Death is swallowed up in victory.

O death, where is thy sting? O grave, where is thy victory?

The sting of death is sin; and the strength of sin is the law.

But thanks be to God, which giveth us the victory through our Lord Jesus Christ. 1 Cor. 15:54-57.

Through all the controversy, Satan has attempted to justify himself, and to prove that heaven was responsible for the rebellion; but before his destruction, he will be convinced of the everlasting goodness of the Father; and bowing before the throne, he will confess the justice of the sentence pronounced against him. God's wisdom, His justice, and His goodness, stand vindicated before the universe. The whole universe, both the lost and the redeemed, will at last pronounce their own sentence in the words, "just and true are Thy ways, Thou King of saints, . . . for Thy judgments are made manifest."

Sing, O ye heavens; for the Lord hath done it: shout, ye lower parts of the earth: break forth into singing, ye mountains, O forest, and every tree therein: for the Lord hath redeemed Jacob, and glorified himself in Israel. Isa. 44:23.

That at the name of Jesus every knee should bow, of things in heaven, and things in earth, and things under the earth.
Phil. 2:10.

John looked again toward the temple; for while he had prophetically seen the culmination, the end had not yet fully come. He sees the seven angels waiting, and to them are given, by one of the four living creatures, seven vials of wrath. So complete is the acknowledgment of the justice of all God's ways that when Christ proclaims, "He that is unjust, let him be unjust still: and he which is filthy, let him be

*And the temple was filled with smoke from the glory of God, and from his power; and no man was able to enter into the temple, till the seven plagues of the seven angels were fulfilled.*
*Rev. 15:8.*

Rev. 22:11, 12.

filthy still: and he that is righteous, let him be righteous still," there is no longer any opportunity for man to change his course, or retrace his steps, the vials which contain destruction for the wicked, are placed in the hands of the angels by one of the four living creatures, representing man in the court of heaven. Man is judged by fellow-man, and the universe proclaims the justice of the law of God. Christ steps out; the temple is left to the Father alone. "The thresholds moved at the voice of Him that cried, and the house was filled with smoke." The seven angels await the command of Jehovah. The closing work of earth is about to begin.

If the tree fall toward the south, or toward the north, in the place where the tree falleth, there it shall be. Eccl. 11:3.

For in the hand of the Lord there is a cup, and the wine is red; it is full of mixture; and he poureth out of the same: but the dregs thereof, all the wicked of the earth shall wring them out, and drink them.

But I will declare for ever; I will sing praises to the God of Jacob. Psa. 75:8, 9.

For he hath looked down from the height of his sanctuary; from heaven did the Lord behold the earth. Psa. 102:19.

# CHAPTER XVII.

## THE SEVEN LAST PLAGUES.

THE inner veil of the earthly sanctuary was rent in twain when Christ on Calvary uttered the words, "It is finished." These words announced to all the waiting universe, that the service in types and shadows was forever at an end; for type had met antitype. When Christ rises from the judgment throne in "the temple of the tabernacle of the testimony in heaven," the holy of holies, and cries so that His voice reaches the utmost bounds of creation, saying, "It is done," the Father's glory fills the temple, and all other beings are excluded. Men on earth may continue to plead for forgiveness; they may still think there is time to make peace with God; but like the Jews, who did not see in Christ the antitype of the lambs they had slain, and continued to minister in the temple, there is no longer any virtue in their service. Neither

Matt 27:50, 51.

In the midst of the week he shall cause the sacrifice and the oblation to cease. Dan. 9:27.

He that is unjust, let him be unjust still: and he which is filthy, let him be filthy still: and he that is righteous, let him be righteous still: and he that is holy, let him be holy still.

And, behold, I come quickly; and my reward is with me, to give every man according as his work shall be. Rev. 22:11, 12.

Behold, the days come, saith the Lord God, that I will send a famine in the land, not a famine of bread, nor a thirst for water, but of hearing the words of the Lord:

And they shall wander from sea to sea, and from the north even to the east, they shall run to and fro to seek the word of the Lord, and shall not find it. Amos 8:11, 12.

Behold, your house is left unto you desolate. Matt. 23:38.

will prayer avail after Christ says, "It is done." His declaration is final; probationary time will then be at an end. For thousands of years men have heard the voice of God, but they have passed on without regard. All men hear the preaching of the everlasting Gospel, but many turn a deaf ear to Jehovah's voice.

Humanity takes all its physical life, all its power and energy from God; for "in Him we live, and move, and have our being;" and yet while every pulse beat is under the direct control of the God of life, and He knows about and makes possible, every breath that is drawn, men will deny His very existence; or, while feebly acknowledging that there is a Supreme Power, they claim that they are wholly independent of that Power, and have the right to follow the dictates of a perverted intellect. Time will be given for these philosophers to prove their theory. When grace and mercy cease to reach earthward, the prince of this world will have full control of the wicked.

When man says by word and act that he will not obey, and those who do obey are gathered into little companies overshadowed by the glory of God, then the restraint is removed, and man feels the effect of a life without Christ. Having waited to the extreme limit of time given for mercy, God calls at last from the temple to the seven angels having the seven vials full of the wrath of Jehovah, and bids them go forth. The seven angels come to the earth one at a time; that is, God's overruling Spirit is withdrawn from one element after another, until utter destruction results. Her plagues [shall] come in *one day*, the prophet says, or one year of literal time.

They come unto thee as the people cometh, and they sit before thee as my people, and they hear thy words, but they will not do them: for with their mouth they shew much love, but their heart goeth after their covetousness.

And, lo, thou art unto them as a very lovely song of one that hath a pleasant voice, and can play well on an instrument: for they hear thy words, but they do them not.
Eze. 33:31, 32.

For in him we live, and move, and have our being; as certain also of your own poets have said, For we are also his offspring.
Acts 17:28.

In whose hand is the soul of every living thing, and the breath of all mankind. Job 12:10.

The fool hath said in his heart, There is no God. Corrupt are they, and have done abominable iniquity: there is none that doeth good.
Psa. 53:1.

Now as Jannes and Jambres withstood Moses, so do these also resist the truth: men of corrupt minds, reprobate concerning the faith.
2 Tim. 3:8.

He maketh his sun to rise on the evil and on the good, and sendeth rain on the just and on the unjust.
Matt. 5:45.

Is there any number of his armies? and upon whom doth not his light arise? Job 25:3.

Every good gift and every perfect gift is from above, and cometh down from the Father of lights, with whom is no variableness, neither shadow of turning. Jas. 1:17.

The Lord will create upon every dwelling place of mount Zion, and upon her assemblies, a cloud and smoke by day, and the shining of a flaming fire by night: for upon all the glory shall be a defence.

And there shall be a tabernacle for a shadow in the daytime from the heat, and for a place of refuge, and for a covert from storm and from rain. Isa. 4:5, 6.

The first angel went, and poured out his vial upon the earth.

The first angel went, and poured out his vial upon the earth. Ever since the divine fiat uttered on the third day of creation week, the earth has been an obedient servant; and since the creation of man, she has never refused to respond to his call for food. Whatsoever a man sowed that he expected to reap; and the grains and the herbs have been for the service of man and beast. The foods which the earth brings forth nourish the human frame, and disease is repelled. But the first angel poured out his vial upon the earth. "Alas for the day! for the day of the Lord is at hand, and as a destruction from the Almighty shall it come." "The seed is rotten under their clods, the garners are laid desolate, the barns are broken down; for the corn is withered. How do the beasts groan! the herds of cattle are perplexed, because they have no pasture; yea, the flocks of sheep are made desolate." Habakkuk says that "The fig tree shall not blossom, neither shall fruit be in the vines; the labor of the olive shall fail, and the fields shall yield no meat; the flocks shall be cut off from the fold, and there shall be no herd in the stalls." "The heaven over you is stayed from dew, and the earth is stayed from her fruit."

A short drought, over a small area, has

For the day of vengeance is in mine heart, and the year of my redeemed is come. Isa. 63:4.

Isa. 34:8.
Gen. 1:11, 12.

*And I heard a great voice out of the temple saying to the seven angels, Go your ways, and pour out the vials of the wrath of God upon the earth.*

*And the first went, and poured out his vial upon the earth; and there fell a noisome and grievous sore upon the men which had the mark of the beast, and upon them which worshipped his image.*
*Rev. 16:1, 2.*

Joel 1:15-20.

Therefore shall the land mourn, and every one that dwelleth therein shall languish, with the beasts of the field, and with the fowls of heaven; yea, the fishes of the sea also shall be taken away.
Hos. 4:3.

Hab. 3:17.

For the mountains will I take up a weeping and wailing, and for the habitations of the wilderness a lamentation, because they are burned up, so that none can pass through them; neither can men hear the voice of the cattle; both the fowl of the heavens and the beast are fled; they are gone.

And I will make Jerusalem heaps, and a den of dragons; and I will make the cities of Judah desolate, without an inhabitant.
Jer. 9:10, 11.

Hag. 1:10.

A thousand shall fall at thy side, and ten thousand at thy right hand; but it shall not come nigh thee. Psa. 91:7.

Rev. 16:2.

And I heard the number of them which were sealed: and there were sealed an hundred and forty and four thousand of all the tribes of the children of Israel. Rev. 7:4.

The third angel followed them, saying with a loud voice, if any man worship the beast and his image, and receive his mark in his forehead, or in his hand,

The same shall drink of the wine of the wrath of God, which is poured out without mixture into the cup of his indignation; and he shall be tormented with fire and brimstone in the presence of the holy angels, and in the presence of the Lamb. Rev. 14:9, 10.

In the last day, that great day of the feast, Jesus stood and cried, saying, If any man thirst, let him come unto me, and drink. John 7:37.

Because thou hast made the Lord, which is my refuge, even the most High, thy habitation;

There shall no evil befall thee, neither shall any plague come nigh thy dwelling. Psa. 91:9, 10.

Isa. 33:16.

And gavest them bread from heaven for their hunger, and broughtest forth water for them out of the rock for their thirst, and promisedst them that they should go in to possess the land which thou hadst sworn to give them. Neh. 9:15.

Hab. 3:18.

Hab. 3:19.

Psa. 91:6, 7–10.

He shall deliver thee in six troubles: yea, in seven there shall no evil touch thee. Job 5:19.

caused untold suffering and disease on the earth. What will it be when the earth ceases to yield her fruits, or when the trees and all vegetation are so full of disease that the cattle starve for lack of pasturage, and man is in no better condition?

"There fell a noisome and grievous sore upon the men which had the mark of the beast, and upon them which worshiped his image." Before the first angel, holding his vial, left the temple, all men had been divided into two classes,—those who are sealed with the seal of the living God, and those who worship the beast, or his image, and bear his mark. The grievous sores come upon those having the mark of the beast. When disease is abroad in the land, it is rebuked only by a strong spiritual atmosphere. Christ was fully charged with life, which is the result of soul union with the fountain head; and as He could touch the leper and cause health to flow from Him to the diseased man, so in the time of the first plague, those who are clothed with spiritual life will resist disease. Even the physical man will be protected by the strength of the soul union with the Father. Their bread and water will be sure, and habits of simple diet have become so fixed during their time of probation that though there may be a drought, God can feed them as He did Israel in the wilderness. In the midst of this terrible suffering, the little companies will sing and rejoice. "I will rejoice in the Lord, I will joy in the God of my salvation. The Lord God is my strength, and He will make my feet like hinds' feet, and He will make me to walk upon mine high places." "Thou shalt not be afraid

. . . for the pestilence that walketh in darkness. . . . A thousand shall fall at thy side, and ten thousand at thy right hand; but it shall not come nigh thee. . . . Because thou hast made the Lord, which is my refuge, even the most High, thy habitation; there shall no evil befall thee, neither shall any plague come nigh thy dwelling."

I will sever in that day the land of Goshen, in which my people dwell, that no swarms of flies shall be there; to the end thou mayest know that I am the Lord in the midst of the earth.

And I will put a division between my people and thy people: to morrow shall this sign be.
Ex. 8:22, 23.

As the Lord put a division between Israel and the Egyptians after the first three plagues had fallen upon the land of the Pharaohs, so in the time of trouble He says, "Come, My people, enter thou into thy chambers, and shut thy doors about thee: hide thyself as it were for a little moment, until the indignation be overpast. For, behold, the Lord cometh out of His place to punish the inhabitants of the earth for their iniquity." "The Lord will create upon every dwelling place of Mount Zion, and upon her assemblies, a cloud and smoke by day, and the shining of a flaming fire by night: for above all the glory shall be a covering."

**The creatures of the sea.**

The vial of the second angel was poured upon the sea, and the creatures of the sea died, for what was once life became poison. There is but a step between life and death. A change of a few degrees in temperature, would kill all life, both animal and vegetable; deprive an animal of the life-giving oxygen, and in a few moments, life is extinct.

*And the second angel poured out his vial upon the sea; and it became as the blood of a dead man: and every living soul died in the sea. Rev. 16:3.*

And the fish that was in the river died; and the river stank, and the Egyptians could not drink of the water of the river; and there was blood throughout all the land of Egypt. Ex. 7:20, 21.

The deliverance of Israel from the land of Egypt, and their guidance through the wilderness, is a type of God's care for His sealed

For it is the day of the Lord's vengeance, and the year of recompenses for the controversy of Zion.
Isa. 34:8.

Thou art wearied in the multitude of thy counsels. Let now the astrologers, the stargazers, the monthly prognosticators, stand up, and save thee from these things that shall come upon thee.

Behold, they shall be as stubble; the fire shall burn them; they shall not deliver themselves from the power of the flame: there shall not be a coal to warm at, nor fire to sit before it. Isa. 47:11-14.

ones during the year when the plagues are falling. This will be a time of trouble such as never was since there was a nation, and the strength of God's people will consist in their pressing close to Him. Deep anguish will often oppress them, but as the light of the promises breaks in, they sing praises for their deliverance.

The rivers become blood.

During the falling of these plagues, men of science, who have advocated the power of the human intellect and the wisdom of man, will doubtless offer scientific reasons for the disease on land and sea. The magicians of Egypt first imitated the wonders which came by the hand of Moses; and when they could no longer do that, they gave a reason for each miracle, assigning some natural cause; and as soon as the plague was removed, Pharaoh would say in his heart, "I thought for a time it was a divine providence upon the land, but doubtless, as the magicians say, it was due to such and such a cause," and Pharaoh hardened his heart. As men did then, so will they do in the end of time; for men's hearts are the same in all generations. The repentance of Pharaoh was like that of Cain,—it was sorrow for suffering, not sorrow for sin. This will be the same in the days of the last plagues.

*And the third angel poured out his vial upon the rivers and fountains of waters; and they became blood.*

*And I heard the angel of the waters say, Thou art righteous, O Lord, which art, and wast, and shalt be, because thou hast judged thus.*

*For they have shed the blood of saints and prophets, and thou hast given them blood to drink; for they are worthy.*

The third angel withdraws the life-giving spirit from the rivers and the fountains of water, and they become blood. Since the days of creation,

God has, by the flowing streams and the wells of water, typified salvation, which is full and free. As a teacher on earth, Christ used the waters of Jacob's well, to illustrate the life of the Spirit, which wells up into everlasting life. The smitten rock in the wilderness, from which flowed the water for the thirsty millions in Israel's camp, was God's voice saying, "Come unto Me and drink." In the sanctuary service, on that last great day of the feast, the silver trumpets called the people together in the early morning; and the priests, bearing flagons of water from the brook Kedron, ascended the steps of the temple singing, "Our feet shall stand within thy gates, O Jerusalem." "Jehovah is my strength and my song; He also is become my salvation. *Therefore with joy shall ye draw water out of the wells of salvation.*" These words will again be sung by those who are preserved in the time of the third plague. Those who have exchanged life for death, will see the rivers turned to blood,—a type of the blood of Christ, which they have spurned; and the lives of saints which they have lightly regarded.

Heaven is bending near the earth, even through its time of trouble; and angels, having watched the workings of evil, uphold the purpose of God, and pronounce His judgments true and righteous. The sun, which has shone alike upon the just and the unjust, which, in its very beams, is a reflection of the smile of God, becomes, when His Spirit is withdrawn, a heat which scorches men as with fire. God, whose countenance is life to those who are in harmony with Him, is a consuming fire to His enemies.

*And I heard another out of the altar say, Even so, Lord God Almighty, true and righteous are thy judgments. Rev. 16:4-7.*

Behold, I will stand before thee there upon the rock in Horeb; and thou shalt smite the rock, and there shall come water out of it, that the people may drink. And Moses did so in the sight of the elders of Israel. Ex. 17:6.

Isa. 48:21.
Psa. 105:41.
Psa. 78:15, 16.
Isa. 12:2-5.

He shall dwell on high: his place of defence shall be the munitions of rocks: bread shall be given him; his waters shall be sure. Isa. 33:16.

2 Kings 3:17, 22.

For they have shed the blood of saints and prophets, and thou hast given them blood to drink; for they are worthy. Rev. 16:6.

Heb. 10:29.
Mal. 3:5.

Zion heard, and was glad; and the daughters of Judah rejoiced because of thy judgments, O Lord. Psa. 97:8.

Matt. 5:45.
Job. 25:3.

Unto you that fear my name shall the Sun of righteousness arise with healing in his wings. Mal. 4:2.

The Lord said, My Spirit shall not always strive with man. Gen. 6:3.

Who among us shall dwell with the devouring fire? who among us shall dwell with everlasting burnings? Isa. 33:14.

Psa. 18:14.
Zech. 9:14.

*And the fourth angel poured out his vial upon the sun; and power was given unto him to scorch men with fire.*

*And men were scorched with great heat, and blasphemed the name of God, which hath power over these plagues: and they repented not to give him glory.*
*Rev. 16:8, 9.*

The lightning has been chained, and when kept within its circuit, is the obedient servant of man, even administering to his physical being; but uncontrolled, it is an instrument of instant death. Thus the sun becomes an agent of destruction, and under the fourth plague its rays scorch men. In the wilderness a cloud overshadowed the camp by day. God was as a

**Men blaspheme God and repent not.**

For death is come up into our windows, and is entered into our palaces, to cut off the children from without, and the young men from the streets. Jer. 9:21.

Therefore shall evil come upon thee; thou shalt not know from whence it riseth: and mischief shall fall upon thee; thou shalt not be able to put it off: and desolation shall come upon thee suddenly, which thou shalt not know.
Isa. 47:11.

Job. 1:16.
Num. 14:14.
Psa. 91:1.

A fire devoureth before them and behind them a flame burneth: the land is as the garden of Eden before them, and behind them a desolate wilderness; yea, and nothing shall escape them.
Joel 2:3.

Who will have all men to be saved, and to come unto the knowledge of the truth. 1 Tim. 2:4.

For God speaketh once, yea twice, yet man perceiveth it not.
Job 33:14.

"shadow of a great rock in a weary land." "He that dwelleth in the secret place of the most High shall abide under the shadow of the Almighty." But those without a shelter, who suffer from the intense heat, which withers every living thing, and prostrates man and beast, blaspheme God and repent not.

As long as probation lingered, God dealt with men in various ways to cause them to repent, He sent warnings by the prophets, He spoke through His providences, He gave blessings and then removed them, He gave health, and when that did not bring repentance, He sought by a bed of sickness to gain recognition. When probation has closed, it will be seen that no power in heaven or in earth, could have turned the worldly-wise to the source of all true wisdom. "Ephraim is joined to his idols: let him alone."

Signs of the coming of the Son of man were given in the earth, the sea, and the sky. Those were unheeded, and in the plagues, terrors come from those same places.

The fifth vial was poured upon the seat of the beast. The developments in the last days, reveal the persecuting spirit of the beast and his image. All the world wondered after the beast, and looked to his man-made power in preference to the God of light and love. Thick darkness covered all the land of Egypt for three days, so that men could not leave their homes. This was a type of the darkness of the fifth plague. Men scoffed when they heard that the darkening of the sun in 1780 was a token of the approaching day of God. Some of these men will be living, when the sun refuses to shine upon the whole earth. They blaspheme because of the heat of its rays; and then gnaw their tongues in anguish during the bitter night which settles upon the earth.

"The great day of the Lord is near, it is near, and hasteth greatly. . . . That day is a day of wrath, a day of trouble and distress,

Immediately the angel of the Lord smote him, because he gave not God the glory: and he was eaten of worms, and gave up the ghost. Acts 12:23.

2 Sam. 24:17.

Christ Jesus, who of God is made unto us wisdom, and righteousness, and sanctification, and redemption. 1 Cor. 1:30.

There shall be signs in the sun, and in the moon, and in the stars; and upon the earth distress of nations, with perplexity; the sea and the waves roaring. Luke 21:25.

*And the fifth angel poured out his vial upon the seat of the beast; and his kingdom was full of darkness; and they gnawed their tongues for pain,*

*And blasphemed the God of heaven because of their pains and their sores, and repented not of their deeds. Rev. 16:10, 11.*

Moses stretched forth his hand toward heaven; and there was a thick darkness in all the land of Egypt three days:

They saw not one another, neither rose any from his place for three days: but all the children of Israel had light in their dwellings. Ex. 10:22, 23.

Knowing this first, that there shall come in the last days scoffers, walking after their own lusts,

And saying, Where is the promise of his coming? for since the fathers fell asleep, all things continue as they were from the beginning of the creation. 2 Pet. 3:3, 4.

A day of darkness and of gloominess, a day of clouds and of thick darkness. Joel 2:2.

Therefore wait ye upon me, saith the Lord, until the day that I rise up to the prey: for my determination is to gather the nations, that I may assemble the kingdoms, to pour upon them mine indignation, even all my fierce anger: for all the earth shall be devoured with the fire of my jealousy. Zeph. 3:8.

Prince of the power of the air, the spirit that now worketh in the children of disobedience. Eph. 2:2.

Great is the wrath of the Lord that is poured out upon us, because our fathers have not kept the word of the Lord, to do after all that is written in this book. 2 Chron. 34:21.

a day of wasteness and desolation, a day of darkness and gloominess, a day of clouds and thick darkness. . . . And I will bring distress upon men, that they shall walk like blind men, because they have sinned against the Lord. . . . Neither their silver nor their

**The light shines only upon the houses of Israel.**

Isa. 2:20.

Riches profit not in the day of wrath: but righteousness delivereth from death. Prov. 11:4.

Yet thou in thy manifold mercies forsookest them not in the wilderness: the pillar of the cloud departed not from them by day, to lead them in the way; neither the pillar of fire by night, to shew them light, and the way wherein they should go. Neh. 9:19.

Now all these things happened unto them for ensamples: and they are written for our admonition, upon whom the ends of the world are come. 1 Cor. 10:11.

As it was in the days of Noe, so shall it be also in the days of the Son of man. Luke 17:26.

It shall be, when thou hast made an end of reading this book, that thou shalt bind a stone to it, and cast it into the midst of Euphrates: Jer. 51:63.

gold shall be able to deliver them in the day of the Lord's wrath; but the whole land shall be devoured by the fire of His jealousy: for He shall make even a speedy riddance of all them that dwell in the land." Terrible is the wrath of God; He has but to hide His face, and all men are put to confusion. Satan, once light bearer in the heavenly court, claimed that light dwelt in him. This will be a time for him to manifest his power; but the world finds that its prince, with all his followers, is enshrouded in the same dense gloom. The light shines only upon the houses of Israel. Each little company is still overshadowed by that cloud which is a protection from the heat and a light in the night. It is the same cloudy pillar which guided ancient Israel.

The wonderful records of deliverance, scattered through the holy Word, are types of the final deliverance of God's people when the earth itself is destroyed, together with the workers of iniquity. Each overthrow of nations is a symbol of the final destruction of all things at the second coming of Christ. These three witnesses,—individual experience, national life, and the written Word, have spoken constantly; but though an angel from heaven should speak in thunder tones, men would not change.

Even during the falling of the plagues, men go on in the way of the world. Governments do their business, men seek gold and fame, nations prepare for war, and the controlling powers of earth,—the beast and his image—still plan the extermination of the hated, persecuted sect upon whom they lay the blame of the famine and the pestilence. As Elijah, the prophet, was called the troubler in Israel, so the commandment-keeping people are pointed out as the cause of tribulation.

The beast and his image seek to control all nations. Satan works in a way never before known. The principles which made Rome the most oppressive government, are revived and strengthened. The miracle-working power of Spiritualism adds strength to the oppression. Paganism (the dragon), the papacy (the beast), and fallen Protestantism (the false prophet), join hands. Urged on by the unclean spirits, deadly decrees are issued by this threefold union, and Satan himself appears in person. The angels loose the winds of strife; and marshaled by the great commander of the legions of darkness, the nations gather for the great battle of Armageddon. Hitherto the hand of God has controlled in battle. His voice

And thou shalt say, Thus shall Babylon sink, and shall not rise from the evil that I will bring upon her: and they shall be weary. Thus far are the words of Jeremiah.
Jer. 51:64.

He said unto him, If they hear not Moses and the prophets, neither will they be persuaded, though one rose from the dead.
Luke 16:31.

He had power to give life unto the image of the beast, that the image of the beast should both speak, and cause that as many as would not worship the image of the beast should be killed.

And he causeth all, both small and great, rich and poor, free and bond, to receive a mark in their right hand, or in their foreheads.
Rev. 13:15, 16.

It came to pass, when Ahab saw Elijah, that Ahab said unto him, Art thou he that troubleth Israel?

And he answered, I have not troubled Israel; but thou, and thy father's house, in that ye have forsaken the commandments of the Lord, and thou hast followed Baalim. 1 Kings 18:17, 18.

*And the sixth angel poured out his vial upon the great river Euphrates; and the water thereof was dried up, that the way of the kings of the east might be prepared.*

*And I saw three unclean spirits like frogs come out of the mouth of the dragon, and out of the mouth of the beast, and out of the mouth of the false prophet.*

*For they are the spirits of devils, working miracles, which go forth unto the kings of the earth and of the whole world, to gather them to the battle of that great day of God Almighty.*
*Rev. 16:12-14.*

I saw the beast, and the kings of the earth, and their armies, gathered together to make war against him that sat on the horse, and against his army. Rev. 19:19.

*Behold, I come as a thief. Blessed is he that watcheth, and keepeth his garments, lest he walk naked, and they see his shame.*

*And he gathered them together into a place called in the Hebrew tongue Armageddon.*

*Rev. 16:15, 16.*

He shall plant the tabernacles of his palace between the seas in the glorious holy mountain; yet he shall come to his end, and none shall help him. Dan. 11:45.

Sisera gathered together all his chariots, even nine hundred chariots of iron, and all the people that were with him, from Harosheth of the Gentiles unto the river of Kishon.

And Deborah said unto Barak, Up; for this is the day in which the Lord hath delivered Sisera into thine hand: is not the Lord gone out before thee? So Barak went down from mount Tabor, and ten thousand men after him.

And the Lord discomfited Sisera. Judges 4:13-15.

Judges 5:19.

In his days Pharaoh-nechoh king of Egypt went up against the king of Assyria to the river Euphrates: and king Josiah went against him; and he slew him at Megiddo, when he had seen him. 2 Kings 23:29.

The archers shot at king Josiah; and the king said to his servants, Have me away; for I am sore wounded.

His servants therefore took him out of that chariot, and put him in the second chariot that he had; and they brought him to Jerusalem, and he died, and was buried in one of the sepulchres of his fathers. And all Judah and Jerusalem mourned for Josiah.

And Jeremiah lamented for Josiah: and all the singing men and the singing women spake of Josiah in their lamentations to this day, and made them an ordinance in Israel: and, behold, they are written in the lamentations.

2 Chron. 35:23-25.

has said, "Thus far, and no farther;" and although His hand was not recognized, it has guided even heathen armies. This is a truth plainly shown in the wars of Israel, recorded in the Old Testament.

But when the sixth plague is poured out, there is no restraining hand. The Turkish power designated as the River Euphrates, which has separated between the East and the West, gives way; and like the rushing together of mighty storm clouds, the armies of the earth, striving for the territory, meet in the valley of Jehoshaphat,—the ancient meeting place for Egypt and Assyria, known in the Hebrew as Megiddo, and in Greek as Armageddon. The word itself means "the place of the troops," and the history of battles fought there, typifies the last great contest between nations under the sixth plague. In the days of Deborah, the prophetess, the armies of Israel fought against Jabin, the king of the Canaanites whose captain was Sisera. God wrought for Israel, and the victory called forth the song of Deborah and Barak. "The kings came and fought, then fought the kings of Canaan in Taanach by the waters of Megiddo; they took no gain of money. They fought from heaven; the stars in their courses fought against Sisera." In the valley of Megiddo, Josiah, king of Israel, was slain by Pharaoh Nechoh, who was passing by that valley to the stronghold of the Abyssinians on the Euphrates. The death of the Jewish king caused great lamentation, called "the mourning of Hadadrimmon"; and looking forward to the time of the end, the prophet Zechariah says, "In that day there shall be a great mourning in Jerusalem, as the mourning of Hadadrimmon in the valley of Megiddo.

While the nations are gathering for this great contest, the seventh angel pours out his vial in the air. The elements, which had heretofore mingled in giving life to man, clash together; and above the tumult, the mighty peals of thunder, and the flashes of lightning, the voice of Jehovah Himself is heard saying, "It is done." "All the host of heaven shall be dissolved, and the heavens shall be rolled together as a scroll: and all their host shall fall down, as the leaf falleth off from the vine, and as a falling fig from the fig tree. For my sword shall be bathed in heaven. . . . For it is the day of the Lord's vengeance, and the year of recompences for the controversy of Zion. And the streams thereof shall be turned into pitch, and the dust thereof into brimstone, and the land thereof shall become burning pitch." "The Lord is slow to anger, and great in power, and will not at all acquit the wicked: the Lord hath His way in the whirlwind and in the storm, and the clouds are the dust of His feet. He rebuketh the sea, and maketh it dry, and drieth up all the rivers. . . . The mountains quake at

**It is the day of the Lord's vengeance.**

*And the seventh angel poured out his vial into the air; and there came a great voice out of the temple of heaven, from the throne, saying, It is done. Rev. 16:17.*

O sing unto the Lord a new song; for he hath done marvellous things: his right hand, and his holy arm, hath gotten him the victory.

Psa. 98: 1.

*And there were voices, and thunders, and lightnings; and there was a great earthquake, such as was not since men were upon the earth, so mighty an earthquake, and so great.*

*And the great city was divided into three parts, and the cities of the nations fell: and great Babylon came in remembrance before God, to give unto her the cup of the wine of the fierceness of his wrath.*

*And every island fled away, and the mountains were not found.*

*And there fell upon men a great hail out of heaven, every stone about the weight of a talent: and men blasphemed God because of the plague of the hail; for the plague thereof was exceeding great.* Rev. 16:18-21.

Nahum 1:1-3

Who among us shall dwell with the devouring fire? who among us shall dwell with everlasting burnings? Isa. 33:14.

Him, and the hills melt, and the earth is burned at His presence, yea, the world, and all that dwell therein. Who can stand before His indignation? And who can abide in the fierceness of His anger? His fury is poured out like fire, and the rocks are thrown down by Him." "For, behold, the Lord cometh forth out of His place, and will come down, and tread upon the high places of the earth. And the mountains shall be molten under Him, and the valleys shall be cleft, as wax before the fire, and as the waters that are poured down a steep place. For the transgression of Jacob is all this, and for the sins of the house of Israel."

**In the night when a holy solemnity is kept.**

"Come, behold the works of the Lord, what desolations He hath made in the earth. He maketh wars to cease unto the end of the earth; He breaketh the bow, and cutteth the spear in sunder; He burneth the chariot in the fire." "A great earthquake, such as was not since men were upon the earth," shakes the earth to its very foundation. "And every island fled away, and the mountains were not found."

When the wicked have no shelter, then are heard songs of deliverance from the little companies. "God is our refuge and strength, a very present help in trouble. Therefore will not we fear, though the earth be removed, and the mountains be carried into the midst of the sea; though the waters thereof roar and be troubled, though the mountains shake with the swelling thereof."

In the midst of the trouble, a peace which

passeth all understanding rests upon the people of God; for they have heard the voice of God, proclaiming the hour of the Saviour's coming. "Ye shall have a song, as in the night when a holy solemnity is kept; and gladness of heart, as when one goeth with a pipe to come into the mountain of the Lord, to the mighty One of Israel. And the Lord shall cause His glorious voice to be heard, and shall show the lighting down of His arm, with the indignation of His anger, and with the flame of a devouring fire, with scattering, and tempest, and hailstones." And yet with it all, when "there fell upon men great hail out of heaven, every stone about the weight of a talent," men still "blasphemed God because of the plague of the hail."

The wicked, with hearts like adamant, see not the signs of His coming, but blaspheme, and to them He comes as a thief.

During these closing scenes, heaven is active with preparations for the second coming. Christ gathers His host about Him. After the Father's voice is heard saying, "It is done," His throne moves. Upon the earth preparations are still going forward to destroy the saints. The decree has been passed, and the time is fast approaching, when with one uprising, the followers of God are to be put to death in one day. As the voice of God echoes through the earth, the earth trembles; the graves open, and those who have fallen asleep under the sealing message, come forth glorified, ready to receive the touch of immortality when Christ appears. Some of the wicked also come forth; for they who pierced Him shall see Him when He comes as King of kings.

The earth shall quake before them; the heavens shall tremble: the sun and the moon shall be dark, and the stars shall withdraw their shining:

And the Lord shall utter his voice before his army: for his camp is very great: for he is strong that executeth his word: for the day of the Lord is great and very terrible; and who can abide it?

Joel 2:10, 11.

How that they told you there should be mockers in the last time, who should walk after their own ungodly lusts.

These be they who separate themselves, sensual, having not the Spirit. Jude 18, 19.

There was a great earthquake, such as was not since men were upon the earth, so mighty an earthquake, and so great.

Rev. 16:18.

Every mountain and island were moved out of their places.

Rev. 6:14.

From the uttermost part of the earth have we heard songs, even glory to the righteous. But I said, My leanness, my leanness, woe unto me! the treacherous dealers have dealt treacherously; yea, the treacherous dealers have dealt very treacherously. Isa. 24:16, 17.

Psa. 46:1-3.

Whose voice then shook the earth: but now he hath promised, saying, Yet once more I shake not the earth only, but also heaven.

And this word, Yet once more, signifieth the removing of those things that are shaken, as of things that are made, that those things which cannot be shaken may remain. Heb. 12:26-28.

DELIVERED AT MIDNIGHT.

The final plague which released Israel from Egypt came at midnight.

Ex. 11:4, 5; Ex. 12:29, 31, 42.

Midnight is given as one of the times when we may expect the Lord.
Mark 13:32-37.

At midnight there was a cry made, Behold, the bridegroom cometh; go ye out to meet him.
Matt. 25:6.

In a moment shall they die, and the people shall be troubled at midnight, and pass away: and the mighty shall be taken away without hand. Job 34:20.

Psa. 119:61, 62.
Nah. 1:7.
Zeph. 3:17.
Isa. 25:9.

Now know I that the Lord saveth his anointed; he will hear him from his holy heaven with the saving strength of his right hand.
Psa. 20:6.

The Lord hath opened his armoury, and hath brought forth the weapons of his indignation: for this is the work of the Lord God of hosts in the land of the Chaldeans. Come against her from the utmost border, open her storehouses: cast her up as heaps, and destroy her utterly: let nothing of her be left.
Jer. 50:25, 26.

In those days, and in that time, saith the Lord, the iniquity of Israel shall be sought for, and there shall be none; and the sins of Judah, and they shall not be found: for I will pardon them whom I reserve.
Jer. 50:20.

Because he hath set his love upon me, therefore will I deliver him: I will set him on high, because he hath known my name.
Psa. 91:14.

It is at midnight that God chooses to deliver His people. Suddenly the storm ceases, the darkness disappears, and the sun bursts forth in all its glory. With blanched faces the wicked behold the small cloud in the east,—a cloud about the size of a man's hand, which gradually increases. Songs of triumph arise from the waiting ones. "The Lord is good, a stronghold in the day of trouble; and He knoweth them that trust in Him." "The Lord thy God in the midst of thee is mighty; He will save, He will rejoice over thee with joy; He will rest in His love, He will joy over thee with singing."

The advancing cloud is greeted with the words, "Lo, this is our God; we have waited for Him, and He will save us: this is the Lord; we have waited for Him, we will be glad and rejoice in His salvation."

Babylon, the nation of the earth which has long made nations drunk with the wine of her fornication, comes in remembrance before God in her threefold nature, as paganism, papacy, and apostate Protestantism, and is made to drink of the wine of the wrath of God.

"Our God is a consuming fire" to all who are out of harmony with Him, but those who are spiritually one with Him, are caught up to meet the Lord in the air, "And so shall we ever be with the Lord."

This time of trouble is but a short distance ahead of us. A soul longing to-day to be near the Saviour, will insure a hiding place beneath the wing of the Almighty during that time.

# CHAPTER XVIII.

## BABYLON, THE GREAT MYSTERY.

THE seventeenth chapter of Revelation is a divine history of the power represented by the beast, which John saw arising from the sea, and which is distinguished from all other beasts by its seven heads and ten horns with crowns. The prophet Daniel wrote the history of the world from the standpoint of nations. He mentions religion, and especially the people of God, but he deals primarily with nations. On the other hand, the history presented to John on the isle of Patmos was primarily an ecclesiastical history. In order to understand thoroughly the record of events which have taken place on earth, it is necessary, therefore, to study together the two prophecies of Daniel and Revelation, for one is the complement of the other. However, in the last days of the world's history, there will be such a close union between the church and the state that, in order to comprehend the outpouring of the judgments of God in the plagues, John was given a view of

Who is like unto the beast? Who is able to make war with him?
Rev. 13:4.

These great beasts, which are four, are four kings, which shall arise out of the earth.
Dan. 7:17.

Go and take the little book which is open in the hand of the angel which standeth upon the sea and upon the earth. Rev. 10:8.

So he carried me away in the spirit into the wilderness: and I saw a woman sit upon a scarlet coloured beast, full of names of blasphemy, having seven heads and ten horns. Rev. 17:3.

For he doth not afflict willingly nor grieve the children of men.
To crush under his feet all the prisoners of the earth,
To turn aside the right of a man before the face of the most High,
To subvert a man in his cause, the Lord approveth not.
Lam. 3:33-36.

I have written to him the great things of my law, but they were counted as a strange thing.
Hos. 8:12.

They have turned unto me the back, and not the face: though I taught them, rising up early and teaching them, yet they have not hearkened to receive instruction.
Jer. 32:33.

Though Babylon should mount up to heaven, and though she should fortify the height of her strength, yet from me shall spoilers come unto her, saith the Lord.
Jer. 51:53.

POWER AND WORK OF ANGELS.

Heb. 1:14. They minister to mankind.
Rev. 14:18. Power over fire.
Rev. 16:5. Power over water.
Rev. 21:12. Gatekeepers.
Dan. 10:16, 20, 21; 11:1. Control affairs of nations.
Acts 12:23. Power over disease.
Dan. 6:22; Dan. 9:20-23; Num. 20:15. Answer prayers.
Rev. 14:6, 8, 9. In charge of the gospel message.
Rev. 15:7. In charge of the plagues.
Matt. 24:31. Gather the righteous.

He increaseth the nations, and destroyeth them: he enlargeth the nations, and straiteneth them again.
Job 12:23.

A fool despiseth his father's instruction: but he that regardeth reproof is prudent. Prov. 15:5.

Let favour be shewed to the wicked, yet will he not learn righteousness; in the land of uprightness will he deal unjustly, and will not behold the majesty of the Lord.
Isa. 26:10.

both the church and the state. The seven last plagues come as the result of a certain course of action. God does not arbitrarily withdraw His mercy from the earth, and torment men because He has the power to do so. Divine law has been revealed to man age after age; and yet, contrary to that law, men and nations have paved the way for their own destruction. In the history of every nation which has arisen and fallen, God has given an object lesson to the world of the ultimate results of continued disobedience to laws which rule in the universe, and in harmony with which, alone, the universe itself continues to exist.

After showing John the destruction which comes when the last cord of mercy binding heaven and earth is broken, one of the angels, holding the vial, in which was one of the plagues, came to the prophet, to give him a reason for the terrors which had just been portrayed. This angel controls certain elements, the proper working of which, preserves life. From the beginning of history, he has watched the growth of nations. He has seen them rise in beauty and strength, prosper for a period, and suddenly disappear, as if the earth had opened and swallowed them; and immediately in the same place another nation would arise, repeat the same deeds, and after a brief space, cease to be. Yet man did not learn wisdom, although God sought by these providences, and by His whole system of revelations, to warn him against certain pitfalls. Only a few scattered individuals from each generation have heard the voice of Heaven, and have been saved.

One of the seven angels which had the vials

" I saw a woman sit upon a scarlet colored beast."

full of the wrath of God, carried John into a secluded spot, where, undisturbed, he could understand the history, viewing it as from a mountain peak, where each object was seen in its relation to every other object. And he saw a whore, a prostitute woman, arrayed in gorgeous apparel, in purple and scarlet color, decked with gold and precious stones and pearls, carrying a golden cup in her hand full of abominations and filthiness of her fornication.

Woman was the crowning work of the Creator, when she came from the Maker's hand, God Himself pronounced her *very good*. She who was the highest, falls the lowest in sin, and as her power for good is unlimited when God directs, so she drags men to the brink of hell when her heart is possessed by Satan. A pure woman represents the church of Christ; a prostitute represents this church when it turns from its lawful husband, and commits adultery with the kings of the earth. "Fine linen, clean and white," is the apparel for the wife of our Lord, but when the character is lost, earth's eye is attracted by the purple and scarlet colors, the gold and precious stones. Purity of life is what God wants; royal apparel and wealth are what the world seeks. The whore sitteth upon many waters, wielding a wide influence, causing multitudes to worship at her shrine; for, said the angel, "The waters which thou sawest, where the whore sitteth, are peoples, and multitudes, and nations, and tongues." From all the earth come those who pay their money to this base creature, and drink from the golden cup which she holds in her hand. Some have drunk once as an experiment, but having tasted her wine,

*And there came one of the seven angels which had the seven vials, and talked with me, saying unto me, Come hither; I will shew unto thee the judgment of the great whore that sitteth upon many waters:*

*With whom the kings of the earth have committed fornication, and the inhabitants of the earth have been made drunk with the wine of her fornication.*

*So he carried me away in the spirit into the wilderness: and I saw a woman sit upon a scarlet coloured beast, full of names of blasphemy, having seven heads and ten horns.*

*And the woman was arrayed in purple and scarlet colour, and decked with gold and precious stones and pearls, having a golden cup in her hand full of abominations and filthiness of her fornication.* *Rev. 17:1-4.*

God saw every thing that he had made, and, behold, it was very good. Gen. 1:31.

For I am jealous over you with godly jealousy: for I have espoused you to one husband, that I may present you as a chaste virgin to Christ. 2 Cor. 11:2.

The king's daughter is all glorious within: her clothing is of wrought gold.

She shall be brought unto the king in raiment of needlework: the virgins her companions that follow her shall be brought unto thee. Psa. 45:13, 14.

Blessed are the pure in heart: for they shall see God. Matt. 5:8.

O thou that dwellest upon many waters, abundant in treasures, thine end is come, and the measure of thy covetousness. Jer. 51:13.

Rev. 17:15.

Babylon hath been a golden cup in the Lord's hand, that made all the earth drunken: the nations have drunken of her wine; therefore the nations are mad. Jer. 51:7.

they are intoxicated. The picture is that of the orgies of ancient Babylon or the mysteries of Greece. "The kings of the earth have committed fornication, and the inhabitants of the earth have been made drunk with the wine of her fornication."

On the forehead of the woman was a name written, "*Mystery, Babylon The Great, The Mother Of Harlots And Abominations Of The Earth.*" This is the mystery of iniquity, which Paul said was at work in the days when he wrote to the Thessalonians.

The apostolic church is represented as a chaste virgin clad in white linen. The history of the seven churches of the second and third chapters of Revelation, describes the decline. The first love was lost, and that made it easy to commit fornication. The church tolerated those who held false doctrines, and certain sects of philosophers who applied the reason of the Greeks to the study of God's Word. The simplicity of early days was changed for worldly habits, teachings, and ways of living. The inward change may be read in the outward manifestations in the churches of Pergamos and Thyatira. Paganism walked bodily into the church, and the leader of Paganism claimed the once pure church as his bride. A false spirit of prophecy, false interpretation of the Scriptures, the exaltation of reason, the love of worldly ways, the desire for money and positions in the government, and finally a demand for the crown itself,—these are what wrought the change from purity, simplicity, and gentleness, to the condition of the prostitute.

The change was not wrought in a day. For

Ye adulterers and adulteresses, know ye not that the friendship of the world is enmity with God? whosoever therefore will be a friend of the world is the enemy of God. Jas. 4:4.

*And upon her forehead was a name written, MYSTERY, BABYLON THE GREAT, THE MOTHER OF HARLOTS AND ABOMINATIONS OF THE EARTH. Rev. 17:5.*

I saw, and behold a white horse: and he that sat on him had a bow; and a crown was given unto him: and he went forth conquering, and to conquer. Rev. 6:2.

Nevertheless I have somewhat against thee, because thou hast left thy first love. Rev. 2:4.

So hast thou also them that hold the doctrine of the Nicolaitanes, which thing I hate. Rev. 2:15.

Rev. 2:12–29.

For I know this, that after my departing shall grievous wolves enter in among you, not sparing the flock.

Also of your own selves shall men arise, speaking perverse things, to draw away disciples after them. Acts 20:29, 30.

Elymas the sorcerer (for so is his name by interpretation) withstood them, seeking to turn away the deputy from the faith. Acts 13:8.

Their word will eat as doth a canker: of whom is Hymenæus and Philetus;

Who concerning the truth have erred, saying that the resurrection is past already; and overthrow the faith of some. 2 Tim. 2:17, 18.

I wrote unto the church: but Diotrephes, who loveth to have the preeminence among them, receiveth us not. 3 John 9.

five centuries after Christ sent out His first disciples, the transformation was going on. Again and again during that time, Christ, like a true husband, sought the return of His church. "Thou hast played the harlot with many lovers; yet return again to Me, saith the Lord. Lift up thine eyes unto the high places, and see where thou hast not been lien with. In the ways hast thou sat for them, as the Arabian in the wilderness; and thou hast polluted the land with thy whoredoms and with thy wickedness. Therefore the showers have been withholden, and there hath been no latter rain; and thou hast a whore's forehead, thou refusedst to be ashamed. . . . And I said after she hath done all these things, turn thou unto Me." Hearken unto the pleading of Jehovah with His church, and judge whether or not He views the plagues with pleasure. "Return, thou backsliding Israel, saith the Lord; and I will not cause Mine anger to fall upon you: for I am merciful, saith the Lord, and I will not keep anger forever." But the church heeded not the call to return. Through the days of Constantine she made greater advances until she took her seat on the beast. "This was Mystery, Babylon the Great, the mother of harlots, and abominations of the earth." She who had once been a golden cup in the Lord's hand, filled with the wine of His love, which heaven through her had offered to the world, turned from Him, decked herself with worldliness, and held to the lips of her admirers a golden cup full of poison. She had fallen, and those who drank of her wine fell also.

For twelve hundred and sixty years the

O Israel, return unto the Lord thy God; for thou hast fallen by thine iniquity.

Take with you words, and turn to the Lord: say unto him, Take away all iniquity, and receive us graciously: so will we render the calves of our lips.

I will heal their backsliding, I will love them freely: for mine anger is turned away from him.

Hos. 14:1, 2, 4.

Jer. 3:2-7.

Cursed is the ground for thy sake; in sorrow shalt thou eat of it all the days of thy life. Gen. 3:17.

The earth also is defiled under the inhabitants thereof; because they have transgressed the laws, changed the ordinance, broken the everlasting covenant. Isa. 24:5.

Say unto them, As I live, saith the Lord God, I have no pleasure in the death of the wicked; but that the wicked turn from his way and live: turn ye, turn ye from your evil ways; for why will ye die, O house of Israel? Eze. 33:11.

For their mother hath played the harlot: she that conceived them hath done shamefully: for she said, I will go after my lovers, that give me my bread and my water, my wool and my flax, mine oil and my drink. Hos. 2:5.

*And I saw the woman drunken with the blood of the saints, and with the blood of the martyrs of Jesus: and when I saw her, I wondered with great admiration.*

*And the angel said unto me, Wherefore didst thou marvel? I will tell thee the mystery of the woman, and of the beast that carrieth her, which hath the seven heads and ten horns.*

*The beast that thou sawest was, and is not; and shall ascend out of the bottomless pit, and go into perdition: and they that dwell on the earth shall wonder, whose names were not written in the book of life from the foundation of the world, when they behold the beast that was, and is not, and yet is.* *Rev. 17:6-8.*

*And here is the mind which hath wisdom. The seven heads are seven mountains, on which the woman sitteth.*

whore, from her capital at Rome, the seven hilled city, controlled the nations of Europe. She offered them her wine, Most men drank

*And there are seven kings: five are fallen, and one is, and the other is not yet come; and when he cometh, he must continue a short space.*
*Rev. 17:6-10.*

He shall wear out the saints of the most High.
Dan. 7:25.

**Rome, the seven-hilled city.**

Wheresoever the children of men dwell, the beasts of the field and the fowls of the heaven hath he given into thine hand, and hath made thee ruler over them all. Thou art this head of gold.
Dan. 2:38.

All that dwell upon the earth shall worship him, whose names are not written in the book of life of the Lamb. Rev. 13:8.

He opened his mouth in blasphemy against God, to blaspheme his name, and his tabernacle, and them that dwell in heaven.
Rev. 13:6.

Who opposeth and exalteth himself above all that is called God, or that is worshipped; so that he as God sitteth in the temple of God, shewing himself that he is God.
2 Thess. 2:4.

Thus saith the Lord, Learn not the way of the heathen, and be not dismayed at the signs of heaven; for the heathen are dismayed at them.

For the customs of the people are vain. Jer. 10:2, 3.

Take heed to thyself that thou be not snared by following them, after that they be destroyed from before thee; and that thou inquire not after their gods, saying, How did these nations serve their gods? even so will I do likewise. Deut. 12:30.

freely, and partook of her sins without restraint; but when man, or nation refused, he paid the penalty with his lifeblood. "The woman (was) drunken with the blood of the saints, and with the blood of the martyrs of Jesus." "The woman which thou sawest is that great city, which reigneth over the kings of the earth." It was the power which dominated Europe for forty-two months, of which Daniel, the prophet, says, "He shall speak great words against the most High, and shall wear out the saints of the most High, and think to change times and laws; and they shall be given into his hand until a time and times and the dividing of times." This is an inspired picture of the church which started out pure, but soon mingled the true religion with paganism. She first asked aid of the nations, then took the reins of government, and ruled both kings and nations. God calls this church a whore, "Mystery, Babylon the Great, the mother of harlots."

Governments are ordained of God, and rulers are His ministers to execute wrath upon evil doers, and to minister good to those who do right. As long as sin exists on earth there will be governments, but their province is to deal with acts, not thoughts and motives. To the evil doer only, they are divinely appointed a terror. In all pagan nations the religion is under the government, and the gods are worshiped because the government so ordains. This was true in all the heathen kingdoms, Babylon, Persia, Greece, and Rome, until after the birth of Christ. So in each of these monarchies, the devil sought to destroy the truth, and those who adhered to it. The history of these nations is but the record of this attempt. Each government was an attempt on the part of Satan to rival the government of heaven, and the utter failure of the attempt put the prince of this world to open shame before the rulers of other worlds, when Christ came into His own territory, and built up a spiritual kingdom within the hearts of the subjects of Rome itself. When at the crucifixion of Christ, Satan was cast from the council of the representatives of worlds, knowing that his time was short, he revolutionized his former methods, and made governments subject to the religious organization. This revolution was a slow process. It was begun soon after the death of Christ. The master hand, which had swayed nations since creation, worked in two directions, hoping that when his forces met he would have accomplished what he had failed to accomplish heretofore.

Let every soul be subject unto the higher powers. For there is no power but of God: the powers that be are ordained of God.

Whosoever therefore resisteth the power, resisteth the ordinance of God: and they that resist shall receive to themselves damnation.

For rulers are not a terror to good works, but to the evil. Wilt thou then not be afraid of the power? do that which is good, and thou shalt have praise of the same.
Rom. 13:1-3.

A drought is upon her waters; and they shall be dried up: for it is the land of graven images, and they are mad upon their idols.
Jer. 50:38.

The king spake, and said, Is not this great Babylon, that I have built for the house of the kingdom by the might of my power, and for the honour of my majesty?
Dan. 4:30.

Jesus answered, My kingdom is not of this world: if my kingdom were of this world, then would my servants fight, that I should not be delivered to the Jews: but now is my kingdom not from hence.
John 18:36.

Now is the judgment of this world: now shall the prince of this world be cast out. John 12:31.

For we wrestle not against flesh and blood, but against principalities, against powers, against the rulers of the darkness of this world, against spiritual wickedness in high places. Eph. 6:12.

As concerning the rest of the beasts, they had their dominion taken away: yet their lives were prolonged for a season and time.
Dan. 7:12.

There are seven kings: five are fallen, and one is, and the other is not yet come; and when he cometh, he must continue a short space.
Rev. 17:10.

In his estate shall stand up a vile person, to whom they shall not give the honour of the kingdom: but he shall come in peaceably, and obtain the kingdom by flatteries.
Dan. 11:21.

I saw a woman sit upon a scarlet coloured beast, full of names of blasphemy, having seven heads and ten horns. Rev. 17:3.

After this I saw in the night visions, and behold a fourth beast, dreadful and terrible, and strong exceedingly; and it had great iron teeth: it devoured and brake in pieces, and stamped the residue with the feet of it: and it was diverse from all the beasts that were before it; and it had ten horns.

I considered the horns, and, behold, there came up among them another little horn, before whom there were three of the first horns plucked up by the roots: and, behold, in this horn were eyes like the eyes of man, and a mouth speaking great things. Dan. 7:7, 8.

Isa. 13:1, 2.
Jer. 51:24, 25.
Zech. 4:7.
Rev. 17:12.

Whereas thou sawest the feet and toes, part of potters' clay, and part of iron, the kingdom shall be divided; but there shall be in it of the strength of the iron, forasmuch as thou sawest the iron mixed with miry clay.

And as the toes of the feet were part of iron, and part of clay, so the kingdom shall be partly strong, and partly broken. Dan. 2:41, 42.

The Roman nation was the recognized mistress of the world in the days of the Saviour. In its development, all the known forms of administration had been tested, and the very essence of the strong features from each of the preceding kingdoms had been combined in the Roman Empire. The changes from the rule of a king to the consuls, the tribunes, the decemvirs, and then to the triumvirs, and finally the revolution which turned it into an empire, had each placed the nation more completely under the control of the principles of that prince who strove to exalt his throne above God. The history of Rome shows this to be true. The complete suppression of individuality, and the exaltation of the state, were as nearly accomplished in Rome as in any earthly government.

Then the mystery of iniquity changed the church from a pure woman to a harlot, and seated her on the beast. The beast had seven heads and ten horns, identifying it with the government of the Western Roman Empire, described in the thirteenth chapter of Revelation and in the seventh chapter of Daniel. Moreover, the angel gave John the interpretation; for, said he, "The seven heads are seven mountains," mountains being a familiar symbol of governments used by Isaiah, Jeremiah, and Zechariah. The seven forms of government have already been mentioned. "The ten horns . . . are ten kings which (in the days of John) have received no kingdom as yet." These are the ten divisions of the Roman Empire, prophesied of in the eighth chapter of Revelation, and symbolized by the mixture of iron and clay in the image of Dan. 2:42–44, which helped to prepare the beast to be ridden by the woman, the church, when she was ready to mount it. The ten divisions were formed before A. D. 476. Between A. D. 533, when Justinian published his decree, recognizing the head of the Roman diocese as head of the government of Rome, and A. D. 538, when the last obstacle in the form of a rival power was taken out of the way in Italy, the woman mounted the beast. Henceforth lordly Rome, which, like Babylon of old, had prided itself upon the fact that it was the master of the world, was guided and controlled by a *prostitute woman.* This in the eyes of nations would be considered the basest of things. The woman who would so rule, would have gone beyond all bounds of propriety, and the nation so ruled would be pitied for its absolute loss of self-repect. If this is true in the actual relationships of life, how must it have appeared in the eyes of heaven, when the very principles in accordance with which nature was created, were so revolutionized as to make this condition of things possible? But the devil was foiled. This was his masterpiece. Amalgamation of species, a thing contrary to divine law, and self-destruction in the end, was practical in Rome. The woman became the mother of harlots. The ten horns, or kingdoms, have one mind with the beast, and give their strength unto the beast.

The woman was drunk with the blood of saints; this was represented by the *scarlet* color of the beast upon which she rode. Rome, as a pagan nation, often shed blood; all the universal

The ten horns out of this kingdom are ten kings that shall arise: and another shall rise after them; and he shall be diverse from the first, and he shall subdue three kings. Dan. 7:24.

Luke 2:1.

**Justinian.**

As for my people, children are their oppressors, and women rule over them. O my people, they which lead thee cause thee to err, and destroy the way of thy paths. Isa. 3:12.

For the leaders of this people cause them to err; and they that are led of them are destroyed. Isa. 9:16.

Whosoever lieth with a beast shall surely be put to death. Ex. 22:19.

For they have shed the blood of saints and prophets, and thou hast given them blood to drink; for they are worthy. Rev. 16:6.

It was given unto him to make war with the saints, and to overcome them: and power was given him over all kindreds, and tongues, and nations. Rev. 13:7.

*And the beast that was, and is not, even he is the eighth, and is of the seven, and goeth into perdition.*

*And the ten horns which thou sawest are ten kings, which have received no kingdom as yet; but receive power as kings one hour with the beast.*

*These have one mind, and shall give their power and strength unto the beast.*

*These shall make war with the Lamb, and the Lamb shall overcome them: for He is Lord of lords, and King of kings: and they that are with him are called, and chosen, and faithful.*

*And he saith unto me, The waters which thou sawest, where the whore sitteth, are peoples, and multitudes, and nations, and tongues.*

*And the ten horns which thou sawest upon the beast, these shall hate the whore, and shall make her desolate and naked, and shall eat her flesh, and burn her with fire.*

*For God hath put in their hearts to fulfil his will, and to agree, and give their kingdom unto the beast, until the words of God shall be fulfilled.*

*And the woman which thou sawest is that great city, which reigneth over the kings of the earth.*

*Rev. 17:11-18.*

The earth helped the woman, and the earth opened her mouth, and swallowed up the flood which the dragon cast out of his mouth.

Rev. 12:16.

I saw three unclean spirits like frogs come out of the mouth of the dragon, and out of the mouth of the beast, and out of the mouth of the false prophet.

For they are the spirits of devils, working miracles, which go forth unto the kings of the earth and of the whole world, to gather them to the battle of that great day of God Almighty. Rev. 16:13,14

Wherefore they came again, and told him. And he said, This is the word of the Lord, which he spake by his servant Elijah the Tishbite,

kingdoms came into power by the shedding of blood; but neither the lion, the bear, nor the leopard were scarlet colored. The nation was painted red with the blood of martyrs when the government submitted itself to the ecclesiastical power, and the church made war with the saints. During the twelve hundred and sixty years of tyranny, the church claimed that it never took the life of a single individual. The church merely decided who were heretics,—so they argue,—and the *state* executed the judgment. The beast ridden by the woman cannot do otherwise than carry out her will. Thus Rome became a scarlet beast.

That there might be no mistaking the scarlet colored beast, the angel explained still further. He spoke of it to John as "the beast that was, and is not, even he is the eighth, and is of the seven." Throughout the history of the first five heads, paganism was the prevailing element; in the sixth, the empire, it was still the ruling principle; during the papacy, the seventh, it disappeared to all outward appearances, but was nevertheless the controlling power; for the papacy is *baptized paganism.*

Following the Reformation, when the whore was hated by the horns, the papacy was crushed; but in the last days the principles of paganism as shown in Spiritualism, the supreme manifestation of which will be the personal appearance of the devil, who claims to be the Christ; and of the papacy and of the false prophet, the daughters of Babylon, the mother of harlots, will all stand forth in the earth as persecuting powers to oppress the people of God. These forces will gather at Armageddon, and upon these the plagues fall. They ascend out of the bottomless pit; for they are foreign to God and have no place in heaven; they go into perdition; for they have defied the God of heaven; they have turned from every principle of life, and they die the death of a harlot, cursed by their own course of action, having contaminated all with whom they came in contact.

The entire existence of these governments has been in open conflict with the Lamb. God has sent unto them prophets and wise men, and even His own Son, and they have slain them all. But at His coming they are slain by the brightness of His countenance. Truth, when allowed to shine forth in its strength, consumes error, and the beast and the image and the false prophet go into the lake of fire, together with the Dragon, that old Serpent, and Satan, who has inspired all against the God of truth and love. This is the history, and this is the end, of the union of Church and State.

saying, In the portion of Jezreel shall dogs eat the flesh of Jezebel. And the carcase of Jezebel shall be as dung upon the face of the field in the portion of Jezreel: so that they shall not say, This is Jezebel. 2 Kings 9:36, 37.

Hear the word of the Lord, ye children of Israel: for the Lord hath a controversy with the inhabitants of the land, because there is no truth, nor mercy, nor knowledge of God in the land. Hos. 4:1.

Which of the prophets have not your fathers persecuted? and they have slain them which shewed before of the coming of the Just One; of whom ye have been now the betrayers and murderers.
Acts 7:52.

The beast was taken, and with him the false prophet that wrought miracles before him, with which he deceived them that had received the mark of the beast, and them that worshipped his image. These both were cast alive into a lake of fire burning with brimstone.
Rev. 19:20.

# CHAPTER XIX.

## BE YE SEPARATE.

How is the faithful city become an harlot! it was full of judgment; righteousness lodged in it; but now murderers. Isa. 1:21.

From the sole of the foot even unto the head there is no soundness in it; but wounds, and bruises, and putrifying sores: they have not been closed, neither bound up, neither mollified with ointment. Isa. 1:6.

By the word of God the heavens were of old, and the earth standing out of the water and in the water: Whereby the world that then was, being overflowed with water, perished. 2 Pet. 3:5, 6.

The Lord said unto Noah, Come thou and all thy house into the ark; for thee have I seen righteous before me in this generation. Gen. 7:1.

Noah lived after the flood three hundred and fifty years. Gen. 9:28.

THE vileness of a union of the Christian church with the state, is depicted in chapter seventeen. When the church that was once pure, united with the government of Rome, and was known as the papacy, God called her Babylon the Great, the Mother of Harlots, He showed by the angels who hold the vials of His wrath, that, as loathsome disease is the physical penalty paid for the life of a harlot, so the seven last plagues are the natural results of the spiritual fornication of which the church is guilty when the name Babylon is applicable to her.

This name carries the mind back to the origin of the expression, in the first century this side of the flood. The earth had been depopulated because of the vileness of its inhabitants, and Noah and his sons alone remained alive. Noah was still living when his descendants gathered in the valley of the Euphrates and founded a city. God told them to scatter over the face of the earth, but they congregated in one place. They began building the tower with the idea of defeating the God of heaven, should He again attempt to destroy man by a flood. The spirit of self-exaltation, born of Lucifer himself, took possession of the men of the valley of the Euphrates, and they openly defied their Maker.

Their iniquity reached unto heaven, and God came down to visit them. His coming brought confusion and consternation; and the languages of men were confounded so that they could not understand one another. Then the name Babel was applied, which means confusion.

But the devil determined not to be defeated in his purpose of exaltation; and surrounding the site of this ancient monument, which never reached completion, he built, sixteen hundred years later, the city of Babylon, which became the capital of the world. This kingdom is used to illustrate the evil of the state church in the end of time The sins of the ancient city are repeated by the last church, and its overthrow is the object lesson, to the world, of the final destruction of the whole world when Christ comes down, because her iniquity has reached heaven. The figure is followed throughout the eighteenth chapter of Revelation; and by comparing scripture with scripture, the grevious sins of modern Babylon stand out in such awful distinctness that they justify the judgments of God as meted out in the plagues. Such a study opens the mind to the meaning of the cry of the mighty angel, referred to in verses one and two.

The sins of Babylon are almost beyond number; but some are pointed out with distinctness by the spirit of inspiration. God's dwelling

They said, Go to, let us build us a city and a tower, whose top may reach unto heaven; and let us make us a name, lest we be scattered abroad upon the face of the whole earth. Gen. 11:4.

Gen. 9:1.

ORIGIN OF NATIONS.

Every family formed the nucleus of a nation and had a language of their own. The descendants of Japheth formed ten nations.

By these were the isles of the Gentiles divided in their lands; every one after his tongue, after their families, in their nations. Gen. 10:5.

The descendants of Ham formed twenty-six nations.

These are the sons of Ham, after their families, after their tongues, in their countries, and in their nations. Gen. 10:20.

The descendants of Shem formed twenty-three nations.

These are the sons of Shem, after their families, after their tongues, in their lands, after their nations.

These are the families of the sons of Noah, after their generations, in their nations: and by these were the nations divided in the earth after the flood. Gen. 10:31, 32.

Rev. 14:8.
Isa. 21:9, 10.

*And after these things I saw another angel come down from heaven, having great power; and the earth was lightened with his glory.*

*And he cried mightily with a strong voice, saying, Babylon the great is fallen, is fallen, and is become the habitation of devils, and the hold of every foul spirit, and a cage of every unclean and hateful bird.*

*For all nations have drunk of the wine of the wrath of her fornication, and the kings of the earth have committed fornication with her, and the merchants of the earth are waxed rich through the abundance of her delicacies.*
*Rev. 18:1-3.*

Isa. 47:7-9.
Zeph. 2:15.
Hos. 2:19, 20.

*And I heard another voice from heaven, saying, Come out of her, my people, that ye be not partakers of her sins, and that ye receive not of her plagues.*

*For her sins have reached unto heaven, and God hath remembered her iniquities.*

*Reward her even as she rewarded you, and double unto her double according to her works: in the cup which she hath filled fill to her double.*

*How much she hath glorified herself, and lived deliciously, so much torment and sorrow give her: for she saith in her heart, I sit a queen, and am no widow, and shall see no sorrow.*

*Therefore shall her plagues come in one day, death, and mourning, and famine; and she shall be utterly burned with fire: for strong is the Lord God who judgeth her.*

*And the kings of the earth, who have committed fornication and lived deliciously with her, shall bewail her, and lament for her, when they shall see the smoke of her burning,*

*Standing afar off for the fear*

place is in the humble, contrite heart; "For thus saith the high and lofty One that inhabiteth eternity, whose name is Holy; I dwell in the high and holy place, with him also that is of a contrite and humble spirit." Babylon made the boast, "I sit a queen, and am no widow, and shall see no sorrow." God claimed the church as His wife, but she forsook her lawful husband, and played the harlot with the kings of the earth. Then she said boastingly, "I sit a queen." This was literally true of the city of Babylon, which was known as the queen of the earth. But in the same proportion that she had highly exalted herself, so was her fall, when the Lord withdrew His supporting hand. God never intended that the church should have anything to do with governments. His life on earth is a living example of what His followers should do and be. He reigned over a spiritual kingdom, when physically He had not a place to lay His head; He was clothed with the garments of righteousness, spotless and pure, although physically, He had but a travel stained robe; or was clothed by the mocking priests in a cast-off purple garment, and crowned with a crown of thorns. Union with the kings of earth, made it necessary to put on the apparel of the world; for an earthly queen is supposed to dress as royalty dress; and when supported by all the kings of the earth, the wealth at her command was unbounded. What need had she for the spiritual wealth which comes through Christ?

**Crowned with a crown of thorns.**

The city of Babylon was called the golden

city, "The beauty of the Chaldees' excellency," "the exactress of gold." She ruled over all the nations. "Wheresoever the children of men dwell, the beasts of the field and the fowl of the heavens hath He given into thine hands." The commerce of the world was controlled by this one power; and the wealth of the East and the West was laid at her feet. She sent ships to the islands for their spices and to the land of Ophir for its gold. The elephants of India and Ceylon yielded their ivory for her palaces and the ships of Tyre brought metals from the mines of Spain and the shores of the Mediterranean. Her lofty structures were built by slaves from captive nations. Her kings, like all Oriental monarchs, were absolute in their authority, and the bodies and souls of men were in bondage to great Babylon.

Her treatment of the Jewish race, who for seventy years were held as slaves, was rewarded by the complete downfall of the kingdom. First, it fell into the hands of a stronger power; but the prophecies concerning her downfall depicted complete ruin, and travellers to-day corroborate the words of Isaiah, "Babylon, the glory of kingdoms, the beauty of the Chaldees' excellency, shall be as when God overthrew Sodom and Gomorrah. It shall never be inhabited, neither shall it be dwelt in from generation to generation: neither shall the Arabian pitch tent there; neither shall the shepherds make their fold there. But wild beasts of the desert shall lie here; and their houses shall be full of, dolefull creatures; and owls shall dwell there and satyrs shall dance there. And the wild beasts of the islands shall cry in their desolate

*of her torment, saying, Alas, alas that great city Babylon, that mighty city! for in one hour is thy judgment come.*

*Rev. 18:4-10.*

The devil said unto him, All this power will I give thee, and the glory of them: for that is delivered unto me; and to whomsoever I will I give it. Luke 4:6.

That thou shalt take up this proverb against the king of Babylon, and say, How hath the oppressor ceased! the golden city ceased!

Isa. 14:4.

*And the merchants of the earth shall weep and mourn over her; for no man buyeth their merchandise any more:*

*The merchandise of gold, and silver, and precious stones, and of pearls, and fine linen, and purple, and silk, and scarlet, and all thyine wood, and all manner vessels of ivory, and all manner vessels of most precious wood, and of brass, and iron, and marble,*

*And cinnamon, and odours, and ointments, and frankincense, and wine, and oil, and fine flour, and wheat, and beasts, and sheep, and horses, and chariots, and slaves, and souls of men.*

*And the fruits that thy soul lusted after are departed from thee, and all things which were dainty and goodly are departed from thee, and thou shalt find them no more at all.*

*The merchants of these things, which were made rich by her, shall stand afar off for the fear of her torment, weeping and wailing,*

*And saying, Alas, alas that great city, that was clothed in fine linen, and purple, and scarlet, and decked with gold, and precious stones, and pearls!*

*For in one hour so great riches is come to nought. And every shipmaster, and all the company in ships, and sailors, and as many as trade by sea, stood afar off,*

*And cried when they saw the smoke of her burning, saying, What city is like unto this great city!* *Rev. 18:11-18.*

Her cities are a desolation, a dry land, and a wilderness, a land wherein no man dwelleth, neither doth any son of man pass thereby. And I will punish Bel in Babylon, and I will bring forth out of his mouth that which he hath swallowed up: and the nations shall not flow together any more unto him: yea, the wall of Babylon shall fall.
Jer. 51:43, 44.

Jer. 50:39.

houses, and dragons in their pleasant palaces: and her time is near to come, and her days shall not be prolonged."

This was literally fulfilled in the earthly kingdom, Babylon; and it is placed on record in the inspired Word, that men may there read the result of such principles as were brought into practice in Babylon the Great.

**Supposed site of ancient Babylon.**

Moreover, to Jeremiah was given a message from God for Babylon, which he wrote out, and sent by the hand of the chief chamberlain of the captive king of Jerusalem as he went into Babylon. This, the chamberlain was bidden to read in a public place; and having read it, he was to tie a stone about the book, and cast it into the river Euphrates, saying, "Thus shall Babylon sink, and shall not rise from the evil that I will bring upon her." Since these things are repeated in the divine description of the woman on the scarlet colored beast, it is evident that every detail preserved in the record of ancient Babylon and its destruction, is to be fulfilled a second time in, and for, modern Babylon, the church that became a whore. So much for the city whose history is so vividly portrayed in the Word.

Jer. 51:49, 58.

And thou shalt say, Thus shall Babylon sink, and shall not rise from the evil that I will bring upon her: and they shall be weary. Thus far are the words of Jeremiah.
Jer. 51:59-64.

As God overthrew Sodom and Gomorrah and the neighbour cities thereof, saith the Lord; so shall no man abide there, neither shall any son of man dwell therein.
Jer. 50:40.

There is another source of information which

shows the repetition of the sins of the city Babylon, as the church entered the Middle Ages. The Roman See gained power gradually. It was at first a simple church the same as all others, which arose as the result of the preaching of the early apostles. Constantinople was for some time a rival of the rising queen; she, too, was seated upon seven hills; but finally, the rise of Mohammedanism in the East so occupied the eastern division of the empire that Rome was quite unmolested in her ambitious designs. The invasion of the West by the barbarians of the North, extended the power, and increased the wealth and influence of Rome.

There, barbarians, "after being satiated with blood and plunder, lowered their reeking swords before the intellectual power that met them face to face; recently converted to Christianity, ignorant of the spiritual character of the church, and feeling the want of a certain external pomp in religion, they prostrated themselves, half savage and half heathen as they were, at the feet of the high priest of Rome." One by one, the barbarians, ancestors of all the nations of modern Europe, bowed the knee to Rome, and crowned her queen of the earth. From each nation, throughout the period of her supreme rule, she gathered her stores of wealth.

For years England, as a government, paid to Rome a tribute of a thousand marks. Likewise from each country, Rome drew the money which was needed for national defense. The poor were robbed by the payment of penance and the buying of indulgences. During the time of the Crusades, nations arose as a whole people, at

To all that be in Rome, beloved of God, called to be saints: Grace to you and peace from God our Father, and the Lord Jesus Christ.
First, I thank my God through Jesus Christ for you all, that your faith is spoken of throughout the whole world. Rom. 1:7, 8.

Thus saith the Lord; For three transgressions of Judah, and for four, I will not turn away the punishment thereof; because they have despised the law of the Lord, and have not kept his commandments, and their lies caused them to err, after the which their fathers have walked. Amos 2:4.

Their works are works of iniquity, and the act of violence is in their hands.
Their feet run to evil, and they make haste to shed innocent blood: their thoughts are thoughts of iniquity; wasting and destruction are in their paths. Isa. 59:6, 7.

Behold, it is written before me: I will not keep silence, but will recompense, even recompense into their bosom,
Your iniquities, and the iniquities of your fathers together.
Isa. 65:6, 7.

Yea, truth faileth; and he that departeth from evil maketh himself a prey: and the Lord saw it, and it displeased him that there was no judgment. Isa. 59:15.

The woman which thou sawest is that great city, which reigneth over the kings of the earth.
Rev. 17:18.

As troops of robbers wait for a man, so the company of priests murder in the way by consent: for they commit lewdness.
Hos. 6:9.

Woe unto him that saith to the wood, Awake; to the dumb stone, Arise, it shall teach! Behold, it is laid over with gold and silver, and there is no breath at all in the midst of it. Hab. 2:19.

How is the gold become dim! how is the most fine gold changed! the stones of the sanctuary are poured out in the top of every street.

The precious sons of Zion, comparable to fine gold, how are they esteemed as earthen pitchers, the work of the hands of the potter!

Even the sea monsters draw out the breast, they give suck to their young ones: the daughter of my people is become cruel, like the ostriches in the wilderness.

The tongue of the sucking child cleaveth to the roof of his mouth for thirst: the young children ask bread, and no man breaketh it unto them.

They that did feed delicately are desolate in the streets: they that were brought up in scarlet embrace dunghills.

For the punishment of the iniquity of the daughter of my people is greater than the punishment of the sin of Sodom, that was overthrown as in a moment, and no hands stayed on her. Lam. 4:1-6.

My father made your yoke heavy, and I will add to your yoke: my father also chastised you with whips, but I will chastise you with scorpions. 1 Kings 12:14.

PROPHECY OF HUSS.

John Huss did more: prophetic words resounded from the depths of his dungeon. He foresaw that a real reformation of the Church was at hand. When driven from Prague, and compelled to wander in the fields of Bohemia, where he was followed by an immense crowd eager to catch his words, he exclaimed: "The wicked have begun by laying treacherous snares for the goose. (The word Huss in Bohemian signifying goose.) But if even the goose, which is only a domestic fowl, a tame creature, and unable to rise high in the air, has

the bidding of Rome. Relics, the bones of saints and martyrs, bits of the cross, the nails, —all such things were exchanged for gold.

The treatment of Columbus by the Spanish government, one of the daughters of Rome, is an illustration of the tyranny exercised over body and mind. Gallileo, who introduced the truth of astronomical discoveries into Italy, incurred the displeasure of Rome, and was pursued by the Inquisition. Later, after the supremacy of Rome was broken, and the queen sat a widow, her children carried out the same principles. England had not lost the spirit when she taxed her colonies, and impressed their seamen. France has never fully recovered; for she still bears arbitrary rule over her possessions. Italy, once a wealthy kingdom, was drained of its wealth by the papacy. Examples might be multiplied without number. It is enough to say that nations have been oppressed. The pagan Roman Empire was lordly and dictatorial; but oppression before the days of the papacy, sank into insignificance, when compared with the tyranny of the woman clad in purple and scarlet, seated upon the scarlet colored beast. Claiming to be the vicegerent of God on earth, Rome held souls in her grasp, and assigned them at will, to heaven or hell, or demanded the payment of any price for their release from purgatory.

The messages sent to Babylon, the city, concerning its overthrow, were repeated to Rome in the person of the martyrs. Wycliffe, Huss, Jerome, Luther, Melanchthon,—these, and hundreds of others, God used as a mouthpiece to proclaim the impending fall of Rome. But so self-confident was the queen that she said, "I sit a queen, and am no widow, and shall see no sorrow. "Come down, and sit in the dust, O virgin daughter of Babylon, sit on the ground. . . . Thy nakedness shall be uncovered, yea, thy shame shall be seen: I will take vengeance. . . . Thou shalt no more be called, The lady of kingdoms."

The wounding of the head of the beast in 1798, the beginning of the time of the end, dethroned the woman for a time, but she was the mother of harlots, and the education, as well as the hereditary tendencies of her children, has enabled them, although in many ways restricted, to continue the practices of the mother. To each of the kingdoms of Europe, the Reformation came as a light and deliverance; but to-day, without exception, those nations are returning their allegiance to the dethroned queen, who only waits the opportune moment to resume her seat and her crown.

Church of St. Peter, Rome.

The hatred which Europe once manifested toward the central ecclesiastical power is fast disappearing; and before the outpouring of the plagues, there will be general agreement to exalt Rome. Rome to-day stands as the arbiter of nations. She is regaining her crown by the

yet broken their snares, other birds, whose flight carries them boldly toward heaven, will break them with much more power. Instead of a feeble goose, the truth will send forth eagles and keen-eyed falcons." The reformers fulfilled this prediction.—*Daubigne's History*.

He that leadeth into captivity shall go into captivity: he that killeth with the sword must be killed with the sword. Rev. 13:10.

We would have healed Babylon, but she is not healed: forsake her, and let us go every one into his own country: for her judgment reacheth unto heaven, and is lifted up even to the skies. Jer. 51:9.

Because ye were glad, because ye rejoiced, O ye destroyers of mine heritage, because ye are grown fat as the heifer at grass, and bellow as bulls;

Your mother shall be sore confounded; she that bare you shall be ashamed: behold, the hindermost of the nations shall be a wilderness, a dry land, and a desert.

Because of the wrath of the Lord it shall not be inhabited, but it shall be wholly desolate: every one that goeth by Babylon shall be astonished, and hiss at all her plagues. Jer. 50:11–13.

They say unto him, Cæsar's. Then saith he unto them, Render therefore unto Cæsar the things which are Cæsar's; and unto God the things that are God's.
Matt. 22:21.

Woe unto them that join house to house, that lay field to field, till there be no place, that they may be placed alone in the midst of the earth! Isa. 5:8.

They covet fields, and take them by violence; and houses, and take them away: so they oppress a man and his house, even a man and his heritage. Micah 2:2.

Woe unto them that call evil good, and good evil; that put darkness for light, and light for darkness; that put bitter for sweet, and sweet for bitter! Isa. 5:20.

For the time will come when they will not endure sound doctrine; but after their own lusts shall they heap to themselves teachers, having itching ears;
And they shall turn away their ears from the truth, and shall be turned unto fables.
2 Tim. 4:3, 4.

Which say to the seers, See not; and to the prophets, Prophesy not unto us right things, speak unto us smooth things, prophesy deceits:
Get you out of the way, turn aside out of the path, cause the Holy One of Israel to cease from before us.
Isa. 30:10, 11.

Since the day that your fathers came forth out of the land of Egypt unto this day I have even sent unto you all my servants the prophets, daily rising up early and sending them. Jer. 7:25.

same method by which she at first received it. One nation after another bows before her throne, and recognizes the woman's right to ride the beast. The wealth of all nations is about to be given into her hands.

In the United States, the formation of the image to the beast, will place the unbounded resources of this country in the hands of the same power. Protestantism repudiates its fundamental principles, the complete separation of church and state, and performs the works of the beast. Society, once democratic throughout, is gradually revolutionized in the formation of the image; as it was done in the growth of the beast. The distinction between the rich and the poor, becomes more marked; the corporations and trusts control the money, the produce, and the laboring classes. Democracy gives way to a king,—the coal king, the oil king, or the money king. A few men dictate to the masses. The independence once gained by war, is lost in America, as in Europe, through false methods of education.

The Protestant churches, once simple in habits and customs, now bid for the most popular minister, pay high prices for pews, listen to paid singers, who know nothing of the power of soul music; and the sermons to which the wealthy listen, are such as will please the ear, but do not convert the heart.

God has sent message after message to save the world. Such are the messages of the three angels of Rev. 14:6–12. The first one was rejected; and the second angel proclaimed the fall of Babylon. The spirit of discernment is lost, and that which came from God, is passed by unheeded. Babylon, devoid of the Spirit which controlled and kept vice in check, becomes as the house which was empty, swept, and garnished. It becomes "the habitation of devils, the hold of every foul spirit, and a cage of every unclean and hateful bird," and the condition of Babylon in the last days is worse than in former times.

Saul, when he could receive no word from the Lord, because he had hitherto rejected divine counsel, sought out a witch, and consulted the spirit of devils. The end of Saul was death by suicide. The churches that reject the message of the judgment and the Saviour's second coming, reject the Spirit of God, and are given over to the control of evil spirits, a miracle working power, which binds men by supernatural manifestations until they are prepared to receive Satan himself, who comes in the name of the Lord.

As Babylon the city, became the home of the bittern and the owl, birds of prey, so Babylon the church, takes the spirit of the carrion birds, and watches to destroy souls. What Rome of the Middle Ages accomplished under the cover of darkness, modern Babylon will repeat in the full blaze of intellectual life. The third angel's message offers life to those who are bound by the fetters of false doctrines, and warns them against the beast and his image.

God's judgment waits until the last end of time,—until there is no longer any who will repent. Before the close of probation, an angel is seen to come down from heaven, and join the third angel. Together, their glory enlightens the world. This is the loud cry. Men acknowledge

When the unclean spirit is gone out of a man, he walketh through dry places, seeking rest, and findeth none.

Then he saith, I will return into my house from whence I came out; and when he is come, he findeth it empty, swept, and garnished.

Then goeth he, and taketh with himself seven other spirits more wicked than himself, and they enter in and dwell there: and the last state of that man is worse than the first. Even so shall it be also unto this wicked generation.
Matt. 12:43-45.

Jer. 51:37.

So Saul died for his transgression which he committed against the Lord, even against the word of the Lord, which he kept not, and also for asking counsel of one that had a familiar spirit, to inquire of it.
1 Chron. 10:13.

Now the Spirit speaketh expressly, that in the latter times some shall depart from the faith, giving heed to seducing spirits, and doctrines of devils. 1 Tim. 4:1.

Therefore the wild beasts of the desert with the wild beasts of the islands shall dwell there, and the owls shall dwell therein: and it shall be no more inhabited for ever; neither shall it be dwelt in from generation to generation.
Jer. 50:39.

The thing that hath been, it is that which shall be; and that which is done is that which shall be done: and there is no new thing under the sun. Eccl. 1:9.

Flee out of the midst of Babylon, and deliver every man his soul: be not cut off in her iniquity; for this is the time of the Lord's vengeance; he will render unto her a recompence. Jer. 51:6.

Behold, I will send for many fishers, saith the Lord, and they shall fish them; and after will I send for many hunters, and they shall hunt them from every mountain, and from every hill, and out of the holes of the rocks.
Jer. 16:16.

It shall come to pass in the last days, saith God, I will pour out of my Spirit upon all flesh: and your sons and your daughters shall prophesy, and your young men shall see visions, and your old men shall dream dreams. Acts 2:17.

Isa. 24:14–16.

In the first year of his reign I Daniel understood by books the number of the years, whereof the word of the Lord came to Jeremiah the prophet, that he would accomplish seventy years in the desolations of Jerusalem.

And I set my face unto the Lord God, to seek by prayer and supplications, with fasting, and sackcloth, and ashes. Dan. 9:2, 3.

Rev. 8:3, 4.

Num. 14:20, 21.

Then the priests the Levites arose and blessed the people: and their voice was heard, and their prayer came up to his holy dwelling place, even unto heaven. 2 Chron. 30:27.

Jude 9.

Rev. 14:9.

Thou tellest my wanderings: put thou my tears into thy bottle: are they not in thy book? Psa. 56:8.

Rev. 5:8.

Not because I desire a gift: but I desire fruit that may abound to your account.

But I have all, and abound: I am full, having received of Epaphroditus the things which were sent from you, an odour of a sweet smell, a sacrifice acceptable, well-pleasing to God. Phil. 4:17, 18.

Rev. 18:4.

the sins of Babylon, and some even of the kings of the earth repent. The loud cry will reach the corners of the earth; thousands will be converted in a day, as they were in the days of Pentecost. As the oppressions of Babylon become more galling, most fervent prayers will be offered for release. The Jews in ancient Babylon near the close of the seventy years' captivity, symbolized the people of God in modern Babylon as the time of the plagues draws near. As Daniel prayed with fasting and heart searching, that he might know the time of deliverance, and that no sins might be left on the books against Israel, so the people of God will plead in these last days. The prayers that Daniel offered, will be answered more fully in the end of time than it was possible for them to be answered in the days of his natural life. The prayer which Moses offered when Israel sinned, and he, their leader, pleaded for their forgiveness, was partially answered then. The Lord said, "I have pardoned according to thy word: but as truly as I live, all the earth shall be filled with the glory of the Lord." Moses waits over three thousand years for the answer to that prayer. From his dwelling place in heaven, he will see the answer in the loud cry of the third angel's message. Other prayers long delayed will then be answered. These requests have been bottled in heaven and when Satan manifests his greatest power, the Gospel of Jesus Christ is preached with a spirit which enlightens the world. Time is about to close, and the vials of sweet odors held by the four living creatures about the throne, will be emptied before the sanctuary work closes.

There will be a voice heard from heaven saying, "Come out of her, My people, that ye be not partakers of her sins, and that ye receive not of her plagues. For her sins have reached unto heaven, and God hath remembered her iniquities." As the angels took Lot by the hands, and hurried him out of Sodom, bidding him not to look back, so angels will hurry the sincere and true-hearted out of Babylon, for her destruction cometh like the burning of Sodom.

This message from God, the Great Shepherd, comes from heaven, and souls respond. To the Jews in Babylon, the same call was given and those who were true to Jehovah, fled to the mountains, that they might not be partakers of her impending destruction. Some had lived so long in the city, that they hesitated about leaving. Lot had sons and daughters who would not leave Sodom; and the family ties were so strong that Lot's wife, the mother, turned to look back, and destruction overtook her. The loud cry will cause many a heartache; will lead to the severance of many a fond tie. Husbands will have to decide whether they will cling to their families, and remain in spiritual Sodom, or whether they will heed the voice from heaven. Mothers will have the same decision to make. This is the time when Christ says, "He that loveth father or mother more than Me is not worthy of Me: and he that loveth son or daughter more than Me is not worthy of Me."

While the work of separation is going on, the power of the beast and his image, grows more intolerable. The believers are obliged to seek shelter in rocks and caves of the mountains.

Depart ye, depart ye, go ye out from thence, touch no unclean thing; go ye out of the midst of her; be ye clean, that bear the vessels of the Lord. Isa. 52:11.

Jer. 51:6.
Gen. 19:16, 17.

The same day that Lot went out of Sodom it rained fire and brimstone from heaven, and destroyed them all.
Even thus shall it be in the day when the Son of man is revealed. Luke 17:29, 30.

The men said unto Lot, Hast thou here any besides? son in law, and thy sons, and thy daughters, and whatsoever thou hast in the city, bring them out of this place:
For we will destroy this place, because the cry of them is waxen great before the face of the Lord; and the Lord hath sent us to destroy it.
And Lot went out, and spake unto his sons in law, which married his daughters, and said, Up, get you out of this place; for the Lord will destroy this city. But he seemed as one that mocked unto his sons in law. Gen. 19:12-14.

Then shall two be in the field: the one shall be taken, and the other left.
Two women shall be grinding at the mill; the one shall be taken, and the other left. Matt. 24:40, 41.

Luke 17:34-36.
Matt. 10:37.

He shall dwell on high: his place of defence shall be the munitions of rocks: bread shall be given him; his waters shall be sure. Isa. 33:16.

The sword is without, and the pestilence and the famine within: he that is in the field shall die with the sword; and he that is in the city, famine and pestilence shall devour him. Eze. 7:15.

But they that escape of them shall escape, and shall be on the mountains like doves of the valleys, all of them mourning, every one for his iniquity. Eze. 7:16.

Luke 21:12, 16–18.
Rev. 18:7, 8.

*And they cast dust on their heads, and cried, weeping and wailing, saying, Alas, alas that great city, wherein were made rich all that had ships in the sea by reason of her costliness! for in one hour is she made desolate.*

*Rejoice over her, thou heaven, and ye holy apostles and prophets; for God hath avenged you on her.*

*And a mighty angel took up a stone like a great millstone, and cast it into the sea, saying, Thus with violence shall that great city Babylon be thrown down, and shall be found no more at all.*

*And the voice of harpers, and musicians, and of pipers, and trumpeters, shall be heard no more at all in thee; and no craftsman, of whatsoever craft he be, shall be found any more in thee; and the sound of a millstone shall be heard no more at all in thee;*

*And the light of a candle shall shine no more at all in thee; and the voice of the bridegroom and of the bride shall be heard no more at all in thee: for thy merchants were the great men of the earth; for by the sorceries were all nations deceived.*

*And in her was found the blood of prophets, and of saints, and of all that were slain upon the earth. Rev. 18:19-24.*

Rev. 18:24.
Matt. 23:34, 35.

For, lo, thine enemies make a tumult: and they that hate thee have lifted up the head.

They have taken crafty counsel against thy people, and consulted against thy hidden ones.

Some will be thrown into prison. Then the plagues begin to fall. "How much she hath glorified herself, and lived deliciously, so much torment and sorrow give her. . . . Therefore shall her plagues come in one day (or one year), death, and mourning, and famine; and she shall be utterly burned with fire."

During this time of trouble, many who rejected the messages when they were given remember the call of God, and when it is too late, seek to recall His messengers. "Behold, the days come, saith the Lord God, that I will send a famine in the land, not a famine of bread, nor a thirst for water, but of hearing the words of the Lord: and they shall wander from sea to sea, and from the north even to the east, they shall run to and fro to seek the word of the Lord, and shall not find it."

There is no word of God in Babylon; for she is the one who exalted self above Jehovah, who caused the two witnesses to prophesy in sackcloth for forty and two months, and who thought to change the eternal times and laws of the universe. "And in her was found the blood of prophets, and of saints, and of all that were slain upon the earth." Those who love the Word of God have withdrawn from her midst, and during the time of trouble, are hidden from the wrath of man and the fury of the plagues. As probation has closed, "the light of a candle shall shine no more at all" in Babylon. The voice of joy is turned to mourning; the social gatherings and the marriage feasts no longer offer any attraction; merchants and the great men of earth fail because of the destruction of great Babylon. The earth is literally turned upside down, and it reels to and fro like a drunken man; for great Babylon has come in remembrance before God. Her iniquities have reached unto heaven, and God comes down to reward her double according to her works.

As the ancient city of Babylon was overthrown because she forsook the way of life, so modern Babylon dies. None need partake of her plagues; for all had an opportunity to separate from her midst. God is to-day making up His spiritual kingdom. His subjects are on the earth, and by the strong magnet of His love He is drawing to Himself all who prefer a spiritual life to one of earth.

The story of Babylon the city, and again of Babylon the church, is the picture divinely given of a worldly life under the dominion of the power of the prince of this world. The little church, hidden from trouble during these last days, may seem to have lost much by following the Man of Nazareth; but their love of truth links their hearts with God, and they taste the joys of an endless life. The great controversy still continues; it ends in the overthrow of Babylon, the mother of harlots, and the confusion of Babel is replaced by the divine harmony, which, for six thousand years, has been marred by sin.

They have said, Come, and let us cut them off from being a nation; that the name of Israel may be no more in remembrance.

For they have consulted together with one consent: they are confederate against thee. Psa. 83:2-5.

Behold, the Lord maketh the earth empty, and maketh it waste, and turneth it upside down, and scattereth abroad the inhabitants thereof. Isa. 24:1.

Isa. 24:17-21.

Wherefore come out from among them, and be ye separate, saith the Lord, and touch not the unclean thing; and I will receive you,

And will be a Father unto you, and ye shall be my sons and daughters, saith the Lord Almighty. 2 Cor. 6:17, 18.

Yea doubtless, and I count all things but loss for the excellency of the knowledge of Christ Jesus my Lord: for whom I have suffered the loss of all things, and do count them but dung, that I may win Christ. Phil. 3:8.

# CHAPTER XX.

## THE TWO SUPPERS.

Isa. 55:1.

Jesus answered and said unto her, If thou knewest the gift of God, and who it is that saith to thee, Give me to drink; thou wouldest have asked of him, and he would have given thee living water.

But whosoever drinketh of the water that I shall give him shall never thirst; but the water that I shall give him shall be in him a well of water springing up into everlasting life. John 4:10, 14.

"Ho, every one that thirsteth, come ye to the waters, and he that hath no money; come ye, buy, and eat; yea, come, buy wine and milk without money and without price."

Isa. 55:2.
Isa. 55:3.
Isa. 55:4.
Isa. 55:5.
Isa. 55:6.
Rev. 3:18.
Rev. 3:20.

"Wherefore do ye spend money for that which is not bread? and your labor for that which satisfieth not? Hearken diligently unto Me, and eat ye that which is good, and let your soul delight itself in fatness."

"Incline your ear, and come unto Me: hear, and your soul shall live; and I will make an everlasting covenant with you, even the sure mercies of David."

For I am not ashamed of the gospel of Christ: for it is the power of God unto salvation to every one that believeth; to the Jew first, and also to the Greek. Rom. 1:16.

Gen. 3:1-6.

The everlasting Gospel, the power of God unto salvation, has, throughout all generations, held out this invitation to the people of the earth. From the fall in Eden to the last generation on earth, guests are chosen for the marriage supper of the Lamb. This will be the great gathering time for the heavenly family,—the first reunion of all the creatures of God's hand. God the Father will gather His children in the New Jerusalem, the mother of us all; and Christ the eldest Son and Brother, the Bridegroom, will come forth, and serve the guests. Christ at the marriage feast in Cana looked forward to the time of His own marriage supper, when sin would be forever blotted out; when His bride, adorned in the righteousness of God, and the guests, arrayed in the wedding garments, would await the coming of the Bridegroom. The changing of the water to wine was typical of the transformation wrought in the character of those who would become guests, when at His word mortality was changed to immortality.

In His talk with Zacchæus, the Publican, the Saviour explained His marriage and the supper. "Because they thought that the kingdom of God should immediately appear. He said therefore, A certain nobleman went into a far country to receive for himself a kingdom, and to return." "And ye yourselves [are] like unto men that wait for their Lord, when He will return from the wedding; that when He cometh and knocketh, they may open unto Him immediately. Blessed are those servants, whom the Lord when He cometh shall find watching: verily I say unto you, that He shall gird Himself, and make them to sit down to meat, and will come forth and serve them."

When the Saviour entered the inner apartment of the heavenly temple, He went to make up the subjects of His kingdom. He "came to the Ancient of Days," the Father, "and there

For this cause I bow my knees unto the Father of our Lord Jesus Christ,

Of whom the whole family in heaven and earth is named.
Eph. 3:14, 15.

Jerusalem which is above is free, which is the mother of us all.
Gal. 4:26.

For whom he did foreknow, he also did predestinate to be conformed to the image of his Son, that he might be the firstborn among many brethren. Rom. 8:29.

Rejoice ye with Jerusalem, and be glad with her, all ye that love her: rejoice for joy with her, all ye that mourn for her:

That ye may suck, and be satisfied with the breasts of her consolations; that ye may milk out, and be delighted with the abundance of her glory.

For thus saith the Lord, Behold, I will extend peace to her like a river, and the glory of the Gentiles like a flowing stream: then shall ye suck, ye shall be borne upon her sides, and be dandled upon her knees. Isa. 66:10–12.

1 Cor. 15:51–54.
Luke 19:11, 12.
Luke 12:36, 37.

When the king came in to see the guests, he saw there a man which had not on a wedding garment:

And he saith unto him, Friend, how camest thou in hither not having a wedding garment? And he was speechless.

Then said the king to the servants, Bind him hand and foot, and take him away, and cast him into outer darkness; there shall be weeping and gnashing of teeth.

For many are called, but few are chosen. Matt. 22:11–14.

Dan. 7:14, 27.

And sent his servant at supper time to say to them that were bidden, Come; for all things are now ready. Luke 14:17.

The lord said unto the servant, Go out into the highways and hedges, and compel them to come in, that my house may be filled. Luke 14:23.

He saith unto me, Write, Blessed are they which are called unto the marriage supper of the Lamb. And he saith unto me, These are the true sayings of God. Rev. 19:9.

They refused to hearken, and pulled away the shoulder, and stopped their ears, that they should not hear.

Yea, they made their hearts as an adamant stone, lest they should hear the law, and the words which the Lord of hosts hath sent in his Spirit by the former prophets: therefore came a great wrath from the Lord of hosts. Zech. 7:11, 12.

Jer. 7:13, 14.

I also will choose their delusions, and will bring their fears upon them; because when I called, none did answer; when I spake, they did not hear: but they did evil before mine eyes, and chose that in which I delighted not. Isa. 66:4.

Blessed are those servants, whom the lord when he cometh shall find watching: verily I say unto you, that he shall gird himself, and make them to sit down to meat, and will come forth and serve them. Luke 12:37.

Rejoicing in the habitable part of his earth; and my delights were with the sons of men. Prov. 8:31.

was given Him dominion, and glory, and a kingdom." "And the kingdom and dominion, and the greatness of the kingdom under the whole heaven, shall be given to the people of the saints of the most High, whose kingdom is an everlasting kingdom." This is the marriage of Christ, and the work of the sealing angel is to put a sign upon those of the last generation who are prepared for the wedding supper. The voice from heaven, which, during the loud cry, says, "Come out of her My people," gathers guests for this supper from the very last people of earth. Probation closes when the last guest has accepted the invitation.

John, in the Revelation of Jesus Christ, had been brought a number of times to this great gathering. In the sixteenth chapter are recorded the plagues which fall upon those who turn from the invitation; the eighteenth chapter describes the character of the church and the governments which attract the minds of men from the call of God, and so infatuate them with the feasts of the whore that they lose the privilege of eating at the table of the Lamb. John saw these things, and understood why the time of trouble came; and then the curtain was drawn aside, and from the scenes of debauchery and destruction, which earth presents, his eye rested upon the heavenly gathering at the great supper of the Son of God.

He saw the hosts of the redeemed from earth mingling with angels and the inhabitants of other worlds. And he "heard a great voice of much people in heaven," the greatest chorus the universe ever heard; that in which all voices unite in singing, "Alleluia; salvation, and glory, and honor, and power, unto the Lord our God." Salvation is the one theme throughout creation. Worlds, long held in suspense because of sin on earth, raised their voices in the universal anthem. They had witnessed the judgment of God; and they who had followed the dealings of Satan on earth, and who knew of his repeated attempts to overthrow the throne of God, saw the final destruction of the wnore, that masterpiece of iniquity. When the last trace of sin was gone, and the smoke of the final burning had ascended up forever and ever, they burst forth in unrestrained accents, saying, "True and righteous are His judgments." And the four beasts and the four and twenty elders bowed before the throne crying, "Amen; Alleluia." These were close beside the throne; and as the command came to praise God, off to the limits of space, rolling on and on like the voice of many waters, sounded the words, "Alleluia: for the Lord God omnipotent reigneth. Let us be glad and rejoice, and give honor to Him: for the marriage of the Lamb is come, and His wife hath made herself ready."

Sometimes it may seem that man is alone; but one glimpse of heaven shows that the whole universe is watching, intently watching, and salvation is the thought of every heart. As their lives are more sensitive than ours because sin has not dulled their sensibilities, so their suffering in sympathy with man, is intense beyond description. Love, eternal love rules the universe, and when the conflict is over, a shout resounds through creation, "The Lord God omnipotent reigneth." Then from boundless space the creatures of His love come to witness

*And after these things I heard a great voice of much people in heaven, saying, Alleluia; Salvation, and glory, and honour, and power, unto the Lord our God:*

*For true and righteous are his judgments: for he hath judged the great whore, which did corrupt the earth with her fornication, and hath avenged the blood of his servants at her hand.*

*Rev. 19:1, 2.*

Then shall he say also unto them on the left hand, Depart from me, ye cursed, into everlasting fire, prepared for the devil and his angels.

Matt. 25:41.

Psa. 112:7, 8.

Rev. 16:7.

Rev. 19:4.

Is there any number of his armies? and upon whom doth not his light arise? Job 25:3.

Rev. 19:7.

Elisha prayed, and said, Lord, I pray thee, open his eyes, that he may see. And the Lord opened the eyes of the young man; and he saw: and, behold, the mountain was full of horses and chariots of fire round about Elisha.

2 Kings 6:17.

*And again they said, Alleluia. And her smoke rose up for ever and ever.*

*And the four and twenty elders and the four beasts fell down and worshipped God that sat on the throne, saying, Amen; Alleluia.*

*And a voice came out of the throne, saying, Praise our God, all ye his servants, and ye that fear him, both small and great.*

*And I heard as it were the voice of a great multitude, and as the voice of many waters, and as the voice of mighty thunderings, saying, Alleluia: for the Lord God omnipotent reigneth.*

*Let us be glad and rejoice, and give honour to him: for the marriage of the Lamb is come, and his wife hath made herself ready.*

*Rev. 19:3-7.*

Mark 14:25.
Matt. 26:29.

When one of them that sat at meat with him heard these things, he said unto him, Blessed is he that shall eat bread in the kingdom of God. Luke 14:15.

Zech. 14:4.

They shall not hunger nor thirst; neither shall the heat nor sun smite them: for he that hath mercy on them shall lead them, even by the springs of water shall he guide them.

And I will make all my mountains a way, and my highways shall be exalted.

Behold, these shall come from far: and, lo, these from the north and from the west; and these from the land of Sinim.

Sing, O heavens; and be joyful, O earth; and break forth into singing, O mountains: for the Lord hath comforted his people, and will have mercy upon his afflicted. Isa. 49:10–13.

Isa. 62:4, 5.

I will rejoice in Jerusalem, and joy in my people: and the voice of weeping shall be no more heard in her, nor the voice of crying. Isa. 65:19.

Zech. 3:4.
Isa. 61:10.

*And to her was granted that she should be arrayed in fine linen, clean and white: for the fine linen is the righteousness of saints.*

*And he saith unto me, Write, Blessed are they which are called unto the marriage supper of the Lamb. And he saith unto me, These are the true sayings of God.* *Rev. 19:8, 9.*

Luke 15:22–24.

the gathering at the marriage supper of the Lamb. In the city of God, the silver table, many miles in length, is spread with the fruits of the new earth. The city which Christ has prepared for the redeemed, rests on the site of ancient Jerusalem which has been purified by fire. It is Eden restored. "His feet shall stand in that day upon the Mount of Olives . . . and the Mount of Olives shall cleave in the midst thereof toward the east and toward the west, and there shall be a very great valley; . . . and the Lord my God shall come, and all the saints with Thee." "Thou shalt no more be termed Forsaken; neither shall thy land any more be termed Desolate: but thou shalt be called Hephzi-bah (that is, my delight is in her), and thy land Beulah (married): for the Lord delighteth in thee, and thy land shall be married. . . . As the bridegroom rejoiceth over the bride, so shall thy God rejoice over thee."

Everywhere will be seen the character of Christ. The city reflects it, the land speaks of purity, and the redeemed are clothed in the wedding garments, linen clean and white, which is the righteousness of Christ worn by the saints. And as the prophet marveled over the grandeur of the scene, and the glory of redemption completed, Gabriel, thinking still of those on earth who should make up that company seated about the table, said, "Write, Blessed are they which are called unto the marriage supper of the Lamb"; for the things which thou hast seen are true. Though still future, John had seen things as they will be when sin is a thing of the past.

John, overcome with inexpressible joy and

gratitude, fell at the feet of Gabriel, to worship him; but he who stands in the presence of God, a channel of communication between God and man, raised the prophet, and pointing toward the throne, said "Worship God!" I, though Gabriel, am but one of His creatures, drawing life from Him and am thy fellow servant and the fellow servant of all who have the Spirit of Prophecy." Gabriel, as the angel of prophecy, feels a tender regard for those with whom he has had open communion; and as he sees the redeemed at the marriage supper, he is able to trace their history and salvation, through their adherence to the Spirit of Prophecy. And he, the servant of God, in bearing light, is a fellow worshiper with all who have received the light; for it is the Spirit of Prophecy which brings all to the unity of the faith.

Dan. 10:21.

Luke 1:19, 20.

*And I fell at his feet to worship him And he said unto me, See thou do it not: I am thy fellow-servant, and of thy brethren that have the testimony of Jesus: worship God: for the testimony of Jesus is the spirit of prophecy.*
*Rev. 19:10.*

If ye will not believe, surely ye shall not be established.
Isa. 7:9.

Hear me, O Judah, and ye inhabitants of Jerusalem; Believe in the Lord your God, so shall ye be established; believe his prophets, so shall ye prosper.
2 Chron. 20:20.

He gave some, apostles; and some, prophets; and some, evangelists; and some, pastors and teachers;
For the perfecting of the saints, for the work of the ministry, for the edifying of the body of Christ:
Till we all come in the unity of the faith. Eph. 4:11-13.

Beginning with the eleventh verse, the closing scenes of earth's history are again opened before John. This time he sees heaven's hosts marshaled,—ten thousand times ten thousands of angels, arrayed as warriors under their Commander. "The Lord hath opened His armory, and hath brought forth the weapons of His indignation: for this is the work of the Lord God of Hosts."

*And I saw heaven opened, and behold a white horse; and he that sat upon him was called Faithful and True, and in righteousness he doth judge and make war.*
*Rev. 19:11.*

Jer. 50:25.

At the head of the forces, rode the Commander in chief of all the hosts of heaven. He was clothed in a vesture dipped in blood. Satan the opposing general, had bruised and wounded Him; but His sacrifice only endeared Him to His own troops, and they became His loyal subjects for eternity. He was seated on a pure white horse, a sign of royalty. On His head He wore many crowns in token of the victories

Who is this that cometh from Edom, with dyed garments from Bozrah? this that is glorious in his apparel, travelling in the greatness of his strength? I that speak in righteousness, mighty to save.
Isa. 63:1.

One shall say unto him, What are these wounds in thine hands? Then he shall answer, Those with which I was wounded in the house of my friends. Zech. 13:6.

Judges 5:10.

THE BIBLE DESCRIPTION OF SOME OF THE MANY CROWNS.

Rev. 2:10. Crown of life.
Rev. 14:14. Crown of gold.
1 Pet. 5:4. Crown of glory.
2 Tim. 4:8. Crown of righteousness.
1 Thess. 2:19. Crown of rejoicing.
Psa. 103:4. Crown of loving-kindness.
Heb. 2:7, 9. Crown of glory and honour.
Prov. 14:18. Crown of knowledge.
1 Cor. 9:25. Incorruptible crown.

*His eyes were as a flame of fire; and on his head were many crowns, and he had a name written, that no man knew, but he himself.*

*And he was clothed with a vesture dipped in blood: and his name is called The Word of God.*

*And the armies which were in heaven followed him upon white horses, clothed in fine linen, white and clean.*

*And out of his mouth goeth a sharp sword, that with it he should smite the nations: and he shall rule them with a rod of iron: and he treadeth the winepress of the fierceness and wrath of Almighty God.*

*And he hath on his vesture and on his thigh a name written, KING OF KINGS, AND LORD OF LORDS.*
*Rev. 19:12-16.*

Heb. 13:20.

Even he shall build the temple of the Lord; and he shall bear the glory, and shall sit and rule upon his throne; and he shall be a priest upon his throne: and the counsel of peace shall be between them both. Zech. 6:13.

Whosoever shall fall on this stone shall be broken: but on whomsoever it shall fall, it will grind him to powder.
Matt. 21:44.

I will declare the decree: the Lord hath said unto me, Thou art my Son; this day have I begotten thee.

won. To His devoted followers, the name of the Commander was "Faithful and True." On His vesture and on His thigh, was written, "King of Kings, and Lord of Lords"; but aside from these letters He had a name known only to Himself and the Father,—a name expressing the depths of divine character which even eternity cannot interpret. Since each redeemed one has an inner experience with Christ, which is a secret between two, so the Father and His eldest Son know each other as none others can know them. To His Father, Christ is the Word of God. The completest union is here signified. God has spoken through Christ in all His creation, and the name Word of God is an eternal reminder of the everlasting covenant into which the Two entered when Christ received that name. It was the Word of God which was made flesh, and dwelt among us. It is the Word that saves, and it is this same Word that destroys. To the one who obeys the Word, it is a healing balm of all the ills to which human flesh is heir. When disregarded, it becomes the stone of stumbling, and rock of offense over which men fall and die.

For the first time in all ages, Christ goes from heaven as a warrior, clad with helmet and sword; for the first time, He comes to rule with a rod of iron. For six thousand years He has been the gentlest of the gentle. He is the shepherd that carries the lambs in his bosom; the father who pities his child. "Can a woman forget her sucking child? . . . yea, they may forget, yet will I not forget thee." But when He comes at the end of the time, to meet the armies of earth that are in battle array on the plains of Armageddon, His eyes flash flames of fire, which burn through the souls of men; and out of His mouth goeth a sharp sword, and with it He smites the nations.

He whose Word has been the saving grace through time, now holds aloft the Word of God, and men are condemned by their own hearts. To the righteous, waiting ones, He comes on a white cloud, and they are caught up to meet Him in the air; but, while to one company, His coming brings immortal life, to the other, who have scorned the Word when it was spoken in human language, that Word, as it comes from Jehovah Himself, becomes a consuming fire.

There is a great earthquake, the earth opens and reveals a lake of fire. This is the first revelation of the lake of fire, which the center of the earth now holds in keeping until the day when Christ treads "the wine press of the fierceness and wrath of Almighty God." The fire from the mouth of Christ slays the remnant of the wicked. They who were prepared to slay the people of God, fall, as did the Roman guard when the angel of the resurrection drew near to the earth. The beast in Europe and the false prophet in the United States, having blended their forces for the accomplishment of their one desire,—the destruction of the remnant of God's people,—fall before Him who sits on the white horse. His name is the Word of God, and He is followed by the armies of heaven, clothed in robes of dazzling purity, each riding a pure white horse. The world is marshaled under the beast and the false prophet and these both are cast alive into the lake of fire. "A sound of battle is in the land, and of great destruction. How is the hammer of the whole earth cut

Ask of me, and I shall give thee the heathen for thine inheritance, and the uttermost parts of the earth for thy possession. Psa. 2:7, 8.

He shall feed his flock like a shepherd: he shall gather the lambs with his arm, and carry them in his bosom, and shall gently lead those that are with young. Isa. 40:11.

For the word of God is quick, and powerful, and sharper than any twoedged sword. Heb. 4:12.

Psa. 103:13.
Isa. 49:13-17.

With righteousness shall he judge the poor, and reprove with equity for the meek of the earth: and he shall smite the earth with the rod of his mouth, and with the breath of his lips shall he slay the wicked. Isa. 11:4.

For a fire is kindled in mine anger, and shall burn unto the lowest hell, and shall consume the earth with her increase, and set on fire the foundations of the mountains. Deut. 32:22.

A fire goeth before him, and burneth up his enemies round about.
His lightnings enlightened the world: the earth saw, and trembled.
The hills melted like wax at the presence of the Lord, at the presence of the Lord of the whole earth. Psa. 97:3-5.

Isa. 63:1-6.
Isa. 64:1-3.
Matt. 28:3, 4.
Jer. 25:33.
2 Thess. 2:8.

I beheld then because of the voice of the great words which the horn spake: I beheld even till the beast was slain, and his body destroyed, and given to the burning flame Dan. 7:11.

He was clothed with a vesture dipped in blood: and his name is called The Word of God.
And the armies which were in heaven followed him upon white horses, clothed in fine linen, white and clean. Rev. 19:13, 14.

Jer. 50:22–24.

For, behold, the Lord will come with fire, and with his chariots like a whirlwind, to render his anger with fury, and his rebuke with flames of fire.

For by fire and by his sword will the Lord plead with all flesh: and the slain of the Lord shall be many. Isa. 66:15, 16.

Psa. 50:3–6.

The anger of the Lord was kindled against this land, to bring upon it all the curses that are written in this book. Deut. 29:27.

*And I saw an angel standing in the sun; and he cried with a loud voice, saying to all the fowls that fly in the midst of heaven, Come and gather yourselves together unto the supper of the great God;*

*That ye may eat the flesh of kings, and the flesh of captains, and the flesh of mighty men, and the flesh of horses, and of them that sit on them, and the flesh of all men, both free and bond, both small and great.*

*And I saw the beast, and the kings of the earth, and their armies, gathered together to make war against him that sat on the horse, and against his army.*

*And the beast was taken, and with him the false prophet that wrought miracles before him, with which he deceived them that had received the mark of the beast, and them that worshipped his image. These both were cast alive into a lake of fire burning with brimstone.*

*And the remnant were slain with the sword of him that sat upon the horse, which sword proceeded out of his mouth: and all the fowls were filled with their flesh. Rev. 19:17-21.*

Jer. 25:30–33.

Then shall that Wicked be revealed, whom the Lord shall consume with the spirit of his mouth, and shall destroy with the brightness of his coming.

2 Thess. 2:8.

asunder and broken! How is Babylon become a desolation among the nations! I have laid a snare for thee, and thou art also taken, O Babylon, and thou wast not aware: thou art found, and also caught, because thou hast striven against the Lord." These all are slain, and at the end of the thousand years, are burned in the lake of fire which purifies the earth. "Our God shall come, and shall not keep silence: a fire shall devour before Him, and it shall be very tempestuous round about Him. He shall call to the heavens from above, and to the earth, that He may judge His people. Gather My saints together unto Me; those that have made a covenant with Me by sacrifice. And the heavens shall declare His righteousness: for God is judge Himself."

From time immemorial, the prophecies have foretold this day of vengeance, and warned the inhabitants of the earth to flee from the wrath to come. But men were lovers of their own selves. To Jeremiah the Lord said, "Prophesy thou against them all these words, and say unto them, The Lord shall roar from on high, and utter His voice from His holy habitation; He shall mightily roar upon His habitation; He shall give a shout, as they that tread the grapes, against all the inhabitants of the earth. A noise shall come even to the ends of the earth; for the Lord hath a controversy with the nations, He will plead with all flesh; He will give them that are wicked to the sword. . . . And the slain of the Lord shall be at that day from one end of the earth even unto the other end of the earth: they shall not be lamented, neither gathered, nor buried; they shall be dung upon the ground."

The culmination of all destruction comes at the appearing of Christ as Commander of the hosts of heaven. And when the slain cover the earth from one end to the other, a mighty angel is represented as standing over against the sun, and crying so that the fowls of the whole earth hear, saying, "Come and gather yourselves together unto the supper of the great God; that ye may eat the flesh of kings, and the flesh of captains, and the flesh of mighty men, and the flesh of horses, and of them that sit on them, and the flesh of all men, both free and bond, both small and great." It is over. Those who sought to slay the truth,—men from every kindred, representing all classes, lie dead, slain by the Word which they rejected. And while Christ returns to heaven with the redeemed, the fowls of the heavens devour the bodies of the slain. This is one supper,—a feast of death. What a contrast to the marriage supper of the Lamb! It is the last feast, even for birds of prey, whose very existence typifies the devouring nature of sin. The earth is soon without form and void! Even the life of birds is destroyed; for the elements melt with fervent heat; the heavens roll together as a scroll, and the atmosphere is dissolved.

All are called to the marriage supper of the Lamb; all may be there, but those who have rejected the Word will be smitten when He comes as a consuming fire.

He shall smite the earth with the rod of his mouth, and with the breath of his lips shall he slay the wicked. Isa. 11:4.

For these be the days of vengeance, that all things which are written may be fulfilled. Luke 21:22.

**The fowls of the heavens devour the bodies of the slain.**

For wheresoever the carcase is, there will the eagles be gathered together. Matt. 24:28.

I beheld the earth, and, lo, it was without form, and void; and the heavens, and they had no light.

I beheld the mountains, and, lo, they trembled, and all the hills moved lightly.

I beheld, and, lo, there was no man, and all the birds of the heavens were fled.

I beheld, and, lo, the fruitful place was a wilderness, and all the cities thereof were broken down at the presence of the Lord, and by his fierce anger.

For thus hath the Lord said, The whole land shall be desolate; yet will I not make a full end. Jer. 4:23-27.

# CHAPTER XXI.

## THE JUDGMENT OF THE WICKED.

Thus saith the Lord; Behold, I set before you the way of life, and the way of death. Jer. 21:8.

Amos 5:14.

He that is not with me is against me; and he that gathereth not with me scattereth abroad. Matt. 12:30.

Josh. 5:14.

He brought me to the banqueting house, and his banner over me was love. Song Sol. 2:4.

Who said, Let us take to ourselves the houses of God in possession. Psa. 83:12.

No servant can serve two masters: for either he will hate the one, and love the other; or else he will hold to the one, and despise the other. Ye cannot serve God and mammon. Luke 16:13.

THE history of our little planet reveals the conflict between two opposing characters. The good and the evil, the true and the false, have made this the battle field of contention. The contest has been over two principles, and every individual has enlisted on one side, or on the other. There has been no middle ground. Christ is General of the forces of heaven, and love and truth have been the banners under which His people have fought. Satan has commanded the other army, and it has been his plan to overthrow not only those who fought with Emmanuel, but to blot out the government of God. To this end he has fought; and in the contest of six thousand years, only two minds have controlled. Men who have not accepted Christ have been enrolled in the army of the enemy. The life history of Satan is sad beyond measure. It is the record of one who took a position for self, for false hood, and for tyranny. In the whole course of its progress, it has been a succession of defeats. Seeming victory for a time, was but the herald of a more overwhelming rebuff, when the end was known. In wisdom, the arch enemy excelled all in the universe, except the Father and the Son; in beauty, he outshone the angelic hosts; in power, he stood next to Christ. He is thus described by inspiration: "Thou sealest up the sum, full of wisdom, and perfect in beauty . . . every precious stone was thy covering. . . . Thou art the anointed cherub that covereth; and I have set thee so: thou wast upon the holy mountain of God; thou hast walked up and down in the midst of the stones of fire. Thou wast perfect in thy ways from the day that thou wast created, till iniquity was found in thee."

Then from this exalted place as covering cherub, whose wings overspread the throne, and through whom the eternal glory shone, he fell through pride. "Thine heart was lifted up because of thy beauty, thou hast corrupted thy wisdom by reason of thy brightness." Jealous of Christ, the only one united with the Father in the councils of heaven, Satan raised rebellion. This was the beginning of self-exaltation, and all iniquity has since flowed from this fountain head. "There was war in heaven: Michael and His angels fought against the dragon; and the dragon fought and his angels, and prevailed not." This was the first defeat, the first step toward his complete destruction. He left his position by the throne to set up a rival government. Satan and his angels were cast out of heaven. "Neither was their place found any more in

Eze. 28:17.

Thus saith the Lord God; Because thine heart is lifted up, and thou hast said, I am a God, I sit in the seat of God, in the midst of the seas. Eze. 28:2.

Ye are of your father the devil, and the lusts of your father ye will do. He was a murderer from the beginning, and abode not in the truth, because there is no truth in him. When he speaketh a lie, he speaketh of his own: for he is a liar, and the father of it. John 8:44.

Thus saith the Lord God; Thou sealest up the sum, full of wisdom, and perfect in beauty. Eze. 28:12.

FIRST FALL OF SATAN.

Eze. 28:15. Was perfect when created.

Eze. 28:12. Full of wisdom.

Eze. 28:12. Perfect in beauty.

Eze. 28:14. Covering cherub.

Eze. 28:17. He first became proud of his beauty.

Eze. 28:17. His pride ruined his wisdom.

Isa. 14:13. He coveted a higher position.

Isa. 14:14. Coveted the throne of God.

Rev. 12:7. Other angels were affected by his course.

Rev. 12:7. Christ and the loyal angels fought against Satan and his angels.

Rev. 12:8. Satan was defeated.

Isa. 14:12. Satan cast out of heaven.

Rev. 12:9. His angels were cast out with him.

Rev. 12:9. They were cast to this earth.

Gen. 3:1–6. He caused our first parents to sin.

Rom. 6:16. Gained Adam's dominion.

Eph. 2:2. Prince of the power of the air.

John 14:30. The Saviour called him the prince of this world.

Pride goeth before destruction, and a haughty spirit before a fall. Prov. 16 : 18.

Now the serpent was more subtile than any beast of the field which the Lord God had made. And he said unto the woman, Yea, hath God said, Ye shall not eat of every tree of the garden? Gen. 3 : 1.

SECOND FALL OF SATAN.

1 Kings 22 : 19–22. Although Satan and his angels had been cast from heaven, they still could appear in the councils of the Lord at the gate of heaven.

Job 1 : 6. Satan met with the sons of God.

Luke 3 : 38. Adam as prince of this earth was called a "son of God."

2 Pet. 2 : 19. Satan usurped Adam's position.

Job 1 : 7. He represented the earth in the council.

Job 1 : 9, 10. He accused God of being arbitrary.

Job 1 : 12–22. When given power he only destroyed.

John 14 : 30. Satan has no part in Christ. He was a son of Adam but never sinned.

John 12 : 31–33. Christ said His death would judge Satan.

John 12 : 31. Christ's death cast Satan out of his place.

Luke 10 : 18. He fell as lightning from heaven.

Rev. 2 : 10. A shout rang through heaven when the accused was cast out.

2 Pet. 2 : 19. Christ overcame Satan, and is now the representative of this world.

Heb. 2 : 17. Instead of an accuser now at the gate of heaven, we have a merciful High Priest.

Heb. 4 : 14–16. One who loves to be merciful to us.

As Moses lifted up the serpent in the wilderness, even so must the Son of man be lifted up:

That whosoever believeth in him should not perish, but have eternal life. John 3 : 14, 15.

heaven." This was the first casting down of Lucifer.

Cast out from the presence of God, Satan was allowed to make the earth the seat of his power, that God might vindicate His law and His government in the sight of all the universe. The devil, therefore, became the prince of the earth and the air, and as the prince of the earth, he met with the representatives of other worlds before the gate of heaven. Year after year, he stood in that assembly as the accuser of Christ and the brethren. He still basely accused God of injustice, and laid upon Him the blame of the rebellion. On earth, he was exerting every effort to establish a government that would not be overthrown; in the council, he was striving to prove that his lack of success was due to interference with his plans by the God of heaven.

In the fullness of time, the Prince of Peace came to the earth. In the heart of the government of the enemy He lived a sinless life. The will of God was done by Him as it is constantly done in heaven. But the sinless One was slain: the cross was the reward of virtue, when Satan meted out the judgment. Unfallen worlds watched and wondered; and as Christ hung upon the cross, the assembly at the gate of heaven decided that Satan should no longer enter there. "It is finished," the Saviour cried, as His gaze pierced the gloom. "Now is the judgment of this world: now shall the prince of this world be cast out"; and seeing the triumph of the cross, He said, "I, if I be lifted up from the earth, will draw all unto Me." "And I heard a loud voice saying in heaven,

Now is come salvation, and strength, and the kingdom of our God, and the power of His Christ: for the accuser of our brethren is cast down, which accused them before our God day and night. And they overcame him by the blood of the Lamb." Thus Satan, at the crucifixion, was shut out of the council of worlds. Christ said, "I beheld Satan as lightning fall from heaven." This was his second casting down.

He said unto them, I beheld Satan as lightning fall from heaven. Luke 10:18.

The blood of Jesus Christ his Son cleanseth us from all sin. 1 John 1:7.

Since the resurrection of Christ, Satan, knowing that his time for work was short, has put forth all his strength in gaining subjects for his kingdom. He goes about to-day as a roaring lion, seeking whom he may devour. The kingdoms of the earth are becoming more and more under his power. The churches, once controlled by the Spirit of God, now render allegiance to the prince of this world. A miracle working power is abroad in the earth, deceiving, if possible, the very elect. The little company who preserve the knowledge of God in the earth, are hunted and persecuted on all sides; but finally the Saviour will appear to take these to the city which He is now preparing for them. The wicked are slain by the brightness of His coming, and are scattered over the face of the earth,—a feast for birds of prey; or are swallowed up in the mighty earthquakes. The earth, broken and torn by the reelings to and fro in the seventh plague, is dark and dismal. It is with-

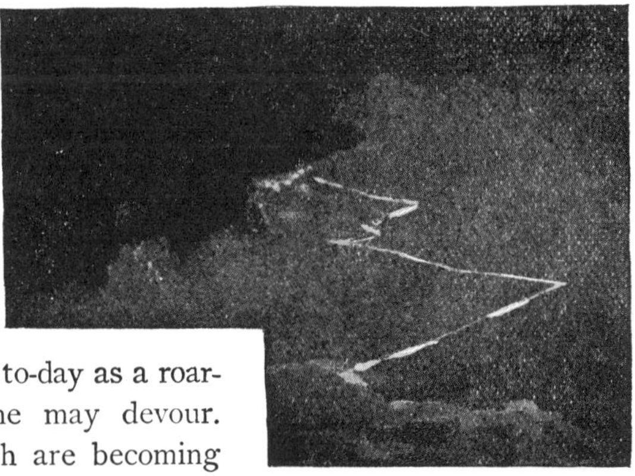

**I beheld Satan as lightning fall from heaven.**

For we can do nothing against the truth, but for the truth. 2 Cor. 13:8.

Who did no sin, neither was guile found in his mouth. 1 Pet. 2:22.

Him, being delivered by the determinate counsel and foreknowledge of God, ye have taken, and by wicked hands have crucified and slain. Acts 2:23.

The God of our fathers raised up Jesus, whom ye slew and hanged on a tree. Acts 5:30.

And they shall be gathered together, as prisoners are gathered in the pit, and shall be shut up in the prison, and after many days shall they be visited. Isa. 24:21, 22.

*And I saw an angel come down from heaven, having the key of the bottomless pit and a great chain in his hand.*

*And he laid hold on the dragon, that old serpent, which is the Devil, and Satan, and bound him a thousand years,*

*And cast him into the bottomless pit, and shut him up, and set a seal upon him, that he should deceive the nations no more, till the thousand years should be fulfilled: and after that he must be loosed a little season. Rev. 20:1-3.*

THIRD FALL OF SATAN.

Rev. 20:1-3. It does not take Christ or a host of angels to overcome Satan now, one angel can bind him.

Rev. 20:3. He is confined to his own territory.

Jer. 4:23-26, Isa. 24:19-21. Sin has made the earth a dark abyss.

1 Thess. 4:16, 17. The righteous are in heaven.

Jer. 25:31-33. The wicked are all dead.

Rev. 20:3. Satan is alone with the evil angels for one thousand years.

Rev. 20:5. The wicked live again at the end of the thousand years.

Rev. 20:7. This gives Satan work and he is said to be "loosed."

Rev. 20:8. He deceives the wicked.

Rev. 20:9. As they gather for battle they are all destroyed.

Heb. 2:14. Christ died to destroy Satan.

Rev. 20:10. As long as Satan lives in the fire he suffers torment.

Eze. 28:18, 19. Satan becomes ashes upon the earth in the sight of all the righteous.

Mal. 4:1-3. Ashes on the new earth is all that remains of Satan and sinners.

out form, and void, and darkness is upon the face of the deep, as before God spake forth the creation of light. It is chaos, the bottomless pit, or the abyss of Rotherham's translation. "And I saw a messenger coming down out of the heavens; having the key of the abyss, and a great chain over his hand. And he seized the dragon, the ancient serpent, which is Adversary and Satan, and bound him for a thousand years, and hurled him into the abyss, and fastened and sealed [it] up above him, that he might not deceive any longer the nations." He is cast into the abyss, and it is sealed above him; so for one thousand years, Satan is confined to the earth. He no longer has liberty to visit other worlds; but alone on the earth, from which all life is gone; alone with his own thoughts, he has time to contemplate the record of the past six thousand years of rebellion against the throne of God. He is no longer the beautiful covering cherub, the leader of the angel choir, the sweet singer of heaven, sealing up the sum full of wisdom and beauty. The glory has faded, and the countenance, once lighted with the love of God, now betrays the scheming wickedness of six thousand years of crime. This is the third casting out of Satan. At the end of the thousand years, "he must be loosed a little season"; and then comes the final destruction, the blotting out of the last trace of sin.

The question sometimes arises, "What will take place during the thousand years between the binding of Satan and his being loosed for a little season?" To John was revealed the event which would take place during that time.

"I saw the souls of them that were beheaded

Satan on the desolate earth.

for the witness of Jesus, and for the Word of God, and which had not worshiped the beast, neither his image . . . and they lived and reigned with Christ a thousand years. But the rest of the dead lived not again until the thousand years were finished. This is the first resurrection." When Christ appears on the white cloud, "He shall send His angels with a great sound of a trumpet, and they shall gather together His elect from the four winds, from one end of heaven to the other." Paul saw the same scene, and thus describes it: "The Lord Himself shall descend from heaven with a shout, with the voice of the archangel, and with the trump of God: and the dead in Christ shall rise first: then we which are alive and remain shall be caught up together with them in the clouds, to meet the Lord in the air: and so shall we ever be with the Lord." This is the first resurrection, when the righteous dead will come forth at the sound of the voice of Christ, and with the living righteous, meet the Lord in the air. "Blessed and holy is he that hath part in the first resurrection. . . . They shall be priests of God and of Christ, and shall reign with Him a thousand years."

"And I saw thrones, and they sat upon them, and judgment was given unto them." During the thousand years, the saints live in the New Jerusalem, the city of God; and as priests of God and of Christ, they sit in judgment on the cases of the wicked. "Do ye not know," wrote Paul to the Corinthians, "that the saints shall judge the world? . . . Know ye not that we shall judge angels?" Peter had this judicial work in mind when he wrote that "God

*And I saw thrones, and they sat upon them, and judgment was given unto them: and I saw the souls of them that were beheaded for the witness of Jesus, and for the word of God, and which had not worshipped the beast, neither his image, neither had received his mark upon their foreheads, or in their hands; and they lived and reigned with Christ a thousand years. Rev. 20:4.*

Matt. 24:31.

Gather my saints together unto me; those that have made a covenant with me by sacrifice. Psa. 50:5.

The Lord shall roar from on high, and utter his voice from his holy habitation; he shall mightily roar upon his habitation; he shall give a shout, as they that tread the grapes, against all the inhabitants of the earth. Jer. 25:30.

1 Thess. 4:16, 17.

Marvel not at this: for the hour is coming, in the which all that are in the graves shall hear his voice,

And shall come forth; they that have done good, unto the resurrection of life; and they that have done evil, unto the resurrection of damnation. John 5:28, 29.

Rev. 20:6.

Do ye not know that the saints shall judge the world? and if the world shall be judged by you, are ye unworthy to judge the smallest matters?

Know ye not that we shall judge angels? how much more things that pertain to this life? 1 Cor. 6:2, 3.

For if God spared not the angels that sinned, but cast them down to hell, and delivered them into chains of darkness, to be reserved unto judgment. 2 Pet. 2:4.

Jude 6.

spared not the angels that sinned, but cast them down to hell, and delivered them into chains of darkness, to be reserved unto judgment."

While the world has been making history, heaven has been keeping the records. "For God shall bring every work into judgment, with every secret thing, whether it be good, or whether it be evil." "Be not deceived; God is not mocked: for whatsoever a man soweth, that shall he also reap."

"But I say unto you," said Christ, "That every idle word that men shall speak, they shall give account thereof in the day of judgment. For by thy words thou shalt be justified, and by thy words thou shalt be condemned." During the life of each individual, angels are recording the thoughts and the acts. These things are placed in a book, called by Malachi, the "Book of Remembrance." This is the daybook of heaven, and in it are recorded not only the words and deeds, but the circumstances and motives which prompted the acts. The place in which a man is born is put on record as of importance in meting out justice. "Jehovah will relate in the records of the peoples: [that] This One was born there." "I will mention Egypt and Babylon among those who acknowledge Me. Behold, O Philistia, and Tyre, together with Cush, This one shall be born there." (Spurrell.) David prays, "Recount Thou my griefs! Put my tears into Thy bottle! Are they not recorded in Thy book?" (Spurrell.) Every heartache caused by sin or oppression, every longing for a higher spirituality, a closer walk with God,—these are all written in this Book of Remembrance, in which are no false entries, for the records are divine.

Also now, behold, my witness is in heaven, and my record is on high. Job 16:19.

For though thou wash thee with nitre, and take thee much sope, yet thine iniquity is marked before me, saith the Lord God. Jer. 2:22.

Eccl. 12:14.
Gal. 6:7.
Matt. 12:36, 37.

Suffer not thy mouth to cause thy flesh to sin; neither say thou before the angel, that it was an error: wherefore should God be angry at thy voice, and destroy the work of thine hands? Eccl. 5:6.

Then they that feared the Lord spake often one to another: and the Lord hearkened, and heard it, and a book of remembrance was written before him for them that feared the Lord, and that thought upon his name. Mal. 3:16.

Psa. 84:4, 6.
Psa. 56:8.

For the Lord's portion is his people; Jacob is the lot of his inheritance.
He found him in a desert land, and in the waste howling wilderness; he led him about, he instructed him, he kept him as the apple of his eye.
As an eagle stirreth up her nest, fluttereth over her young, spreadeth abroad her wings, taketh them, beareth them on her wings:
So the Lord alone did lead him, and there was no strange god with him. Deut. 32:9-12.

"I have spread out My hands all the day unto a rebellious people, which walketh in a way that was not good. . . . Behold, it is written before Me. . . . Therefore will I measure their former work into their bosom."

Isa. 65 : 2, 6, 7.

These are some of the things which are written over against our names in the daily records of heaven All nature teaches the same lesson. There is a record kept in heaven; and there is an account just as accurate, kept in the body of

A naughty person, a wicked man, walketh with a froward mouth.
He winketh with his eyes, he speaketh with his feet, he teacheth with his fingers;
Frowardness is in his heart, he deviseth mischief continually; he soweth discord. Prov. 6 : 12-14.

Rev. 20 : 12.

The judgment was set, and the books were opened. Dan. 7 : 10.

**There is a record kept in heaven.**

I saw the dead, small and great, stand before God; and the books were opened: and another book was opened, which is the book of life; and the dead were judged out of those things which were written in the books according to their works. Rev. 20 : 12.

each individual. The acts of each day shape the character, shape the vessel which contains the spirit, as truly as the clay is shaped on the wheel in the hands of the potter. The facial expression, the language, the gestures, every thing about a person, can be read as an open book, by the keen eye of Jehovah; and this life record which each man carries with him to the time of death, is as true as the one in heaven. The two will exactly correspond in the day of judgment, when the books are opened, and the dead small and great stand before God. Man may deceive his fellow man as to his character,

The shew of their countenance doth witness against them; and they declare their sin as Sodom, they hide it not. Woe unto their soul! for they have rewarded evil unto themselves. Isa. 3 : 9.

Thou hast filled me with wrinkles, which is a witness against me: and my leanness rising up in me beareth witness to my face. Job 16 : 8.

Jer. 18 : 4-6.

He that hideth hatred with lying lips, and he that uttereth a slander, is a fool. Prov. 10 : 18.

I will praise thee; for I am fearfully and wonderfully made: marvellous are thy works; and that my soul knoweth right well.

My substance was not hid from thee, when I was made in secret, and curiously wrought in the lowest parts of the earth.

Thine eyes did see my substance, yet being unperfect; and in thy book all my members were written, which in continuance were fashioned, when as yet there was none of them. Psa. 139:14-16.

Now, lo, if he beget a son, that seeth all his fathers sins which he hath done, and considereth, and doeth not such like,

That hath not eaten upon the mountains, neither hath lifted up his eyes to the idols of the house of Israel, hath not defiled his neighbor's wife,

Neither hath oppressed any, hath not withholden the pledge, neither hath spoiled by violence, but hath given his bread to the hungry, and hath covered the naked with a garment,

That hath taken off his hand from the poor, that hath not received usury nor increase, hath executed my judgments, hath walked in my statutes; he shall not die for the iniquity of his father, he shall surely live. Eze. 18:14-17.

I entreat thee also, true yokefellow, help those women which laboured with me in the gospel, with Clement also, and with other my fellowlabourers, whose names are in the book of life. Phil. 4:3.

Luke 10:20.

The Lord said unto Moses, Whosoever hath sinned against me, him will I blot out of my book. Ex. 32:33.

When a righteous man turneth away from his righteousness, and committeth iniquity, and dieth in them; for his iniquity that he hath done shall he die. Eze. 18:26.

Gal. 6:7, 8.

but this is only because of his brother's inability to read. Every page is unwritten at birth; but with the first breath, the recording angel begins to write. If only one life were effected by the acts of to-day, they might be lightly passed; but our daily thoughts and deeds are reproduced tomorrow in a new generation. God, seeing the influence of heredity, passes judgment upon the one who is truly to blame. In earthly tribunals, many a man suffers for the crimes of his ancestors. In the final judgment, this will not be so; for the Book of Remembrance is the record of an infinite Being. He sees the end from the beginning, and knoweth our thoughts from afar off.

Besides the Book of Remembrance there is the Book of Life. This is referred to many times in the Scriptures. On its pages, appear the names of all who have ever professed the name of Christ; all who have reached heavenward for help. The Saviour gently rebuked His disciples when they gloried over the success which attended their first missionary trip, and said, "Rather rejoice because your names are written in heaven." Those who remain true to God have their names retained in the Lamb's Book of Life; and the good deeds from the Book of Remembrance are written opposite these names. Those who grow weary, and turn away from the Lord, have their names blotted out of the Book of Life; and at the same time, the record in the Book of Remembrance, shows only the sins they have committed. When a name is enrolled in the Book of Life, the name of Christ is taken, and by faith the works of Christ are imputed to the believer. When man forsakes Christ, there is no record of good deeds, for without Him we can do nothing; and the page is soon filled with a record of pride, selfishness, and all the works of the flesh. "For he that soweth to his flesh shall of the flesh reap corruption."

On the other hand, when a soul repents, it matters not what the past record of sin may have been, his name is entered on the pages of the Book of Life; those sins are covered by the blood of Christ, and are finally blotted out. "Repent ye therefore, and be converted, that your sins may be blotted out, when the times of refreshing shall come from the presence of the Lord."

The third book is the Book of Death, and in it are the names of those who might have had life, but who chose death. Over against each name, is the list of sins, to which flesh is heir when it stands to battle with the world and the devil, without the aid of Christ. "For though thou wash thee with nitre, and take thee much soap, yet thine iniquity is marked before Me, saith the Lord God." This Book of Death is referred to when Hosea says: "The iniquity of Ephriam is bound up; his sin is hid." And Job said: "My transgression is sealed up in a bag, and Thou sewest up mine iniquity."

These three books,—the Book of Life of the Lamb, the Book of Remembrance, and the Book of Death are often referred to by the inspired writer. When the investigative judgment began in 1844, the Book of Life was opened; and before the Father, Christ pleaded His own blood for every name for which pardon was written. The Book of Remembrance told of sins committed by these, but Christ's righteousness was

THE THREE BOOKS OF JUDGMENT.

I. BOOK OF REMEMBRANCE.

Mal. 3:16. Records every word.

Matt. 12:36, 37. Idle words.

Psa. 56:8. Tears of repentance.

Psa. 87:4-6. Birthplace and environments.

Eccl. 12:13, 14. Every secret act.

1 Cor. 4:5. Counsels of the heart.

II. BOOK OF LIFE.

Luke 10:20. Names written in heaven.

Luke 10:19, 20. To be enrolled in the book of life is the highest honor given mortals.

Phil. 4:3. Names of faithful workers recorded.

Ex. 32:33. The names of those that cling to sin will be removed.

Rev. 3:5. Names of the faithful retained.

Rev. 13:8; 17:8. Wicked are not recorded.

Rev. 20:15. None will be saved whose names are not recorded in the book of life.

Isa. 4:3 [margin.]

Psa. 69:28; Eze. 13:9.

Heb. 12:23; Dan. 12:1.

III. BOOK OF DEATH.

Jer. 17:13. Those that forsake God are written in the earth.

Jer. 2:22. Sins all recorded.

Job. 14:17. Sins sealed up.

Deut. 32:32-36. The sins of the wicked are all "laid up in store' until the day of punishment.

Hos. 13:12. Sin bound up.

When he hath made an end of reconciling the holy place, and the tabernacle of the congregation, and the altar, he shall bring the live goat:

And Aaron shall lay both his hands upon the head of the live goat, and confess over him all the iniquities of the children of Israel, and all their transgressions in all their sins, putting them upon the head of the goat, and shall send him away by the hand of a fit man into the wilderness:

And the goat shall bear upon him all their iniquities unto a land not inhabited: and he shall let go the goat in the wilderness.

Lev. 16:20-22.

His mischief shall return upon his own head, and his violent dealing shall come down upon his own pate. Psa. 7:16.

*But the rest of the dead lived not again until the thousand years were finished. This is the first resurrection.*

*Blessed and holy is he that hath part in the first resurrection: on such the second death hath no power, but they shall be priests of God and of Christ, and shall reign with him a thousand years.*

*And when the thousand years are expired, Satan shall be loosed out of his prison. Rev. 20:5-7.*

Rev. 20:6, 7.

Thy dead men shall live, together with my dead body shall they arise. Awake and sing, ye that dwell in dust: for thy dew is as the dew of herbs, and the earth shall cast out the dead. Isa. 26:19.

a covering, and the sins were transferred to Satan's account in the Book of Death. This was the work of Christ in the most holy place of the temple in heaven. It was typified by the work of the high priest in the earthly sanctuary on the day of atonement. On that day the priest came out of the sanctuary, and laid his hand on the head of the scapegoat, in the outer court and confessed the sins of the people upon its head, in type transferring them to the goat, which was then led into the wilderness by the hand of a "man of opportunity" This represented the work brought to view in the twentieth chapter of Revelation. When Christ finishes His work in the temple, the sins of Israel will all be laid upon Satan; and during the thousand years on the earth, alone and desolate, the sins which he tempted the redeemed to commit, will rest heavily on his heart. His name heads the list in that Book of Death, and it is followed by the multitudes innumerable as the sands by the seaside who have chosen him as leader. During the thousand years the righteous reign with Christ, and with Him, go through the Book of Death, awarding punishment to those whose names are written there.

"Blessed and holy is he that hath part in the first resurrection: on such the second death hath no power. . . . And when the thousand years are expired, Satan shall be loosed out of his prison."

At the voice of God, the earth gave up the dead, who have long slept in her bosom. "The sea gave up the dead which were in it; and death and the grave delivered up the dead which were in them." They rise to see the holy city come down from God out of heaven. The Mount of Olives cleaves asunder and the city with all its inhabitants rests there,— the wicked behold the reward of the righteous. Then Satan marshals the hosts of the wicked who have been resurrected, and inspires in them a hope that the city of God can be taken. His army is innumerable; it is composed of men from all ages,—giant intellects, heroes and the great men of earth, kings, rulers, and mighty men of wealth, come forth from their graves with the same selfish ambitions with which life closed. These, the number of whom is as the sands of the sea, are perfectly organized and thoroughly drilled. In battle array, they march over the broken surface of the earth, toward the holy city, which stands beautiful and glorified. As the hosts approach the holy city, with its glittering foundations and gates of pearl, shrouded in the light of its King, the gates are closed, and on a great white throne, high and lifted up above the city walls, in full view of the unnumbered hosts, sits the King of Kings, holding aloft the law of God. Those in harmony with this foundation truth are within the city. Those who have rejected this, and chosen the leadership of Satan are without. For a brief time the wicked behold the glories which they have lost. Christ is seen in all His beauty. The story of redeeming love from the fall to the end, revealed by the cross, flashes vividly before every mind. "His horn shall be exalted with honor. The wicked shall see it, and be grieved; he shall gnash with his teeth, and melt away: the desire of the wicked shall perish." "There shall be weeping and gnashing of teeth,

I will set my glory among the heathen, and all the heathen shall see my judgment that I have executed, and my hand that I have laid upon them. Eze. 39:21.

His feet shall stand in that day upon the mount of Olives, which is before Jerusalem on the east, and the mount of Olives shall cleave in the midst thereof toward the east and toward the west, and there shall be a very great valley; and half of the mountain shall remove toward the north, and half of it toward the south. Zech. 14:4.

For, lo, thine enemies make a tumult: and they that hate thee have lifted up the head.

They have taken crafty counsel against thy people, and consulted against thy hidden ones.

They have said, Come, and let us cut them off from being a nation; that the name of Israel may be no more in remembrance.

For they have consulted together with one consent: they are confederate against thee. Psa. 83:2-5.

*And shall go out to deceive the nations which are in the four quarters of the earth, Gog and Magog, to gather them together to battle: the number of whom is as the sand of the sea.*

*And they went up on the breadth of the earth, and compassed the camp of the saints about, and the beloved city. Rev. 20:8, 9.*

I saw a great white throne, and him that sat on it, from whose face the earth and the heaven fled away. Rev. 20:11.

The Lord hath made known his salvation: his righteousness hath he openly shewed in the sight of the heathen. Psa. 98:2.

The heavens declare his righteousness, and all the people see his glory. Psa. 97:6.

Thine eyes shall see the king in his beauty: they shall behold the land that is very far off. Isa. 33:17.

when ye shall see Abraham, and Isaac, and Jacob, and all the prophets in the kingdom of God, and ye yourselves thrust out." Christ is exalted in the presence of that host; every knee is bent before Him, and every soul in that multitude, of the condemned, renders praise to Jehovah. Satan himself is obliged to witness to the triumph of truth in the Son of God. The righteous, within the city, who have looked into the life records of those without the walls, see, as this host marches in battle array, that the spirit of destruction still possesses their hearts, and they acknowledge that the judgments of God are true and righteous altogether.

He shall snatch on the right hand, and be hungry; and he shall eat on the left hand, and they shall not be satisfied: they shall eat every man the flesh of his own arm:

Manasseh, Ephraim; and Ephraim, Manasseh: and they together shall be against Judah. For all this his anger is not turned away, but his hand is stretched out still.

Isa. 9:20, 21.

Wherefore God also hath highly exalted him, and given him a name which is above every name:

That at the name of Jesus every knee should bow, of things in heaven, and things in earth, and things under the earth;

And that every tongue should confess that Jesus Christ is Lord, to the glory of God the Father.

Phil. 2:9-11.

**The ark in the flood.**

Then from His throne, God breathes upon the assembled multitudes. Fire comes down from God out of heaven, and mingles with the fire which comes from the interior of the earth; and it devours them. "The devil that deceived them [the nations] was cast into the lake of fire and brimstone, where the beast and the false prophet are." "And death and hell were cast into the lake of fire. . . . And whosoever was not found written in the Book of Life was cast into the lake of fire." This is the second death. Here, the words of the Psalmist are fulfilled: "The righteous shall be recompensed in the earth: much more the wicked and the sinner." The city of God, like the ark in the flood, rides safely on the billows of flame. The elements melt with fervent heat, and the earth, with all its works is burned up. The

*And fire came down from God out of heaven, and devoured them.*

*And the devil that deceived them was cast into the lake of fire and brimstone, where the beast and the false prophet are, and shall be tormented day and night for ever and ever.*

*And I saw a great white throne, and him that sat on it, from whose face the earth and the heaven fled away; and there was found no place for them.*

*And I saw the dead, small and great, stand before God; and the books were opened: and another book was opened, which is the*

wicked become ashes under the soles of the feet of the righteous. The last act in the shadowy service of the tabernacle,—the placing of the ashes of the bullock in a clean place,—has met its antitype. The earth is cleansed by fire; sin, and all its blasting effects are destroyed. The controversy is at an end. The enemy of truth, together with all who have championed his cause, is forever blotted out of existence: the earth is ready to be renewed by the presence of God, and repeopled by those who have been snatched by the love of Christ from the ruin which threatened to engulf the race. The struggle was a terrible one; the victory was dearly bought, but looking upon the company, gathered about the throne, Christ sees the travail of His soul and is satisfied.

*book of life: and the dead were judged out of those things which were written in the books, according to their works.*

*And the sea gave up the dead which were in it; and death and hell delivered up the dead which were in them: and they were judged every man according to their works.*

*And death and hell were cast into the lake of fire. This is the second death.*

*And whosoever was not found written in the book of life was cast into the lake of fire.*

*Rev. 20:9-15.*

What do ye imagine against the Lord? he will make an utter end: affliction shall not rise up the second time. Nah. 1:9.

He shall see of the travail of his soul, and shall be satisfied: by his knowledge shall my righteous servant justify many; for he shall bear their iniquities. Isa. 53:11.

# CHAPTER XXII.

## THE GLORIES OF THE NEW JERUSALEM.

**"In the beginning God created the heaven and the earth."**

WHERE wast thou when I laid the basis of the earth?
Declare: if thou art acquainted with understanding.
Who planned her measurement, if thou knowest?
Or who stretched forth the measuring line upon her?
Into what were her sockets sunk?
Or who laid her key-stone,
While the morning stars exulted together,
And all the sons of God shouted for joy?
Or who enclosed the sea within doors
When it burst forth as if issuing from the womb?
When I used the clouds for its vesture,
And thick darkness for its swathing band?
When My decree brake silence over it,
When I established its bars and its doors;
When I said: Thus far shalt thou come, but no further,
And here appoint I the boundary of thy tossing wave?

*Spurrell's translation of Job 38:4–12.*

In the beginning, when all things in the universe perfectly obeyed the divine law; when worlds performed their revolutions throughout space in perfect unison, and in the universe of God there was not one note of discord, then He spake, and our world came into existence; He commanded and it stood forth, and a shout rang from the sons of God; for they saw another work of His hands. Man upon it was as truly in harmony with the law of God as nature itself; and God pronounced all things very good. In innocency man was placed here in a home prepared of God, and there was but one thing for him to accomplish,—this was strength of character, which would link humanity and divinity into one. With the fall of man, a cloud rested on the face of the whole earth: the first glory was shrouded, and the world itself, was, at the time of the flood, turned out of its course. At creation, the waters filled the earth and there were no rains; but the ground was watered from beneath, by a mist which arose. At the flood, the fountains of the great deep were broken up, and the waters poured forth in great streams. Since that time, a large portion of the surface of our world, has been covered with vast seas. This was not so in the beginning. When sin filled the earth, God destroyed Sodom and Gomorrah by fire from heaven. Those two cities in the plain of the Jordan were destroyed for an object lesson of the destruction of the earth; and since that time, there has been fire within the earth,—the elements of its own destruction, pent up, awaiting the command of Jehovah, to perform their appointed work. At the end of the thousand years, fire will destroy the

By the word of the Lord were the heavens made; and all the host of them by the breath of his mouth.

He gathereth the waters of the sea together as an heap: he layeth up the depth in storehouses.

Let all the earth fear the Lord: let all the inhabitants of the world stand in awe of him.

For he spake, and it was done; he commanded, and it stood fast.
Psa. 33:6–9.

Gen. 1:31.

The Lord God commanded the man, saying, Of every tree of the garden thou mayest freely eat:

But of the tree of the knowledge of good and evil, thou shalt not eat of it: for in the day that thou eatest thereof thou shalt surely die.
Gen. 2:16, 17.

There went up a mist from the earth, and watered the whole face of the ground. Gen. 2:6.

Psa. 82:5.
Job. 9:5.

Hast thou marked the old way which wicked men have trodden?

Which were cut down out of time, whose foundation was overflown with a flood.
Job 22:15, 16.

Gen. 7:11.

Even as Sodom and Gomorrha, and the cites about them in like manner, giving themselves over to fornication, and going after strange flesh, are set forth for an example, suffering the vengeance of eternal fire. Jude 7.

Gen. 19:24, 25.
Deut. 32:22.

The heavens and the earth, which are now, by the same word are kept in store, reserved unto fire against the day of judgment and perdition of ungodly men. 2 Pet. 3:7.

*And I saw a new heaven and a new earth: for the first heaven and the first earth were passed away; and there was no more sea. And I John saw the holy city, new Jerusalem, coming down from God out of heaven, prepared as a bride adorned for her husband.* Rev. 21:1, 2.

earth together with the wicked. "And I saw a new heaven and a new earth: for the first heaven and the first earth were passed away; and there was no more sea." Through the open heavens, Christ and the saints beheld the "New Jerusalem, coming down from God out of heaven, prepared as a bride adorned for her husband." Jerusalem is a name interwoven with all the history of the chosen people from the days of the establishment of the nation in the land of Palestine. The name means "possession of peace;" and when the heathen were driven from its strongholds, and it became the capital of the Jewish nation, the promise was given that should Israel adhere to the commandments of God, Jerusalem would become an everlasting city. But the conditions were unheeded, and that city, which in the days of Solomon, was raised to the highest pinnacle of fame as the capital of the world, has been degraded, desecrated and burned, until to-day the very ground about it seems unable to support life; and the city itself is in the hands of the Mohammedans, the smoke of the bottomless pit. Here the Prince of heaven was crucified; here, on the site of the cross, He will at last erect His throne.

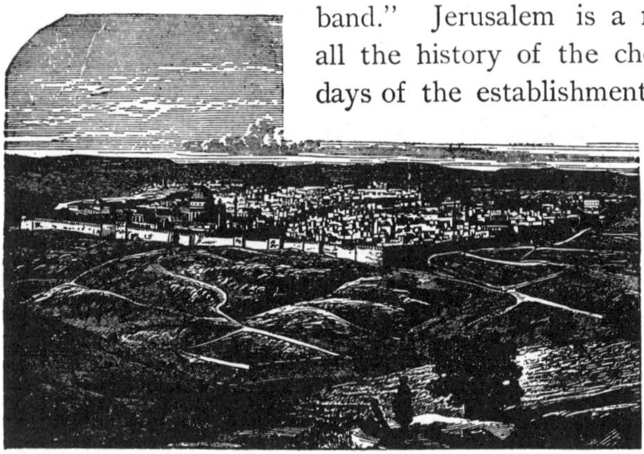

**Jerusalem.**

JERUSALEM.

Josh. 15:8. The ancient Jebusi or Jebus.

Josh. 10:5-23. King slain by Joshua.

Josh. 18:28. Allotted to Benjamin.

Judges 1:21. Never conquered by Benjamin.

2 Sam. 5:6-8. Conquered by David.

2 Sam. 5:9. Made the royal city.

2 Chron. 6:6. Specially chosen by God.

Jer. 17:20-25. God promised if they hallowed the Sabbath, Jerusalem would remain forever.

Jer. 17:27. Destruction threatened if they broke the Sabbath.

Jer. 39:1-8. Destroyed by Nebuchadnezzar.

Lev. 25:2-4. God had commanded that the land should rest every seventh year.

If the plan of God had been followed, the Garden of Eden would have become the center of the city of God. That plan failed; and the

Jews had the privilege of making their city the house of Jehovah. They failed, and Christ ascended to heaven, there, to prepare a city, the New Jerusalem, as the capital of the universal kingdom. The New Jerusalem will be located on the precise spot where the city once stood. The Mount of Olives parts asunder, one half moving to the north, and one half to the south; and on the great plain between the peaks, the capital of the new earth will rest. Christ's mission to the earth was to save that which was lost. Sin robbed man of the beauties of Eden; sin defeated the plans for the Jews; and what man might have done, but did not do because of evil, Christ does through the power of His love. In spite of the delay caused by sin, the final triumph will be greater than it could have been, had sin never entered the world. Such is the infinite depth of redeeming love.

The story of Jerusalem is salvation's story; and throughout eternity, that glorious home of the saved, will tell to every saint who enters there, and will proclaim to all the universe, the cross of Christ and life through Him. When the city descends as a bride adorned for her husband, the redeemed receive it with shouts of triumph, and Christ receives it as the trophy of His struggles. Christ and His followers enter the city, and there is spread for them the marriage feast of the Lamb.

From heaven the voice of Jehovah proclaims: "Behold, the tabernacle of God is with men, and He will dwell with them, and they shall be His people, and God Himself shall be with them." In Christ the God-man, Jehovah tabernacled. His name was Emmanuel, which means

Lev. 26:33-35. God had warned them that if they did not let the land rest every seventh year He would take them out of it.

2 Chron. 36:21. They sinned, and the Lord let the land keep her Sabbaths for seventy years, which would cover four hundred and ninety years they had neglected letting the land keep Sabbath.

Neh. 13:17, 18. Breaking the weekly Sabbath of the Lord led to the neglect of the Sabbath for the land.

Jer. 17:25. God designed Jerusalem would remain forever.

Rom. 8:3. The sins of man destroyed the city. Christ came to give back what was lost.

Heb. 11:16. Man failed to keep Jerusalem, so Christ has prepared a city for him.

Gal. 4:26. This city is in heaven.

Rev. 21:1, 2. It will come to the new earth. It is called the New Jerusalem.

Zech. 14:4. The new city will occupy the site of the old Jerusalem.

Jer. 17:24, 25. God's original plan that the Sabbath should be hallowed by all who dwelt in Jerusalem will be fulfilled.

Rev. 22:14. Those who enter the new Jerusalem will keep all of the commandments, and in so doing will hallow the Sabbath.

*And I heard a great voice out of heaven saying, Behold, the tabernacle of God is with men, and he will dwell with them, and they shall be his people, and God himself shall be with them, and be their God.* *Rev. 21:3.*

Behold, a virgin shall be with child, and shall bring forth a son, and they shall call his name Emmanuel, which being interpreted is, God with us. Matt. 1:23.

"God with us." In the human form, divinity was veiled by the same cloud which sin cast over the face of Eden; but in the New Jerusalem, the people meet God face to face, with no dividing veil between. From the most exalted position in the kingdom of God to utter destruction; this is the story which sin has written: from death to life immortal; from degredation to the capital of the universe; this is the story of redemption.

What wonder that those who have passed through these experiences sing, "Great and marvelous are Thy works, Lord God Almighty; just and true are Thy ways, Thou King of nations." "Alleluia: for the Lord God omnipotent reigneth!" There is no longer cause for sorrow and weeping; for the former things have passed away. Tears came when sin entered the dominion of God. There were no tears before that; and when the traces of sin are gone, tears will have forever passed away. "Let us be glad and rejoice, and give honor to Him."

Words cannot express the fullness and beauty of the law of compensation which is revealed in the entire history of salvation. This will be partially understood by those who gather in the city, and behold all things made new; those who see Christ as the Alpha,—Him who first created; the Genesis, in which was hidden the fullness of God's love; and the Omega, the final completion, which rising above the fall, and having banished every trace of sin, sits as King of kings, surrounded by subjects who are better able to appreciate the spiritual nature of Jehovah and His kingdom than they could have been, had sin never entered. This is infinite

Where sin abounded, grace did much more abound. Rom. 5:20.

*And God shall wipe away all tears from their eyes; and there shall be no more death, neither sorrow, nor crying, neither shall there be any more pain: for the former things are passed away.*
*Rev. 21:4.*

He will swallow up death in victory; and the Lord God will wipe away tears from off all faces; and the rebuke of his people shall he take away from off all the earth: for the Lord hath spoken it.
Isa. 25:8.

As it is written, Eye hath not seen, nor ear heard, neither have entered into the heart of man, the things which God hath prepared for them that love him. 1 Cor. 2:9.

*And he that sat upon the throne said, Behold, I make all things new. And he said unto me, Write: for these words are true and faithful.*

*And he said unto me, It is done. I am Alpha and Omega, the beginning and the end. I will give unto him that is athirst of the fountain of the water of life freely.*
*Rev. 21:5, 6.*

When all things shall be subdued unto him, then shall the Son also himself be subject unto him that put all things under him, that God may be all in all. 1 Cor. 15:28.

*He that overcometh shall inherit all things; and I will be his God, and he shall be my son.*

*But the fearful, and unbelieving, and the abominable, and murderers, and whoremongers, and sorcerers, and idolaters, and all liars, shall have their part in the lake which burneth with fire and brimstone: which is the second death.*
*Rev. 21:7, 8.*

love, the character of our God and His Christ. And above all, as the most supreme manifestation of that love, is the promise that he that overcometh through Christ, shall inherit all these things. The new earth is not awarded like charity gifts, parceled out to the poor of earth; it is not bought, but men are born into the family of God, and as joint heirs with Jesus Christ, they receive the new earth as an inheritance. Christ spoke to Nicodemus of the new, the spiritual birth, which brings the inheritance. The soul hungering and thirsting in this life opens the springs of heaven, and Christ Himself gives unto those who are athirst of the water of life freely.

If children, then heirs; heirs of God, and joint-heirs with Christ; if so be that we suffer with him, that we may be also glorified together. Rom. 8:17.

John 3:5.

Blessed are they which do hunger and thirst after righteousness: for they shall be filled. Matt. 5:6.

Behold, God is my salvation; I will trust, and not be afraid: for the Lord JEHOVAH is my strength and my song; he also is become my salvation.

Therefore with joy shall ye draw water out of the wells of salvation. Isa. 12:2, 3.

Num. 21:17, 18.

Every well of water has been a token of this promise which will be fulfilled in the new earth. The living fountains there will contain the water of life which will give eternal life and unbounded wisdom. Rivulets flowing from that eternal fountain bring life to the earth to-day, and those who drink now, have a pledge that they shall drink in the kingdom of God. This is the wine of the living grape, typified by the cup given at the Passover table on that last night of the Saviour's life, when He said: "I will drink no more of the fruit of the vine, until that day that I drink it new in the kingdom of God." This new wine will be given to the guests at the marriage supper of the Lamb.

She is a tree of life to them that lay hold upon her: and happy is every one that retaineth her. Prov. 3:18.

If thou knewest the gift of God, and who it is that saith to thee, Give me to drink; thou wouldest have asked of him, and he would have given thee living water. John 4:10.

I am the true vine, and my Father is the husbandman.

Every branch in me that beareth not fruit he taketh away: and every branch that beareth fruit, he purgeth it, that it may bring forth more fruit. John 15:1, 2.

Matt. 26:29.
John 13:1–3.

"Let not your heart be troubled," said the Saviour, and John was one of the number to whom He spoke: "In My Father's house are many mansions: if it were not so, I would have told you. I go to prepare a place for you. And if I go and prepare a place for you, I will

Father, I will that they also, whom thou hast given me, be with me where I am; that they may behold my glory, which thou hast given me: for thou lovedst me before the foundation of the world. John 17:24.

*And there came unto me one of the seven angels which had the seven vials full of the seven last plagues, and talked with me, saying, Come hither, I will shew thee the bride, the Lamb's wife.*

*And he carried me away in the spirit to a great and high mountain, and shewed me that great city, the holy Jerusalem, descending out of heaven from God,*

*Having the glory of God: and her light was like unto a stone most precious, even like a jasper stone, clear as crystal;*

*And had a wall great and high, and had twelve gates, and at the gates twelve angels, and names written thereon, which are the names of the twelve tribes of the children of Israel:*

*On the east three gates; on the north three gates; on the south three gates; and on the west three gates.*

*And the wall of the city had twelve foundations, and in them the names of the twelve apostles of the Lamb.*

*And he that talked with me had a golden reed to measure the city, and the gates thereof, and the wall thereof.*

*And the city lieth foursquare, and the length is as large as the breadth: and he measured the city with the reed, twelve thousand furlongs. The length and the breadth and the height of it are equal.* Rev. 21:9-16.

Surely there is a vein for the silver, and a place for gold where they fine it.

Iron is taken out of the earth, and brass is molten out of the stone.
Job 28:1, 2.

Thou shalt make the breastplate of judgment with cunning work; after the work of the ephod thou shalt make it; of gold, of blue, and of purple, and of scarlet, and of fine twined linen, shalt thou make it.

Foursquare it shall be being doubled; a span shall be the length thereof, and a span shall be the breadth thereof.

come again, and receive you unto Myself; that where I am, there ye may be also."

After a life on earth with the Saviour, and after being shown the sorrows through which man must pass before the end, John was prepared to appreciate the city which Christ had gone to prepare. One of the seven angels who carries the vials of God's wrath, revealed to the prophet the beauties of the New Jerusalem.

The city lieth four square, perfect in its dimensions, measuring three hundred and seventy-five miles each way, with a wall of precious stones. This wall measures in height, one hundred and forty-four cubits, or between two hundred and sixteen and two hundred sixty-six feet. The city in all its details represents salvation; also the people within its jasper walls, represent the salvation of God. At creation the gold, the silver, and the precious stones, lay on the face of the earth. Men used them for selfish purposes; and for this reason at the time of the flood, they were buried beneath the surface, and are brought to light only as the result of hard labor. In the New Jerusalem, they will be so arranged as to tell the story of infinite wisdom and love.

Some have given the following imaginative interpretation to the various colors of the stones: "At the base is the crimson jasper, typical of the suffering and death of the Saviour slain from the foundation of the world. Above this, is laid the sapphire, like a blue flame of truth. In the pure white chalcedony is reflected the purity of the Christ life. The emerald green, like the rainbow about the throne, offers hope to those who rest upon the others. The sardonyx reflects many colors, but above it, is the deep red sardius, covered by the chrysolite. This is overlaid by the beautiful blue beryl, whose light mingles with the blazing topaz in telling the story of joy and peace in the Lord. The eleventh is the purple of royalty, crowned with the purity of the amethyst." The foundation, composed entirely of precious stones, is beautiful beyond description; but besides this, it is ornamented, or garnished, with *all manner of precious stones.*

Stones have voices, although they speak in tones seldom heard by men. Christ told His disciples that if men held their peace, the very stones would cry out. The story which they tell is the old, old story; and as they form the walls of the New Jerusalem, and the glory of Christ and the Father shines on them, they will not meet the eye with a dull, lusterless surface, but with a glory known only in the purity of a spiritual world. Inanimate nature partook of the curse of sin; but the foundation of the city of our God, like all things in the earth made new, will shine in its original splendor. On these twelve foundations are written the names of the twelve apostles, the pillars of the Christian church. The prophet on Patmos had been condemned, his name recorded on the books of Rome as a criminal and an exile; what joy, then, must have come to him, when he saw in heaven his name engraved on one of the foundations of the city. Here is the difference between human and divine judgment.

The streets of the city are of pure gold,—so pure that they are transparent like crystal. The light from the countenance of Christ falls

And thou shalt set in it settings of stones, even four rows of stones: the first row shall be a sardius, a topaz, and a carbuncle: this shall be the first row.

And the second row shall be an emerald, a sapphire, and a diamond.

And the third row a ligure, an agate, and an amethyst.

And the fourth row a beryl, and an onyx, and a jasper: they shall be set in gold in their inclosings.

And the stones shall be with the names of the children of Israel, twelve, according to their names, like the engravings of a signet; every one with his name shall they be according to the twelve tribes.
Ex. 28:15-21.

*And he measured the wall thereof, an hundred and forty and four cubits, according to the measure of a man, that is, of the angel.*

*And the building of the wall of it was of jasper: and the city was pure gold, like unto clear glass.*

*And the foundations of the wall of the city were garnished with all manner of precious stones. The first foundation was jasper; the second, sapphire; the third, a chalcedony; the fourth, an emerald;*

*The fifth, sardonyx; the sixth, sardius; the seventh, chrysolyte; the eighth, beryl: the ninth, a topaz; the tenth, a chrysoprasus; the eleventh, a jacinth; the twelfth, an amethyst.*
*Rev. 21:17-20.*

Gen. 31:45-52.
Gen. 28:18-22.
Rom. 8:22.

And are built upon the foundation of the apostles and prophets, Jesus Christ himself being the chief corner stone. Eph. 2:20.

Gal 2:9.

Notwithstanding in this rejoice not, that the spirits are subject unto you; but rather rejoice, because your names are written in heaven.
Luke 10:20.

O thou afflicted, tossed with tempest, and not comforted, behold, I will lay thy stones with fair colours, and lay thy foundations with sapphires.

And I will make thy windows of agates, and thy gates of carbuncles, and all thy borders of pleasant stones.

And all thy children shall be taught of the Lord; and great shall be the peace of thy children.

Isa. 54: 11, 13.

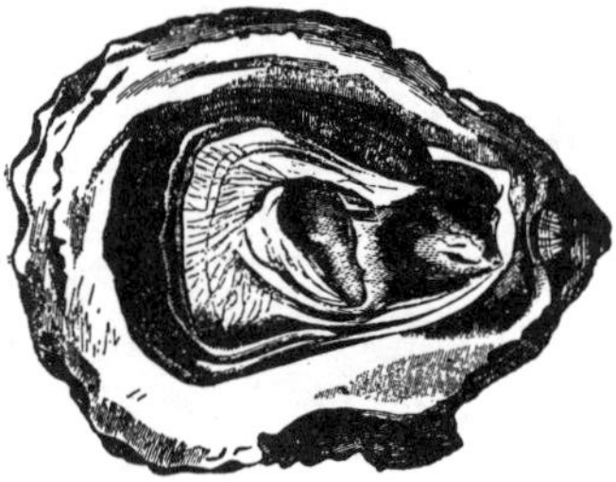

**Pearl oyster.**

*And the twelve gates were twelve pearls; every several gate was of one pearl: and the street of the city was pure gold, as it were transparent glass. Rev. 21:21.*

Thou wilt say then, The branches were broken off, that I might be graffed in.

Well; because of unbelief they were broken off, and thou standest by faith. Be not highminded, but fear:

For if God spared not the natural branches, take heed lest he also spare not thee. Rom. 11: 19-21.

I heard the number of them which were sealed: and there were sealed an hundred and forty and four thousand of all the tribes of the children of Israel. Rev. 7:4.

Blessed are the pure in heart: for they shall see God.

Matt. 5:8.

They shall see his face; and his name shall be in their foreheads.

Rev. 22:4.

upon the beautifully blended colors of the wall, and then is reflected again and again on the polished streets. Men have lavished wealth on buildings, but no earthly edifice ever equaled the beauties of this capital city. In this wall are twelve gates; in number the same as the twelve tribes of the children of Israel,—the twelve patriarchs, whose names appear graven in living characters upon them. Each gate is a single pearl. The pearl, as we know it, is formed by the life fluid of the oyster covering a foreign substance. The pearls of heaven represent the abundant righteousness of Christ called forth by sin; but which, flowing full and free, covers every blemish in the character to which it is applied.

As the redeemed enter the city, they are arranged according to the tribes of ancient Israel, character forming the basis of division. The twelve taken together reflect the fullness of Christ. The character portrayed in the blessings pronounced upon the sons of Jacob, reveals the many sides of the life of the Son of God, as manifested in redemption.

In the city, the saints meet Jehovah face to face. Even God veiled His glory during the reign of sin; and not until the work of Christ is entirely finished, and He leaves the temple in heaven preparatory to coming to earth, does the undimmed glory of the Father burst forth. This was typified in the sanctuary service, by the veil which protected the Shekinah from the gaze of the people, and by the cloud of incense, which went up before the priest when he ministered in the inner apartment on the day of atonement. Had it been otherwise, the consuming glory would have slain all. In the New Jerusalem, there is no veil, no temple; but God and Christ are the light of it. The veiling of Jehovah's glory is likewise typified by the sun and moon in our own heavens. The light of these bodies seems intense to mortal eyes; but in the new earth, the sun will shine with a light seven times brighter than to-day and the moon will be as our sun. Even then, their light is hidden by the glory of celestial rays. Day and night, that light of life shines forth throughout eternity. This light causes spiritual life, just as our sunshine makes the earth to bring forth and bud.

*And I saw no temple therein: for the Lord God Almighty and the Lamb are the temple of it.*

*And the city had no need of the sun, neither of the moon, to shine in it: for the glory of God did lighten it, and the Lamb is the light thereof.*

*And the nations of them which are saved shall walk in the light of it: and the kings of the earth do bring their glory and honour into it.*

*And the gates of it shall not be shut at all by day: for there shall be no night there.*
*Rev. 21:22, 25.*

The glory is not wholly confined to the city; for the earth itself is Eden restored. The redeemed have houses outside the city. The earth brings forth in abundance, and labor is a pleasure. As it was God's plan to people the earth, and have all nations come to the Garden of Eden, so in the new earth the nations, or tribes, under their kings, bring their glory and honor into Jerusalem, coming there to meet with God.

**Day and night, that light of life shines forth throughout eternity.**

Christ was manifested that He might destroy the works of the devil. God placed man in a perfect earth, and bade him subdue it; in other

*And they shall bring the glory and honour of the nations into it.*

*And there shall in no wise enter into it any thing that defileth, neither whatsoever worketh abomination, or maketh a lie: but they which are written in the Lamb's book of life. Rev. 21:26, 27.*

words, to make the whole earth like Eden; but Satan thwarted the plan, and for six thousand years he has reigned on the earth. When the earth is restored, it will not be as it was in the beginning, but far more beautiful. It will be as it would have been in the same length of time, if sin had never entered. All the works of the devil will be destroyed. The work that man would have done, if sin had not entered, Christ will do. Instead of their home being simply a garden, there will be the beautiful city enclosing the garden.

The human mind can but faintly grasp the idea of spiritual existence; and the best that mortal man can do, is to compare the glory of eternity with those things which are divinely appointed to foreshadow the things of the eternal world.

The ear of man catches but the smallest proportion of the sounds which are everywhere about him; his eye sees but little that light in reality reveals; so narrow is the sphere in which we live. God has spoken of the other world, and He has described it in human language. There are things which eye hath not seen, nor ear heard, but God hath revealed them by His Spirit; so of the glories beyond, one can truthfully say, The half hath not been told.

Through eternity those whose names are written in the Lamb's Book of Life will receive new revelations of Jesus Christ; and they themselves will reflect more and more of the divine character. Then it will be known what life really is. As the Saviour leads to fountains of wisdom, men will know that He is "the way, the truth, and the life."

For this purpose the Son of God was manifested, that he might destroy the works of the devil.

1 John 3:8.

Be ye glad and rejoice for ever in that which I create: for, behold, I create Jerusalem a rejoicing, and her people a joy.

And I will rejoice in Jerusalem, and joy in my people: and the voice of weeping shall be no more heard in her, nor the voice of crying.

Isa. 65:18, 19.

Now unto him that is able to do exceeding abundantly above all that we ask or think, according to the power that worketh in us,

Unto him be glory in the church by Christ Jesus throughout all ages, world without end. Amen.

Eph. 3:20, 21.

Father, I will that they also, whom thou hast given me, be with me where I am; that they may behold my glory, which thou hast given me: for thou lovedst me before the foundation of the world.

John 17:24.

All the treasures of the universe will be open to the study of God's redeemed. Unfettered by mortality, they wing their tireless flight to worlds afar,—worlds that thrilled with sorrow at the spectacle of human woe, and rang with songs of gladness at the tidings of a ransomed soul. With unutterable delight the children of earth enter into the joy and the wisdom of unfallen beings. They share the treasures of knowledge and understanding gained through ages upon ages in contemplation of God's handiwork. With undimmed vision they gaze upon the glory of creation,—suns and stars and systems all in their appointed order circling the throne of Deity. Upon all things, from the least to the greatest, the Creator's name is written, and in all are the riches of His power displayed.—*The Great Controversy Between Christ and Satan.*

# CHAPTER XXIII.

## THE NEW EARTH.

THE book of Revelation is a great signal, pointing to the New Jerusalem and the earth made new. Growth in character is all that hastens one along the road that leads thither. Human history has been like the ebb and flow of the tide. The waves break, break, break, on the sands; but only an occasional one reaches beyond the level of its fellows. David had a good opportunity to watch the fluctuations in human progress, and the backward steps; the stumblings led to the writing of many psalms. Thus came the prayer "Create in me a clean heart, O God; and renew a right spirit within me." The Revelation of Jesus Christ is a double history; it shows the love of Jesus Christ which has met man, and the church, as it has pursued its zigzag course; and it portrays a character, that by the grace of

Set thee up waymarks, make thee high heaps: set thine heart toward the highway, even the way which thou wentest: turn again, O virgin of Israel, turn again to these thy cities. Jer. 31:21.

Grow in grace, and in the knowledge of our Lord and Saviour Jesus Christ. To him be glory both now and for ever. Amen. 2 Pet. 3:18.

Eccl. 1:5-8.

I would hasten my escape from the windy storm and tempest. Psa. 55:8.

Hosea 4:9.
Hosea 11:7.
Hosea 4:16.
Psa. 45:1.
Psa. 51:10.

Rev. 1:19.
Psa. 5:8.
Heb. 12:13.
Isa. 35:8, 9.

He that receiveth you receiveth me: and he that receiveth me receiveth him that sent me. Matt. 10:40.

Rev. 8:13.
Rev. 11:15.

I will make them one nation in the land upon the mountains of Israel; and one king shall be king to them all. Eze. 37:22.

Or else how can one enter into a strong man's house, and spoil his goods, except he first bind the strong man? and then he will spoil his house. Matt. 12:29.

Rev. 14:9, 10.

Hearken to me, ye that follow after righteousness, ye that seek the Lord: look unto the rock whence ye are hewn, and to the hole of the pit whence ye are digged. Isa. 51:1.

Rev. 5:9, 10.
2 Pet. 3:7, 13.
John 14:1, 2.
Rev. 20:9, 10.

God, made a straight path from earth to heaven. The way which He trod, is the road to the New Jerusalem. The seven churches began where His life closed, and their work closes only where the gates of the city are open to receive them.

The seven seals portray the sufferings of the slain Lamb in the body of His people; and the seventh leaves heaven in silence while angels gather the redeemed from the earth. The seven trumpets are blown in the hearing of all nations; all the world records the story of the Son of man, and the seventh gives the kingdoms into the hands of Him who reigns as King of kings on the earth, with Jerusalem for His capital.

The birth of Christ, the crucifixion, and the work in heaven since the ascension,—all point to the kingdom restored. The history of the beast, and of the image to the beast, both record the persecution of a people who will be loyal subjects of the King of earth. If the one hundred and forty-four thousand are studied, they are found to be the Remnant, snatched from the very pit of destruction, to reign in the earth as kings and priests, throughout eternity. The plagues are but the sign of the self-destruction of all forces opposed to the law of God; and they pave the way for the cleansing of the earth by fire, preparatory to the restoration of the paradise of God.

Christ prepares the capital city in heaven; while on earth He molds the character of His subjects. City and people meet on the new earth. The many paths traced in the book of Revelation, lead unto the thoroughfare which ends at the gates of that city. The last chapter of the book,—a fitting close for such history as is revealed in the other chapters, gives a description of the earth rescued from all sin,—the Eden restored.

The first Eden remained on earth one-fourth of the period of earth's history. With its closed gate, and an angel guard at the tree of life, it was a wonderful lesson to the inhabitants of the world before the flood. Before the destruction of the earth by water, the garden was transported to heaven, and the promise since has been, "To him that overcometh will I give to eat of the tree of life, which is in the midst of the paradise of God."

In Eden the tree of life grows on the banks of the river of life. As long as Adam and Eve ate of the fruit of that tree, life was eternal. The waters were life-giving. This virtue has been lost by the rivers of earth, through the curse of sin, yet every flowing river is a reminder to man, of the river of life which proceeds from the throne of God. The source of this river is God,—the fountain, or head waters of all truth; and flowing from Him, who is infinite and eternal, it signifies the spread of truth through the earth. In Eden that water typified Christ; and there, they communed with Him as freely as they drank of the clear flowing waters. Rivulets from the throne have always watered the earth, but there never have been channels sufficiently strong for an over abundant flow. On the new earth, that river will be restored. Christ Himself will lead His people to the fountain of living waters. "Thou shalt make them drink of the river of Thy pleasures. For with Thee is the fountain of life." "Ho, every

For the Lord shall comfort Zion: he will comfort all her waste places; and he will make her wilderness like Eden, and her desert like the garden of the Lord; joy and gladness shall be found therein, thanksgiving, and the voice of melody.
Isa. 51:3.

Rev. 21:1–27.

Gen. 3:24 [margin.] Adam was driven from the garden of Eden 4004 B. C.

Gen. 7:11 [margin.] The flood was in 2349 B. C.

Sixteen hundred and fifty-five years intervened between the two events.

2 Cor. 12:4.
Rev. 2:7.

By the river upon the bank thereof, on this side and on that side, shall grow all trees for meat, whose leaf shall not fade, neither shall the fruit thereof be consumed: it shall bring forth new fruit according to his months, because their waters they issued out of the sanctuary: and the fruit thereof shall be for meat, and the leaf thereof for medicine. Eze. 47:12.

Gen. 2:8, 9.
Dan. 12:5, 6.
Dan. 8:2.
John 1:4, 9.

The Spirit and the bride say, Come. And let him that heareth say, Come. And let him that is athirst come. And whosoever will, let him take the water of life freely.
Rev. 22:17.

Gen. 3:8.
Eze. 47:2.

He leadeth me beside the waters of quietness.
Psa. 23:2 [margin.]

Psa. 36:8.
Isa. 55:1.

one that thirsteth." "The Spirit and the bride say, Come. . . . Let him that is athirst come." Jesus said: "Whosoever drinketh of the water that I shall give him shall never thirst." "If thou knewest the gift of God, and who it is that saith to thee, Give Me to drink; thou wouldest have asked of Him, and He would have given thee living water."

For I will pour water upon him that is thirsty, and floods upon the dry ground: I will pour my Spirit upon thy seed, and my blessing upon thine offspring. Isa. 44:3.

John 4:10, 14.

John was fond of the figure, and seemed to catch the words uttered by his Master, as none of the other disciples caught them. Perhaps this was caused by the fact that before writing the gospel, he had seen such a clear portrayal of the new earth that certain sayings of Christ came vividly to his mind.

The gospel of John was written one year after the Revelation.

Every river is a type of the river of life; and every tree that grows will remind the one who listens for the voice of God, of that tree of life, which grows on either bank of the river. The real tree of Eden was transported to heaven; but its boughs are represented as hanging earthward, and its fruit, in type at least, has been plucked by those who had soul hunger and who reach upward for it. It will blossom in reality in the new earth, bearing its fruit every month, twelve manner of fruit which will supply every want of the spiritual being. There will be no lack. "The leaves of the tree were for the healing of the nations," and "the leaf thereof for medicine." All the war and strife of nations have come because man ate not of the fruit of the tree of life. The whole controversy of six thousand years originated when man ate of the fruit of the tree of the knowledge of good and evil. That tree will not be found in the earth made new, and the fires of the last days will con-

Now when I had returned, behold, at the bank of the river were very many trees on the one side and on the other.
Then said he unto me, These waters issue out toward the east country, and go down into the desert, and go into the sea: which being brought forth into the sea, the waters shall be healed.
Eze. 47:7, 8.

*And he shewed me a pure river of water of life, clear as crystal, proceeding out of the throne of God and of the Lamb.*
*In the midst of the street of it, and on either side of the river, was there the tree of life, which bare twelve manner of fruits, and yielded her fruit every month: and the leaves of the tree were for the healing of the nations.*
*Rev. 22:1, 2.*

Rev. 22:2.

Unto you that fear my name shall the Sun of righteousness arise with healing in his wings; and ye shall go forth, and grow up as calves of the stall. Mal. 4:2.

sume all nations who have continued to eat of its fruit. "The scars and bruises" [Ez. 47:12, mar.] caused by eating its fruit will be healed by the leaves of the tree of life.

Christ is the tree of life, the bread of life and the water of life: man will live in Him; and yet in the new earth as in this world, nature will, in all its features, symbolize what Christ really is to man. As the redeemed partake of the fruit of the tree of life, to their souls, will come redemption's story. By individuals, and through nations, God has attempted to demonstrate the possibility of living under the shadow of the tree of the knowledge of good and evil, and yet eating of the fruit from the tree of life. This is the life of faith, and those who gather about the real tree in the new earth, will be those who have partaken of that fruit when the other was near, and was held out as a tempting morsel.

In Israel, as a nation, God wished to illustrate the truths of heaven; and had they followed where He led, He would, through them, have shown to all other nations that the tree of life could blossom on earth, and that a nation could be healed by its leaves. Israel, not willing to eat only of the food of God, mingled the good with the evil, and became like all other nations. In the earth restored, all nationalities, all tribes, and peoples will, for the first time, gather together and with one common language worship our God. The fruit and the leaves of the tree of life bring all together. Christ came "to seek and to save that which was lost." In the river of life and the tree of life, together with the blessing each insures, much is restored that was lost by the entrance of sin.

By the river upon the bank thereof, on this side and on that side, shall grow all trees for meat, whose leaf shall not fade, neither shall the fruit thereof be consumed: it shall bring forth new fruit according to his months, because their waters they issued out of the sanctuary: and the fruit thereof shall be for meat, and the leaf thereof for bruises and sores.
Eze. 47:12 [margin.]

Prov. 3:18.

The fruit of the righteous is a tree of life; and he that winneth souls is wise. Prov. 11:30.

I am the living bread which came down from heaven. John 6:51.

John 7:37, 38.
John 6:35, 47.

Jesus said unto her, I am the resurrection, and the life: he that believeth in me, though he were dead, yet shall he live:

And whosoever liveth and believeth in me shall never die. Believest thou this?
John 11:25, 26.

It shall come to pass, that whosoever shall call on the name of the Lord shall be delivered.
Joel 2:32.

Why gaddest thou about so much to change thy way? thou also shalt be ashamed of Egypt, as thou wast ashamed of Assyria. Jer. 2:36.

For then will I turn to the people a pure language, that they may all call upon the name of the Lord, to serve him with one consent.
Zeph. 3:9.

Luke 19:10.

*And there shall be no more curse: but the throne of God and of the Lamb shall be in it; and his servants shall serve him.*
*Rev. 22:3.*

Isa. 65:17, 18.

God setteth the solitary in families: he bringeth out those which are bound with chains.
Psa. 68:6.

For the husband is the head of the wife, even as Christ is the head of the church: and he is the Saviour of the body. Eph. 5:23.

If ye then, being evil, know how to give good gifts unto your children, how much more shall your Father which is in heaven give good things to them that ask him?
Matt. 7:11.

Isa. 49:15–17.
John 3:16.
1 John 4:19.

He that loveth not knoweth not God; for God is love.
1 John 4:8.

I will spare them, as a man spareth his own son that serveth him.
Mal. 3:17.

Psa. 65:2.

When his kinsmen heard of it, they went out to lay hold on him: for they said, He is beside himself.
Mark 3:21 [margin.]

The angel said to John, "There shall be no more curse." "Former [things] shall not be remembered, nor come upon the heart. But be ye glad and rejoice for ever in that which I create: for, behold, I create Jerusalem a rejoicing, and her people a joy." The presence of joy implies the restoration of families; and in this, is one of the most beautiful promises of the new earth. Sin has marred family relations: the curse has entered all families, if not in one form, it has come in another. The family has been the closest tie between heaven and earth. In the midst of sin and deep degradation, the unselfish devotion of mothers for their offspring, has spoken of the love of Christ in a language which has reached all hearts, from that of God on the throne to the infidel who scorns the name of God. The truth that "We love Him, because He first loved us," still remains; and when a touch of love has been born in the mire of sin, it is the reflection of Heaven's love. In the new earth such love will meet its reward; for He "setteth the solitary in families: He bringeth out those which are bound with chains."

"Oh, Thou that hearest prayer, unto Thee shall all flesh come." To-day many families are divided. Some members wish to eat of the spiritual bread, and others prefer the food which nourishes the nations of the earth. This makes a line of separation; for those who are spiritual stand on one plain, and the physical man stands on another. "He that soweth to his flesh shall of the flesh reap corruption; but he that soweth to the Spirit shall of the Spirit reap life everlasting." When the separation comes, as it will at the end of time, God sets the spiritual souls in families,—families of which they would have been members had sin never existed. Love of parents for their children is a type of the Father's love for humanity; and to comfort the hearts of mothers, there is the promise that little children lost on earth, will be restored to their parents in the new earth. The promise was made to Israel: it will be fulfilled to those who are Israelites indeed. The sorrow of a mother over her dying child is felt in heaven. "A voice was heard in Ramah, lamentation, and bitter weeping; Rachael weeping for her children refused to be comforted for her children, because they were not." "Thus saith the Lord; Refrain thy voice from weeping, and thine eyes from tears: for thy work shall be rewarded, saith the Lord, and they shall come again from the land of the enemy." This prophecy of the weeping mothers was fulfilled in the mothers of Bethlehem, weeping for their children in the days of Herod, and was a type of every mother in Israel called to mourn the death of her infant. In it is also a pledge of the resurrection of children.

For the flesh lusteth against the Spirit, and the Spirit against the flesh: and these are contrary the one to the other: so that ye cannot do the things that ye would. Gal. 5:17.

Gal. 6:7, 8.

**"Oh, Thou that hearest prayer, unto Thee shall all flesh come."**

Thus saith the Lord; Refrain thy voice from weeping, and thine eyes from tears: for thy work shall be rewarded, saith the Lord; and they shall come again from the land of the enemy.

And there is hope in thine end, saith the Lord, that thy children shall come again to their own border. Jer. 31:16, 17.

Mal. 4:2.

For, behold, I create new heavens and a new earth: and the former shall not be remembered, nor come into mind.

But be ye glad and rejoice for ever in that which I create: for, behold, I create Jerusalem a rejoicing, and her people a joy.

And I will rejoice in Jerusalem, and joy in my people: and the voice of weeping shall be no more heard in her, nor the voice of crying.

There shall be no more thence an infant of days, nor an old man that hath not filled his days: for the child shall die an hundred years old; but the sinner being an hundred years old shall be accursed.

Isa. 65:17-20.

When the Son of righteousness arises with healing in His wings, these "shall grow up as calves of the stall." "There shall be no more thence [in the new earth] an infant of days, nor an old man that hath not filled his days;" for the curse is removed, and there shall be no more death. The child shall grow as a "calf of the stall," and no man in that land of life will ever die. Before the earth is renewed, the child of a hundred years shall die, and the sinner will be accursed. Over there, they have access to the tree of life, and they drink of the water of life, and live throughout eternity. In place of the curse of death, there will be the throne of God and the Lamb. God's throne is a living throne.

Psa. 8:4, 5.
Psa. 80:7.

For the first time since creation, God can be seen face to face. Man was created inferior to the angels for a little time. While on earth we pray, "Cause Thy face to shine; and we shall be saved." Then the full light of His countenance will be open to the gaze of man, "and His name shall be in their foreheads."

*And they shall see his face; and his name shall be in their foreheads.*

*And there shall be no night there; and they need no candle, neither light of the sun; for the Lord God giveth them light: and they shall reign for ever and ever.*

*And he said unto me, These sayings are faithful and true: and the Lord God of the holy prophets sent his angel to shew unto his servants the things which must shortly be done. Rev. 22:4-6.*

Genesis is the first unfolding, in human language, of the plan of salvation. Each following book of the Bible is a further explanation of the truths stated in Genesis. Revelation is the Omega,—the gathering together of all the threads of truth,—a meeting of all the ways. The twenty-second chapter is a summary of the book of Revelation. As if John found it difficult to comprehend the scenes he beheld, Gabriel repeats, "These sayings are true and faithful." To all appearances, the earth was not ready for paradise when it was spread out in panoramic view before John: likewise, as the human eye

Thou hast put all things in subjection under his feet. For in that he put all in subjection under him, he left nothing that is not put under him. But now we see not yet all things put under him.

Heb. 2:8.

measures circumstances, the world seems further from that time to-day; but "The Lord God of the holy prophets sent His angel to show unto His servants the things which must shortly be done. Behold, I come quickly." And John seeing and hearing these things, again fell at the

"The Lord God of the holy prophets sent His angel to show unto His servants the things which must shortly be done."

Rev. 22:6, 7.

The Revelation of Jesus Christ, which God gave unto him, to shew unto his servants things which must shortly come to pass; and he sent and signified it by his angel unto his servant John:

Who bare record of the word of God, and of the testimony of Jesus Christ, and of all things that he saw. Rev. 1:1, 2.

When I speak with thee, I will open thy mouth, and thou shalt say unto them, Thus saith the Lord God; He that heareth, let him hear; and he that forbeareth, let him forbear: for they are a rebellious house. Eze. 3:27.

Thou shalt speak my words unto them, whether they will hear, or whether they will forbear: for they are most rebellious. Eze. 2:7.

Thou therefore gird up thy loins, and arise, and speak unto them all that I command thee: be not dismayed at their faces, lest I confound thee before them. Jer. 1:17.

Bless the Lord, ye his angels, that excel in strength, that do his commandments, hearkening unto the voice of his word.
Psa. 103:20.

Dan. 12:4.

Stay yourselves, and wonder; cry ye out, and cry: they are drunken, but not with wine; they stagger, but not with strong drink.
For the Lord hath poured out upon you the spirit of deep sleep, and hath closed your eyes: the prophets and your rulers, the seers hath he covered.
And the vision of all is become unto you as the words of a book that is sealed, which men deliver to one that is learned, saying, Read this, I pray thee: and he saith, I cannot; for it is sealed:
And the book is delivered to him that is not learned, saying, Read this, I pray thee: and he saith, I am not learned. Isa. 29:9-12.

For the time is come that judgment must begin at the house of God: and if it first begin at us, what shall the end be of them that obey not the gospel of God?
1 Pet. 4:17.

Rev. 22:11.

*Behold, I come quickly: blessed is he that keepeth the sayings of the prophecy of this book.*
*And I John saw these things, and heard them. And when I had heard and seen, I fell down to worship before the feet of the angel which shewed me these things.*
*Then saith he unto me, See thou do it not: for I am thy fellow-servant, and of thy brethren the prophets, and of them which keep the sayings of this book: worship God.*
*And he saith unto me, Seal not the sayings of the prophecy of this book: for the time is at hand.*
*Rev. 22:7-10.*

feet of Gabriel to worship him; and again the angel said, "See thou do it not." Gabriel professes himself a fellow servant of John, and of all who keep the prophecies of this book. Angels, as well as men, obey the word of God revealed to the prophets, for the prophecies are an unfolding of the law of God.

Reference has been made more than once to the prophecies of Daniel, which Gabriel commanded that prophet to seal until the time of the end. The Revelation prophesies the unsealing of that book, and Gabriel distinctly tells John that the words which he had written were not to be sealed; for the time of their fulfillment was at hand. The expression is both literal and prophetic, for the record began with the life of John, and extended into eternity. The coming of Christ is near; the signs preceding His coming have already appeared.

In 1844 prophetic time closed; this was the end of the twenty-three hundred days of Dan. 8:14. It was the beginning of a new work; and when the judgment then begun is finished, which event the prophecies say is near at hand, Christ will rise from His judgment throne, with the words, "He that is unjust, let him be unjust still: and he which is filthy, let him be filthy still: and he that is righteous, let him be righteous still: and he that is holy, let him be holy still." When these words are spoken, the heavens prepare for His second coming. "Behold, I come quickly." While mercy lingers, man, by turning to Christ, may have his heart purified; his mind made a channel for divine thoughts. Only those who are His servants to this extent, can be said to have received His name in the forehead. All others are filthy, and are numbered with the family of Satan who is the father of lies.

Rev. 14:6, 7.
Matt. 24:14.

At the close of prophetic time Christ came in judgment. To-day the message is going to the earth; and it is swelling into the loud cry, "Behold, I come quickly; and My reward is with Me, to give every man according as his work shall be." He who has been sowing to his flesh, will reap his reward which is death. He who has submitted himself to the ruling power of the Spirit, will of the Spirit, reap life everlasting. The subjects of the judgment of the world, the reward of the righteous, and the punishment of the wicked, are threads in the web woven in eternity's loom.

Talk no more so exceeding proudly; let not arrogancy come out of your mouth: for the Lord is a God of knowledge, and by him actions are weighed.
1 Sam. 2:3.

*He that is unjust, let him be unjust still: and he which is filthy, let him be filthy still: and he that is righteous, let him be righteous still: and he that is holy, let him be holy still.*

*And, behold, I come quickly; and my reward is with me, to give every man according as his work shall be.*

*I am Alpha and Omega, the beginning and the end, the first and the last.* *Rev. 22:11-13.*

Eden and the new earth clasp hands in the expression so oft repeated in the book of Revelation, "I am Alpha and Omega, the beginning and the end, the first and the last." "I know whom I have believed, and am persuaded that He is able to keep that which I have committed unto Him against that day." "Being confident of this very thing, that He which hath begun a good work . . . will perform it until the day of Jesus Christ." The work, planned before the foundations of the earth were laid, is accomplished without an alteration, notwithstanding the introduction of sin. The only difference there will be, is in the strength of character which is developed during the journey through the valley of the shadow of death.

For ye shall go out with joy, and be led forth with peace: the mountains and the hills shall break forth before you into singing, and all the trees of the field shall clap their hands. Isa. 55:12.

2 Tim. 1:12.
Rev. 1:4, 8, 11.
Rev. 21:6.
Rev. 22:13.
Phil. 1:6.

Now unto him that is able to keep you from falling, and to present you faultless before the presence of his glory with exceeding joy. Jude 24.

In Eden, God's word was made known to man by angels at the tree of life. Upon obedience, rested the right to eat of the fruit of that tree. Satan made it appear that obedience to the

1 John 3:8.
Titus 1:2.
Rom. 16:25, 26.
Eph. 3:9.

If thou wilt enter into life, keep the commandments.
Matt. 19:17.

*Blessed are they that do his commandments, that they may have right to the tree of life, and may enter in through the gates into the city.*

*For without are dogs, and sorcerers, and whoremongers, and murderers, and idolaters, and whosoever loveth and maketh a lie.*

*I Jesus have sent mine angel to testify unto you these things in the churches. I am the root and the offspring of David, and the bright and morning star.*

*And the Spirit and the bride say, Come. And let him that heareth say, Come. And let him that is athirst come. And whosoever will, let him take the water of life freely.* *Rev. 22:14-17.*

Rev. 22:14.

Keep my commandments, and live; and my law as the apple of thine eye. Prov. 7:2.

For the commandment is a lamp; and the law is light; and reproofs of instruction are the way of life. Prov. 6:23.

For verily I say unto you, Till heaven and earth pass, one jot or one tittle shall in no wise pass from the law, till all be fulfilled. Matt. 5:18.

Rev. 22:16.
Rev. 14:12.

*For I testify unto every man that heareth the words of the prophecy of this book, If any man shall add unto these things, God shall add unto him the plagues that are written in this book:*

*And if any man shall take away from the words of the book of this prophecy, God shall take away his part out of the book of life, and out of the holy city, and from the things which are written in this book.*

*He which testifieth these things saith, Surely I come quickly. Amen. Even so, come, Lord Jesus.*

*The grace of our Lord Jesus Christ be with you all. Amen.* *Rev. 22:18-21.*

commandments was a tyrannical request, and at the tree of the knowledge of good and evil, proclaimed that man should be as gods. The error of all time,—the hope of eternal life by some other means than obedience to the commandments,—is the subject of the controversy. In Eden, at the beginning; the commandments and the tree of life were placed together. Christ in His personal teaching and in His life, linked them again, saying, "The words that I speak unto you, they are spirit, and they are life"; and John, writing for those who stand at the gateway of the New Jerusalem, says, "Blessed are they that do His commandments, that they may have right to the tree of life, and may enter in through the gates into the city."

Jehovah's law is a law of life; those who are sealed, are commandment keepers; and the last struggle of earth, will be over the question of the immutability of the law. This then, is another thread, so often miserably twisted and knotted, which is woven into its proper place, in this closing chapter. Without are dogs and sorcerers, false prophets, murderers, and all, who, in word, bear false witness, or by life, belie the name of Christ; but to the church He says, "I Jesus have sent Mine angel to testify unto you these things." "Here is the patience of the saints: here are they that keep the commandments of God, and the faith of Jesus." As the offspring of David, He speaks with the authority of the rightful ruler of the earth. There, His commandments are the foundation of His throne and the law of His kingdom. He is the bright and morning star, and leads the universe; He heralds a new day, when time will be no more, and eternity will be unbroken. The new day is about to begin; it is ushered in by the marriage supper of the Lamb. The invitation to that feast is given by the Spirit, the Bridegroom, and the bride. There is power in the word, "Come"; for the Spirit breathes it, and whatever is God-breathed is. Here is the same experience that Peter had on the stormy sea. The Master said, "Come," and while the disciple believed the waves formed a solid footing. When he doubted he began to sink. To-day the Spirit says, "Come"; and he who believes in the power of God unto salvation, will be carried through by the one word, "come." It is a living word, like the word spoken during creation week. As the trees have continued to grow year after year, each oak bearing acorns, which in time produce other oaks, so the word "come" has been repeated by those who heeded the sound, and whosoever will, has drunk of the fountain of life. Those in whom the Word lives, become living voices who repeat the invitation, "Come," "Ho, every one that thirsteth, come."

"What thing soever I command you, observe to do it." This is the divine voice speaking. "Ye shall not add unto the word which I command you, neither shall ye diminish ought from it, that ye may keep the commandments of the Lord your God."

Peter answered him and said, Lord, if it be thou, bid me come unto thee on the water.

And he said, Come. And when Peter was come down out of the ship, he walked on the water, to go to Jesus.

But when he saw the wind boisterous, he was afraid; and beginning to sink, he cried, saying, Lord, save me.

And immediately Jesus stretched forth his hand, and caught him, and said unto him, O thou of little faith, wherefore didst thou doubt?

Matt. 14:28-31.

**When he doubted he began to sink.**

Add thou not unto his words, lest he reprove thee, and thou be found a liar. Prov. 30:6.

Trust in the Lord, and do good; so shalt thou dwell in the land, and verily thou shalt be fed.
Psa. 37:3.

God's Word is pure; every word contains eternal life; and he who crushes one word to earth, will find that it will rise against him, to blot out his name from the Book of Life.

The words of the Lord are pure words: as silver tried in a furnace of earth, purified seven times.
Psa. 12:6.

The whole of the Revelation of Jesus Christ, by the angel Gabriel to the prophet John, tells of the unspeakable love of our Father and our Brother; and of longing in the courts of heaven, for the completion of the conflict with sin; and of the restoration of man to his place around the throne. Christ's parting words are concerning His coming. He speaks them Himself, as if to make them doubly impressive. "Surely I come quickly." "Lo, I am with you alway," fell as a parting blessing as the cloud received the risen Saviour; "Surely I come quickly" is the personal message sent to us who are to-day waiting for the consummation. And our hearts respond, as with John we say, "Even so, come, Lord Jesus."

Behold, what manner of love the Father hath bestowed upon us, that we should be called the sons of God: therefore the world knoweth us not, because it knew him not.

Beloved, now are we the sons of God, and it doth not yet appear what we shall be: but we know that, when he shall appear, we shall be like him; for we shall see him as he is.

And every man that hath this hope in him purifieth himself, even as he is pure.
1 John 3:1-3.

# CHAPTER XXIV.

## THE SANCTUARY AND ITS SERVICE.

THE book of Revelation is a revelation of Christ's work in the heavenly sanctuary. The first chapter presents Him walking in the midst of the seven candlesticks, guarding and directing His people. In the fourth chapter, we have a view of the throne of God in the heavenly sanctuary, with the seven lamps of fire burning before the throne. The eighth chapter reveals our great High Priest adding *much* incense with the prayers of His people, as He presents them before the throne. The eleventh chapter opens the most holy place and reveals the ark of God's testament containing His law. With these facts before us, a study of the book of Revelation is not complete without a chapter on the sanctuary and its service.

I saw seven golden candlesticks; And in the midst of the seven candlesticks one like unto the Son of man. Rev. 1:12, 13.

These things saith he that holdeth the seven stars in his right hand, who walketh in the midst of the seven golden candlesticks. Rev. 2:1.

There were seven lamps of fire burning before the throne, which are the seven Spirits of God. Rev. 4:5.

Another angel came and stood at the altar, having a golden censer; and there was given unto him much incense, that he should offer it with the prayers of all saints upon the golden altar which was before the throne.

And the smoke of the incense, which came with the prayers of the saints, ascended up before God out of the angel's hand. Rev. 8:3, 4.

Who serve unto the example and shadow of heavenly things, as Moses was admonished of God when he was about to make the tabernacle: for, See, saith he, that thou make all things according to the pattern shewed to thee in the mount. Heb. 8:5.

Thou shalt set up the court round about, and hang up the hanging at the court gate. Ex. 40:8.

Heb. 9:7.

Neither by the blood of goats and calves, but by his own blood he entered in once into the holy place, having obtained eternal redemption for us. Heb. 9:12.

They (the priests) shall keep thy charge, and the charge of all the tabernacle: only they shall not come nigh the vessels of the sanctuary and the altar, that neither they, nor ye also, die. Num. 18:3.

For if the blood of bulls and of goats, and the ashes of an heifer sprinkling the unclean, sanctifieth to the purifying of the flesh:

How much more shall the blood of Christ, who through the eternal Spirit offered himself without spot to God, purge your conscience from dead works to serve the living God? Heb. 9:13, 14.

Aaron shall burn thereon sweet incense every morning: when he dresseth the lamps, he shall burn incense upon it.

And when Aaron lighteth the lamps at even, he shall burn incense upon it. Ex. 30:7, 8.

Num. 1:53.

The earthly sanctuary was a type of the heavenly one. In it, men divinely appointed by the Lord served "unto the example and shadow of heavenly things." The sanctuary was surrounded by a court. In this court the people assembled and the offerings were slain. No blood was ever shed within either the holy or the most holy place. This was the type, and plainly revealed the antitype. Christ came and offered His life in the antitypical court,—this earth,—where His people, dwell. He then entered the heavenly sanctuary with His own blood, to present it before the Father in man's behalf. The people could enter only the court of the earthly sanctuary; none but the priests entered the holy places.

The people of God to-day are in the outer court,—the earth, and by faith follow their High Priest who officiates for them in the holy places.

There was virtue in every service of the ancient sanctuary to the one who by faith cooperated with the priest in the service. Those priests served "unto the example and shadow of heavenly things," and our High Priest is now performing the *real* work, of which that was a shadow, and every individual, who will by faith follow Him in that service, will be blessed. Every morning and evening the high priest in the ancient sanctuary entered the holy place and placed fresh incense upon the fire which was constantly burning upon the golden altar. Sufficient incense was placed there each morning to last all day, and at evening the supply was sufficient to keep the fragrant smoke ascending through all the dreary hours of the night. As Israel encamped about the taber-

**Those earthly priests served " unto the example and shadow of heavenly things."**

nacle, each sleepless one could detect the fragrance of the incense of the sanctuary as it was borne upon the breezes of the night. While the priest was placing the incense on the sacred fire, and the dense volume of fragrant smoke ascended, the prayers of the whole multitude ascended with the smoke. What could more fitly represent the real incense,—Christ's righteousness,—which He adds to the prayers of His people from the golden altar before the Father's throne in heaven? The earthly priests served "unto the example and shadow of heavenly things." Those who believe this may *know* that every morning there is an abundant supply of Christ's righteousness offered, and as they pour out their soul before God, their prayers will not ascend alone; for the great High Priest will add "*much incense*" with them, and the Father, looking upon the righteousness of His Son, will accept the feeble petitions of His child. All day and all night the incense ascended; it represented a never failing supply, and testified that whenever a sinner cries out for help there is righteousness for him.

The temple of God was opened in heaven, and there was seen in his temple the ark of his testament. Rev. 11:19.

Looking unto Jesus the author and finisher of our faith. Heb. 12:2.

According to the custom of the priest's office, his lot was to burn incense when he went into the temple of the Lord.

And the whole multitude of the people were praying without at the time of incense. Luke 1:9, 10.

Rev. 8:3, 4.
Rev. 5:6, 8.

Let my prayer be set forth before thee as incense; and the lifting up of my hands as the evening sacrifice. Psa. 141:2.

For therein is the righteousness of God revealed from faith to faith: as it is written, The just shall live by faith. Rom. 1:17.

He shall burn incense upon it, a perpetual incense before the Lord. Ex. 30:8.

He put the table in the tent of the congregation, upon the side of the tabernacle northward, without the vail. Ex. 40:22.

I am the living bread which came down from heaven. John 6:51.

Heb. 7:25.

Thou shalt take fine flour, and bake twelve cakes thereof: two tenth deals shall be in one cake.

And thou shalt set them in two rows, six on a row, upon the pure table before the Lord.
Lev. 24:5, 6.

Upon the north side of the holy place stood the golden table, bearing its twelve loaves of bread. This bread was called "bread of the presence." Ex. 25:30. (Young's Trans.) Christ is the "living bread," who ever liveth to make intercession for His people. As the bread was ever before the Lord, so Christ ever liveth in the presence of the Father, as the representative of fallen man. The twelve loaves into which the bread was divided, represented the

**Bread placed on the tables on the Sabbath.**

Thou shalt set upon the table shewbread before me alway.
Ex. 25:30.

He said unto them, This is that which the Lord hath said, Tomorrow is the rest of the holy sabbath unto the Lord: bake that which ye will bake to day, and seethe that ye will seethe; and that which remaineth over lay up for you to be kept until the morning.
Ex. 16:23.

twelve tribes of ancient Israel, and also the twelve thousand of each of the twelve tribes which form the one hundred and forty-four thousand, who follow the Lamb wheresoever He goeth. God gave a strict command that bread used on the Sabbath should be baked on the sixth day, that there be no baking done on the Sabbath; but this "bread of the presence" was made on the Sabbath, placed upon the tables on the Sabbath, and the old bread that was removed was eaten on the Sabbath day. Everything connected with the service of the table of shew bread was Sabbath service. It must surely teach that Christ has special blessings for His people on the Sabbath, and that fresh supplies of His Word, the "bread of life," should be placed upon His table; and as the priests ate the same bread the following week which they had placed fresh on the table, and it was assimilated and became a part of themselves, so Christ would have every one of His followers who sets forth afresh the bread of life each Sabbath day, eat the same bread themselves and let it become a part of their own lives. The people of God are "an holy priesthood," embassadors for Christ, representing Him upon the earth.

The golden candlestick represented the church of God. It was of beaten work, many heavy strokes of the hammer were necessary to blend the pieces of gold into one complete whole and form the perfect candlestick. In like manner, it takes many trials and chastisements to eradicate pride, envy and covetousness from the people of God, and blend them into one complete church, "without spot, or wrinkle, or any such thing." The candlestick upheld seven lamps; these lamps in the earthly sanctuary, were a type of the "seven lamps of fire burning before the throne in heaven, which are the seven spirits of God."

Christ says of the church, "Ye are the light of the world." The Spirit of God shines forth upon the earth through the church. The

The sons of the Kohathites, were over the shewbread, to prepare it every sabbath. 1 Chron. 9:32.

Every sabbath he shall set it in order before the Lord continually, being taken from the children of Israel by an everlasting covenant.

And it shall be Aaron's and his sons'; and they shall eat it in the holy place: for it is most holy unto him of the offerings of the Lord made by fire by a perpetual statute.
Lev. 24:5-9.

So the priest gave him hallowed bread: for there was no bread there but the shewbread, that was taken from before the Lord, to put hot bread in the day when it was taken away. 1 Sam. 21:6.

Isa. 56:2, 3.
Isa. 58:12-14.

Let no man despise thy youth; but be thou an example of the believers, in word, in conversation, in charity, in spirit, in faith, in purity.
1 Tim. 4:12.

Be ye clean, that bear the vessels of the Lord. Isa. 52:11.

1 Pet. 2:5.
2 Cor. 5:20.

The seven candlesticks which thou sawest are the seven churches.
Rev. 1:20.

And thou shalt make a candlestick of pure gold: of beaten work shall the candlestick be made.
Ex. 25:31.

Beloved, think it not strange concerning the fiery trial which is to try you, as though some strange thing happened unto you.
1 Pet. 4:12.

For by one Spirit are we all baptized into one body, whether we be Jews or Gentiles, whether we be bond or free; and have been all made to drink into one Spirit.

For the body is not one member, but many.

But now are they many members, yet but one body.
1 Cor. 12:13, 14, 20.

Aaron shall burn thereon sweet incense every morning: when he dresseth the lamps, he shall burn incense upon it.

And when Aaron lighteth the lamps at even, he shall burn incense upon it, a perpetual incense before the Lord throughout your generations. Ex. 30:7, 8.

**The candlestick was one whole piece.**

For every one that asketh receiveth; and he that seeketh findeth; and to him that knocketh it shall be opened.

If ye then, being evil, know how to give good gifts unto your children: how much more shall your heavenly Father give the Holy Spirit to them that ask him? Luke 11:10, 13.

If we confess our sins, he is faithful and just to forgive us our sins, and to cleanse us from all unrighteousness. 1 John 1:9.

If he be not able to bring two turtledoves, or two young pigeons, then he that sinned shall bring for his offering the tenth part of an ephah of fine flour for a sin offering. Lev. 5:11.

If his offering be a burnt sacrifice of the herd, let him offer a male without blemish: he shall offer it of his own voluntary will at the door of the tabernacle of the congregation before the Lord.

And he shall put his hand upon the head of the burnt offering; and it shall be accepted for him to make atonement for him. Lev. 1:3, 4.

Thou shalt call his name JESUS: for he shall save his people from their sins. Matt. 1:21.

church, the candlestick, upholds the light, guiding souls to the Lord. The candlestick was one whole piece. An individual that is out of harmony with the body, the church, is not a part of the candlestick. The work of dressing the lamps every morning and evening was not given to the Levites; but Aaron, the high priest, the one who represented Christ in the fullest sense, cleaned and refilled the lamps. He served "unto the example and shadow of heavenly things." In the heavenly sanctuary, every day Christ performs the work of which this was a type. It is the privilege of every child of God to believe, as each morning he pleads for strength and wisdom for the day, that Christ in heaven is pouring out an abundant supply of His Holy Spirit to meet every need. At the close of the day, as he reviews his failures and mistakes, he may know that as on earth the high priest lighted the lamps every evening, so Christ, the great High Priest, is giving of His Holy Spirit to cover all the work of the day.

Throughout the year the service was conducted in the first apartment of the earthly sanctuary. Provision was made for high and low, rich and poor, to bring an offering for sin, and by so doing show their faith in the "Lamb of God" that would take away the sins of the world.

The sinner brought his innocent offering to the door of the tabernacle, and laying his hands upon its head, confessed his sins, thus in type and shadow, transferring them to the offering. What could more fitly represent the one who, realizing that he is a sinner, confesses his sins, laying them all on Jesus, the only One who can save His people from their sins?

In some offerings, a portion of the blood was taken by the priest into the holy place and presented before the Lord. In every sin offering where the blood was not taken into the holy place, a portion of the flesh was eaten by the priest in the holy place. The flesh was assimilated and became a part of the priest, thus typifying Christ, who "bare our sins in His own body on the tree." Christ entered the heavenly sanctuary with the same body that hung upon the cross; He also entered with His own blood. It was necessary in the type to carry both the flesh and the blood into the sanctuary to fully represent the work of Christ. It took all the offerings to represent the complete work of Christ. Each offering typified some special portion of His work.

Lev. 4:5, 6.

Wherefore have ye not eaten the sin offering in the holy place, seeing it is most holy, and God hath given it you to bear the iniquity of the congregation, to make atonement for them before the Lord?

Behold, the blood of it was not brought in within the holy place: ye should indeed have eaten it in the holy place, as I commanded.
Lev. 10:17, 18.

Lev. 6:30.
1 Pet. 2:24.
Heb. 9:12.
Lev. 4:8–10.
Lev. 4:31.

Innocent offerings.

After either the blood or the flesh was presented before the Lord in the holy place, the fat was separated from the offering by the sinner, and the priest burned it upon the brazen altar, thus typifying the final burning of sin. It was a sweet savor unto the Lord; for it represented the burning of sin without the sinner. The remainder of the blood was poured out upon the ground at the base of the brazen altar, thus typifying that the earth would be freed from the curse of sin by the blood of Christ. Day by day throughout the year, this service was carried on in the first apartment. The blessing of the Lord attended it, and at times the bright

The wicked shall perish, and the enemies of the Lord shall be as the fat of lambs: they shall consume; into smoke shall they consume away. Psa. 37:20.

Thou hast bought me no sweet cane with money, neither hast thou filled me with the fat of thy sacrifices: but thou hast made me to serve with thy sins, thou hast wearied me with thine iniquities.
Isa. 43:24.

Lev. 4:30.
Num. 35:33.

At the door of the tabernacle of the congregation before the Lord: where I will meet you, to speak there unto thee. Ex. 29:42.

And there I will meet with the children of Israel, and the tabernacle shall be sanctified by my glory. Ex. 29:44.

Lev. 16:29, 30.

Into the second went the high priest alone once every year, not without blood, which he offered for himself, and for the errors of the people. Lev. 9:7.

Lev. 16:11-14.
Lev. 16:7, 8.

**The earthly high priest.**

Then shall he kill the goat of the sin offering, that is for the people, and bring his blood within the vail, and do with that blood as he did with the blood of the bullock, and sprinkle it upon the mercy seat, and before the mercy seat:

And he shall make an atonement for the holy place, because of the uncleanness of the children of Israel, and because of their transgressions in all their sins: and so shall he do for the tabernacle of the congregation, that remaineth among them in the midst of their uncleanness.

glory, representing the visible presence of God, would fill the first apartment, and the Lord would commune with them at the door.

The tenth day of the seventh month was the crowning day in the tabernacle service. This was the only day when the service was carried past the second veil into the most holy place.

Before the priest offered the sin offerings for the day, he offered a bullock for his own sins and for those of his household. Two goats were chosen and lots cast upon them, one lot for the Lord, the other for Azazel, the evil one. The goat upon which the Lord's lot fell was offered for a sin offering; the high priest entered the most holy place with this blood, and sprinkled it upon the mercy seat eastward, seven times. He then came out to the golden altar that had been touched so many times during the year with the blood of the sin offerings and with the blood of the Lord's goat, cleansed it from all the uncleanness of the children of Israel. When he had made an end of cleansing the sanctuary, when every confessed sin had been removed from the sacred place, the high priest came forth, bearing the sins of the people, and laid his hands upon the head of the scapegoat, confessing over it all the sins of the children of Israel. Then the goat, bearing the sins, was led away into the wilderness, and the people were free from the sins forever.

The type was a beautiful service, but the antitype is far more beautiful. Christ our High Priest officiated in the first apartment from His ascension into heaven until the end of the two thousand three hundred days of Dan. 8:14, when the heavenly sanctuary was to be cleansed. This period ended in the autumn of 1844; at which time Christ entered the most holy place of the heavenly sanctuary. In the type all trace of sin was removed upon the tenth day of the seventh month. This day was called the day of atonement, or at-one-ment, because the sins that separated God and His people were then removed.

In the antitype, Christ forever removes the sins of His people, and in order for this to be done, there must be an examination of each case. Daniel saw the books of heaven open, and John says the dead were judged out of those things which were written in the books. Removal of the sins necessitates an examination of every individual case. Since 1844, Christ and the heavenly beings associated with Him, have been examining the records of heaven. The name of every one who has ever confessed his sins, will come up in review before the Father. The words come back to earth, "He that overcometh, the same shall be clothed in white raiment; and I will not blot his name out of the Book of Life, but I will confess his name before My Father, and before His angels." When every case is decided, Christ closes His work and leaves the sanctuary. He then lays all the sins of His people upon Satan, the antitypical scapegoat, and he is left upon the desolate earth during the thousand years.

In the type, after the sins were laid upon the scapegoat, the priest cleansed the court; the bodies of the offerings were burned in a clean place. When the sun set on the eve of the day of atonement, the ashes in the clean place were all there was left of that which represented sin

And there shall be no man in the tabernacle of the congregation when he goeth in to make an atonement in the holy place, until he come out, and have made an atonement for himself, and for his household, and for all the congregation of Israel.

And he shall go out unto the altar that is before the Lord, and make an atonement for it; and shall take of the blood of the bullock, and of the blood of the goat, and put it upon the horns of the altar round about.

And he shall sprinkle of the blood upon it with his finger seven times, and cleanse it, and hallow it from the uncleanness of the children of Israel.

And when he hath made an end of reconciling the holy place, and the tabernacle of the congregation, and the altar, he shall bring the live goat:

And Aaron shall lay both his hands upon the head of the live goat, and confess over him all the iniquities of the children of Israel, and all their transgressions in all their sins, putting them upon the head of the goat, and shall send him away by the hand of a fit man into the wilderness:

And the goat shall bear upon him all their iniquities unto a land not inhabited: and he shall let go the goat in the wilderness.

Lev. 16:15-22.

Heb. 4:14.
Heb. 9:24.

Repent ye therefore, and be converted, that your sins may be blotted out, when the times of refreshing shall come from the presence of the Lord. Acts 3:19.

Dan. 7:9, 10.
Rev. 20:12.

Rev. 3:5.
Psa. 7:16.

For the bodies of those beasts, whose blood is brought into the sanctuary by the high priest for sin, are burned without the camp.

Heb. 13:11.

Even the whole bullock shall he carry forth without the camp unto a clean place, where the ashes are poured out, and burn him on the wood with fire: where the ashes are poured out shall he be burnt.
Lev. 4:12.

Ye shall tread down the wicked; for they shall be ashes under the soles of your feet in the day that I shall do this, saith the Lord of hosts. Mal. 4:3.

I will bring thee to ashes upon the earth in the sight of all them that behold thee.

All they that know thee among the people shall be astonished at thee: thou shalt be a terror, and never shalt thou be any more.
Eze. 28:18, 19.

Praise ye the Lord. Praise God in his sanctuary. Psa. 150:1.

and defiled the sanctuary. In like manner, when the great antitypical day of atonement closes, all there will be left of sin, sinners, and Satan, will be the ashes under the soles of the feet of the righteous on the new earth. After Satan's long conflict with God and His people, he will be destroyed, and his ashes, fertilizing the new earth, will only add to its beauty.

Thus ends the long conflict. Never again will the harmony of the universe be marred by sin. Sorrow and pain will no longer be felt by the beloved of the Lord; but throughout the ceaseless ages of eternity songs of praise and rejoicing will come from lips touched with eternal youth. "Let everything that hath breath praise the Lord. Praise ye the Lord."

# QUESTIONS FOR STUDY.

NOTE.—For the benefit of those who may wish to use "The Story of the Seer of Patmos" as a text-book in either the family or the school the following questions have been prepared.

## CHAPTER I.

### THE SEER OF PATMOS.

1. What is said of the men through whom God communicates with earth?
2. What is the best gift? What is the church exhorted to do?
3. What is necessary in order to view scenes still future? Have there been any of this class?
4. What is said of those chosen to be prophets? How are they purified?
5. What is the book of Genesis called? What does it contain?
6. When and by whom was it written?
7. What relation does Genesis sustain to the rest of the Bible? What is the Revelation?
8. How does the preparation of Moses compare with that of John?
9. When did Daniel live? What was revealed to him?
10. Give in brief, what was shown to Daniel.
11. Who predicted the time of Christ's baptism? Describe the scene of the baptism.
12. Who witnessed the baptism?
13. How did the preparation given Daniel compare with that received by John?
14. How are they both represented to-day? How did the Saviour foretell that John would be a latter-day prophet?
15. What is revealed in the prophecy given to John?
16. What is the book of Daniel? What is the Revelation? When are nations mentioned in the Revelation?
17. What is shown by the lives of Daniel and John? Who were represented by them?
18. What was the active element in both their lives?
19. Give the particulars in regard to Zebedee and Salome.
20. In what business were James and John engaged?
21. Describe the home life.
22. Why did the two brothers visit Enon? Who accompanied them?
23. What did they see and hear at Enon?
24. What course did John and Andrew pursue? Describe their visit with Jesus.
25. Of what was this the beginning? What formed the union?
26. Describe Andrew's course of action.
27. Give the experience of Peter.
28. Describe John's connection with the Master.
29. What was the result of this union? Was it ever broken?
30. What incident is given as proof that the union was sometimes broken?
31. Describe John's visit to the wilderness to seek Jesus. Also his visit with Mary.
32. Why was John chosen to care for the mother of Jesus?
33. Was John naturally mild and gentle? What name did Jesus give James and John? What was revealed by the name?
34. With what were the natural inclinations replaced? For what were these experiences a preparation?

35. What did John become? How many had the same gift?
36. What does the history of John become?
37. Mention four facts in regard to John's Christian experience. Who will have a similar experience?
38. Give two illustrations showing John's natural disposition.
39. What request was made by John's mother? Give the Saviour's reply.
40. What enabled John to comprehend the answer?
41. Name the various ways in which John showed his love for the Master.
42. What opportunity did John fail to grasp? Why?
43. Describe John's conduct on the night of the arrest and trial.
44. Describe the scene at Calvary.
45. What would have prevented their disappointment?
46. In what way did John recognize the risen Saviour?
47. Where did John go after the resurrection? Why?
48. Who sought him? What commission was given him?
49. Give the future of Peter and John as revealed by the Saviour.
50. What is given of John's history after the ascension? What became of James?
51. What was done by the Romans?
52. Why was John banished?
53. What was he permitted to see? What was given to John?
54. What enabled John to become the link that connected heaven and earth?
55. Who appeared to John? For what purpose?
56. State what is said of Genesis and Revelation. Who guided the pen of the writers?
57. What comparisons are given between Moses and John?
58. What are the two mountain peaks of Biblical history?

## CHAPTER II.

### THE AUTHOR OF THE REVELATION.

1. What is the first chapter of Revelation?
2. State what is said of the first three verses.
3. What is said in regard to the title of the book? What does John call himself?
4. State what is given in regard to the names, "Christ" and "Jesus."
5. What was opened to John? Of what is the book of Revelation an explanation?
6. Give what is stated in regard to the union of Divinity and humanity in the plan of salvation.
7. What is contained in the history of the church?
8. State what is said in regard to the name "Emmanuel." What was revealed to John by Gabriel?
9. When did Gabriel visit John? For what purpose? State three things of which John "bare record."
10. Upon whom is a heavenly benediction pronounced? Of what is this an evidence?
11. To whom is the book of Revelation addressed? Who will study the book? How much is contained in it?
12. What came into John's mind as he looked towards the shores of Asia?
13. What was each one of the seven churches taken to represent?
14. State the position held by Asia in the spread of Christianity.
15. What position did Palestine occupy? What did Asia Minor become?
16. State what is said of Ephesus.
17. Name the three Beings that unite in sending a blessing to the church.
18. Give five statements made in regard to Christ.
19. What have men been made to acknowledge?
20. To whom does all power belong? For what are men exhorted to pray?

21. What two positions are given to the followers of Christ? State what is said in regard to their holding these positions.
22. Relate six scenes that were revealed to the prophet.
23. What expression is used four times in the first chapter of Revelation.
24. What day was especially dear to John? Describe the Sabbath after the crucifixion.
25. What two events are commemorated by the Sabbath?
26. What is the central truth in giving the life of Christ? What did the Sabbath bring to John?
27. Who appeared to John? Give the words that were spoken.
28. What did the voice resemble? Describe the personal appearance of the Saviour.
29. What is expected of those who reveal Christ in the earth? What is said of the church?
30. Who spoke to John? How was John affected by the glory of Christ's presence?
31. What was laid upon John? Repeat the words that were spoken to him. What is said of the message given?
32. Where was Christ walking? What symbolized the churches? What did He hold in His hand?
33. Describe God's care for His church. What is completed by the church?
34. Repeat the last quotation given in the chapter.

## CHAPTER III.

### THE MESSAGE TO THE CHURCHES.

EPHESUS.

1. How much time is covered by the message to the seven churches?
2. What is said of the Divine Presence in the earth? How does heaven regard the earth? To what is the church compared?
3. Who is found with Christ in the midst of the church?
4. To whom was the first message addressed? State several reasons why Ephesus was taken to represent the first period of church history.
5. What met in open conflict? Describe the condition of Ephesus when entered by Paul.
6. What is said of Paul's preaching? In what place were the first meetings held? How long did they continue? Why were they discontinued?
7. Where did Paul then go? How long did he teach in this place? What was accomplished by his teaching?
8. What is said of the Greeks? What exchange did Paul offer them? Repeat 1 Cor. 1:22, 23.
9. How did they show their faith in the teachings of Paul? What is said of students from the school of Tyrannus?
10. What caused an uprising among the people? Describe it. Who was Diana? What came into open and bitter conflict?
11. Give the first words addressed to Ephesus. How did those labor who received the Spirit on the day of Pentecost?
12. What is said of Christian churches and schools? What effect did this have upon paganism?
13. What two classes were found among the new converts? Was the church able to detect imposters?
14. Name two individuals who had a ready spirit of discernment. What is said of Apollos?
15. Who had instructed Aquila and Priscilla? What met face to face?
16. What three things were met by Christianity? By what two methods of work was the church raised up at Ephesus?
17. Was John acquainted with the work at

Ephesus? What did the angel say to the Ephesus church? Who sent the message? What power attended the Gospel? Why?

18. How did Christianity appear to the heathen? Why?
19. What was accomplished in thirty years?
20. Who heard the glad tidings? Who ruled the world? Did any of the royal household hear the message?
21. What did God say of the workers of that period? What was the impelling power?
22. What did many of the Greek converts retain? How did they interpret the Scriptures?
23. What did the converted philosophers try to do? What was the result? What message did God send to the church?
24. Who were the Nicolaitanes? State their belief. With what did it conflict? To what did it lead? Were there other errors?
25. What does God say of the Nicolaitanes? Give the closing words of the message.
26. What promise is held out to the overcomer? Who may accept?
27. What is said of the tree of life? What choice must every individual make?

SMYRNA.

28. How far was Smyrna from Ephesus? How did they compare commercially and financially?
29. What was a drawback to the Ephesus church? In what did Smyrna's wealth consist?
30. Through whom did persecution come? What is said of the true Jew? Who belong to the synagogue of Satan?
31. What is the devil's counterfeit of salvation through faith in Christ?
32. What is made clear by the allegory given to the Galatians? Who were represented by Ishmael? Whom did Isaac represent?
33. What comforting message was sent to Smyrna? By whom was it signed? To what did Gabriel call attention? Why?
34. To whom was the message to Smyrna sent?
35. What three classes embraced the faith? How did this affect the church?
36. What was gradually lost? What result followed? What foundation was laid? What became popular?
37. What was respected in the Roman world? What were the Christians?
38. Relate the course pursued by the Christians. What was the result? What did the Christians often bring upon themselves? Give an illustration.
39. What edict came as a result of this course? How long was it enforced?
40. How does the death of a martyr affect the Father? Give the definition of Smyrna. To whom is this name applied?
41. Did God reprove this church? What is said of the over zealous?
42. What is said of the second death? What does the Smyrna church follow?

PERGAMOS.

43. What may we learn from the message to the Pergamos church?
44. What caused a reaction? What did Constantine espouse? Why? What was the effect upon the church?
45. What is the meaning of Pergamos? State the condition of the church.
46. Name five churches which sought for supremacy. Which one was acknowledged to be the head of the Christian church?
47. Who was watching the church? What message was sent to the Pergamos church?
48. Of what two sins was the church guilty?

What character from the Old Testament is taken to represent this period?

49. Give the substance of the quoted paragraph. How is the exact history portrayed?
50. Give the steps that led to the union of church and state.
51. Give the substance of the second quoted paragraph. What was Balaam's scheme?
52. Between what years were the church and state united? What exchange was made? What was introduced into the church?
53. Define idolatry. Also fornication.
54. What would have saved them from the temptations of the Moabites?
55. What was the doctrine of the Nicolaitanes? How did it affect the church?
56. To what period does the message to Pergamos apply? To whom is it a warning?
57. With what must the history of this period correspond? What does the history of Balaam become?
58. What warning was given the Pergamos church?
59. Quote the promise given. State what is said in regard to the manna.
60. How does a union of church and state affect the church?
61. What is the lesson for the church? The home?
62. What is written on the white stone? What was Zerubbabel called? To whom may it also apply?
63. State what is said of the "new name." Give Jacob's experience.
64. How were the children anciently named?

THYATIRA.

65. With what date did the Pergamos period close? What was consummated by this time?
66. What separation took place? Describe the two companies. What led to the apostasy?
67. Give the substance of the message to the Thyatira church.
68. What was absorbed by the church? Who was amenable to this power?
69. What was advocated? Why? What means was invented to atone for sin?
70. What did the masses think? State the reproof given Thyatira.
71. What character is taken to represent the church of Thyatira?
72. Relate what is given in regard to Jezebel? What is said of the history of Jezebel?
73. What came as the result of the doctrine of justification by works?
74. Describe the condition of things at this time. Who had full control?
75. How was Jezebel's using the king's name repeated.
76. Give three events in Jezebel's life that were repeated in the history of the church?
77. When and how was the power of the papacy broken? What continues?
78. What will be the fate of Babylon and her daughters? Of what is the death of Jezebel a symbol?
79. Describe the experience of those who separated from the main body in the early days of Thyatira.
80. To whom are these compared? Name some of these faithful ones.
81. What message is given these faithful ones? Define Thyatira. To whom does it appear to have direct application?
82. What had the church lost?
83. What broke the power of the papacy? What was given the people of the sixteenth century?
84. Name three important subjects that were presented. Why were they not accepted at this time?

85. Who opened the Scriptures? How was the light received?
86. What else was seen by the faithful of this period? Why was this sign given?
87. What promise does Christ give?
88. State what is said in regard to the light. Give the effect of the fires of persecution.
89. To what was the Thyatira church pointed? With what is this message in harmony?
90. What should be remembered? What will be repeated?
91. Give two conditions that will follow the union of church and state.
92. Of what was Elijah a type? What words were often repeated?

## CHAPTER IV.

### THE MESSAGE TO THE CHURCHES.—Con.

SARDIS.

1. To whom was the Sardis message addressed? What period was covered by the message to Thyatira?
2. Describe the change in the condition of the church. Who were the forerunners of Protestantism?
3. When was the darkness first broken? How long before the sun shone in its splendor? How long had darkness reigned?
4. How did the change affect the world?
5. Where did God prepare a cradle for the newborn cause of Protestantism? What nations failed to shelter it?
6. What nation became the center of the movement?
7. Define Sardis. To whom is the name especially appropriate? What is Protestantism? Of what is it the result?
8. What is the result of teaching justification by faith? What gives a death blow to tyranny in government? What comes with freedom of conscience?
9. What opportunity was given Europe in the days of Luther? Give the result. What reason is assigned for the failure?
10. What had existed since the days of Wycliffe?
11. Give the history of Protestantism in England
12. Was freedom always granted in America? What gradual change was made?
13. What is said of the Constitution of the United States? When did God place His sign in the heavens?
14. How did the breaking of the papal power affect the countries of southern Europe?
15. What can you say of the first fifty years of Protestant principles in America? What was offered each denomination?
16. Give the particulars in regard to William Miller's experience.
17. What line of prophecy did he study? With what results?
18. Give the condition of the churches. What does the Lord say of the condition of Sardis?
19. How had the life been taken from Protestantism?
20. What had been the experience of Christianity and paganism? When was the experience repeated?
21. Describe the experience of Protestantism and the papacy. What were they bidden to do?
22. What were they admonished to remember?
23 How long did William Miller wait before he proclaimed the message? Why? When did he begin preaching? To what church did he always belong?
24. What two events are recorded for the year 1833 A. D.? By what two ways was God calling to the Sardis church?
25. What class of men helped to spread the advent message?

26. Tell what you can of the "Missionary to Asia."
27. Who proclaimed the message in England? In South America? Relate the experience of Gaussen.
28. How was the message given in Scandinavia?
29. What was published in 1838? Give the particulars in regard to this prophecy.
30. How extensively was the advent message proclaimed? What was said to Sardis?
31. What two sins were found in the church at that time?
32. What is the white raiment? Give the closing words of the message to Sardis.
33. Whose name will be retained in the Book of Life? What was revealed to Daniel? At the end of what period was the judgment opened?
34. With what did this work correspond? What mistake was made? What is said of the mistake?
35. How long will this message be given? Who will see the second coming of Christ?

PHILADELPHIA.

36. What did the Saviour find? What was said of this class? What was offered by the advent message?
37. What was the experience of those giving the message? Define Philadelphia.
38. What two motives caused many to accept the message? Who composed the Philadelphia church?
39. How does Christ regard the Philadelphia church? Why?
40. What took place when the call was given, "The Bridegroom cometh"? To what was the door an entrance? How was this shown in type?
41. Where was the glory of God seen in the earthly sanctuary? Where is the attention directed?
42. Who opened the most holy place? When? What message is sent to all?
43. How many may enter the door? What is possible to the one whose faith centers in Christ?
44. What came in the autumn of 1844? What did further investigation reveal? How was the waiting time spent? What inquiry was made?
45. Who received light? When? What course did others pursue? Who were left in darkness? What class received a flood of light?
46. What was seen through the open door? What became the test from this time? Who was leading the people? How?
47. What was opened to the understanding? What became the message for the world? What was portrayed in vivid colors? State what is said of the law and the Sabbath.
48. What effect did the proclaiming of the Sabbath have upon the churches? Of what should every open door remind us? Who compose the synagogue of Satan?
49. What comparison is made between the first advent of Christ and 1844? Who will finally be seated on thrones?
50. What opportunity was given the faithful ones in 1844? What promise is given them? How will patience be developed?
51. What was the message to Thyatira? What message was given the Philadelphia church? How did the light of Thyatira compare with the light of Philadelphia?
52. What is said of the crown? Who only can enjoy heaven? How long have the angels been waiting?
53. What will some of the Philadelphia church become? To what period does the Philadelphian message extend?
54. What will characterize those who sit on the right of the throne?

LAODICEA.

55. Name the three churches, whose messages extend to the end of time. Who gave the message to Laodicea?
56. What was in progress during the period of the Laodicean message?
57. What contrast is given between Christ and Satan? When was the cry, "Babylon is fallen," first given? What is necessary?
58. Where did the light of the sixteenth century come from? What two important truths were made known at this time? What is said of the Sabbath?
59. What was repudiated by the church? By the state? What did some proclaim?
60. What is said of the remnant? What does Christ say of them? For what are heaven and earth waiting?
61. What two forces are preparing for the struggle? What is the only power that can retard the work?
62. What command does the Saviour give? For what are the Lord and the angels waiting?
63. What does the true Witness say of the church? What danger lies before those who have sacrificed for the truth? What will they say?
64. What is their true condition? Who pities the church? What counsel is given them?
65. Describe the white raiment offered. Who receive it? What is said of the life of the one in touch with heaven?
66. What remedy is offered for spiritual blindness? What is said of Satan's work?
67. What counsel is given by the heavenly Merchantman?
68. For what will many be reproved? What are at stake? To what time does the Laodicean message extend?
69. Describe Christ's attitude towards those who have not accepted Him. If admitted, what does He promise to do?
70. What honor will be conferred upon the remnant? What place will they fill?
71. From the lowest depths to what is man exalted? What is said of the place occupied by the redeemed?
72. Who are watching for the consummation? Give the closing words of the message.

## CHAPTER V.

### A GLIMPSE OF HEAVEN.

1. What is said of John's experience? What was opened before him?
2. Relate what is said of Stephen. What touched the heart of Christ? What invitation was given to John?
3. Who only can view heavenly scenes? Who describes the throne of God? Did John have a view of the throne?
4. How long has the throne of God been connected with the sanctuary? How should one feel when studying heavenly scenes?
5. What is said of the plan of Redemption? How are the heavenly beings employed? Describe the One upon the throne.
6. Of what is the rainbow a symbol? With whom did the plan of Redemption originate? Give the details of the plan.
7. Who clasped hands over the covenant? What power was bestowed upon Christ? What is said of the work of the angels?
8. What will be sung throughout eternity? What is nature?
9. What is said of the rainbow? What separates man from God? What are the tears of the penitent?
10. What does God remember when He looks upon the rainbow? Of what does the rainbow remind man?
11. Who were seated about the throne? Describe their appearance. Who

are the four and twenty elders? Where is their work described?

12. What is said of the throne of God? What is accomplished by the power centered there?

13. What is said of the work of the angels? State what is said of the voice of God.

14. Mention three times when the voice of God was heard by men. What was typified by the seven lamps in the earthly tabernacle? Where were they? What is said of the Spirit?

15. What does Jeremiah say of the throne of God? How does Ezekiel describe it?

16. What was in the midst of the throne? What is represented by these four living creatures? Describe each of them.

17. What shows that the New Testament is an unfolding of the Old?

18. Where were the four natures combined? What is said of Judah? How is the kingly nature represented?

19. What was shown by the genealogy in Matthew? State what is said in regard to Christ. Of what is every firstborn a type?

20. What was represented by the face of the calf? State in full what is said in regard to the Levites. Of what is every heavily laden beast a reminder?

21. State what is said in regard to the Gospel of Luke.

22. What does the keen eye of the eagle represent? How does John present the Saviour? What does he portray more fully than any other writer?

23. Give the substance of the last paragraph in the chapter.

## CHAPTER VI.

### WHO IS WORTHY TO OPEN THE BOOK?

1. Where had John been taken? What was described in the fourth chapter? In the fifth chapter?

2. Describe the close connection between God and His people. What did John see? State what is given in regard to the book. What is the mystery of the Gospel?

3. What challenge was given by the angel? How was John affected by the scene? Describe the scene in heaven.

4. Who broke the silence? Give the experience of the elder. What did he say to John? What two things were taken to represent God's power? Describe the power of the root.

5. What is said of the Root of David? Who only can be trees of righteousness? With what had John been familiar from childhood? What promise was familiar to the Jews?

6. Give the quotations from Jeremiah and Zechariah. Who had used these same symbols in John's presence? What is said of Christ?

7. What comparison is given?

8. For whom did the angel call? What was written in the book? Where is it revealed?

9. Who did John see in the midst of the throne? Describe the scene.

10. State the change wrought in the earth by sin. What covenant had been made? How did man show his faith in this covenant?

11. What is said in regard to all animal life? How did the offerings affect the Father?

12. What caused the death of Christ? With what is heaven well acquainted?

13. What is said of the Lamb? What is indicated by the "seven horns and seven eyes"?

14. Who took the book? From whence came the power? Who unite in all the work of Redemption?

15. Who worshiped the Lamb? Give in full the work of the elders and the living creatures.

16. What is said of the incense in the earthly tabernacle? What is being offered now in heaven? Why is repentance a sweet odor? What is said of the morning and evening prayers?
17. State what is said about the unanswered prayers. What will finally be known?
18. What can the sinner behold? State what is said in regard to the work of the elders.
19. What is sung? What is sung by the elders? Why? To what do the redeemed in heaven look forward?
20. What will be the grand chorus when the redeemed are gathered?
21. To what does heaven look forward?
22. What two companies join in the song? What is sung by each company?
23. Give the chorus. Who join in this? Who closes the song? How did this affect the elders?
24. What will enable man to repeat the songs of heaven? Towards what are all the angels looking? Are you?

## CHAPTER VII.

### HISTORY IN THE SEALS.

1. How is Revelation introduced? What is said of the first five chapters? Of the sixth chapter?
2. What is held in the right hand of the Father? Who alone can read the scroll? What do the seals reveal? What period is covered by the seals? Who only knows all the secrets of the life?
3. Who announced the opening of the first seal? What is said of the living creatures? In whom are they interested?
4. What did John see when the first seal was opened? What does Zechariah say of horses? For what is God's Spirit seeking? What church was given a double portion of the Spirit?
5. What was represented by the white horse? What was manifested in the church of the first century? What separation was made?
6. What is said of the crown? Describe the success of the work as represented by the crown. Give Peter's experience.
7. To what was the church compared? What was its most attractive feature? What is said of its connection with the living water?
8. To what do the writers of that age witness? What was written to the Romans? What statement was made to the Colossians? How long did it take to complete this work? By what power was it accomplished?
9. What does the Gospel bring if received? What if rejected?
10. Who announced the opening of the second seal? What was said of the red horse? State what actually took place.
11. What period was covered by this seal? With what church does it correspond? State how the experience of God's people looked in the eyes of the Lord, and in the eyes of the world.
12. What was the result of the sacrifice of lives? What gave strength to the people? Why? Give the result of an act performed in behalf of Christ.
13. What is necessary for spiritual life? What change came in the church at this time? How did Satan accomplish the work?
14. Who announced the opening of the third seal? What was seen? When do men become self-appointed judges? Is this the Spirit of Christ? What did Moses pray?
15. What follows disobedience to the law of God? What is said of the "mystery of iniquity?" What spirit is manifested in this power?
16. What is said of the balances? Who

has oversight of the weighing? What divine command is given? Of what were the oil and wine symbols?

17. What was done by the church during the fourth and fifth centuries? What change was made during this period?

18. What was seen when the fourth seal was opened? What was indicated by the pale horse? Give some facts in regard to the persecution at this time.

19. What is the result of the church being clothed with civil power? What follows? Who watches over every soul?

20. Who suffered with the martyrs? What was necessary at the crucifixion of Christ? With whom does Christ identify Himself?

21. What was seen when the fifth seal was opened? Where are the names of the martyrs? Explain how the earth is the altar.

22. Who fell before the one who sat upon the pale horse? Name some of the martyrs. Who else was persecuted? Why?

23. Of what does the earth bear witness? What is said of this witness? What question was asked, when the history of nations was revealed to Daniel? Give the effect of the curse of sin. What voice is heard by the ear of Jehovah?

24. What did John see? What is said of those who have given their lives for the sake of truth? How will their number be increased? What will be repeated?

25. When will they in reality receive the white robes? How are they regarded at the present time?

26. Who receives the most benefit from the history of the seals? When does the period of the sixth seal close? How does it differ from the first four seals?

27. Who will welcome the Saviour under the seventh seal? What will be the fate of those who will not heed the signs?

28. How did the sixth seal open? State what is given in regard to the earthquake. How may we know which events to accept as signs?

29. How many Bible writers mention the signs in the sun, moon, and stars? Name the four that wrote before the time of Christ. Name those who mentioned these signs in the New Testament.

30. How many peculiarities are mentioned? When does Matthew tell men to look for the signs? What is meant by the "tribulation of those days"? Give dates for the beginning and ending of this period. Why was the persecution shortened?

31. When was the persecuting power broken? Could the sun be darkened as a sign before 1776?

32. Give Mark's testimony. Definitely locate the time when the sun must be darkened to be a sign. Give the fulfillment.

33. What is said of Luke as a writer? What is shown by the manner in which he states the facts? What effect would the signs have upon the people of God? What were they to know?

34. How near is the Saviour's coming? What is stated in Joel 3:15? When was the sun darkened? Describe the event.

35. Give the prophecy of Amos and the fulfillment.

36. Give Isaiah's prophecy, also Amos 8:9. What does Ezekiel record? Which is the only dark day that fulfills all the specifications given in the Bible?

37. Give the substance of the quotation from "Our First Century." How did the sun appear?
38. What prophecy had been given in regard to the moon? Describe the fulfillm nt.
39. How were the stars to fall? Give the date of a shower of stars that fulfilled this prophecy. Describe the scene.
40. Give date for the opening of the sixth seal. What four statements are made concerning this period? What two classes are mentioned?
41. To what does the sixth seal look forward? Describe the change wrought in the earth by sin.
42. How will the voice of God affect the earth? Who will then seek to hide from the Lord?
43. What dates are clearly marked? "Who shall be able to stand?"

## CHAPTER VIII.

### THE SEALING WORK.

1. What does the seventh chapter of Revelation contain? What is said in regard to the signs? What was to follow the signs in the heavens?
2. Locate the seventh chapter of Revelation chronologically. What did John see? What is said of these angels and their work? Of what was the wind a symbol?
3. What two principles changed the condition of the world? Define each. What besides the churches was affected by the Reformation? What was required?
4. Where did civil and religious liberty blossom and bear fruit? State how the United States was regarded by other nations.
5. What was the condition of Europe? What is said of France? Describe the condition in all the European countries. Where did the trouble first break out?
6. Give an account of the uprising in France. What followed in other European countries?
7. What three important events in English history are mentioned?
8. When did the climax come? State in full the particulars of the trouble in France. Give the changes wrought in Germany, Prussia, and Austria.
9. What took place in a brief period of time? Describe the calm which followed. What was practically a thing of the past? What could now ripen?
10. What is said of the closing work in the earth? What is now going on?
11. What did John see? How are nations represented? What question is asked? What is always true of God's people?
12. What was given to Abraham? What is given to the seed of Abraham living in the end of time? How is the seal received? What is this sign or seal? Give the words of Paul.
13. Give a full definition of the seal. Between what two parties is the Sabbath a sign? Of what is it a sign? Who only can enjoy the spiritual rest in the Sabbath?
14. Where is the seal placed? Who only can read it? Can civil law enforce Sabbath-keeping? Why not?
15. Whose life reveals true Sabbath-keeping? Which day is the Sabbath? Name the three steps taken in making the Sabbath.
16. What does every seventh day of the week contain? What three things are necessary in the seal of every earthly ruler? Where is the seal usually attached to a legal document?
17. Where is the seal placed in the law of God? Repeat the fourth commandment. Point out the three specifications of God's seal as given in the fourth commandment.

18. When the fourth commandment is omitted, has the law any seal? What two things are mentioned as being revealed in the fourth commandment?
19. What call was given in 1848? Since that time, what message has been going to the earth? How did the work commence? What is said of the extent of the work?
20. How many receive the seal of God? How are they divided? What is the basis of the sealing work?
21. To whom was the promise of the new earth made? Who inherits the promise? What position will the adopted children occupy?
22. What is said of the names of the twelve tribes? What class is represented by the name of Issachar? State what is said of Naphtali. What contrast is given? Are both classes necessary?
23. What is said of Levi? Of Reuben? Who are represented by Judah? What tribe is left out? How is the number made up? What was said of Dan? What gift was given Dan? How did he pervert the gift? What did he become?
24. Who has the gift of judgment misdirected? Will those who continue to criticize others ever enter heaven? Why not?
25. Who did John see before the throne? What is said of this company? Of what do they sing?
26. To what other company was their attention directed? What is said of this company?
27. What was Satan forced to acknowledge? What is their reward?
28. What position was held by Lucifer? Who fell with Satan? Who will finally occupy the place formerly filled by Satan?
29. Who compose Christ's body-guard? State what is said of this company.
30. How will the sunlight on the new earth compare with the present state? Describe the effect of the glory of the angel upon the Roman guard.
31. What is said of those who walk in the presence of God? Give the substance of the last paragraph in the chapter.

## CHAPTER IX.

### THE TRUMPETS.

1. What is the closing work of earth? For what is the universe now waiting? What can hinder this work?
2. What is said of Christ's kingdom and the subjects? When will the overcomer inherit the kingdom?
3. What was shown to John? When does the sixth seal close? What is said of the opening of the seventh seal?
4. What is said of God's dwelling place? Who carries the announcement that the work is done? Mention four events that follow the announcement.
5. Describe the coming of Christ. What promise will then be fulfilled? Describe the reunion that will then take place.
6. How much time is spent on the journey home? What is said of this company?
7. Of what is the giving of the law a symbol? Give the words of Moses.
8. Who only will hear the law spoken a second time?
9. What was given the prophet? Give what is said of the messages to the churches. Give in full what is said of the seven seals. What other phase of history is given?
10. How much time is covered by the seven trumpets? What three lines of prophecy are mentioned as extending into eternity?
11. Of what is the trumpet a signal? What is the history of the trumpets? Why is it left on record?

12. What work is introduced before the trumpets? Why? How is Christ presented? Give in full what is said in regard to the incense.
13. Of what was the incense a type? What is said of the supply? What does the High Priest offer? What is said of recorded prayers? How surely will they be answered? What are the angels doing?
14. Will any reject light? How and when will the prayers be answered? What takes place in heaven when the sealing work is finished?
15. What is Satan's studied plan? What effect will this plan have upon individuals and the church? By whom was this lesson taught? How was the lesson taught the Roman Empire?
16. What is said of the Roman Empire at the time of Christ? When was Rome divided? Give capital of each division. Give what is stated in regard to the three divisions.
17. What followed the sounding of the first angel? Give the historical fulfillment.
18. When and by whom was the Eastern Roman Empire invaded? Describe the invasion. When was Italy invaded? Describe the invasion. Give the particulars in regard to the capture of Rome.
19. Give date of Alaric's death. What is said of his successor?
20. Quote Rev. 8:8. Where and by whom was this fulfilled? Who led the Vandals? What is said of him? Give the particulars in regard to the Vandals being in Africa.
21. How did the Vandal conquests in Africa affect Rome? What other conquests followed? What happened in June, 455? Describe the pillage of Rome. How did it compare with the sack of Rome by the Goths?
22. Describe the view of the mountains given to the prophet. With what does this agree? Describe the Vandal conquests and give their extent.
23. What measures were taken by Rome? What was prepared? Who united in these preparations? Describe the destruction of the fleet.
24. How was Genseric recognized? What did he live to see? Give date. What change was taking place in Rome at this time?
25. Quote Rev. 8:10. What is said of the Huns? What took place in the days of Ætius? What course did Theodosius pursue? What did the Senate do? Of what was this a fulfillment?
26. Who became rulers in 433? What is said of the conditions of peace? Give the substance of the conditions of peace.
27. What was Rome made to realize? What course did Attila pursue? Give the result.
28. Describe Attila's invasion of Italy. How did Rome escape? What is said of the "wormwood" and the "star"?
29. When did Attila die? Was Rome delivered? Who was in the heighth of his power at this time? How long did his work continue?
30. What is said of Roman power? Who occupied the throne of Rome. What was necessary to complete the overthrow?
31. Quote Rev. 8:12. How many emperors ruled during the last twenty years of the Roman Empire? Relate what is said of Nepas, Orestes, Augustulus, Odoacer, and Zeno.
32. Give particulars in regard to Odoacer's reign. In what condition was Rome? Who had prophesied of this?
33. How long will Rome remain divided? When did the Middle Ages begin?

What is said of the next few years? Give the fulfillment of Dan. 7:8.

34 Where did the people seek safety? What power was constantly increasing? What is said of the church?

35. How did the Saviour appear to His followers? What is said of the fall of Rome? Of what is its fall a type? What is said of the history of the four trumpets? How is Rome next presented?

36. Quote Rev. 8:13. What is said of barbarian warfare? How does heaven look upon these scenes? What is especially designated as woes?

## CHAPTER X.

### THE BEGINNING OF WOES.

1. What bitter struggle is mentioned? What is said of the devil's counterfeits? How has God used these deceptions? What should be kept in the mind?
2. What is said of God's plan and Satan's working? Who was seen by the Infinite One?
3. What did the "mystery of iniquity" find? What shows the foresight and wisdom of the Saviour? What is said of Satan's schemes? How shown?
4. What is said of the barbarian hordes? In what condition was the Eastern Empire? Quote Rev. 9:1. What had gone forth from northern Asia? From central western Asia?
5. When and where was Mohammed born? From whom did he claim descent? What is said of the faith he founded?
6. What does Gibbon say of Arabia? Who were gathered in Arabia? How did Mohammed become acquainted with these people?
7. What is said of Mohammed? What is said of his flight from Mecca? Give date. How did the religion of Mohammed compare with the faith of others? Give some facts in regard to their worship.
8. What was the single rule of action? How do the Mohammedans regard Jesus? By what was the Bible replaced? In what respect did Mohammedanism seem to be a reform? What is the foundation of a Mohammedan's faith? Compare it with the papacy.
9. What is said of the ancient history of the Arab? What did Mohammedanism do for them? To what was the rapid progress of the Saracen arms due? What was the result?
10. Give the result of the fall of modern Persia. Quote Rev. 9:3. What are the Saracens called? Show how the eighth Egyptian plague describes their work.
11. What did Solomon say of the locusts? Show the parallel in the history of the Saracens. How did Mohammed first gain adherents? What change was made? In a few years what conquests were made? Describe their mode of conquest.
12. Give Abubeker's instruction to his chiefs. Who were protected? Who destroyed? When was the conquest of Egypt begun? When and by whom was an attempt made to conquer Africa? When were the Moors conquered?
13. When did the Moslems reach the Pyrenees? What did they hope to do? When and by whom was their progress checked? Give an account of their work in Spain. What was preserved by them?
14. What change was made in their mode of conquest in the South and West? Was this true of the East? State what is said of their warfare in the East.

**15.** When did they attack Constantinople? What inducement was held out to the army? What dismayed them? How long did they continue the siege?

**16.** What was done in 677? What took place between 716 and 718? State how the two Saracen armies were defeated. Why did they give up the second attempt to capture Constantinople?

**17.** In what way did the Saracens resemble the locusts? Why did they fail to capture Constantinople? State what is said of the Arabian horse.

**18.** What is the Arab's crown? What is said of their customs and personal appearance? State what is said of their mode of warfare.

**19.** With what were the Arabs armed? Quote Rev. 9:11. Give the historical fulfillment. What is said of Othman?

**20.** What was done by the Crusades? What was approaching? When did Oth man invade Nicomedia? What does Gibbon say of the date?

**21.** How long were the Saracens given power to hurt men? Five prophetic months equal how much literal time? Give dates for the beginning and end of the 150 years.

**22.** What does Gibbon state of Othman's work? What demand was given and obtained by Orchan? What was accomplished between 1360 and 1389.

**23.** State what you can of the fourth king? What was the condition of Constantinople? With what other foes did the Turks have to contend? Did the Byzantine court gain strenght? Quote Rev. 9:12.

**24.** For what was God waiting? How was the sixth trumpet opened? What altar is here referred to? Quote Rev. 9:13, 14. When on the verge of victory, how was the Turkish force abated?

**25.** State in full what took place in 1448 How were the "four angels" loosed? Name the four Sultanies. What was soon gained by the Turks?

26. What change of rulers was made in 1451? Relate in full what is recorded of Mohammed II.

27. When was the siege formed? What is said of the army? Give the result. How did the Moslems treat the religion of Rome? What was affected by the fall of Constantinople?

28. What followed the fall of Constantinople? By what had the breastplate and scimiter been replaced? How did the discharge of the firearms appear to the prophet? Who does Isaiah say is the "tail"?

29. What is said of the military valor of the Turks? What other factor was equally potent? What prophetic period began July 27, 1449? State what is said of this period. How was the end marked?

30. Give date for the end of this prophetic period. Give the four waymarks in the history of Constantinople.

31. What conclusion was drawn by Josiah Litch and Wm. Miller? Was this published? Relate the historical facts that led to the fulfillment. What four powers held a council? When?

32. What did the Turkish ruler volunteer to do? Give the substance of the official document

33. When was this signed by the Turkish ruler? How has Turkey been known since that time?

34. Give Daniel's prophecy concerning Turkey. When will the Turks leave Europe? Of what will this move be a sign?

35. To what should these things lead us?

In what two places will we look for changes? What takes place in heaven when the capital of Turkey is removed to Palestine?

36. What is said of the closing words of the ninth chapter? Of what is the fall of nations a symbol? How are men affected by these things? Who are precious in the sight of the Lord? What work is being done to-day?

## CHAPTER XI.

### THE VOICE OF THE MIGHTY ANGEL.

1. What was seen by John? What are mingled in God's dealings with men? When did a thrilling message come to the world?
2. Describe the angel that brought the message. What is said of the message? What was the significance of the cloud? What enables individual to penetrate the cloud?
3. To whom is the rainbow a reminder of the everlasting covenant? Give the history of the rainbow. Who behold the bow? When was the rainbow first placed in the sky?
4. What is said in regard to God's looking upon the rainbow? What does every cloud contain? What is said of the dark clouds? Of what should every cloud be a reminder?
5. What was shown by the rainbow about the head of the angel? What is said of the insignia of earthly potentates? What did the angel bind together?
6. What two events were prophesied of by Daniel? What was Daniel's prophecy? What was he told to do? At what time, and by whom would it be understood? What was the line of prophecy Daniel sought to understand? What is the only sealed message of the Word?
7. Describe the book in the angel's hand. When did the angel set one foot on the sea and one on the land? Describe the condition of the world How much was embraced in the message? How was the message given? What was the result? What was seen on the brow of the angel?
8. How did nature respond? Give the oath of the angel. How was Jewish history divided? State what is included in the two thousand three hundred days of Daniel 8:14.
9. When did men begin to study the prophecies of Daniel? What conclusion was drawn? To what did they think the cleansing of the sanctuary referred? How was it preached? Who led the work in America? In England? In Asia?
10. How was the work carried forward in Sweden? What interpretation was given Rev. 9:13–21? What took place in 1840? How were people affected by it? What message was given at this time? From whom was it sent?
11. What did the angel sware? Describe the messenger. What was the effect of preaching the message? What did the school children repeat?
12. Quote Rev. 10:7. What is said of the seventh trumpet? What will be finished in the beginning of the seventh trumpet? When did the sixth trumpet end? When was the loud cry of the mighty angel given? When did the seventh trumpet begin to sound? What is the mystery of God?
13. When was the truth in regard to the heavenly sanctuary discovered? What began in 1844? Where did Christ go at that time? What was begun when the first case was decided?
14. What was this period? With what are the sixth and seventh verses of the tenth chapter of Revelation parallel?

15. How was the advent message received? Quote Rev. 10:8. Did the angel close the book? Quote Rev. 10:9 What does eating the book imply? How did Jesus use the figure?
16. When was there a deep searching of the Scriptures? Describe the condition in the spring of 1844. Give the particulars in regard to the decree of Artaxerxes.
17. What was the effect of eating the little book? What is said of the disappointment? To what is it compared? What was the effect upon the churches? What message was given as the result?
18. How were the expectations of many defeated? Quote the words of the angel. What is said of this message?
19. How many will hear this message? What is the message? When did the bitter disappointment pass?

## CHAPTER XII.

### THE THIRD WOE.

1. What is contained in the three preceding chapters? In the eighth chapter? Give the outline of the ninth chapter. What is given in the tenth chapter of Revelation?
2. What is said of the eleventh chapter? State the condition of Rome in 476 A. D. Name the ten tribes that were settled within the borders of the Western Empire. What three were "plucked up"? When? Why? What was developed from the other seven tribes?
3. What does a study of the Eastern Empire necessitate? What was claimed by the western division of Europe? What is said of the attempt of Mohammedanism to conquer Western Europe? How did the West stand?
4. What was born in the West? What commission was given Western Europe? For what was this a preparation?
5. What was given John? What was he to do? What is said of the one absolute rule by which actions are measured? Give the conclusion of the whole matter. What was the measuring reed?
6. What was shown John? Whose wisdom was given him? For what purpose? Of what is God's law an expression?
7. What is said of the temple? What story was told by the measuring of the temple? When John measured the altar what was seen? What is said of the love of Christ? How long will it be studied? What does it reveal? How many dimensions does it have? What does it all read?
8. How many classes are measured by the law? What is the test? What is the standard? Describe the character that is accepted. What develops a character that will stand the test?
9. What was revealed under the third seal? What contrasts are given? To what place was the attention of the prophet called? What was to be left out? Why? For how long a time was the holy city to be trodden under foot?
10. Where is the scene located? Quote Dan. 7:25. Explain the twelve hundred and sixty days. When was the papacy established? What was this period called? What is said of it?
11. What two powers brought darkness? Describe the work of Mohammedanism. What two powers bore sway in the East? Describe the thraldom in the West.
12. What day did the Mohammedans substitute for the Sabbath? What did the "man of sin" think to change? By what was the Bible replaced in the East? Quote Rev. 11:3. For how

long a time was the Bible suppressed in the West? What does history prove?

13. What was believed by the one that held the balances? What was God doing at that time?

14. What are the "two witnesses"? What is told by the Old Testament? By the New Testament? How is the same mystery revealed to individuals? Relate the incident at Jacob's well. When will the testimony of the two witnesses be accepted?

15. What is said of the two olive branches? How is the church represented? From where does the oil come? What is said of the oil?

16. How is the unity of the candlesticks typified? Of what is this a beautiful picture? From whence does life flow? What brings spiritual death? Does this affect the tree?

17. What is said of the two witnesses? What is the only channel through which man may receive light? What is said of the power of the two witnesses? What does Elijah's experience illustrate? When was the restraining power of God withdrawn? What followed?

18. What was removed by the Reformation? What was accomplished by Wycliffe's translation? How was the light spread? Give illustrations. What formed the basis of all instruction? What followed?

19. To what do all historians witness? What is stated by Ranke? What prevented the overthrow of the papacy? What is said of the Jesuits?

20. Through what means did the Jesuits work most efficiently? What was the result? What is said of France? What is said of the Jesuit teaching? When did the beast make war against the two witnesses?

21. What is said of the Counter-Reformation? In what does France stand alone? State what is said in regard to the worship of the "Goddess of Reason."

22. When was the Bible prohibited in France? How long did this condition exist? What was repeated in France? What else was found there? What did France do?

23. What was established in France? Describe the scenes which followed? How did other nations look upon it? What resolution was passed by the convention? Describe the condition of the nation.

24. Who called a halt? What was seen by the nations? What has been exalted? Which nations have taken the lead? What is said of copies of the Word of God? Give the rise of the British Bible Society. Tell of the American Bible Society. What is the result?

25. When did modern French history begin? What was the great earthquake? What did the beast receive? What changes were wrought? What follows the exaltation of the Scriptures?

26. Who place themselves on the verge of a precipice? What is being repeated in the twentieth century? What is exalted by education without God?

27. What took place on earth in 1840? In heaven? Who was sent forth? What response was made on earth? Why was the seventh angel held in heaven? Quote and explain Rev. 11:14.

28. What was John told in the tenth chapter of Revelation? Quote Rev. 11:15. What three things are necessary to make up a kingdom? What is the work of the investigative judgment? Explain when the three parts

of the kingdom will be given to Christ.

29. When and by whom is the enrollment for the kingdom made? State in full what is said of this work. What takes place when the work is completed? What is said of the elders and their song? To what do they look forward?

30. When did the third woe begin? When does it end? Name five events which take place during the sounding of the third woe.

31. When did Christ's ministration in the most holy place begin? Quote Rev. 11:19. When was the sacredness of the law revealed? What was seen about the fourth commandment? How did the seal of the law stand out?

32. What filled the people with reverential awe? Who saw light? Upon whom was the seal placed? What do they compose?

33. What will be seen in the sky? What will be the condition of the earth when the third woe closes?

## CHAPTER XIII.

### THE GREAT CONTROVERSY.

1. What is said of the salvation of souls? State the object of all creation. Through whom has God revealed the plan of salvation? How have the angels shown their interest in the work?

2. What plan is given to reveal God's love? What is said of the ministration of angels? By what are the Father's blessings offset? To what did every offering point?

3. How was the real object of the service often hid? For what were God's people anxiously looking? How did they always picture the Coming One? For whom did the self-righteous Jew look? What had no charm for the Jew? What was portrayed by the prophecies?

4. With what is Satan familiar? With what did he try to absorb the minds of the people at Christ's first advent? What was the condition of the world when Christ was born?

5. What was the condition of the race? State what is said of Zacharias and his wife. How were their prayers answered?

6. What is said of Nazareth? What message did Gabriel bring? How was the message received?

7. How many have been mentioned who were true to God? Who else is mentioned? What is said of Anna? In what condition were these faithful ones said to be?

8. How are these faithful ones represented? What was represented by the moon? What met in the child that was born?

9. What was shadowed forth and taught by every sacrifice offered? What did the sinner see by faith? What did the service typify?

10. What kind of a foundation has God placed under His church? From what is light emitted? What is said of the twelve stars?

11. What is said of the birth of Christ? Into whose territory did He come? How? What was the wonder that appeared in heaven? What is stated in Rev. 12:9?

12. What was done by Rome during the reign of paganism and papacy? Who gained control of Palestine? Relate what is said of Herod. Of what scripture was this the fulfillment?

13. When did Herod die? How was one third of the stars cast to the earth? What other event was described by these words?

14. Describe Satan's attempt to destroy the

infant Jesus. Who guarded the child? Name some of the ways Satan attempted to overcome the Saviour during His lifetime.

15. What five names are given to Christ? What was said of Judah? How was this fulfilled? What did the Father say of Christ?
16. Who only has been given the right to rule with a rod of iron? Quote the decree given.
17. State what is said of the Saviour's life and death. Give two instances when heaven resounded with shouts of triumph. How many years before the papal tyranny?
18. Give the three steps from the typical service to the day of triumph. What was brought to the mind of the prophet?
19. When was there war in heaven? How did it originate? What was the result? What is said of Justice, Mercy, and the rainbow?
20. What did Satan claim? Where was he granted a trial? At what cost? Through what did Satan work? What did our planet become? State in full what is said of the council at the gate of heaven.
21. What part did Satan act? What two cases are mentioned? To what have the angels listened? What four events in the life of Christ were watched by the heavenly host?
22. Quote the words of Christ as He looked forward to the cross. What was sealed at the cross? Describe the scene. What stood face to face at the cross? For what had Christ lived? What had Satan manifested?
23. What was heard in heaven when Christ died on the cross? What assurance did this bring to Christ? Quote Rev. 12:10. What triumph was gained at the cross?
24. What was formed by the life of Christ? Quote Rev. 12:11. How did the sealed sepulcher affect the disciples? Contrast this with the feelings of the angels. Quote Rev. 12:12.
25. What effect did all of this have upon Satan? What new scheme did he invent? When was the papacy established?
26. How long did the papacy hold power? Give the condition of the world during this period.
27. How did God break the power of the papacy? What three instances are mentioned? What is still felt in the earth? Who have the privilege of giving the Gospel to the earth?
28. What is contained in the tenth and fourteenth chapters of Revelation? Give in full the two characteristics of the Remnant Church.
29. How will Satan work at this time? What was given to John? What is added? What will be obeyed by the Remnant Church? What is said of the book of Revelation?

## CHAPTER XIV.

### THE BEAST FROM THE SEA AND THE BEAST FROM THE EARTH.

1. When can the world's history be rightly understood? What was seen in the history given John? What is revealed in the history of nations? What is contained in the twelfth and thirteenth chapters of Revelation?
2. Describe Patmos. How were the scenes of nature connected with the teachings of Christ? Quote Rev. 13:1. Describe the beast. Where do we find the same symbols?
3. How much of the world's history is covered by the four beasts shown to Daniel? State what is said of Babylon. Give the character of the Medes and Persians. What example of tyranny is given?

4. What new scheme was presented through Greece? What was the result?
5. From whence did the beast come? What was combined in it? Describe the body.
6. How many heads did the beast have? Give in full the six different forms of government introduced into Rome before the advent of Christ.
7. How was the pagan empire of Rome affected by the preaching of Christ? Where did paganism hide itself? What did this establish? Into how many divisions was Rome divided? Into what did seven of these divisions develop?
8. What is shown by the crowns on the horns? How many horns were set aside to make way for the seventh head? What was written upon each of the seven heads? What did it indicate? What is said of the seventh head?
9. What took place in 330 A. D.? What is said of the pope's throne? Who laid the foundation of the papacy? When and by whom was the edifice completed? What three powers opposed the bishop of Rome?
10. When did Justinian's decree go into effect? What began in 538 A. D.? Quote Rev. 13:6. What power was claimed by the church?
11. What attempt was made? How did this affect the Sabbath? What change was made in the decalogue? What was the result? Who found death a welcome relief?
12. How widely was the Gospel preached? How many will feel the oppression of the seventh head? What was accomplished by the seed of the woman? When and where was the last public persecution?
13. What took place in 1798? What is said of the wound? Is the work of the seventh head completed? What was believed? What is said of the life of the beast? What decision will be made before the end?
14. What four things are said of those whose names are in the book of life? Who receive the mark of the beast?
15. Who will be destroyed? Who will reign as king? What follows the beast? Why is such a power tolerated? What will be seen in the closing days? Who will meet these things?
16. What is said of the twelve hundred and sixty years? State three ways in which it has been viewed. What is the noontide of the papacy? What will be repeated? When? What is given in the last half of chapter sixteen?
17. What is said of the Reformation? In what two ways must the papacy be considered? To what did the Reformation give birth? Give the fulfillment of the words, "The earth helped the woman."
18. What more definite view of the help given by the earth was shown John? When did this power arise? Contrast the rise of the two powers. When and by whom was it brought into existence?
19. When did Europe hear the reports of a land beyond the sea? What motives inspired the navigators? What was God's purpose in the discovering of the United States of America? To what country did Protestantism pass after Germany refused full liberty?
20. What country gave free scope for the development of these principles? What course did the British finally pursue? To what country did these principles of liberty then pass? What freedom did America give its people?
21. In what particular place did Protestantism and Republicanism struggle for

existence? What did the principles of monarchy strive to do? What was the result of perseverance and strong determination?

22. How did Boston show its freedom? To what place did Thomas Hooker emigrate? What was the result of this move? What was it that gave Rhode Island its existence? How does it stand in the Union to-day?

23. In what other place was this battle fought? What took place in 1776? What led to the forgetting of all internal strife? What was the danger that now awaited the people? When some men advocated to return to former principles, how did God interfere?

24. What important move was made in 1787? What was the result? What did Gladstone say of this document? Upon what principles was this new government founded? Of what was this an outgrowth? What then was restored to their proper place?

25. How long had darkness covered Europe? At the end of this period, what arose out of the earth? What was then planted in congenial soil? What did this nation become to all other nations? What has become the model for the reorganization of nations? How did it affect the monarchs of Europe?

26. Is the world free from the influence of the dragon? What is necessary to successfully carry out these principles? What has been the real support of the nation? What philosophy has supplanted the truths of God? What is the result of the philosophy of Greece on the education of children and youth? What does it develop in the character? What is its effect upon society?

27. How does the dragon's voice sound through all the earth? Who dictates to thousands? In what way is the voice of oppression heard? What does the prophecy teach us concerning America? What are the words of the prophet?

28. What is the Protestant nation imitating? What is seen more and more in the nation? How is it affecting the nations of Europe? How and where will the deadly wound be healed? Where is the home of Protestantism?

29. What is the character of her churches? What are they rapidly doing? What two things will characterize the remnant? To whom do these two characteristics belong?

30. What did the beast do that is seen in the image? What is the object of the Spirit of Prophecy? How is it counterfeited? Through what agency does the devil seek to imitate the work?

31. How will Satan himself finally appear? What will he have power to do through human instruments? What does Christ say will arise? What did the dragon seek to do at the birth of Christ? When Christ was caught up to heaven, what did the dragon do to the church? What will be his most daring act?

32. Where did Spiritualism arise? When Satan thus appears, what will he demand? What people will the laws then imitate? What was demanded by the decree of Xerxes? Will these scenes be repeated?

33. Where will the sign of loyalty be required? What will bring every individual under the eye of the government? What condition of things that once seemed impossible is now in existence?

34. Why is the history of the beast repeatedly given? How has America once

taken the lead, and what will she do? How is the image compared with the real in the thirteenth chapter of Revelation? Explain Rev. 13:18.

35. What is now right upon the world? Where will be the battle-field for the final struggle? What will go forth from its borders? With whom will the members of this church join?

36. What is fast approaching? What will succeed the downfall of nations? What will be developed in this struggle? When will this be accomplished? What will be demonstrated before the universe? What should be the prayer of all?

## CHAPTER XV.

### THE THREE ANGELS' MESSAGES.

1. When was John's attention called to scenes where the conflict was ended? What is said of the Lamb? What choice did He make? Locate the city of God.

2. When did Christ enter the first apartment of the sanctuary? What took place in 1844? When do the events in the last part of chapter thirteen take place? What is the condition of the ruling powers of earth during the time of this sealing work?

3. What is said of the one hundred and forty-four thousand? What took place in 1848? When is the wound of the beast healed? Where is the image to the beast formed? How much power was given it? What class is oppressed by the image?

4. What nations control the world? How many are reached by the sealing angel? What contrast makes the work of redemption seem wonderful? From whom is the last company chosen? Why are they chosen?

5. Who receive the name of the Father in their foreheads? How are they designated? Where are they seen? What place do they occupy? From where do they come?

6. Quote Isaiah 6:1. What figure is taken to represent Christ and the true church? What is said of apostate churches? Upon whose foreheads is the name of the Father placed? How will they be shielded?

7. What is said of the character of this company? How does the possession of the mind of Christ affect men? Is it possible to walk with God today? Give the character of those who are sealed. How did they overcome?

8. Who only can enter the temple? Where are the new names written? What position does this company occupy throughout eternity? How are they described?

9. Define music. Who will sound the clearest notes? What will each chord tell? To what are heavenly voices compared?

10. What will the hundred and forty-four thousand sing? Who only can join in the song? What is said of the music?

11. Give the title of their song. Of what class is Moses a type? Who claimed the body of Moses? Who will have a special resurrection? Why? With whom does this company join their voices? Of what victory will they sing?

12. Quote Rev. 14:6. What is given in the tenth chapter? Of what is Rev. 14:6–12 a further development? To what period of time did the angel refer? When was the message given? What marked the close of the two thousand three hundred days? How was this change announced on earth?

13. How extensively was the message given? What was proclaimed? What has

long been the point of controversy? By what was this gospel covered? What came as the result of this?

14. By what did Satan try to hide the gospel in the days of Babylon? How has it been treated through all time? What did Christ put in a new setting? How did His questions affect the learned doctors? What had been accepted by the world?

15. What is said of the sixteenth century reformation? Where was light seen? What is said of Protestantism? Describe the parasitic vine. What message was proclaimed while this vine was growing? To what did men turn? What book was studied?

16. Quote Dan. 8:14. When did this period end? How many times is the word "sanctuary" used in the Bible? Does it ever refer to the earth? What mistake was made? How was Dan. 8:14 interpreted? By whom was this message proclaimed in America, England, and Asia?

17. Describe the disappointment. What was said by the faithful? While studying the Scriptures, what did they receive? What did they see by faith? What had they truthfully given? What work commenced at that time?

18. What message was heard throughout the earth? Explain the fulfillment of Zech. 9:9. If the people had known all, would the message have gone with power?

19. How long will the first angel's message sound? How was it given in 1843 and 1844? When will it again swell into a loud cry? Who will join in giving the everlasting Gospel?

20. Give the second angel's message. In what two ways was the preaching of the everlasting Gospel received by the people? What class was pronounced fallen? Who drank of the pure water of life? What position was taken by the churches after 1844?

21. What kingdom was taken as a symbol of the churches? What mixture is offered men in place of the everlasting Gospel? What union is formed? What attempt is made? When did the second angel's message begin? How long will it continue? Why are the words "is fallen" twice repeated?

22. To what is this warning given the churches compared? Who will heed the call? When will the message swell into a loud cry? What two classes are mentioned? What was done by the first angel? What has been invented by the devil? What warning is given by the second angel?

23. When was the sealing work begun? What is said of the law of God? Is there a countersealing? What does Jehovah recognize in the lives of His people? What are the three characteristics of the seal? Does the enemy's seal possess these characteristics?

24. What does the image to the beast enforce? Which commandment has the papacy thought to change? What power are those obeying who choose to keep the first day of the week as the Sabbath?

25. What will the law compel men to receive? What prophecy will then become a reality? What will take place in the close of earth's history? What will happen to those who accept Jehovah as King?

26. What did another angel flying in the midst of heaven proclaim? How extensive was the first angel's message? What relation do the second and third angels sustain to the first? How many will hear the warning of the

third angel? In what can each individual honor the Creator? How much light will each receive?

27. What will those who reject the warning receive? What does the Lord say of those who will heed the warning? Who will drain to the dregs the cup of God's wrath? What has Satan claimed? In what condition are those from whom the Sun of Righteousness withdraws His shining? What is this time called? How is man left to contend with disease and death?

28. What are the plagues in the sixteenth chapter of Revelation? Can man who lives in the light of the sun realize what it would be to have it blotted out? How does this illustrate the time of the plagues? What will the seventh plague accomplish?

29. When will the wicked be called forth from their graves? What then takes place? Who will live without an intercessor? How are the righteous hidden? How are they described? Where are their eyes turned? What are they awaiting? Who only are the living representatives of God on the earth?

30. What is watching and waiting? What did God say to John? What did He tell him to write? What did the Spirit say? What will those be free from who fall asleep? Who completes the good work they have begun?

31. What change is made in Christ's garments? What is placed upon his brow? Who draws near? What does the angel say that comes from the temple? What does the angel say who had power over fire?

32. What two vines have been growing in the earth? Which vine is the most luxuriant? How are its grapes described? Where are the clusters thrown?

33. Why does nation rise against nation? What great battle is fought? What flows for miles around the city? What takes place at last? What is seen in the East? What is seen as the cloud draws near?

34. What is in the hand of the King? Who are drawn upward? What will be reunited? Who meet? What song does all creation take up?

## CHAPTER XVI.

### PREPARATION FOR THE PLAGUES.

1. Of what has inspiration given us a vivid description? Why cannot human language describe it? What is the New Jerusalem called? Where is it located?

2. Between what two periods did Christ minister in the first apartment of the heavenly sanctuary? Where was the lamb slain?

3. When did the two thousand three hundred days of Dan. 8:14 end? What does the tenth chapter of Revelation make known? What began when Christ entered the most holy apartment? How long will the judgment continue? When this work is over, what does Christ do and say? How many will then have heard the everlasting gospel?

4. With whom will those in the last generation be numbered? What does Christ at this time cast upon the earth? What does He lay aside? What bursts forth in all its splendor?

5. In what way did Christ minister in heaven? What was veiled? When Christ utters the triumphant shout, "It is finished," what takes place? How does this glory flash forth? When and how was this typified?

Who then, with Christ, leaves the temple?

6. What does John see standing before the altar? What was given to the seven angels? What is under the control of mighty angels? Who has had a partial control of these forces? Who now stands waiting the command of Jehovah?

7. To whom does John now have his eyes turned? From where does this company come? While Christ and the angels are without the temple, who alone remains within? How do they pass the time of the plagues? What affect did the deliverance of Israel have upon the nations? What song did they sing?

8. How did the sea of glass appear to John? What music is then heard? What song did they sing? What has Satan sought to do through all this controversy? Of what will he finally be convinced? What will he confess? Who finally pronounces his sentence? What does Christ then proclaim?

9. In what condition are the wicked at this time? What is moved at the voice of God? What is about to begin?

## CHAPTER XVII.

### THE SEVEN LAST PLAGUES.

1. What veil was rent in twain when Christ died? What did the words "It is finished" announce to all the universe? Where is it that Christ rises from His judgment throne? What voice then reaches the utmost bounds of creation? Whose glory fills the temple?

2. What may men continue to plead? Who are they like? Will prayer any longer prevail? What will be forever at an end? To what has man turned a deaf ear?

3. From whom does all life emanate? What do men deny? What do they claim? Who will have the full control of the wicked at this time? In what condition are the people of God?

4. From where does God's call come at the last time? What does He say to the seven angels? What has been withdrawn from the earth? How long a period of time will the plagues continue? Where did the first angel pour out his vial?

5. Has the earth ever refused to respond to God's call for food? In what way will the day of the Lord come? What will be the effect of this first plague? How does the prophet Habakkuk describe it? What is the condition of the cattle and man? What comes upon men?

6. How many classes are there then upon the earth? What is the only rebuke of disease? What would the touch of Christ accomplish when upon the earth? Who alone will resist disease? What will be sure to the people of God? In the midst of this terrible suffering, what will the little companies sing? Will any plague come upon them? How many plagues came upon the Egyptians before the Lord put a division between them and His people?

7. What does the Lord say to His people? What does He create upon every dwelling? Where was the vial of the second angel poured? What was the effect?

8. What was a type of God's care for His people at this time? In what does the strength of God's people consist? What will men say during the falling of these plagues? What example have we of this? How did it affect Pharaoh? Whom did Pharaoh's re-

pentance resemble? Will it be the same at this time?

9. What is the effect of the third angel's pouring out his vial? What do flowing streams and wells of water typify? What is God's voice to man in the flowing water? When the priests bore the flagons of water from the brook Kedron, what did they sing? Who will sing these words again?

10. What is bending near the earth in the time of trouble? What will be the effect of the heat of the sun when God's Holy Spirit is withdrawn? What is God to His enemies? Of what does the sun become an agent? What is taught by the cloud over? shadowing the camp of Israel by day? What is the affect of the sun then upon the earth?

11. What has the Lord done during the lingering of probation? What will be seen? Where did the fifth angel pour out his vial? What developments of the beast are manifest in the last days? What does all the world do at this time?

12. What was a type of the darkness of the fifth plague? At what have men scoffed? What does God bring upon men, and how does it affect them? What cannot deliver them? When God hides His face, how does that affect men? Where only does the light shine? What is destroyed with the earth?

13. Of what is the overthrow of nations a symbol? What three witnesses have spoken constantly? How will men go on during the falling of the plagues? What was Elijah called? How will the people of God be pointed out? What do the beast and his image seek to do?

14. What adds strength to the oppression? What urges the people on? What do the angels loose?

15. For what are the nations gathered? Upon what is the sixth plague poured out? What does Armageddon mean? What noted battles were fought in Megiddo, or Armageddon? Who fought against Sisera in the valley of Megiddo? Where was Josiah slain?

16. What does the prophet say there will be in Jerusalem? Where does the seventh angel pour out his vial? What is its effect? What is the voice of Jehovah heard to say? How does this affect the heavens? Where does the Lord have His way? When He rebukes the sea, what is the result? How will it affect the hills and the earth?

17. What does He say to the world? What becomes of the mountains? What will the righteous sing? What will the Lord cause to be heard? Where will His anger be made manifest? What will fall upon men? What happens after God says, "It is done"? What is fast approaching? Who come forth from their graves? At what time does God deliver His people? What is seen in the East?

18. What song arises from God's people? With what words do they greet the advancing cloud? What comes up in remembrance before God? How will Babylon then appear? To whom is God a consuming fire? What is a short distance ahead of us? What will insure a hiding-place beneath the wing of the Almighty?

## CHAPTER XVIII.

### BABYLON, THE GREAT MYSTERY.

1. Of what is the seventeenth chapter of Revelation a history? What distinguished the beast that John saw rise from all other beasts? From what

standpoint did Daniel write his history? What does he mention in connection with the nations?

2. In order to get a thorough understanding, what two prophets should be studied together? What will be in the last days? How does John describe it? What is the cause of the seven last plagues? Does God arbitrarily withdraw His mercy from the earth?

3. What has God revealed to man age after age? How have men treated the divine law, and what has been the result? How has God given an object lesson of the ultimate result of a violation of His law?

4. What follows the breaking of the lats chord of mercy binding heaven and earth together? What does this angel control? What has been his work from the beginning of history? How has it been with the nations? Did man learn wisdom by this experience? Of what should these revelations have warned him?

5. Who has heard the voice of God in this? Where was John carried by one of the seven angels? How could he view these events? What did he see?

6. What relation did woman sustain to the work of creation, and what did God pronounce her? What is the influence of woman for good or evil? What does a pure woman represent? What does a prostitute woman represent?

7. What is the apparel of the wife of our Lord? When the character is lost what attracts the eye of the church? What does the Lord want? What does the world seek?

8. Where, and for what purpose does the whore sit? What do waters symbolize in the Scriptures? Who pay their money to this base creature? From what do they drink? When they have drunk once, what effect does it have? Of what is this a picture?

9. How does John describe the nations? What was on the forehead of the woman? What does Paul say of the "mystery of iniquity"?

10. How is the Apostolic church represented? What does the history describe? What was their attitude towards those who held false doctrines? How could the inward change be read?

11. In what way did paganism come into the church? In what way did they treat the Scriptures? What did they finally demand?

12. What was going on for the first five centuries after Christ? What does He say of His people? Did the church heed this call? How did she deck herself?

13. For how long a time did the capital of Rome control the nations of Europe? How does God describe the woman? Who was represented by the woman? How does Daniel describe this power? What did she first do that led her into this condition? What does God now call her?

14. For what purpose are governments ordained of God? What is the province of government? How is religion maintained in all pagan nations?

15. What has the devil ever sought to destroy in nations? What is the history of nations? What did Satan attempt to do in each government?

16. What did Christ do when He came into His own territory? How did the death of Christ affect Satan? What change did Satan then make in civil government? When did this change begin?

17. In how many directions has Satan

worked to accomplish his object? How was the Roman nation recognized in the days of the Saviour? In its development, how many forms of administration had been tested? What were these changes of rule called? What was suppressed, and what was exalted?

18. What change did the "mystery of iniquity" accomplish? How many heads and horns did the beast have? With what do the seven heads and ten horns identify the beast? What further explanation does John give of the seven heads?

19. What do mountains symbolize in prophecy? How is this divided state described in Daniel 2? Before what year were the ten divisions formed? When did Justinian publish his decree recognizing the Roman diocese as the head of the government?

20. In what year was the last obstacle removed? From this time onward, what position did Papal Rome occupy? By whom was she controlled? Did the devil succeed in his plans?

21. What did the woman become? With what was she drunk? How did kingdoms come into her power? Was the lion, bear, or leopard scarlet? What painted this nation red? When was this nation red with the blood of martyrs?

22. What did the church claim during this 1260 years? What did the church do? Who executed the judgment?

23. What further explanation did the angel give? What prevailing element existed in the government during the reign of the first five heads? What was the principle during the sixth head?

24. When did paganism disappear to all outward appearances? What is real papacy? What followed the Reformation?

25. What will take place in the last days? What will be the supreme manifestation? Where will these forces gather? What will fall upon them? From where do they come? Why do they go into perdition? What is the nature of the death they die?

26. With whom have these governments been in conflict? What has been their crime? When and how are they slain? What will consume error?

27. Where will the beast and his image finally go? Who will go with them?

## CHAPTER XIX.

### BE YE SEPARATE.

1. What is depicted in chapter seventeen? What name did God call the church of Rome? What did He show by the angels who hold the vials of His wrath? What are the natural results of spiritual fornication?

2. To what period is the mind carried back for the origin of the expression, "Babylon"? What caused the depopulation of the earth at the time of Noah? Where did the descendants of Noah gather together? What had God told them? What did they begin to do? What spirit took possession of the men?

3. What was the result of their iniquity reaching unto heaven? What was the origin of the languages? What term is applied to them? How did the devil show that he was determined not to be defeated? What happened sixteen hundred years later?

4. How was this kingdom used by the inspired penman? Of what is its overthrow an object lesson? Through what chapter is this figure followed?

To what does such a study open the mind?

5. Where is God's dwelling place? What boast did Babylon make? What did the church do? What was literally true of ancient Babylon? What did God never intend that the church should do? How did He reign when upon the earth? With what was He clothed? What made it necessary to put on the apparel of the world? Why?

6. What was the city of Babylon called? Who at this time controlled the commerce of the world? What wealth was laid at her feet? Where did she send her ships for spices? From where did she obtain her ivory? From where did the ships of Tyre bring her metals? Who built her lofty structures?

7. What was the character of her kings? How long was the Jewish race held as slaves? How was Babylon rewarded? Do travelers to-day corroborate this downfall?

8. What message did God give Jeremiah? Why was this detail preserved in the record of ancient Babylon? When were these sins repeated?

9. How did the Roman see gain her power? What was for sometime her rival? What other city besides Rome is situated upon seven hills? From what directions did the Barbarians come? With what were the Barbarians satiated? What power met them face to face? Of what were they ignorant? What was their condition when they prostrated themselves before the church?

10. What did all nations do to Rome? From whom did she gather her stores of wealth? What tribute did England pay to Rome? For what was their money needed? How were the poor robbed?

11. How many rose at the bidding of Rome? What was exchanged for gold? How is this tyranny illustrated? Who received the same principles? How did England show she possessed the same spirit? What nation has never fully recovered?

12. What other nation was drained of its wealth? What spirit did the Pagan Roman Empire have? What claim was made by Rome? How did she treat the souls she had in her grasp? Who bore God's message to Rome? What reply did Rome make?

13. When did the wounding of the head of the beast take place? Of what period did that mark the beginning? What brought the light to each of the kingdoms of Europe?

14. What are the nations of Europe doing to-day? What is fast disappearing? What agreement is made before the outpouring of the plagues? How does she stand before the nations of the earth to-day? How is she regaining her crown? What is about to be given into her hands? What will place the unbounded resources of this country in her hands?

15. What will Protestants then repudiate? How is society revolutionized? What becomes more and more marked? In what way is this shown? Through what means is this obtained? How is this shown among the Protestant churches?

16. What messages are sent to save the world? How are the churches described when devoid of the Spirit of God?

17. To whom did Saul go when he was rejected by divine counsel? What was his end? To whom are the churches given over? Who are they

prepared to receive? Of what did Babylon become the home? How is this applied to modern Babylon?

18. What does the third angel's message offer? How long will the judgments of God wait? Who join the angel? What is this enlightenment in the world called? What will be the effect of the loud cry? What will cause fervent prayers to be offered?

19. How was it with the Jews in ancient Babylon? How did Daniel pray at the time of deliverance? When will Daniel's prayers be most fully answered? What other prayer for forgiveness was partially answered? From what place does God hear and answer prayer?

20. What takes place when Satan manifests his greatest power? What will be heard from heaven? What will the angels of God do? Who escaped the destruction that came upon Babylon anciently? Why did they not all leave the city of Babylon?

21. What was the occasion of Lot's wife looking back? What crisis will be brought upon families in the loud cry? What scripture is applicable to this time?

22. When do the beast and his image grow more intolerable? Where will the believers seek shelter? How long a period will be covered in the falling of the plagues? What scripture describes those who reject the message?

23. How long did the "two witnesses" prophecy clothed in sack-cloth? What was found in Babylon? What has become of those who loved the Word of God? How does God describe the closing of probation? What no longer offers any attraction?

24. How are the merchants and great men of earth affected? How will the earth itself be affected? What has reached unto heaven? What is the result? What is God doing to-day? What is He doing to all those who prefer a spiritual life?

25. Of what is the story of Babylon a picture? How will the controversy end?

## CHAPTER XX.

### THE TWO SUPPERS.

1. What Scriptural invitation is given? What is the everlasting gospel said to be? During what time are the guests chosen? Who will be gathered in this great reunion? How are the guests arrayed?

2. What was typical of the transformation of the character? How was this explained to Zacchæus, the publican? How are the people of God described?

3. For what purpose did the Saviour enter the inner apartment of the heavenly temple? To Whom did He come? What was given Him? What is this event called? What voice at this time comes from heaven? To what people is this voice addressed?

4. What is recorded in the sixteenth chapter? What does the eighteenth chapter describe? After the closing scenes of the eighteenth chapter, what did John then see? What did he hear?

5. What is the one theme throughout creation? What had Satan repeatedly attempted to do? What followed these attempts? After the sinless beings had seen all this, what did they say? Who bowed before the throne, and what did they say?

6. What does one glimpse of heaven show? Whose intense sympathy for man is beyond description? When the conflict is over, what shout resounds throughout creation? Who come to witness the gathering of the mar-

riage supper of the Lamb? Describe the table.

7. Upon what site does the city rest? What is the effect of Christ's feet standing upon the Mount of Olives? What will never more be said? Where, and how will be seen the character of Christ?

8. What does Gabriel say of those invited to the marriage supper? What did he say to John? How does he feel toward those through whom he has communicated? With whom does the angel Gabriel class himself?

9. How is this view again presented before the prophet? How does he speak of Christ's vesture? What endeared Him to His own troops? What do they become to Him? Describe Christ's coming. What was written on His vesture and on His thigh? What name did He have?

10. How is the experience of the redeemed described? What is Christ to the Father? Of what is the Word of God an eternal reminder? What was the Word of God made? Where did He dwell? What is the Word of God to those who obey it? What does it become when disregarded?

11. In what way does Christ come for the first time? What has He been for six thousand years? Describe His eyes. How do they affect the souls of men? How is His word described, and what is its effect on the nation? How are men condemned?

12. How does He come to the righteous waiting ones? What does He bring to His people? What does He become to the wicked? How is the earth affected by His coming?

13. What is here first revealed? What does Christ tread? How will His coming affect the remnant of the wicked? What are they prepared to do? How are Europe and the United States represented? How are the armies in heaven clothed? How is this scene described?

14. What takes place at the end of the thousand years? Quote Psa. 50:3–6. What prophecies have come to us from time immemorial? With what words does Jeremiah prophesy? Of what is this a culmination?

15. What does the angel standing in the sun cry? Where are those now who sought to slay the truth?

16. Who accompanies Christ to heaven? What is in contrast with the marriage supper of the Lamb? What does this typify? What will become of the heavens? How many are called to the marriage supper of the Lamb?

## CHAPTER XXI.

### THE JUDGMENT OF THE WICKED.

1. What does the history of our little planet reveal? What are these two opposing characters? How many will be enlisted on one side or the other? Under whose generalship have God's people fought? Who has commanded the other army, and what has been his plan?

2. How many minds have controlled men? What is the character of the life and history of Satan? Of what is it a record? Of what has the whole course been a succession? How great has been the wisdom of the arch-enemy? What was his position in heaven? How does the prophet describe him? What was the cause of his fall? Of whom was he jealous? Of what was that a beginning? Who fought with him, and what was the result?

3. What did this defeat point forward to? From what place was he cast out? Where was Satan permitted to make

the seat of his power? Why did God permit this? What did Satan therefore become? Where, and for what purpose did he meet the representatives of other worlds? How did he stand in that assembly? Upon whom did he lay the blame of the rebellion? What was he seeking to establish upon the earth?

4. What did Satan try to show was the cause of his lack of success? What happened in fulness of time?

5. How did Christ live in the heart of the government of the enemy? What was done by Him on earth? What was done to Him? Who watched and wondered at the controversy? What were the Saviour's last words? What did He say concerning Satan? What did He exclaim at the triumph of the cross?

6. What did John hear at this time? From what place was Satan then shut out? How does Christ describe Satan's fall? What has been Satan's condition since the resurrection of Christ? What is becoming more and more under his power? What was once under the control of the Spirit of God that now renders allegiance to Satan?

7. What working power is abroad in the earth, and what is being accomplished by it? What does the little company of commandment keepers do? How are they treated? Where will the Saviour finally take them? What becomes of the wicked?

8. How will the earth be affected by the seventh plague? How does Rotherham render the translation of Rev. 20:1–3? What cannot Satan do, and where is he now confined? How does his countenance now appear?

9. What will take place at the end of the thousand years? What will be the last act in the drama? What question is here answered?

10. What did John say he saw? When Christ appears on the white cloud, what does he do? How does Paul describe this scene? What is this called? Who are here blessed?

11. Who will be priests of God and Christ for a thousand years? What did John see? Where are the saints during this time? What does Paul say the saints will do?

12. How does Peter describe the fallen angels at the present time? While the world is making history, what is heaven doing? What will God finally do? What does Christ say about the words men speak?

13. What are angels doing during the life of each individual? Where are these records placed? What is this book called? What is placed in this book? In view of this, what does David pray? What is written in the Book of Remembrance? What teaches the same lesson?

14. What is the influence of each day upon the individual? What shows that character is being formed by the daily life? What two records will correspond in the judgment? When is every page unwritten?

15. What shows that our deeds live when we die? What is the difference between God's judgment and man's judgment? Who keeps this record?

16. What other book is mentioned besides the Book of Remembrance? What appears upon its pages? How did the Saviour rebuke His disciples when they gloried over their success? What will be the reward of those who remain true to God? What will be the reward of those who grow weary and turn away from the Lord?

17. When the name of Christ is taken, what

is imputed to the believer? Why is it that when a man forsakes Christ there is no record of his good deeds? With what are the pages then filled?

18. How is it when a soul repents? What is the third book called? What is over against each name? How does Hosea refer to this book? How does Job speak of it? What three books are often referred to by the sacred writers?

19. When was the Book of Life opened? When the sins are blotted out of the Book of Remembrance, where are they transferred? Where is this work carried on? How and when was it typified on earth?

20. What did the priest do with the scape-goat on the day of atonement? What did this represent? When Christ finishes His work in the temple, what will become of the sins? Whose name heads the list in the Book of Death? In what are the saints engaged during the thousand years? When this period expires, what takes place? What occurs at the voice of God?

21. When the wicked rise from the dead, what do they see? What happens to the Mount of Olives and the dead who are buried in that country? What does Satan then do with his host? How great is his army, and of whom is it composed? How great is the number, and how are they organized?

22. As they approach the holy city, what do they see? Where are those who are in harmony with the truth? Where are those who have chosen Satan? What flashes vividly before every mind? Who will the wicked who have died in Jerusalem then see?

23. How many bow before Christ at this time? What possesses the hearts of those who march in the battle of Satan? What will they acknowledge? What then comes from God as He sits upon His throne? Who is then cast into the lake of fire and brimstone? What is this final end called?

24. What are the words of the Psalmist in describing this scene? How will the city of God be preserved? What will become of the earth? What will become of the wicked?

25. What was the last act in the shadowy service of the tabernacle? What has become of the defiled earth? Who are blotted out of existence? What will then take place? What has been the nature of the struggle? When it is all complete, what does Christ see?

## CHAPTER XXII.

### THE GLORIES OF THE NEW JERUSALEM.

1. What seven questions did the Lord ask Job? When did all things in the universe obey divine law? What did God do at that time? How did it affect other worlds?

2. In what condition was man when God first created him? What did God say? What one thing was to be accomplished by man himself? What was the effect of man's fall? What took place at the time of the flood? How was the earth watered until the time of the flood? How has it been since?

3. What did God do when sin filled the earth? Of what was the destruction of Sodom and Gomorrah an object lesson? What has there been in the earth since then?

4. What will take place at the end of the one thousand years? What will the righteous then see? With what people has the name "Jerusalem" been interwoven? What does the name

mean? What promise was given? When was the city raised to its highest pinnacle of fame? How has it been degraded?

5. In whose hands is the city, and what happened there? What will the Lord finally do? What was God's original plan with the garden of Eden?

6. What was the privilege of the Jews? What was one reason for Christ ascending to heaven? Where will the New Jerusalem be located? What was Christ's mission on earth?

7. What robbed man of the beauties of Eden, and defeated the plan for the Jews? In spite of the delay caused by sin, how will be the final triumph? What does this show?

8. What, and for how long will be the lesson of the story of Jerusalem? To whom will it be proclaimed? When Jerusalem descends from heaven, how will it be received?

9. What is proclaimed by Jehovah from heaven? How did God tabernacle with man? How was divinity veiled? How will it be in the New Jerusalem?

10. How was the story of sin written? What will those who have passed through these experiences sing? Why will there be no more sorrow nor weeping? What can words not express? By whom, and when will this be partially understood?

11. Who sits as King of kings, and what has been accomplished by Him? Who can better appreciate the kingdom because of sin? In this how is the love and the character of God shown? Who will inherit all these things?

12. In what way is the earth given to man? Who opened the springs of heaven? What has been a token of this promise, and when will it be fulfilled? What kind of life will the fountains in the new earth give? Who has a pledge that they will drink in the kingdom of God? How was this typified?

13. What was the Saviour's promise to the disciples? When was John prepared to appreciate this city? Describe the city. Where were these precious stones at the creation? How did men use them, and what was the result? What story will they tell in their arrangement in the New Jerusalem?

14. Relate the description of the stones as imagined by some. Of what is the foundation composed, and how is it ornamented? What story will these stones tell? When the glory of Christ and the Father shines upon them, how will they meet the eye of the saints?

15. What with man partook of the nature of the curse of sin? How will the foundation of the city of God shin What is written on the twelve foundations? How is the difference between human and divine judgment shown? How does the light of Christ's countenance affect the streets of the city?

16. How does the city compare with earthly edifices? How many gates to the city? Whose names are written on the gates? Compare the earthly and heavenly pearl. In what order are the redeemed arranged as they enter the city?

17. What is revealed in the blessings pronounced upon Jacob? When will the undimmed glory of the Father break forth? In what two ways was this typified in the earthly sanctuary? Why? What will be the light of the New Jerusalem?

18. How is the veiling of God's glory typified by the sun and moon? What will hide their light in the new earth? What will be caused by the celestial

light? Will the light be confined to the city? Why not? Describe the new earth. Who will bring the glory and honor into the city? Why was Christ manifested?

19. What was the original plan of God, and what has sin done? What is the best the human mind can do? What can the ear of man catch and his eye see? How has God described the other world? What can be said of the glories beyond?

20. What will those whose names are in the Lamb's Book of Life receive in the kingdom? When will it be fully known that Christ is the way, the truth, and the life?

## CHAPTER XXIII.

### THE NEW EARTH.

1. Of what is the book of Revelation a great signal? What hastens one along that road? What is human history like?

2. What did David have a good opportunity to watch? What did his stumblings lead him to do? What did they lead him to pray?

3. What does the book of Revelation show and portray? Where in history did the seven churches begin, and where will they end?

4. What do the seven seals portray, and where does the seventh end? Where are the seven trumpets blown? What takes place under the seventh?

5. To what do the birth and crucifixion of Christ point? What is recorded by the beast and his image?

6. What will be found by studying carefully the hundred and forty-four thousand? Of what are the plagues a sign? To what do they pave the way?

7. Where does Christ prepare the city? At the same time what does He do upon the earth? Where do the city and the people meet?

8. To what do the different lines of prophecy in Revelation lead? What does the last chapter of this book give?

9. How long did the first Eden remain on the earth? What was a wonderful lesson to the antediluvians? When was the garden transported to heaven?

10. What promise is made to the overcomer? Where does the tree of life grow? What was the nature of the tree of life? What was the nature of the waters of the river of life? Why was man excluded from the benefits of the literal tree of life and the water of life?

11. Of what is every flowing river a reminder to man? Who is the fountain-head of all truth, and what does it signify? What did the Edenic waters typify? What has always watered the earth? When will that river of life be fully restored?

12. Where will Christ lead His people? What will He make them drink? Who invites all to come? If we knew the gift of God, what would we ask of Him? What would naturally lead John to use figures concerning this gift of God?

13. Of what is every river and tree a type? How is the real tree in Eden represented? When will it blossom in reality? How many manner of fruit will it bear? What is said of the leaves of the tree?

14. What is the cause of the war and strife among the nations? When did this controversy originate? Why will not that tree of knowledge be found in the new earth?

15. What will all nature in the new earth symbolize? What will come to the

redeemed when they partake of the tree of life in the new earth? What has God sought to demonstrate in this earth? Who will gather about the real tree in the new earth?

16. What did God seek to illustrate in Israel? Had they faithfully followed Him, what would He have shown to other nations? What was the result of Israel refusing to eat only of the food of God?

17. When, for the first time, do the leaves of the tree of life bring all together? What did the angel say to John? What is the testimony of Isaiah? What does the presence of joy imply?

18. Where has sin entered? What has been the closest tie between heaven and earth? What can be seen in the midst of sin and deep degradation? Where pure love is seen, of what is it the reflection? Where will such love meet its reward?

19. What will God do to the lonely ones on the new earth? To whom shall all flesh come? What makes separation in families to-day? What will every man reap?

20. What reunion takes place in the new earth? What is a type of the Father's love for humanity? To whom will little children lost on earth be restored? What comforting words does the prophet speak to weeping mothers?

21. What was a type of every mother in Israel? How will the people grow physically in the new earth? What will there never be in the new earth? Why will this be so? To what will the inhabitants of the new earth have access through all eternity? What will be in the place of the curse of death?

22. What is the nature of God's throne? What for the first time is seen? How was man created? Where will the Father's name be placed?

23. What is found in the book of Genesis? What relation do the other books of the Bible sustain to the book of Genesis? What is the book of Revelation? What do we find in the twenty-second chapter? When John could not comprehend these sayings, what did Gabriel say? Why was it necessary for the angel to assure John that these things were true? How did these words affect John? What did Gabriel say to him?

24. What are prophecies? To what prophecies does the angel Gabriel refer John? What does Gabriel distinctly tell John? When did prophetic time close? What prophetic period ended in 1844? What began at that time?

25. When Christ rises from His judgment throne, what does He say? For what do the heavens then prepare?

26. While mercy lingers, what may be accomplished? Who only, at this time, will have the Father's name in their foreheads? What is said of the other class?

27. What message is sounding to-day? What will be the reward of the two classes of sowers? What are the threads woven in eternity's loom?

28. How much is comprehended in the expression, "Alpha and Omega"? What is now accomplished? What has been developed through this long journey?

29. What was the privilege of man in the Garden of Eden? What did Satan claim? What did he proclaim to man? What has been the false hope of man ever since?

30. What were placed together in the Garden of Eden? In Christ's personal teaching and His life, how did He

link together the tree of life and the commandments? What does John say to those who stand at the gate of the New Jerusalem?

31. What is God's law, and who are sealed? Over what question will be the last struggle on earth? Who are without the city? How does John describe the last people on earth?

32. How does Christ speak as the offspring of David? What relation do His commandments sustain to His throne? What is Christ called? Why? What ushers in that new day?

33. Who gives the final invitation? What kind of an experience will the people of God have?

34. How long were the waves a solid footing to Peter? What one word will carry the righteous through? What is the nature of that word? How is this word "come" illustrated? Who will repeat this invitation? What does the divine voice say? What is the nature of God's Word? Whose name will be blotted from the Book of Life?

35. Of what does the whole book of Revelation tell us? What were Christ's parting words with the disciples? What personal message is sent to us? With what do our hearts respond?

## CHAPTER XXIV.

### THE SANCTUARY AND ITS SERVICE.

1. Of what is the book of Revelation a revelation? How was Christ represented to John? What do we have in the fourth chapter? How does the eighth chapter reveal Christ? What does the eleventh chapter reveal? With these facts in view, what is necessary?

2. Of what was the earthly sanctuary a type? With what was the sanctuary surrounded? What was done in the court? Was any blood ever shed in the holy or most holy place? Where did Christ offer His life? Where did He then enter, and for what purpose?

3. Who alone entered the holy places on earth? Where are the people of God to-day? How do they follow their High Priest? To whom was there virtue in every service? To what did those priests serve?

4. What is our High Priest now doing? For what purpose did the high priest enter the holy place in the earthly sanctuary? How much incense was placed on the altar morning and evening? Who could detect the fragrance of this incense? What was ascending when he was placing this incense on the fire? What did this incense fitly represent?

5. What does Christ add to the prayers of His people? What may those who believe this know? Upon what will the Father look?

6. What stood upon the north side of the holy place? What was this bread called? Who is our living bread? Whom does Christ represent in the presence of the Father? Whom did the twelve loaves represent?

7. When were the children of Israel to prepare their bread for the Sabbath? When was this shewbread prepared? What must it teach us? What lesson is to be derived from the priest eating of that bread?

8. What would Christ have every one of His followers do? What kind of a priesthood are the people of God?

9. What did the golden candlestick represent? How was it made? What lesson is there in this? What did this candlestick uphold? What did the seven lamps signify? What does Christ say of the church? How does

the Spirit of God shine upon the earth?

10. When an individual separates from the church, what relation does he sustain to the candlestick? Who dressed and filled the lamps, and what is its lesson? What is the privilege of every child of God to believe?

11. For how long a time was the work performed in the first apartment? For how many was this provision made? What did this sin offering show? What ceremony did the sinner perform when he brought his offering? Upcn whom does the sinner now lay his sins by confession? In what way was the sin conveyed to the sanctuary? When the blood was not taken in, in what other way was the sin conveyed to the sanctuary? How was this fulfilled in Christ?

12. In what way did Christ enter the heavenly sanctuary? In what two ways was it necessary for the sin to be conveyed into the typical sanctuary? How many offerings did it take to represent the complete work of Christ? Who separated the fat from the offering? What did the priest do with it, and what did it typify? What made this a sweet savor to the Lord?

13. Where was the remainder of the blood poured out? How often was this ceremony performed? In what way did the Lord show He approved of it?

14. Where did the Lord meet and commune with those who brought the offering? What was the crowning day in the tabernacle service? Was this the only day that the service was carried within the second veil?

15. What must the priest do for himself and household? How many goats were chosen, and for what purpose? For what purpose was the Lord's goat offered? What did the priest do with its blood?

16. Describe the cleansing of the golden altar. After the high priest had made an end of cleansing the sanctuary, what did he do with the sins? What became of the goat that bore the sins?

17. When did Christ, our High Priest, enter the most holy place? How long did Christ officiate in the first apartment? What was removed from the earthly sanctuary? What was this day called? Why?

18. What is necessary in order for Christ to accomplish His work? What did Daniel see? What does John say? What does the removal of sins necessitate? What has been going on since 1844? Whose names will come up before the Father? What words come back to earth? What is done when every case is decided? What does He then do with the sins of God's people?

19. Where is Satan during the thousand years? After the sins were laid upon the scapegoat in the type, what did the priest then do? Where were the bodies of the offerings burned? What was there left of that which represented sin and defiled the sanctuary?

20. In the antitypical day of atonement, what will be left of sin, sinners, and Satan? What important relation will Satan then sustain to the new earth?

21. Will the earth ever again be marred by sin? Will sorrow and pain ever again be felt?

22. What will come before the Lord throughout the ceaseless ages of eternity? What will everything that hath breath do?

# INDEX OF MARGINAL REFERENCES

## *Genesis*



## *Exodus*



## *Leviticus*



## *Numbers*



## *Deuteronomy*

## *Proverbs*



## *Ecclesiastes*



## *Songs of Solomon*

## *Isaiah*



## *Jeremiah*

## *Lamentations*



## *Ezekiel*



## *Daniel*

## *Mark*



## *Luke*

## *I Corinthians*



## *II Corinthians*



## *Galatians*



## *Ephesians*



## *Philippians*



## *Colossians*



## *I Thessalonians*



## *II Thessalonians*



## *I Timothy*